Jane Pace and The Tapetia Mortis

A Jane Pace Novel

E.V. Comfort

Warning

This title contains the following:
Graphic language, sexual content and violence.

JANE PACE AND THE *TAPETIA MORTIS*

This book is a work of fiction. The names, characters, places, and incidents are products of the write's imagination or have been used fictitiously and are not to be construed as real. Any resemblance to persons, living or dead, actual events, locale or organizations is entirely coincidental.

ISBN: 978-0-9858603-4-9

Cover Art by George Lovesy

JANEPACE.COM

Dedication

To Kristi for her infinite patience and encouragement,

To Micah who provides clarity and believes in interactive novel writing,

And to a Family that makes everything worthwhile.

Contents

Book 1:

Jane of Pace-Pallon

PREFACE

My name is Jane Pace and I am a freak and not a freak of nature. I am a fairly notorious high powered Telekinetic who lives on Terra 1, *a space station orbiting Terra. If you are reading this you have probably read the book written about me (with names changed, etc., so that I couldn't sue the bastard who wrote it) so you have, I would guess, 23% of my story. The rest of that book is a combination of imagination and shit. So, I got to thinking that I would take down my version of my story, mostly for my own amusement.*

I was...born (created would be a better word) on Pace 4, the fourth planet of the system of Pace-Pallon. Pace-Pallon (named after the two lead colonists) had been founded 700 years ago by Terrans who were eager to attain genetic freedom. That is, they wanted to mess with human genes without all those pesky regulations. So, they left and settled the system with its 4 planets and small yellow sun. They had started out with the best of Terran technology to allow space travel, exploration, etc., but faster than light ships fell into disrepair, then were junked. Planetary defenses were minimal. Pace-Pallon was an adequate system in the middle of nowhere. We were visited by Terran military vessels twice a year. They came, checked in, then left unimpressed. We wanted to be left alone and we were. We had turned our eyes inward. We were "improving" the human race and we wouldn't be bothered until we were ready.

I have been able to gather some personal logs, some journals and, occasionally, some official reports to help reconstruct certain things that happened. Some of these came from other students at The School I attended (we were instructed to always keep journals). Those other students were also freaks. It was a freak school, though they weren't all the same flavor of freak. Our School trained us to be political (as well as actual) weapons and we were very good at being just that.

Ironic, though, that 700 years of genetic meddling were absolutely no help when real danger appeared.

Some Terran once said that all wealth is biological. The Scientist Class of Pace-Pallon would have agreed completely. But on June 29th, 2869, I would have given anything for the universe's biggest gun.

ENTRY 1-1-1

04:00 – School Dormitories, June 29th, 2869

Something slammed into the ground near the center of the Quad. Then another something. Then two more impacts, all hard. Always sensitive to any movement (a strange manifestation of my Telekinesis) I was out of bed and on my feet in an instant. It was still dark, but it didn't matter. In an attempt to calm myself I put my brain through my morning routine. Sense the room. Room-mate Atalanta was still abed, breathing slowly. I could sense her heartbeat was still in the calm of sleep.

Moving about the room, I felt the rather indistinct heartbeats of my School dorm-mates. I felt the slow turn of Pace 4, my home planet, beneath my feet. I took a deep breath and moved my mind into the Quad. The ground still shuddered from the impact of…something. Something large. And more than one.

Atalanta sat up in bed.

"Something's wrong. Worry. Fear." Atalanta got out of bed and turned on the light. She started dressing. Even half asleep she was beautiful. Never not beautiful. Little bitty dark, stacked goddess. And she's my room-mate. Not fucking fair. Atalanta was a Manipulative Empath (a MEmp) and could sense mass emotions and channel or change them at will. But right now she just listened.

"What have you got?" she asked as she pulled on her boots.

"Something big hit the ground hard outside in the Quad. I have to get closer." I threw on some clothes as well.

"General check," Atalanta said as she headed for the door. I nodded. Whenever we worried about anything (at least in the last year that General Armstrong had been our School's Dean or "Keeper") one of the MEmps would go scan him to see how worried we should really be.

Suddenly movement. Someone was running. Running toward our room. Atalanta read my fear and we both backed away from the door. I concentrated on the heartbeat, breathing pattern of the runner, trying to feel if I could recognize it. We Macro TK's were supposed to be learning to do that instantly with anyone we knew. I was still getting the hang of it, but I hadn't been too worried about it. I wasn't quite 18 and had 3 more years of School training before graduation. Atalanta was just 21 and within days of graduating. Therefore, she knew everything.

Heartbeat, familiar. Breathing pattern reads "fit" and "male." Slight limp on left foot…oh, I knew who this was… It was…

Arthur, 18 and also a Macro TK, stopped running at the doorway.

"Arthur," I said weakly. Fuck.

"You're a genius." Atalanta smirked. "What's the word?"

"They want all the TK's in the Quad. They think it's a meteor shower…" Arthur wiped the sweat off his forehead.

"How many?" That was Atalanta.

"Four," I answered, then I shook my head. "No, they're metal. Not meteors. I can't tell if they are solid, though. Not from this distance. You?"

"I didn't even get "metal" from them."

Atalanta raised her eyebrows in disbelief at our combined incompetence and sauntered towards the door.

"I'll be with the General," she purred as she left.

"Lucky bastard," Arthur sighed. I whacked him on the arm.

"First of all, the General doesn't fuck students. Second of all, even *she* isn't beautiful enough to wash away the stench of bitch. Can we go?" I threw on my jacket as Arthur looked sheepish. And now you know why we broke up.

A Note on School Student Classifications

There are 3 main groups of supernormals at the School:

Manipulative Empaths (MEmps), like Atalanta.

Telekinetics (T.K.s), like me, who…move things. I can throw a man across a room, crumple an LPG (Laser Projectile Gun), or shatter a femur all with the twitch of my fingers (though I get points off for the twitching). By age 20 I should be unstoppable in most situations. That is the point of the training, though I could do a tremendous amount of damage right now. The difference being that the havoc I could wreak today might be accidental.

There are two kinds of TK's. One is rare, the other REALLY rare. A Macro TK (which is what I am) is the strong man of the extrasensory universe. He/She is the tornado that can throw a shuttle 100 meters away, hold up a roof while people escape, or divert a missile. A Macro TK gets to put on a good show. Now the Micro TK is a totally different story. A Micro TK Assassin is trained like a doctor (in terms of anatomical study). He/she learns the subtle ways to immobilize, kill, or create pain. Some are traceable, some not, but the effect and the evidence are always planned, always deliberate. If this artery can be held closed Telekinetically for, say, 4 seconds, we can induce a stroke. Sometimes that is enough. For 8 seconds (or whatever is appropriate) we can cause death. No obvious weapon, no evidence. Unfortunately, there isn't much crossover between Macro and Micro. It's like asking a house painter to use his roller to paint a miniature water color, and vice versa.

That being said, I am a Macro TK with some sensitivity for the Micro. Even this is highly unusual, but I have no control in the Micro. For me it's like saying, "OK, now concentrate really hard and, without moving, wiggle your pancreas." I am a strong Macro, however, though still rough.

We also have a big crop of Telepaths (TPs) of varying strengths and abilities that can read minds superficially or deeply delve into innermost thoughts. Some Telepaths can even rearrange or change memories, depending on their abilities.

There have only been two students (long since graduated) at the School who had EVER had both TP and MEmp abilities. And while the TK's (including myself) were all bred with a basic resistance to being "read" by a TP, the geneticists have been unable to create a TK-TP.

The resistance to being scanned by a TP was done out of necessity to make living with TPs bearable. The geneticists knew (from long experience) that no one likes having their thoughts read all the time. And everyone hates TPs.

Arthur and I raced out to the Quad to find it teeming with people, both students and military personnel. The metal Objects were all being cordoned off by official looking people. Each Object was a dull metallic black, their surfaces pitted as if they had been damaged coming through our atmosphere. Each was about the size of a ground car. There was one near the center of the Quad, one on the sidewalk by the kitchen (that should make getting meals interesting), one in the fountain by the back door and the last one was out of sight, having smashed its way through the roof and first floor. I assumed it was somewhere in the old choir room.

The teachers ferreted around, enjoying their extra ordering-around abilities. Our self-defense instructor, Arrow Peters, 5'4," copper-skinned and lethal, paced around the center Object looking worried. She saw us and immediately bridled.

"Stay back. Orders."

I stepped closer anyway, just as Arthur was obediently backing up. Since he was in front of me, we bumped into each other. I sighed and kept moving toward the Object. Arrow, never one to give orders more than once, assumed a fighting stance as a last warning.

I closed my eyes to concentrate (my teachers found that habit lazy and annoying, but it worked). I felt the coiled energy of her coming strike and prepared to move, but that was a secondary concern. I was reaching out to sense the Object. I felt quiet from it. Like sleep. Not nothing (like a lump of rock) and not actual movement.

"Arrow!" Suddenly all movement stopped in the Quad. Arrow's body lost its tension. Everyone focused on the newcomer. I stayed as I was. There was no mistaking that voice.

General Samuel Armstrong entered the Quad and made his way to the center. Coming near to me he spoke to me in a low voice. "What do you get from this?"

"It's not a rock. And it's not a meteor. I feel layers, like a shell or egg. And something very small is happening in there. So small I can barely feel it. Like…a thought, or …something." I opened my eyes and looked up at him. Even at my 5'10" he had a good 4 inches on me. "I don't know what it is, Sir."

The General nodded. He turned to Atalanta, who had just caught up with him. A man, in an instructor's uniform, was close behind. The man, Stuart, was the School's top Telepath and newest instructor, just returned from his Tour.

"Scan it."

Atalanta nodded and took a deep breath. She cocked her head to one side, as if listening to a song played very far away. She looked suddenly up and around at the other 3 Objects. She frowned.

"It's strange, Sir. I'm not getting anything from the Object individually, but when I move a little bit myself I get sort of a feeling…"

The General looked from the Objects back to Atalanta. "A feeling, an actual emotion?"

"No, Sir. Not exactly. Like a low tone, or almost invisible white noise. But it is from all of them together, not one individually."

"Invisible white noise," the General repeated, unsatisfied. Atalanta looked embarrassed. It shouldn't have made me happy, but it did. The General turned to Stuart.

"I get a similar reading. Definitely no conscious thought, but not nothing," Stuart said seriously.

Arrow stepped forward. "Do we evacuate, General?"

The General thought for a second, then shook his head. It was then we noticed a crumpled piece of paper in his hand.

He stood up straighter and cleared his throat.

"Attention, boys and girls. Obviously, we have had a bit of excitement here this morning, but there is no need to panic. Well, there may be plenty of reason to panic in future, but we just don't have enough information to do so right now. So, go back to your rooms and try to get some rest. We are back to business as usual in the morning. The old choir room is off limits indefinitely and so is the Quad. And, yes, I will find some way of getting food from the kitchen to the refectory." Some students smiled at this last, but it was only the younger ones. The Quad immediately started to clear out.

The General turned to Arrow. "I want a TP, a Micro, a Macro and a MEmp on duty in the Quad at all times. 4 hour shifts. And a guard on each Object at all times. I want everyone to be paying attention in case anything changes."

But Arrow was nothing if not persistent. "But why not evacuate? We have no idea what these things are capable of. They could be some kind of alien bomb, or seed pods, or disease carriers…"

"I agree it is potentially dangerous, but," and he held up the crumpled yellow paper, "according to this communique we have nowhere to evacuate to. Satellites estimate that over 5 million of these things blanketed the planet tonight."

My stomach knotted up. The others looked similarly afflicted with fear. Arrow, however, showed nothing.

"We could go to Pace 2."

The General shook his head again. Suddenly his face looked tired. Not a handsome face even on the best of days, he looked haggard. As if he already grieved for something.

"Apparently Pace 2 got hit about 4 days ago, Pace 1 two days ago, Pace 3 a little over a day after that."

Stuart crossed his arms over his chest. "And we've been waiting for the other shoe to drop, so to speak, on Pace 4?"

The General nodded. "Stuart, Jane, Atalanta, you take the first watch. Arrow, find Wilby and get him out here, too. Organize a schedule. Everyone will take a turn, but make sure someone with experience is in charge of every shift. We don't want some baby missing something."

Arrow nodded and went off to find Wilby. Wilby was a Micro TK, 25, and really, really good looking. Could make any girl (or boy) drop his or her pants with a look and a smile. Probably even me and I couldn't stand him, not that he'd noticed me. But I think I may be one of a handful of people (male or female) he hadn't screwed during his years here. I'd like to say that he'd asked and I'd turned him down, but he hadn't. There is something depressing about being ignored by a sexual compulsive. He was really gifted, though, supernormal-wise. And Micros were incredibly rare.

Once Wilby arrived we did our four hours. Nothing changed, at least nothing that we could perceive. The next gang of four relieved us and we all went off to our respective rooms and got ready for class.

Classes at the School were like classes at most other prep schools. We had teachers, lessons and tests. Some of us were good at some things, not so much at others. And like in a dance class, there was no hiding anything. Everyone knew what everyone else could do.

We were here to work for the Government. We were paid by the Government. And we were here to uphold the needs and desires of the Government agenda. The two main differences between this and other prep schools: We had been genetically engineered to be here and were thus "owned" by the School (our very existences being illegal—see Five Gene Rule below), and we were being trained to kill. Anyone at any time. With no visible weapons beyond our own bodies and minds. We were *the weapons.*

A Note on THE FIVE GENE RULE

After centuries of abusing their ability to alter the genetic code of anything (with the expected disastrous consequences) the Scientists of the Pace-Pallon Genetic Review Council of 2720 (150 years ago) placed a Rule for genetic engineering that was paired with extremely nasty penalties for violation. Too many horrors (including those of deformity, sterility and disease) had come of unbridled tampering. With that, the centuries of Pace-Pallon being a limitless genetic playground were over. No more ten foot tall people with seven fingers (for basketball), no more women with four breasts and 3 clitorises (pity), or men with 2 foot penises (yikes), no more children with dog snouts, no more gills (which had never really functioned properly, whole batches drowning), no more humans who never needed to shit (oh, my god, that was more disgusting than I can say), no one had mink fur all over anymore, and no more prehensile tails. In retrospect, it seems a shame that the Scientist Class that had pushed so hard for genetic freedom—hard enough to start a colony just to do it—didn't have higher goals than, "Hey, let's try that." But we on Pace-Pallon have never been accused of being very deep. Anyway, back to the Rule...

Once the Rule was established (after having been overwhelmingly ratified by a terrified Coalition Government) it was law. Any genetic alterations must be documented and listed as part of the identification number of every citizen's live birth record (i.e., once a human came out of the tubs—there have never been any body births on Pace). That number would follow them their entire lives and could become a privacy issue, since it would (if one knew how to interpret the numbers) tell what *you were. Extrasensory alterations were only allowed by special order and were* never *allowed of civilians under any circumstances. Parents were allowed to pick 5 (non-extrasensory) genetic tweaks for each fetus. A panel and the geneticist performing the tweaks would then sign off on them. Parents caught doing more than the 5 or doing any of the illegal ones would have a lifetime reproductive ban, the geneticists would lose their licenses and go to jail, and the fetus would be destroyed.*

Since every student at the School had the very same extrasensory tweaks that were so very illegal, we were all illegally alive. It was the main reason to not run away; once we lost the protection of the Government we would be destroyed. Personally, if it came to that I would be averse to letting them. After all, I have skills. All of us do. Which is why our Daddy Government needs us, and is always a little afraid...

09:00 – Telepathy Instruction (Stuart)

Arthur, 10 other Macros, a Micro, Gladys, and I waited in the large classroom. We were on the lower level of the Quad by the kitchen and could see the Sentry guarding one of the Objects. Stuart, our instructor, walked in with, surprisingly, Wilby and Atalanta.

Stuart stood in front of the class. We liked Stuart, even though he was a TP, and we paid attention.

"Today we are going to work further on identifying, identifying people we know."

One of the Macros, whom I will call Smart Ass, pointed at Stuart and said, "Stuart!"

Stuart sighed and nodded. "Right." He looked up at the small observer's window near the ceiling. "Make it dark."

Instantly shutters dropped on the windows and the lights went out, shrouding the room in pitch black darkness.

I fought the urge to panic at the sudden change, and started deep breaths. I felt the slow turn of Pace 4 beneath my feet. I felt around the room with my mind. I started counting bodies. That was always the first thing he asked.

I heard Stuart's voice. "How many people are in this room?"
I knew that there were 16 once Stuart and his friends had arrived, but was pretty sure that this was a trick question. I counted again. No, there were 16.

"Sixteen." I volunteered at the same time as two other people.

"Correct." Stuart had moved closer to the rest of the students. "You all need, by hook or by crook, to be able to tell where everyone is in a dark room like this. You should be able to tell how many, but you also need to know *who* is in the room." He paused, apparently thinking of Smart Ass. "No one is going to ask me to turn on the lights to help with that?"

"Man, I fucking hate the dark. I'm just waiting for this to be over." Smart Ass's voice came from the far wall, where he had retreated.

Stuart chuckled, "I am going to pair you off and I want you to use your senses to try to figure out who your partner is. No touching and no talking. Everything else is on the table."

I could hear his footsteps in the absolute darkness. I had the feeling he was making more noise than usual in an effort to keep from getting stepped on. I could feel him moving people around. Gentle hands rested on my shoulders and he moved me a few paces to the side, near the closed windows. He'd never touched me before. I could tell his hands were powerful, but his touch was delicate. Like he was afraid he'd break me. His hands went away and I was sorry.

I realized I was standing across from someone.

Stuart's voice sounded from the front of the room again. "How many people in the room?"

I felt around again. "16." Half a dozen of us answered that time.

"Good," Stuart's voice was moving again. "Now, who are you standing across from? 5 minutes."

I closed my eyes to "listen." Silly in the dark, but what can you do? It was my way. I started at the air vent at the top of the room and followed the movement as it came towards me and my unnamed friend. After a second I could feel a shape, like a footprint from where the air wasn't. Tall. Wide shoulders and narrow hips. A man. His breathing was calm, in control. Too tall to be Stuart. Thinking, thinking. I crossed my arms on my chest in frustration. At that moment, something in his chest (his diaphragm???) spasmed in a …laugh? Arrogant pig, laughing at me…WILBY!

Stuart was at the back of the room, now. "Three questions: Do you know who your partner is?"

All of us answered, "Yes." Wilby's voice still had a laugh in it. Shmuck.

"Second question: How many people are in this room?"

We all answered "16" again.

"Good." Stuart was moving again. "Third question: Are they the same 16 people?"

Wilby laughed again, this time a real chuckle. I shook my head in dismay. How the fuck would I know? I could barely tell it was Wilby.

I could feel the others moving around, agitatedly, as discouraged as I was. Wilby walked away, still amused at the stupidity of us youngsters. When Stuart spoke next, he was right next to me.

"Relax. Tomorrow we will review the basics of identification. Tricks of the trade. It looks like you were all able to identify your partners in the dark, which is good, but you had 5 minutes, which is an incredibly long time. You need to be able to know who you're dealing with in seconds, not minutes. Those extra minutes can screw your mission and get you and your team killed. So, we will work on it. By the end of the week you should be able to identify everyone you know in the dark inside of 5 seconds. This will be intensive training, some group, some individual."

I felt him move closer to me, his lips near my ear. He smelled like aftershave. He smelled good.

"Don't worry. You'll get it." He whispered. The lights slowly came up and he was up talking to Wilby and Atalanta. As I left, I put my hands to my cheeks. I was blushing.

Excerpt from Atalanta's Journal dated June 29, 2869

Strange Objects hit the ground all over Pace 4 today. Didn't get us out of fucking class, though. Even the end of the world couldn't prevent that. God forbid. Can't wait to get off this fucking planet. Can't wait to meet some actual normal people. I am so sick of supernormals. Rivalries. One-upping each other all the fucking time. Superdickheads.

At least Arthur keeps things amusing. Idiot drools so much I'm sure he'd lose his load if I touched him. As if I would. And it looks like Stuart has picked his piece of ass for the semester. He likes them 17. 17 is just old enough to keep you from being a pervert and young enough that your prey doesn't know any better. Must be a real drought in the pool for him to single Jane out, though. I bet his technique hasn't changed a bit. I mean, it works, right?

Unfortunately for Jane, I don't think she is hot enough in the sack (or at all) to keep him quiet. He's OK until he starts trying to convince you to overthrow the government. Creep.

13:00 – Hand to Hand Fighting (Arrow)

My least favorite class. We were a smaller group, about half a dozen of us (including Arthur and Atalanta), because the class was supposed to be advanced. I was only in this particular group because I had been held back too many times in the beginners group and the instructor had hated me.

Arrow Peters stepped onto the practice floor. Copper skin, dark hair and eyes. Small and angular with a figure that was lean and strong. She moved like a hybrid of an assassin and a dancer. In her way she turned as many heads as Atalanta (though 'Lanta was more empirically lovely) when she entered a room. The difference was that while men were drawn to Atalanta, men backed up when they saw Arrow. She had a definite 'don't fuck with me' vibe.

I didn't fuck with Arrow, at least not on purpose. But that didn't make me good at fighting. At least not without 'help.'

Arrow looked us all over, her face expressionless. I knew she was sizing us up, both as students and as threats. She had to be the best "normal" fighter alive. I outweighed her by 40 pounds and was over six inches taller than she and she put me on the matt before I'd even touched it. Every time.

"Pair off," she said, and we obediently did. I was now standing across from Arthur. Being in the same class had been so exciting and fun when we were on the verge of dating and when things had been going well. After that it sucked.

Arrow led us in standard warm ups. Stretches, stances, etc. I had done these a million times before and my mind started to wander. I thought about the identification exercise we had all failed so embarrassingly in the morning. I had a good view of Arthur's ass in front of me as we warmed up. Fine, I thought. I'll start with him.

I closed my eyes, still going through the motions of the warm-ups. Not wanting to get caught out for being distracted, I kept the movements of the group in one corner of my thoughts. Hopefully this would keep me from continuing to exercise while everyone else had stopped. And stared. Not that that had ever happened before. Twice.

Ok. Arthur. His movements were very rhythmic, giving me a good impression of body shape as he repeatedly disturbed the air around him. I felt his breathing. Steady, strong. Faster than normal but not as fast as mine. Is everyone in better shape than I am? Apparently. He continued moving and I found I could feel large muscle groups in his legs and arms give and relax as he moved. Like a living machine. It was fascinating. They gathered up to lift the leg (or arm), carried it to where it needed to go, then let go in the most controlled, beautiful way. Hey, wait a second…

I was so surprised that I opened my eyes and lost the count. Arrow glared at me and I corrected. She walked on by. My mind was reeling. I am a *Macro*. Feeling the pull of muscles is not a Macro thing. That's a *Micro* thing. Like a real Micro thing. Holy shit. I had to know more.

Back to Arthur. I started at his head this time. I moved on immediately. I couldn't understand what I was getting from the brain and then I felt his tongue move as he swallowed. That was kind of gross, so I moved down to his chest. His diaphragm flattened, his rib cage pushed out and I could feel his lungs fill with air. Or at least I thought that's what it was. Yeah, that had to be it. I needed an anatomy class. Speaking of anatomy…

I peeked out of one eye and noticed that Arthur was eyeing Atalanta, who was warming up two couples down. Our uniforms were unisex but not on her. Arthur took sneaking glances at the parts of her generous cleavage that he could see. I closed my eyes again and moved my concentration...lower. I got to his, what shall I call it, ah yes, Man Meat. I was pretty sure I had the outline both from what I could sense and from memory. Yes, I thought something was going on there, though it was a guess.

I felt Arrow moving closer to us and opened my eyes. Arthur, unfortunately, was still concentrating on cleavage and didn't notice until it was too late.

"Something on your mind, Arthur?"

Arthur looked up. His face turned bright red. And his Man Meat deflated so fast I was surprised it didn't make some kind of balloon noise.

I did my best to cover my laugh with a cough.

Arrow, not content and more than a little annoyed, kept going. "While I am sure Miss Atalanta's breasts are fantastic…"

"Thank you, Miss Peters," Atalanta said cheekily.

"…they will not be much defense against attack. Unless they have powers we don't know about…?" Arrow looked over at Atalanta. My god, I think I saw a hint of a smile. Arrow can smile???

"No, ma'am." Atalanta responded pertly.

Arrow glared at Arthur until she felt he had been properly chastised. He knew he'd get his punishment later. She liked to hand out the individual suffering at the end of class. She said that the anticipation of punishment (and of not knowing what it will be) was part of the process. Group punishments were something else. Something worse.

All trace of humor gone, Arrow walked to the side of the room and opened the weapons cabinets.

"Pick your favorites. Standard safety armor and helms. Go until first blood."

Arthur started towards the cabinet with the others. I hesitated, entranced by the way his leg muscles and joints worked together. It was music. This Micro thing was blowing my mind.

"Jane!" Arrow called out. Without thinking, I at once registered that I was behind and did what came naturally. My favorite double daggers and arm shields flew out of the cabinets, toward me. I caught them deftly. And froze.

Everyone was staring at me.

The one thing you never *ever* did in a class with a "normal" teacher was either use or flaunt your powers (unless expressly asked to do so). It was against the rules of the class and, worse, it was showing off. It would be different with a Macro Teacher and an all Macro class. But that wasn't the case here.

I just stood there. I had no idea what to do.

Arrow stalked over to me, controlled fury. I had just taken a dump on her class. I was sorry, but had no idea how to tell her that I was. At least not in front of everybody. Especially that everybody that was probably about to get punished right along with me.

Arrow cocked her head and looked at me.

"I would normally give everyone Pattern 5 drills to run in the Quad. But the Quad is off limits right now." She paced around me. "So, we'll do Pattern 2 drills in here." No one said anything, but you didn't have to be a MEmp to feel the dread coming from the students. "We'll have a "A" Team and a "B" Team. I'll supervise A and Jane will supervise B." Arrow glared at me once again. "Let's go!" Arrow headed to the left side of the room.

I looked at my Team. They hated me. I hated me. Fuck.

I took a deep breath. I figured that since they were going to hate me anyway, we might as well win the drill. At least would be a distraction from thinking about all the shit I was going to get from everyone once class was over. "You heard the lady, let's get to it!"

Funny thing about talents, though. Some are obvious and some are more passive. A Pattern 2 Drill involved a shooting game through a very complicated obstacle course. The course was picked by computer and was different every time. Each Team started at one end of the course, had to get by the other Team somewhere in the middle and make it to the other end. The first Team to get all its members (both alive and 'dead'; we *never* left anyone behind even in practice) to the opposite side won. The thing that made it so hard was the amount of blind alleys, so to speak. Most of the opportunities to fire resulted in casualties. It was expected and usually unavoidable. These drills almost always ended with the two (or three) remaining people on any giving Team racing to carry the eight bodies of their downed team members over the finish line. It sucked.

The thing was that I was really good at Pattern 2. We never, ever did it because it was an indoor-only exercise and all of us (Arrow included) preferred to work in the Quad. As a matter of fact, I wasn't sure Arrow had ever *had* us do Pattern 2. Heh. Heh.

Why was I so good at Pattern 2, when I have gone out of my way to emphasize that I was not very fit, not the greatest fighter and that Arrow, in general, thought that I was a waste of her time?

Because Pattern 2 was done with dyed hard wax bullets. I might not have been allowed to move them (not making that mistake again, at least not today) but I could feel when they were fired, how fast they were going and where they would land. And when I knew it, my Team knew it. They might hate me, but we were going to smoke our opponents.

And we did. And we won. And they still hated me.

Some days you can't win even when you win.

<u>05:00 – Guard Duty, The Quad</u>

Stuart, Atalanta, Wilby and I stood in an awkward semi-circle "watching" the Objects and waiting for the sun to come up. It was cold. Stuart, having seniority, was in charge of our little group. Nothing was happening, though. We were bored.

"Everyone take a reading." Stuart spoke the command softly, not wanting, apparently, to disturb the rest of the sleeping world, but we all obeyed. I paid attention to him for a second as he prepared to scan the Object. I wanted to see if I could sense him scan. He held very still for a second, then took a slow breath. I was suddenly irritated with myself. If these were the obvious changes, what else was I missing? It wasn't light enough to see his expression change and I couldn't distinguish muscles in his face. I didn't have either the skill or the talent. Damn it.

Belatedly, I turned my attention to the Object. Something was very slightly different.

"Report." Stuart looked away from the Object. His breathing was normal again.

Atalanta was first. She shrugged adorably. "Slightly more of that…invisible white noise. Something is changing in there, I'm sure of it."

I nodded, "That tiny movement I felt before has increased, just a bit. There is more to it." Wilby looked at me in surprise and not without annoyance. That report had sounded more Micro than Macro.

Wilby spoke, still semi-glaring at me. "It's like shadows moving. Hundreds of them, but so small, barely corporeal. But there is more to it than yesterday."

Stuart sighed. "And I, on the other hand, felt nothing at all. No conscious thought, no words or ideas. Nothing."

At a head jerk from Stuart, we all moved toward the next Object. I trotted to catch up with Wilby. I didn't want to ask his advice, assholes like him were rarely kind, but he was the best Micro we had. He started talking to me before I had even reached him.

"There are no Micro/Macro hybrids. It's never happened before." There was a frown on his beautiful face. I don't think I'd seen him frown before.

"I can't imagine that I'm a true hybrid, Wilby, but if what I'm sensing gives me an advantage on a mission, I need training."

"Training for what exactly?" That was Stuart. We all stopped walking. Wilby looked even more annoyed.

"I'm reading things, recently, that I don't understand. Or I'm guessing and I have no real way of knowing whether I'm right." I folded my arms across my chest and glared a Wilby for being the jerk I knew he'd be.

"Like what?" Stuart looked thoughtful. Atalanta stopped near him suddenly, staring at him in surprise. She had scanned him by accident, I could tell. I'd seen her do it before.

"Yesterday, I felt muscles…"

Wilby snorted. "Really, Jane, your private life is…"

"Shut up, Wilby." I kept going, focusing only on Stuart. "I mean, I felt them gather and pull a leg bone up, hold it, then put it back with a controlled release. I don't understand any of the internal stuff I've been getting, but I really think that I read that right."

"Shit." Wilby said to himself. He sat down. On the next Object.

"Wilby, really." Stuart tried to wave him up and off.

"It's not going anywhere, Stuart. I've already scanned it and it's the same as the other one."

I stared at Wilby, who was avoiding my gaze. "I'm not supposed to be able to do that. I'm a Macro with a hint of Micro. That wasn't just a hint."

Stuart chewed his bottom lip thoughtfully. I couldn't tell what he thought about my problem. He didn't look happy, that was for sure. "Keep paying attention. Test yourself in as many situations as you can to make sure this isn't some kind of fluke. And I'll arrange for you to test off site as well—or at least as far from those Objects as we are allowed to get."

"You think they might be affecting my abilities?" I eyed the closest Object warily. Wilby suddenly looked like he'd rather that he wasn't sitting on one, but knew it would look very uncool if he got up right then.

"Considering how little we know about them, who can say?" Stuart beckoned Wilby off the Object. Wilby complied while trying not to show how relieved he was. "Now, let's check this one and move on."

"Stuart..?" I implored. Stuart's expression softened a bit.

"Give it a week, Jane. If your abilities stay like this, then we will have you tested. After I talk to the General, of course."

I nodded. Wilby wouldn't look at me. We scanned the second Object (which was acting like the first, just as Wilby had said), then started to move on to the Third.

I thought I caught Stuart watching me when he thought I wasn't watching. I'd never read Stuart in an in depth way. It had seemed both unnecessary and disrespectful before, but now I was curious.

I skipped his head, which I knew would only confuse me and moved to his chest. Good regular breathing and … some other stuff that I couldn't make sense of that seemed to be chugging along just fine. I modestly skipped down lower to his legs and admired the pull and stretch of his muscles as he walked. I doubted I would ever get tired of that motion. It was too cool. We were nearing the entrance to the choir room to check on Object Three.

I couldn't help it. I scanned his … Man Meat. Just then he gave me one of his quick looks. And the Man Meat became much, much larger.

Oh my.

ENTRY 2-1-2

A Note on Language

Some people might wonder at certain expressions used in writing this record, as well as noticing how very Anglicized a good portion of the character names are. There is a reason for this. All people on Pace-Pallon were raised bi-lingual. Our original colonists were all from Terra (over seven hundred years ago) and the only contact we had outside our system was with Terran war ships twice a year.

The Founding Scientists felt that it was important to keep Terran Standard alive on the colony, while at the same time creating a language for us to speak in our daily lives that more resembled the sounds bats make when they fuck. (Pace-Pallon really enjoyed being different merely for the sake of being so.) The (very) artificial Pacey language was dropped, for the most part, as soon as we'd left Pace-Pallon for good. Some of us made a full record of it for the Terran Linguistic database and did our best to never speak it again. There would be times over the years when it would come in handy, I will (very) grudgingly admit, but even so it was still god-awful to use. A real horror show.

Since Pacey was deliberately untranslatable and phonetically bizarre, I have, more often than not, simply given people/places/things/organizations in these stories names that I chose myself (I am partial to Terran English literature). Some of the survivors chose their own names (and I have used those) and some of those had used theirs for decades (the Armstrongs, for example, who had had many years of contact with Terrans). If some of the names used are laughable, don't blame me. Blame the idiots who picked them for themselves.

06:24 – The Quad, June 30, 2869

Stuart, Atalanta, Wilby and I stood next to Object 1, scanning. I could tell that Stuart was still reading nothing—no conscious thought, anyway, or language.

The rest of us, however, had a lot to see.

I started, as always, with the solidity of Pace 4 under my feet then moved over to the ground under the Object. The ground remained unchanged, placid. I moved my gaze up to the Object. All the layers and layers I had sensed before were humming with tiny, tiny movement. I felt warmth, energy, all so very small that it would have been easy to miss.

I looked sharply over at Wilby whose face registered shock. He met my eyes, then we both turned to Atalanta.

"More. There's just more of everything." Atalanta looked very worried. "This is bad." She looked at Stuart. "What does it mean?"

Stuart shook his head. "I'll make the report to the General." He started for the Guard Tower. "The rest of you stay here and keep watch."

I hesitated a second then followed Stuart.

I didn't speak until we were in the stairwell on our way up to the Tower. Stuart, lost in disturbed thought, only noticed me when he turned a corner.

"What are you doing here?" He was irritated and didn't try to hide it.

"Have you told him that you can't read the Objects?" This diplomatic conversation starter did nothing to lessen his irritation.

"He knows." Stuart scowled. "Now, go back."

"No, that you *still* can't read them? Now that they are so much more…awake, I mean."

He stopped on the stairs, now genuinely pissed off.

"No, Jane, I didn't tell him. I never go out of my way to remind my boss that not only was I once useless, but that I am *still* just as useless."

He started up the stairs again and I followed. "I think the fact that you aren't getting anything may be significant, Stuart." We reached the top and entered the Guard Tower. "I'm sorry your ego is bruised, but this could be important…"

"How so?" But it wasn't Stuart who had said that. Ah, that voice. The General looked up from where he was sitting, leaning back, boots up. The Guard Tower was a round, glassed in room at the top of the School complex. It was more administrative office than actual guard tower, but it still had a great view of everything.

The General was out of his office, as he usually was, sitting at the huge desk that typically accommodated the entire administrative worker pool. Unfortunately for them, this was his favorite place to sit. He could see the whole Quad as he leaned back in the chair with his boots up. The pool just made way. I could see them camping at other desks, inconvenienced but accepting.

Stuart glared at me. I could see the "ego" comment still rankled. The General, apparently, could see that, too.

"My office." The General led the way. We followed obediently. I snuck a look back at the main room just as the office door shut. Everyone was moving back to their original places, ready at a moment's notice to clear out if he wanted his favorite spot back. I liked that. But I liked the General. I had assisted him for a few months when he had first taken the post a year ago and hadn't seen anything wrong with him, despite his intimidating manner. Most people never got past that. Including, apparently, Stuart.

"What." The General sat on the edge of his desk.

Stuart took a deep breath, but the General immediately interrupted.

"And don't even think about scanning me, boy. I've gotta couple of memories in here that will give you nightmares the rest of your life and I promise you that that is *all* you will get from me." The General folded his arms on his chest. "We clear?"

"Yes, sir." It was weird seeing Stuart cowed like that. And the General had done it so efficiently. And he was a "normal." Interesting. "Well, Sir, we have detected more activity in each of the Objects. It's all still on a very small scale, but it is increasing exponentially."

"Uh huh," the General said. "But that's not all, is it?"

I knew this was my cue, "One other thing we noticed, General…"

Stuart talked over me, "Sir, shouldn't we be calling the Council or the military Governors? Or something? Aren't there going to be experts here any second? Haven't the people in charge been reading our reports?" His voice got smaller. "Isn't anyone going to help?"

The General stared at Stuart for a moment in wry astonishment. "So, now you want Big Daddy to step in and fix everything." He shook his head. "Thank god I am not too old to appreciate irony."

I did not have a clue as to what was going on. The General stood up and paced.

"Truth is, son, no one's coming. Every report you give me I've already gotten 50 different times from all over the planet. Every on-duty supernormal has been assigned to as many of these damn Objects we can find. The big brass are trying to figure out how to communicate with these things to find out what they want, but its slow going."

Stuart paled. This news didn't make me feel any better either. The General leaned against a window.

"So, Jane, what do you have for me?"

"Stuart can't read the Objects," I blurted. Stuart went from pale to red. "And I think that the fact that he can't get language, advanced thought or even images from these things is significant."

"How?" The General's posture looked the same (from the outside) but I could sense muscles tensing.

"I think he isn't feeling thought because there isn't any to feel. What if these Objects contain things that are alive but aren't sentient? I can feel thousands of little things moving, growing. But no one can sense consciousness." I faltered a bit. "Or have they?" I asked the General.

He shook his head.

"If there is no consciousness, there can be no rational thought. No rational thought means no language, therefore no communication. If we can't talk to them we won't be able to ask them what they want. Or tell them to go away."

Stuart spoke in a small voice, "So we probably won't know what they want until…"

"…they are ready to get it," the General finished.

"How many Objects have landed on Pace 4, General?" I had to know.

He shrugged, "We estimate just over 5 million."

If I'd thought Stuart was pale before, I had been wrong. "Holy fuck," I said softly.

The General chuckled in spite of himself, "Poetically put."

"Sorry, Sir." The General waved off my apology.

"So," he said, thinking out loud, "5 million Objects, growing, how many did you say? Right, thousands of …somethings in each one. We are infected and surrounded at the same time." He pushed himself off the wall.

"Stuart, I need you to take Jane to see our friend on the mountain today."

"Huh?" Stuart was trying to show how surprised he wasn't with little success.

"Cut the crap, kid, I know you were going to take her sometime this week, but I need you to go today. Ask him about the Objects and about Jane's new Micro abilities and see what he says." The General seemed genuinely amused at Stuart's flummoxed behavior. Stuart's mouth kept opening and closing like a terrified fish. "I'd go myself," the General continued, "but there are things I know that I'd rather he didn't."

The General went to sit behind his desk. He flicked out his hand in a gesture of dismissal to Stuart.

"Make your arrangements. Top priority."

Stuart left quickly. I started to follow, but stopped at the door. I looked back and saw the General looking at me with a twinkle in his eye.

"Sir, how did you…?"

He gave a low laugh. "I love supernormals, Jane. They're so busy looking for some super advanced threat—you know, the next big brain-changing thing that will render everything else obsolete—that they overlook the obvious."

He looked up at the corners of the ceilings suggestively. I instinctively scanned and found small metal...boxes with…aha. I smiled.

"Idiots never heard of microphones?" He shook his head. "Now git."

"Yes, Sir." And I got.

Our excursion got going very fast. 15 minutes after our meeting with the General Stuart and I were walking out across the school grounds. Strange as it may sound, this may have only been one of a half dozen times I'd left the School since I'd come to live there over two years ago. It was a beautiful day and the grass (a soft mossy vegetation) glistened in pretty yellows and blues.

We approached the transportation shed. Stuart reached for the door and I suddenly put my hand on his to stop him.

"I thought we were walking," I said nervously.

"Too far," he responded easily. I didn't budge. "What's wrong, Jane?"

I swallowed convulsively. "I've never flown. I don't think I can do it."

He smiled at me. I could tell he thought I was cute, like an errant toddler. I had never been closer to decking him. "It'll be fine. Flying is fun and it's just a shuttle. No big deal."

I removed my hand from his wrist and backed up. He really didn't get it.

I tried again, "You don't understand, I think the motion will..."

He opened the door to the shed and beckoned. "I'll walk you through every step. Nothing to be afraid of."

I realized that I wasn't willing to cause a scene, so I walked in. The huge shed was close to dark with scattered work lights here and there on the ceiling. Stuart was walking towards a small shuttle. I followed tentatively knowing that this was going to suck (and in no hurry to get to it). He pressed some buttons on the outside of the shuttle and the hatch opened. He turned to me, his brown eyes soft and wide in the darkness. He took a step towards me. I could smell the aftershave again. I breathed deeply.

Stuart took another step, then kissed me. His mouth, his delicious smell and his hands in my hair were so intoxicating that I lost my balance. He pulled me to him as I wrapped my arms around his surprisingly muscular back. He stopped for a second and smiled at me. I was too dazed to smile back but just looked back at him in a sort of wonder.

He leaned in to kiss me again and pressed another button on the side of the shuttle. The huge doors of the transportation shed opened dramatically as his mouth covered mine.

The heavy doors were almost completely open, machinery humming as it moved them. My whole body was humming, too, and I wasn't together enough to even try to sense what his body was doing. Though there were signs...

The shed was filling with light. A gorgeous vista of countryside lay before us and the shuttle gleamed in readiness. He ended the kiss with a smile just as the doors finished moving.

"Let's go."

The timing, the view and the kiss had been so perfect, somewhere in the back of my head I wondered if he had done that move before.

<u>*Excerpt from Atalanta's Journal dated June 30, 2869*</u>

More scanning of those damned Objects. They've certainly changed—from a drag to terrifying. I went to read the General again. I'm doing that at least once a day, now. It's stupid, I know, but he's the only one in this place that seems to know anything. And I don't like unnecessary worry—it makes lines.

The funny thing is; he lets me scan him. He hates being scanned but he lets me every time.

Today I found him right after he had sent Idiot Stuart and Sexless Jane off on their errand. He was laughing. I asked him what was so funny. He said kids were always the same. The world could be ending, everything is going to hell, but a kid only wonders how it will affect his chances of getting laid. He smiled at me and I felt better.

Funny, I don't remember him ever trying to make me laugh before. I was all the way back down in the Quad before I realized that I had forgotten to scan him.

We buckled ourselves in. The shuttle was Ok, I thought nervously. Sure. As long as it was in the hanger. Stuart started the engines. They made a rather pleasant rumbling and I spent a minute trying to sense how the engine was using its energy, what was channeled where and how the movement created changes in the metal of the ship it was attached to. All this was fine.

Stuart gently told the shuttle to lift off the shed floor. I threw up.

It was all downhill from there.

Fifteen minutes later we landed. Stuart couldn't get the shuttle hatch opened fast enough. I threw myself out the door and landed on some kind of gravel path. I had nothing left to vomit anymore, but dry heaved anyway. I took two breaths, attempting to calm down, and reached my mind out to feel the blessedly slow movement of Pace 4. There it was. Home. My stomach settled almost immediately. Oh, my god that had been fucking awful.

Stuart was off to the side, taking long breaths of clean air. That shuttle reeked and was beyond disgusting. Vomit bags would have been nice. No longer standard on shuttles, apparently. I had a feeling Stuart would have that changed within 10 seconds of our return home.

I looked up and around and noticed that we were near the summit of a small mountain. Valleys stretched out majestically on either side of us. No cities were in sight and nothing moved but the occasional tree stirred by the wind. Very quiet and peaceful.

<u>A Biographical Note on Irrfan</u>

He was 54 (The General's generation) and one of the illegal experiments with genetics. In this case, however, he was a renegade even from the government. Government agents had tried to roust him from his mountaintop den once—he'd let one survive to bring home the message that he wouldn't kill any more people if he was left alone. As long as he kept to himself, they pretended he wasn't there.

Like all citizens of Pace-Pallon, Irrfan, was a genetic experiment, but for Irrfan the Scientists had overreached and what resulted was a disaster. It was immediately clear that he was a freak above all other freaks.

There is a story (possibly apocryphal) that the geneticists, realizing their mistake, had tried to euthanize him in his cradle. He had read their lethal thoughts and had acted on instinct. They were dead before they had crossed the room.

"So, Stuart, this is your pretty friend," an extremely loud voice boomed. I belatedly put my hands over my ears. I looked over at Stuart who shook his head. I lowered my hands again. Was that noise inside my head??

"Sorry, children," the voice continued at a more reasonable level, "I can't always tell how loud I am."

"Who are you? And where?" I asked. Stuart touched me on the shoulder.

"You don't need to vocalize. Think the words and he will hear you."

"You, whoever you are, can read me? But Stuart still can't?" I was still looking around, figuring the speaker had to be fairly close, but I could see nothing.

"Correct, Jane. I can read every thought you've ever had." He must have felt my instinctive revulsion at the idea and I could tell he was chuckling wherever he was. "Don't worry, my dear, you only think you have secrets at 17." He paused. Taking a breath, I guessed. "My name is Irrfan. Part of a genetic experiment our benighted Scientist Class will never admit they made. In my body lie the remnants of 25 or so clever ideas implemented by people with more brains than sense."

"I can't stop you from reading me?" I felt at once excited and violated. Maybe my brain was more interesting than I thought if he wanted to scan it.

"Yes, your brain *is* more interesting than you thought. The thoughts themselves are…adequate, but what you can *do* with your thoughts is quite fascinating." The Voice seemed to find this invasion of privacy quite commonplace.

"You've already scanned me?"

"Darling, I scanned you before you landed in that wretched shuttle. Sorry about the nausea. We Telespatials are exceptionally sensitive to any kind of movement. Movement that affects us directly is especially disturbing."

There was a pause. The Voice spoke calmly, "Stuart, you must speak out loud or the little lady won't hear you."

Stuart cleared his throat, "Jane doesn't know about that classification."

"Ah. Telespatials are relatively new, say within the last 100 years or so. The talent only occurs (when it does) to Macro TK's. It allows them not just to move Objects through space but to understand and feel movement in all its forms." The Voice laughed. "It's why Jane is unbeatable against any projectile weapons and why that shuttle ride made her so miserable."

"You know the General sent us." I stood up on the gravel path. "Do you have any information that can help us?"

There was a pause. "Perhaps," the Voice said thoughtfully. "You should be ashamed of yourself, Stuart. Even the General was appalled at the way you clung to the idea of government intervention in this catastrophe."

I silently wondered what that scene had looked like to the Voice as he had read it in Stuart's mind. Or in mine, come to think of it.

Stuart lifted his chin, embarrassed but still a bit defiant. "You can't say that they caused *this* mess, can you?"

"No," the Voice responded. "I never thought that our doom as a people would come from the outside. It figures that we can't even self-destruct properly."

"Doom?" I asked fearfully. All my quiet worries that I had been suppressing and rationalizing away seemed to crystalize into terror at that word. He had said it with such authority, almost as a throw away. "It can't be." I tried to mask the desperation creeping into my voice, but I wasn't doing a very good job. "Not just like that. I know you both hate the government, but you can't believe that they are so irresponsible as to have no plan, no strategy to save us…"

Another pause.

"I'll bring you in."

Stuart looked up in complete surprise. "But, Irrfan…"

The Voice sounded tired, "I'll survive. Jane, focus on the solidity of the ground. Keep it as a constant and I will try to keep it slow. Try not to vomit on or in my house." And with those cryptic words he went silent.

I looked over at Stuart, nervous. He didn't look too calm himself. "Just keep it together," he said quietly, but I wasn't sure if he meant that for himself or me.

I felt myself being lifted off the ground. I saw Stuart being lifted at the same time and felt another dry heave coming. I remembered what the Voice, Irrfan, had said and closed my eyes, feeling for the solid ground of Pace 4. I had never tried to feel it without standing on it, but it was there. We were up, I guessed, about 100 feet in the air now. I kept my eyes closed, just concentrating on the air moving past me, the earth below and the steep slope of the mountain as we moved up.

I was too focused on everything to pay attention to Stuart, but I heard him say, as if to himself, "I love flying…"

Then after about, I guessed, two miles I felt my body getting lower towards the mountain. The trip was almost over. My feet touched the ground and I opened my eyes. Stuart landed beside me, a sort of awed smile on his face. I looked around and saw a small, low house built into the side of the mountain. It looked abandoned and the yard, such as it was, was littered with discards. A busted shuttle here, a motor bicycle with a wheel missing there. Trash and weeds were the only things to flourish. A truly depressing place.

"Come on in." This time the voice was real, I mean, not in our heads. "Slowly, please. Slowly."

Stuart started carefully up the walk. I matched his slow pace, staring around me in wonder.

"That's the same man I heard in my head?" I asked.

"Yes," Stuart answered.

"But we were at least 2 miles away and way out of sightline. How could he have reached us at that distance *and* been able to scan us so easily?"

Stuart picked his way gently up the broken stone path to the front door. "Irrfan is…special."

"Stuart, wait." Stuart paused and turned back to me. I rubbed my forehead, trying to take all this in. "He's a Macro, obviously, a Telespatial (assuming that is a real thing), and the most powerful Telepath…ever?"

"Something like that."

I took a step closer to him, grabbing gently onto his jacket lapels to make him focus on me. "And he is your friend, this Super-Super? What else can he do? What is he capable of?"

Stuart leaned closer to me and kissed me. "That's not the question, Jane. He can do more than you can possibly imagine. The real question is," he took my hand and we started up the path again, "what he can't do and why."

A Note on Pace and Pallon

Seven hundred years ago a married couple, Atticus Pace and Indira Pallon, created a charter to allow them to gather money and people in order to start a colony. They had managed to escape prison for the 6th time that year and were eager to go somewhere where they could stop feeling harassed. It was disgruntled parents and children that were (in most cases justifiably) harassing them, but justice was never a concern for either Pace or Pallon; they just wanted to be left alone to do their thing.

Pace and Pallon were the two foremost genetic scientists in the Terran Confederation. Geniuses who had worked tirelessly for decades eradicating genetic disorders, birth defects and disease. They were as famous as geneticists could have been and considered almost saint-like by the media and, thus, the public. For a while.

The year Atticus Pace turned 50 he realized that he was tired of putting out genetic "fires." He thought it was high time that the human race was improved. His 56 year old wife, having just gone through the enormous hormonal and physical changes of menopause, had started exhibiting latent Telepathic powers. That gave both of them a direction, a focus for their research. Never content to move slowly, they started genetic experiments in utero, then moved on to create fetuses out of raw DNA.

The parents of these engineered children were willing (for the most part) initially, but most became disillusioned when their children turned out "different" (sometimes in the most disturbing ways). Everything seemed fine at first, but when children started being born with say, Telepathic abilities but blind, or could self-levitate but were allergic to their own skin, the flaws in the research were exposed. Both Pace and Pallon lacked any sort of patience, taking a hundred fetuses, altering one gene in each, seeing what the change did to them/for them for a year, then immediately moving to the next step with fresh fetuses. In effect, there was no actual research to their research.

The next ten years were full of work, then arrests, then time in court, more work, more arrests... Money, and they had buckets of it, had thus far kept them out of prison, but they knew it was only a matter of time. They also had, unbelievably, acolytes that supported their every move. Many of these were parents of the children who had (accidentally) won their spin on the genetic roulette wheel. As the geneticists headed towards seventy, they realized that they needed more freedom. A good lab and a planet of disciples seemed a dream they could realize when the government opened up the bidding for the next colony ship. They poured all their vast fortune into the charter and into recruiting. Indira's Telepathic abilities (which were a closely held secret) were invaluable in fundraising.

Two years later, Atticus Pace, Indira Pallon and 10,000 other souls (some of whom were the results of previous experiments, not all of them successful) set out for a small 4 planet system with a yellow sun.

The most interesting colonists they had with them, however, didn't want to be there at all. A small contingent of Telepaths, Telekinetics, and Empaths were along for the ride. Some of these abilities were naturally occurring, some engineered. None of them was welcome on Terra. One of the reasons the Pace-Pallon charter had been approved (when it really shouldn't have been) was that the government at the time was thrilled that it now had a place to send all the supernormals it didn't know what to do with. Some of these supers were fleeing a life of persecution and secrecy; some were sentenced to the colony. All were freaks.

And there was no place on Terra for freaks.

Stuart and I slowly surveyed the wreck that was Irrfan's house. Except for the far corner of the structure which sported a broken roof and side wall, the house seemed to suffer more from neglect than anything else. Most windows had boards over broken glass. The paint was chipped and weathered to the point of colorlessness. Once through what had been the front door we made our way through piles of refuse to what appeared to be a living room. To one side was an enormous and surprisingly pristine plate glass window that showed the view from the mountain in all its glory.

On the opposite wall, almost leaning against it sat a large, morbidly obese man. This was Irrfan. He was oily, slovenly and the smell emanating from him was appalling. I had the horrible feeling that his chair also had a built in toilet, because it looked as though he hadn't stood up (or thoroughly bathed) in years. I flicked a glance at Stuart, but Stuart was acting as though this was all quite normal and that the gross stuff was to be ignored. I did my best, but the smell was overpowering.

"Welcome, Jane, Stuart. I am Irrfan." His voice was softer and at normal volume. If you closed your eyes (and nose) it was a very nice voice.

"How do you do?" I asked, not really sure how to proceed.

"Ill, actually. Dealing with living creatures makes me quite sick. Too much motion. Too many thoughts. In view of that we will keep this brief." Irrfan took a deep breath as if trying to calm nausea.

"The Objects you are worrying so about (and I think you should be worried) are changing inside. Things are growing, many thousands of them. Telepaths can't read them, but TKs can, as can your pet MEmp. You are right, Jane, they are alive but have no consciousness. They exist, they have a drive, but they do not think."

"What is the drive?" I took a step forward, despite the stench. Irrfaan blanched at the movement, looking pale green, and I froze.

"Thank you. What are the usual things that drive living creatures? Stuart?"

Stuart spoke softly, as if afraid even talking would make Irrfan feel worse. "Traditionally, they are shelter, sex and food, among other things."

"A place to start, my friends. Since we are pretty sure that these creatures exist more on a viral level than anything else, I think that any attempt they make to get either shelter, sex or food (or god knows what else) from us will be ugly, if not fatal to our race."

I spoke more gently, following Stuart's lead. "You've scanned one of these things? Up close I mean."

Irrfan laughed gently, then looked like he regretted it. "Look in the left corner of the room."

We both turned our heads and saw, under the debris of a partially caved in roof, an Object.

"He has been my companion these 3 days. Not much of a talker, but very entertaining nonetheless."

I had to ask the question the General had really sent me to ask. "What do you think will happen?"

Irrfan shifted uncomfortably in his seat. "I think that each of the 5,454,631 Objects covering our benighted planet is gestating thousands of creatures. When they are full grown they will come out and do whatever it is they want. I am calling them the *tapetia mortis*, which is Latin for "carpet of death." He smiled. "I used my Terran language translator and got ten different versions of *tapetia mortis*, like *teppi dauða* (Icelandic), *tapiŝo de morto* (Esperanto) and the one in Afrikaans which was *tapyt van die dood.* I toyed for a second with calling them "Dood" but it made me giggle, and that wasn't the feeling I was trying to evoke."

He paused. His color was not improving. I had the feeling that he would pass out if we stayed with him long enough. What else was I supposed to ask about? Oh, yes...

"Yes, Jane, you seem to have some latent Micro Telekinetic abilities." Right. He can see everything I am thinking. Stuart looked very uncomfortable at Irrfan's statement.

Irrfan looked annoyed at Stuart for the first time. "Don't be a fool, Stuart. Being the most powerful supernormal in every relationship isn't all it's cracked up to be." Stuart started to protest, clearly embarrased that Irrfan was bringing this up in front of me, but Irrfan stared him down.

"Tell General Armstrong that you need training and quick. It may not help you now, I'm not sure anything can, but I think it will be very useful in the future." He started tapping his fingers gently, rythmically on his arm rest. He was clearly growing agitated. He flicked his fingers out, dismissing us. Stuart and I turned slowly, but I had one burning question. I thought it a loudly as I could in hopes that he would answer it in spite of himself.

When he answered it was a whisper in my head as we slowly passed out of the house and down the broken path into the yard.

"I exist, Jane, in this squalid solitude, because it is the only way for me. My creators took gene mods by the handful, trying to create the next leap in evolution. They had no regard for whether or not a person could stay sane with all the "gifts" being forced on him.

"I stay away from people because I can't stop reading their thoughts. I can't block it out. Anywhere within 5 miles, I am forced to know everything. Whether your lunch agrees with you, or you are angry with your room-mate, or in Stuart's case, whether your balls itch. But the Telespatial part of it is the worst and I can never escape *that* no matter where I move. While I am being bombarded with your unwanted thoughts I am also being overwhelmed with the sounds of blood moving through veins and arteries, the squeak of joints, the rubbery sounds of tendons, the great sloshings of the heart—and don't even ask about the bowel sounds. Every step or breath you take has those noises, but also the sort of extreme motion sickness you felt in the shuttle. I feel it with everything that moves. Everything."

"I'm sorry," I thought gently.

"Thank you, my dear." His voice faded away. Stuart and I walked out the yard and started the two mile trek back to the shuttle.

Thankfully, Stuart had left the hatch open and the fans on, so the shuttle was only half as disgusting as I had expected it to be. Better prepared this time, I concentrated on the ground as we lifted off. Stuart wasn't looking at me much. He seemed embarrased.

"Should we fly faster or slower? Which will help, do you think?" He was making a show of adjusting controls as we hovered for a second.

"Gently, thanks." And Stuart guided the shuttle with a soft touch. I was still queasy, but was having a much better time controlling it.

"Jane?" It was Irfaan in my head again. I looked quickly at Stuart, but he gave no sign. "Everyone has their limitations. Even me. Even you and Stuart. Soften the cold eye of youth." I attempted to digest this, not really sure what that meant, but he continued. "And tell Sam to call his son. Today."

Irrfan's voice faded. The General has a son? I was so surprised I completely lost my concentration on the planet's surface...and vomited. Gross.

23:00 – Guard Tower

I was showered, scrubbed, teeth scoured and thoroughly cleansed after returning from that vile shuttle flight. I stepped into the Quad, running my hand through my half dry hair. I was supposed to meet Stuart in the Armory and I was late. I was halfway past one of the Objects when I noticed that one light still shone in the Guard Tower.

We had radioed in Irrfan's words to the General in between my dry heaves. I had heard a dead quality in the General's voice that scared me. And the way he had repeated, "Call my son. He really said that? Call my son?" Since I had been the only one to hear that part of Irrfan's message I had had to confirm it over and over. He seemed dazed.

I did not want him to be dazed. If he wasn't OK, how would any of us be OK?

I changed course and went up the stairs.

I found the General sitting in his favorite spot at the big community desk. His boots were up, his uniform jacket unbuttoned. It was his standard attitude, but... I scanned him. He was all tension, his heart beat was kind of...slow and lumpy. I saw the half empty bottle of spirits next to him. No cup.

I stood there for a minute or two, waiting for him to notice me, but he seemed lost in thought. Or drink. Or both.

"Sir?" I stepped into the light.

"Come in, Jane. Pull up a desk." He didn't turn, or even shift position. I walked over and, after a moments consideration and seeing no chairs handy, sat on the desk next to his booted feet.

"I wanted to see if there was anything I could do for you." He turned his head towards me and I could see his eyes for the first time. Huge, in the near darkness, they would have been handsome eyes if they hadn't looked so defeated. He reached for his spirit bottle and took a swig. He offered the bottle to me and I took it. I took a swig. Nasty, yes, but this is what grownups drink, right? I handed it back.

"There's nothing to do, Jane." He resumed staring out at the dark countryside.

"I didn't know you had a son, Sir."

The General put his feet back on the ground and straightened his uniform a bit. "Hadn't spoken to him in over a year, until today." He seemed to fall into a reverie. I gathered from this that the conversation had gone badly.

"Do you have many secret children, General?" I asked, awkwardly trying to lighten the mood.

He looked over at me, giving me his full attention for the first time. It was like he was trying to read me, but without the extra talents. I smiled. He grimaced and we both took another swig.

"You mean with a girl in every port?" He stood up, buckling his jacket. "No, I only have the two."

Confused yet again, I replied with, "Two?"

He headed for the stairs. "Good night, Jane."

"Good night, Sir."

23:30 – Armory

I opened the door to the Armory and slipped in. The room was dark, with a bit of moonlight coming through the skylight. I couldn't see Stuart, but I could feel he was there.

"Why are you so late?" He was moving towards me quickly. I could feel the tension running through his body, washing over me. I could sense his arousal and my own body responding.

"I had to be sure I was really clean. Took longer than I thought."

Suddenly he was kissing me, my mouth, my breasts, urgently pulling off my clothes. I threw his jacket on the floor and started on his belt when he paused.

"Have you been drinking? You taste like…different."

I shook my head and unbuttoned his shirt. Unbidden, I pictured the General's face as he had looked just a few minutes ago in my mind. So sad, almost lost.

Stuart kissed me again. "I like it."

He sat me on a munitions locker and was inside me before I knew it. But I couldn't shake the image of the General, so defeated, until, at last, our mutual release made coherent thought impossible.

ENTRY 3-1-3

A Note about The Tour and the constituents of the Pace-Pallon System

Pace-Pallon was composed of 4 planets orbiting a yellow sun, with their functions dictated by their geography and resources. Pace 1 was the largest, with the best climate and an enormous amount of arable land. Pace 3 was a hellhole with dangerous seismic activity that contained a tremendous amount of minerals and metals. Pace 2 was the industrial center where everything was manufactured from ships to hairnets. Pace 4, my home, was the center of government and the military and had very limited access for civilians.

Every citizen of Pace-Pallon did Compulsory Service (one year each on Pace 1-3) and then was allowed to choose where they would settle. Compulsory Service (known as The Tour) started on each citizen's 22nd birthday. On your 25th birthday a citizen who had satisfactorily completed his/her 3 years got a free trip to Pace 4 (for most people it was the only time they would get there) and they could either have been recruited by the military or government service or been allowed to choose their planet.

Pace 2 was the most populated at about 30 million as it constantly needed people for its factories, etc. The second most peopled world was Pace 4, not surprising since 4 was comprised of the military, governmental and administrative workers for all four worlds. Then there was Pace 3, where the toughest souls went, living in domes and onboard orbiting ships. The denizens of Pace 3 were the best compensated of all the workers on all the worlds (it was the only way they could get anyone to go there). And lastly there was beautiful Pace 1 with its farms, grasslands, mountains and lakes.

We, the supernormal students, were all created on 4, the tubs that grew us were on 4 and we expected to live our whole lives on 4. The only chance we would ever have of seeing our other worlds was through The Tour unless we were on assigment. Either way we would never have gotten to choose our home. Being illegally alive in the first place, that was not an option for us.

Every person on every Pace planet did The Tour, even normals. The supernormals were usually "buddied" with at least one other super, but other than that would live as normals. This was a really exciting prospect for most of us; like a Prince getting to live as a commoner for 3 years. This secrecy was vital for the clearest of reasons: most of us were being trained to be either spies or assassins. The powers above needed to know who wasn't capable of living in secret. Also, the relationships supers established with normals could be used later in cementing false identities. Every School graduate was given a new identity and background and then dropped into the deep end.

I was really looking forward to my Tour. Stuart had spoken rapturously about the beauties of Pace 1. Fields of grain and whole miles of flowers in color coordinated rows. The wind captured the combined scents and caressed the countryside with their perfume. I wanted to see it. Better yet, I wanted to smell it.

Both Stuart and Wilby had completed their Tours successfully. Stuart had requested (and had been chosen) to be a School instructor and Wilby was on Pace 4 marking time before his first assignment. At this point Atalanta was about a half year away from her Tour and I was over four years away from mine. Arthur was somewhere in between. Arrow Peters had been back from her Tour for 2 years. The General's Tour was so long ago, he told me once, that he barely remembered it. I don't know that I believed him.

<u>09:00 – School Infirmary, July 1, 2869</u>

"Ready, Jane." Wilby sounded vaguely annoyed, but I was starting to think that that was just his normal mode. We were in the triage unit of the Infirmary. Standing next to him was an older man who wore nothing more than a very tiny pair of shorts.

"This is Anson. He is a Grade 6 Assassin for our beloved Government and has come here today for your first anatomy lesson in the Micro Track." I looked at Anson and he nodded at me. Words were apparently unnecessary for a Grade 6 Assassin.

Wilby walked over to a blank wall and pulled down a chart of the human body. He pointed at the red lines running through the human outline.

"Arteries."

I nodded.

"I will name each artery and you will see if you can feel it within Anson's body. He will assist you. New Micros tend to lack control, so he will also be able to protect himself if you lose control inside him."

I looked from the chart to Anson, who waited calmly. "What am I looking to feel? How will I know that I've got the right thing?"

Wilby nodded, clearly having expected this question, "Most of us learn to differentiate the feel of the walls of the arteries (and veins) from the surrounding tissue. It is a matter of practice. But, I think, you should also look for…" he hesitated for a second, but I couldn't think why, "the motion of the blood cells."

Anson looked sharply at Wilby who pointedly ignored him and continued, "If you can feel *that*, you will have many clues as to where the blood is going. Arteries take the flow downward, veins take the flow upward and have valves to help. Once you know what you are doing, finding the heart will be a piece of cake, but the heart is rarely the goal. You may be looking for something very subtle. The veins and arteries can lead you where you want to go if you can recognize them for what they are."

I was impressed, despite myself. "Can all Micros do all this?"

Wilby shrugged, but I could tell he was warming to the subject. "Each of us has, say, natural preferences in identification. My specialties have always been the nervous system and, like you, muscle groups. You said something about 'hearing the music' of the muscles?" He grinned, actually grinned. It was blinding. If he was handsome perpetually annoyed, smiling made him dazzling. "I can feel that, too."

I found myself smiling back unintentionally. "Could you always do that?"

He shrugged again, but this time modestly, "As long as I can remember. Took a while to figure out what it was I was sensing, but I can't think of a time when I didn't feel it." He took a breath, returning to the lesson at hand. "The nerves and all the other systems, pulmonary, vascular, respiratory, digestive, endocrine, immune, lymphatic, vestibular, musculoskeletal, etc., I learned."

"Like this?" I gestured toward Anson, who watched me warily. Was it that Telespatial hint Wilby had given him, or had I grown horns?

"Like this," Wilby said firmly. "Now, we will start with," and he pointed to the diagram, "the vertebral artery."

I closed my eyes and concentrated, trying to match the artery on the diagram with the appropriate area on Anson's neck. I started with the skin, which felt like rubber and had no movement I could detect. I tried to force my mind through, breaking past the skin. Immediately I was awash with sensations: blood moving fast, in pulses, rubbery tubes that were probably veins and arteries, the gentle movement of shoulder and neck muscles, the quiet scraping of the neck vertebra as he turned his head slightly… It was fascinating. I confess that I lost myself for a minute, enjoying the sensations.

"Jane." Wilby was calling me back to myself.

I moved my focus back to the part of the neck where the artery was supposed to be. There it was, or something was. A tiny fleshy sort of tube filled with rushing water, not blood. It was moving down fast, but in spurts. I widened my scan for a second. Ah, with the heartbeat. Cool. I concentrated harder, trying to discern more about the blood when Anson cried out. I stopped and my eyes flew open.

"She was about to burst the artery. I could feel the walls thinning." Anson looked pale and sat down heavily on a nearby chair.

"I am so sorry," I started, but Anson waved me off.

"Did she get it?" Wilby had a hand on Anson's shoulder. Anson nodded. Wilby looked over at me.

"That was very good, Jane. You just need to know your own strength. Next time you will test yourself to find out how little effort you can put into the scan to get the same results."

"I am really sorry, Wilby." Wilby had already moved on, unconcerned. Anson stood up again, apparently ready for the next round.

"This is training, Jane, and that is why we have Anson here. He is better at this than you can imagine and he would have taken you out before you could seriously damage him."

I looked at Anson with interest, "How?"

Anson smiled, but Wilby answered, "All in good time. Now, a couple of things to think about for your next try. I spoke to some of your teachers and they all commented on your habit of closing your eyes when you scan."

"They hate it when I do that."

"They are right to. Listen, part of the foundation of knowledge you are getting here is for attack, but the other is for defense. You can be all-seeing and all-knowing in a controlled classroom environment, but out there you have eliminated one of your most valuable weapons."

I knew I shouldn't be defending my crutch, but I couldn't help it. "But if I can sense the movement, I can do without regular sight."

Wilby shook his head. "There are threats that can be seen but not felt. What if something dangerous is immobile until ready to strike? Do not depend on movement and mass alone. I'm glad you can fight without sight, but why take it away when you don't have to?"

I looked at the floor. I felt petulant, but knew he was right. Wilby continued, having made his point. "Another reason to combine sight and scan is that it can be another guidepost, as can touch." He looked at Anson, who cocked his head to the side, waiting. "The Femoral artery, for instance, in the upper leg."

Dutifully, I started to concentrate on where I thought it was (eyes open this time), but Wilby shook his head and I desisted. I could feel the tension in him as he scanned, looking at Anson's upper leg, right side.

"Now I have the femoral artery." Anson nodded confirmation. Wilby continued, "If I give the artery a little squeeze for a second, then let go, squeeze, then let go and on and on, I can, if you put your hand there, make a pulse."

I gently put my hand on the ...almost naked man's thigh. Anson's eyes twinkled at my discomfort, "You have to press harder, or you'll never feel it." Good grief, that was a line.

Grimacing, I pressed down firmly on Anson's thigh. And there it was. An artificial pulse in the artery. I looked up at Wilby.

"This sort of trick is used to impress upon people that we have control over their bodies. It is subtle, but works for those with good imaginations. Of course there are also the old standbys of pinching the Achilles tendon…" Anson sucked in his breath sharply. "Or pressure on the sciatic nerve…" Anson let out a small groan. "Or the old classic of the descending colon squeeze." Anson doubled over in pain, but then straightened up again a second later, sweating.

Wilby continued, oblivious, apparently, to the agony he had just caused so casually, "Seeing the effects of your actions gives you all kinds of useful information. It also lets you know when your victim," and he gestured towards Anson, "could use a break. Not everyone's pain tolerance is the same and not everyone's mental tolerance for...prodding is the same."

"So, we are learning how to torture?"

Wilby stepped closer to me and looked in my eyes. "No. And yes. We are learning skills to protect ourselves and the people we have been assigned to defend. If a murderer, for example, is going to kill more people but knowing what he knows will save them, what would you NOT do to get that information?"

I shrunk back from him, but he went with me, this time taking my hands. His grip was strong.

"Would you let innocent people die because you are squeamish?"

"No?" I said as I looked up at him, silently pleading with him to end this uncomfortable conversation. He dropped my hands and turned away from me, slowly pacing.

"What's the problem, Jane?"

I thought about it for a long minute. I didn't want to see someone writhe in agony, us both knowing that I had caused it. I didn't want the smell of sweat, of fear as I tortured someone. I didn't want to get carried away and kill. But when it really came down to it, I didn't want the look on their face as I made them scream. "I guess I don't want the memory of hurting someone to stay with me forever."

Wilby stopped pacing. "There are worse things. Can you think what they might be?"

Oh, yes, I knew. I knew now that this was where the entire lesson had been heading from the beginning. "The pictures of the faces of all the people that died because I did nothing."

Wilby stepped closer again, his eyes fierce. "No, not because you did nothing, because you didn't do your *job*."

Now Anson spoke, this time in a more fatherly manner. "We, and all supernormals, were bred solely to fulfill the duties of taking care of our people in ways that normals can't. We are special. Different. We will never *be* normal, no matter how that damn Tour tries to convince us. We will never fit in and the normals will never completely trust us."

"Great." This might have been the worst conversation I'd ever been part of. Seeing the horrified look on my face, Wilby shot a look at Anson.

"But," Wilby continued for Anson, "we can be useful, we can help and we can earn respect. Remembering our duty is the key."

I digested this for a second. "But you work for the Government."

"We do."

"Stuart hates this Government. He says they own us and that we have no freedom." And now I sounded like a whiny teenager. Wilby and Anson seemed light years beyond me. I had never really thought about my duty. Duty to what? To whom?

"Without this Government, we wouldn't exist. Without this Government, we wouldn't have an education or a job or a purpose. Without this Government we would be hunted as freaks."

"Like on old Terra," I said to myself. "But we protect the normals that fear us, who would hunt us down if they could? Why?"

Anson took that one. "We are all humans and we all deserve survival. Not all normals hate us."

I shook my head in wonder. "Just most."

Wilby nodded agreement. "Our Government is flawed and it has made some whopping mistakes, and it will make more, but with this Government we are valued and needed. Stuart is a fool if he wants to be freed from that." He moved back to the chart of the human body. "We are where we were designed to be. We are not accidents and we are not lost and left to fend for ourselves. How many normals can say that?"

I didn't answer and it seemed as though an answer wasn't required.

Wilby pointed at the next artery. "Right common carotid."

I concentrated, this time eyes open.

Excerpt from the Journal of General Samuel Armstrong, July 1, 2869

The Objects didn't land on all four of our planets at the same time. Some planets were closer and some were further away from the Objects' entry point into our system. Pace 2 was hit first, then 1, then 3 and then 4. Even though the landings were a little spaced out, they all managed to happen within 2 days of the initial hit on Pace 2. I am hoping that this means that Pace 4 has a 2 day window before those Objects open and discharge whatever the hell is in them. This assumes, of course, that they won't wait for each other to mature and all open up at the same time.

So now anyone that can is watching Pace 2 as our test planet. Some here hold the hope that even if Pace 2 is lost that we will be able to learn from what happens to it and save the later planets. The Government is evacuating as many people off 2 as they can, but there will still be a lot of people left. Besides, where can they go? To another planet with more Objects?

We are all so screwed.

11:30 – Guard Tower

I climbed the stairs to the Guard Tower slowly. Two and a half hours of Wilby's Micro class had been much more tiring than I'd expected. My brain hurt. Once I reached the main room I noticed that the General was not at his usual perch at the communal desk. One of the administrators divined from my glance who I was looking for and jerked his head in the direction of the General's office. I nodded my thanks and headed that way.

I raised my knuckles to the door and was on the verge of knocking when I heard, "Come in, Jane," from inside. I opened the door and went in. The General was sitting at his desk staring at a monitor that I hadn't seen there before.

"Sir, how did you know..?"

"Cameras, Jane, cameras. Come sit over here." The General beckoned me to a seat next to him behind the desk. Once I had sat down I had full view of the monitor the General had been watching.

"What are we watching?" On the monitor was what looked like a town center teeming with people going about their business. There was a fountain in the center of the square and in the fountain sat an Object. No one was paying any attention to it.

"This is a live feed of the main square of Oblea, a factory town on Pace 2. The Objects on 2 have been in Pace-Pallon the longest, so we are keeping an eye on 'em."

We sit in silence for a minute or two, staring at the monitor.

It was weird sitting in purposeless silence with the General. "Wilby said you wanted to see me, Sir, after the lesson?"

He nodded. "You did well, today, Jane, real well." He grinned, still looking at the monitor. "You didn't kill Anson—or even seriously injure him." He reached for the coffee cup he had sitting on the desk. He caught my eye. "I won the pool."

"The pool," I repeated, surprise written all over my face.

"Always have a pool for the first lesson Micros. Legend is that Abernathy, the Keeper at the time Wilby started here, won over 10,000P after his first anatomy class."

That was a fucklot of money. "So, I take it that Wilby…"

"Accidently killed the Assistant? Oh, yes." The General, still grinning, took a swig of his coffee. He was looking amused enough that I wondered what was really in the mug. "They were using normal Volunteers at all lessons then, even the initial ones." His grin turned to a grimace, "That may not have been the best idea. They switched to experienced Micros (until students gain some control) about 8 years ago. Cut down the casualties by quite a bit."

I leaned back in my chair. I would probably have killed Anson if Anson had been a normal. Good god. I was messing with some scary shit.

The General settled into his chair and put his feet up. "Took a hell of a lot of fun out of the pool, I can tell you."

"I appreciate your confidence in me, Sir." I said weakly, wondering where he got that confidence and where I could get some.

"And Anson. We were lucky to get him for your next two lessons with Wilby. After that you'll have normal Volunteers."

"Right. Normals." At that last word the General put his coffee cup down and...seemed to stop what he had been going to do. I scanned him and felt the tension in his shoulders and legs. I thought that he had been about to stand up, but now he was trying very hard to look casual. Funny, I thought. And I would have bought it, too, if I hadn't been able to read him.

"I know, Jane, that you don't know a lot of what you supers call normals." I could feel him trying to force his shoulder muscles to relax. It wasn't working.

"Just you, Sir, Arrow and some of the administrative staff."

"I just want to caution you that this is Pace, not Terra. *All* of us have been genetically engineered. All of us came out of the tubs altered. The supernormals are rare, true, but not so unique."

There was a knock at the door that made me jump. The view on the General's monitor momentarily switched to show the corridor outside the office door. It was Atalanta. The monitor switched back to the town square.

"Come in, Atalanta." The door opened and Atalanta sashayed in, stopping suddenly when she saw me sitting with the General. The General ignored our mutual surprise at seeing each other in this context. "Report."

Atalanta stood up straighter. "We are fully scanned and processed up until 22:00 today. Nothing really of interest, mostly general worries about the Objects. I left the detailed findings and," she smiled her beautiful smile, "scuttlebutt with your Assistant."

"Good. Dismissed." The General started to turn back to the monitor but Atalanta paused at the door.

"See ya round, General," She cooed and undulated out the door, closing it behind her.

He looked at me out of the corner of his eye, as if both amused and embarrassed.

"Subtle, isn't she, Sir?" The words were out of my mouth before I realized it. But his grin was back, as if he was relieved that I had acknowledged her blatant come on—and thought it was a joke.

"Like a shuttle crash."

"You were saying, Sir?"

"Ah, yes." He put the mug down and rested his elbow on one of the arm rests of his chair. There it was again, I thought, the attempt to look casual. Why? "Just because a normal doesn't have a big sign over his head screaming out his modifications doesn't mean that he doesn't have any worth paying attention to. As a warrior, as a fighter you must *never* assume that you know all the weapons that your enemy has. That will mean failure of your mission and death for you and your team."

His heart was beating faster and the tension in his shoulders was acute. This was very serious for him. Serious for him, then serious for me.

He took a deep breath and looked at me intently. "There are normals and there are true normals. A true normal is something you've never seen in your life."

"Yes, Sir. But you've seen them?"

"Twice a year when the Terran war ships come and check in."

"Do they seem very different to you?"

The General shrugged, "Well they can't lift shuttles with their minds, but other than that they seem like all the other people we know."

"That bad, Sir?"

The General let his amused twinkle be his answer as he turned back to his monitor. The tension slowly drained out of him. He flicked his fingers at me in his favorite gesture of dismissal. I got up and headed for door. I was not hurrying because I had never once left that office without his having the last word. I was not disappointed.

"Jane?"

"Sir?" I turned back. He looked especially thoughtful; his dark eyes were unfocussed as if his mind were somewhere else.

"Never underestimate anyone." He leaned back in his chair, boots up again. "There are no normals on Pace."

I nodded and left, my mind full of his warning. Why did he want me to know that now? And why was *he* telling me? Why didn't he have Wilby do it?

I checked my watch. Fuck. I was late for History and I'd missed lunch. We need to breed people that don't need to eat, I thought as my stomach growled.

The Quad bell sounded. I really was late now. I moved faster.

<u>*A Note on Normals*</u>

There was a certain arrogance that supernormals had when it came to their non-super counterparts. We tended to think that, as the General implied, that normals were purely ordinary. Pacey normals, however, were anything but. All were engineered for extra longevity (life expectancy for all *Paceys was 150 years) and extreme disease resistance.*

In some respects the supernormals were at a disadvantage since almost all of their 5 gene allotment was devoted to their extrasensory powers. Normals had quicker reflexes, better sight, smell and hearing. Some normals could see the different light spectra. There was even an experiment, I've been told, that allowed those bred to be soldiers to see heat signatures. Some could even track the footprints of their prey using the heat their feet had left behind.

Each designer usually tried to put in one "special" extra improvement to each normal fetus. There was one geneticist, Dr. Swithin Bishop, who was known for giving his embryos the ability to see at night, like a cat, but with human (as opposed to cat) eyes. Actual animal-human hybrids were a whole other story and had been outlawed 30 years ago when the current Government had taken over. More on that later.

These "secret" talents, while never obviously super, were usually kept private by the humans that possessed them. Everyone knew how badly the supernormals had been treated before they were outlawed and paranoia had turned into custom.

The only way to tell (without asking) what extra gift(s) a person had was by knowing their ID number which, if you knew how to read it, would give you all kinds of information.

For example: 3-2-325-11-86-2852-889431

The 3 means the third child of the genetic father (sexist, I know), the 2 means female, the 325 means she was born on Pace 3 in the 25th town (Dembiec on the main land mass), the 11 was the code for the supervising geneticist (our Dr. Swithin Bishop), the 86 meant augmented sight (in this case she could look at things miles away or microscopically, depending), 2852 was the year she left the tubs and she was the 889431st person to be "born" in Dembiec.

People used only part of the numbers for everyday things like shuttle licenses, military or government ID or to apply for travel papers. This girl would have used 325-2852-889431.

Full ID numbers were always kept confidential. Only your boss or your CO would know the whole number and then only if it was relevant to the job. Knowing someone else's full number without their permission was considered a serious privacy violation and was punishable by law. No one had a sense of humor about the ID numbers. No one.

<u>17:00 – Dormitory</u>

I walked in and flopped down on my bed, exhausted. Two more hours before I had to meet Stuart. Atalanta emerged from our bathroom wet and wrapped in a towel. She went to the mirrored bureau and started brushing her damp black hair. What was it I had wanted to ask her? Oh, right.

"So, you are the one that listens to all the recordings of everything that goes on here?"

Atalanta stopped brushing. She froze, actually. I had never seen her surprised. She always seemed to know everything—of course now I knew why.

"What are you talking about?"

"I know the whole School is wired. I just hadn't figured out who was listening until today."

She turned and looked at me; fear was in her lovely eyes.

"I repeat, what are you talking about?"

"The General told me that there are microphones everywhere. You had to know I would figure out what you were doing when you made your report in front of me today."

"Don't be ridiculous, Jane. I haven't seen you since guard duty this morning."

Puzzled, I scanned her, but it didn't help. I didn't know if her tension was from lying or from confusion. Aaah, I need more training.

"In the General's office? When I was there with him looking at the monitor of Pace 2? You did see the General today, didn't you?"

Atalanta turned back to her reflection and resumed combing her hair. "I did see the General today, if you must know, but you weren't there. He was alone."

I stood up and walked closer to her. This was unbelievable. "You're kidding, right?"

She gave a small laugh. "Do I kid?"

No, she didn't. What the fuck was going on? She really didn't remember seeing me there? How in the name of god was that possible?

"And by the way, don't get the idea what Wilby likes you just because you're both Micros now."

What? Now that was a change of subject. "Wilby doesn't like anyone but Wilby," I said, mind reeling.

Atalanta smiled alluringly at herself in the mirror. "Not always."

I could feel…Arthur coming along the corridor to our room. Hearing footsteps Atalanta looked over at me questioningly.

"Arthur," I answered the unspoken question unthinkingly. Then I mentally kicked myself. Why am I giving her information if she hates me so much?

Arthur burst through the door. He never knocked. Always trying to catch a glimpse of…something.

"Hey…" Arthur got a look of Atalanta wrapped in her towel. Wet. And lost the power of speech.

Atalanta looked from him to me. "I thought Arthur was more your type."

I ground my teeth. "I'm with Stuart."

Atalanta rolled her eyes at my choice of boyfriend. "Oh, right. *Him.*"

Arthur had recovered enough to speak. "We're doing a lifting contest in the Armory. Placing bets. Wanna come?"

Atalanta gave another little laugh. "Oh, how did you let this one go, Jane?" She cocked her head to the side. "Are you sure you are done with him, I mean for good?"

I thought for second. I couldn't have been more done with Arthur. Yuck. But I was curious what she would do to try to make me jealous. We both knew that I was no competition for her. Or did we? What was all that about Wilby? Hm?

I lowered my eyes and forced a blush (I can do that, but I doubt that ability was one of my 5 gene mods). "Of course. Don't be an idiot, Atalanta." I put as much "secret yearning" as I could into my tone.

Arthur looked confused. This was not unusual for him.

Atalanta pasted an innocent look on her face and raised her hands to her hair, ostensibly to put it in a ponytail. Her towel slipped down a bit revealing her large perfect breasts. She coupled this revelation with a look to Arthur.

His jaw hit the floor and he casually tried to bend a knee and sort of cross his legs (while standing, which was awkward) to conceal his erection. Atalanta giggled and dropped a hand to one breast suggestively. Arthur paled.

"Oh, knock it off, 'Lanta. He's going to faint."

"Fine." Her voice was hard again and she covered up, tucking the towel firmly around her. She started to walk back into the bathroom. "Stay away from Wilby." The door shut behind her.

Arthur looked at me. It was clear he would fuck anything at this point just to get some relief. Really makes a girl feel special.

I got up from the bed. "Don't even think about it, Arthur." And I left.

<u>22:00 – The Quad</u>

I had been wandering the Quad aimlessly for about an hour. I could hear the Lifting Contest that had gone on despite Arthur being, apparently, a no-show. From the cheers and shouts it sounded like a Macro, Paulette, had won. I enjoyed the competition and I usually did all right. I'd won once, but a lot of the stronger people hadn't come that night. But hey, a win is a win.

I walked by the first Object, scanning it absently. I stopped walking. Those tiny things that had been moving felt different. They had…feet! Or legs or something. And it wasn't a vague feeling of individual movement anymore, there were thousands of individual creatures, small (but not as small as they had been even this morning) and moving in all different directions. I felt dizzy with the movement. Feeling nauseous, I quickly disengaged.

I took a step back and did my centering routine to calm down. I felt Pace 4 solidly beneath my feet. I moved up from it, trying very hard to keep my eyes open, and was once again assaulted by movement, movement and more movement. Now thoroughly panicked, I disengaged and backed far away from it. Was it just this one? I had to know. I didn't *want* to know at all, but I had to find out.

Feeling disinclined to moving closer to Object 2 I reached out to see if I could scan it long distance. As soon as my mind touched it I was again overwhelmed with the motility of these, what did Irrfan call them? Oh, yes, *tapetia mortis*. The carpet of death. If they grow at all this is going to be one huge fucking carpet.

The other 3 Objects read the same. They were all teeming with…life?

I was on the stairs to the Guard Tower before I even knew what I was doing.

<u>22:10 – Guard Tower</u>

The General was leaning back, boots up as usual, at the communal desk in the main room. A large bottle stood next to him, mostly empty. I noticed that it was a different type of spirits than he had shared with me yesterday.

I caught a quick look at his face before fear compelled me to speak. His expression was desolated, his eyes sad.

"They have legs, Sir. Or feet. They're individuals now!" I blurted.

He looked up at me and smiled sadly. "I know, Jane."

I sat down on the desk, deflated. Of course he knew. I'm an idiot.

He took hold of his bottle and handed it to me. The guy really seems to hate glasses. What the hell, I thought, and took a swig. It burned going down but I didn't mind.

"It's happening to all the Objects on all the other Paces, some more and some less." His voice was clear, but I could tell from the slow response of his muscles and the slow tracking of his eyes that he was pretty drunk. I took another swig, resting the bottle on my leg as I sat.

"Pace 2 still leading the way?"

"Yep." The General awkwardly reached for the bottle his large hand brushing my thigh as he took it. My breath caught. I was sure it was the spirits affecting me and not his touch …because that would be really weird. Right?

"The Government must have figured out a lot about these things by now, right Sir? All their experts must be able to tell us something?"

He shrugged. "We know that the Objects seem to be impervious to just about anything we can dish out—or rather that we are *willing* to dish out. They've tried drowning them (inconclusive), setting them on fire (they didn't burn) and nuking them, sort of."

"They *nuked* them?" I asked, incredulous.

He nodded. "Well, they tried to. In the middle of the Wastes. They'd been prepared to do it, but pulled the plug at the last minute. Problem was that if they'd used the explosive force they felt they needed to make a dent in that shell, the bomb itself (and it would have had to have been pretty fucking powerful one) would have created enough fallout that we'd have to abandon the planet anyway. Especially if it turned out they would have had to use one bomb for every Object."

"But there are millions…"

"…on each planet. I know. It seems a very clear case of win the battle/lose the war." The General took another swig, clearly depressed by this reiteration.

"Why not just pile all of them up together and nuke that?" I took the bottle back from him and drank.

"They are afraid to move them. They're afraid not to. What if what's inside is waiting for one good crack from outside to come out and…do whatever it is they're gonna do?" His fingers brushed mine as he took the bottle back again and I felt a little sort of thrill. What the hell is wrong with me? "They even tried super-heating them, then vibrating their insides to a pulp, but that seemed to make the little things inside move faster, possibly speeding up the maturity rate, so they stopped that experiment, too. Someone else apparently suggested just crushing them completely flat, but they were afraid of that, so it was never tried." The General sighed. "So now their policy is 'wait and see.'"

"That's insane. Sir." I was a little embarrassed by my own temerity, but this did seem crazy to me.

"You'll get no argument from me, Jane. And, hindsight being what it is, it seems to me that we have fewer options now than we did two days ago." I looked up in surprise. "What was just an almost completely solid Object is now a shell holding *somethings*," he explained. 'Wait and see' will be our undoing, mark my words."

I looked at him in horror. He seemed to come out of his haze long enough to realize he was scaring me probably more than he needed to. "It isn't all the Government's fault. Mostly, but not all. I don't have any sure-fire solution either. But maybe, if we pay attention, we'll see something or sense something no one else has. Maybe that will help."

I could tell he was pacifying me, but I was willing to take it. I *wanted* to have confidence in my Government and in the General himself. "I hope so, General."

"Samuel. When we're alone you can call me Samuel," the General said, obviously relieved that he had thought of a way to change the subject. "You know I realized the other day that no one calls me that anymore?

I'm just The General or Sir or, sometimes, Dad, but never Samuel. And, dammit, I want someone to call me by my real name. You know, like a person, not just a job." He nodded to himself as if approving his own decision to share his first name. I started to protest, but he cut me off. "And don't go thinking I won't remember in the morning. I never forget anything." He took a drink. "Unfortunately."

"Samuel," that sounded really wrong to me, but whatever, "it's very late. You should go to bed." And then I blushed, this time naturally. Those are not the words you use to your boss.

Samuel laughed. "I suppose you are right, Jane. And you have a date." He stood up unsteadily. I reached out to help him but he waved me off. "Enjoy it now. That sort of thing is harder to come by when your name is 'Major' or 'Colonel.'"

"You see that for me, Si…Samuel?" I was surprised. Surprised that someone I respected had given more thought to my future, to my career, than I had.

"I do." He took a hesitant step towards me, but seemed to change his mind and turned towards the stairs. "Good night."

"Goodnight, Samuel," I said softly to myself.

23:00 – The Armory

I stood in the darkness, waiting for Stuart. He was late. Or I was early. I didn't know but I fully understood how Arthur had felt a few hours ago. I needed something and right now. My body was on fire. My heart was racing. I needed Stuart to show up. Or did I? Well, Stuart was the most likely to show up so that was good enough.

I heard the door open in the darkness. I sensed it was Stuart and that he wasn't quite in the state that I was in. I wasn't tremendously experienced, but I figured that it wouldn't be too hard to catch him up. I unbuttoned my shirt and dropped it to the floor.

Stuart stepped into the half-light. "Sorry I'm late." He stopped and stared. I definitely had his attention.

"It's all right." I unbuttoned and removed my pants.

He took a step closer to me. I took off my bra. I was no Atalanta, but breasts were breasts. I scanned him again. Ah, there we go.

He crossed the room to stand close to me, as if drinking me in. He stood there for second, not touching me, not doing anything. The anticipation was driving me crazy.

"Stuart?" I tried to keep the plea out of my voice without success.

He kissed me gently, cupping my breasts in his hands. That was nice, but my patience was already exhausted. I kissed him hard and his pants were undone and on the floor in a second. Earlier I had maneuvered an exercise mat to the floor near us and I now pushed him down on it.

I'd never taken the initiative before, but he wasn't complaining so I kept going. I kissed him deeply, then moved down to kiss his chest, then lower. He reached for me but I pulled back and carefully lowered myself down. My god. Fuck yeah.

He groaned in pleasure and we began to move together, first slowly, then urgently. When we once again reached the state where thought was useless he cried out, "Jane!"

And when I came a few seconds later a small voice in my head whispered, "Samuel."

ENTRY 4-1-4

Excerpt from the Journal of General Samuel Armstrong, July 2, 2869

Last night, in a clear breakdown of...sense I told my favorite Macro to call me by my first name when we were alone. I guess all this must be getting to me because I can't think what else would prompt me to do that. It has been a long time. A very long time.

The problem is, aside from the breach of discipline, Jane is young enough to be my daughter. And that wishful statement stretches the boundaries of the space/time continuum. I know that sort of thing isn't supposed to matter on Pace, but it bothers me. *Four years of Terran prejudices. I guess they'd sunk in more than I'd thought.*

But it felt good to have a woman call me by my name. Even if that woman is only a girl.

I must be losing my mind.

Well, at least the world is ending soon and none of this will matter.

I need help.

10:00 – Listening Post, Guard Tower

I stuck my head around the door to see Atalanta seated at a desk, earpieces on, apparently going over the last few hours of information gathered by the microphones. She looked up, surprised, and pressed a button on her console.

"What." Atalanta did not have a welcoming expression on her face. I ignored that fact.

"Two questions."

"Busy," she said as her hand hovered over the console.

"Just two." I came in the room and closed the door behind me. I could see that her curiosity was getting the better of her.

She leaned back in her chair. "Make it quick."

I pulled out the chair next to her and sat, uninvited. "One: are there microphones in the Armory?"

Atalanta smirked. "That room gets more action than any other part of the School. Nice work, by the way," as she patted my knee condescendingly, "in discovering your inner slut."

I have the power to blush at will, but, unfortunately, I don't have the power to *not* blush at will.

"I was just listening to last night's recording," Atalanta continued, "I'm glad you came in. Tell me what was happening…" and she put one of the ear pieces on my ear, “here.” Dear god it was Stuart and I in the middle of…aaaaah! My cheeks were burning. Like actually on fire.

“I am not going to fucking tell you anything.” I stood up and got away from her. Atalanta laughed and waited in silence. Waited for me to get the quid pro quo. I really wanted my second question answered.

“Well,” I started hesitantly, “he was putting his…” and I trailed off, mortified.

“His...?” Atalanta really was enjoying this, the bitch.

I was looking everywhere in the room but at her and the demon ear piece. “His Man Meat inside…”

I was interrupted by gales of laughter from my torturer. She laughed so hard, so unkindly, and for so long that tears poured out of her big dark eyes.

“Darling,” she said between gasps of laughter, “you must never, ever call it that again. It makes you sound like a teenager.”

“I *am* a teenager,” I murmured.

“Sorry, an idiot teenager.” She corrected herself. “Call it a cock or a member or even, if you must, a penis, but never Man Meat again.”

I let her laughter die down. “You done?”

She wiped the lingering tears from her eyes. “Oh yes, that was so much better than I had hoped for. What is your second question?”

“Can you give me the General’s ID code? The full one.”

Atalanta sat up abruptly, all evidence of mean spirited humor gone from her face. “Why do you need that? Who do you want it for?”

I sat back down. “No one. For myself.”

“Why?” She looked at me piercingly. I knew she was trying to scan me and was grateful that she couldn’t.

“None of your business. Will you help me?”

Atalanta looked away, chewing her lip. Weighing her options, I guessed.

“Wilby.” This was a statement. She stared at her screen, waiting for my answer.

“Yours,” I answered readily.

She nodded. “I can’t give you that number. Even looking at it is illegal.” She typed something into her console, then typed something else that looked like a whole mess of passwords. I made a bit of a show of looking away, to show her that I didn’t want anything else that was a breach of security protocol. She reached a particular screen then stood up and headed for the door.

“Wait until I’m gone, then go.” And she left.

Clever. She had to make sure that if she was read by a TP strong enough to override our built-in blocks to scanning that she hadn’t actually shown me anything herself. A cast iron bitch, yes. Stupid, no.

I found the number on what appeared to be the General's Personnel File. I read it over and over until I had it memorized and then I got the hell out of there.

All the way back to the dormitory I kept thinking 1-1-401-44-97799-2814-264 over and over, terrified I would forget it. I started going over what the numbers meant in my head.

First child, male, born on Pace 4 (none of this was unusual so far) but the 01 after the planet code meant...Bane, the capital of 4 and thus the capital of Pace-Pallon itself. This brought me up short. No one was born in Bane. Bane was a military base, essentially. And since there had never been any body births on Pace-Pallon his birth there couldn't have been an accident. I'd heard of stories of Terran women going into birthing contractions at the oddest times and places, but that just didn't happen here. How could he have been born there?

And the next number, 44, was supposed to be the number of the head and supervising geneticist. Who the hell was 44? I should be able to figure that out. Numbers were never reused, though they were supposed to be assigned randomly. That said, though, we had been out of double digits for hundreds of years. My geneticist, Dr. Anne deCardenas, was number 7833. That 44 was either an old number reserved ages ago, a special or a fake number, if there even was such a thing.

And what the hell was this 97799? I had never seen that many numbers in a custom designation. It could be something really kinky, too. Supernormals had been outlawed for over 100 years by the year the General was born, but people were still trying to sneak through some cool stuff. What did they give the General?

The 2814 was self-explanatory and put the General at 55 standard. That was not revelatory, but then there were the last numbers of the ID to send me into confusion again: 264. So that means that at some point there were 263 other impossible births in Bane. And they must have been viable when released from the tubs because anything non-viable (still births, serious malformations, etc.) would never have been assigned a number.

This was a really weird ID number, much weirder than I had expected. What did they do to him, to Samuel? What great secret was he harboring?

The bell rang. Class. Right.

<u>10:30 – Telepathy Instruction (Stuart)</u>

Arthur, 10 other Macros, a Micro, Gladys, and I waited in our usual large classroom. I'd missed a class or two (due to my new Micro training) and knew Stuart was touchy about that sort of thing. I was hoping that my girlfriend status would get me a pass on that. Stuart walked in, all tension and avoiding my gaze. Great. I was wrong. Wilby followed him in. I stared at him in surprise but he only smirked at me.

Stuart took a position at the front of the room. "As those of you that bother to come to class know, we have been working on identification. Now, I think it is time for a Pop Quiz."

What I was thinking now was that he was being an asshole.

"There are 15 of us here *today*," Stuart went on. I restrained myself from rolling my eyes. "You have ten seconds to stand in front of each person here, get the info you need to identify them, then move on to the next person. At the end of the approximately 2 minutes the Quiz will begin." He threw me a glance. "Good luck."

We stood in a sort of elongated circle and shuffled from person to person at ten second intervals. One by one I tried to get something from each person. Arthur, easy, too much information on that one, Gladys, slight hand tremors, Allison (Macro), rumbling nervous stomach, Garrett (also a Macro), convulsive swallowing, and on and on. Finally I was standing in front of Wilby, whom I read by the steadiness of his heartbeat, not to mention his height, and the strength of his smirk muscles (or something like that). Then I was in front of Stuart whom I identified by his combination of anger and partial erection. Geez. He wouldn't meet my eyes.

The timer went off. Stuart raised his voice, "Make it dark."

And it was dark, very dark. I could sense Stuart and Wilby moving people around in preparation for the Quiz. Stuart's hands were on my upper arms as he shifted me two steps to the left. His fingers gently grazed my right breast. Instinctively I slapped him. It was a quiet room and the sound carried across the quiet room.

"What was that?" Arthur asked.

"Quiet!" Stuart responded angrily. He moved away from me as quickly as he could. I could feel the waves (so to speak) of silent laughter coming from Wilby. It's so nice that I can make the people around me laugh, I thought sourly.

"Subvocalize for your answers." Subvocalization was a great trick for communicating with Telepaths when they were otherwise unable to read you. It was a ploy we used sometimes at school. The effort needed to say words (but at much lower than standard sounds levels) pushed the word-thought over the anti-Telepath block we'd all been bred with. "Five seconds each," Stuart continued, "for identification starting…now."

I focused on the test. In front of me stood my first test person.

"Allison," I said subvocally. I moved to the next.

"Arthur."

"Lee."

"Stuart." Man he was still really pissed.

"Gladys."

"Paulette."

"Indus."

"Francis." Etc., etc., until I reached Wilby.

I shook my head, silently taking him to task for laughing at me, knowing that he would be able to read my head shaking as disapproval. "Wilby." He started his silent laughter again. I moved on again to…

"Paulette." Again. Great, now Stuart was messing with me. Or maybe he was doing this with everyone.

And Wilby again. "Wilby." Even Wilby was less amused this time, I could tell.

Annoyed, I subvocalized, "We done yet, Stuart?"

We stood in darkness for another few seconds.

"Lights!" and the room returned to its original brightness. But Wilby had said it, not Stuart. Stuart was trying to remain calm and professional. Neither Wilby nor I was buying it, I could tell from Wilby's face, but some of the others might have believed. Not that I cared, really.

"You'll have your marks at our next class. Enjoy a free period as a reward. See you tomorrow." And with that Stuart smiled painfully and walked out of the room.

Wilby and I stayed behind for a second.

"I was going to try to get you out early for your second Micro lesson. Thought if I offered to assist him, Stuart would be more inclined to let you go." Wilby rubbed his chin ruefully.

"What do you think of that theory now?" I said in a not unfriendly tone.

Wilby shrugged. "Are you free now?"

I nodded. He gestured for me to precede him and we left.

The Biographical Information I have on General Samuel Armstrong

Let me start off by saying that a lot of this bio is based on hearsay, opinion and gossip (at the time I asked around about the General, I mean Samuel, I hadn't yet developed my later intense distaste for such things). I also was able to get an official CV for him by the simple means of asking for it from his assistant. I was clearly destined to be a super spy.

According to his CV he was born on Pace 4, but in Homestead, not Bane. He had left the tubs in 2814 and was still 55 Standard years old. His genetic parents had been Derek and Heike Armstrong and they had lived, according to this, in Homestead their entire lives. They had been Government workers (but not for this Government) and had died, apparently, in the coup. The fact that they had had last names was significant because that usually meant regular contact with offworlders. People like that would hardly have stayed in a little shit town like Homestead either—aside from the fact that they would never EVER have run across any offworlders there. There were no details on their potential extra abilities, but I hadn't expected to find any. That was private stuff.

Samuel was an only child, but that was neither here nor there. Some people would make a gene mod choice and when the kid was born love the mod so much that they would breed as many as possible with it. Sometimes, when the opposite happened, they would give up. And sometimes the people just wanted one kid. He had been raised by his parents which, while fairly common for a Pace normal, never happened for the supernormals. Stuart said that that is because the Government never wanted us to be more loyal to people than to It. Sure, why not.

Samuel had done brilliantly in school and had been moved into a military track even before his Tour. While on Pace 1 he met his wife, Ruth, and they married before his Tour was over. According to one of his admin's Ruth had been a real nut. She loved the outdoors and farming. Once she'd married Samuel she suddenly realized her future was going to be either a life by herself while he was shipboard or at his side in confined spaces with recirculated air. (Why she hadn't had the sense to see that coming defies explanation). The admin had never met Ruth, but she was sure Ruth had been a beautiful woman with more passion than sense. Sounded believable to me. Samuel had immediately been assigned as first officer on a merchant vessel that shuttled goods and people between planets. Ruth had gone with him, dutifully, and stayed with him for a year, even after he had been promoted to Captain.

Mallory, our Weapons Mistress, had known the General before the coup and told me that he had seen it coming and suggested that Ruth cook up their son and return to Pace 1 and safety. Ruth had reached Pace 4, gotten the embryo started and then took the tub with her back to Pace 1. This had been highly unusual and extremely difficult (those tubs were huge, complicated and extremely heavy, apparently), but she had done it. Their son, Ian Armstrong, had been released from his tub while his father was assuming command (at 26) of the insurgent forces.

Samuel's tactics were brilliant and the bloodshed minimal and they had won the day. The Government was now the Government. Brian, the wizened old security guard, told me that nobody beyond Pace 4 had really given a rat's ass about the coup. The only people that cared were the ones doing it. That seemed to be stretching it, but I wasn't one to look a gift source in the mouth.

Samuel the war hero was promoted to Colonel (skipping Major altogether) and given command of the space borne military (sub-light) fleet around Pace 1. This kept his marriage together a bit longer, but 3 years later he was given an offer that he couldn't refuse. Twice a year and for over 700 years the Terran military had sent a ship to Pace-Pallon to check in/up on them. They did this with all their colonies. For some ships, this was all they did. So one visit the Captain Berenice Lachailles offered Samuel a trip to Terra and advanced tactical training at the Confederation's much vaunted Blevins College. This was too good of an offer to pass up, so he went. He was gone 4 years. Ruth divorced him as soon as he'd left.

Once he had returned to Pace he had immediately been given command of the entire Pace-Pallon space-side military complex. He was now The General. He'd pushed relentlessly for resumption of our long defunct faster-than-light ship building program. It was amazing that he had even gotten the 6 ships built that he did, considering how little interest there had been in the project. The biggest and best one, the Scylla, *was the most impressive ship Paceys had ever made. It was almost as fast as...the weakest of the Terran ships. He had, according to our Infirmary Nurse, George, been immensely attached to these ships. He'd even been aboard the* Edo *when the drive had malfunctioned and the ship had exploded. George had been on duty in the Bane Great Infirmary when the General had been brought in. Samuel had come very close to death and it had taken him nearly a year to fully recover. A year no one seemed to know anything about.*

That Lost Year had puzzled me, I admit. It was skipped in the CV. None of my sources, such as they were, had known anything beyond the fact that no one had any proof of his having left Pace 4 during that year.

Once Samuel was ready, though, he'd gone back to work and stayed there until last year when he had abruptly retired. Retired and then became Keeper (Dean) at our School. Why he'd chosen that was beyond me and beyond all my sources, too. Mallory and George just shrugged at me and Brian squinted and said, "He'd been on those there ships for decades going strange places. Maybe he has Space Herpes." Now who could argue with that?

So, the questions remain:

Why is it a secret that he was born in Bane, when no one is born in Bane?

What happened in that Lost Year?

Why did he abandon his career to come here?

Oh, yes, and what is his top secret gene mod?

I wasn't sure how much I'd learned from all this.

<u>11:58 – Triage Ward, School Infirmary</u>

"To review: There are two main parts to the human nervous system, central and peripheral. The central consists of..." Wilby prompted.

"The brain and spinal cord," I answered. We were nearing the end of the lesson. I was tired, Anson, tiny shorts and all, looked tired and Wilby looked fresh as a daisy. Easy to do, I supposed, when one isn't either causing pain or receiving it.

"And the peripheral..?"

"Is everything else. Nerve-wise, that is." I sat down on one of the exam tables. Wilby walked over to the current chart and studied it for a second.

"Last thing. I want you to tell me what nerve I am affecting in Anson's body." Anson looked up in surprise, but didn't say anything. I guess he wanted to see if I could do it, too.

I nodded and felt Wilby's body tense up the way it usually did when he either scanned or manipulated something. I moved my scan to Anson, starting at his feet and moving up. I was already much more comfortable with all the weird little things the body did that were considered normal. I even knew what some of those functions were called. Feet, no. Legs, no. Man m… genital area, no. I moved out to the fingers, then up the arms. Wait. A little pulse in the… elbow. Ha!

"Ulnar nerve," I said, a hint of triumph in my voice. Wilby smiled and I heard Anson let out the breath he was holding. He rubbed his elbow. Oh, right, that would have hurt a lot.

"Good. Let's call it a day," Wilby said. I got down from the table to leave. "I hear there is going to be a fighting exhibitition this afternoon."

"Really," I said. That sounded cool. They hadn't had one of those since I had been at the School.

"It's in the Armory. Your favorite room." Wilby's smirk was back.

What the fuck? I tried not to blush, but then remembered that the Armory was everyone's favorite room at one time or another. At night that place saw more action than a bordello.

"But during the day, it's just an Armory, Wilby." I thought I had managed to sound detached and cool as I turned towards the door to go.

"According to the tapes I've seen, though, both your technique and Stuart's stamina have improved greatly," he said to my back.

I stopped walking as my life flashed before my eyes. I thought I'd been embarrassed before, but I'd been wrong. Involuntarily I put my hands to my cheeks. Cold as ice. Well, I thought ironically, I've figured out how to beat the blushing thing. Complete mortification always does the trick. Then my logic caught up with my brain. Tapes? Fucking Atalanta. What a bitch. I could only hope that Wilby was the only asshole she'd shown them to.

"Thanks," I said as I took another step towards the door. Wilby hurried and got in front of me, smiling willingly. I wished that he was ugly. Really fucking ugly. My wish did not come true.

"I'm sorry, Jane, I tend to take a more, shall we say, technical view of sex. Isn't that right, Anson?"

Anson was putting on his trousers. "Yes, it's true." He caught Wilby's eye and smiled ruefully.

Is there anyone, besides me, that Wilby isn't sleeping with???

"I don't think the natural sex act is something to be embarrassed about, Jane, but not everyone feels the same way." Wilby ran his hand through his perfect hair. Despite myself I felt I could watch him do that all day.

He looked at me expectantly. I have to say something? What would an actual sophisticated grownup say? How the fuck would I know that? So, I went with some version of the truth. "I don't know how I feel about that."

Wilby nodded wisely. "Quite normal at your age. I guess this whole topic was a rather awkward way of suggesting a kind of …trick that we Micros use."

Anson looked up sharply. Wilby gave him a blinding smile. The conversation paused for a second as the two of them seemed to stare each other down. In the end Anson shrugged.

"You mean a …sex trick?" They had those?

"Oh, yes," Wilby said happily. "It only works on men, unfortunately, but it, if used at just the right time, can make for a mind blowing orgasm."

Ah, there was a word I'd never heard anyone say out loud. He seemed even worldlier to me now.

"Isn't that right, Anson?" Wilby asked this without looking at him. Wilby kept his pretty eyes on me.

"Mind blowing. Absolutely." I noticed that Anson had removed his clothes again. This time all of them. And there was his…penis. Or member. Or cock… no, I wasn't ready to for that word.

"We haven't gone over the anatomy of the penis because it is part of the reproductive system and technically not really useful to our work. *But* the most important nerve in male sexual arousal is the dorsal nerve." Wilby gestured over the top of Anson's penis.

Wilby turned to me. This was really strange, but somehow fascinating. Do all adults sit around trading or, god forbid, demonstrating their sex tips? I thought not, but I was still curious.

"Try to feel for the nerve." And there was that look again from Anson to Wilby.

I felt for it and there it was. There was actually quite a bit of stuff going on down there. And more seemed to be happening every second that passed.

"Now," Wilby was next to me, gleam in his eyes, "give the nerve a hard squeeze."

I did and Anson gave a small cry of…pleasure? Or was that agony? I couldn't tell.

Wilby smiled again. "Just like that. Do that right as he is about to come and you won't believe the response."

I looked at Anson for my second opinion. "And it's really that good?"

"Unbelievable." I noticed that Anson was not putting his clothes on. He looked at Wilby. Wilby looked at him. I suddenly felt like I should be gone.

"Thanks," I said and I got out of the room. The door closed and I stood outside it for a second, thinking about this very, very odd lesson. My stomach rumbled and I started towards the Refectory, but reflexively glanced back and through the glass window in the Infirmary Door.

Naked Anson stood in there, eyes closed. Wilby was on his knees in front of him, his head blocking view of…

All right then, gotta go. And I went.

<u>14:00 – Practice Floor, Demonstration Room and Gallery</u>

I entered the second floor Gallery with a couple of dozen other students. We were going to get to see "real" fighting. I took a quick scan of the area and had to immediately disengage. Everyone was too excited and I didn't have enough control yet to know how to turn down the volume. I was excited myself. I wondered who was going to fight.

I saw the General standing off to the side, talking to Mallory, the Weapons Mistress. The Quad bell tolled fourteen times and The General made his way to the center of the practice floor. All the crowd sounds extinguished themselves within seconds.

"Today, boys and girls, we will have a little exercise in underestimation. I have a Pace normal who will fight a TP as well as a TK Micro and a TK Macro. I know most of you think that that should be a piece of cake and that no normal, even a Pacey normal can stand up to a super. We shall see if this is true today. The Pacey normal is…unusual, but that is really the point. Normals have been messed with just as much as you have and their talents are much easier to hide."

Some hands raised, but the General shook his head. "I won't tell you what the hidden gifts are of this normal. And you may never figure it out. But she'll give you a run for your money." At that *she* whispered excitement spread across the students both on ground and in the gallery where I was. There was only one woman who would stand a chance of making the point he was trying to make…

He took a couple of steps back and held out his arm theatrically, "Children, I give you Arrow Peters!"

Arrow stepped out of the shadows and on to the mat. She wore something tight and black that showed off her preternaturally toned copper arms and legs. Her black hair was in a tight knot at the base of her neck. She moved her small frame with lean power, like some ancient Terran predator. For the first time I was struck by how beautiful her severe, almost architectural body was. She was the anti-Atalanta who was all softness and breasts. Well, at least the two women had not liking me in common. Arrow ignored the crowd, her focus intense. Her black eyes alternated between the General and the door that would bring her opponent.

The General spoke again, “There will be three matches, unless someone taps out…”

Arrow audibly snorted at the idea. The General’s mouth twitched in amusement and …pride? I blinked in surprise. Is that what I saw? All of a sudden I was overwhelmed with admittedly inappropriate jealousy. Does she call him Samuel, too? Funny how I’d become so quickly attached to something that hadn’t seemed correct at the time. I calmed down. Sort of. So, I told myself, the first name thing was still a compliment. Take it for what it actually is, idiot.

“One more thing, kids, we have rules for hits, especially in the Micro match. A hit only counts if both the Micro *and* his victim acknowledge it. What I mean is, I can say I broke Arrow’s arm but if she didn’t feel either pressure or mild pain in her arm and acknowledge it, it doesn’t count. Now, we expect some real injuries, but serious ones imply a loss of control that *will* be punished.”

He held his arm up again, “Our first challenger is our resident Telepath Instructor, Stuart!”

Stuart, looking calm but pale came through the door and stood on the mat a respectful distance from Arrow. I was still annoyed at him, but pitied him as well. Even if he won he was going to have his clock cleaned. I scanned him and was shocked (almost literally) to feel his body swimming in adrenaline. He looked taller, handsomer, more bad-ass, standing there, waiting for the Ok to fight.

The General backed off the mat, watching the antagonists closely.

“Fight!” The General bellowed.

Stuart and Arrow started circling each other slowly, sussing each other out. Arrow’s body was taut but calm (how she did that was beyond me) and her well-toned heart beat steadily. Stuart wasn’t as calm as she was, but not nearly as panicked as I would’ve been in his shoes. This was partially because he was scanning her as he was moving.

Suddenly she kicked her leg at his chin and he ducked just in the nick of time, immediately swinging his fist at shoulder level towards her face. She blocked with her arm, but his motion continued as he swept a leg to knock her feet out from under her, which he did. She fell easily, too easily, and rolled like some kind of dancer assassin coming up with a roundhouse punch to his gut.

It hurt, I could tell, but Stuart hid it and backed up, prepping for his next attack. She coiled down like an unholy spring, pressing her advantage. She whipped behind him, punching his kidneys. He turned and grabbed her around the neck. He was taller and heavier than she and they both paused for a second with his arm around her throat.

In a flash she turned around in his grip and head butted him, breaking his nose. Stuart, backing up, released her and held up his hand in surrender.

We all broke into cheers as the General declared Arrow the winner. Arrow allowed one of her rare smiles as she shook Stuart's hand before he went off to the Infirmary.

"We will take a 5 minute break and then continue with the second fight." Arrow went to the side of the room and sat drinking water.

I reviewed the fight in my mind. Stuart had been trying to read her and anticipate her moves. Why hadn't he been able to do that more successfully? That was really the only extra defense a Telepath had in a fight. Actually, now that I thought about it, he should have lost by a lot less. He had looked pretty hot kicking ass (or attempting to) like that, though. I hadn't seen him fight before. I'd never really thought of him as dangerous. Hm.

The General was back in the center of the practice floor with Arrow, who looked none the worse for wear from her first bout.

"Our second challenger, about to embark upon her Tour and winner of the July Heavy Lifting Contest, Macro, Paulette!" The General held out his arm again and Paulette emerged from the door. She looked older and tougher than her 22 years. Her arms and legs were muscular like a gymnast's, contrasting strongly with Arrow's leanness. I would not want to fight Paulette. Of course I'd take her over Arrow, but still…

The General was already off the mat. "Fight!"

Arrow was immediately thrown across the room and slammed into the far wall. She dropped hard to the floor. As she hit, though she yelled, "Make it dark!"

Suddenly the room was pitch black. A couple of spectators screamed. Pussies. I felt around the room, reading Arrow and Paulette. I could feel Arrow force herself to stand. I could tell by the careful way she moved that she was glad no one was watching. She hurt. The room was deathly quiet. We could hear Arrow's labored breathing. But then her breathing sounded more normal, then disappeared into silence.

I could feel the tension emanating from Paulette's body. I knew she was realizing that she had screwed up; she should have 'killed' Arrow immediately. Now she was flying blind and no longer in her position of strength. Talk about adrenaline.

There was a small noise in a far corner of the room. I felt Paulette make a sweeping motion with her arm. Several people (spectators, not Arrow) cried out in pain. Far away from this action Arrow made her slow, stealthy way towards Paulette. She hit a chair and it scraped on the floor. Paulette reached her hand out, but didn't do anything.

"Lights," Paulette said and the lights came up. Arrow was 40 feet from Paulette with many, many chairs and people in front of her. Medics rushed over to the far corner where the spectators had been hurt. Arrow limped back to the practice mat. The General joined them.

Paulette looked at him. "Couldn't take her out without taking everyone else out, too. Can't be accurate if I can't see. She beat me."

Arrow shook her head. "You would have gotten me eventually one way or another. Too many noisy obstacles. I have to concede."

The General looked at both of them. "I think we have learned a lot from this little encounter. I declare this a Draw!" He gestured for them to shake hands, which they did, with grudging respect. "Ten minute break."

Arrow did her best not to collapse into her chair. She knew everyone was watching. Paulette had disappeared out the door, upset with her lack of victory.

Before anyone knew it the General was back on the mat with Arrow, who looked almost recovered. "And our final contender, just about to take his first assignment with the Churchill Intelligence Unit on Bane, Master Micro, Wilby!"

Arrow looked up, literally, as the very tall Wilby strode towards her. He looked serious; not a smirk in sight.

The General backed quickly away as he shouted, "Fight!"

Wilby gave her a look and Arrow immediately doubled over in pain. She dropped to the floor, but quickly rolled out of sight into the spectators. And about 30 seconds later many of them (nearly half, but not all together) suddenly stood up and started randomly moving around. With this she became virtually invisible. That couldn't be coincidence, but how did she do that?

I concentrated, trying to find Arrow among all the other people. Ah, I see. Very good. Wilby was moving systematically through the audience, scanning, scanning for her body signature. But she kept low and kept moving, and her blockers also kept moving, making it much harder for him to get a lock. She was always one step ahead.

I focused harder on Arrow. Then I felt the vibration. She was subvocalizing. To the Telepaths, asking them to run interference for her. I assumed that only the Telepaths that weren't fans of Wilby were helping her. Yep, that was pretty much every one of them here.

Wilby's heart rate was very high. I was pretty sure he'd picked up on the sub vocalization. He kept moving, getting closer and closer to her. Her movements were very deliberate; she was letting him do this. What was her plan?

Suddenly all her blockers *moved* en masse at Wilby. Wilby turned, Arrow emerged from the crowd of Telepaths and streaked like lightening towards him and…

Wilby had Arrow pinned to the floor, in the aisle between chairs.

"Fuck!" Arrow cursed quietly.

The Telepaths she had corralled were still sort of standing around. Arrow looked pissed though resigned to her fate, but Wilby looked more thoughtful than triumphant. He tried to help her up, but she shook him off. They clasped hands for a second then Arrow stalked away as quickly as she could. Wilby watched her go, still thinking, until the congratulations of others had to be attended to.

The General was off in the corner talking to Arrow, his hand on her small shoulder. I think he was trying to make her feel better. Seeing him touch her was not making *me* feel better, though. Wait a minute. I am *not* jealous. No, Sir, I am not. No way. Not at all. And my thoughts continued on this track for quite some time.

A Note on Allowances within the Breeding Program

All peoples of all the Pace Worlds are effectively sterile, meaning that the Government (or, depending, the Government) had taken steps so that not only did no one get pregnant by accident, but that no one got pregnant at all. 700 years ago conception control was relegated to a mandatory implant that all girls received when they were 10 standard years old. The implants were not perfect, unfortunately, and there were occasional accidents. Also, it was pointed out that the policy made birth control a woman's responsibility and this really pissed women off. They'd had enough of that on Terra.

Over time a conception control enzyme was created, by Indira Pallon herself, and introduced into the water supply. Few smart asses stopped drinking water and got pregnant just to spite the system. Two months later the enzyme was added to ALL foodstuffs and into the fertilizer that grew them. There were no more body births on Pace-Pallon. That was 687 years ago.

Pace and Pallon, surprisingly, had stopped short of actually sterilizing the population, either with mass surgical procedures or with genetic engineering. This was a rather surprising bit of circumspection from a couple not known for it.

Every person on Pace-Pallon had their eggs or sperm harvested at age 17. The ostensible idea was that this was to preserve their DNA when it was at its freshest in case something happened down the road. What was never mentioned was how the Government made use of this huge cache of genes (it had been rumored for years, though, that there were people out there who were created solely for and by the Government. Nothing had been proved however). These harvested eggs and sperm were also used for the (non-secret) donor program.

Because Paceys didn't have to worry about pregnancy, and disease, including the sexual variety, had been virtually eliminated sex had never had the criminal or dangerous elements to it that it has had on Terra or on most of the colonies. Pretty much anyone could sleep with anyone, at any time and in any way with no physical repercussions.

When a couple decided to reproduce, they brought their genetic material to the main Center on their planet of residence. (Military personnel, like the General, were the exception and were required to use the Center on Pace 4. The Military kept a stringent eye on the genetic implications of its officers' offspring.) Everyone submitted their material for scanning and, on a rare occasion, were denied permission to breed (at least, with the material at hand). When this happened, one of the potential parents simply applied for a donor egg (or sperm), they were then re-screened and, assuming that passed muster, were allowed to create their embryo.

Couples were never told why they were denied. The Founding Scientists thought that knowing why would cause friction within existing committed relationships. They reasoned that since the real problems that had created most taboos were a) either someone being too young for sex (age of consent on Pace-Pallon was 15 and was rigidly, even violently enforced), b) or having too close a family relationship, or c) of both members of the couple being of the same sex. Pace and Pallon reasoned that, while you couldn't breed a half-brother to a sister or first cousin to first cousin or uncle to an adult nephew (or worse), it didn't mean they couldn't have a happy relationship if they couldn't *reproduce. So why spoil it by telling them?*

Same sex couples got around the age old breeding problem with the help of Atticus Pace who was able to alter the sex of the mother or father's egg or sperm (depending) so that it could combine with that of its partner.

The good news was that most people knew who their parents were and never gave a thought about anyone's possible illicit relationships. And some people were really stumped when they went to the Center and were denied.

<u>19:00 – The Quad</u>

I was walking back to the dormitory after dinner when I bumped into Stuart, not quite literally. He had some kind of tape over the bridge of his nose and I could see the beginning of some major bruises under his eyes. I smiled at him, but he was in no mood for it.

"Did you enjoy seeing me get my ass kicked?" he said with a combination of anger and self-pity that I found unexpectedly intriguing.

"Not at all." He relaxed a bit. I continued, "I had never seen you fight before." I leaned in a little and straightened his collar. "I like the way you move."

He looked down at his feet, trying not to show how pleased he was with my comment. "Hey, you know I'm sorry I've been a jerk today." Stuart took a couple of steps closer and pulled me to him.

"Thanks," I said inadequately, since I was pretty sure that he didn't even really know *why* he had been pissed at me in the first place. But then again I wasn't going to ask for miracles. He leaned in and kissed me gently. I still had the image of him fighting, editing out the part where he lost to someone half his size and weight, and I kissed him back.

"Armory? 23:00?" Stuart's hands were under my shirt and we both knew that my answer was yes. He kissed me again and left. I stood for a second. The Armory. The most public private place in the School. Well, I had an idea about that. And, actually, that reminded me of Wilby's trick. Might be fun.

22:45 – Quad Outside Guard Tower

I was early to meet Stuart, but, truth be told, I had been hoping that I could check in with the General, I mean, Samuel. There was no light at all in the Guard Tower. Damn. I stood in the Quad for a moment, debating. If he was in his office I couldn't use the excuse that I had seen his light on from the Quad because his window is on the outside of the school. I should let it go. But I wanted to see him. But what excuse for coming up would I give?

Oh, fuck it, I'm going up.

His office door was ajar and his light was on. The monitor was on his desk, still showing that town center in Pace 2. He wasn't sitting back in the chair, but there was a half empty bottle on his desk. He was searching for something in the cabinets. He seemed upset and there was urgency to his quest.

Samuel looked up at me, "Jane, help me."

I was at his side in a second. "What are we looking for?"

"Picture frame. Picture frame. It's gotta be somewhere in here." He pulled open another drawer and then made like he was going to pull it completely out and dump it. I put my hand on his wrist and stopped him.

"Let me look, Samuel." Hearing his name seemed to both calm him down and change his focus. He watched me as I went through the contents of the drawer.

"Your boyfriend did all right, today." The General leaned back in his chair and took a swig of his bottle. He offered me one, which I took as I paused in my search. I rested the bottle on my thigh, this time deliberately. I wanted to see what would happen if he touched me again. Maybe it had been a fluke before. "Arrow did better, of course, but I think we all knew she would. Even Stuart."

Annoyed at the mention of Arrow, I handed the bottle back. I turned back to the drawer. "She's really something."

He took another drink, his expression falling. "She's a pistol."

I felt something under some papers. The frame. I pulled it out of the drawer and handed it to him.

"Ah, there she is." The General held the frame up so that we could both see its picture. It was the General as a boy with a large canine. The General was grinning and the canine, or dog, was licking his face. "That was my Melly, Melanie, and she was my best friend growing up." He handed me the picture. "I wanted you to see this. A little reminder of where we've been as a people."

I couldn't think why. "Thanks?"

The General chuckled, but then turned serious again. "You know that the current Government outlawed animals 30 years ago."

I nodded. We had covered that in Political Science two years ago. "There had been so much interbreeding of animal DNA into our own that people were starting to panic again. They were afraid that the children being born with cat's eyes, a dog's sense of smell or a monkey's ability to leap (all directly borrowed from the actual animals) were changing us into something less than human."

"It was a terrifying time. I wasn't around 150 years ago when the first Panic happened—even I'm not that old—but this was scary enough. The three years leading up to the coup were a very paranoid time. The old Government had started rounding up children and adults with the animal DNA. They never came back." Samuel shook his head sadly. "The old Government was desperate to fix or erase this horrible lapse of judgment on the part of the geneticists that had approved all these mods. Those geneticists were executed, and rightly so, I might add, but not by the old Government. We did that as soon as we took over." He took a sip and handed it back to me as I sat on the desk.

I looked again at the picture in my hand. I took a drink. "What happened to Melly?" I handed him the picture but kept the bottle.

"Thankfully she'd died of old age two years before the coup."

I took another sip, trying to justify my possession of the bottle. "Did any of the part-humans survive? They never told us in class."

"Yes, many of them did. They weren't allowed to breed, not with their own DNA at least, and there are still some around today."

Samuel reached for the bottle, but I held it for a second, his hand slipping down the bottle and resting on my thigh. What was my question again? Oh yes, "Why was it a good thing that Melly died before the coup?"

He firmly pulled the bottle from my grasp with one hand, the other he left on my knee to steady himself as he drank. It was very hard for me to concentrate when he did that. "You know why. They told you *that* in class at least."

I looked over at the picture of Melly. "They slaughtered all the animals in the whole system to prevent this from ever happening again. They took DNA from every breed of every type of creature first, of course, especially the food animals so that their proteins, fats, etc., could still be synthetically produced to feed us, and then wiped them all out."

"My parents died protecting their horses." Samuel took a really long drink after that revelation. He looked so sad that I boldly (for me) took his hand and squeezed it.

"I'm so sorry, Samuel." There were tears in his eyes. He looked at me and smiled.

"Thanks." He brought my hand up to his mouth and kissed it. My vision blurred for a second and my heart raced. He let go of my hand, then, and stared as if appraising me. "Now git. I have this bottle to finish and you are late for your date."

I stood up a little unsteadily, a combination of booze and a sensation I'd rather not name in relation to the General.

"Goodnight, Samuel." I headed for the door and paused for the last word. I looked back at him and I realized that I really didn't want to go. But that was crazy and…

Samuel took another drink. He looked at me, then back at his monitor.

"Arrow's my daughter." And he flicked his fingers in a gesture of dismissal.

I was now really, really happy and I refused to examine why.

I practically ran down the hallway. Samuel had been right, I was late for Stuart. I took a short cut that would take me to the stairwell closest to the Armory when I passed the Listening Room. I was almost completely past it when I heard noises within. I paused. The door was cracked and movement caught my eye. There was Wilby, pants around his ankles...impaling Atalanta as he bent her over her desk. Her eyes were closed and she let out a moan as he pounded her. Wilby looked up when he saw me move by the door and winked at me. He then closed his eyes as he increased the rhythm.

I shook my head and moved on.

23:20 – Armory

Stuart was on top of me as we writhed together under the protection of one of the army tents kept in the Armory (my brilliant idea to foil the cameras). I was getting closer and closer to coming and I could feel his orgasm building as well. I quickly located his dorsal nerve as my body started to shake. I felt him start to come, focused on the dorsal nerve and gave it the squeeze Wilby had said would make Stuart's orgasm unforgettable. And unforgettable it was.

Stuart pulled out with a scream of agony, rolling back on the floor, cradling his genitalia and rocking back and forth in misery.

I knew I had to make a decision. I knew I could always apologize later if I had to, but I had bigger fish to fry.

"What happened?!?" I asked, all innocent concern.

"I started to come and suddenly there was this unbelievable pain. Like I'd been stabbed or something." He was still holding his crotch, but was able to sit up. I took this as a good sign.

"Does it hurt now?" I asked, knowing it shouldn't and hoping I was right.

"No." He picked up his now limp penis and studied it. It looked perfectly ordinary to both of us.

"I'll scan it." I focused on the internals of the thing, especially the dorsal nerve, and everything seemed undamaged. Well, that Micro trick was surely good at making somebody suffer. And speaking of suffering, I am going to beat the crap out of fucking Wilby. "Everything seems fine." Stuart's color was returning to his face and he looked OK now. "Why don't you go lie down."

"Shouldn't I get this checked out? What if it happens again? What if this happens every time I have sex?" He looked a bit panicked. I didn't blame him, but when he said 'sex' all I could picture was Samuel and I had to admit that I'd been picturing Samuel, and not Stuart, when I'd come.

"I think that getting your penis checked out by Doc Wells will give the gossips a lot to talk about." No fucking kidding. And that was why Atalanta and Wilby had been marking time waiting in the Listening Room. Fuck. "What I think you should do is trying fucking another girl and see if it happens again. I doubt it will. It might be some freaky Micro thing that I haven't learned about yet. It might be my fault." Oh, he had no idea. With luck he would never know. Those chances were slim, I knew, but I wasn't in the mood to deal with it now.

"Fuck another girl? What are you talking about, Jane?" Stuart looked puzzled for a second and then his expression cleared. "Oh."

"It's been great, you know, but I think we're done." I nodded to add emphasis.

He looked momentarily outraged, confirming my secret theory that he had never been decently dumped. "But what if I…"

I cut him off as I lay down, mock seductively. "Or would you like another go?"

Stuart shivered. "No."

I smiled and kissed him on the cheek. I threw some clothes on and was out of the tent in a second.

I was relieved, to be honest, that I was free of Stuart, but that feeling passed quickly as I walked back towards the dormitory. Soon all my thought was focused on how much pain I was going to cause that Atalanta fucking son-of-a-bitch.

Wilby, you pissed off the wrong Macro.

ENTRY 5-1-5

05:00 – The Quad, July 3, 2869

As we had every morning for the past 5 days, Stuart, Atalanta, Wilby and I stood next to Object 1, getting ready to scan. The sky was dark and the air was cold, but these things were a stark contrast to the energy and activity within the Object. The creatures inside were big enough that even Stuart, who went first, could get a reading on them. He told us that it was how he imagined scanning the mind of a small animal or crab. Since none of us, including him, had ever even seen a small animal or crab in real life, we only had to assume he was correct.

I scanned the Object myself, starting from the solidity of Pace 4 then moving up as I always did. I listened hard, turning up the "volume" in my head as high as it could go, thinking there would be a lot of little details to read. I was immediately assaulted with thousands of fully developed…creature-crab things, scurrying, running frantically from place to place all…eating?? I took several involuntary steps back. Wilby caught me before I fell.

I looked at him. "Did you feel that? Are they *eating*?"

Wilby straightened me up and let go. He looked pale. "I think they are eating out the inside of the Object."

Stuart took a half step back, but remained silent.

But Wilby's voice was deadly serious. "There is less mass inside the Object than there was yesterday and the creature-crab things are much bigger."

Stuart rubbed his law unhappily.

"The creatures are eating both to grow and to make room for themselves," Wilby concluded reluctantly. This had been my conclusion, too, and it made my stomach hurt.

"Welcome to our worst nightmare," Stuart murmured to himself. I couldn't have agreed more, even though it was the last thing I wanted to do.

"I keep hoping this will all go away," Atalanta said in a small voice. I would have felt sorry for her if she weren't such a bitch. But she was.

"How is the General scanning lately?" Wilby frowned also, clearly as unnerved as anyone.

Atalanta's frown disappeared. "He's fine. I mean he's concerned, of course, but very calm. I haven't read any panic." Her face clouded briefly, "At least not yet."

This did not sound like Samuel. It did sound like the General, however.

"No sadness, or anxiety? No overpowering worry? Nothing like that?" I asked. How could she not get that from him, when I could tell he felt like that without any of her abilities?

"Nothing so extreme," Atalanta said, apparently very reassured by her report. "I mean, yes, I got bits of that. Well, some of that. He'd be crazy not to be a little stressed out with all of this." Atalanta sounded defensive. Defensive of him or of her reading? Both, probably. She didn't want to panic and having her leader stay calm enabled her to stave off fear.

The General I knew was afraid, sad, very worried and under a tremendous amount of stress. The only time he wasn't, I guessed, was late at night with his bottle of spirits. But why couldn't she read him properly? What she was getting from him was soberly appropriate. So perfect. Almost textbook from the perfect leader. Hm. And the other day when Atalanta had had a different memory of her report to the General than I had. That was interesting, too. Who was being messed with, her or me? The evidence pointed to her. The reason was obvious, but who was doing the tampering? And then I knew. Holy shit. I remembered what Samuel had told me. There are no true normals on Pace. That included Samuel himself. Wow.

But I was supposed to be paying attention to this stupid Object of Death in front of me.

"Jane, are you there?" Stuart sounded annoyed. I could not have given a rat's ass. I suppose I should have, given the fact that I had nearly squeezed his man meat (yes, *man meat*, Atalanta) off last night. That, of course, wasn't exactly what happened, but I liked putting it that way in my head.

"Sure. What were you saying?"

Stuart shook his head. "I think we can all agree that this Object is getting closer and closer to expelling its contents. I wish we had an idea when."

"The General is watching Pace 2," I said without thinking. "He'll know when those Objects open up or whatever, before we do."

Everyone stared at me. Wilby raised an eyebrow in my general direction. I guess my knowledge of this was too…intimate for this crowd. "None of you noticed the monitor on his desk?" Atalanta shrugged. She'd noticed it. "Didn't anyone bother to ask what was on it?" I asked, not hiding my exasperation. "It isn't a secret. Apparently people on all four Paces are watching this town in Pace 2 to see what and when things are going to happen." I said all this with calculated indifference, hoping that they would chalk it up to my being annoyed with them as opposed to something illicit going on with me and the General. Thank god I hadn't called him Samuel by accident; I'd never hear the end of it. "And you people think *I* don't take an interest in what's going on."

Wilby was silent, as were Stuart and Atalanta. This was all very bad. Stuart took a deep breath.

"I'll report this to the General right away." We nodded and moved on to the next Object. We wouldn't want to miss a chance to be re-terrified, I supposed.

Wilby sidled up to me as we made the short walk. "So, how was the Armory last night?" If I hadn't already decided to bide my time and pick my moment to punish him, this alone might have set me off. And the fact that he now pretended he knew nothing about what happened last night annoyed me even more. The attempt was so patently lame I decided that he was only doing it to get under my skin. Unfortunately, it was working. I was lining up coy responses and trying to think of ways to blow him away with my icy wit (this was not, admittedly, a good plan considering my usual level of wit) when I had an idea. I glanced over at Atalanta who was pretending to scan the Object again.

I walked up to Wilby, standing close. I cocked my head to the side and looked up at him. His face reflected his surprise. I placed my hands on his chest and pressed against him. "Why?" I asked teasingly. "Sorry I wasn't with you?" I looked at him doe-eyed. His expression was distrustful, but I could tell he was responding anyway. I wasn't the only one.

I felt a small hand on the back of my shirt as I was pulled roughly away. Suddenly Atalanta was between us, looking rather like an enraged hornet.

"Were you? Sorry, I mean?" Atalanta's voice was pitched low but still held a vast amount of venom. Wilby cast me an annoyed glance, but had to focus on Atalanta who was vibrating with fury.

I got the hell out of there while Atalanta was still staring him down. I was almost out of the Quad before I heard Wilby burst into tears, sobbing loudly. MEmps don't have the flashy skills like us Macros, but no grown man likes to be forced to cry in public. Especially a know-it-all snark like Wilby.

Well, I laughed to myself, we may be a prep school for supers, but we are still as juvenile as any other prep school. And like any regular almost 18 year old, I still wanted my revenge on that bastard. But right now I had a class to get to. Fuck the Objects. They could watch themselves.

Excerpt from Captain Ian Armstrong's Journal dated July 3, 2869

P.S. Scylla *finished its long patrol today and now we are hauling ass to Pace 4. Unfortunately we are way too close to use jump engines and way too far away for sub-light to be anything but frustrating.*

I'm still going over the General's call in my head. Old bastard is so used to people just following orders—it killed me that I couldn't say no.

But if he says come and that it's a matter of life and death, you come. Even if that's the last place you want to be.

Fuck fuck fuck FUCK!

<u>09:00 – Weapons Training, Practice Floor, Demonstration Room and Gallery (Mallory)</u>

Mallory, the School's Weapons Mistress, was 50, scarred, lethally fit, and had skin like shoe leather. She was unusual, however, (and in more ways than even I had known about at the time) in that unlike most of our instructors, who had only fought in simulated battles, Mallory was an actual veteran of the coup 30 years before. She had even served under the General himself when he had led his people to victory. On top of that she was also an excellent instructor; managing to be both indomitable and likeable, which was impressive.

We were a small class of Macros only. Arthur, myself, Paulette and Felix, 25, stood on the practice mat expectantly. I'd known Felix from other classes and remembered him vividly. He was small, wiry, really fucking ugly and, like Arrow, let people underestimate him because of his size.

He had a hell of a temper, though, and an affinity for violence that scared some people. I liked him. As far as I could tell he really didn't give a shit about much except maybe Mallory. She'd helped make him even more lethal. The jury was still out on whether that was a good thing.

Mallory walked, well, stalked was more like it, to the front of the room then stood, weight on her toes, arms bent at her waist, hands in fists, knees slightly bent. She stood this way all the time. When she was preparing to fight. At lunch. At cocktail parties. She was always ready to fight. We knew from experience that she was a deadly opponent and an intelligent teacher, but the fact that she was Arrow's mentor was her local claim to fame.

She walked over to a table full of weapons and picked up a military-grade Laser Pulse Gun. It was large and heavy but she tucked it under her arm with ease. Without a word she turned and fired it directly at me.

I dropped to the floor. She fired again, but I had collected myself and I, concentrating, raised my hand, wrenching the gun out of her grasp and into the air. I pinched my fingers together and bend the gun's nose up and back on itself. The gun was effectively disabled. I stood up, annoyed with myself as I mentally lowered the ruined gun to the floor. I was alive, yes, but I had done about 40 things, well 3 or 4, wrong.

Mallory just looked at me, waiting. I grimaced. "I waited too long to get the gun away from you, I didn't pick up anything to use to attempt to divert, or stop, the pulse, and I used physical movement as a crutch during a fight."

"But you kept your eyes open for the first time." Felix said saucily.

"And you're alive." Mallory crossed her arms over her chest. "Your analysis was correct, Jane, but don't think you aren't improving. As I recall your first response to that test was…" she prompted.

"…putting my arms over my head and screaming?" I answered. Felix chuckled, but it wasn't an unfriendly sound. Paulette, whose sense of humor seemed to have been removed in the tubs, didn't respond. Arthur laughed, though. Mallory turned to him.

"And what was your first response, Arthur?" Her voice was stern but her eyes twinkled.

"Oh, I ran like the wind." Arthur said confidently. He'd come a long way, actually, and he knew it.

I shook my head, ruefully, and grinned at him for the first time in I don't know how long. "At least you weren't screaming," I said as an aside.

"I was afraid the pulse would follow the sound," he responded quietly, amused.

"*Anyway*," Mallory interrupted, "there is one other problem," she saw my face fall and then quickly added, "and it's one we haven't discussed before." That's one of the reasons students liked her. She didn't sugar coat your mistakes, she knew it wouldn't help you in the long run, but she still managed to be kind. Rare, that.

"Today we are going to talk about Wasted Effort, also known as Conserving Energy." Mallory paced in front of us like a Terran cat. "On a mission or in a fight you will always, *always*," and she shot a look at the muscle-bound Paulette, "use the least amount of energy to accomplish your goals. Do not block like this…" Mallory brought her forearm up in a sweeping, showy gesture, "when you can do this." Mallory simply brought her forearm up. "Minimizing your effort is a way to reduce the energy expended. Why could this be important?" She looked at us expectantly.

We thought about it. "The fight may not be over," Felix responded. "Even if *you* think it is."

Mallory nodded. "I have seen so many people die because they had worn themselves out, often by celebrating their victory. A surprise attack at the last minute, even long after the battle is over, and a fighter can be too tired, sleepy or, very often, too drunk to respond properly. And they die." She stepped closer to us. "These are errors, my friends. *Unacceptable* errors."

Mallory walked back to the table and picked up another Pulse Gun. She tucked it under her arm, like she had the previous, then looked back at us. "And there's always some joker who thinks that conserving energy in a fight means doing as little as possible." She turned to face us to make sure that we were getting it. "Conserving is not laziness. You're saving your energy in order to help your team and your mission. You'll be able to do more, contribute more if you stop wasting strength on things you don't need to. Laziness is always punished, one way or another."

Mallory held the Pulse Gun out for us to see. "Now, I want ideas on 5 ways this gun can be disabled quickly. Go."

"Smashing it into a wall after I yank it out of your hands?" Felix offered.

"Inelegant but effective in a pinch. What else?" Mallory started pacing slowly in front of us, holding the Pulse gun.

"I can crush the trigger mechanism," I mimed smashing my hand upwards. "It also might smash the gun into the user's chin when I do it. Could either distract him or knock him out if I'm lucky."

"Or I could just," Felix held his hands up as if they were around a basketball, "break his neck." He turned his hands to demonstrate.

"Which wouldn't disable the gun," I argued.

"Or I could just throw him out the window," Felix continued. He smiled. "I just love throwing people out windows. Especially if they are trying to kill me."

"I get that. I do, but it isn't subtle. What if we need subtlety?" I pressed him.

Mallory then broke in, amused. "What Felix is trying to say, I think, is that if we need something that no one will notice we should…send someone else."

He threw his hands out in mock exasperation. "You think I can't be subtle? Hah. I can be subtle all day long. You want 5 ways a Macro can disable that gun subtly? I got 'em…"

And he did. He detailed his methods for the next 5 minutes. He was right, too. He was too good. I didn't know if I would ever be *that* good, but I didn't have time to worry about it now. Class was over and I needed to see a man. Well, I needed to see two, but one had to wait. Now it was off to the Guard Tower.

10:15 – General Armstrong's Office, Guard Tower

Once again I heard "Come in, Jane" before I'd even knocked. I went in, shutting the door behind me. The General seemed wholly engrossed in the Pace 2 monitor on his desk. He was sitting up, staring, his body radiating tension.

"What do you have for me?" he asked, not looking up.

"I had a question for you," I said hesitantly, "but I'll come back later."

"Jane, take a look at this, please." Samuel got up from his chair and indicated that I should take it. "I want your opinion."

I walked over and sat. The chair was warm from his body. I allowed it to distract me until I looked at the monitor and forgot everything else.

There was the Town Square. No people. Nothing moved. The Object that was in the fountain was cracked open down the middle and now appeared empty. The place was desolate. The businesses along the square were gutted, roofs caving in, glass broken. Even the fountain was dry.

"Fuck me," I breathed softly. The General looked like he was about to say something but held his tongue. He watched me take all this in, like I was a test subject in civilian reactions, which I guess I was.

Then I saw something. I pulled the chair in closer and noticed hundreds of shapes, things, scattered all over. They didn't move either.

"When did they open?" I asked quietly, still watching.

He sat down on the desk next to me, a reversal of our usual positions, his left knee by my shoulder. "Late last night. There were a million calls for help," he rubbed his face with his hand, "but they stopped within a few minutes. Long before anyone off planet could come."

I looked up at him. "Was anyone going to come, Samuel?"

He paused a second, sadly, "No. All we did was watch them die. Right here," he pointed at the monitor, "in the comfort of my own office, I got to watch this town, and by extension the whole planet, get massacred."

"Mother of god," I whispered, suddenly overwhelmed by grief and fear. Instinctively needing comfort I leaned against his leg, resting my head against his knee. I heard his quick intake of breath and I immediately stiffened realizing that I crossed yet another line, but I didn't want to yield my position. He'd have to say something to get me to move. But he didn't say anything. I think he was as surprised as I was that I had done this. I relaxed, as much as I could, against his knee.

"Why can we still see the feed? Wouldn't they have disabled it?" I asked softly, wanting to know, but not wanting to break the spell.

He answered me gently, as if taking his tone cue from me, "The creatures don't seem to be interested in the technology. They ignore it. I think they are just there to eat."

"I wonder if a whole world was enough," I said to myself. I looked away for a second, resting my face on his knee. Samuel said nothing, but reached down and started stroking my hair. Suddenly I could hardly breathe. I assumed that he was only trying to comfort me, but I was not feeling comforted. Everything I had been denying to myself just fell away with that touch. I pictured myself standing up and kissing him, touching him everywhere. Yes, I wanted him. Oh my god, I wanted him bad. But my wanting him would not magically make him want me, too.

His large, rough hand, so strong, so powerful was petting me gently, lovingly. I'm like a daughter or a niece to him. He's being nice to me.

That might be, but his touch was incredibly sexy. My body was reacting even though my head knew it completely wrong to do so. I closed my eyes, trying to distract myself. He had to stop soon, I thought, or I may come right here in the chair. Stop, Samuel. But don't.

"What was it you wanted to ask me?" His voice sounded funny, like he was getting control of it. He mercifully stopped stroking my hair. Thank god. Dammit.

"Oh. I just wanted to know if you are able to control the images, thoughts and emotions that people get when they scan you? Can you make them see or feel anything you want?"

Samuel gave a chuckle. "Yes."

"Samuel?"

"Yep?"

I left the comfort of his knee and turned partially around to face him. "Why did you lead me to that? About you. I mean, aside from the whole 'don't ever underestimate normals' thing? Why? And why me?"

He looked away. "I don't know, Jane. I don't know."

He looked back at me and it was at that moment that we both came to the realization that, now that I was turned around, I was basically sitting between his legs in close proximity to his crotch. I felt my cheeks turn red. Samuel looked embarrassed, too.

"Coffee?" He got up and walked across the small room.

"Sure." I looked back at the screen and attempted to collect myself as my eyes fell on the monitor screen again. I leaned forward in the chair. Something about that image was bothering me. "Why aren't the creatures moving? Are they resting?"

Samuel walked back over to the desk, handing me a full coffee cup as he reached me. "I've been talking to people about that since early morning. No one seems to know. We have a survey team heading out to Pace 2 right now, but it won't arrive until tomorrow."

I looked up at him. "Could they be dead?"

He shrugged. "I don't think we could be that lucky. I think they're just resting. That was a hell of a meal." He started to take a sip of his coffee, but it seemed to disgust him. He put the cup down on the desk.

"Can we move the camera in closer?" I moved my face up to the monitor, trying to see more. Something about those still creatures just struck me as wrong. Samuel watched me for second, deciding if I was serious. When it was clear I was he picked up the phone.

Twenty minutes later the camera slowly zeroed in on two of the creatures. The sun was fading for Pace 2 and the beauty of sunset washed over both the ruins and the creatures. Now the 2 crab-creature things filled the screen. Parts of the…skin (?) of the things were smooth and hard looking and parts were jagged. But only jagged on what looked like their belly..? Why?

The General sat down on the desk again. "Maybe that jagged underside, assuming that's the underside, is natural to their…breed. I think all of them have it. I've been staring at the larger picture for hours and I'm sure I'm right on that."

"I don't know. Maybe..." Stumped, I just kept staring at the close up image. I knew I was missing something.

Just then rays of the setting sun illuminated the creatures—literally. The sun filled them with light, and it could only do that because...

"They're hollow!" Samuel and I said at the same time. I stood up and started pacing. Samuel dropped back onto the desk.

"So those are, those are..." I stopped. This knowledge had implications that didn't make me any happier.

"Shells, Jane. Shells." Samuel kicked his legs out from the desk, then did it again and again restlessly. "They ate, they grew and they shed their skin, like a Terran snake."

I gave him a horrified look. "So how fucking big are they now?"

Samuel got off the desk and headed for the door. "I don't know. But the question that's really worrying me is," and he held the door open for me to go, "where *are* they now?" He smiled apologetically, "I've got calls to make. Thanks, Jane. You were a big help."

I smiled thanks and walked down the hallway. Yes, that's me. Helpful. Useful like a sexless niece. No, wait, that didn't sound right. Anyway, I needed to go.

<u>*A Note on the Education of Supernormals*</u>

After Pace normals were born, they went to schools within their home towns or the closest cities, and at 15, transferred to the prep school that best suited their abilities and aptitudes (or the abilities the Government wanted them to have). Then they stayed at that school until their Tour. Supers, on the other hand, went to a series of schools that each, in turn, became their sole home. The schools raised them, offered parental figures (though not actual parents) and taught them everything they knew. All Supernormals were created in Foundry, a town on an isolated bit of continent on Pace 4. Foundry was entirely supported by the Government with no other purpose than to create and nurture supernormal children.

Foundry-1 was the nursery where the children stayed until they were 3 standard years old. Most adult supers barely remembered this. Next they were moved to a different complex called Foundry-2, for ages 3 to 10. Here they started their actual education and the rudiments of controlling their extra abilities. Kids were informally labeled and classified according to the abilities they actually exhibited as opposed to the abilities that they'd been designed *to have. (Not every mod came through.) The transition from 1 to 2 was important for screening as well as social development. The kids that had the genes but not the expected talents were very often adopted out to interested normals on Pace 4 (usually Government workers), never knowing why. Those children were loosely monitored for the rest of their lives, however, and once in a long while someone developed their talents late and was pulled back into the fold.*

Another screening happened at the transition between Foundry-2 and 3. For the first time the kids were officially rated in terms of their talents. (Unofficial ratings had, of course, been occurring their entire lives among both staff and peers). There were actually two separate Foundry-3s. Foundry-3B (known informally as "Baker") for Telepaths and MEmps and Foundry-3C (or "Charlie") that housed Micro and Macro Telekinetics. (Telespatials were not recognized as official Supernormals.) Kids were sent to Foundry-3 schools between ages 10 and 11 and stayed there until age 15 when they had to apply (or audition, more like) for their prep school. The best, most secret of these schools on Pace 4 took the most powerful, talented, brightest (though intelligence was not always a requirement) students on the planet. It didn't have any name other than the School. The other 3 prep schools, Globus, Keith and Dunnicliffe had their share of good people and existed in remote corners of Pace 4. But the top kids always ended up at the School, 100 miles outside of Bane. Students came here after their 15th birthday and stayed until they left for their Tour. (As a side note, the prep schools used to accept students when they were 14, but the teachers had gotten fed up with policing the students at night, so 20 years ago the age was raised to 15—the legal age of consent. Problem solved.)

Each level of school (and each school itself) was administered by a Dean or Keeper, who was responsible for all aspects of education, training, indoctrination and security. In a perfect world this job would have been held by an experienced Super who would be counted on to keep the "baby" supers in line. Unfortunately, the program was just under 30 years old and any really gifted adult supers were needed in the field. So Pace normals were used, even with their obvious disadvantages. The trick in finding people willing to take on this rather difficult responsibility, though, was that the schools were secret, the jobs technically didn't exist, and the students were not only illegal, but could gut (literally) an unsuspecting normal both mentally and physically pretty quickly if they didn't like or respect him/her. You had to know the job existed (which no one did) and then actually want it *(which few would).*

No one understood why General Samuel Armstrong had become Keeper. Even his son, Ian, Captain of the P.S. Scylla, *who knew the reason, didn't understand.*

14:45 – Quad Outside First Year Classroom

I walked towards my lesson with Wilby, thinking thoughts of revenge. I had a very solid, I thought, plan to make him suffer and was going over it carefully when I heard laughter. Unconsciously I reached out to scan the surrounding area. There. On the other side of the pillar was…Felix, I thought. I walked around it and there he was, watching the first years, the new crop of 15 year olds, practice their Macro skills. I stared into the classroom in time to see a young boy pick up one of the foam practice blocks, get distracted (I remembered that exercise, it was all about keeping focus) and…drop it on his partner's head. Felix laughed again.

"I love the new kids. Endlessly entertaining." Felix grinned and lit up a tobacco roll. He inhaled deeply.

"You know you'll get in trouble if they catch you smoking that," I started to say, but then he looked at me with a raised eyebrow. Right, this was *Felix* I was talking to. "Sorry."

He shrugged. He smoked in silence for a second, but looked like he had something on his mind, so I waited. I had a little time before I was going to kick Wilby's ass.

"I understand why you hate Atalanta so much." He never took his eyes off the kids in the class, but he sounded serious.

Atalanta? Was she sleeping with him, too? Of course she was. "You probably do. Why do you care?" I folded my arms across my chest, mentally defending myself from this unexpected attack.

He looked at me. "I'm not fucking her, Jane."

"If you say so, Felix, but I can't see why anyone would care about her if they weren't." While I was saying exactly what I thought, the words sounded harsher coming out of my mouth than they had sounded in my head.

"That's a pretty cold thing to say." Felix was right and I was suddenly ashamed. "I'm not saying she's not a bitch at times."

Now I had to give *him* a raised eyebrow in incredulity. He kind of laughed to himself.

"Or most of the time. But," he took a long drag, "I've known her since we were kids in the same class at Foundry-2. She's had to come a long way, figuring out how to deal with being…"

"…the most beautiful woman anyone has ever seen?" I snorted and then added sarcastically, "That *would* be rough."

"At times, yes. People have wanted her for as long as she can remember."

"Sure." I agreed, not sure where this was going.

"Imagine being 8 standard and being able to feel lust from your 45 year old history teacher. And then your Keeper who kept asking you, at 10, to help her after hours with lesson plans for the staff. And on and on and on." Felix dropped his tobacco roll in disgust and stepped on it, extinguishing the fire.

I recoiled in disgust. "How many..?" I couldn't finish the sentence. I wanted to vomit.

He took a deep breath. "A couple got to her before she'd learned to defend herself with her talent."

"I've seen her do it. Subtle but effective."

He laughed again. "Well, she must have liked whoever it was because I have seen her wield emotion like the hammer of god. She needed to do it to survive. And the rest of the time she keeps people at a distance by…"

"Being a bitch." I felt sorry for her, but I couldn't get over how mean she had been to me. He started to walk away, but I had one more question. "Why you, Felix? Why are you her only friend?"

He walked back to me, standing closer than before. "Not because I'm ugly." I started to protest, even though that had been exactly what I was thinking. He held up his hands to forestall my equivocation. "I was the only one who couldn't lust after her. She really liked that about me. Still does."

I just stared at him, wanting to know what the hell that meant, but not wanting to say another insensitive thing. At least not so close to all the other insensitive things I'd just said.

He stepped closer, for privacy. He was, actually, very close to me, but I read no sexual…anything from him. Nothing, like he was…oh. Crap.

"They took that away because they wanted the gene for strength instead. And they thought it would make me a more dangerous fighter. More focused."

More angry, I thought to myself. No sex, no release, no passion, no lust. I was overcome with sadness for him. Felix read this in my eyes and set his jaw, angry at my pity.

"And *that* is why I don't tell anyone." He stepped back from me. "My frustrations are my problem. I just wanted to...stand up for my friend."

Felix started to walk away, but then turned back. "There is a difference between being a bitch and being evil. Please keep that in mind, Jane." And he walked away.

"I will," I said to no one.

Excerpt the Journal of General Samuel Armstrong, July 3, 2869

Jane's discovery that these creatures had shed their skin has finally lighted a fire under the assholes in Bane and they are sending an "expert." A real true-blue member of the Scientist Class, Dr. Ivor Bayliss, will be here in the morning to help. With what I could not fucking tell anyone.

We lost contact with Pace 1 today. The feed must have been disabled by accident, since the one on Pace 2 is still running just fine. We should be getting a sub-light ship or two of refugees late tomorrow or early the next day. They are fools to come here while we wait for the other shoe to drop.

I just hope Ian can get here in time.

I think I'm done with this stupid fucking journal.

15:00 – Quad outside Infirmary Triage Room

I stood outside the Triage Room, going over my plan for the 100th time. Wilby was in there alone. Anson must be late. Good.

I walked in. Wilby looked at me, smirking. "I straightened things out with Atalanta." He shook his head. He was annoyed, though he was trying to conceal it. "Pretty juvenile move."

"I have a lot of those up my sleeve." I sat down on one of the tables. Yes, I am relaxed. I am so friendly, aren't I? Believe it, asshole. "Why go to all that trouble, Wilby? Are you *that* bored?"

He chuckled and walked over to me. "Bored, yes. But I had another goal." Wilby stepped really close, insinuating himself between my legs as I sat on the table. I mentally shook my head in wonder at my past self, thinking of all the times I had wanted him to be this close. And now I couldn't enjoy it because I knew he was a creep.

Wilby slowly traced my collar bone with his finger. "You are the only Macro/Micro Hybrid anyone's ever heard of. You are one of a kind."

I forced a blush and looked away modestly. "So, you noticed me," I said softly.

Wilby nodded, his hand moving slowly down from my collar bone. "And you looked like the monogamous type, so I needed to…move up the date of your break up with Stuart." And he leaned in and kissed me urgently.

I felt the solidity of Pace under my feet. I felt the weight of his body with my mind.

I 'picked him up' and 'threw' him across the room. He hit the wall hard, a beautiful look of complete shock on his face. I saw and felt the focus behind his eyes, knowing he was about to strike back, but I was way ahead of him. I turned him upside down and started spinning him against the wall. I remembered the pain I had put Stuart through and I realized that I was even madder than I'd thought.

Wilby screamed, putting his hands to his head as if that would stop the spinning.

I 'pulled' him from the wall, spinning him round and round in the air like a top.

I 'slammed' him against the wall again, and screamed, "You…"

Slam, "…arrogant…"

Slam, "…motherfucker!"

At this point Anson ran in the room, apparently having heard Wilby's screams. Anson froze, looking up at Wilby as he continued to spin around. Then Anson realized what was going on as he looked at me, fear in his eyes. He made for the door.

I looked at him with loathing. "I hope you enjoyed the blow job you got for helping this fuckhead trick me, because it may be a while before you'll want to use your dick for anything."

With that I located his dorsal nerve and 'squeezed.' He collapsed on the floor in agony.

Wilby vomited in midair and I stopped 'spinning' him, lowering him to the ground. I knew he was in no shape to retaliate now. I was done. Spent.

I was feeling pretty good when I heard that unmistakable voice behind me.

"What the fuck is going on here, Jane?!?" Samuel was behind me, correction, the General was. I didn't need to see him to tell how furious he was. I turned around and saw his face and backed up several paces. He was beyond furious. George, the nurse, and several other medics appeared behind him and he waved them in. They swarmed around Anson, who I knew from experience would be all right, and Wilby. I tried to scan Wilby as they lifted him out, but there was too much movement for me to get anything beyond the fact that he was conscious and breathing.

The General still had to be dealt with, however, and he advanced on me in such a menacing manner that I backed all the way up into a table.

"I repeat, what the fuck was going on here?"

I couldn't speak. I hadn't factored the General into my plan at all. I hadn't counted on his seeing any of it. A blind spot, I guess. Deep down I must have realized that I couldn't get my revenge and keep his respect at the same time. I wished my unconscious mind had let me know.

"And I suppose that this is all the explanation I am likely to get?" I had to look away. I could see the disappointment in his eyes and I couldn't take it. I wanted to disappear.

He folded his arms on his chest. He wasn't as angry, I could tell, but the disappointment was unwavering. I felt nothing but shame.

"Brig. Now." And the General walked away. Just like that. He didn't even escort me there. He knew I'd go. Like the stupid child I was. And I did.

Excerpt from Atalanta's Journal dated July 3, 2869

So, Jane went crazy and tossed Wilby, the asshole, around like a rag doll and made him puke himself. Quite a temper on that little sexless goat girl. Wilby's still in the Infirmary with a broken shoulder blade. My guess is that the shit hit on her after tricking her into pinching her (then) boyfriend's dick nerve. This is the gift that keeps on giving. I would have been happy with just the dick pinching. That was one of the funniest things I have ever heard in my life. Disappointing that she'd blocked the camera and we'd only had sound, but I'm not greedy.

I suppose I should be grateful to Jane for punishing him not only for that little prank, but for attempting to cheat on me. I may give her a pass the next time she does something incredibly stupid in front of me. Or I may not.

Arthur says she's in the Brig for the night. 'Brig,' ha. Before the General got here it was called 'detention.' The room doesn't even have bars, just a door that doesn't even lock because it used to be a supply closet.

They should put Wilby in there with her. Then she could finish the bastard off. Or at least make him shit himself. Asshole.

23:00 – The Brig

I walked into the Brig and sat on the bed, numb from a victory that had ended in surprise defeat. For the first few minutes I just sat, thinking little but feeling miserable. I wished I could do it all over, but that didn't help. I was just an idiot that's all there was to it. And Samuel… I stopped that train of thought, not ready for it. Too sad.

I head boots coming down the hall. The walk was angry, furious, even. It was a military walk made by a commander who needed to rip a new one to a subordinate. I backed away from the door. The boots marched right up to it. The General was here to put me in my place.

But he stopped, hand on the doorknob. He stood there a second, then marched down the hallway, his hesitation seemed to make him madder and he marched even faster. I crept back to the door, scanning him as he went by again and again. His blood pressure was high, skin flushed and his knee joints were protesting with every stomp of his feet. He paced in front of the door for an hour like that.

I went back to sitting on the bunk, still stunned by my own lack of judgment. I started mentally reviewing more acceptable methods I could have used to get my revenge. Like simple humiliation. Starting a nasty rumor. Or that 'cutting wit' plan that I could never seem to pull off. And still he paced.

Another hour passed. The General's angry pacing, even though it was starting to feel slightly less angry, was starting to get to me. I supposed that I could try to kill myself with something in the room. Not that I wanted to die, but I thought maybe I could get some points for sympathy. Maybe Samuel would forgive me if he felt sorry enough for me. Maybe he would like me again. Maybe he would stop fucking pacing himself into the grave.

I knew this suicide thing was not a good plan and just about as immature as my revenge plan had been, so I was relieved when I found nothing in the room designed to help me in my fake suicide attempt. Besides, I reasoned, he was too close by. That sort of (fake) thing really only worked if he was far away and had to run to my side. He would need several terror-filled minutes (though hours were preferable) to realize how much I meant to him. I supposed that I could do it silently, though how I didn't know, so that he could be right outside but only the security people could see that I was in trouble and smash the (unfortunately unlocked) door down to save me, all the while Samuel could lament that he had been just on the other side of the door…

Then I had a thought and checked the room for cameras. None. So no one to save me at the last minute in my silent suicide attempt. And the try had to be serious enough to scare people. No cameras meant that I would have a serious chance of ending up dead. I might have been immature, but I was not stupid. So much for *that* terrible plan.

When we reached hour two his pacing had slowed. He was succumbing to fatigue. I felt his headache and his posture slumping. I still heard the tread of his boots, but it seemed as though he had worn out most of his anger. Soon his pacing was a slow walk. I wished I could see his face. I wondered what he was thinking about, still out there for all those hours.

Now that his walking was nearly silent I had nothing to distract me from the thoughts I had been avoiding. I'd lost someone so special to me and finally, seriously admitting that brought nothing but pain. I couldn't stand remembering that look in his eyes. Unbidden big tears rolled down my cheeks. I lay down on the cot and let them drip into the pillow. Just then he stopped walking completely. He was outside the door again. I could feel his breathing.

A minute later I finally heard the door knob turn. The door opened silently and he came in. I stood up immediately, then felt foolish. What's next, saluting?

He took another couple steps into room and stopped, as if unsure of himself. I couldn't look him in the eyes. I just kept imagining how stupid he must have felt even liking a fool like me. I had been glad when he'd stopped the angry stomping, but now I was afraid that he had sunk into calm indifference. That was much worse. Much. He didn't look at me. He'd written me off. I wish he'd say something and get this over with.

"Are you all right?" Samuel asked softly and looked me in the eye. I saw kindness there in his face, the last thing I'd expected.

It was too much. I turned away, fresh tears coursed down my face. He walked around and got in front of me. He bent down to see my face clearly, brushing my hair back with his hand, his expression distressed. He took a handkerchief out of his breast pocket and dried my tears. I looked up at him, more tears welling up and he pulled me to him, wrapping me up in his strong arms. I clung to him. He rocked me gently.

"It's all right, Baby." He said in my ear. "It's gonna be all right."

In his arms I was safe. I was so happy. He didn't hate me. For that moment I was satisfied, especially since, up until a few seconds ago, I'd thought I'd lost everything. I buried my face in his chest as he held me.

I felt something in him change. I realized that I had been so…connected to him that I had been scanning him without realizing it. I felt his hands moving in a sensuous rhythm on my back. He was breathing faster, like I was. Our bodies had changed in their orientation to each other and we'd made that change unconsciously. What had been a hug was now an embrace.

I felt him hard against me as my body ached for him. I pulled back from him a bit so that I could look in his eyes.

"Samuel," I whispered, putting a wealth of longing into the name.

And he kissed me. I gave myself over to his mouth with a pleasure so intense I thought I was going to faint. He tasted like spirits. He tasted like Samuel. His hands were in my hair as I unbuttoned his shirt. I ran my hands over his chest and he shuddered.

He seemed hesitant to go further so I took his hand and kissed his palm. He was watching my face as if afraid of…what? I ran his hand down from my mouth to my collar bone and then to my breast. He inhaled sharply and I kissed him again. His other hand tentatively touched my backside. I put mine on his, pulling him closer. He moved his hands slowly and I let out a small moan. My hands arched under his shirt now, moving up his well-muscled back.

Then I brought one hand back and brushed fingertips over the front of his trousers, feeling his hardness.

"Jane," he groaned. He kissed my mouth then moved lower to my neck. Then lower again. Oh my god.

It was bliss and I wanted more, more, more.

I started to unbuckle his belt and suddenly his hands were holding mine, stopping me.

I looked up in total surprise. For a second I didn't even understand that he *was* stopping me. And when I did I just stood there, staring at him.

"I can't, Jane. I'm so sorry." He let go of me and backed away. I felt bereft, cheated, but mostly confused.

"You're still angry with me. You should be."

He shook his head. "No. I don't care about that anymore. I'm just a selfish old asshole." He looked at me, so sad. "I've wanted to do that for a long time."

"Me, too," I breathed. This made him smile, but didn't make him look any less sad.

"But I can't make love to a student. I'd lose my job and I have to be here."

"For Arrow." I sat down on the bed, my mind reeling. He knelt next to me and took my hand.

"For Arrow and for all of you kids." At the word 'kids' I tried to pull my hand back but he wouldn't let it go. "I said I was selfish and you know I'm right." I didn't say anything. "But I wanted to be close to you before everything went to hell. I couldn't help myself."

I brought his hand up to my mouth and kissed it, the way he had kissed my hand just a day or two ago. He'd closed his eyes when I'd delivered the kiss as if savoring the contact. "Please Samuel. Stay with me. Please?"

I followed his face with my eyes as he rose, buttoning his shirt. He shook his head. I could see tears forming in his eyes and could feel the lump in his throat. He started to speak but I held up my hand to stop him.

"It's all right. I think I understand."

With infinite sadness he turned to leave, but a thought occurred to me. Something he'd said.

"Samuel?" He looked back from the doorway. "When exactly *is* everything going to hell?"

I hadn't thought his expression could have gotten any more despairing, but it did as he answered, "Tomorrow, Baby." He gave me one last longing look and left.

I sat on the bed and stared at the wall until dawn.

ENTRY 6-1-6

06:00 – Dormitories, July 4, 2869

I opened my eyes in the near dark. I felt around for movement in the room. Atalanta was sleeping soundly, her breathing regular. Then I realized what had woken me; it was the change in the room's air pressure. The door had opened and closed. I felt him moving quietly towards me. I reached out my hand to touch his face. He paused, his eyes almost luminous in the darkness. I had so hoped he would come to me. I didn't want to wake Atalanta but I thought his name exultantly, "Samuel!" Then he was over me in the bed.

He leaned down to kiss me as I happily surrendered to his need and mine. I pulled off his shirt, at last getting to trace his muscles, his chest. Now my top was off, too, and he tasted everything, driving me crazy. He pulled off my pants and then, finally, his. I could hardly breathe, the anticipation was killing me. I reached a hand down to guide him and he let out a small groan as he moved inside me for the first time. Our bodies were electrified as we made love; the rhythm taking care of itself. And as we came he kissed me again and whispered, "Baby."

I sat up suddenly. Sunrise was filtering into the room, but there was no Samuel. I was drenched with sweat and my body still gave off little spasms as it recovered. I may have been alone (dammit) but that was one hell of an orgasm. Now that I was relaxed (*really* relaxed) I noticed that my room-mate was not. She scanned like she was…no, how was that possible?

I looked over, then immediately felt I should look away, but I didn't. Her beautiful face was contorted in ecstasy; her right hand was out of sight under the sheet, her left cupped one of her bare breasts. Within seconds she came with a whimper, took a deep breath and smiled her beautiful smile. Atalanta looked over at me and giggled. "Morning, sunshine."

I didn't know how to react to all this. I was disappointed that my time with Samuel had been a dream, a fucking awesome dream, yes, but still not real. And I was unsure how I should handle having just watched my room-mate come in front of me. I had to admit, though, that I was glad that I had just come myself because that had been pretty hot and I was fairly sure that coming *because* of my room-mate would've been the only way this situation could have been more awkward. Turned out I was wrong, but that was what I'd thought at the time.

Atalanta, unlike me, seemed really happy. She stretched in her bed and sat up, pulling her top down over her breasts. She shook out her hair, still smiling. I was at a loss as to what to say so I said nothing. She seemed to find this amusing, too. "Well, that was fun, Jane. Thanks for the awesome orgasm."

Just when I had thought I couldn't be more uncomfortable. "Excuse me?"

She got out of bed, tying her hair up in a ponytail. "That was intense. You must really want him." She peered at me, "Or her. It didn't feel personal enough to be me, or was it?"

Dammit, now I was blushing. "No, it wasn't you, 'Lanta." I got out of bed and straightened my own clothes. "And what the hell kind of coincidence was that?"

"No coincidence, sweetheart." She stepped into the shower to turn on the water then returned. "You know how our TP's can read super strong thoughts that override our built-in barrier?" I nodded. "With MEmps it's strong emotions. I can block them pretty easily when I'm awake, but it sneaks up on us when we sleep. That was some dream. Hit me like an avalanche. Your lust invaded my dream and became my lust as well. And because I wasn't awake to control things, at least not when it started, my lust became yours again and so on. Like a feedback loop."

I sat back down on the bed and rested my head in my hands. No matter how many times I've been embarrassed, it always feels like the first time. "Has this ever happened before? With me?" I said through my hands.

"Not like that."

Just fucking shoot me. Atalanta walked over and sat next to me. "Jane, it doesn't mean anything. It's just sex and I don't mind. I needed it, actually. And so, apparently, did you." She walked back towards the shower. "Trust me, you wouldn't believe the shit I've had to dream because of room-mates. Night terrors, falling, being murdered, rape dreams—and not the fun ones. I'll take a rocking orgasm any day of the week over any of that."

She stripped, dropping her clothes on the floor as she moved. Most people looked better in clothes than out. Atalanta did not have that problem.

I looked up. "Why are you being so nice to me?" I had to ask. This was not usual charming Atalanta I knew.

She thought for a second, then her smile returned. "Because you didn't fuck Wilby, and then you fucked *with* Wilby. Wish I'd seen it."

I dropped my head in my hands again. This was not a good way to start what was sure to be an impossibly awful day. Atalanta had the shower door open and was stepping into it when the School Announcement System beeped on. I'd forgotten we had one. I stood up, listening and Atalanta turned the shower off and started dressing.

"Children," it was the General's voice, Samuel's voice, amplified. I felt my throat tighten, still confused about last night, unwilling to believe all he'd said. But the General was speaking, "We will attempt to evacuate the School today to someplace safe off planet. You may bring one, and I mean *one*, bag with you of standard service size. You will pack now and then keep it with you *at all times* until further notice. You go to the can, you take it, to the refectory, you take it, to the Armory for a nooner (something that I would *not* advise today), take it. Or drop it in the center of the Quad and someone will try to get it to the shuttle. There will probably be no notice from our ride and no going back for anything or anyone. I will keep you informed of anything else you'll need to know as the day progresses. That is all."

Atalanta and I stood in silence for a second. I looked at her. "I'll find the service bags." She nodded and began opening bureau drawers and pulling stuff out. I looked under my bed and there the bags were. I pulled them out, tossed her one and we got to work.

Atalanta and I were dressed and carrying our bags out the door when we heard a giant thump. The ground shook with the impact of whatever it was and we immediately ran out into the Quad along with about a hundred other people. We dropped our bags on a pile of other bags and looked ahead of us in surprise.

A ground car sat in the middle of a grassy area and several "baby" Macros were clustered around it. Felix prowled around behind them, obviously supervising. His expression brightened when he saw us coming towards him. He had a smile for me, but a wink for her. She winked back. Wow. She actually likes someone. I suddenly wondered who the object of Atalanta's dream had been. Hm.

Felix turned back to his charges and took a breath to say something when he was interrupted.

"I need you, Felix, Paulette, Arthur and Jane over here with me." It was the General, all controlled stress and focus. Felix quickly told his charges to stand still and do nothing and we headed over to our Keeper who was standing on the other side of the ground car. I was sure that to the unfamiliar he looked just like a tired version of himself, but I knew better. He looked like shit. He scanned full of adrenaline, his eyes were trying not to be bloodshot, and his usually military posture was slightly stooped. I looked at him, full of concern. He must have sensed it. He caught my eye and gave a microscopic shake of the head.

Paulette and Arthur caught up with us and we stood around the ground car. The General walked in front of it so that we could see him.

"This is the deal. I need you each to gently, and I mean *gently*, Paulette, lift an Object over the School and set it down as far away from it as you can get it. Without dropping it. You can practice on this ground car. We think, though don't know for sure, that the size, mass and weight will be comparable to that of an Object." We Macros stood in silence for a second, taking this in. The General continued, "I cannot express how important it is that this be done *gently*." Paulette discreetly rolled her eyes. "Dropping your Object or even setting it down too hard may open it prematurely. That would be a terrible thing, don't you agree?"

The General walked to the back of the group, standing behind me. "One of you will lift and the other 3 will be spotters. Control is key. You 4 are our most powerful experienced Macros. We are depending on you all." He checked his watch. "You have 10 minutes to practice."

He stepped away from the Macros, checked his watch again and shouted, "Stuart!"

"On my way, General." Stuart spoke from the far side of the Quad.

I quickly walked over to the General. He had his hands on his hips, impatiently waiting for Stuart.

"There a problem, Jane?" His eyes scanned the Quad restlessly, then stopped as he watched Paulette half drop the ground car. The resulting thud made everyone jump.

"I know, *gently*," Paulette yelled out before anyone could say anything. The General closed his eyes in mortification.

"Sir?" I asked, a little insistent. He nodded, not looking at me directly. "Did Pace 3 go down?"

"At 5 this morning." He rubbed his face with both hands, clearly fighting off fatigue.

"Did any ships get away?" Even though he'd said exactly what I had expected him to say, it was too horrible to process. Millions of people gone.

"Five. They're heading out of the system now. Someone finally understood what a stupid fucking idea sending everyone here was." Now the ground car was lifted high over everyone's heads, then gently put down. That had to be Felix. He really was good. "Anything else?"

I saw Stuart approaching and knew time was short. I dropped my voice. "You need to keep an eye on what you're projecting. One way or another your stress will be ours." The General looked over at me, right at me, angry, I think, that I was adding to his burden. I didn't blame him, but I was still right.

Stuart walked up. "He won't talk to me. He almost smashed the camera, he was so annoyed I'd turned it on." The General snorted, apparently not surprised at this news. "And Dr. Bayliss's shuttle will be here in an hour."

We looked over and saw Arthur lift and then put down the ground car in a satisfactory manner. Atalanta stood between the General's group and Felix's. She took her relaxing breath, then slowly turned her eyes on the General. She scanned him quickly then walked away, her expression serious but not out of her mind terrified. Thank god. The General flicked me a glance.

"Shouldn't you be lifting something?" he said, then he and Stuart walked a few steps away to talk with more privacy. He may be annoyed, I thought, but the kid was right, wasn't she?

"Jane!" Felix called out. My turn, apparently.

Seconds later I was standing in front of the ground car. I started with Pace 4 then moved up to the ground car, running over its bulk and estimating its mass in my mind. The trick was to convince my body not to try to lift it. My mind needed to do all the work, my body should be at rest. Way easier said than done, especially with something this large.

The car lightly lifted off the ground. It weighs nothing, I kept telling myself. Nothing at all. But the higher I lifted it, the heavier it seemed to get. I could feel the muscles in my shoulders tightening into rock. I forced myself to lower the car gently to the ground before I hurt myself.

There was some small applause. Felix looked concerned and stepped close to me. "I'm worried, Jane. You've got power to spare but you have to let go of the physical or you're going to get hurt.

I looked down, acknowledging his point, but then looked up with a grin, "At least I kept my eyes open."

He smiled back and patted me on the shoulder, "Full marks for that, Jane." He walked over to Atalanta who had been watching us, looking …distressed. Sad? I liked Felix and was happy that he liked me, but she had no reason to be jealous. I knew Felix's secret and I only had eyes for Samuel, whether or not Samuel wanted me. But there was none of the fury she'd directed at Wilby, just loss? Why?

Stuart seemed to appear out of nowhere, heading right for me. "We'll lift the first Object in 5 minutes." He looked over at Felix who nodded. "Jane, the General needs you." Stuart took me away as Felix stepped back in front of the ground car.

"Let's try this again..." He looked at Paulette.

She held up her hand, "Don't say it." And Felix didn't.

07:00 – The General's Office, Guard Tower

Stuart and I arrived at the top of the stairs. We could hear yelling through the General's Office door. This made me move faster. Stuart, however, just shook his head and didn't alter his pace at all.

"Listen, you goddamn son-of-a-bitch, we're sending a shuttle and getting you out of there if we have to kill you to do it!" the General roared at his desk monitor. Who the hell was he talking to? Or at? The General saw Stuart and me enter and waved us over.

"Jane, talk to him," the General waved me over to the monitor. I sat down in the General's chair and looked at the screen.

Irrfan. Mad as a hatter and still filthy. He looked all right otherwise though his house was even more derelict than when I'd been there last week. He saw me and smiled, immediately becoming calm.

"Jane, dear." Irrfan chuckled. "General Armstrong thinks you will help him convince me to come with you in your grand escape. He doesn't realize that you are the one person who can understand why that will never be."

Shit. Really? That's why I'm here? And for the second time today I was wishing for someone to shoot me. I gave out a defeated sigh. The General, as surprised as I was, but for very different reasons, moved closer to the monitor, and thus very close to me.

"What the fuck does that mean, Irrfan?" The General looked from his image to me. It took every bit of will I possessed not to shrink away from him and his anger. I may not be happy about this, I thought to myself, but I'm not a coward. Or I won't allow myself to be.

"As a courtesy, I will lay out the top 3 reasons I am not coming with you. We both know that you cannot make me, but I find myself suddenly wanting to spend a few minutes of my remaining hours talking to others. Most out of character for me."

The General straightened up and turned away, looking at Stuart who just shook his head sadly.

Irrfan was the only one of us who looked even remotely happy. "Your goal for evac is to get at least into orbit if not out of the system as soon as possible, then wait for the Terrans to rescue all of us and take us to Earth itself, correct?"

Stuart and I both looked at the General. I don't think either of us had thought that far ahead. The General had, apparently. "Yes," he responded.

Irrfan nodded. "One: Being around people makes me both intensely ill and intensely crazy, a fact which tends to get innocent people hurt. Two: The motion of the ship will be difficult, if not impossible, for me to adapt to." Irrfan stabbed a fat finger in the General's direction. "You boys will need to help Jane with that. It won't be as bad as it would be for me, but it won't be easy for her." That directive was meant for both Stuart and the General, but only the General nodded. I could feel it. "Three: If I am a freak here in the land of freaks, on Terra I will be a monster. I *will not* go through that again and worse." Irrfan leaned towards the camera. "Believe me, Sam, I *will not go*." He relaxed. "Tell him, Jane."

Oh great, he'd remembered me. The General turned my chair partially around so that I was facing him. Stuart was watching and I could tell he was scanning mercilessly, trying to figure out this obviously weird room dynamic.

"Tell me what?" The General folded his arms on his chest.

I cleared my throat, then went for the direct approach. "Even if we could take him, Sir, we would be taking him to a life of misery and madness. He would rather die quickly than live for months or years, first violently ill onboard ship and assaulted by the thoughts of all of us, then studied and prodded as some kind of science experiment on Earth." I stood up trying to catch his eye, but failed. "I know it is anathema to leave a man behind, but he needs to choose for himself." And then I added. "The way a man should." He looked at me then.

Irrfan let the silence hang for a second or two, then broke it with, "I won't be left behind for long, Samuel. Besides, I saved your and your kids' lives last week when I told you to call Ian. You chose to call him. Let me choose not to."

The General sat down on the credenza behind him. "I won't risk sending anyone for you." Irrfan smiled. "But, I think I'll be able to ask you one more time."

"Not for me, Sam. You know what I'll say."

"For my conscience, then, you weirdo."

"Fair enough," Irrfan smiled. He then called out "Stuart!" I'd forgotten he was there. Stuart stepped forward and I surrendered the chair. I sat next to the General on the credenza. Stuart dropped into the chair, his eyes were red. He'd been crying while we'd been arguing. I felt so sorry for him. And Irrfan.

"Stuart, listen to me," Irrfan spoke soothingly. "This is the only way, which you knew before you spent an hour this morning trying to convince me to accept rescue. You have been a good friend to me, but I need you to move on."

I watched Stuart, worried for him as he shook his head at the image of his friend. I'd never seen him so upset. In agony, yes, upset, no. He swallowed hard, clearly temporarily silenced by emotion.

Irrfan's large and filthy face softened further. "Use your assets to your advantage. And don't give up, Stu, you are a good man. I will miss you."

"Jane," the General's voice was quiet but insistent. I turned to look at him, fighting the urge to reach for him even though I shouldn't. "Jane, make sure you get on that ship. No matter what." That wonderful voice of his was full of fear, now that there was only me to hear it. "Irrfan's made his choice. But we will leave no one else," he looked at his hands, speaking even more softly, "and especially not ..." He couldn't seem to go on. We just sat in our own silence as Stuart recovered his voice and started arguing with Irrfan again.

I tried to read the General but I couldn't get anything that made sense. His heart rate read as calm, his breathing regular, but I knew that was wrong just by looking at him. Then I got it. Hey. Bastard was blocking me, messing with my reading. I don't think he'd ever done that before. What was he hiding from me? How upset was he? And then I had a quieter thought. He's really terrified that I won't make it on board, but doesn't want me to know it. I looked at his careworn face but he deliberately stared straight ahead.

"Pretty soon we'll be all that's left of Pace," he said bleakly.

He said this so matter-of-factly, that the fear I'd been suppressing suddenly overwhelmed me. I must have turned white or held my breath or something because he finally looked me in the eyes. "Don't let fear get in the way of doing what's right. Use your strength and I'll see you on that ship. Yes?"

I took a deep breath, nodding quickly, trying to convince my fear to back off. "Yes, Sir," I whispered. My affirmative seemed to help him regain control. The General stood up.

"Stuart," the General called, "We're gonna go lift some Objects. Back in a few."

"Thank you, Sir."

The General and I left the office and headed for the stairwell. He stopped for a second with his foot on, surprisingly, a step going up, not down to the Quad. "By the way, Jane, I'm stationing all the Macros on the roof for the lift."

I stared at him in disbelief. "Because having us haul giant, heavy, deadly Objects several stories in the air and put them down without breaking them and killing everyone wasn't enough of a challenge? Now we need to be on the *roof*?"

The General paused a second as if trying to decide whether to be amused or annoyed with me. Apparently amusement won because he snorted. "Line of sight, Jane. We need to be able to maintain line of sight for the whole move."

That made sense. Fuck. The roof just seemed awfully high. "Sorry."

For a second I saw the old twinkle back in his eye. "I think that's the latent sarcasm gene," he said dryly.

I swatted him on the arm. "My secret weapon." He nodded thoughtfully to himself, twinkle already gone, as we reached to top of the stairs and the sunlight.

The Macros were there, plus Atalanta and, surprisingly, Wilby who was still bandaged up on his chest and shoulder. Felix talked quietly with Atalanta, but moved over to the General and me when we arrived.

"We're ready, Sir."

"Good," the General responded. "You first." Felix nodded.

Felix, his compact form exuding confidence, walked to the part of the roof closest to Object 1 and that had a good view of the field we hoped the Object would land in. He planted his feet solidly on either side of the pinnacle of the sloped roof. I scanned him, trying to catch his process. He took a breath and made his body calm. He folded his hands in front of him at waist height. He turned his head to the left and looked at Object 1.

Belatedly I realized that I was supposed to be spotting as I noticed Arthur and Paulette concentrating as well.

I could feel the ease with which Felix lifted the thing, like it was an empty egg instead of a multi-ton Object of Death. No grunting or straining. It was as if it had become buoyant. He brought it to the second story level and students both on the ground and on other levels watched it go by warily. Then it was up over our heads, hovering for a second as Felix changed his physical orientation from the left (where it came from) to right (where it was going). The Object floated serenely out over the School out-buildings and landed ever so gently in the field.

We all, including Felix, exhaled in relief. Unfortunately, this was too serious a moment for clapping; the brief enthusiasms of the early morning had made way for cold reality.

"Good work, son."

"Thank you, Sir." I noticed that Felix's face was slick with sweat. So, he'd just made it look easy. I was even more impressed with him now. Atalanta walked over to him, beaming and gave him a kiss on the cheek. I saw Wilby off to the side looking as if he'd just bitten into a turd. I wondered which of the three of us he hated most. Had to be me.

Arthur was next and I walked over to Atalanta and Felix while he picked his spot.

"What is Wilby doing here?" I asked them.

Felix looked away, suddenly very absorbed in where Arthur was standing. Atalanta shrugged her adorable shoulders.

"No idea, but I heard the General order it. I think he is monitoring the Macros."

"What on Pace for? Proper liver function?" I did not understand, but then I guessed that my understanding was not required.

People had been talking but then silence fell as Arthur quickly lifted his Object into the air. His style was more dramatic, less obviously controlled, but I could feel that his grip on that sucker was secure. He was doing very well. The Object zoomed over the roof and out to the field, only slowing down just when it was time to set down. He put it down gently and smiled with relief.

The General smiled at him, too. "Good job, Arthur. Paulette, get in position."

I walked over to Arthur and gave him a hug. He was really sweaty and breathing hard. Felix and Atalanta caught up with me.

Felix asked, "How was it?"

Arthur tried to catch his breath. "Fucking heavy."

Felix clouted him on the shoulder. "No, Arthur. You feel the mass, then let it go. It wasn't supposed to be heavy at all. I can't believe…" But then Felix saw the look on my face and changed his tone. "Great work, man. You really showed control."

Arthur brightened. I laughed inside my head. Trust Arthur to do something really good, then spoil it by talking about it—yet another reason we'd broken up.

By now Paulette was in position for Object 3. Felix, Arthur and I stood in a semi-circle behind her. With a Herculean effort she hoisted the Object into the air. Felix shot me a look and we both concentrated on the Object, trying to soften the movement. I felt Wilby moving up behind us. Why? But I had no time to wonder further as the Object lurched over us. Atalanta gave a small squeak of fear, but immediately subsided as, I am assuming, people glared at her to be quiet. The Object made it over the roof and was speeding towards the field with the other Objects. Too fast. I thought Paulette was in trouble. I walked over and saw the look of total terror on her face. She looked at me for a second.

"I can't put it down right. I can't do it," she whispered. I looked at Felix, who shot a glance at the General.

"Jane, take it," the General commanded. Great.

With the greatest care, I took the load from Paulette. I could feel Felix and Arthur, gently helping. It *was* heavy, but I tried to let the weight go, with some success. I felt the creatures inside it, disturbed by the movement, moving like crazy. I took a step back, repulsed.

"Jane..?" Felix said softly, calling me back to the job at hand. I nodded unconsciously. I refocused on the Object and gently brought it down on the field.

People were smiling at me in congratulations, but I wanted to run away. I felt like I'd just touched an infestation of ...a cancer, something horrible. I stood off to the side, wringing my hands. I wanted to scrub my mind free of all those little moving horrors. I saw the General take a step towards me, but he was stopped by Wilby, who spoke low. They called Felix over and conferred for a second. The General looked unhappy but nodded his approval.

It was now time for my official lift. I was the one to get the Object out of the old choir room. Tricky, I thought, but doable. I just wished I could avoid feeling the creatures inside. Made my skin crawl.

Felix approached me. "Wilby said that your shoulder muscles are tensed to the point of breaking your scapula. May I?" Surprised I nodded and he walked behind me putting his hands on my shoulders. He was right. So, Wilby was there to monitor *me*? Right, the freaky Macro/Micro chick. Fucking great. "Now force yourself to relax," Felix said as he massaged my shoulders. It felt really good. I tried very hard not to picture Samuel doing this. That seemed like a bad idea right now. I caught Samuel's face out of the corner of my eye. He looked really unhappy and Atalanta not much happier. I needed Felix to stop touching me, much as I liked it, or things were going to get ugly. All of this made me oddly pleased, though, and I did relax.

"I know this is weird," Felix said in my ear, "but we're going to stay like this during the lift to remind you not to hurt yourself."

"But," I started, dismayed and embarrassed.

"General's orders." Felix sounded calm, like the natural teacher that he was. I shot the General an annoyed look. He ignored it. Time to lift, then.

I started with Pace 4, then up to the School building I was standing on, then down in the hole to the room that had been our old choir room. Not that we'd ever had a choir. I felt the Object, picturing the weightlessness that Felix had done so easily. I felt Felix's hands on my shoulders, and immediately tuned them out. I focused on detaching from the physical. The Object floated easily up out of the building, bits of concrete and wood falling as it lifted. Suddenly the Object was free and over our heads. I had it and I didn't strain, I didn't tense. I had it right. I ignored the creepy infestation inside it. I was in control more than I'd ever been. I moved it away from the School and over to the other Objects, setting it down as delicately as anyone could have asked for. I could feel the big grin on Felix's face as he let go of my shoulders and hugged me.

He let me go, still grinning. "You did it, Jane!" People were smiling at me. Not Atalanta. Not Wilby. Barely the General, but other people. Wilby walked away, his job clearly done. The General appeared, expression blank, but trying to look approving. He awkwardly reached out and patted my shoulder.

"That was good, Jane. Very good." He attempted a smile, failed, and walked away.

I saw Atalanta shoot him a look of complete shock, then look back at me. Dammit. He'd been upset enough, dare I say, jealous enough for him to lose track of what emotion he was projecting to whom. A fool would have merely been confused by that reading. Unfortunately, as I've said before, Atalanta was no fool. She stared at me a second, cocked her head to the side as if trying to take it in. She shrugged (at my taste, at his, who knew) and moved away. But she didn't look pissy any more. She hugged Felix again.

I watched them for a second, then made an observation of my own, *without* empathic talent. Even without, I was sure I was right. So, the hottest babe in the world, loves Felix, I thought. Ah, Mother Irony.

We had all started down the stairs when I froze. The General stopped, then they all stopped because he did.

"Something's coming." I sensed something flying through the air towards us. "I think it is that Doctor's shuttle. The General nodded and we all started down the stairs again. The General let everyone pass him and I slowed down. Soon we were alone. We just stood there. He was upset, I could tell, and so tired. Much as I'd enjoyed his moment of jealousy, I couldn't bear him thinking I wanted anyone else.

I walked close to him, but he was too tall for me so I went up a step. "Samuel," I whispered as I kissed him tenderly on the cheek. He had no response, he just kept looking away. "Baby," I said softly. "I'm with you even…" and I paused, considering the sad truth, "when you don't really want me."

He looked up, hurt in his eyes. I found it hard to breathe. He exhaled sharply and reached for me, pulling me to him and holding tight. In his arms I found I could breathe again.

"I want you, Jane. God help me, but I do," he said as he buried his face in my neck.

I closed my eyes, happy, so happy, breathing him in. We just stood there for a second, wrapped up in each other. I spoke softly in his hear and felt his body shudder as I did so. "Let's just focus on getting everyone on the ship and worry about the rest tomorrow."

"On the ship," he agreed. He sighed and I could feel the vibrations through his chest as he said reluctantly, "That prick's shuttle must have landed by now."

Much as I didn't want to leave his embrace (and I really, really didn't) I nodded. "Then let's go, Samuel." And we went.

A Note on the Scientist Class of Pace-Pallon

The one true aristocracy on Pace-Pallon was the Scientist Class. They controlled our genetic future and whether our offspring survived and thrived. They set the tone for the whole system. Pace and Pallon had set it up this way with the idea that scientists would be above the sort of petty power-grabbing that normal politicians and royalty would have been prone to. This was a typically oblivious choice made by two people who had started an entire colony as a massive power grab. But they'd believed in it and had set it in stone.

700 years later we had a firmly entrenched power structure with brilliant, if pampered, Scientists ruling all. These Scientists were almost exclusively geneticists with a smattering of engineers who looked after agriculture and metallurgy and we'd even had one (one!) who designed faster than light engines. He was a Terran import who had been delighted by some of our customs (he'd brought his sister with him, don't ask) and shocked by others. He had helped the General create the fleet of 6 FTL ships (well, 5 after the Edo *was destroyed). Unfortunately, he'd died on the* Edo *and the General's dream of an exploratory fleet had died with him.*

There were levels of influence within the class itself, of course, the highest being the Alphas. There was a reshuffling the rare times the government had changed over and that was the only time anyone had the opportunity to upgrade their status. The higher strati were usually vacated by that age-old equalizer of execution, as when the current Government had taken over 30 years ago.

The breeding programs for Scientists were extremely top secret and highly illegal. There was none of the stringent oversight that attended Pace normal births. The Scientists were smart enough to realize that their children at least needed to look *like everyone else (blue and green people with glowing hair really were a relic of the past), but on the inside they could be a crazy quilt of ideas, some good, some bad. The "Doctor" in front of their names had long ago become an inherited title. They went to special schools, lived in special towns and were the only humans on all four planets who could opt out of The Tour if they wished. Pace was their playground. Some people resented this power but most just accepted it.*

Dr. Ivor Bayliss, a low level functionary (an Omega, if you will), was sent to Pace 4 that last day with what he felt was an exciting discovery. Typical of his class he was a kind of thoroughbred; brilliant, highly strung and spoiled. He'd engineered his first humans just over 25 years ago and had talked parents into all kinds of "improvements" that had, for the most part, improved little and created misery. But in the tradition of his idols Pace and Pallon, he'd never looked back, only forward, and never gave a thought to having to pay for his mistakes. Of course, cosseted in his laboratories, rarely venturing out, he'd never actually met *any of his mistakes.*

09:00 – The Quad

All of us stood around as we watched Dr. Ivor Bayliss's shuttle's cargo hold open and start to disgorge its contents onto the field just outside the School. Some of the General's soldiers pulled open the Quad's double doors (that I'd never seen fully opened) and we watched the back hatch of the shuttle unbutton and something massive, a giant metal crate, being powered out. I looked at Felix questioningly, but he only shrugged.

A man emerged from the shuttle and started walking energetically towards us. He was medium height, blonde with a short beard and blue eyes. He walked with a spring in his step and was very expensively dressed. He seemed very…merry for someone whose world was about to end.

The General straightened his uniform and posture. "Fucking Scientists," he murmured for those of us closest to him. He then left us, meeting the visitor in the middle of the Quad. The General stuck out his hand in greeting. The visitor hesitated a second (I got the feeling that no one was ever allowed to touch a Scientist) but then smiled good-naturedly and offered his. They shook.

"Dr. Bayliss, welcome to our School," the General said in an appropriate if not actually warm tone.

"General Armstrong, I am *delighted* to be here." Dr. Ivor Bayliss's accent was clipped and formal and he bobbed forward on his toes in emphasis of his delight. Oh, god, I thought. What an ass. "I've always wanted to see this School and meet our next generation of secret protectors." He looked us over with friendly condescension.

I could tell from the tension in the General's neck that he was trying not to shake his head in horror. It almost made me laugh, but I knew that would not go over well.

"What's wrong?" I heard Atalanta whisper to Felix. I looked over, scanning him as I did so. Wow. Tension, blood pressure through the roof, muscles locked, fists clenched. I'd seen Felix pissed off, but never truly angry like this. Atalanta looked at me, worried. Felix just stared, stared at Dr. Bayliss.

"I say, could I borrow one of your famous Macros? I have a surprise for all of you but it's too heavy to move without help. Any volunteers? I mean, if that is all right with you, General?" Dr. Bayliss smiled at everyone.

Felix took a step forward but Atalanta and I pulled him back. He shook us off, but quit trying to move forward. The General was looking at us, trying to pick someone.

"Fe…" he started to say but changed his mind when he saw Atalanta and I shake our heads no. "Arthur, help the Doctor and Jane be spotter."

Dr. Bayliss rubbed his hands together in glee. "You won't believe what I've got here, General. It's the most amazing thing I've even seen."

The General gave him a half-hearted smile, but this did nothing to dim the Doctor's enthusiasm. I wasn't sure anything would have at that point. Arthur and I walked over to the large crate. The General and the Doctor followed. The shuttle crew was packing up and preparing to take off. The General looked over at the Doctor, alarmed.

"They're not leaving?" The General looked appalled.

The Doctor laughed, "Oh, don't worry. They said they'd be back for me tomorrow."

The General, Arthur and I all stared at the shuttle pilot, who grinned maliciously and dove into the cockpit. Within seconds the shuttle was in the air and gone.

The Doctor clapped the General on the shoulder (reaching up to do so), "Don't worry, dear fellow, I won't be on your hands for long."

The General closed his eyes. I could read both tension and…nervous laughter bubbling up in him. Boy, this had to be bad. We were going to be stuck with this fop forever, weren't we?

The Doctor stood aside from the crate. "Gentleman, Lady, would you please? Into the middle of the grassy area in the School's Quadrangle, if you would?"

Arthur and I nodded. Arthur prepared then gently lifted the crate. He smiled for a second. "Not nearly as heavy as the Objects." The crate floated a few feet away from us when I belatedly remembered that I was supposed to be spotting, not that Arthur needed it. He'd really come into his own. When, I didn't know, but he had. I gently felt for the mass of the thing but did not interfere. I positioned myself so that I could catch it if it fell. The four of us walked slowly together as Arthur expertly guided the crate. I continued my scan of the crate, admittedly curious as to its contents.

Suddenly I felt hard shell, legs tapping the bottom of the crate, internal organs moving all wrong. Wrong and wrong again. My good god, he had one of those creatures in there. I backed up so fast I fell down. Our progress stopped and the General, concerned, helped me up. He read the panic in my face and grabbed my shoulders to steady me. I started wringing my hands convulsively and rubbing my arms, trying to rub the creepy crawly feeling off of me.

The General's eyes were wide, afraid for me, "Jane, what is it? Is it what's in the crate?"

I nodded, my hand-wringing not abating. He stared at my hands, moving, moving. He looked from me to the crate then at Dr. Bayliss. He got it. "That pompous son of a bitch brought one of those things to my *School*?" He made sure I was steady on my feet and then strode over to Arthur who was still lifting the crate.

"Arthur, take that to the Transport Shed. You don't need a spotter."

"Yes, Sir." Arthur looked confused, but immediately changed his course.

The Doctor was overwhelmed with disbelief. "I say, General, I want all the children to see this." The General ignored him, following Arthur and the crate to the Shed. "It's really quite a find," the Doctor continued. "We've only managed to capture a half dozen at great expense to life and limb…" His voice trailed off as he, too, followed the crate.

I was no longer wringing my hands, but I was still upset. Why *would* that son of a bitch bring that thing here? Oh, right. They've probably done everything they could to it in their labs and now needed to see what the freaks had to say. I needed to scan it again, even though the thought of actually doing it was abhorrent. We needed to know what was inside it. Once we knew *that*, then maybe we'd know how to kill it.

A few minutes later a bunch of us were assembled in the Shed. Wilby for the Micros, Arthur and myself for the Macros (Felix being mysteriously absent), Atalanta for the MEmps, Stuart for the Telepaths, the General for the people with sense and Dr. Bayliss representing the damn fools (at least that's how I saw it).

Dr. Bayliss danced around, barely able to contain his excitement. He'd made sure we were paying attention then stepped in front of the crate that now rested on a large work table.

"Ladies and gentlemen," he said theatrically, "I give you…" Then the Doctor said as an aside to the General, "We used the name your friend Irrfan came up with. We couldn't come up with anything better." He started again, so pleased with himself, "I give you… *tapetia mortis*!" He pressed a button on the side of the crate and some kind of sight barrier within the clear outer substance comprising the cage dropped down on all sides. Inside stood a horrible crab-like creature, in mass the size of a large canine. It had twelve legs and a hard shell. It was unclear how it could see, or if it needed to, because there were no visible eyes. The shell was mottled brown and black and some kind of puss appeared to ooze out of the joints. It sat there calmly, as if evaluating us as much as we were evaluating it.

I clasped my hands together, trying to retrain myself from wringing them together. It helped that the thing wasn't currently scurrying around.

"It was very lucky. We happened to have a Survey Team on Pace 1 right after they'd…" Dr. Bayliss paused as if reluctant to say what the creatures had just been doing.

"…just devoured every living thing on the planet?" I finished, barely concealing my anger at this folly.

"Right," the Doctor sounded relieved to have had someone else say it, "and it had just shed its skin. Seems that is a very vulnerable time for the creatures. So they captured it and eventually we found that this transparent alloy really slows him down."

The General stepped forward to get a closer look. Stepping closer was the last thing I wanted to do, but he was a lot braver than I. "Slows him down you say?" At that statement the creature vomited something that smelled appalling and made the alloy in the floor steam slightly. The General looked over at Dr. Bayliss. "That cage is transparent Tenorium alloy. We use that for visibility in our jump ships. That stuff is almost impenetrable."

"Well, so we thought." The Doctor shook his head ruefully, "I find that these crates last about 2 days." We looked at him horrified. "Don't worry, the lads picking me up are bringing a new one tomorrow."

"What's that in the corner?" Arthur asked, pointing. In the far corner was a black insect nest-shaped thing attached to the walls. It looked like a work in progress, building up to the top of the cage.

"Yes, well, he seems to be building something. It's incredibly strong. It's impervious to…everything."

"How do you know that?" Atalanta finally spoke quietly. Dr. Bayliss lit up, delighted to be talking to the very pretty girl.

"Well, we had another creature, another *tapetia mortis* and we were able to get…access to its cage." He looked a little uneasy, but Atalanta clearly wanted him to keep talking so smiled at him and touched his lapel. I bet she was projecting something, too.

"Sounds dangerous, Doctor Bayliss. However did you do it?" She looked up at him, doe-eyed.

"It was quite thrilling, actually. The Marines were able to destroy that particular creature with a flame thrower." We could all tell he was spinning this as fast as he could.

The General closed his eyes as if asking for strength. "And why did the Marines have to destroy it?"

"To protect the Scientists, of course." Atalanta had tucked Dr. Bayliss's arm through hers and he was oblivious to how upset the General was getting.

"Because it'd escaped," the General said with a sigh. He looked at me and I shook my head. "How many people did it consume before you killed it?"

"Half a dozen, give or take. I wasn't there, of course, but I saw it all on monitors later."

Needing a distraction from the recital of lethal incompetence I was hearing I started scanning the cage. The cage itself was as expected, an inert solid Tenorium alloy. The vomit was clearly corrosive but I couldn't get anything else from it. I turned my attention to the hornet's nest like structure in the back corner.

"Do you know what the structure is made of, Dr. Bayliss?" I asked.

"Feces," he answered promptly, which prompted Atalanta to assume an adorable expression of disgust. A put on, of course. Dr. Bayliss looked at her and attempted to soothe her wounded sensibilities. I nearly laughed but held it in. The Atalanta I knew was hardly the delicate flower she was pretending to be.

"You mean this thing is building a nest, or whatever, out of its own shit?" Arthur burst out.

Dr. Bayliss gave him an annoyed look. "It's very efficient. Disgusting by our standards, of course, but efficient. Nearly indestructible, as I said, and perfectly evolved in its utility. Look, there it goes."

The creature made a scissor-like motion several times then excreted a black tarry mess, about a cup full, though it was hard to really tell. The room immediately filled with the most noxious smell and it was hard not to retch.

"Vile, isn't it? You get used to it," the Doctor said pleasantly.

The creature then scooped the semi-liquid mess and added it to the nest in the corner of the crate. It moved quickly and added, conservatively, a quarter inch to the height of the thing. By the time it had finished, the nest already looked dry and hard. The creature then vomited into the top of the structure. The whole process was thoroughly gross.

"But what's it building?" The General asked patiently.

"We don't know. Not yet, anyway."

The General turned to Wilby and me. "Get a feel for what is inside, if you can."

Wilby and I walked over to the far side of the cage and started scanning. As soon as my mind was inside I immediately felt burning, like acid, which I assumed was the vomit, but also a pressure. A building pressure.

"Do you feel that?" I asked Wilby.

Wilby looked at me with contempt, "Of course I feel it. You don't need to ask that every time, Jane. I've been doing this a lot longer than you."

Oh, good, he was back to form. "Sounds like you need a slap against the wall…"

He stepped closer to me, menacing, but I'd made him puke in midair and he lacked the power to scare me. "You have no idea how much pain I can cause…"

"Or how much I enjoyed seeing you tossed around like a rag doll. I hope you skipped breakfast this morning." I smiled up at him super sweetly.

"Wanna get started?" He stepped even closer. I held my ground. I only had eyes (and not in the romantic sense) for Wilby and I was going to clean his clock. Again. What I didn't see (or didn't register until I'd reconstructed it later) was Atalanta giving a worried look to the General. He caught it and Atalanta pretended to stumble to distract Dr. Bayliss. All I saw was the General appear out of nowhere.

"Really, children?" he growled softly. We stepped back from each other.

"Bitch," Wilby muttered under his breath.

"Cunt," I breathed back under mine.

The General put his fingers on the bridge of his nose, clearly asking a higher power for patience. "Report, Wilby."

"There is a reservoir of the acidic vomit within the nest. The thing that is puzzling is the pressure that seems to exist when this large of a quantity of the vomit is stored like this."

"Meaning…" The General prompted.

"It bubbles, Sir. Like it's boiling." I answered before Wilby could.

"Any thoughts, Doctor?" The General turned to the Doctor who was doing his best to catch a peek down Atalanta's shirt.

"Sorry?"

"Never mind." The General gestured to Stuart, who had been hovering in the background. I wondered idly if he was thinking of the last time we'd been here in the Shed together. I hoped not. "What have you got?"

"I've been scanning since we walked in and, as before with the creatures in the Objects, I'm not getting conscious thought. There are very strong drives going on there, but I would venture to say they are emotion-based, not thought-based." Stuart gave a deferential look to Atalanta who nodded. She deftly disengaged herself from the Doctor and moved back towards us. Her girlish manner was gone and she was back to all business. I found it a relief, personally.

"I'm getting a couple of things. Instead of "hunger," I am getting "full" or "sated" and an intense drive to build. It was very strong right before it dumped and then carried into the building and subsided when the feces were used up. It seemed, I don't know, like it was part of the species, a biological imperative. An overwhelming imperative." Atalanta looked thoughtful.

"Good. See if it happens again. Keep a Micro with you. Keep Wilby." Wilby looked thrilled. "Doctor, would you be so good as to supervise while I go check on some things?" The General was extra gracious.

Dr. Bayliss, realizing Atalanta would be staying, nodded cheerfully. "Carry on, General. Thank you," and dismissed him.

The rest of us, Stuart, Arthur, the General and I left the Shed and headed back to the school. There was silence for a moment.

"I swear I'm gonna deck that moron," the General said through clenched teeth. Stuart grinned at this and then we all did. We reached the doors and Stuart made a bee line for the Guard Tower stairs. I assumed he was going back up to Irrfan, lost cause that that was. The General made to follow him when Mallory ran up to him breathless.

"It's Arrow, Sam. Something's wrong," she said in a low urgent voice. The General paled, then started to follow Mallory. He took two steps then beckoned with his hand.

"Jane," he called. I turned and caught up with them.

Within a minute we were in Arrow's apartment within the School complex. She was huddled on the floor, sitting up with her long arms wrapped around her legs. Her breathing was shallow and her face tear-streaked. She looked up only for the General.

"Arrow. What is it?" the General's voice was very gentle, as if he were talking to a distressed child.

Her eyes were wild when she looked up at him. "They're about to break free, Sir. Break free and consume us. They will spread out like a carpet of death over everything and then everything will be gone."

"When, sweetheart, when?" He knelt next to her. She closed her eyes and two tears leaked out.

"Soon. Too soon. I've seen so many die. So many friends just…eaten. Poor Arthur." And Arrow, tough, steely Arrow burst into tears. What did she mean, poor Arthur? Arthur was fine.

The General gently took her hands and made her look at him. "The ship. Did you see the ship?"

Arrow shook her head, her expression one of pure misery. Wait a minute, I thought, she's a pre-cog? And she's seen Arthur die already? And no ship? That can't be true. I needed to get out of there and I ran out into the hallway. I could feel a scream building, but I couldn't let it happen. I could scream later, I told myself, when we're all dead.

Through the open door I could hear the General say to Mallory, "Give her a sedative and make absolutely damned sure that she makes it on that ship." It was an order, but his tone was pleading.

There was a brief pause. "You can count on me. You know that," Mallory said gently.

He exhaled as if just the act of giving this task to Mallory assured its success. Which it probably did. "Thank you, Mal."

"Any time, Sam."

A minute later the General walked out into the hallway and leaned against the wall next to me. By then I'd gotten a hold of myself.

"No Pace normals are normal, eh, Sir?"

He laughed a sad laugh. "Nope."

"Is Arrow always right? When she 'sees' things?"

He pushed away from the wall. "Yes, but she can't see everything." He reached over and squeezed my hand. "I need you to monitor the Objects from the Shed roof. I think you're as much advanced warning as we'll get. And by the way," he let go of my hand and stood in front of me, hands on hips, "can you leave off the pissing contest with Wilby? Talk about wasted energy."

I looked up at him, amused. "Until we're on the ship. All right?"

We started walking out of the dorm. "No, but it is as good as I'll get right now."

"Bet your ass. Sir."

The General let out a laugh. "Now git, and make sure you get on that ship when it comes." He tossed me something which I caught out of reflex. It was a radio. "That will transmit to everyone and will allow me to contact you if anything changes on my end. Go." I nodded as I grasped it tightly and headed for the shed.

A few minutes later I stood on the shed's roof, my dislike of heights all but forgotten as I prepared to concentrate on the Objects in the near distance. I felt Dr. Bayliss, Atalanta and Wilby below me in the Shed. They seemed fine, so I threw my awareness out to the Objects.

Frantic movement. Digging, clawing. They were attempting to force their way free of the Objects. I could feel the Objects' outer skin weakening. I suppressed my terror as I tried to keep my focus. I felt a crack in one of the shells. I picked up the radio.

"The shells are cracking!" I yelled into it, panicked. I heard my words echo throughout the School. I felt people begin to move faster like a disturbed ant hill. I looked below me and saw the Doctor, Wilby and Atalanta running out and away from the Shed towards the School. Atalanta looked back and saw me, waving for me to follow.

The radio beeped. It was the General. "Jane, get out of there!" I nodded, though there was no one to see it, and started climbing down the ladder on the side of the building. Another shell cracked. My hands were shaking as I grasped the rungs. But two feet from the ground everything changed.

I felt something. High in the atmosphere. Something huge. The ship! It was coming!

I picked up the radio again. "The ship is coming! I feel it!"

Another shell cracked. "Jane, run!" It was the General again on the radio.

I threw myself down the ladder and ran as fast as I could to the School and into the Quad. A dozen people slammed the massive double doors shut as soon as I ran past them. Without thinking I ran for the steps and up to the Guard Tower. My only thought was to get to Samuel, to make sure he got on the ship. I just hoped it would get here in time.

I reached Samuel's office in time to feel the sonic boom that could only be the ship entering the atmosphere. But the only person in the office was Stuart. Stuart, pleading with Irrfan.

"Please. Let us come for you. The ship is almost here. Jane felt it."

By this time I was next to Stuart. Irrfan looked up at the camera. "Too late for me, dear boy. Get to your ship."

Irrfan turned to his Object, waved his hand and broke it open. A thousand horrible crab-creatures poured out like enormous spiders. They weren't particularly fast, but they were relentless. Irrfan grinned and made a grand sweeping motion with one fat arm—and a couple hundred crabs were swept out of the house and off the mountain.

The next batch approached. He made a fist and slammed it down and they all flattened, dead. He cackled in delight.

He stared at the next wave intently, concentrating. And one by one, every one he stared at popped apart, like popcorn.

For the next wave he put his hands on his hips and suddenly two axes floated next to him, one on either side. He grinned and set the axes to work at blinding speed. Crab body parts flew everywhere.

The next group was picked up and two by two smashed in on themselves.

Another wave came, then another. Irrfan kept going. He was brilliant, but we could see he was getting tired.

Then Irrfan started turning the crabs inside out, which was quite disgusting. After that he started tossing them one by one trying to get them back in the Object. He awarded himself points depending on accuracy, style, etc.

But they kept coming. Apparently, play time was over.

Irrfan held off the horde with one hand and started sweeping in great circles above his head with the other.

Stuart and I leaned closer to the monitor, trying to figure out what he was doing. Then it became clear as bits of house started coming apart and flying away. Even the abandoned and empty Object was gone, lost down the side of the mountain.

The sweeping motion became stronger. "Woohoo!!" Irrfan screamed as the wind he had created knocked his house into bits and blew them away. He only left one part of one wall—the one with the camera.

He was now unprotected on the bare mountain. He stood up and let his chair blow away. He had the most maniacal look on his face as he paused, clearly concentrating. The crabs he'd thrown down the mountain were climbing back up. The thousand crabs he hadn't killed were closing in. He was unconcerned. He concentrated harder and harder.

Suddenly the ground under his feet bubbled. And another part behind him seemed to be pushing upwards. The crabs were within a foot of him, their millions of legs making ugly tapping sounds on the rock. The sounds sent shivers down my spine, but Irrfan was unaffected, his concentration unbreakable.

A crab touched his foot. Irrfan looked at the camera, grinned like a loon and yelled, "Take a look out your back window, kids!"

Without thinking we both turned to the General's back window.

And Irrfan's mountain exploded.

Stuart let out a cry of anguish. The monitor went black. The ground shook and the top of the mountain was sheared completely off. What a talent, I thought. Holy shit.

At the same time the ground shook *again* with a gigantic *thump*. I ran into the hallway to an interior window and looked down into the Quad. An enormous shuttle had landed right in the center of the School. I let out a gasp of relief. I shook Stuart.

"The ship is here. We have to go, Stuart." He did not go. "STUART!" He stayed put, apparently too grief-stricken to care. I scanned him for mass, then lifted him roughly with my mind. I ran for the stairs, Stuart 'dragging' behind, a few feet off the ground. He hit a few walls, but I didn't have time to care. We emerged from the stairwell to see a short gangway leading into the back of the gigantic shuttle. I hadn't known a shuttle could *be* that big. People were running, scrambling up to get in.

I ran up the gangway, still 'dragging' Stuart. I got inside and dropped him, then ran back down. I stepped out of the way of the panicking mob and reached out to feel for the Objects. What I could feel scared the crap out of me: they were empty.

And then I felt something else.

I felt the ground outside the Quad move.

Mother of god. "They're coming!"

I could feel thousands and thousands of creatures, carpeting the fields and surrounding us, heading towards our School, towards food. The panic I felt was rising. Then I remembered something. Some*one*. Arthur.

Atalanta and Felix ran past me up the gangway. "Where's Arthur?!?" I yelled.

"I'm sure he's on board, Jane. Come on!" Felix yelled. They disappeared into the crush of evacuees in the shuttle. But I knew Arthur wasn't up there with them.

"Arthur!" I screamed impotently.

Then I heard it. Chewing. Scraping. I looked at the double doors that separated us from the outside world. Those things were eating them. It was as if the universe just stopped for a second. And then they were through. The few remaining humans that weren't on the shuttle screamed and ran for it. I started up the ramp but felt something and stopped.

A man, a soldier I'd never seen before bellowed at me, "Get up the goddamned ramp! I have to retract!"

Then I saw it. A small group of people running for the ship, Arthur among them.

"Wait!" Arthur shrieked just as the creatures swarmed his group, running over them like they were nothing. It all happened in a second and they were gone. Arthur was gone.

The soldier, a captain I thought, sprinted down the small gangway and picked me up like a sack of potatoes, flinging me over his shoulder. He reached the top and slammed his fist into a button on the wall. I felt the doors close and the gangway retract at rocket speed.

"Get us in the air, Janowski!"

"Aye, Sir."

The ship rumbled and shot straight up. And as it shot up I fainted.

I woke up in Samuel's arms, being carried like a child. I felt around gently, trying to sense the size of the ship I was on. This one felt like it was the size of a city. At least we were off that cursed shuttle. I looked around me. I seemed to be in some kind of officer's lounge with wide windows on the bottom of the larger ship. The ship moved smoothly and I was grateful. Pace 4 became blanketed in night as we crossed the terminator. Below us I was surprised to see some cities still lit up.

Samuel sat down in one of the chairs by the window, resting me on his lap. He saw my eyes were open and kissed me on the forehead.

"Arrow? Wilby?" I had to know.

"They're here, Baby. We lost about fifty people including Arthur and Paulette." I felt the lump in my throat and tears in my eyes. He gestured to the view outside the Tenorium window and turned me a little so I could see it better. I could feel others pressing forward catching a look at the planet below.

"Take a last look, children. Our home is lost." The General looked around him, his face a mass of loss and defeat. "We are all that is left, now. All that is left of Pace-Pallon."

No one said anything. The room was deathly quiet except for some quiet sniffling.

A lighted city went dark, then another. A minute later another. I couldn't look anymore. I buried my face in his chest and sobbed quietly.

When the last light on Pace 4 went out Samuel pulled me closer and wept.

July 4, 2869

END OF BOOK ONE

Book 2:

Jane of the *P.S. Scylla*

Book 2 Preface, as written by Felix Pace

When I suggested to my dear friend Jane that she write her story (in order to counteract the damage done by the book those vermin 'journos' wrote), it never occurred to me that work for *me* would be involved. But I would do anything for Jane.

So, in case you are coming late to the party, this is Book 1 in *very* broad strokes:

Where we are:
Pace 4, the Government-run planet of a four-planet system surrounding a yellow star. The system, our home system, is called Pace-Pallon. Jane and her friends (myself included) live at an educational institution for supernormals, not so cleverly called 'The School.'

What we are:
There are three major types of genetically enhanced supernormals at the School: Telekinetics (Macro and Micro), Manipulative Empaths (MEmps) who can sense both individual and group emotions, channeling and changing them at will, and Telepaths.

Who we are:
Jane is 17, almost 18, and a Macro-Telekinetic; she can lift big things with her mind. She also, over the course of the period of time covered in Book 1, realizes that she may be a supernormal rarity—a Macro/Micro hybrid—which may allow her to sense and move things that are also very, very small like blood vessels or water molecules; things assassins find fun.

Felix, that would be me, is 25 and recently returned to the School as the Macro-Telekinetic instructor, though I pretty much end up teaching everyone. I am a Macro-Telekinetic myself.

Atalanta, a 21 year old MEmp, Jane's room-mate, my friend and the most beautiful woman in the entire universe.

Wilby, 25, ridiculously handsome slut and genius Micro-Telekinetic. Asshole.

Arrow Peters, 29, a pre-cog who teaches our self-defense classes. Tiny and lethal.

General Samuel Armstrong, 55, the Keeper (or Dean) of our School, and a 'normal.' Good man.

Of course, at this point the General would say that there is no such thing as a Pacey 'normal.' He'd be right. He usually is.

And, last but not least…

What the hell happened:

Book 1 covers a one week period, starting with the landing of the carriers (or Objects) of the deadly crab-like *tapetia mortis* on our home planet (Pace 4) on June 29th 2869 and ending with the destruction of all life on the four planets of the Pace-Pallon system on July 4th, 2869.

The five million or so Objects that blanket Pace 4 (and the other three planets in our system) are inert in the beginning but slowly change as creatures inside them start to move and then eat the insides of their carriers. It becomes clear that they are going to get bigger and stronger and then eventually break out of their shells and escape. This is a very bad thing.

Wilby, to his annoyance, is assigned to give Jane Micro lessons (now that she can do the Micro 'thing') and she learns fast. He, rather surprisingly (at least *I* was surprised), talks to her about the importance of duty and of doing a job well in order to protect those who do not have our gifts—even prejudiced assholes who hate freaks. Apparently this includes most 'normal' Paceys and all Terrans.

Pace 2 (the first of the four Pace planets to have been hit by the *tapetia mortis* Objects) falls. Millions upon millions of humans are devoured by the creatures in the space of a few hours.

Somewhere amidst all this I try to get Jane to like (or at least be able to stand) my childhood friend, Atalanta. She takes some convincing since Atalanta was, at least at that time, really bitchy. But I knew Atalanta was special; I'd come back to the School just to be near her. I wanted the two of them to be friends; since I wasn't sure my Atalanta *had* any friends. So I pushed a little and waited to see what would come of it. A lot, as it turned out, but that is getting ahead of the story.

Arrow Peters, the pre-cog, tells us the future is really bad. Unfortunately, she is right.

Pace 1 falls, then 3. Just us left now, but not for long.

Ian Armstrong, Captain of the *P.S. Scylla* (one of Pace's 5 faster than light ships) and the General's son, swoops in and rescues most of us supers, planning to keep us all in space until the Terrans can come and re-rescue us.

The Pace 4 *tapetia mortis* eat. The last millions of planet-bound Paceys die.

We few are all that is left of Pace-Pallon.

So, some final thoughts:

I know I didn't mention them in the above little summary, but the Scientist Class (our very own Pacey aristocracy of spoiled fuckhead entitled geneticists) controls everything we do—not to mention controlling our very existences since they were the ones who had created and now own us.

They are evil, either actively or passively. Scientists. Evil. Remember that.

Wilby is a shit but *not* actually rotten. Same goes for my Atalanta.

While the *tapetia mortis* may have eaten every living thing on Pace-Pallon we aren't done with them.

The General Armstrong family (which includes Ian and Arrow, his publicly unacknowledged daughter) is really…unusual.

The 55 year old General and the almost 18 year old Jane are irresistibly drawn towards each other. Moths to flame.

So now you should be caught up (or caught up enough). If you need more details, go back and read the fucking book again.

Hope you enjoy *Book 2: What The Hell Else Bad Is Going To Happen To Jane (and her friends)?*

Godspeed, everyone.

Felix Pace
Three Furies Fleet
August 19, 2889

ENTRY 1-2-7

10:00 – *P.S. Scylla*, July 10, 2869

It had been a week since the fall of Pace-Pallon. The ship was in a low orbit around Pace 4 and since we had nowhere to go, it looked like it would be for a long time. Or until the Terrans rescued us, assuming they did. I'd spent that first night in Samuel's arms, sitting in that officer's lounge. I'd slept at some point but I was sure Samuel hadn't. Once the ship's clock told us that it was morning (we'd apparently seen our last sunrise for quite a while) we'd separated, too numb to talk. His son, Captain Ian Armstrong, the soldier who'd saved my life during the evacuation, had insisted that his father take the Captain's cabin, so that is where Samuel went.

No, I'm wrong. Samuel had spoken to me. He'd given me the door code to his cabin. Then he'd left. I was glad he'd spoken to me, but I'd barely registered what he'd said.

Not really knowing what the next step was, I went and found Atalanta. She would at least tell me what to do—whether or not I felt like doing it was something else.

I found her assigning quarters. Even Atalanta showed the effects of shock. She was almost a different person; eyes dull, hair unbrushed, careless of her clothes. If I'd been more myself I would have been gratified that she had shown evidence of a heart at last. Instead I just wanted her to give me a bed.

A Note on the P.S. Scylla

The Scylla *had been built with grand dreams of long term space travel and exploration, a ship that would be teeming with scientists and soldiers and, eventually, colonists of Pace-Pallon itself. This was the brainchild of the General and his Terran engineer, Chow Lin. Unfortunately, Government interest had only extended to the building of the ships themselves. There had been no supporting programs to create the personnel necessary to fully staff these large ships. No exploratory programs. Few Scientists had wanted to move past genetic engineering and no one had encouraged their children to do so.*

Chow Lin, however, had at least made sure that there were people trained (almost entirely miners from the fiery Pace 3) to maintain the engines and the ships.

Some of these people turned out to be quite brilliant, but had not been born Scientists and had no "Doctor" before their name, so were considered only grunts. There was even a fledgling fighter program with 16 single-man fighters completed. Dozens more had been planned, but the Government had decided the fighter project would be secret, so no one knew about it, and no one had learned to fly.

The Scylla *was the largest of the five remaining faster than light ships. After the* Scylla *came the* Wayne, *the* Newton *(a carrier), the* Trafalgar *and the* Hastings. *Since the staffing and training of full crews had not happened, the 5 ships were minimally staffed and almost eerie in their emptiness.*

Captain Ian Armstrong had been promoted to the command of the Scylla *about a month after his father had resigned from fleet command. The Captain had felt that any chance of exploration, while remote when the General was there, had died when he left. The Captain was then in charge of ship that could technically go anywhere, but now had no chance of it.*

Crew quarters on the *Scylla* were configured in four bunk sets. Two bunks on each side of the room with drawers, etc., below and on the far wall. The room was divided by a privacy curtain, though considering how small the rooms were it was doubtful that much privacy would be gained by using it. Atalanta had put herself and Felix on one side and me on the other, leaving one bunk empty. Felix had been surprisingly difficult to convince, but had yielded in the end to Atalanta's insistence. I got my door code, grabbed my service bag (that had somehow made it to the shuttle, though I couldn't imagine *how* it had), and took off for my new home.

I was glad to have Atalanta as my roommate again, much as I could be glad about anything. I wasn't completely convinced that we were going to continue getting along, but felt a "better the asshole you know than the asshole you don't" philosophy was prudent in this case. I got in, found my bunk and slept for 10 hours.

21:00 – Loading Bay, *P.S. Scylla*

That evening I found myself standing in the loading bay with all of my fellow supernormals. We'd been called to an assembly. I'd slept but didn't feel any less tired. At least I didn't actually feel bad. I didn't feel anything. Intellectually I knew that this wouldn't last, but I was in no hurry to get to the grief that awaited me. I put all thoughts of Arthur out of my mind. The numbness let me do that and I was grateful. I wished it could last forever.

Atalanta appeared next to me as we all waited. She looked tense. I suddenly felt guilty for contributing nothing. That feeling quickly passed. Then I thought of something.

"Why didn't Felix want to room with us?" I asked.

"With me. He has no problem with you." Her expression was both bitter and resigned.

"But you two are so..." What to call it? "...close."

"Yes. Sometimes too close." Atalanta ran her fingers through her hair. "He'd been away for a long time. He'd only gotten back about 2 weeks before this," she gestured around, "started happening."

I looked at her, but still didn't get it. "So?" I said undiplomatically.

"We fight. A lot. It all starts out great. We get along like a house on fire, we draw closer and then we run into the same fucking roadblock every time."

Sex. Right. "Have you tried projecting on him?"

Atalanta turned on me in sudden fury, "Of course I've tried projecting on him, you idiot. I've tried everything I can think of. Nothing works. And then he gets jealous with my work..."

Her work. What the hell did that mean? "I'm sorry? Work?"

Atalanta shook her head and looked annoyed with herself. I guessed that that had been a slip of the tongue.

"Then why not let him go off on his own. There are plenty of Macros he could room with."

"Because he..." Atalanta swallowed. "I have to stop him."

"From what?"

"From killing Dr. Bayliss."

There was no chance to follow up on that cryptic remark as General Armstrong had stepped to the front of the loading bay. Behind him assembled Captain Armstrong, Mallory, Doc Wells, some man we'd never seen before, Felix, Wilby and Arrow. From the way the General's son was glancing at her, it looked like he was a planet too close to Arrow. Arrow, however, appeared cool and focused.

I felt a rush of excitement in seeing Samuel even if he was fully the General at this moment. The few times I'd seen him over the past week he had been distant and professional. I'd reasoned that he was very busy, which he was, and still reeling from the loss of Pace, which he had to be. I missed him. But I didn't know what he was thinking anymore. I had his door code, but didn't know what would be waiting for me on other side of it. Anyway, he started speaking.

"Good evening, Children." The General looked less beaten down, tired but purposeful. Once the worst had happened, there was nowhere to go but up, I thought. "I've called you all here to talk to you about your futures. There is a lot for you to think about over the next month or so. A lot has changed and will keep changing. I, we," he gestured to the group of people standing behind him, "want you to be as prepared as possible." He stood at parade rest, hands behind him and scanned the crowd, his eyes resting on me for (I was pretty sure) a second longer than they had to before moving on. "Our hope is that we will be meeting up with the Terrans by August and that they will take us with them to Earth itself. We should all be thinking of ways that we can make it our home."

There was some murmuring in the crowd, which surprised me. The rumor mill had been talking about nothing but Earth for the last week. At least, that's what Atalanta had told me when I'd been pretending to listen.

"The best way to make the transition will be to have something to offer." He crossed his arms on his chest, frowning. "You are all worried about the prejudices of the Terrans and rightly so. As a group they will not take to us, whether we are supernormals or Pace normals. However," and he leaned forward for emphasis, "I have found that individual Terran people can be won over. We are all human, whether or not everyone's comfortable admitting it, and on some level we can understand one another." The man I'd never seen before nodded behind the General.

"I have discussed this with my advisors," he gestured to the group behind him, "and we agree that the best way to be made welcome is, as I said, to have something to offer—preferably something no one else has." Some people in the audience nodded. "What makes us freaks will make us valuable. They have rules against making people like us, and I mean the Pace normals, too, but there are no rules against using us if we already exist. We need them to want us first, grow to understand us later. To that end we will be stepping up training for all supers. This will be intensive and exhausting but will hone your skills and make you all that much more of an asset."

Gladys, a Micro from one of my old classes, raised her hand. The General nodded at her to speak. "Does this mean, Sir, that we will get to *choose* what we do?"

There was a pause as everyone took in this rather mind-boggling query. Even I, who had been wrapped up in my own thoughts and barely paying attention, had to take a moment to consider the implications. *Choose?* Really choose? And not just predetermined choices A and B, but *anything*? I didn't know how to take that in. I looked at Atalanta who chewed her lip thoughtfully.

The General waited for the murmurs to die down a bit. "While you are on the *Scylla*, or any of the Pace fleet's ships you are considered under my protection, like you were at School, and subject to my authority." He paced slowly in front of the crowd. "When we are rescued you will be free," voices rose in excitement but he raised his hand for silence, "but this is a freedom you aren't used to and it comes with a price. You are free to, once we reach Earth, run off and do whatever you like. And starve to death if you cannot afford food or find work. You are free to try to find a commission in the Terran military, but you will be subject to their orders, like you now are to mine. You can start a business, you can travel to other colonies—assuming you can afford to do that.

"You can also," and suddenly the General's face was deadly serious, "choose to use your talents in ways that conflict with Terran law. I would not advise this, kids. You may think that because there are no acknowledged Terran Telepaths or Micros that you can get away with anything, but you would have underestimated them. They are smart and they are much more likely to catch you than you think—especially if you are being hunted by another one of our supers."

There was silence. The group of teenage boys who had been grinning when the General had mentioned a life of crime were no longer grinning. The General started to say something else but seemed to think better of it and turned, gesturing to his 'advisors.'

Gladys raised her hand again. The General indicated she should ask another question. "What if we choose to stay, Sir? On Pace, I mean."

This time there was silence. What if we didn't have to go? What if the creatures died or left? What if we could go home? I felt lifted by hope for a second until I looked at the bleak expression on the General's face.

"There is no way to know at this time whether Pace-Pallon will ever be habitable again. We are proceeding as though it will not be. We do not have enough supplies to orbit indefinitely. Once the Terrans arrive you may make arrangements, if you can, to stay on a ship, if any decide to stay. But I would advise you to think long and hard against doing that." That wonderful voice of his dropped lower. "Our home has been destroyed. It isn't the place we knew even two weeks ago. And the people we lost will not be waiting for us if we go back."

He looked at Gladys with sympathy as she nodded her understanding like a small child. Tears dripped off her nose. The General straightened his shoulders as if trying to shake off the sadness that had come with that question. He gestured to the people lined up behind him.

"I would like to introduce to you the Captain of the *P.S. Scylla*, Ian Armstrong." Captain Armstrong was tall, like his father and had the same military bearing, but where Samuel was lined and careworn, Ian was strong-featured and smooth with clear blue eyes to Samuel's brown. The General continued his introductions. "Mallory, who is staying on as our Weapon's expert. You'll be seeing a lot of her." He smiled at her, she smirked back. "Doc Wells, whom you all know so well." The short, fat man with the enormous beard who had been our Doc at the Infirmary waved to us.

The General skipped the unknown man. "Felix, who has accepted the position of head Macro instructor for the remainder of our time on the *Scylla*." Atalanta smiled at him and so did I. Felix looked both wary and proud. "Wilby, who will remain as our head Micro trainer." Wilby smiled in cocky acknowledgement. Oh, good, he's back to his usual asshole self. Isn't training going to be fun? "Arrow Peters, who will continue as our hand to hand instructor, among other duties." Arrow gave us all a look that was clearly meant to remind us not to cross her. Not that we would. And I found myself wondering how her pre-cog talent affected her fighting.

The General stopped pacing and stood in front of us again. "And lastly, I would like to introduce the official Terran Observer for the *P.S. Scylla*, Doctor Sahil Singh." The strange man stepped forward, his face serious. He was of medium height, dark skinned and dark eyed with long curly black hair and looked to be about 40 standard. "There is no Scientist Class on Earth. Doctor Singh *earned*," the General gave Dr. Singh a conspiratorial look which caused the Doctor to chuckle, "his degree on the Lunar Colony and has been stationed on the *Scylla* and also Pace 4 for the past 2 years observing our genetic science." The General took a step back, yielding the floor to Dr. Singh.

Dr. Singh took a step forward, his manner now serious. "Good evening." He paused, gathering his thoughts, then launched in with, "Truthfully, living among Terrans will be a challenge. While they all are, whether they admit it or not, products of some form of genetic engineering, there is a predominant feeling that mods such as those found on Pace-Pallon are unnatural. Each of you will have to decide how to deal with expressing your talents; whether to be bold or to hide them. General Armstrong is correct in saying that you will probably have more success in getting along on an individual, rather than a societal, level.

"There are," Dr. Singh continued, "by the way, naturally occurring Telepaths, Telekinetics and Empaths within Terra and the Terran colonies, but they're rare and elusive. The irony is, of course, that it looks like human evolution is starting to embrace the genetic codes that lead to the natural creation of supernormals. You all, unfortunately, were created a couple of hundred years too soon." Dr. Singh looked as though he were done speaking, but apparently thought of something and spoke again.

"I will be on this ship until we rendezvous with my people. I would be happy to answer any questions you might have, but I need to offer a word of advice and warning to you all..." Dr. Singh leaned forward, very intent on making his point. "You all must assume that the humans you will meet will have no defenses against you. You can scan them, read their minds, feel their emotions, move their bodies, invade them as you wish. But you must *not*. All prejudices begin with fear, and if you remind them why they are scared of you they will act. So, please, be respectful and be disciplined about it. I cannot stress how important this is." In fact, Dr. Singh looked worried as though we hadn't gotten it and was about to say it again when the General put his hand on Dr. Singh's shoulder to stop him. The gesture was a friendly one.

I turned to Atalanta with raised eyebrows.

She answered my unsaid question in a low voice, "Confidence in himself and a great deal of worry." I nodded.

Dr. Singh was finishing up. "Earth can be very beautiful and the people have good hearts. Mostly. I hope you will put every effort into fitting in and making a contribution. We are all humans. We should be able to work together." His voice had faltered a bit on that. I shot another glance at Atalanta.

"Not as much confidence in that statement."

I gave her a small smile. "Even *I* picked that up."

"Will wonders never cease?" but her tone was teasing.

Dr. Singh had stepped back from his speaking position and there was a pause as the General turned to his colleagues, clearly discussing something.

"By the way," Atalanta continued softly.

I looked at here inquiringly. Atalanta stepped a bit closer to me to whisper, "Much as I enjoy your dreams and I have never been one to question a good come, don't you think it's time you went and saw him?" She flashed her eyes in the direction of the General.

Fuck. So I'd done it again? Yes, Sir, that's me, Dream Slut. At least my room-mate was ok with it. Of course, I realized, I had more than one room-mate now.

"Did Felix..?" I asked, then wished I hadn't.

Atalanta's mouth drew into a thin line. "Slept right through it the first two times..."

The first two times?? "And the other?" I said as I prayed that there was only one other time.

Atalanta gave me a look, divining my thought. "Don't worry about it, Jane. He can handle it. It doesn't bother him. Of course, that's the problem, but it is what it is."

Dream slut? Dream destroyer, more like.

"I'm sorry, 'Lanta."

She looked at me annoyed, well pissed was more like it, but stopped herself from saying something nasty. I could tell. I'd seen that expression way too many times to mistake it. "I'm new to this whole friend thing. Is there a way that I can tell you to fuck off without ending our friendship?"

I was charmed and grinned at her. "Go ahead. I'll give you a freebie."

She nodded, "Fuck off, Jane."

I laughed, "Would that I could."

The General had stopped conferring with his people and stepped into speaking position again.

"Your intensive schedules will start tomorrow morning." He crossed his arms on his chest again. "One more thing. You will all need to have chosen last names by the time we meet with the Terrans. You will be registered, sampled, retina-scanned, etc., and you will need a last name to go in your file. Think carefully, this will be the name you are known by on

Earth and its colonies. Until then you may call yourself what you want. That is all."

We disbursed.

<u>*Excerpt from Indira Pallon's Journal—April 8, 2172*</u>

Experiments are going on as planned. I'm still getting used to being able to research without having some evil bureaucrat breathing down my neck, even though we've been here for almost 3 years. The problem I am running into, though, time and time again is that I can't do things quickly enough.

Take Pace 3. We lucked out with 3 being so rich in minerals and fuel, but the few colonists we can get to go there are dying like flies. The heat, the lack of decent atmosphere, the higher gravity—it's wearing them out if not outright killing them. Our initial domes were too thin and we're reinforcing, but it's taking months. Months of not *mining,* not *producing. We've had to throw out tons of DNA from Pace 3 colonists because the place is so toxic that it is...changing it. It doesn't seem to matter that much, though, because the colonists whose DNA it is are usually dead before they can try to use it. What a waste.*

In light of a Pace 3 problem, I just put in a new batch of embryos with increased muscle mass and vastly improved oxygen synthesis but they take years to grow into adults. Why can I give them extended life, excellent health, faster reflexes and not speed up maturity? And I don't have time to figure out how to do that because I have too many fires to put out.

Atticus is no help. He's spending all his time on the cosmetic stuff. The Exotics, we're calling them. Purple skin with green blood or some nonsense. 10 foot tall athletes. Hands with claws for wall climbing. I do love the prehensile tail idea, though. I didn't tell him that. He doesn't need encouragement.

I think I've talked him out of the three breasts concept, though you never know with Atticus. The thing is that even with 3 tits, it will be 15 years from birth until he can legally play with them. He did support that 15 Standard Age of Consent Law and thank god for that. And he'll stick to it like everybody else. I'll make him.

The Exotics will be interesting to watch grow up and interact with the normal-looking colonists. This will be a good lesson for everyone, a social experiment on a grand scale. I will make everyone be fair. We will teach our people that we are all freaks—and that we are all brothers and sisters to one another. Even to the most freakish freaks of all.

21:30 – Command Center, *P.S. Scylla*

I walked through the Command Center on my way to meet Felix and Atalanta at the Officer's Lounge. I walked through there as often as I could in an admittedly pathetic attempt to catch a glimpse of Samuel. While he'd been there about half the times I'd been through, he'd never acknowledged me, so it was with great surprise that I heard him call my name when I entered the room. He was standing with his son and Dr. Singh.

"Ian, Sahil, this is Jane. She's our Macro/Micro hybrid." The General's voice was cool. I scanned him and found nothing unusual. No burning passion, no sadness, no longing. Nothing. Damnit, he was blocking me again. I shook hands with both men, then smiled at Ian.

"You saved my life." The General looked up, surprised that I had a…mortal connection with his son. He looked like he'd tasted something bad. "On the shuttle gangway." Then I was sad, remembering Arthur. "Thank you."

Captain Ian Armstrong thought for a second, then got it. "My pleasure, Jane. I'm very sorry about your friend." He really did have the most startling blue eyes. Startling but not cold.

I fought the lump in my throat, "We've all lost someone."

Dr. Singh spoke up, "Sam says you are the first hybrid anyone has heard of. When did you figure it out, if I may ask?" It seemed fitting somehow that the Terran who had reminded us to use good manners with non-Paceys would have impeccable manners himself.

I grimaced. "About 2 weeks ago. I scanned a leg and felt the pull of the muscle. It was…" I searched for a word and found nothing impressive, "really neat."

Captain Ian grinned. "You must tell us about it sometime."

"I'm sure you'll have plenty of time on the shuttle tomorrow." Ok? I looked at him questioningly. The General continued. "There are some isolated areas that may not have been hit. Or at least not yet. Any refugees you find will be assigned amongst the fleet."

My memories of shuttles were not happy ones. I swallowed, already feeling nauseous. "Who else will be there, Sir?"

"The Captain, Atalanta, Felix, Doc Wells and a pod of my men. These people are likely to be terrified and may be injured and suffering from exposure. Ian has been sending shuttles out every day since we got here and we've only found a handful of people, but there are some other places I think we need to try before we give up the search. Report at 06:00 tomorrow."

I nodded. He did his finger flick dismissal thing, which Captain Ian seemed to find amusing. I turned to leave, then turned back. "And why me, Sir?"

"Some of these people have lived on their own for a long time. They may be…untrusting of Pace normals and…" he let the sentence peter out.

So I finished it for him. "You wanted to send a good quality freak to make them feel at home? Is that right, Sir?"

For a second I saw Samuel looking at me, sour expression on his face. Then he was the General again. "Yes, Jane, that's right."

I turned to leave again as I heard Captain Ian say, "I'm turning in. First watch in the morning." Ian gave a joking salute to his father and Dr. Singh and walked in the direction of the Officer's Quarters. I caught the General's eye as I hurried after his son. I had no intention of actually catching up to Captain Ian, but the General didn't know that. And then I felt it. The tightness in his chest, the stab of pain behind his eyes. I looked back at him in alarm and caught his eye. He looked right at me and straightened up, the gesture somehow defiant, and turned back to his work. He may or may not be jealous, I thought. But he sure wasn't happy.

I made it quickly to the Officer's Lounge, having passed Captain Ian as soon as we were out of the sight of his father. I saw Atalanta at a table alone. No Felix. There were a lot of glasses in front of her. She was resting her chin heavily on her hands and looked miserable. I walked slowly over to the table knowing that what was coming was not going to be good. I was not wrong.

I sat next to her and she looked over at me fuzzily. I tried to head her off.

"Want to go back to our quarters?"

Atalanta laughed. "That's not what you want to know, Jane." Her words were only slightly slurred but she was still plenty drunk. "You want to know if I've had a fight with Felix. Well, I sure did." She picked up a mostly empty glass and drained the few final drops. "A real humdinger." She looked around her at the other patrons. "Caused a scene. Just like the old days." She looked sadly into the empty glass.

I should have offered to take her to bed again, but I was too curious. "Why would you fight, 'Lanta? You know he's crazy about you."

She laughed again, but there was no mirth in it. "That's why we fight. I've a mission now and he hates it. Hates it." Her beautiful face was sad.

"You're going to look for survivors with me tomorrow. Why would that bother him?"

Atalanta was pouring all the bits of spirits from different glasses (and different drinks) into one glass. This, apparently, took all her concentration; she only answered when she was done. She put the semi-full glass down and put a finger to her lips, making a shushing sound. She dropped her voice to a sloppy whisper. "If we find survivors they will go here and there in the fleet, right? So I go to the *Hastings* with them, that's the one the Scientists and their lackeys are on, and I do what I do." She ran her hand down the neck of her low cut blouse, absently brushing her magnificent cleavage. Oh. Now I got it. Or close enough.

Now I was intensely curious. "Felix knows it's your job, right?"

She sat up, indignant. "It doesn't mean he wants me manipulating and fucking a bunch of Scientists. But this time Felix is going, too, to control things. Talk about picking the right person on paper, but the insanely wrong one in real life…" Then she looked contrite, clearly ashamed that she had just bad-mouthed Felix. "Felix's not stupid, you know, he knows what I have to do sometimes, but he's never had to watch..." Her eyes filled with tears and Atalanta had to pause to collect herself. She regained a semblance of control, but her pretty face still showed her emotional torture. "And he's not unpatriotic or whatever," she said defensively. "The General needs to know what's going on there. He said I could refuse, but I wouldn't. He said Felix could, too, but Felix wouldn't either. Masochist." She shook her head at this folly, "The General's trying to protect us."

"Protect us from what?"

But Atalanta was on another line of thought. Her eyes were filling with tears again. She looked at me. "Felix would protect me with his life. He told me. He told me tonight."

I took her hand and squeezed it. "He loves you, very much."

"I know," she sobbed. I let her cry for a minute, patting her hand. Then I heard a sound. Sniffling to the right of me. Then soft crying on the far side. Then outright wailing right behind us. I quickly scanned the room. Everyone was in distress. The bartender as wiping his eyes on a bar napkin. If we don't get out of here, I thought, the whole bar's going to commit suicide.

"We're going home, sweetheart." I reached down to put my arm around her tiny waist and helped her up. She looked up at me.

"I wanna go home, Jane." She leaned against me. I knew what she meant. It was just then that the wave of sadness caught up with me.

"Me, too," I said softy as I tried not to cry myself. I took her to our quarters and tucked her in. Felix was not there and I was relieved.

I missed Samuel. I started thinking about him and found myself despairing—and then realized I needed to get out of that room at least for a while. Maybe she'd get her control back after the spirits wore off. I hoped so. I already had enough sadness to deal with without having more imposed upon me.

<u>*Excerpt from Captain Ian Armstrong's Journal, July 10, 2869*</u>

We seem to have configured a kind of fleet over the last week. Most of the survivors are from Pace 4, since they'd had the most warning, most money and most access to ships. The Alpha Scientists are on the Hastings *and the rest of the aristocracy has commandeered the* Trafalgar. *A lot of normals were saved from death merely by being servants. The Scientists, who seem to demonstrate no regard for human lives beyond their own were very insistent that their lackeys be saved. The few survivors of 2 are on the* Wayne *with many more from 1 filling out the space. Almost all of the sub light fleet, around 300 ships, was able to get away. We will start going ship to ship making lists of survivors, tending to wounded, shuffling personnel, etc., once we have finished looking for stranded humans plane-side.*

There are a dozen or so mining ships from 3 that are in orbit for the first time. Really weird looking ships. The 3 Paceys won't communicate with us except let us know they know we're around. Pacey 3's have always been strange. And I know strange. And the Scylla *has all the supers. And Dad. And Arrow.*

Dad's worried about the high proportion of Scientists to everyone else. He's sending that gorgeous MEmp over tomorrow to figure out what they're thinking, assuming they're thinking anything at all. He's sending the ugly Macro with him to guard her. What a couple.

I don't know how much longer I can avoid Arrow. I've hardly seen her this week, but she'll start teaching tomorrow and will have to be more visible. I can barely look at her. I keep seeing him *in her big brown eyes. I'd never seen that before. I wish I didn't know she's my half-sister.*

22:00 – Command Center, *P.S. Scylla*

I'd decided to head back to the Officer's Lounge for the drink I'd never gotten and out of habit took my favorite route of passing through the Command Center.

I glanced at the command chair as I passed and saw dark haired man leaning back in his chair with his boots up. My heart jumped. Samuel stuck to his quarters now unless in a meeting with someone, what was he..? I walked closer and had second shock. It wasn't Samuel, it was Captain Ian. He saw me as I was moving by. I was practically running now, internally mortified (and a little creeped out) at my own mistake.

"Jane?" Now I had to stop. I turned and forced a smile. That drink was looking further and further away. And I really needed it now.

"Sir?"

Captain Ian rose quickly from his chair. His movements were energetic, athletic. He seemed to have energy to burn. His father had great physical power, but at a cost, somehow. He held out a yellow communique.

"I wanted your opinion on this." He brought the paper closer so that I could read it. "It's from the Survey Teams monitoring the *tapetia mortis* on all four planets."

The communique read:

The tapetia mortis *seem to be engaged in building large hive-like structures in various places on the planets in our system. We estimate that there are tens of millions of creatures on each planet. We have found some evidence of dead ones in vastly underpopulated areas. There was a cluster of 4 Objects found to be situated in the Hassan Wastes on Pace 1. The Objects are all open but a hundred thousand* tapetia mortis *lie dead around them. Our guess is that they starved to death. And unlike other reports of empty shells and molting, these creatures died within their shells.*

Another problem area for the creatures is the inhospitable Pace 3. We have to judge this by the number of hives, or nests being built. There are 38 on Pace 4, 27 on Pace 2, 18 on Pace 1 and only 5 on Pace 3. There have been many instances of fire being used as a weapon against them and one has to conclude that the dangerous conditions of Pace 3 had been their natural enemy.

There will be another report in 8 hours.

-Ezra Emminger, Pace-Pallon Survey Captain

"But didn't they analyze the nests? They have to get someone close enough to scan them," I said excitedly, thinking out loud. "When we saw the nest that crab-thing built in its cage, Wilby and I could feel the pressure building up inside it. If we could feel that on the *small* scale, I can only imagine the pressure that would be building up if they were trying it on the larger."

Captain Ian regarded me thoughtfully and not patronizingly, which he was certainly within his rights to do. "We need to figure out how many creatures it's taking to build each hive…"

"…and we need to have a firm idea of how large these hives are." I was pacing, my brain on fire with possibilities. I looked up at him. "We need to know the scale." I sat down on the edge of the desk. "And we need to know what they are going to do with all that pressure."

Captain Ian nodded. "We'll swing by as many of those hives as we can during our rescue operations tomorrow."

"Good," was what I said. What I *did* was shiver involuntarily. Captain Ian gave me a questioning look. "Sorry, Sir. Scanning those things makes me feel like they are crawling all over me. It's incredibly disgusting."

He shivered, too, at the thought. "I can believe it." He scratched the back of his head and stifled a yawn. "I was actually in bed when this came in." He smiled, his blue eyes twinkling. Like his dad's did in a different color. Aaaaah. I have to stop comparing like that or I'll go crazy. "I'm going for a drink instead of bed. Were you heading in that direction earlier, or did I imagine it?"

Oh, what the hell. "A drink is that I want," I said. And oh, so many more things, like your father's…never mind. "Sounds good."

A few minutes later we were seated in the Lounge, drinks in front of us. He leaned back in his chair, appraising me as I sipped my spirits. Watching him watching me, I raised my eyebrows. He smiled. He smiled so easily, I thought. What *didn't* happen to him that he can do that?

"I'm trying to figure you out," he said. My eyebrows went even higher. "I knew you were the one who'd sussed out the molting thing. Dad had it in his report." Captain Ian reached for his glass and took a drink. "So I told him that I thought you should have a look at the info we were getting on the creatures."

"Seems reasonable, even though the General and I figured out the skin shedding thing at the same time. Couldn't hurt, right?" I tried to feel more relaxed with each sip. No, this wasn't weird. Nope. Not at all.

"That's what I thought, but he told me to leave you alone," he said. I put my glass down. He did what? Captain Ian continued, "That you needed time for your transition to space and were under tremendous pressure. And to use you, your talents I mean, sparingly."

Abruptly I was angry. Samuel was ignoring me and trying to sabotage my working relationship with his son who was also, at least in theory my *boss*. Telling the Captain to use me sparingly, indeed. What the fuck was Samuel doing?

"Jane?" Captain Ian interrupted my reverie.

I snapped out of it. "Sorry, Sir. The General is trying to look out for me, which I appreciate," bullshit, "but I am available like any other student." I laughed. "I think he may have confused me with some of our more high maintenance supers."

Captain Ian's twinkle had returned. "Like who?" A man who liked gossip. Fun.

"Atalanta, for sure. I love her, but she can be a real pain in the ass." I took another sip and considered. "Gladys, that red-headed Micro. The one with all the questions. She likes to make you choke if you are beating her in an argument," Captain Ian looked startled, unconsciously putting a hand to his throat. "But only if she outranks you," I added. "And then there's Arrow. She's a whole other story."

In a split second his open expression closed like a shutter. The Telepaths will have a field day with him, I thought, unless he has some of his father's ability to block. Arrow, eh? Now my curiosity was aroused and I kept going as if innocently. "It's not that she throws tantrums or anything like that. She just…has ways of letting you know you need to back off." I casually took another drink. "She scares a lot of people."

He played with his glass. "Does she scare you?"

I shrugged. "As a fighter she terrifies me." He looked up. "Too controlled, too perfect." He nodded unconsciously. I pushed a little with, "You've fought her, I take it."

"A long time ago." Ian seemed lost in thought. I suspected something, but it was just a feeling. I tried to think how I could confirm my theory without getting into trouble.

"Then maybe you can tell us about her. She's a mystery to us, you know. Never talks about herself. Doesn't socialize." I reviewed her in my head and started wondering about her for the first time. It was a mystery why she was so…non-existent except when she was fighting. "I only saw her upset the one time…" Then I stopped myself. Fuck. I really had to start paying attention to what I was saying.

He seemed to withdraw further. He drained his glass and turned it over on the table. "And I bet you saw her lose it right before something really bad happened." He turned his blue eyes on me. "Like before this," he gestured grimly around him, "happened."

I nodded slowly. His knowledge of her was even more intimate than I had guessed. Right in line with my theory, though.

He stood up to go, all joviality gone. He looked sad and tired. *That* I was used to in an Armstrong. "You know a lot more about her than I thought anyone here would, Jane, given how close Arrow is with her secrets. I hope I'm the only one you've let that slip to."

"Yes…" I said hesitantly, not wanting to perjure myself. I hadn't told anyone else, but that didn't mean that no one else knew.

"I know Arrow. You'd never see her show it, but she'd be mortified if anyone knew."

"I'm sorry it slipped out. I was surprised you knew." I proceeded carefully. I needed to bring him to the proper place, out of fairness, but I had to tread lightly. I was pretty sure I didn't know how to do that. So I bunted. "Were you together long?"

He looked down at me, surprise on his face, then his expression softened with relief. "It was a long time ago, or at least it seems that way. I barely remember it." Well, I could tell that was a lie. Poor sucker. "I'm going to bed, Jane, and I hope I can trust you to keep that to yourself. It doesn't matter now anyway." He leaned in for emphasis. "The important thing is that Arrow's secret remains that way. Right?" He forced a friendly smile. I tried to smile back, but I knew I was an asshole for what I was about to do. But I had to do it. "Goodnight."

He had taken two strides away from me when I called to him. My heart was pounding, my system full of adrenaline. This was going to be ugly. He turned around, a little annoyed, but trying to hide it, and came back.

"Yes?"

I leaned close to him. I could smell the spirits on his breath. They reminded me of…oh, stop it. It was time. I had to warn him.

"I'm sorry, Sir, but that isn't her only secret." And I looked into those beautiful eyes trying to send my knowledge to him without having to say the words, "I know she's your half-sister." It took him a second, then he recoiled like I'd struck him. I held his gaze as he looked at me with horror and…embarrassment since he'd pretty much admitted that he'd fucked her in the past.

"Who told you that?" he asked, incredulous. He could tell that I knew that he had already known. But *my* knowing meant anyone could know and that was clearly terrifying. I felt his heart hammering, the muscles in his fists straining, his blood pressure skyrocketing. I had set a bomb off inside him and I'd meant to do it. I told myself it was kinder he heard from me that the secret was out…but looking at his handsome miserable face I quailed.

Now I could feel his body chemistry shifting as his shock was turning to anger. He leaned in close, teeth bared. Too close. I 'moved' him back with a hand movement, using enough force to make sure he felt it. This only stopped him for a second. "You keep that bit of information to yourself or I'll…" His voice trailed off threateningly.

Unfortunately for him, I *really* didn't like being threatened.

Now I leaned in. "You've had a shock and you're my superior so I'll give you a break on this one." I made my voice as cold as I could. "I wished to warn you for your own good. I don't plan on telling anyone else who doesn't already know." I let that sink in. He went paler.

"But if you think you can threaten me, superior or no, you are *mistaken*." I dropped my voice lower but made sure he could still hear me. "I could shatter every bone in your body with less effort than it takes to sip my drink." This was a large exaggeration, but he didn't know that. I sipped my drink. "Goodnight, Sir." And I flicked my fingers in the gesture of dismissal.

He slowly stood up straight again and left without another word, unkind or otherwise.

I laughed ironically to myself as I waited for my heart rate to return to normal and my hands to stop shaking. And to think that just a few minutes ago I was mad at *Samuel* for sabotaging my working relationship with his son. As if I'd needed his help. Oh, fuck it.

I ordered more spirits.

Excerpt from Atalanta's Journal, July 10, 2869

Everything is shit. Our home is destroyed and we may never get to go back. We have to refugee with Terrans who will hate us. Felix is jealous of my assignment. Well, not that I got it, but of what it is. And fucking

Jane. I know she can't help it. I know that. But she just dreams all over me all the time. If I was alone, even though I am technically *alone, I would be enjoying it. I haven't fucked anyone since fucking Wilby. And yes, that is a double entendre.*

The first two nights Felix was on the top bunk and slept right through it. The third night I think he suspected something was up, but tried to go back to sleep. And so on until last night.

Jane was out very late. I'd assumed she'd finally hooked up with her General and that we could all get some rest. We'd gone to sleep, separately, but Felix woke up screaming, terrified of something. A night terror. He was inconsolable and I couldn't bear it. He wouldn't tell me what it was, but he was frightened and deeply ashamed of something. I tried every MEemp trick I could think of to calm him down. But what worked was just as simple as touch. I took him into my bed, as I'd done before when this had happened. And he slept. Eventually I slept, too.

But sometime in the middle of the night Jane came home. She had not seen her General and was as sexually frustrated as ever. So she dreams and her dream lust becomes mine, and back and forth like always. But this time I'm sharing my bed with Felix and before I am even conscious I have touched him and kissed him like…a woman touches the man she loves. And he couldn't respond, because he can't *and we both felt like freaks. He retreated to his bed and we couldn't even look at each other in the morning.*

And now we've got that fucking mission.

Maybe I'll become numb from all this suffering. Or maybe I'll just go mad. Both options sound wonderful.

Oh, and I found out that Dr. Bayliss had been sent to Hastings *to give his report on the supers, which is why we haven't seen him in the last few days. Unfortunately, they're sending him back. They said that he was needed as an "interface." Which means they don't want him. If only I could just let Felix kill him. Except it would ruin Felix's life—not that he'd care. He has me to care on his behalf.*

And thus we add one more thing to the misery that is Felix and Atalanta. Numbness can't come too soon.

<u>23:00 – The General's Quarters, *P.S. Scylla*</u>

I stood outside the General's quarters, thinking. I'd had a drink or two more at the Lounge to calm my nerves. It hadn't really worked, but I was here anyway. I put Captain Ian out of my head. That was a problem for tomorrow. Samuel was the immediate problem.

I pressed the door chime. No response. Again. And again nothing.

I entered the door code and the door opened. I walked in and took a look around me. A bed on one corner of the medium sized room, bathroom on the other. In the center of the room stood a large desk with Samuel sitting at it, feet up, bottle of spirits. No glasses. He looked up at me.

"Jane?" He put his feet down. "What's wrong?" He stood up. He stood up very steadily. Then I noticed that his bottle was unopened. He was stone sober. Bad luck for me. This was also not at all what I'd thought he'd greet me with. I'd expected him to tell me to leave or pretend he had a lot of work to do to get rid of me, or something. I felt foolish.

"Nothing. Everything's fine." I took a few steps further into the room. "I just wanted to see how you were."

"I'm fine." Samuel started to sit down but then thought better of it. I guessed that he thought that if he sat then I would sit and stay longer. I scanned him and was blocked again. He had clamped down on what he was projecting so severely that he read as barely alive. Well, I reasoned, he was hiding something.

My eye glanced at the unopened spirits bottle. He was keeping control. For me? I wondered how many nights of the last seven he had spent sitting here, in control, waiting for me to show up so that he could prove…what? That he could exist without a pulse? Or that he could exist without *me*.

Well, he could try to convince me that he felt nothing, but I didn't have to believe him.

"I don't see how you could be, after last week. None of us is." I looked him in the eye. "Samuel." My saying his name made his pupils dilate. Well, he wasn't completely made of stone, no matter what he was projecting.

Samuel walked out from behind his desk. "You shouldn't be here, Jane."

"Why?" I asked boldly. I took a step closer to him. He took a step back and was stopped by the desk.

"You don't understand."

I got closer. "Explain then."

He looked uncomfortable. "This can't work. It would be difficult on Pace, but it will be impossible on Terra."

I was inches from him now, not touching him, but almost. I looked up into those sad brown eyes. "Why?"

Suddenly he was angry with me for being deliberately obtuse. "I'm too old for you, Jane."

I looked at him critically. "You are old, yes, but not too old. If I was 100 and you were 138 no one would give a shit."

Samuel took my hands impulsively. "But we're not."

I would not give up. "You still want me, Samuel. You still do or you wouldn't be projecting yourself into a coma right now. Your desk chair has more life signs."

He laughed in spite of himself and I pulled my hands from his grasp and placed them on his chest. His whole body stiffened. "Jane, please don't."

I shook my head and leaned up against him. His arms had dropped to his sides. He didn't overtly respond, but I could *feel* his heart pounding even if I couldn't sense it. But he didn't touch me. He didn't do anything. Suddenly I was stabbed with a sort of terror that I'd lost him. I guessed I had.

I stepped back. He walked away from the desk. I rested my hands on it, sad, embarrassed, and dreading having to feel the grief of losing him on top of all the other grief. Well, if he didn't want me enough to overcome the age thing, then he didn't want me enough. And I should let it go.

"I'm sorry," I said at last. "I'll stop bothering you."

He didn't respond. I should've gone immediately, but I knew that I would never be here with him again. As uncomfortable as it would be to stay I just couldn't face leaving.

I gave him a quick glance over the shoulder and an attempt at a smile. "So, how about a drink?" I reached for the bottle and started to open it when I was assaulted with everything Samuel had been holding back. His heart rate, his breathing, his…everything.

Then he was behind me, pressed up against me. He moved one hand to caress my breasts, the other much lower. I felt light headed and almost drugged, his touch was so intoxicating. I reached a hand back to cradle his head as he kissed my neck. "This changes nothing, Jane." His voice was rough as he growled in my ear. So damned sexy. "This will just make it worse later."

I felt him hard against me and said what I'm sure he knew I'd say, "Then let's make it as bad as it can be."

I turned around and kissed him, devouring his mouth as he devoured mine. I unbuttoned his shirt and touched his chest, finally feeling his skin, his scars under my fingertips. In a moment my top was off and his mouth, his tongue... Good god. I reached for his belt, but stopped, painful memories intruding of the last time we had been this close.

He brought one hand up to his face and kissed the palm. He then quickly unbuckled his belt and I used my other hand to help drop his pants and shorts to the floor. I reached out to touch him.

"Baby," he moaned. Within a few seconds the rest of my clothes were also on the floor. He lifted me onto the desk and kissed me. Feeling his strong hard body against mine, flesh to flesh, was ecstasy all by itself, but I knew it would get even better. He held onto me tightly as he moved inside me for the first time. We came very quickly in that first frenzy and took our time the second. And it was when we were together that second time and Samuel said my name so tenderly as he came that I realized I loved him.

He was right, I thought as I eventually curled up to sleep, my head on his chest. Sometime soon everything was going to be much worse. I brushed the hair off his forehead as he slept. But, I smiled to myself as he unconsciously shifted my body to fit with his, not today.

ENTRY 2-2-8

A Note on Dre Orwan Wix-Thomas (2679-2813)

Dre Orwan Wix-Thomas was an agitator and fame-seeker who was a vociferous supporter of supernormal rights. He wrote, he spoke, he appeared wherever and whenever he could to 'get the word out.' At least, that was what he had spoken about in his youth. But over time either his views had changed or he'd realized that he could get more publicity with more radical opinions and the tenor of his message had shifted to that of supernormal superiority.

Wix-Thomas was largely forgotten by the time the tapetia mortis *landed on Pace-Pallon. But his work had never really disappeared. There were always some disaffected supernormal teens, persecuted and full of self-loathing, who would find a battered copy of a compilation of his essays and cling to it for dear life.*

An excerpt from Dre Orwan Wix-Thomas's essay entitled "A Hard Look" published in the August 2718 issue of Chaos Magazine *(two years before the institution of the Five Gene Rule and the outlawing of the creation of supernormals): "And the question becomes, should we let them curtail our genetic freedoms? Should we bow to the inferiority of the normals? Should we submit to rules that will keep us from altering our children so that they can attain the ideal of human perfection? Why are we willing to hand over the final genetic decisions to the Scientists? And make no mistake, friends, if this 'Five Gene Rule' becomes law that is exactly what we are doing. And if I want my daughter to be superior shouldn't I be allowed to try to make her so? As her father isn't that my right? Am I not allowed to take the same risks that Pacey parents for 600 years have been allowed to? And I know there are children that have been abandoned as too deformed or strange and I say that their parents should pay for their cruelty. But if you* are *willing to pay the price when it doesn't work you should be allowed to take the risk. We can make the human race perfect one child at a time. And down the line when we are perfect, we supernormals, will be able to lead and the remaining normals will* want *us to lead."*

It may be noted that dissatisfied adolescent supers aside, Wix-Thomas's effect wasn't quite the same on paper as it was in person. Historians believe, though it was too long ago to prove now, that Wix-Thomas may have been the first (and only) naturally occurring Manipulative Empath. There were some supernormals, even some former supporters, who were disgusted that he had been unwilling, apparently, to identify himself as such for the record. More cynical people think that he had just been waiting for the most opportune time to spring his 'surprise' and win ultimate fame. No one will ever know. Wix-Thomas went into seclusion after the 2730 Five Gene Rule decision and was rarely seen again. He was found dead, alone at age 134. He had no children.

Wix-Thomas did gain a measure of the immortality he'd so desperately craved, however. Most historians give him a good chunk of credit for fanning the flames of fear and (unintentionally, of course) getting the Five Gene Rule passed years before it would have, if it would have at all.

04:45 – General Armstrong's Quarters, *P.S. Scylla*, July 11, 2869

I woke up suddenly. I knew I wasn't in my bunk and I had the feeling like something huge had happened to me, I just couldn't remember what it was. Then he shifted closer to me, resting his sleeping face in my neck and it all came back. Samuel and Samuel and Samuel. It hadn't been a dream. I found myself almost overcome with emotion and took a minute to collect myself. I pulled his arm around me and willed myself back to sleep.

It took about 30 seconds for me to realize that that was not going to happen. I was too happy, too excited, too astonished at my luck. I rolled over to face him, studying that wonderful lined face. He was frowning in his sleep and I gently smoothed his forehead. I watched him for another minute, now acutely aware that the alarm would be going off in a little over ten minutes. Yep, I needed him awake. And I had an idea. I carefully disengaged myself and slipped down his body and under the sheet. I was in the process of executing my plan when I heard Samuel say…

"Oh, fuck me."

I popped my head out from under the sheet. "Sir?"

He was propped up on his elbows now, body (well, most of it) still half asleep but his eyes awake. "You are insatiable, woman."

I rested my chin on his hip and attempted to look innocent, which, in that particular location, was a real trick. "So, you don't like your wake-up call?"

He laughed, "All men like *that* kind of wake-up, Jane." He reached down and stroked my hair. "Good morning, Baby."

I kissed his hand and smiled. "Morning, Samuel." And then I thought of something. "Hey, you called me 'woman.' Are you saying I've been promoted from 'kid'?"

He laughed again and stretched. "I'm saying that everyone deserves a promotion after last night."

Just when I'd thought I couldn't be happier, I was. "Whatever you say, Mr. President," I smiled at him and then disappeared again under the sheet.

06:00 – Shuttle Bay, *P.S. Scylla*

I arrived at the Shuttle *Valencia* just in time. I knew military people hated tardiness, but my morning routine had been completely shattered by being at Samuel's place. Shattered in the best, hottest, way, but shattered nonetheless. I had a feeling that Captain Ian was going to make this ride weird, one way or another, and I didn't want to start on the wrong foot by being late.

Atalanta, Felix and the pod of soldiers were already there. We were apparently waiting for Doc Wells and Captain Ian. Atalanta flashed me a brilliant smile and put up her hands as if warding something off.

"My god, Jane. You're making me giddy."

I blushed but was too happy to be actually ashamed. Nice, that.

She moved closer to me conspiratorially. "So, I guess you finally sealed the deal?" I started to say something but she just laughed. "You don't need to tell me. It's hard to miss." Felix was watching us, puzzled, but not intruding.

I glanced from Felix to Atalanta. "Everything OK?"

She shrugged, her smile faded slightly. "Quiet. No drama."

"I'm glad," I said, since it seemed that that was the best they were going to do. The Captain, Doc Wells and the General arrived. The Captain and the General seemed to be arguing about something.

"Well, then I'll just take them. We can't put it off and she's the best one to go. You said that yourself, Ian." The General sounded annoyed. I tried not to stare, but that was impossible. He saw me and caught his breath. Samuel, my Samuel.

Next to me Atalanta muttered, "All this joy is making my head hurt." I looked at her quickly but she just smirked at me.

"I just think she's a disruptive influence. Sir." Ian added that last. He looked tired and petulant.

The General was getting more annoyed by the second. I could feel his tension. He dropped his voice lower, but I could still hear him. "You need to get over whatever personal problem you have with Jane." He looked over at me and I instantly knew that a full report would be expected the next we were alone. Well, *that* would be interesting. "We have a schedule to keep and missions to carry out. Now, get to work or let someone else do it. That's an order, Captain."

Atalanta shot me a look but I shook my head to stop her unspoken question. Captain Ian hesitated for a fraction of a second, then headed for the *Valencia*, sparing one last glare for his father.

"Let's load." The Captain was first on and we all followed dutifully. I got one quick look at the General as I boarded.

"Don't forget your vomit bags." He said softly. Ah, Jane, your lover says the prettiest things. I nodded, they were in my pack. They were pretty much all that was in my pack. I got on.

The soldiers buckled themselves in the back with Doc Wells. Captain Ian was already in the pilot's seat and he'd gestured Felix into the co-pilot's seat. I didn't know if Felix could fly anything, but I wouldn't put it past him. Atalanta and I found spots next to each other on the wall and strapped ourselves in. I recognized the shuttle because of its terrific size; the Captain had saved our lives in it. How many people was he expecting to rescue today, I wondered.

The shuttle bay was emptied and depressurized. The bay doors opened in front of us, revealing Pace 4 below us. We were given immediate clearance for launch. I pulled out a vomit bag from my pack, holding it ready. Atalanta stared at the bag nervously and I guessed that she was rethinking her proximity to me. I didn't blame her. I dreaded being near me, too.

Captain Ian gently powered the shuttle off the deck, slid her forward and then shot her like a crazed bullet out of the ship and into space. I puked. And kept puking as he flew the shuttle like a deranged fighter pilot around other fleet ships and towards the atmosphere. I could hear, in the small breaks I had between spasms of retching, others gasp and quietly protest at this unnecessarily rough ride. Then one of the soldiers puked on the floor. And another.

"Captain Armstrong?" That was Doc Wells.

Captain Armstrong didn't answer, seemingly locked in some sort of angry zone.

"Captain!" Doc Wells insisted.

Captain Ian looked back and saw, then smelled the floor that was now covered with this morning's breakfast rations. The shuttle straightened out. He offered no apology. My stomach started to settle.

"Preparing to enter atmosphere." The Captain's voice was cold and professional.

Atalanta looked from him to me. "What did you do to him? Why is he so angry?" Then her eyes widened, "Does he know about…?"

"Not as far as I know." I leaned a little closer, trying not to breathe on her. "We had an argument at the bar after I put you to bed last night." I considered what to say. "About a point of family history. His."

"Something you learned from the General?"

I nodded. Atalanta waited for me to be forthcoming, but I stayed silent. She started to say something, but stopped. Opened her mouth to speak again, but closed it. She seemed to be having an argument with herself.

"I could probably work on you until you told me, you know that, right?" she said, frowning.

Now, despite everything, I was curious. "How?"

She started to retort when she realized that I wasn't challenging her. I actually wanted to know. She calmed down, mollified in spite of herself.

"I start by moving up your guilt..."

"I'm sorry, 'moving up'?"

Atalanta turned towards me. "For MEmps all emotions are on the equivalent of dials in someone's mind. So I could move up, or dial up, your guilt, play up your affection for me, amp up your natural fear of being disliked, etc. Then I could turn down your worry that *he* will be angry, even try to develop your dislike for the Captain, assuming you have any."

I gave a half laugh. "I don't dislike him. I just want him to stop being a dick."

"Agreed." Atalanta ran her hands through her hair. "So, that would be my plan before I scan you. Every plan has to change once you are inside, of course. People can have the strangest feelings about things. I'm always surprised what people feel."

"And you've tested all this on the Volunteers?" I remembered Wilby had mentioned them but I'd never gotten to try myself on them. The world getting destroyed had pretty much nixed that.

Atalanta looked away, "Among others."

"But I have that resistance thing, right, so you can't just do that to me?"

Atalanta sighed. "It's not that I can't do *anything*, it's just much, much harder unless you are very emotional. That makes it easier to get in."

Despite the nausea and the Captain being pissed at me and having to keep a secret from my friend, I was still higher than a kite from being with Samuel. I concentrated, trying to make my emotions diminish. After a second, Atalanta put her hand on my arm.

"Stop, Jane." She laughed at me. "It takes years of practice to be able to do that successfully. All you just did was make it look like you were taking a dump."

"Thanks," I said sarcastically. "So, are you going to use your magic on me or what?"

"No." The she thought of something and looked serious. "Unless this secret affects me—or Felix. Does it?"

I shook my head.

"And you'd tell me what it was if it didn't have to do with the family of your boyfriend, right?"

I let out a sigh of relief, which I managed to blow away from her.

"Yes."

"Ok, then." We sat there for a second, feeling the shuttle rumble as we got closer and closer to the ground. She turned to me suddenly, "You are so full of shit. There is no way you'd let me scan you. You'd throw me out of the shuttle before you let anything like that happen—while we were still in orbit." She play slapped my shoulder. "And you just let me show off like that. For shame."

"I wanted to know." I noticed we were getting to an altitude where we might be able to see something. "And I would've waited until the shuttle was on the ground. Probably." I smirked and she shook her head, a motion that combined annoyance and amusement.

"Approaching Destination 1," Captain Ian said seriously.

All talking, all sounds stopped. Below us lay a gray-brown expanse of nothingness. No plant life, no habitation, just an occasional random pile of wood or stone to indicate a former dwelling. Miles and miles of it. Brown and gray and dead. The only true evidence that humans had ever lived there were the streets and roads, dicing up the landscape. Roads ready to take a race of people anywhere they wanted to go. Only there were no people anymore.

"Where are we, Sir?" I asked.

"Village of Agyekum. We are going over to the side. Prepare to bank left, Jane."

"Thank you, Captain."

The Captain banked left easily and with a skill that truly proved how much of an asshole he'd been earlier, throwing us around like that. Since I was prepared for the move I didn't vomit and I was pretty sure that everyone on the shuttle was grateful.

"Rising to altitude 9,000 feet."

I couldn't see why we were rising. The ground looked just as flat and dead as it had before. We rose and rose until we must have been at 9,000 feet and we still flew. We entered a low cloud, were enveloped in white then burst free of it…and almost flew into a mountain.

"Grab your bag, Jane!" the Captain yelled as he pulled up, up, up on the throttle. The mountain rushed towards us.

Without appearing to consider, Felix put his hand out to stop the mountain. "Jane!" he called to me, and I belatedly did the same. "Repel the mountain. Pushing off the mountain should give the shuttle the cushion it needs to stop the crash."

It was as if everything had slowed down. I could feel the dual engines at the back, whining in protest at the aspect change. I felt the incredible velocity of the shuttle itself and the absolute immobility of the sheer rock face we were about to hit—I could feel it but it wasn't right in front of us. It was further away—how could that be? I wanted to trust my sensing, but my eyes told me we were going to die if we didn't do something. I went with my eyes. I sensed the Captain peripherally and he was full of adrenaline and his heart was racing, but he was in control of himself. Still in slow motion I saw the wall of rock coming.

I reached out and pushed, just to test my strength. The shuttle kept going unaffected. I looked at Felix with alarm.

"Push stronger but with control." The wall was too close. I pushed strong and imagined myself actually moving the mountain. I could feel Atalanta next to me holding in a scream. The wall zoomed closer, closer. I could see rock in detail. We were going to hit.

"Felix! Push!" We pushed as hard as we fucking could.

The ship whipped by the rock and missed the mountain but flipped over and over and over. Some people were screaming. The ship fell like a toy, spinning round and round as we fell.

"I can keep us from crashing if we can stabilize." Captain Ian yelled. He was telling us Macros. I could tell Felix was concentrating, but it wasn't helping. Why couldn't he fix it? Felix was good at everything Macro.

Then I got it. This wasn't just a Macro problem. It was a *Telespatial* problem.

I flung my consciousness down to Pace 4 for stability, then back up to the out of control shuttle. I instinctively judged the speed of the spinning. I closed my eyes and concentrated. It was like reaching out your hand to stop a top from going round. The ship stopped whirling around so suddenly that we all would have been hurt, hurled like rag dolls against the shuttle walls, if we hadn't been strapped in.

The shuttle engines quit their complaining and sounded normal again. We flew for a few seconds in silence.

"Anybody hurt?" Captain Ian asked. We waited as Doc Wells walked up and down, checking people.

Doc Wells answered, "Bruised rib or two from the harness. Some cuts and other bruises. Nothing serious."

"That wall wasn't there." The Captain looked to Felix. "Seriously, it wasn't there. The sensors put that mountain a quarter mile to the west of where we found it. That should not have happened."

Felix scratched his small beard. This bothered him, too. I was just so glad not to be dead, I wasn't really thinking at all. "Jane, how long did you have to push before you felt resistance?"

I thought about it. "A while. Much longer than I thought I'd have to. It scanned like it wasn't there, but I *saw* it. You?"

Felix nodded. "Captain, can you tell us where we were supposed to be going?"

Captain Armstrong pointed to a place on the computer's chart. "Enclave. Extremely isolated."

"And these are people who are paranoid about the Government finding them. Are any of them supers?" Felix asked.

The Captain nodded. "Unconfirmed, but the General suspects there are. Why?"

Felix grimaced. "I'm saying that your sensors were right. What looked like a wall wasn't. If it had been we would have been able to push off of it—and you would have read it and we wouldn't have come out of the cloud there. My guess is that the illusion was put there to protect the Enclave."

"So, to find the people we have to..." Captain Ian prompted.

"...go through it," Felix finished.

The Captain gently turned the shuttle around, back to the place we'd nearly died (one way or another). Within a minute we were heading for the same sheer wall of rock. I could see the knuckles on the Captain's hands turning white.

"What do your sensors say, Captain?" Felix asked quietly.

"That we're not flying head first into a wall of rock," he responded tightly.

And it was coming closer and closer. Atalanta closed her eyes, but Felix and the Captain and I kept ours open.

And just like that we were through. In front of us was an enormous cave carved into the sheer cliff face. The cave looked as large as the *Scylla*. Captain Ian picked a likely spot and set us down in one corner. We all debarked and fanned out, looking for survivors. Atalanta and I were at the front, scanning for life. We got nothing.

Then, coming out of an apparently solid rock wall, emerged an old woman. Her hair was wild and knotted, her skin like abandoned leather and most of her teeth were missing. And she was 9 feet tall and thin as a rail. I detected (now) a fast and strong heartbeat, good blood flow and a ...struggle to walk that indicated serious joint pain in her long thin knobby legs. The old woman looked at me, then at Atalanta.

"Go ahead, my lovely, tell me what you sense from me."

Atalanta scanned obediently, then looked at Felix. "She feels intruded upon. She hates that we are in her home."

The old woman smiled her hideous smile. "That's right, dear, and now what do you scan?"

Atalanta frowned, "Happiness. Now, fear. Sadness. Lust." Atalanta crinkled her nose. She stepped back to where Felix and the Captain were standing. "I can't read her."

"Quite right," the old woman said angrily. "Why are you here?"

Captain Ian stepped forward. "The planet has been decimated by alien creatures. We have already evacuated many survivors. We've come to take you away."

The old woman smiled again. "I don't want to be rescued and I don't care about the rest of the goddamned planet. My people came here when I was 5 standard. I've protected it with my pictures ever since and I have no intention of stopping now." She looked at all of us with contempt. "And for those of you who wish to do the math, that was 176 years ago."

"Do you speak for everyone?" the Captain asked respectfully.

"Yes," she answered then she laughed. It was a harsh, ugly laugh.

"May I look around, speak to some of them?"

"Anything you want, handsome, as long as you are out of here in 10 minutes. After that the walls you run into will be real."

He nodded his agreement to the terms and took off down the front of the cave, signaling for the soldiers to follow him. The old woman then turned to those of us left. "Who was it that defeated my pictures?" Felix and I exchanged a look. "Oh, you two. You're the first ones to get through—that I didn't want to get through. I couldn't believe it when that shuttle went spinning around like that. Hell of a ride."

"Why did you come here?" I had to ask.

She held her head up proudly. "They were about to legislate against us. We Exotics. We were going to be catalogued and monitored and taken out of the breeding program because we were strange—despite the fact that we had been made different on purpose. My parents, cousins and some friends all decided to get out before we couldn't. We came here and learned to survive."

I looked around the austere cave, then looked out at the view. It looked like you could see a hundred miles. Hills, rivers, plains and it was difficult to see the devastation from that height. Even gray and ravaged from the *tapetia mortis*, it was truly beautiful. "Is this the real view?"

The old woman nodded. "It is what I see from my *home*. I would not change it—even ruined as it is."

Captain Ian returned. "She is the only one here, assuming that she is letting me see anything actually real. There is a huge and full crypt. There is no one else here."

"Ten minutes are up, pretty boy. Time for you to go." The old woman started walking back towards the deep part of the cave.

We started walking back to the shuttle. My mind was imagining the kind of brutal life she must have been living for so long.

"Hey, you two." She was calling Felix and me. We turned. "You're abandoning your planet without a struggle, that much is clear." I was startled. I hadn't thought of it that way before. To me it was only escape, not abandonment. "But if most of you are dead, that means most of the Government is dead, too, right?"

We nodded. "So you can start over. Don't blame the planet for what's ruined it."

"But everything's been destroyed." I said.

The old lady shrugged. "Do what you want. But you only get one home." She started walked away again.

Captain Ian started for the shuttle. "By the way, for the records, what's your name?"

"Why the hell would that matter?" the old woman called over her shoulder as she disappeared into the darkness.

The ride out of the cave and the mountains was subdued and much less exciting. We stopped at two other remote places but found nothing in either. And I mean nothing. Everything had been consumed. It was like the people had been erased.

"Destination 4 coming up," Captain Ian said as we flew.

"How many after this, Sir?" asked Atalanta.

"Two. I know you have other obligations, but we have to hit the places on the list."

Felix looked quickly at Atalanta, unhappy to be reminded of the second part of their mission. Atalanta herself looked closed off and wrapped up in her own thoughts. "Of course, Sir."

We came upon a large river. So large that it was hard to see from one side to the other. We flew low over it until we came upon a medium-sized island in the middle. We landed on the beach and got out.

There were structures in the distance. Houses and a larger structure that looked like a hall. And something else that looked like a…barn? What the hell was a barn doing there? And then we heard it. A bleat. Then more. I looked at Captain Ian, not sure that I was hearing what I was hearing. Suddenly a flock of sheep appeared, running out onto the beach.

"Well, I'll be damned," Captain Ian said softly.

None of us had ever seen animals, or if we did we didn't remember them. All of them had been destroyed before we'd been born or when we were very small. They were intriguing and abnormal at the same time. And then from behind a stand of trees came something, someones, I should say, even more interesting.

A dozen or so people walked towards us. They were a pale purple with their extremities turning to a deeper purple that was almost black. The whites of their eyes were very white and their pupils pure black. So black that the irises were all but invisible. Some wore their hair long, some had no hair at all. They were taller than average, but no taller than, say, Wilby, and they moved with a fascinating grace. Oh, and they had tails. If these weren't Exotics, I thought, nothing is. I found them at once alien and very beautiful.

None of our party said anything for a minute. Then the Captain stepped forward with his hand outstretched.

"I am Captain Ian Armstrong of the *P.S. Scylla*."

The woman in front shook his hand. "I am Ophelia Glory and you, I presume, are here to rescue us."

"Yes, Ma'am, if you wish to be rescued." I could tell his mind was on the strange old woman.

"Of course." Ophelia turned and gestured to her people with her elegant long fingered hand. "This is some of my family. My parents, children, grandchildren, aunts and uncles. There are 28 of us all together."

Children, she said? My mind was reeling. That was as revolutionary a thought as the sheep. I snuck a glance at our people behind me and was relieved to see them looking as stunned as I felt.

"We will take you and your people to our fleet. We are awaiting contact with a Terran ship and hope to be taken to Earth."

Ophelia sighed. "Yes, I guess that is the only option. Better than dying here."

"I agree," but Captain Ian didn't look like he agreed. He looked like he was sending these people to their deaths. Ophelia seemed to divine his thoughts.

"Pretty soon there will be no food and all the animals will be eaten. Then I will starve myself to feed my children and then they will have the privilege of watching me die. Earth has to be better than that, yes?" And then she smiled at him. Her smile was at once feral and charming.

All at once something streaked out of the trees, aiming for Ophelia, Felix and I both reached out to stop it, but Felix got there first. And there, now hanging in mid-air was a medium to small feline. A cat. And that cat was pissed.

Ophelia and her people laughed, which made the cat even more annoyed. Felix, a little embarrassed, put the cat down. It immediately curled around Ophelia's leg and hissed at him.

"Two conditions, however, Captain, if I may?" Ophelia reached down to scratch her cat's head. We could hear the purring, though the cat never took its eyes off of Felix.

"If I can accommodate you, I will, Ma'am." The Captain looked at her warily.

"Firstly, my family stays together. One ship assignment for the lot of us. If one of us chooses to go off on his or her own, that is fine, but we choose, yes?"

"I will see to it."

"Thank you. The second condition is that we bring our animals." The Captain started to protest, but stopped himself. I wondered if he was remembering the story of his grandparents who'd died protecting their horses over 30 years ago.

"I will do my best." I could see the Captain trying to figure out how that would work in his head. "My best, Ma'am is very good."

She smiled at him again. "I believe it."

Two hours later we took off with 28 Exotics (including 7 children), 5 cats and 49 sheep. We had loaded them in the cargo hold, where all us students had been put for our rescue. I had stood next to Captain Ian as the last of the sheep had been loaded and started to chuckle. And then I found I couldn't stop. Ian looked at me, irritated.

"What's so funny?"

"I'm just picturing the General's face when you turn over the sheep." And then I couldn't help it. I giggled.

He listened to the *baaas* as the back hatch prepared to close. He shrugged. "It was the right thing to do."

"Oh, yes," I agreed.

The hatch shut. He looked at me as I was trying not to smile. "Yeah, I'm still screwed."

"You know it." I laughed and he kind of smiled at me. I thought that it was nice having him not actively hate me for a minute. But I still knew what I knew and I was pretty sure this friendliness wouldn't last.

So now we were off to Destination 4. The Captain's humor faded the closer we got to wherever it was we were going. He kept stealing glances at us as though he felt guilty about something. As we got closer, Felix sort of jumped. He'd recognized something. He looked over at Atalanta and found her staring at him, fear in her eyes. Fear of what? Then I saw it. Ruins. Ruins of our School. Only the foundation was left and the Object shells in the field. The Shed was gone, the rooms, the dormitories, the Guard Tower, the Armory. Even the Quad was bare of grass. I glanced to the far left and saw the remains of Irrfan's mountain.

"The General wanted to make sure we hadn't missed anything." Captain Ian sounded embarrassed.

"Anything we missed they got, Captain." Felix said bitterly. The Captain just nodded.

Suddenly I was seized with an urge to go back to our School, to walk the paving stones and remember. "Could we go there? Just for a minute? Please, Captain?"

Captain Ian didn't answer, but he landed the shuttle. Felix's expression was unreadable but Atalanta looked distinctly unhappy at the prospect. I felt I was being selfish, but I really wanted to be there and feel my planet under my feet for the last time. What would I be without it? *Could* I be without it? Aside from 'pushing' Captain Ian last night I hadn't done anything (off planet) with my abilities since we'd left Pace. Well, I thought, if this is it, I need to say goodbye properly.

I got out and started walking towards the Quad. I pictured the double doors that I should have been passing through and looked back and up to see the Guard Tower that wasn't there. I could envision the place teeming with people, with people like me and my friends. My eyes were now coated with tears but I didn't cry. I just stood there trying to take in the change from my home to this.

I felt Felix and Atalanta and, eventually, the Captain coming up behind me. No one said anything, each apparently lost in his own thoughts. I stopped looking around because there was nothing to look at. Except those 4 shells in the distance. Those shells.

Suddenly I was overcome with fury. Anger so fierce it felt like it was in every crevice of my mind, every part of my body. I heard Atalanta gasp as she picked up my feelings.

And then I was running. Running to those damned shells. *That's* what they leave behind. Not the building, not a roof or a photograph or a person—not even bodies to bury. Not Arthur, not Paulette or 50 others. No, they leave the fucking *shells*.

The others were running to catch up but I was, for once, faster than anyone, fueled by pure vitriol. I stood in front of the shells. I raised my hands over my head and whipped them around. Nothing happened. I did it again and I felt the breeze change. I paused, collecting myself. I, probably for the last time, felt the solidity of Pace 4 below my feet. I relished in its strength, its mass. And while I knew I couldn't actually pull energy out of the ground, that's what it felt like as I summoned every bit of anger I had and threw my arms up again.

Suddenly all four shells were in the air. Atalanta screamed and ducked and I didn't blame her. The detached part of me was pretty sure that my compatriots thought I'd lost my mind. Maybe yes, maybe no. I spared a glance at Captain Ian who was watching me slack-jawed. Mess with me, will you?

I 'whipped' the shells around like I was mixing them in a bowl. The shapes were starting to blur together. I pushed harder for more speed but I only got a little. Apparently, I was no Irrfan. Suddenly I felt Felix behind me.

"May I?" he asked softly. I didn't know what he 'might' want to do, but I nodded. He put his hands on my shoulders. It was only then I noticed my muscles were tensed to iron strength. His touch allowed me to relax and the shells spun faster. He left one hand on my shoulder and raised his other. I could feel his concentration. The Shells spun themselves into a new shape, almost the shape of a missile. "Now let's send those motherfuckers off our goddamn planet and back where they came from." His voice was still low, but I felt the venom in it and knew his fury was as deep as mine. It didn't surprise me. We'd all lost.

Together we held the shell-thing as it spun. "And…now!" Felix shouted and, with a colossal heave we fired it up into the sky. A few seconds later we saw a flash as it hit the atmosphere.

I sat down hard on the grass. Felix returned to Atalanta who was softly crying. Ian stayed where he was, still in shock. After a few minutes spent in silence we returned to the shuttle.

Our flight away from the School grounds was subdued. It was funny, I thought, I wouldn't have believed there was nothing left if I hadn't seen it—felt it for myself. And then I realized that was why the General had sent us there. Proof. And closure, I guessed. I sighed, absently looking out the forward windows. And I stopped dead, my gut clenching in shock when I recognized what I saw.

"Destination 5," Captain Ian said softly to no one in particular.

We were on the far side of Irrfan's mountain and creeping up one of the faces was a massive hive. It was the largest single structure I had ever seen and was shaped like a large sack with a long tube-like neck. It was crawling with the creatures, who swarmed over it like insects. Millions of them. Like the *tapetia mortis* they were. Hundreds at a time made their way to the enormous opening at the top, methodically adding to it.

"We need to get closer to it, Captain," Felix said, concentrating on the creatures.

The Captain skillfully brought us close enough that we could have counted the legs on the things had we wished to. I looked back and saw Doc Wells and the soldiers watching us intently. Watching *us* more than the creatures. Perhaps because we were less terrifying. Or maybe just more familiarly terrifying. Well, I thought, let's give the normals what they're paying for. I looked at Felix and he turned to Atalanta.

She stared out at them, shivering with the mental contact. "The urge to build, then get out of the way. Every creature at the mouth of that thing wants to either defecate then build or puke and then go down."

Captain Ian interjected, "This is what they're thinking, I mean, feeling?"

Atalanta nodded, "It's like it was before; it's an overwhelming urge. The biological imperative. They don't *think*, they just *do*."

"I agree. I get the same movement pattern over and over. But…" Felix hesitated. "They seem a little slower. Just a little. I wish I knew what that meant." Felix looked at me, giving me my cue to scan.

I didn't do more than a cursory scan of the creatures, just enough to confirm Felix's finding, which I was able to do quite easily. They *were* slower, ever so slightly. And then I moved my mind away from them so I could avoid the hand wringing that always came with that mental touch. I went up over the top of the hive and inside.

Bubbles, boiling bubbles and tons of pressure building up. I had to back out, the pressure was too much for me. But I also had to know—where was that pressure going? We, Felix and I, would have felt it if it was being expelled through the main chimney-like opening. I had to go back in. Heat, bubbles, acid burning. Suddenly I was afraid, afraid I wouldn't make it back out. Terrified, actually.

Then I felt a hand holding one of mine and calm washing through me like a cool breeze. Thank you, Atalanta. I took a breath and started looking around. I sensed the shape of the inside of the hive. It was roughly the shape it appeared from the outside except…for the hundreds of holes that had been made into the mountain. Holes. Tunnels, really. I immediately withdrew back into myself and found Atalanta still holding my hand. I squeezed hers.

"Thanks. That place is seriously scary."

Atalanta smiled and Felix looked at me intently. "Well?"

I knew the best way to show what I had learned was to show them. "Captain, would you please take us to the North face of the mountain?"

"Sure," the Captain replied, his expression indicating that he expected to be made unhappy by what I was going to show him there. No fool, he. He turned the shuttle and we flew slowly to the other side of the mountain.

"It isn't a hive," I explained. "'Hive' implies a nest. A home, if you will. This is a construct. I'm guessing that it is almost a device that they are building."

"So, what's in there, Jane?" Atalanta asked.

"Acid and massive amounts of pressure. On a vast scale. And if my guess is correct, it's only keeping together because of what's on the North face."

As I said this, Captain Ian brought the shuttle round so the face in question was in view.

The North face was pitted with holes that spewed what looked like hot gasses and occasional drops of acid. Hundreds of holes with hundreds of thousands of creatures sitting next to them. Alive, we could sense it, but unmoving. Almost like they were waiting. For what? Then I thought I knew. I started to speak, but it was Atalanta who beat me to it.

"So if these holes act as relief valves, essentially, then what happens if they get plugged up? Is that what those crab things are waiting for? That's what it looks like."

Felix answered her, clearly thinking as he spoke, "I would think that once the holes were plugged that anything dropped in from the top would shoot out like a rocket."

"And whatever was put in there would have to be virtually indestructible," I continued.

There was a pause. We all had, apparently, reached the same conclusion as to the nature of the indestructible things.

"So if they make new Objects *this* will be how they get them into space?" the Captain asked. "But how do they make the Objects?"

Felix answered him, "Unknown. They can't use the old ones—and not just because we destroyed those four. They're eaten and grown and are almost twice the size they were when they first got here." He scratched his beard. "But they came from space and assuming we weren't the first planets they've consumed—and their abilities are way too specialized and perfected for me to buy that—then they must be planning to go back out there. Perhaps to find their next meal?"

We all absorbed this for a second.

"Dr. Bayliss will be back from the *Hastings* tomorrow. We can consult with him," the Captain said confidently. Apparently, the Captain had spent very little time with our *tapetia mortis* expert. The Captain steered the shuttle away from the mountain and towards space.

"Great," Felix said sourly. His body had quickly tensed up the way mine did when I was lifting wrong. I began to be afraid he was going to snap something. I waited for him to calm down but he just kept getting more and more tense. I couldn't take it. I gestured for Atalanta to do her calming thing, but she shook her head no. Apparently that was not something that would go over well with him in this particular mood.

I unbuckled and crept up to him as he sat in the co-pilot's chair. Felix looked at me in alarm.

"Jane, you shouldn't be unbuckled…" but I cut him off.

"Felix, you need to relax or you're going to hurt yourself. Do it or I'll knock you out for your own good." He stared at me in astonishment. "Right *now*," I growled.

His blood pressure went even higher as his anger redirected at me. The Captain watched us out of the corner of his eye. I'm sure he was thinking that two Macros fighting each other in a moving shutting was a recipe for death. I was thinking that, too, but I was pretty sure it wouldn't come to that.

"I'm your *instructor…*" Felix started.

"More importantly, you are also my friend. You must calm down. Please, Felix." I stared him down until his expression softened.

He looked at me, his face reflecting his inner pain. "You don't know, Jane."

"I know I don't. But a genius without a conscience can create a lot of pain." I rested my hands on his arm and I could feel him slowly notch down his tension. "We can talk later if you wish. Maybe there is something we can do."

He rested his head against the back of the seat. "There isn't."

"Then maybe we can figure out a way to get revenge."

He looked up sharply at that last. He looked from me to Atalanta who'd been listening intently. She nodded. I had no idea what we were going to do, but Dr. Bayliss must have done something that needed punishing. And I firmly believed in punishment. Just ask Wilby.

A Note on Exotics

In an effort to force the next phase of human evolution Atticus Pace had unleashed wave after wave of cosmetic mods on his embryos. Some of the genetic changes had to be internal as well (you can't have a prehensile tail, for example, without extending the spine to support it, creating nerves designed to handle it, etc.) but for the most part the external was handled by Dr. Pace and the internal by Dr. Pallon. Atticus Pace wanted to be the one to create the two headed child with forked tongues, clawed feet and bright red skin. Indira Pallon wanted to make it fly. The experimentation process always had much more failure than success (two heads were horrifying and the hundreds of fetuses that it had been tried on were put down) but there was always more DNA to work with.

The human race was looking more exotic and, on the whole more beautiful, though some skeptics said that Paceys were becoming less human. Dr. Pace scoffed at this idea. "How can we be less human if we are simply rearranging the building blocks that make us human? If you build a barn out of wood, then tear it down and build a mansion with that same wood, are they not both kinds of houses? Do they not both keep the rain from you? And wouldn't you rather live in a mansion than a barn?"

Dr. Pallon focused on increasing the extrasensory powers of her embryos. She found that since Telepathy was occurring more and more naturally (even on Terra) that it was fairly easy to guarantee it in a newborn. Telekinesis was more difficult. It hardly ever "took" and when it did it wasn't always the same talent. Sometimes the most a subject could do would be to move a glass across a table, but then another subject would be able to lift a train car with nothing more than a look. Some batches of talent mods had been missed entirely, or misread until Dr. Jenna Riley, Dr. Pallon's assistant, noticed that instead of the Telekinetic talent manifesting in big ways (in humans referred to as 'lifters') that it had come through in tiny ways.

After being repeatedly disappointed in lifting tests Dr. Riley had all but given up on one 7 year old girl. Dr. Riley had left the room in frustration and had returned to witness the little girl playing with her dog. The dog kept giving little yelps as if it was in pain and Dr. Riley had gone over to see what was going on. On the dog's back was a line in the fur. At first it looked like it was painted on, but it wasn't. The little girl was pulling out hair after hair in a perfect straight line, one by one, without ever actually touching the dog. That little girl, Alice, was the first confirmed Micro TK. Dr. Pallon was delighted and had Alice show off to everyone until eventually they'd had to get a fresh dog. A similar type of accidental observation had discovered, fifty years or so later, the difference between Empaths and Manipulative Empaths (MEemps). Dr. Pallon was so delighted by the MEmps that she'd discontinued creation of all Empaths from that time forward.

The one thing that Drs. Pace and Pallon never did was have children of their own. Their excuse was that, now that they were on Pace, there was no time and that work was paramount to them. They had decided to dedicate their lives to improving the lives and abilities of other people's children. And thus, weren't all Paceys their children?

Atticus Pace's Will never mentioned his potential personal genetic contribution to Pace-Pallon, but when Indira Pallon's Will was read at her funeral two years after her husband's death, she had specifically stated that while her DNA would be kept as a teaching tool it must never under any circumstances be used to a create a child. No explanation was ever offered.

13:00 – Mallory's Training Room, *P.S. Scylla*

Thirty of us fired Laser Pulse Guns at targets. Mallory paced behind us like a cat. Part of me was amused that I'd compared her to a cat before, but had never actually seen one until today. I watched a second. Yep. Cat.

Lunch had been interesting. Everyone had wanted to hear about the Exotics and I hadn't minded talking about them. Anything was better than thinking about our farewell to Pace 4. People wanted to hear about the Exotics, but what they really wanted to do was see the sheep and cats. Even Wilby had managed to hover close by to hear the details.

The General's expression had been priceless when the animals had been unloaded. He'd recovered quickly, of course, and found a place for everyone. I'd only spoken to him for a few seconds to get clearance to talk about our new additions (which he'd granted). Then I was off to food and then classes.

I aimed my LPG and fired. A few inches off target. I tried to touch the energy inside the gun with my mind and then dropped the gun with a yelp of pain. Mallory was at my side in a second.

"I tried to feel the energy and it…burned me." I felt like an idiot.

Mallory shook her head in wonder. "It's like letting the baby play with a candle."

"Sorry." I picked the LPG off the floor and was surprised to find it wasn't hot. Of course it wasn't hot. My *mind* had been burned, not my fingers. Wow. I *am* an idiot.

"Keep at this and if you hit the center 2 times I'll let you do something you'll really like." Mallory patted me on the shoulder and moved on.

It took an hour and I am pretty sure the second bull's-eye was dumb luck, but I did it. I was the last one and had the joy of having everyone staring at me, waiting for me to finish. But finish I did and Mallory immediately brought out a large leather roll, dropping it heavily on the floor in front of the class. She then kicked the roll open. Metal weapons were attached to the roll in slots.

"These, my friends, are traditional Terran projectile weapons. The original 'guns' if you will." She paced behind them looking lovingly down at them. "These are older models, but updated versions of these are still used all over Terra and the Colonies. They are cheaper and easier to repair than LPGs. While the Terran Military Force, or TerMil, uses LPGs almost exclusively, your average person on the street will use a regular 'gun.' You may each take one—and be careful. They are all loaded."

We all grabbed guns. They were much heavier than LPGs, but not uncomfortably so.

"There are a couple of things to get used to with these. 1) Noise. They are incredibly loud when they fire, especially compared to an LPG. You don't want to lose your concentration by being startled at the loud bang they make. 2) They have a serious recoil or 'kick,' depending on the gun type, and this can hurt, sometimes break bones in your hand if you aren't holding your gun properly. 3) They must be loaded and reloaded with the actual projectiles and have limited continuous firing capabilities and 4) There are about a million types of projectiles, or bullets, that can fit in guns like these. Make no mistake—*what* they fire at you (or you at them) can make as much difference as whether they are firing at you at all."

I raised my hand, intrigued by my little gun friend now. "Types of projectiles, Mallory?"

"I know that you have all used the hard wax bullets that we save for drills. Real bullets are only similar to those in shape and size. Everything else is different. Bullets can be made of a range of materials, from light metals to heavier ones, to ones that heat up with the controlled propulsive explosion and stay hot into the target, to bullets that explode on impact, to ones that are poisoned with every kind of poison you can think of, to ones that disintegrate once damage has been done, or even simple darts that drug. LPGs have been standardized for hundreds of years. We use them, TerMil uses them, the Colonies use them. There aren't a lot of surprises with LPGs. These babies," Mallory held up a beautifully taken care of rifle, "are nothing but surprise."

Mallory gave a signal and the targets were replaced with new paper ones. She then handed out protective vests and ear covers and showed us how to hold the guns.

She walked over behind me, "Now we will let our hardest worker go first." Someone groaned quietly. "Knock it off," she said and there was silence. She turned back to me. "Now raise the gun, finger on the trigger, and aim it using the sights, bracing your shooting hand with the other." I did as I was told and held position until she told me to fire. "Now, Jane, no hocus pocus on this one. Just get a feel for it. And watch out for the kick back."

I tried to make myself as still as possible, aimed then fired. In a split second I felt the powder ignite and the explosion move the bullet out of the chamber, down the barrel and into open air. It was fascinating and much more interesting than firing the LPG. The bullet raced towards the target…and hit the wall. That was bad enough, but the recoil from the gun had made my hand ache.

"Well, that sucked." I muttered.

Mallory laughed. "It's a different animal, as I said. Try again."

I repeated my procedure and had better success the second time. I was about two inches from the center. My hand still hurt and I was astonished, even with my ears covered, how loud the thing was.

"Now the guns we will actually train on next time are more modern versions of these. They're almost silent with no recoil at all. The principals are the same as these, however."

"If these aren't the guns we'll be using, why are we..?" Gladys asked. I hadn't noticed her. Always with the questions.

"…wasting our time with them?" Mallory finished for her. "So that you'll appreciate the difference, the improvements in the newer guns. Also because odds are they'll be used against you at some point and sometimes the only weapon you have is one you took off your enemy. It would be nice to know what to expect from one if you found it. Besides," Mallory checked the sight on her rifle, "they're cool." That seemed a stretch to me, but I didn't argue with Mallory about her weapons. The woman knew her shit.

Mallory turned back to me, "One more time and then we'll move on to Jeremy." Jeremy was a Micro three years ahead of me. He looked eager to shoot.

I aimed, but this time I wanted to see if I could *make* myself accurate. I oriented myself towards the target. I tried to feel the ground, but the ground was now a deck and it was moving. OK, I thought, it's not such a big deal. My confidence wasn't where it usually was, but a lot had happened over the last few weeks, and I chalked it up to that.

I pressed the trigger, felt the propulsion, felt the bullet leave the gun and moved it where I wanted it to go…but it didn't obey. I watched in horror as the bullet flew into the corner of the room at what seemed like light speed, ricocheted off, hit the ceiling…and flew into Jeremy's chest. Jeremy flew backward and landed on the floor spread eagled. Students were screaming, some unwilling to get up from the floor where they had thrown themselves.

I looked at Mallory, whose expression was unreadable. Unhappy unreadable, I should say. Without a word I handed her the gun. "Mallory, I…" I started to say, but she shook her head and pointed at Jeremy who was trying, with assistance, to sit up. I looked at his vest and the remains of the bullet that would have pierced his heart had he not been wearing it. I knelt down.

"Jeremy, I don't know what happened." He looked up at me, a mixture of fear and anger in his eyes. "I am so sorry."

"You are a menace," he growled softly for my ears only. Then louder he said, "An accident, Jane. Could've happened to anybody," but he gave me the look that said that it could only have happened to me. I guessed I was getting a reputation—for exhibiting a combination of violence and incompetence. Wonderful.

I stood up again. Mallory looked at me thoughtfully. "I think you need to talk to Felix as soon as he gets back and see what he thinks."

I left amid the worried glares of my fellow students. And this day hadn't been bad enough already.

21:00 – Felix's Classroom, *P.S. Scylla*

I sat in one of the chairs, waiting for Felix. He hadn't yet returned from his mission with Atalanta and I had wandered the halls of the ship for hours. All I wanted to do was crawl into bed with Samuel and forget this whole fucking day. What was I going to do if I couldn't lift anymore?? We're doing all this work to make ourselves more attractive to the Terrans. If I can't use my talents *what do I have to offer*?

My thoughts ran on like this for a while and by the time Felix entered the room I was fit to be tied. He'd clearly been upset when he walked in, but his expression cleared when he took one look at my panicked face. He moved quickly over to kneel by my chair.

"Don't freak out."

Right. Too late. "Will I get it back once I'm on an actual planet, or am I just screwed?"

Felix actively restrained himself from chuckling, which I appreciated. "No. You still have it. You just have to acclimate to being onboard ship. That's all."

Then I thought of my argument with Captain Ian. "Why was I able to 'push' someone without any problem? Why could I do that and not direct that bullet? I can move projectiles, Felix. I'm good at it. Or," and I took a deep breath, "I *was* good at it."

"A simple push doesn't really need thought or grounding. You did it instinctively, right?"

"Very." I'd enjoyed it, too. Prick'd deserved it.

"The more intricate stuff, the bigger stuff was the sort of thing you had to be oriented to do. Orientation is easy on the only planet you've ever lived on. A ship is always changing in ways you're not used to. You are focusing, unconsciously, on, say, 5 things that ground you. But you really only needed 3 of those things and a modification of another to do it." Then Felix cocked his head to the side, looking at me. "Who'd you push, by the way?"

"It was the…never mind." All I needed was to add to the violent/crazy/incompetence thing. "So you don't have this problem?"

Felix pulled up a chair and sat next to me. "I did. And it wasn't easy. I couldn't move anything the way I wanted, if I could at all. I spent the first week experimenting. Disastrously." He shook his head ruefully. "I felt I needed ground, turn of the planet, physical contact with it, concentration and the ability to feel the mass of the Object I was trying to move."

He looked at me intently and I started to feel less anxious. This was Felix and he did everything well. If he says he's got it, than he has.

"But once I made the 'ground' the deck I realized I didn't need to be on a planet." I looked at him dubiously. "We've been in a stationary orbit this past week and half. The General did that mostly for us Macros, which is why your transition to shipboard life has been relatively smooth, shuttles notwithstanding. But we Macros have to be able to adapt to a moving ship. The General can't be expected to hold still forever, especially with…" he broke off, plainly regretting that last thought. He cleared his throat and went on. "It will take practice, but if I can do it, you can."

That seemed an awfully big assumption and my face must have shown my disbelief because he laughed. Felix got up and stood behind me, placing his hands on my shoulders.

"Now try this." He took a deep breath and I did the same. "Reach out to feel the ship—not the people or the things in it, but the metal bubble that encases us and keeps our atmosphere in and space out." And he added, "Start at your feet the way you did at home."

I started at my feet and felt the metal deck beneath them. It felt hard and strong, but so thin and too pliable, then I was suddenly outside the ship whizzing through space. And I fainted.

I awoke and found myself on the floor leaning against Felix while he propped me up.

"Welcome back, friend." He helped me back up into the chair. "Now try again and this time *stay in the ship*."

I felt the deck and this time instead of going all the way through it, I traced it around, trying to touch the whole outer skin with my mind. I became fascinated by the irregularities in the hull and the places that had those Tenorium windows Samuel liked. I felt the vacuum of space whizzing by but didn't reach out to touch it again. I stood up and moved around the room like a person in a trance. I felt the orientation of the shape change with me as I moved. I was astonished at how much the ship seemed to change when I changed position. Something as large as a planet would never have been affected by a person walking. Flying over it in a shuttle, sure, but as big as this ship was, it was nothing compared to a planet. But I got it. I could feel it now. This was a place to start.

I looked over at Felix and smiled.

"Good. Now what you have begun to do is get the feel of the ship going *this* speed on *this* course." My expression faded a bit. You mean this wasn't all there was to it? Felix continued. "I am going to ask the Captain to run a series of sub light drills for us Macros, trying to get us used to all kinds of variations in speed and direction. I think we will be able to tell how fast and what direction we are going on any ship we're on after a while." This clearly pleased him. I wasn't as pleased. I could picture myself fainting all over the ship. Not a pretty picture.

"Have you been working on this with all the Macros? Or just the ones who fail spectacularly in class?" I'd tried not to sound bitter. Well, I hadn't tried all that hard.

"Starting tomorrow. Your…escapade moved your time table up a bit, yes. I'm assuming Jeremy is all right?"

"Bruised ribs. It'll hurt when he coughs, but other than that he's fine," I said with relief.

"The General is insisting, and I agree with him, that we need to be able to adapt to any reasonable (and some unreasonable) situation. We can't only be Macros on the ground. We have to be able to work anywhere, especially since our most likely employer works in space."

This made sense to me even if I was dreading the training. Fuck those Terrans anyway. Why did they have to make everything so nerve-wracking?

Felix stared me in the eye, his mien now extremely serious. "From now on, Jane, you must never *ever* use your gifts without thoroughly grounding yourself first." I opened my mouth to speak, but he cut me off. "You didn't know this would happen today. This is new for all of us. But you know now. You must take this very seriously. No excuses. Someone will die next time. It's all too easy for people like us." He was clearly thinking of something or someone else as he paused. What had he done? Was that the reason for the night terrors? I liked him too much to pry so I merely waited for him to continue. "We have a responsibility."

"I won't forget, Felix. Not ever."

"Thank you, Jane." And he kissed me on the cheek. "We'll work on this more at the regular time tomorrow. The General has asked you to report to his quarters when we are through here, so I'd go if I were you." Felix's smile was more a smirk. A friendly smirk, at least. I guess Atalanta must have said something.

"I'll see you tomorrow. You're the best, you know." I gave him a generous smile. I felt considerably better; my problem was on the way to being dealt with and I was finally going to see Samuel.

"I know," Felix replied as I flitted out the door. I caught a look at him as I went, his whole posture conveyed dejection. I made a mental note to talk to Atalanta tomorrow. It just wasn't fair.

<u>22:00 – The General's Quarters, *P.S. Scylla*</u>

I entered quickly. There he was, Samuel, boots up, with an open bottle of spirits within easy reach on the desk next to him. He was reading something.

"So, you've saved the lives of everyone in your shuttle, you and Felix sent Object shells into the atmosphere, obliterating them, in the process scaring the shit out of both Atalanta and my son, helped diagnose the possible future plans of our alien enemies, and shot a fellow student." He dropped the paper down at looked at me. "Busy day."

He paused, then I saw the twinkle in his eye. He laughed. Then I laughed, and if mine was tinged with a little bit of hysteria, it didn't matter. He held out the bottle. I approached him, grabbed it and took a nice long drink.

He looked at me appraisingly. "Never boring, are you?"

"No, Sir," I said as the spirits burned their way down my throat. I handed the bottle back and sat in his lap. He put one arm around me and took a swig. He put the bottle down and kissed me gently.

"Happy birthday, Baby."

I looked at him in surprise. I'd forgotten all about my birthday. It seemed such a trivial thing after all that had happened. It only meant something to me now because he'd said it.

"Is there anything you want?" His voice was softer now. I loved him so much I felt my heart would burst.

I nodded and kissed him again urgently. He responded ardently as my hands reached to undo his belt. We made love in the chair first, then he carried me to the bed for more.

In the constant night we moved together and as we came I felt tears coursing down my cheeks. He brushed my hair out of my face alarmed.

"What's wrong, Jane?"

I tried to pull myself together, but it didn't work. I couldn't hide the tremor in my voice. "We'll never see home again, will we, Samuel?"

His face mirrored the loss I felt. "No, Baby."

I nodded, my throat tight from trying not to sob. He lay next to me and wrapped me up in his strong arms. No, I thought. Pace is lost, but right now my home is *here*.

ENTRY 3-2-9

A Note on Religion

One of the first things Pace & Pallon did when establishing their colony 700 years ago was to outlaw churches. This was not surprising considering that church and synagogue (and mosque and temple, etc.) groups had been their most tireless critics. Moral outrage was very easy to come by with Drs. Pace and Pallon constantly toying with human genetics. The churches had also very often ended up taking in and caring for the results of the most spectacularly failed experiments. Outlawing houses of worship, religious meetings and formalized groups did not mean, however, that they had outlawed religion. What they had criminalized was public and group expression *of religion.*

Pace and Pallon had confiscated all existing copies of the Judeo-Christian Bible, the Koran, the Bhagavad Vita and any other accepted religious texts they could think of before anyone had even boarded the ship for Pace. They had then, with typical industry, rewritten them to reflect the values of the new world. Certain accepted taboos disappeared, certain punishments for breaking laws were either softened or deleted and, in a move that shocked the remaining purists among the colonists, the Bible was edited for continuity and sense. The whole concept of holy wars was dropped, but 'love thy neighbor' was kept. The idea of an actual savior was downplayed and the Old Testament God was made gentler. And they had made sure to work in a scene where Jesus explains that a woman or man must not know marital love (sex) until she or he has seen 15 summers, thus reinforcing the Age of Consent.

There were some protests from colonists who had been very attached to the scriptures they had grown up with, but that faded with time. Our founders were confident that if they made all these changes, some clumsy, some subtle, and the Book (as it was known) was around long enough it would become part of the culture. And it did.

They allowed and even pretended to encourage private home worship. The head of the family could be priest/rabbi (or other equivalent) and services could happen whenever. Most home churches were Ju-Cross (Dr. Pace felt that 'Judeo-Christian' had too many moral connotations) based and started with a common prayer book that Indira Pallon had ruthlessly adapted from the English Book of Common Prayer. The word 'God' was made lower case by rule of law. There were other religions or cults that had cropped up naturally within the colony, but even most of those had a similar monotheistic tone, most referred to a god and most had the standard morals. There were never any meetings of multi-family groups; no friends invited for dinner on a religious holiday. Pace and Pallon gave their people religion for the comfort of afterlife protection, but nothing else. It isolated everyone and that was the whole point.

07:00 – General Armstrong's Quarters, *P.S. Scylla,* July 12, 2869

Samuel and I lay as we'd fallen, exhausted after a marathon of lovemaking that had started (I'd looked at the clock) at least 4 hours earlier when he'd been unable to sleep. I tried to catch my breath and realized that, even tangled up in Samuel, I was too relaxed to move. He wasn't moving either so I supposed he was in a similar boneless state. I saw his eyelids droop. So *now* he can sleep. The alarm went off, but we stayed still. It kept buzzing.

"Samuel."

He sighed and sat up, partially knocking me over in the process. He helped me straighten up and brushed the hair out of my eyes.

"We need a vacation," he said as he kissed me.

"What does a vacation look like in space?" I leaned contentedly against his chest. He laughed and I could feel it. Wonderful being this close, I thought.

"Well, if you're not near a planet you pretty much stay in your quarters and do what you want."

"And we weren't doing what we wanted for the last 4 hours?" I pulled the sheet up modestly but he twitched it away.

"But now we have to get up and go to work," Samuel grimaced.

I shook my head. "You're right then. Vacation for sure."

He smiled at me. "On a different subject. Have you seen Arrow?"

Oh, goodie, I thought sarcastically. Well, we knew this conversation was coming eventually. "Not really. She's been keeping to herself even more than usual since we moved to the ship."

"Hm." He pulled himself to the edge of the bed and swung his legs over. "I'm worried about her."

"You should be." He looked at me inquiringly. "You wanted to know why Ian doesn't like me?" I asked rhetorically. "He was asking about Arrow, too." I joined Samuel at the edge of the bed. "I told him that I knew that she is your daughter."

Samuel threw his head back as though I had punched him. "I wish you hadn't done that, Jane."

"Why? It seemed only fair to let him know that there were people who had that information. In case he…" Samuel stood up and started looking for clothes. I watched him intently. "You know about them, don't you?"

Samuel found my underwear and tossed it to me. "He never said anything, he wouldn't, but I suspected. It was the only reason for him to get as upset as he did when he found out."

I put my underwear on and started looking for my shirt. "But they didn't know then."

He pulled on his trousers with unnecessary force. "They do now."

I sighed, annoyed. "Those Terrans really infected you with their hang-ups, didn't they?"

He turned to face me, now really angry. "This isn't a joke, Jane. One whiff of this once we meet up with the Terrans and his career is over." He snapped his fingers. "Just like that."

"No one knows *here*, Samuel. Yes, I agree that the Terran prejudice is an obstacle, but we haven't even seen them yet. Right now we are effectively on Pace. On *Pace* this shit doesn't matter." I frowned. "Or it shouldn't matter. That taboo was for the sake of the gene pool. As long as Arrow keeps from getting pregnant, which won't be a problem as long as we are on a Pace ship…"

"Arrow won't have children no matter who she's with," Samuel said flatly.

I stood before him, still half dressed, arms folded on my chest. "Why? Because you decreed it? Are you punishing her?"

"No!" he said, shocked. "First of all, Arrow won't talk to me, so 'decreeing' anything would be a waste of breath and second of all, it was entirely her choice. It was one of the first things she told me." His anger seemed to fade as he recalled their first meeting. "She didn't even fully believe I was her father at the time." He sat back down on the bed.

"You never told me how you found her." I sat next to him.

He sighed, taking a moment to collect his thoughts. "It was the year I got hurt, when the *Edo* exploded and poor Chow died. He built all these ships," Samuel gestured around him somehow indicating the faster than light fleet. "Something went wrong and over 100 people died, including Chow and almost me." He sighed. "I spent almost a year at the Military Infirmary on Pace 4 at Bane. Recovery was slow and pretty rough. I was really fucking bored. I got to thinking and wondered if they'd already used my file DNA to make any kids. Ian was little then and I liked the idea of giving him a sibling or two. It was clear to me that Ruth and I weren't going to make it so there weren't going to be a full-blooded sisters or brothers."

A shadow of sadness passed over his face. I wanted to comfort him, but let him be, not wanting to interfere with the story. "So I snuck into the archives and, after a lot of searching, discovered that my DNA had been used once, to make a little girl. In fact she was still in the tubs when I was there. I actually got in and saw her there, swimming around, a healthy little baby." He smiled at the memory, but then his face clouded. "She was mine. I couldn't take care of her, or help her—she belonged to the Government. That's why she was born in Bane."

"Like you were," I said without thinking. He looked over at me, this time really shocked. "Why were you born in Bane, Samuel?"

He answered still getting over his surprise at my knowledge, "They'd lost the ability to create 'picture makers'—supers who could make you see anything they chose by projecting it in your mind. Like that old woman in the report. As with so many of these hare-brained experiments, it didn't work. I was reclassified out of being a super and returned to my parents, who managed to love me anyway." At this I took his hand and squeezed it. "They never forgave the Government for throwing me away like that." He turned to me, "Ruth and I chose not to enhance Ian at all." I sucked in my breath. I had never heard of anyone doing that. Ever. "I mean, he has the standard good health, fast reflexes, longevity, etc., but nothing extra. Nothing that *we* would consider mods." He laughed to himself. "It took Ian years to forgive us for that. For choosing to make him normal."

"Why did you do that? I asked incredulously.

Samuel shrugged. "Ruth grew up on a farm on Pace 1. Farmers mess with genes the way everyone used to do it—breeding for the attributes you wanted and trying to lose the ones you don't. She thought, and I completely agreed, that humans had been messed with enough. It wasn't the easiest decision, but we made it." He scratched his neck, thoughtfully. "I think that was the last time we agreed on anything."

"But Arrow had mods. Some pretty intense ones if she was at Bane, right?"

"Well. Yes. But I lost track of her almost as soon as I'd seen her." He looked embarrassed. Well, there was no way I was going to let him get away with not telling me with a lead in like that.

"How?"

"I…snapped. I realized, watching her, that I had handed over something truly valuable to strangers who could use it however they wished. For good or evil. And that I had been criminally irresponsible to do so. And now I had a daughter that didn't belong to me."

"What did you do?" I asked warily.

"I went into the DNA storage room and…set off a couple of dozen impact grenades." He grinned toothily. "I got the whole fucking batch, mine included." I slapped him on the shoulder, impressed. The he gave me a sly look. "I have a feeling you're gonna throw that little episode in my face the next time you do something insane."

I laughed. "I hadn't thought of that, but thank you for the suggestion."

His smile went away. "But unfortunately, they figured out it was me and locked me in my room for a couple of months until I was fully healed and could return to duty. I was a 'war hero,'" Samuel spat out that words with disgust, "and pretty close to untouchable so my career was unaffected.

But it was while I was locked in my room that my daughter was born and taken away."

"When you did find her—*that's* why you became Keeper! That's why you gave up the military…" I let my voice trail off as I absorbed the truth. He must have searched for decades. God, what determination.

"So when did she meet Ian?"

"Around the time she came to teach at the School. She'd been part of the 'Founder Program' but the talents they'd wanted her to have hadn't manifested, so they'd tossed her out like they had me, except that she didn't have any parents to take her in. She was adopted out and watched." His eyes gleamed, "But what they didn't know was that she *was* a super. She'd just hidden it so she wouldn't become property of the Government."

I was impressed again. "Smart girl."

"Too smart by half."

"So she got a job at the School to…see the life she would have had if she'd been found out?" I asked.

"Something like that. Ian wasn't a Captain then, just a top pilot and he flew the previous Keeper all over the place. So, that's where they met."

"And that's where they fell in love," I finished. Samuel looked uncomfortable, as well he might, but it didn't change facts. "Why won't Arrow have kids? Why such an emphatic 'no'?"

"The Founder Program was created to breathe life back into the breed. The Scientists felt that we'd been diluted over the centuries and wanted to return us to our roots. So the 'Founders', after being dead for over half a millennium, became…"

"…parents," I finished, aghast. "So who was Arrow's mother?"

"The Mother of Pace-Pallon herself." Samuel's expression was bleak.

"Not Indira Pallon? That can't be." I tried to wrap my brain around it, but it was too big. "Who knows this, besides Arrow, you, and now me? Does Ian know?"

"I don't think so, but I'm don't actually know for sure. And this program was only implemented 30 years ago, which means that there is a good chance at least one of the Scientists involved is sitting pretty over on the *Hastings*."

"It isn't Bayliss, is it? He's certainly a conscience-free bastard if ever I saw one."

"Agreed, but he's too young and not nearly senior enough. Anyone messing with Indira Pallon's DNA had to be at or near the top."

I thought for a minute. "Samuel, glad as I am to be filled in, why did you tell me all this now? There must be a reason."

He looked away, his posture now awkward as if he was embarrassed. "I was going to ask you to look in, befriend Arrow for me." I looked at him, horrified. "I know she's difficult, but she doesn't have any friends and she won't talk to me unless it's a direct order from the General. I don't want to force her."

"You want *me* to force her." I stood up and found a wall away from him to lean on. He stood up and followed me.

"No. Just be there."

"Why me, Samuel? I only have two friends in the universe and I only made them in the last 2 weeks. I'm not a social," I paused as I forced myself to not say 'girl,' "person."

He stepped very close to me. It was distracting. He knew this of course. Bastard. I liked it, but...bastard. "I don't need her charmed, in fact I don't think she's charmable. She needs someone to be strong and call her on her shit. Someone who isn't afraid to fight back." Then Samuel realized what he'd just said, "Not *actual* fighting back, Jane. I mean it."

"So let me get this straight. You are sending in your," now that I'd started that sentence I really was at a loss as to what to call myself, so I fudged it, "...partner in amorous adventure to talk to your long lost daughter (who hates me, by the way) and ask her what's up?"

Now he was really close, pulling me to him. "I'm worried about her and you are the only person I trust to send. Not Ian, certainly." Proximity to Samuel was getting more and more distracting. "Think about it, Jane, please." I nodded against his chest. "Oh, and don't lie to her about us. She hates having things kept from her."

I laughed, "Partner in amorous adventure it is."

He cradled my face gently in his hands. "Let's just go with the classic 'girlfriend.'"

"So I'm your girlfriend, Samuel?" I sounded like a goddamn teenager, which while accurate, was not at all how I wanted to sound.

He smiled as he kissed me lightly, "What else, Baby?" And he kissed me again and again. Everyone was going to be late to work that morning.

09:00 – Conference Room, *P.S. Scylla*

Dr. Bayliss stood at the head of the conference table alternately leaning back on his heels, then standing on his toes. This was the well-bred man's way of expressing impatience, I guessed. I noted all this as I zoomed around the corner and into the room, ten minutes late. I slammed into a chair and looked up. Captain Ian, Atalanta, Felix, a strange man and, of course, Dr. Bayliss, all stared at me and my explosive entrance. Atalanta took one look at me and rolled her eyes with a giggle.

"Really, Jane," she whispered.

I ignored her. "Sorry, Dr. Bayliss." I thought about throwing in something about being unavoidably delayed or getting caught in... And then realized that anything I said would just make Atalanta laugh more.

"We, I mean, *I* just got word of this meeting a few minutes ago." Yeah, right in the middle of…never mind. Oh, well. And if our timing was correct any second now I should be hearing...

"Morning, Doctor Bayliss." The General arrived, cool and calm. Not so, me, as his voice sent a thrill through my whole body. I pretended to be interested in my chair in an attempt not to give myself away.

"Stop it," Atalanta laughed quietly. "You keep broadcasting like that and I'll have to fall in love with him, too,"

I shushed her. I looked up and found the Captain watching me intently. Fantastic. Well, maybe he was only watching me because he wanted to get close to my room-mate. Wouldn't be the first time. This was an unfortunate train of thought because I could suddenly picture Arthur who'd gone so far as to lose his virginity with me so that he would be better prepared for her. I'd been furious when I'd figured it out, but now it just seemed so...Arthur. Dr. Bayliss was speaking.

"So, according to the hypothesis proposed by Captain Armstrong, Felix, Miss Atalanta and Miss Jane, the *tapetia mortis* are building pressurized launch chambers in which to return their sated selves to space and their future planetary meals. Is that essentially correct?"

We all nodded.

Dr. Bayliss pressed a button and a large monitor lowered down from the ceiling. "Since I had the good fortune to receive Captain Armstrong's report while still on the *Hastings*, I was able to run the hypothesis by several of my esteemed colleagues and take advantage of their inestimable expertise."

The look I saw the General give his son would have melted the shell of any Object in its path. Captain Ian turned slightly red and pretended to pay even more attention to Dr. Bayliss. Too bad we hadn't thought of using parental disapproval as a military weapon.

Dr. Bayliss continued on, oblivious.

"We analyzed the sensor logs that had been sent along with the report and were able to draw some conclusions about what you were seeing." He clicked something and a vat of what looked like the boiling puke appeared on the monitor, bubbling away. "The vomit is a combination of several known acids and two unknown—we were able to analyze samples in the Pace labs before we left. We've been referring to it as *t-melange*, owing to its nature as a mixture. The acids involved do not agree with each other and this constant fighting creates the pressure, thus the bubbles and from that it follows that the greater the amount of *t-melange*, the more explosive it will get."

"Explosive?" Captain Ian asked.

Dr. Bayliss loooked at him with a serious and patronizing expression. "There is no propulsion without explosion, Captain."

"Right." The Captain looked nettled and became silent.

"So the shape of the Hive-looking things is meant to direct the explosion," Felix said intently. It took me a second to realize that Felix had sounded just like the intelligent, rational Felix I knew. But he was speaking to Dr. Bayliss, the man he had sworn to kill. What the fuck?

Dr. Bayliss clicked and the monitor showed an internal diagram of one of the hives, complete with acid, chimney and holes in the mountain. I was immediately distracted from my concerns over the mystery of calm Felix.

"This is a rough model of the structure you saw by your School. We've dubbed it Irrfan-1, after your friend." I laughed a little to myself. Irrfan would have appreciated the irony that his name had been lent to something that would allow the creatures that he'd only been able to kill at the expense of his own life to escape to new worlds and kill more people.

"Thank you," the General said graciously with just a touch of irony. I got the feeling that his thoughts had run along a similar vein.

"The structures, *t-hives* as we are rather inaccurately calling them, are structured to channel the pressure generated in the most efficient way. The pressure is currently being diffused by the relief holes that have been carved out of the mountain. While this is a specific example, we now have surprisingly similar data on nearly all accessible *t-hives* on Paces 1, 2, and 4."

"Not from the ones on 3, naturally," the strange man said, speaking for the first time. We all looked at him, curious. He, though sitting, was easily the largest person in the room. Very tall, very muscular. Probably outweighed even the General by a good 100 pounds of what looked like pure muscle. He might have been handsome once, but his skin was pockmarked and scarred and his face was partially covered by a half-healed burn. "No one gives a crap about 3. Too much trouble."

Dr. Bayliss's expression became one of suffering tolerance. "I'm sorry, may I introduce Senior Engineer Sigmund Van Houton. He was on the *Hastings* when I made my initial report to my fellow Doctors." We could see, and I could feel, Sr. Engineer Van Houton bristle at that reminder that no matter how good or bad he was, he could never ever be a Doctor. Since most of us were willing to embrace anyone that Dr. Bayliss didn't cotton to on that basis alone, we all gave him welcoming smiles. He barely acknowledged us.

"The reason I'm here is because I think our experiences on 3 have relevance to the current problem." He glared at Dr. Bayliss who pretended not to notice.

"And what, in your view, is the problem, Engineer?" The Doctor's voice was full of thinly veiled contempt.

"How do we destroy the creatures before they move on to destroy the next set of worlds?" The Engineer looked appalled that Dr. Bayliss had to ask.

"If we can, of course, but what the real concern is how quickly we can re-terraform our planets and start over once the creatures have vacated."

The rest of us looked at each other in astonishment. Part of me leapt at the very idea of getting to go home again. No more fucking Terrans, no separation from Samuel, assuming he wanted to stay... And another part of me balked at the idea. As scary as the Terrans were to me, there was a certain appeal to being able to do, to choose whatever I wanted. No, I thought. I choose Samuel.

"You're off your fucking rocker, *Doctor*," the Senior Engineer sneered. "Pace-Pallon is finished. It was dead the moment those Objects landed on it. We have no right to selfishly let those monsters free to destroy more worlds when we have even a chance of stopping them."

Dr. Bayliss looked taken aback. No one spoke to a Scientist that way. "I think you have a mistaken impression not only of what the *tapetia mortis* will do, but of our responsibilities in the matter, Engineer."

"It's *Senior* Engineer, and I think it's time to show that simulation you made."

Dr. Bayliss just stood there.

"You had to have made one. Show us what will happen when it is time for the *tapetia mortis*, as you call them, to go."

Dr. Bayliss seemed unable to move. I glanced over at the General whose expression was suspiciously blank. His eyes were twinkling, though.

Van Houton stood up and Dr. Bayliss paled and backed up a pace. Van Houton snorted in contempt and waved Dr. Bayliss to a seat, which the Doctor took almost in spite of himself; the Senior Engineer was a very physically imposing man.

"You all may call me Sig, if you like," he said to us, but then turned to Dr. Bayliss. "Not you." He could have been joking, but he clearly wasn't. Dr. Bayliss gave a tiny nod of assent.

"I went to the *Hastings* yesterday to try to talk sense into our Scientist Masters—not that I expected anyone to listen, it was more for the sake of my conscience than anything else." Sig took a quick look around the room as if testing our reactions. "This is something you all need to see."

Sig took a breath and clicked for the next display on the monitor.

The graphic started with a close-up of Irrfan-1, then slowly backed up to show the other *t-hives* dotting Pace 4. There was a pause as soon as the view was sufficiently far back to show most of them. Then one by one the things started shooting into the sky and leaving the atmosphere for space. The new Objects, for that's what they were, shot out by the hundreds like bubbles from an insane bubble machine. It was horrifying and fascinating to watch as the orbit around 4 filled with Objects. Then I noticed that the Objects were moving in a pattern, closer and closer to each other.

"What are they doing?" I asked.

"We think that they're magnetically attracted to each other, and they have to come together with sufficient speed (and mass) to be able to break orbit. I don't think that it is one mass of them per planet, that would be too large, but several per planet is plausible. They break orbit and are gone."

"Exactly. Gone." Dr. Bayliss seemed to have gotten some of his courage back. He stood up, dwarfed by Sig. "We get our planet back and rare opportunity to begin again."

Sig glared at him. "I know you Scientists don't really believe in the idea of consequences, but don't you feel strange about potentially sentencing other people to death because we let these things go?"

Dr. Bayliss was taken aback but recovered, "If that were to happen, if it was *proved* that it had happened, then I would, of course, feel terrible about it, but these are all hypothetical situations. We have no idea how long these *tapetia mortis* had been travelling through the universe before they landed here. It could be hundreds of years from now before…"

"So, the deaths are OK if they happen hundreds of years in the future?" Sig said caustically.

"No," Dr. Bayliss said suddenly, finally showing his anger. "It is *not* all right, but you are talking about the possibility of permanently destroying our home to kill these things. I cannot condone something as insane as that! We have fought for these worlds, suffered for them and made them our own! We have a right to keep what is ours and let the universe take care of itself!" The Doctor's face was red and his eyes wide. He no longer seemed to care whether or not Sig killed him.

Felix's hand twitched. Jumped, really. I looked with alarm at Atalanta, who was pale and slightly perspiring with effort. I didn't have any idea how to help her, though. It wasn't my area.

Sig himself, however, had not matched Dr. Bayliss's anger. He had, in fact, calmed down and looked over at the General meaningfully. The General sighed and nodded having gotten the point.

I was mulling all this over; we all were, when I had an unhappy thought. "Excuse me?" My voice was quiet but it carried and everyone looked up. I suddenly felt a little intimidated but my courage didn't fail me. "So let's say we let them go and they disappear for 200 years or so, to pick a period of time at random. And we start again, we build, we bring in new colonists, we grow and we prosper."

Sig looked at me, as did the General. It was the Doctor who prompted me with, "Yes, Jane?"

"What's to stop them from coming back *here*?"

Atalanta sucked in a quick breath. Sig stared down Dr. Bayliss who, surprisingly, did not bat an eye. I had a feeling that his display of temper had knocked some of his civilized veneer off and we could see his inner toughness now. What surprised me was the General's expression. He didn't look at all shocked by what I'd said, he looked…proud.

Now I was pretty sure I'd been primed (or the group had been primed and I'd just been the first to get there) to say what I'd said. Didn't make it any less true, but I wasn't entirely comfortable having been manipulated like that. Hey, wait a minute. I turned quickly to Atalanta, while still looking ill, gave me a hint of a smile. Son of a bitch. My eyes found the General's when his expression changed to alarm. He looked from me to Atalanta and back again.

I turned back to Atalanta who, now that I looked more closely, was taking quick shallow breaths like she was fighting pain.

"'Lanta?" I whispered.

Her eyes were closed with concentration. "You have to get Felix out of here, *now*." I looked over at Felix and noticed his calm was quickly receding, his fingers were tapping and though he kept clenching his fists to stop it, he clearly couldn't. I felt a tremor in the table. Any minute things were going to go bat shit. An out of control Macro could, as we all knew, be extremely dangerous. She was right; we had to get him out of here.

"Faint." I whispered.

She pretended to faint. For a split second I thought she'd fainted for real, but then figured out she hadn't since Dr. Bayliss was still alive. I screamed, for effect, and the room dissolved in confusion.

"Felix! Help!" I screamed. Oh, goodie. Now I'm a violent, incompetent drama queen, some part of my brain thought. Captain Ian was closer to us than Felix was and started to move in to assist. His father stopped him, giving Felix time to get to us. Felix and I carried Atalanta out.

As we headed down the hallway I heard Sig say, "Dramatic little group, eh, General?"

The General laughed, "You've no idea. Call me Sam, Sig. Care for a drink?"

"Always."

Good, I thought. Sig is as much of a freak as we are. Maybe he can help us…do whatever it is we're going to do. Whatever the hell that is.

11:00 – Hallway outside Training Room 4, *P.S. Scylla*

Atalanta was still keeping it together, sort of. Felix was walking with us, no longer even pretending to help support her. He was clearly in trouble. Whatever calming effect Atalanta had put on him was wearing off more and more with every second.

"Almost there, Felix." Atalanta said through gritted teeth. We stopped in front of an empty training room. Atalanta gave him a look and he went in, door closing behind him. Then Atalanta collapsed into my arms. I was surprised, having been too focused on Felix, and we ended up on the ground in front of the door.

"'Lanta!" I said, afraid for her.

She shook her head. "It's just strain. I just need to rest."

Both our heads turned quickly towards the sound of a large crash inside the room. I started to leap to my feet but she stopped me. "Let him get it out, Jane. He'll go crazy if he doesn't." I sat back down, then found myself pulling her against my side so I could keep her steady as she started shaking.

"When did you decide to do that, in there? Suppress him, I mean?" I had to know. Considering how strongly Felix felt about Dr. Bayliss, what they'd been able to accomplish had been just short of a miracle.

Atlanta's beautiful face was sheened in sweat. "Yesterday. As soon as it was clear that the meeting was really going to happen." She glared back in the direction of the conference room. "All thanks to Captain Armstrong."

I nodded. "I don't think he had any idea what Dr. Bayliss was until today. And don't worry," and here I had to chuckle evilly, "Samuel will straighten him out as soon as he's finished attempting to charm Sig."

There were many more crashes and bangs inside the classroom. I fought the urge to race in there. It really seemed wrong to just sit and listen, but Atalanta kept her place and I followed her lead. He was her man, after all, when all was said and done.

"Did you tell Samuel, about Felix, I mean? He seemed to know something was up," I asked over the noises of destruction.

"I told him what, but not why. Felix doesn't know that and I would prefer if it stayed that way. The General didn't ask, he just accepted it. I was there to attempt to tip the odds in our favor anyway, so he said it was all right as long as I could keep up the primary mission." Her color was better and she'd stopped sweating. Now she just looked tired.

"Which you did brilliantly. It was incredible." I did not have to fake an awed expression. It *was* incredible.

Atalanta smiled at me, unconsciously preening a little. Funny how I would have found that intensely irritating a month ago and now it just seemed cute. We heard the rhythm of the crashes slow down by quite a bit.

Atalanta stood up and I followed suit. She looked at me, her concern for Felix evident. "Listen, Jane. When the door opens he'll probably want me, but I want you to go in first." I started to protest but she cut me off. "He's very proud and he'll be sorry later if I see him before he's completely in control again." I didn't know what to say. I was nosy enough to really want to know what the hell had gone on in there and I was genuinely worried about Felix. But I really didn't want intrude on their relationship. Then again, she was asking and she wasn't forced to… I nodded. "Another thing," Atalanta continued, "you can reason with him

Macro to Macro in ways that I can't if it turns out he hasn't gotten it all out of his system."

"Good point."

Just then the door opened. The room was trashed. Chairs smashed, computers tossed around. Part of the cloth ceiling cover was down and several of the wall sections were pulled off. The training mat was shredded and the writing boards on the walls were broken into large pieces. And on the far wall Felix sat, leaning to the side, bloody. Dear god.

I turned to Atalanta, "We need medics."

"No. Not yet," she said fiercely. "I'll get a medkit and diagnostics." She waved me in. "Go." Atalanta ran off in the direction of the Infirmary.

I turned back to the ruined room and looked at Felix. It only took me a second to realize how many places he was bleeding on his body. I ran to him and knelt down next to him on the floor. He looked over at me. His eyes were clear; he was lucid despite the pain he must have been in.

"Where's my girl?" he asked softly.

"Getting med supplies." I used my sleeve to absorb some of the blood on his face. He let me, but watched me the whole time.

"Saving my pride. As if that were still possible."

I started feeling his shoulders for breaks. Then his arms and hands. He seemed to find this amusing. "Why, Jane, this is so sudden." His torso and legs seemed fine also.

I smiled at him perfunctorily and his expression grew tragic. "Why did you have Atalanta suppress you, Felix?" I asked. "She could have told you what happened at the meeting. Hell, *I* could have."

He shrugged. "I got paranoid that he would read into it if I wasn't there and I knew I would never make it through on my own. I need to make sure that he doesn't see me as any kind of threat. It could be useful later. What I didn't realize is that he has no idea who I am, and I don't think he would care if he did know."

I thought Felix was probably right, but I persisted. "And Atalanta is perfectly fine with this being a facet of this as yet undetermined revenge plan?"

Felix straightened up against the wall painfully. "She's buying time."

Yes, I could see that. Time to save the man she loves from himself. I looked around the room, then back to the damage on Felix's body. Bloody, yes, but so far all superficial. But a Macro as good, as great as Felix wouldn't have needed to get hit at all. Why? Why get hit?

"I see you putting it together. Something I think only a fellow Macro would really notice. Why all this?" Felix indicated his bloody injuries. His tragic expression increased to the point that I wanted to look away. "Because I wish I was dead."

He took my breath away with that statement. I searched his face and he really seemed to mean it. Then I couldn't see him at all because my eyes were full. It was such an awful thing to say that it actually hurt to hear it. Especially from Felix. He held my hand, saying softly, "But I couldn't do it. I would start something coming at me, something that would end it quick and I always softened it right at the end. So, I am bruised and bloody but still alive. An alive coward, but alive."

I was no Empath, but imagining his pain was torture. He seemed sane, but how could he be? "What stopped you?"

He sat silent for a minute and I could see his jaw clenching as if trying to control emotion. "I'd been thinking about it for the last couple of days, of ending it all. I'd been obsessed with the idea of it being the ultimate release. But Atalanta stood in the way of my easy out. When it came down to it I realized that the only thing that could make this bad situation worse would be to kill myself. My misery is mostly on her behalf. How could I do that to her? How could I put that on her shoulders? So, I didn't."

I nodded, a small sob escaping as tears fell down my cheeks. He immediately looked contrite. "I'm sorry I burdened you with this, Jane. I just wanted to tell a friend…"

"It's all right," I said, pulling myself together. "I didn't know how bad it is with you, Felix, and I'm so sorry."

He shrugged, "I didn't want anyone to know. And there is nothing anyone can do anyway."

I wiped tears off my face with the back of my hand, mindful that Atalanta would be coming back soon. I took both his hands. "Felix, you are my dear friend. With my friendship comes obligations and—and you can't fucking try that shit ever again, OK?!?!?" I'd started off mature and, I don't know, urbane and then just devolved into the profane. More my speed, really.

Felix actually laughed. "I'll do my best, friend."

I kissed his hands and dropped them back in his lap just as Atalanta came in with the medkit. His face lit up when he saw her and I left as soon as she started fussing over him. I wished there was something I could do. What, though?

I had other things I had to focus on now. Like Arrow. I really wasn't looking forward to this.

<u>11:30 – Training Room 8, *P.S. Scylla*</u>

I found Arrow still in her Training Room. Her classes were over for the day (I'd checked) and she was straightening up the room. Long knives, it looked like to me. One of those areas that crossed over between Weapons, which was Mallory's domain and actual fighting, which was Arrow's. There was some blood on a towel she was carrying. Not her blood, naturally, and some on the floor. First blood was such an old tradition, but

Arrow loved it. I had several small scars on my arms, reminders that my defensive moves had been lacking.

"Something I can do for you, Jane?" Arrow said with words that would have been welcoming if they'd been said by someone else.

"The General asked me to see how you were doing." There was no point beating around the bush. This wasn't going to work anyway so I figured I could do my best and get out before she killed me. If I could.

"I'm fine." Arrow kept on straightening up. I guessed she considered that a dismissal. Too bad.

"Your father is worried about you," I said, figuring that would get her attention. It did. She stood up, body taught like a bow string, tension emanating from her.

She hesitated and I had the feeling that she'd been gearing for denial, but changed her mind. "That is information I hope you will have the sense to keep to yourself."

I just stood there, waiting. She was the perfect fighter, but I doubted she had the patience to withstand the sheer irritation of me quietly standing there. Her stress was building exponentially. Arrow looked at me, her gaze dangerous. "Get out."

"He searched for you your entire life and dropped his career once he found out where you were. Couldn't you at least talk to him?"

I saw a shadow of guilt pass over her angular face. "So, you are reduced to hitting me with guilt? Is that all you have? Simple guilt?" Arrow sneered.

"The guilt is hardly the simple kind and no, that isn't remotely all I've got. I was hoping you would be reasonable." Well, not really. But it sounded good.

"All right, Jane. What else have you got?" She raised her chin defensively.

"Why don't you want to have children, when you know your mother is Indira Pallon? I would think that would be an incentive. You know, preserving the bloodline." I'd started out trying to preserve my 'icy reserve' stance to show her she couldn't push me around, but ended up frankly curious.

Arrow reacted the complete opposite of how I thought she would. Her expression fell, some of her defensiveness going with it. She thought for a minute, as if parsing her words. "Imagine that you find out one day, when you are nearly 30, the biological mother you had never been able to identify was Dr. Pallon. You are a super, so have no idea who your parents are, so I'm sure you can imagine it."

I nodded.

"At first you're proud. She was the 'mother of Pace-Pallon' after all and almost a god on Pace. So, since you only know what they taught you at 'normal' school you start doing research on her. To try to find out what fascinating qualities she had and then try to project them onto yourself."

I smiled at this last. That is exactly what I would have done. It had always seemed a little contradictory to me that a system so obsessed with genetics would want to keep its supernormals from ever having an actual living example of them. You know, like a parent.

"But," and here Arrow frowned, "what you learn is how careless she was with human life. How many hundreds of thousands of tubs she'd had drained when things had not gone her way. How many babies and children she'd had put down when they'd turned out strange, frightening or troublesome. How many adults she had experimented on trying to predict genetic decay. And her complete lack of empathy for others."

I was appalled. Arrow was right, Dr. Pallon was a god to us. We'd been taught that our entire lives. Nothing had ever contradicted it. Until this moment. Arrow took note of my expression of horror.

"I read everything she ever wrote. Every journal, every lab notebook, every scrap of paper. At first it was to find out evidence of her greatness and then it became an obsession to prove that she wasn't a sociopath. But I couldn't prove it, Jane. She was a monster. My mother was a monster."

My god, I thought. Every moment Arrow must be wondering when she was going to have to surrender to her genes. She must second guess everything she does. I wondered if she'd attributed her ill-fated love affair with Ian to that, too. Wouldn't have surprised me.

"But you have Samuel's genes, too, and he's a good man." Arrow looked up at my use of his first name. "And you can't think that you are only the sum of your genes. There has to be more to us than that."

"*Samuel,*" she mocked me with her emphasis, "is a good man, I grant you, but I can't take the chance that my children will favor him and not their grandmother." Arrow scratched her chin. I could feel her tensing up again. I think she'd bared too much of herself, or something, but she was getting upset. "So you and the General, eh?"

"Yep." This wasn't going to be good. Her sneer was returning.

"How old are you, Jane, 15?"

What bullshit. She knew exactly how old I was. She'd been one of my first teachers when I'd come to the School 3 years earlier. When I *was* 15.

"18, thanks." She was not going to provoke me. I kept saying. Over and over.

"You really put the *girl* in girlfriend." Arrow said, her voice dripping with scorn.

"Well, you really put the *brother* in brotherly love, don't you?" I said without thinking.

She moved so fast I barely had time to register it. She took my legs out and slammed me (hard) on the matt. Hard enough that it knocked the wind out of me and I was pretty sure something had cracked. She was on top of me, teeth bared in fury, her forearm on my throat. I just lay there, offering no resistance. I didn't want to, anyway. I hurt.

She kept me there for a full minute, then seemed to come out of her angry haze and got off of me. She sat on the matt, lost in her own thoughts.

"Fuck, Arrow, I think you cracked something," I gasped. She snapped out of it and held out a hand to get me to a sitting position. "Thanks." I tried to take some long breaths and found it was getting easier. A bit. "Sorry I crossed the line there, but I got tired of you being such a bitch."

Arrow laughed in spite of herself. She pulled her knees to her chest and hugged herself. "Why didn't you defend yourself? You didn't even try and even *you* aren't that incompetent."

Arrow's people skills really were entirely missing. But she made up for it with lethal force. "A couple of reasons. 1) Samuel made me promise not to fight you. 2) I haven't fought you since I learned you were a pre-cog and I didn't know how that would go, and 3) this wasn't a fight. This was you making a point. The only way to limit it to that would be offer no resistance."

Arrow raised her eyebrows in surprise. "Well-reasoned. But you're telling me you went through all that between my moving for you and your hitting the ground?"

I grimaced, "No. I had two thoughts 1) I promised Samuel and 2) AAAAAAH! The rest of that I worked through just now."

"Fair enough."

I tried to shift my position but pain stopped me. "So, what are you going to do about Ian? He's in bad shape."

"I'm sure he has been. It was a terrible shock. I don't think either of us has fully recovered from it even though we've known for over a year."

"But you have time. A couple a weeks before the Terrans show up and ruin everything. You could talk to him, you could..."

"You don't understand, Jane. That day the General came to the School and told me who he was and who I was, told me about my mother...and Ian, was the day that changed everything for me. I feel tainted by all of it. Ian and I were ruined that day. And even though I know it wasn't his fault, my life was happier before the General had told me anything."

"You'd rather have found out when you applied for a baby?"

"No." She took a breath, "But look what happened. Now there is no breeding program, no genetic files (most likely). Now things are back to basics. I *wouldn't* have known."

"That doesn't seem better to me. You *shouldn't* have a genetic child with Ian. And you *won't* have a genetic grandchild of Indira Pallon."

Arrow seemed to be sinking into her own gloom, but then she seemed to remember something and her face lit up with a gallows smile. It made me want to back up. “That reminds me. My best find during my researching was in Dr. Pallon’s Last Will and Testament. In it she expressly forbade anyone under any circumstances from using her DNA to create a child. She never, ever wanted a child of her own.”

“Maybe she was instinctively trying to protect a child from the horrors of the world she’d created.”

“Or maybe I’ve been rejected by a monster.” She shook her head and got up. She offered me her hand and I took it, pulling myself to a listing stand. “Tell the General I’ll check in with him once in a while. I guess.”

And she left. I took a step to leave, too, but took a minute. Ow.

<u>19:00 – Officer’s Lounge, *P.S. Scylla*</u>

It was dinner time and I was eating alone in the Lounge. I appreciated the quiet. I’d checked on Atalanta and Felix who were asleep wrapped up in each other. The General and Sig had apparently spent the day together, plotting and…whatever Alpha Males did when they tried to become friends. They were eating in the Captain’s Dining Room. I was glad I hadn’t been asked to attend, not that my presence would have been at all appropriate. I was tired and sore and my heart hurt for Felix and, surprisingly, for Arrow.

Doc Wells had immobilized my shoulder with a brace. One of my ribs had been cracked and the shoulder bruised so this was supposed to limit movement and thus the pain. Unsuccesfully. Doc Wells didn’t ask any questions, which was nice. Made it easier to go to him, which was probably why he did it. I just wanted Samuel and sleep, but knew Samuel could be hours. I sighed and tried to eat.

“Jane?”

I didn’t look up. “Is there something I can do for you, Captain?”

“May I join you?” I looked up then to those blinding blue eyes. On the surface he looked better but inside I could tell he was still a wreck.

I didn’t want him to, but didn’t care enough to protest. I tried to shrug but, “Ow,” was all that came out. He took that as an assent and sat.

“Are you hurt?” He looked at me concerned. No, I’m wearing a shoulder brace and just said, ‘ow’ when I tried to move. No, I’m not fucking hurt.

And since he was the last person I wanted to talk to about how I’d gotten injured, I now just wanted him to leave. “I’m fine. So, what’s up?”

“How did you know it was me?” he said, deliberately not answering the question.

“Bio-signature.” Captain Ian looked confused. “Every living creature has similarities with all the others, but the way a body works can be very individual. Heart rate, blood circulation, the way joints move, chronic stomach problems, etc. You can scan someone and then pick out a couple of items unique to them—and they can be unique on their own or in combination. It doesn't matter as long as they allow you to differentiate one person from another. My technique is very unrefined as yet, I need more training," with fucking Wilby, "but I've got the signatures of the major players so far."

Ian smiled confidently at me. "So, what do you see?"

I scanned him again. "You're physically perfect. No joint pain, no headaches, no ulcers. Even your colon is exemplary. Your heart pumps like a machine (it isn't one, in case that made you nervous) and your blood reaches your extremities in the most textbook fashion. You are the healthiest man I've ever scanned. In fact you have the body of an 18 year old and, as far as I can tell, will have for the next 50 years."

Captain Ian sat back in his chair in astonishment. "You can get all that from a scan?"

"Wilby could get more. Prick is a much more accomplished Micro than I am. Or probably ever will be."

Captain Ian absently rubbed his chin stubble. "You'd think we'd all read as 'perfect' as I do. I mean, that was the goal, wasn't it? Perfection?"

"The goal, yes, but the 5 Gene rule has limited a lot of things. A lot of health problems," not to mention mental ones, "come with messing too much with genes. You're lucky your parents chose to focus on health instead of the weird stuff."

Captain Ian sat up straight in his chair as if he'd been electrocuted. I shook my head at myself. That hurt, too. I've got stop doing that.

"How the fuck do you know that? How the fuck do you know *any* of this shit?" He spoke in a low, angry voice, eyes blazing.

I took a second to ponder the correct response to that completely fair question. I'm in love with your father? You father and I fuck like bunnies most of the time and talk in the breaks? There was always the honest, 'your father told me' but that would only delay the real answer by one question. Girlfriend? God, this was awkward. Ok…got one.

"Your father and I are seeing each other." And I took a bite of my neglected meal.

Captain Ian digested that for a minute, then nodded to himself, nagging questions apparently answered. "So you know all these things and warned me and tried talking to Arrow," now it was my turn to be surprised, "because of *him*."

"Because of Samuel."

Captain Ian raised his eyebrows at my use of the General's first name. Then he shrugged. "Well, because of *you*, Arrow spoke to me today for the first time in months."

"What did she say?"

"Not much, but it was a step." The Captain almost looked pleased.

"A step towards, what, Captain?" That was the confusing part, of course, of this doomed romance. Should it just stay unhappy, or was it better to push for temporary bliss (assuming that was even possible) and then torrential misery later, and not even that much later?

"Ian, please. Seems so formal when you seem to know more about me than I admit to knowing about myself. I don't know what we'd be stepping towards." Ian took a sip of his glass of spirits. "I just know that I miss her. All the time."

I nodded. This must be the Ship of Fucking Misery. "I'm sorry, Ian, if that counts for anything. You both got screwed."

Ian laughed softly to himself. "So, true." He took another drink.

"So why aren't you in the 'Captain's Dining Room,' Ian, I mean *Captain* Armstrong?"

"I got sent to the corner for that blunder with Bayliss," Ian said with chagrin.

I couldn't help it, I laughed. Part of it was relief that all the secrets were finally out and part of it was picturing Samuel taking his tall strapping son to the proverbial woodshed for fucking up.

"I didn't know the Doctor was…like that until today. And, as I pointed out to father, Sig would never have made it to the *Scylla* if I hadn't overstepped."

"True." I looked down at my half-eaten dinner. All I wanted was a hot shower and sleep. I stood up to go. "I'm going to bed. Goodnight, Ian."

"I'm sure father won't be done with Sig for a couple of hours." Ian took a large bite of food.

"That's OK. I need some rest," I responded without thinking.

Ian stopped mid-chew. "Gross, Jane."

23:50 – General's Quarters, *P.S. Scylla*

I'd wrapped myself in Samuel's robe after a scalding shower and had fallen asleep in his chair, waiting for him. The shower had helped ease the bruises a bit and sleep had come surprisingly easily.

Much later I woke when I felt the door opening to let him in. He walked in, only slightly unsteady, which amazed me considering that he had probably been drinking all day.

"Jane, what happened?" Samuel asked softly, concerned. Ah, he'd seen the brace in the corner.

I looked up at him. "I'm just sore, Baby. Diplomacy."

I could feel him tense up, manifestation of his anger, "I thought you weren't going to fight her, Jane. You promised."

I turned the chair to face him. That was far easier than turning myself. "I didn't, Samuel. Unfortunately, you didn't make her promise not to fight *me*." That, apparently, didn't help. Now, instead of his anger being directed at the both of us, it was all going to her. "Hey," and I reached out a hand to him. He gave me his reluctantly. "I deserved it and I'll heal. She said she would talk to you sometime soon."

He sat on the desk, still holding my hand. "That's better than I thought anyone could do." Samuel brought my hand up to his lips and kissed it. "Thanks, Jane."

"You're welcome. How did it go with Sig?"

"Went great with Sig. We just need to figure out how to use his expertise."

"To do what?"

"Fucked if I know, Baby. Something." He let go of my hand as he stood. "Let's go to bed."

"Sure." I assented, but I stayed in the chair. He'd taken a couple of steps before he'd realized I wasn't following.

"Coming?"

"I would, but I think I've been in the chair too long and now I can't move." I looked up at him plaintively. "Help?" Before I knew it he was by my side and picking me up as gently as he could to carry me to the bed. The immobility of the last few hours had not been my friend. My back, shoulder and bruised rib felt like they were on fire. He stood me up in front of the bed and took off my robe. I hadn't looked in the mirror but I could tell by his quick intake of breath that it didn't look good.

"My god, Jane," he whispered, anguished.

I turned around, slowly, and held out my arms for him to come to me. He did hesitantly and I put my arms on his shoulders to steady myself. "I had to let her knock me down. It was a tactical decision and it worked."

"She did all this to you by knocking you down *once*?" Samuel said incredulously. He smiled a little, proud of Arrow's prowess. That injured his girlfriend. I laughed, even though it hurt, and took two painful steps closer to kiss him.

It took forever to get back to sleep. Part of the problem was I'd had an idea of how to help Felix and Atalanta, but didn't know if it would help or hurt in the long run. I needed to talk to Atalanta.

Samuel shifted in his sleep and I carefully maneuvered myself so that my injured back was warmed by his chest. It helped. I gingerly wrapped his arm around me and slept.

ENTRY 4-2-10

08:00 – The General's Quarters, *P.S. Scylla*, July 15, 2869

I was partially under the bed, looking for Samuel's second boot. He really was careless with his shoes. Being in love, of course, I found this charming. I felt him walk up and turned to see two socked feet. I sat up. He had his boots in his hands.

"Where?" I asked. He reached out a hand and carefully helped me up. Three days had made a big difference in healing and I only hurt now when I wasn't paying attention and made a mistake.

"One in the closet, one under the desk." Samuel pulled me to him gently. "How are you feeling, Baby?" He nuzzled his face in my neck. The sensations this aroused reminded me (not that I needed reminding) that Doc Wells hadn't cleared me for sex yet. Not that I planned on waiting much longer either way; I just didn't know how Samuel felt about going against the Doc's orders. His hands were starting to wander. I could lie and say I was already cleared, I thought. I'm not a big fan of lying, but I'm a real big fan of what he's doing. "Do you see Doc Wells today?"

"First thing." Thank god.

"Then," He said as he kissed me, "I will see you tonight."

"Not a moment too soon," I said, kissing him even more deeply.

Laughing, Samuel disengaged from me. "Now git. I won't be fit to leave my quarters if you keep that up."

I smiled at him and left.

10:00 – Training Room (Felix), *P.S. Scylla*

I stood in the center of the training room and waited for Felix. Doc Wells had, grudgingly, cleared me so I was pretty pleased. Tonight was going to be a lot of fun.

In the classroom were me, Beno, 25, and Erika, 22. All Macros. I didn't know the other two, both being older than I, especially since Beno was just returned from his Tour. He'd been on Tour with Wilby, so I could assume, among other things, that Beno wasn't a virgin.

In front of us stood what looked like an enormous metal box with a vault-like door on its front. All three of us had been walking around it when the room door opened. In walked Felix, Gladys and Wilby. Why Micros? I wondered. And why Wilby? Isn't it bad enough that I have him for my next class?

The Micros joined the Macros and Felix took up a position by the box. He looked tired to me, but scanned otherwise OK.

"Good morning. Today we will start working with the Box." Felix paced in front of it. "You will find yourselves, at times, needing to get into impossible places in very little time. Doors, locks, seals, etc., can usually be overcome with a combination of practice and proper thinking." His pace quickened. "Each of you, whether Macro or Micro has individual strengths and weaknesses. You must all use your brains to solve problems using your gifts *and*," he said, stopping abruptly and turning toward us, "using the gifts of your team."

He stared us all down to make sure we had it.

"Wilby." Wilby looked up alertly. "Please get this door open." Wilby stepped forward, but Felix held up a hand and he paused. "Walk us through it, please." Wilby nodded grudgingly. I was amused. He couldn't show off his speed if he had to slow down to talk.

Wilby stood in front of the door, concentrating on it. "First feel for any defects in the structure of the door itself. Sometimes you get lucky and the door is flawed enough that you can get it open with a tool instead of by going through the lock."

"How many times has that happened?" Gladys asked.

"Once."

"What tool did you use?"

Wilby smiled, "Felix," and he flicked Felix a smirk. Felix chuckled and waved Wilby back to work. "Next you have to do a broad scan of the lock itself. Then you look internally." He scanned and we all kept quiet. "This is a high level combination-style lock. It has tumblers and pieces that move. This is a jackpot for Micros."

"What other kinds of locks are there?" I asked, now completely interested.

Wilby turned away from the door. "There are two kinds of locks, really. Physical and electronic. Physical can include things like this tumbler lock and the really large ones that guard vaults, etc., and even booby traps. As long as something (besides the lock itself) has to move to make the lock release it is considered a physical lock. The electronic ones are both more complicated and simpler. Retina scans, voice print, finger prints, DNA samples, secret codes all boil down to passwords. They can be beaten, true, but I prefer a less subtle approach which Felix will be demonstrating later."

He turned back to the door. "Now Gladys and Jane, come scan this lock and see if you can sense what I'm doing." Gladys and I stepped forward and focused on the lock. "The key is to feel where the tumblers need to be to release the catch." I felt the outer shell of the lock, then moved inside. It was a fascinating mass of gears all interlocking in patterns. I wanted to spend more time examining it, but Wilby was already moving things. He slipped one gear, shifting it to another position, then another, another, then three more. I could see what he was doing and could feel the clear line he was making. It was really quite elegant. It was funny how he could be as good, potentially, as Felix, but be so much less likable. Well, you can't have everything.

In no time the path was cleared for the catch to move. It did with an audible 'click' and the lock released. Wilby pulled the door open a little, just to prove that it had been unlocked.

"Excellent. Thank you," Felix said as he pushed the door closed again and relocked it. Wilby acknowledged the thanks and stepped back. Gladys and I followed suit. "Most Macros, however, do not have the ability to do this and have to rely more on brute forces than finesse." Felix stepped away from the door. "Who wants to be first?"

Beno stepped forward confidently. Felix nodded for him to proceed then gave us a meaningful look as he backed way up from the Box. The rest of us backed up.

Beno cocked his head to the side, concentrating. I wondered if that was something he did unconsciously or if it was an affectation. Either way, it looked cool. Beno drew in a deep breath and suddenly there was a loud BANG. The doors looked like they'd been punched in with a giant fist. Beno took another deep breath to do it again, but Felix held up his hand for a halt.

"Excellent, Beno. Your control was perfect and you didn't tense up," Felix shot me a glance. He took my shrug and eye roll as a response and moved on, amused. "But while this tactic will eventually smash you through the door, it might take longer than you have. Jane, have a go."

I stepped forward, feeling a bit nervous. That had been a fucking awesome punch and I was envious of his ability to do it without actually moving or even making a fist. For me the fact that it hadn't been showy made it even more impressive. But I had to think. We aren't trying to blow through the door; we are trying to get it *open*. I knew what to do.

I positioned myself in front of the Box. I didn't have to remember to keep my eyes open anymore, which was nice, but I was far from mastering the tensing up problem, as Felix had not so subtly just reminded me. Fuck it. One way or another I was getting that door open. I felt the metal of the door and traced the crack that ran between the door's two sides. I imagined it to be like finding your place in a book. The two doors were like paper. I imagined my fingers prying them apart. No weight, no struggle, just paper. And that is just what happened.

The top of the doors started peeling away at the crack as if little fingers were doing it. Once there was space between the two doors the fingers moved down a few inches, then more and more and more. I got faster as I realized that it was going to work. I could feel, in the back of my mind, Felix holding his breath. Within a minute or two there was a two inch gap between the doors. I stopped manipulating the metal, walked forward and pushed it open. Felix broke into a grin and Wilby looked sour, which I found very encouraging. My shoulders didn't hurt, but I also hadn't been lifting so I didn't really count that as a victory.

"Well done, Jane. Your tactics were good and speed will come with time and confidence." Felix opened the doors as wide as they would go. "You can see now there are multiple layers to the Box. We will be working more with them in subsequent lessons, though not with this particular Box." We all chuckled. "This next demonstration is a bit advanced, but I think people should know and, more importantly, *see* what is possible." This ought to be good, I thought.

Felix stood in front of the Box. I scanned him and he was calm. I didn't know how he did that.

For a second nothing appeared to be happening until I felt something moving in the center of the outer doors. It was swirling like...like a giant drill bit. My eyes opened wide in surprise. I looked quickly over to Felix, but he was focused on the Box. The "drill bit" got bigger and bigger until it was about the size of a dinner plate. The metal of the outer doors was shaving off, the bits falling onto the floor. Felix paused for a second, as if letting us fully understand what he was dong, then it was like he gave the "drill" a giant push...and it drilled through the layers to the back of the Box and out in the space of 3 seconds. The rest of us leaned down and looked through the hole and saw the back of the training room on the other side.

"Holy shit, Felix," I said, unaware that I was speaking aloud.

Felix laughed, "Always the wordsmith, Jane." He turned back to the class. "Everyone's talent can manifest differently, but you each have the potential to do that sort of thing. Normally, of course, you would have been introduced to this closer to your Tour years, but there is no more normal for us. I'll see most of you at tomorrow's lesson." And with that dismissal we filed out, but not before I mouthed a "wow" to Felix. He shrugged modestly, but his cheeks were a little pink with my praise.

It wasn't until I was in the hallway that I remembered that my next class was with Wilby. Bleech.

I was on my way there when I saw the General coming quickly down the hall in the opposite direction. He looked harried and was in his full dress uniform, which was extremely unusual. He saw me and headed in my direction. We were near a conference room and he pulled me inside.

"The Director has called a meeting of all ship representatives in two hours." The General looked even more harried up close. The Director was the Top Scientist and was our equivalent of the Terran President. The current Director was Doyle Jacobi of whom I had only seen pictures. But no Director had ever been a friend to Supernormals. Especially since they couldn't even admit we existed.

"Where?"

"The *Hastings*." His forehead was crinkled with worry. I reached up to smooth it but he caught my hand and held it. "The word was out an hour ago. I have to be there. Ian is in charge here. I don't know when I'll be back tonight."

I nodded. I knew he was worried, but I didn't know why. This wasn't the time to ask, though.

"I have to go." Samuel pulled me close and kissed me on the forehead. "Did Doc Wells clear you?"

"Yes. We have to be careful, but yes." Ah, men, I thought. He saw the amusement in my eyes and divined the reason, but I kissed him before he could react. "I'll be waiting, Baby. Do what you need to do."

Samuel nodded and embraced me quickly and left.

12:00 – Training Room (Wilby), *P.S. Scylla*

I entered the room, not sure what to expect. A torture chamber? Vivisection? A good session of 'let's see how much this hurts' with me as the test subject? None of that would have surprised me.

What I actually saw did, however. It was a work table, a chair and a bowl of fruit. I just stood there, puzzled. A second later Wilby entered. I gave him an inquiring look.

"Today we are keeping things simple." He indicated the table. "Peeling fruit." He opened his jacket and pulled out a small case, opened it and took out a small knife, similar to a scalpel. He handed it to me, handle first and I took it warily.

"Peel the oranges and de-seed the apples." He looked at me seriously. "No hands, as they used to say."

I nodded and took a step towards the table but he stopped me. "Only use the knife on the first orange. It will give you a sense of the pressure involved." As Wilby spoke an orange rose out of the bowl and shed its peel in one beautiful continuous motion. It was quite mesmerizing. The now peeled orange then floated over to Wilby and into his outstretched hand. He broke off a section and popped it into his mouth.

"This is first year Micro stuff. You need to be able to manipulate with this kind of precision to be considered a 'real' Micro." Wilby popped in another section, the chewing barely covering his disdain.

"You mean, as opposed to being considered a novelty act?" I said, annoyed. Well, I guessed I should be flattered that he cared enough to continue to hate me. Prick.

"Exactly." Wilby smiled maliciously. "Not everyone that thinks they're a Micro actually *is* one."

I had the overwhelming urge to stick my tongue out at him, but didn't think that would help. I wished I hadn't been so impressed with his peeling of the orange, but I had been. That was fucking cool.

"You done? Sir?"

He grinned and took another bite. "Yeah, I'm done. Stay until the whole bowl is peeled." He headed for the door. "See ya." And he was gone.

I then very maturely stuck my tongue out at the closed door, then headed over to the table and sat. I picked up an orange and held it, feeling its heft and the skin's texture. I could sense the thickness and the separation point. All that being said, though, I hesitated. There was no big weight issue, so that was good. I was used to sensing small things now, but I didn't think I had the control needed to manipulate the knife. Throw the knife, sure, but make it cut exactly where I wanted it to?

I made the orange float in front of me. It was light, even though that wasn't supposed to matter, and I knew I could keep it there indefinitely. Now I elevated the knife and moved it towards (and above) the waiting orange.

I took a breath and made a gentle downward cutting motion...and the orange sliced right in half, which surprised me so much that I dropped everything. Fuck, that knife was sharp! Who would have thought that that knife would be able to cut like that? Of course *I* would have been able to tell had I bothered to test its sharpness before using it, I thought with chagrin.

I practiced pressure on the two halves until I thought I had it. I put down the knife and made the next orange float up. I then imagined the knife and started to cut. I made it through the skin easily but cut too far and bit into the flesh. As I was mutilating this orange I realized that I was making this harder than I needed to. Oranges are designed to peel, generally. So as long as I could get the peeling started with a cut I could use a blunter shape to actually peel it. By the second orange I could peel it just fine. It didn't look as nice as when Wilby did it, but it was peeled.

Once the oranges were finished I took a small break. I wondered if Wilby's desire to see me fail would be counterbalanced by his pride as a teacher. Tough to say. I sat back down at the table and sighed.

Apples.

15:00 – Command Center, *P.S. Scylla*

Several hours later I was done. Done enough, I should say. I used to love apples. Anyway, I needed Ian. I needed to know what was going on at that meeting. Ian was in the command chair looking over reports. He saw me approaching and smiled. Like a real actual happy smile. I didn't need Atalanta to be blinded by his happiness. I assumed something had happened with Arrow. I wanted to be happy for them, and I was, tentatively, but I knew Samuel would definitely not be.

"Jane!" Ian got out of the chair. "What can I do for you?"

I smiled and stepped a bit closer to speak confidentially. "Has there been any word on that big meeting on the *Hastings*?"

Ian grimaced. "Nothing useful. The meeting started. Dad made it there in time, as did our friend Sig. Bayliss went over on Dad's shuttle."

"Oh, he must have loved that."

"I think I could actually *see* his blood pressure spike."

"Do you know the agenda?"

"Only in general terms. Everyone is supposed to agree on a plan. Are we staying, are we going? Are we going to deal with the *tapetia* threat before it moves on or will we just let it go? Will we wait for the Terrans or move on without them?"

"But I thought we didn't have enough faster-than-light ships to fit everyone," I protested.

"We don't." Ian's expression was bleak.

"You are telling me that there are actually people out there, our people, who want to abandon some of the few of us that are left because their ships are too slow?" I felt the outrage building. Ian held up a pacifying hand.

"The General would never let that happen and I don't think it will come to that with the Terrans on their way. When it comes down to it, we don't really have anywhere we have to be right now."

My anger cooled down rapidly in the light of Ian's confidence. "So, what is Samuel so worried about? I only saw him for a second before he left, but it was all over his face."

Ian shrugged. "What he is always worried about…"

"…his 'kids,'" I finished. "Biological or otherwise."

Ian nodded. "You all are a lot more visible now and there are many fewer distractions to keep the Scientists busy. Dad thinks they are going to legalize the supernormals."

"That's good, right?" To me legalization sounded like freedom. But then I wondered exactly what I wanted freedom *from* besides the Government. Nothing else was coming to mind. I just wanted to 'own' myself. That and be with Samuel. Yes, that seemed to be the whole list. Though I supposed freedom from my owners didn't matter as much now that Pace was gone. Unless, of course, it wasn't.

"Legalize them and then take them under their protection."

I was starting to feel my stomach knot up. "Protection?"

Ian looked at me seriously. "Control."

I felt fear radiating through me. Ian's obvious concern wasn't helping. "What for?"

Ian rested his arm on my shoulders for a second. "I don't want to speculate, Jane. Wait for Dad to get back and tell you. Hopefully he'll tell all of us. I'd at least like to know *why* I'm freaking out."

I did, too.

<u>17:00 – Training Room (Arrow), *P.S. Scylla*</u>

"Attack me." Arrow commanded.

I just stood there. I didn't feel like attacking her. I felt like going to the General's quarters and worrying. Arrow tapped her foot, annoyed.

"Attack me, Jane." She took a step towards me but I still did nothing. "I am an assailant. Not your boyfriend's daughter, not your teacher. I'm going to kill you if you don't." Her body, the finely honed machine that it was, was taught and ready. I felt like pleading for my half-healed shoulder, but knew she'd just laugh. Like assailants waited for you to be ready.

"What weapons?" I asked, stalling.

"Gimme what you've got."

"Everything?"

"Your whole arsenal."

This was a new thought. I'd never fought Arrow with my abilities. It'd always seemed like cheating or, at the very least, bad manners. Of course, with Arrow, I wasn't sure how much of an edge my talents would actually give me.

I started to take a breath as I centered myself on the ship and that was when she moved. She kicked me right in my bad shoulder. I went down with a hiss of pain…and threw her across the room.

She hit the wall, but instead of crumpling she used the hit to propel herself off of it to the ground. She came back and I swept her feet out from under her. She landed on the ground and used the momentum to roll back up to a stand.

I didn't have time to be impressed and she moved close, punching me in my damaged rib. I swore internally and threw her into the air again, this time spinning her like I did Wilby. This gave me a moment to catch my breath, but the spinning got too close to the ceiling and she stopped it forcibly.

She dropped to the ground like a cat, spied a long knife (that I hadn't noticed before) and picked it up. In a movement too fast for even me to see she launched it at me. I 'stopped' it, 4 inches from my chest and let it hover there. I met her eyes…and 'turned' the knife around. She hesitated a second, then charged.

Without thinking about it I reached out and 'squeezed' both femoral nerves. Hard. She cried out in pain and dropped to her knees. Within seconds I had the long knife across the room, hovering at her throat. She froze, staring at it.

I waited for her to yield, but she didn't. I carefully (secretly glad for my earlier knife practice) cut a tiny line in the shallow skin on her throat. I waited for the drops of blood to drip.

"First blood." I said, trying not to sound as breathless as I felt. I lowered the knife carefully, then let it drop to the floor with a clatter.

Arrow stood up, breathing hard herself, and dried her bloody neck with her shirt collar. "That was actually pretty good, Jane. You stopped me."

I nodded, my hands shaking with adrenaline. "You could have killed me with that knife."

Arrow shook her head. "I knew you'd stop it."

Well that made one of us. Oh, I see. "So you 'saw' this whole thing? Beforehand, I mean?"

"I did. I can't control what I see or when I see it, but I try to take advantage of the visions when I have them." She walked closer to me. "You have to be better prepared, Jane. This was a good fight and you've come far, but it took way too long. You hadn't scanned the room or you would've known about the knives, and yes there are several hidden around the room for me to use."

I belatedly scanned the room and felt four other knives scattered around, all out of sight. "Sorry. You're right, of course."

Arrow didn't acknowledge that. Why should she? She knew she was right. Arrow frowned. She looked worried. Everyone looked worried today. I wish I knew what the fuck was going on.

"I saw the General," she said and I idly wondered if she would ever call him 'Dad' the way Ian did. Probably not. Especially not if her boyfriend could call him Dad, too. I shivered involuntarily. How un-Pacey of me, I thought, disappointed in myself. "Right before he left. He told me the supers need to focus on upping their speed in a fight. He was very insistent. Speed and constant awareness."

"Ok." I was puzzled, though. Speed was important, of course, but why be so concerned with it just now. And was 'constant awareness' an actual thing? "I don't understand, Arrow."

Arrow's frown deepened. "I've thought about it a lot. And the only thing I could come up with was as a way to solve a tactical problem."

"What problem?"

"How do you defeat supers that can throw you across a room, or paralyze you with their minds." She looked up at me. "Or turn up your fear level to the point of rendering you useless. Or read your thoughts to learn your weaknesses?"

This was sounding worse and worse. "How?"

"If your goal is to kill them, something as simple as a poison dart grenade in their room as they slept." I sucked in my breath, horrified. "And if your goal is to take them alive (which I think is more likely), drug them and keep them drugged. A thoroughly drugged supernormal becomes just another drugged body that you can do anything to."

I wrapped my arms around myself, unconsciously defensive. "Who would do that?"

She shook her head, as if trying to break her own morbid train of thought. "I have my suspicions, but I don't care to speculate right now. We have to wait for the General."

I didn't say anything and we stood there in silence for a minute. Arrow turned then and headed for the door. "Tomorrow we're going to start drug defenses. All of us need to know how to recognize smells, effects, etc."

"And these things are most likely to come when we're asleep?" I asked quietly.

Arrow nodded. "That's when I would do it. Start training yourself to keep part of your consciousness alert. It takes practice, but it can be done." She paused for a second. "The General can help you. All officers can do it. They must." Then I saw a tiny smile lurking in the corner of her mouth. Her heart beat faster and her face flushed slightly. She was thinking of Ian. *Her* officer who sleeps lightly. Oh, boy. Well, if I didn't know that things had changed from witnessing Ian's happiness; Arrow's blush said it all. I knew better than to voice my suspicions. My shoulder was killing me. Again.

"See you tomorrow, Jane." And Arrow left. She never made any noise when she walked. It was like she just evaporated. The door closed.

"Say hello to Ian for me," I whispered.

A Note on the Governmental Structure of Pace-Pallon

Drs. Pace and Pallon being scientists (before they had designated themselves Scientists, as in the class) had been determined to let science rule the day when it came to writing Pace-Pallon's Constitution. Atticus Pace had started out using the Constitution of the United States of America as his starting point, but he had soured on that document the more closely he'd examined it. There had been too many guarantees of personal freedom, too many inalienable rights for citizens, far too much due process and no room for a created aristocracy.

So, he'd tossed it and started again using the much newer, much more flexible Branaugh-Connoly Constitution that had been bought and paid for (there were actually a couple of firms that had existed solely to manufacture Constitutions for new Colonies) by the starkly beautiful Mottola Colony at the edge of the Alpha Quadrant.

Mottola had an acknowledged aristocracy, a strong military and had been founded by dissenters looking for religious freedom. (As a side note Mottola, however, did not want religious freedom for all on its *planet and had immediately created a state religion with compulsory belief.) Dr. Pace had cheerfully plagiarized the parts of that that he liked and dropped the ones that didn't suit.*

What Pace-Pallon had ended up with was a semi-parliamentary system with two main Houses: Empiric (Scientist) and Commons (everyone else). Each House had a leader that was internally elected. Members were referred to as "Factors." Empiric Factors had their eligibility determined, not by district or by land ownership, but solely by birth and approval by an in-house committee headed by the Director. Factors from the House of Commons were elected by popular vote within their particular districts. The Director appointed all Judges and they were usually Scientist cast-offs. Over time Judgeships became hereditary, too.

The only Office with any power that had ever been up for grabs was the Directorship. And while no Commoner could ever aspire to be Director, every Scientist did. With nasty, cut-throat (sometimes literally) political maneuvering coming from every Empiric party member, the Director always ended up being the canniest, toughest son of a bitch in the 4 planets. In this regard Director Doyle Jacobi was as typical as they came.

01:10 – The General's Quarters, *P.S. Scylla*, July 16, 2869

It was very early morning, but I was awake, sitting in Samuel's chair, watching the *tapetia mortis* simulation over and over. I had tried to sleep but failed. I was too worried and I'd become too used to sleeping with Samuel next to me. The cold empty bed was an unhappy reminder that he would break with me when the Terrans came. He'd told me he wouldn't make himself a joke by staying with me and I knew he meant it. It was those 38 years between us that made him the fool, that would taint his post-Pace career. I understood it intellectually and I guessed I didn't really blame him. Well, I wished I didn't.

I was starting to get upset, already missing him. I tried thinking about something else. I burrowed deeper into Samuel's robe and started the simulation over again.

I heard the door open and looked around. Samuel walked slowly into the room. His uniform jacket was open and he looked generally disheveled. That was nothing, however, to what I felt from him; tiredness and an overdose of adrenaline had made him wired. His eyes were bloodshot and his posture was stooped. He saw me and tried straightening up with some success.

"Well, Jane." I started to get up to go to him but he waved me down. He pulled off his jacket and tossed it on the floor. "We're in the shit, now." He came over and sat on the desk in front of me. I reached out and touched his knee and he gave my hand a squeeze.

"Tell me."

He took a breath and crossed his arms on his chest. "The supposed reason for this meeting was to discuss whether we should evacuate with the Terrans or stay and try to rebuild once the creatures have vacated."

I sat up more fully, dismayed, "But…"

"I know. They are blind to the actual issues, especially to any *responsibility* we might have to other planets. While that is an important concern, that wasn't the main one."

My stomach knotted up again. If that wasn't the main problem, what the hell was?

He sighed unhappily. "They lost most of their gene banks due to denial and general poor planning. Wherever we end up they are determined to start again."

"On a new colony? With more of the same?" I had heard Bayliss say it, but I hadn't really given the idea any credence.

"Exactly. More of the same." He rubbed his face with his hand. Whatever this was, he really didn't want to say it.

"You're scaring me, Samuel."

"I wish…" He looked up and right at me. "They want all the supernormal DNA. *Our* supernormal DNA, to be exact. And they made it very clear that they are willing to take it by force if we refuse."

I felt as if I'd been punched in the gut. "They…they can't do that."

"They can legally, as if that ever meant anything on Pace. Supernormals belong to the Government. The Government, such as it is, exists on the *Hastings*. And sooner or later they will be coming for the supers."

I fell back in the chair. "So that is why you're going to have Arrow train us to deal with gasses and drugs. You suspected even before you left."

He nodded. "Bayliss gave me the first real clue, though I'd had my suspicions before. It was a logical step for them if they were planning a new Colony." He closed his eyes, trying to fight off the fatigue that was now setting in. "There is another problem and it means a change for us."

Now I felt nauseous. I said nothing, but felt my throat tightening and tears forming behind my eyes.

Samuel continued, "I'm afraid I lost my temper a bit when all this came up."

I could imagine it. I almost wished I'd seen it. Almost.

"And I, stupidly, made it abundantly clear that I was the biggest, most vocal opponent to their plan."

"No," I whispered.

He looked at me, his head to one side apologetically. "You and Arrow have extremely rare talents, Jane. Who do you think they'll come for first?" He clenched his fists involuntarily. "After they kill me."

I blinked away tears so that I could see. Not my Samuel. No, no, no, no… And then I knew what was coming.

"So, I'm going to send you back to Atalanta and Felix with a guard. I'll have a guard here as well and we'll just hope that they wait a bit to act. We should be able to come up with some kind of defense fairly quickly if we all work on it." He clenched his jaw. I could feel the physical manifestations of his distress washing over me.

It was clearly time for me to respond. "The guards are fine. They'll want Atalanta and Felix, too, you know. But I'm not going."

Now Samuel was angry. "Jane. This has to be an order."

"No," I said firmly. "I am here as your girlfriend and as your girlfriend you can't order me to do anything. And you know full well you can't *make* me go."

He just sat there. He knew it was true. And he knew I was just dumb enough to prove it. "You will be much safer with your friends."

"Perhaps. But if you think I am abandoning the man I…" and I caught myself, but recovered, "…my boyfriend, however grand he is," Samuel let out a small laugh at that, "to save my own skin then you have no idea who you are fucking dealing with."

Now I was angry and I realized that I had stood up and was pacing. I hadn't even noticed myself doing it. "Would you just leave *me*? Even if I were the old one and you the kid?"

He smiled a little at my word choice. "No."

"Then we don't need to discuss that shit ever again. Right?"

He said nothing for a minute and then sighed. "Right."

I walked up to him. Since he was sitting his face was on the level of mine, which I liked. "Can you sleep?" He shrugged. His face was a mask of sadness and worry. "Is the guard already out there?" He nodded. "Then you sleep and I'll stay awake." I kissed him gently. He pulled me to him.

"It's not that simple, Baby."

I closed my eyes as I buried my face in his neck. "Nothing ever is." We stayed like that for a while until I felt his body start to shut down for sleep. I led him by the hand to our bed and undressed him.

I stayed awake the rest of the night keeping watch and, eventually, he slept.

ENTRY 5-2-11

09:00 – The General's Quarters, *P.S. Scylla*, July 16, 2869

Samuel woke suddenly that morning and looked over at me. He looked at the clock. I saw him register that it was 3 hours later than he usually got up.

"I didn't have the heart to wake you." I said softly. He nodded and kissed me as he got out of bed. I closed my eyes to doze until he left. I heard him turn on the shower.

Then out of my sleepy fog I heard that voice say, "Get some sleep, Baby. I'll push all your lessons back." Then I heard him open the shower door and get in. I smiled and turned on my side. I must have slept for a few minutes but woke when I felt him next to me. I opened my eyes and found him staring at me, thoughtfully. He was partially dressed as if he had changed his mind about leaving.

I started to say something about work but he stopped me with a kiss. He said nothing, just stripped off my clothes carefully and methodically. He kissed me again with urgency and proceeded to make love to me with a tenderness and, frankly, thoroughness that I hadn't seen from him before. He moved slowly. The depth of his intensity was astonishing. No, not astonishing, devastating.

I felt emotion building in my chest to the point of pain. I almost wanted him to stop, but his passion was inexorable and I couldn't have fought it even if I'd tried. It was almost more than I could bear. All the worries about losing him to the Terrans and the newer fears of some assassin taking him away surged to the fore, try as I did to bury them deep down.

He came with something like a sob. I clung to him as my own orgasm rocked me and I found a cascade of tears streaming from my eyes. I wanted to tell him how much I loved him, how much I needed him, but all I said as he brushed the tears off my face was, "Please don't leave me, Samuel." His face was all sorrow as he looked away for a second, thinking. He gently pulled me to him, resting my head on his chest.

I pretended to fall asleep so that he could go. He kissed my forehead and settled me in the bed comfortably. Then he finished getting dressed and left. I let my tears fall into the pillow and soon fell asleep for real; exhausted in heart, body and mind.

11:00 – The General's Quarters, *P.S. Scylla*

I awoke about 2 hours later still…I guessed 'upset' was the best word for it. All through my shower I went over and over Samuel's coming to me that way and how intense he'd been with me. We had never been casual about sex, but that had been something different. I still felt kind of emotionally raw from it and confused. I couldn't let it go. It was as if he'd been trying to use that intimacy to bind me to him. How could he not know that I was already bound? Completely bound? I sighed and put on my boots.

Finally ready to go I headed for the door.

But the door opened onto a sea of activity. I watched fully armed Marines walking up and down the corridors, crew members moving purposefully and the occasional supernormal looking worried. What the hell was going on?

I started to walk down the corridor when I noticed that one of the Marines was following me. Tailing me, more like. I stopped. He stopped. I took two steps. He took two steps. I turned around and found myself confronted with a large, tall man with a rakish smile.

"May I help you?" I asked.

"Yes, Ma'am. I have been assigned to protect you until the current crisis is over."

Oh, goodie. A bodyguard. I was torn between annoyance and acceptance. I knew why he was there, of course, and also knew who had sent him. "And your name," I noted his stripes, "Sergeant, is...?"

"Sergeant George Lee, Ma'am, First Battalion, Pace-Pallon Independent Marines." His rakish smile deepened as he said this. *Independent* Marines? There are Independent Marines? When the fuck did that happen? I looked at Sergeant George more closely. He was tall and muscular, not unusual for a Marine, but while his almond shaped eyes were full of humor, his aura of physical strength was impressive. An ugly scar at his jawline marred what would have been a handsome face. He's seen action, I thought, and recently. That scar is only half healed.

"When did we make an…alliance," I was guessing, but this seemed a safe bet, "with the Independent Marines, Sergeant?"

"This morning, Ma'am." The Sergeant's eyes became hard. "Our battalion escaped Pace 3 on our sublight ship *Hephestra* but our ship was recently damaged. General Armstrong offered us a deal. Muscle for sanctuary."

"Sanctuary from whom, exactly?"

"The Government. We seceded once we were in orbit. They didn't like it and came to…collect us. We resisted, naturally, and beat them off." Now the Sergeant's eyes were full of pain and I wondered how many of his fellow Marines had been lost in the action. "But *Hephestra* was too damaged for us to remain on board for much longer. We sent out a distress call and the *Scylla* came."

"The *Scylla* can't have been the only ship that answered your call, Sergeant." My mind was racing, absorbing the information.

"No, Ma'am." The rakish grin was back full force. "But it was the biggest and the meanest."

I grinned back at him. The General must have been in fine feather. "So, you're my bodyguard? The General assigned you?"

"Yes, Ma'am. The man himself. He wanted someone extra tough to protect his," and here he actually *winked* at me, "special lady."

I was so surprised at this expression that I let out a laugh that somehow turned into a cough. Just picturing Samuel refer to anyone that way, especially me, was so improbable it was funny. I tried not to continue laughing without much success. "Were those his words, Sergeant Lee?"

"Nah, he didn't say anything about that. I just could tell. And you're coming out of his quarters at noon."

"Right." I leaned closer to him. "That fact isn't common knowledge. I would appreciate it if that could be treated as a private matter between the General and myself."

"Understood, Ma'am."

I smiled at him gratefully. "Please call me Jane. I have no official designation, no rank and certainly haven't earned a 'Ma'am.'"

The Sergeant didn't look happy about the informality. "Miss..?"

I shook my head. "Supernormals don't have last names." Then I looked up at him. "They did tell you we are supernormals, didn't they?"

He nodded, suddenly looking a little nervous, which to me was ironic considering that he could rip me to bits with his bare hands. I put my hand on his muscular arm. He flinched but held steady. He has courage, I thought. And that is certainly what we need right now.

And he was a normal, a Pace normal, but *not* a super. I didn't want him to be afraid of me. That would help no one.

"You don't need to worry about me. I am a bi-level Telekinetic," and yes, I did just make that term up, "which means I can move both big and small things with my mind." He nodded, a bit wide-eyed. "I can't read your mind and I can't read your emotions. I can sense internal physical responses and that can sometimes give me a clue as to what a person is thinking, but other than that I have to guess like everybody else." He relaxed a little bit, but I could still feel tension in his shoulders and arms. Part of that was, I suspected, being a Marine and part was me.

I stepped back from him. "If Samuel, the General, picked you, you must be a hell of a fighter. The best."

He nodded again and I could feel him relax a bit more.

"I'm actually barely adequate at straight fighting. Just ask my Instructor." Boy, wasn't that the truth, though I was improving. I smiled confidentially, "I tend to fall apart if I'm not crushing something."

He laughed. "I could show you some tricks, sometime, if you like."

I nodded agreement, pleased, and stuck out my hand. "Jane."

He hesitated for only a second and shook my hand with his massive paw, "George."

13:00 – Loading Bay, *P.S. Scylla*

Well, we were back in the Loading Bay waiting for some kind of announcement from the General. At first supers and Marines had been mixed together as they waited, but it soon became apparent that, especially for the shorter supers, standing behind a Marine was like standing behind a wall. After a few minutes most of the Marines had drifted to the back. Not George, though. He made it clear with a look that he wasn't going anywhere.

I scanned the crowd for people I knew and noticed the family of Exotics standing over to one side, not that they were hard to miss. They each had their own Marines, too. I was pleased to see some of our supernormals standing with them. Maybe the whole 'we're all freaks together' concept could work after all.

I saw Atalanta in the crowd and we made our way towards each other. She was trailed by a very intimidating female Marine.

"Corporal Dawes, this is Jane, my sometime room-mate." Atalanta looked all right. A little sad, maybe, but not in the grips of overwhelming suffering. I felt a pang of guilt. I'd been too wrapped up in my own life to be much of a friend. I needed to fix that.

I nodded a greeting and turned to George. "Atalanta, Sergeant Lee." George's face lit up when he saw Atalanta. She smiled back politely, but not encouragingly. Poor Felix, I thought. I checked the room and felt Felix standing over on one side with his giant Marine guard. The guard made Felix look even smaller. I hoped the Marine didn't try to mess with him. There are some small kids you pick on and some you don't. I wondered why he wasn't with Atalanta. Had something happened?

Atalanta pulled me a little away from our guards and whispered, "Do you know anything?" It took me second to realize she was talking about this meeting and not what was going on between her and Felix. At that moment I saw the General and what looked like a Marine Colonel walk into the room. I held up my finger indicating (I hoped) that we should wait to talk until after we heard what the General was going to say. She nodded.

"Good afternoon, Children and Marines." The General smiled as all of us let out a spontaneous roar of approval for the Marines. I cheered, too, but what I was doing was studying him. The smile was nearly real, but underneath it he looked pale almost…shaken. The knot of worry returned to my stomach.

"Colonel Aleph Gold has agreed to an alliance with us," more cheers from the Marines, "at least until our current problems with the Government have been resolved." The General looked pleased. I looked at Atalanta.

"Confidence and pleasure at the Alliance." Atalanta shrugged. I wonder if she'd guessed the General's secret. I wouldn't put it past her.

"As I am sure you have heard things are difficult now with the Scientists."

"Difficult would be an understatement," A voice said behind me. I turned to see Ian behind me. He looked stressed. Weren't we all?

I leaned back and whispered, "What's the plan?"

Ian put a finger to his lips and pointed at his father who was continuing.

"I have new information. The Director has ordered and is enforcing the taking of mandatory DNA samples from all Pace normals." There was a lot of angry muttering in the crowd. "We know now that Director Jacobi has formal plans to restart the Pace-Pallon colony, either here or on another suitable planet. He lost almost all of his genetic stores when our home was destroyed, but he is actively rebuilding. He's starting with the normals. Unfortunately, he will not stop with them."

Gladys, who could always be counted on for a question or two, raised her hand. The General nodded at her to speak. "Why are the normals going along with this, Sir?" Voices became angrier in the crowd. The General raised his hand for silence and got it.

"I don't agree with a Pace normal's decision to do this, however, I can't really blame them. They're at the mercy of the Government and have been threatened. I suspect that they do not understand how much things have changed. They also don't have our, shall we say, resources." He smiled and this time there were smiles of pride all around and some scattered cheering. He was whipping us up, I thought. Something really bad must be coming.

"From what my sources tell me," his eyes flicked involuntarily to Atalanta, then away, "they're almost finished taking samples of the normal DNA. Their next step will be to come for us." The General let that sink in. "The Director has made it very clear that he will get your sample. You can volunteer or you can protest. Either way he will take it. He claims a legal precedent—supernormals are technically owned by the Government, therefore your genetic sample belongs to them as well."

Atalanta looked at me, a little startled. I nodded. I looked over at Ian who didn't look surprised, just sick. I knew he was thinking of Arrow and her oh-so-rare talent. I leaned close to him to speak softly in his ear. "He, *we*, will never let them take her." Ian looked at me, surprised at the ferocity of my words, but took a breath to try to relax.

The General stepped forward, now emanating power. "I am here to tell you that the taking of your DNA is wrong, with or without your consent. They are taking the building blocks of life and playing with them as they have always done. As we have always *let* them do." He dropped his voice, though it still carried perfectly. "*I will not let them do this. We* will not let them do this. We will fight." There was silence for a second then the murmurs started again, but before they could take hold the General resumed his normal tone.

"The Colonel and his Independent Marines have officially seceded from Governmental control. When I said that they are here to help us, it would be more accurate to say that we are here to help each other. Welcome them, please. They are part of our family now and we of theirs."

"Will we secede, too, Sir?" Gladys asked.

The General took a second. "It was never my intention to separate us from any of our remaining people. But this violation of our rights cannot stand." He searched our faces. "If we vote on it today, it will be a civilian matter, which is fine, but seceding officially now will bring all the wrath of the Director down on us before we're ready. I'd rather wait until we're provoked to do it—leave it as a military decision. It buys us more time. Time we need to prepare."

Gladys looked awestruck at the concept. "So we could...overrule you, General?"

The General gave a small chuckle at her discomfiture. "On civilian matters, yes. On Military ones, no."

Gladys subsided. I watched her expression and wondered if the General hadn't just made a tactical error in giving away this power. Not that he wasn't correct in doing so. I looked worriedly over at Atalanta.

She shook her head. "He wants them invested in this. They need to choose, Jane. You know he'll fight to the death for them even if they don't want him to."

Fight to the death. Suddenly I felt my eyes filling with tears. Of course he would and so would I, but hearing her say it made it seem so much more real. A picture flashed in my head of him lying cold and dead on a slab. I couldn't breathe. Tears spilled down my face. I felt Ian's hand on my shoulder, trying to comfort me. As kind as that was, it made it worse. I was embarrassing myself. Then I felt a small, strong hand holding mine and was flooded with calm. My breathing returned to normal and I wiped the tears off my face with my other hand. I looked down into Atalanta's beautiful eyes, soft with remorse.

"I'm sorry I put it that way."

"No, I'm sorry. I don't know what's wrong with me today." She gave my hand a squeeze and let it go. I smiled a thanks at Ian and he took his hand off my shoulder. I knew exactly what was wrong with me, though. It was being with Samuel this morning. As wonderful and powerful and intimate as it had been, it was too much. I couldn't get my armor back up fast enough. The last thing I wanted to do was give up making love with Samuel, but I didn't think I could handle the complete vulnerability that came with what we did this morning again. At least not right away. What could I do?

The General had been speaking during all this, but I hadn't heard a word. It appeared now that he was wrapping it up. "Please do not panic. Keep to your lesson schedules, unless otherwise instructed to do so. A lot of things will be in flux over the next few days, so just bear with me." His wonderful voice became serious again. "It is very likely that we will make our stand here, on the *Scylla*. Each one of us stands in front of the others, protecting us from the people who would hurt us."

He paused a second, looking a little unhappy about what he had to say next. "Anyone who wishes to transfer to either the *Hastings* or the *Trafalgar* has the freedom to do so. A shuttle will be leaving the *Scylla* in 24 hours for those ships. It isn't much time to decide, I know, but for the safety of everyone involved, it has to be that way. Keep in mind that choosing to leave this ship will probably be the last choice you get to make. That is all."

Atalanta and I, and our guards, walked out of the room through the main door. Ian melted into the crowd.

"He saw that." Atalanta said to me as we walked. That 'he' was the General.

"Saw what?"

"He saw you upset," she said.

Fuck. His emotional child of a girlfriend. "Are you sure?"

She nodded. "I felt his concern, but he didn't break his focus then."

"'Then?" I stopped walking. Atalanta stopped, too and we made a little eddy in the human tide coming out of the loading bay. "When did he break his focus, Atalanta?"

"When Ian put his hand on your shoulder." I blinked at her uncomprehendingly. Atalanta nodded. "He covered it, but not before I read a big spike of jealousy."

"But...but..." I sputtered incoherently.

"He's not an empath, Jane. He's just a man. If he could read you the way I can he would never be jealous of any other man." I blushed. Atalanta looked at me, her expression serious. "You should tell him."

I shook my head.

"Do you want to know how he feels about you? How he *really* feels?"

"No," I said automatically. I thought for a second, then said, "No," again but with more conviction.

Atalanta shrugged. "Suit yourself." She started to move off into the crowd, but I chased after her. I'd had a thought. A way to strike at the people who were threatening us, but I needed help.

"I need your advice, 'Lanta."

"I just gave it to you."

"On something else. I think I have a plan." We walked off together trailed by our giant muscular shadows.

15:00 – Command Center, *P.S. Scylla*

I parted from Atalanta at the entrance and watched her walk off purposefully. She hadn't fully approved of my little plan of retribution, but she hadn't vetoed it outright either. I thought she was hoping someone would improve it before it was put into action. I couldn't have agreed with her more. But right now my job was to find Samuel, I mean, the General. Samuel would be no help at all. I just hoped the General would be at home. I saw him standing by Ian's command chair and made right for him.

"Sir?"

The General looked up in surprise. "Yes, Jane?" Samuel looked at me with concern. I saw Ian watching us, as if trying to determine our dynamic, since he rarely saw us together. The General noticed this and frowned. I didn't need to read Samuel's emotions to see the jealousy. He turned to his son. "Ian, would you give us a moment?" Ian nodded sharply, a little miffed at being dismissed, but he left. Well, I thought, it was for the best.

"Sir, I have an idea that would allow us to get back at the Director where it will hurt him the most. A preemptive strike, if you will."

The General sat in Ian's chair and looked at me appraisingly. "You have a mission plan?"

"Yes, General."

"What sort of personnel would you need?" He pretended to look at his report, but I could tell he had no idea what he was looking at. I could feel his blood pressure building up.

"A pilot, Atalanta and…me. That's all, Sir."

"And I am assuming that this plan would involve you and Atalanta going to the *Hastings*? By yourselves?" His heart was racing now. There was pressure in his chest now.

"Approximately, Sir, but it would be…" I started, though I knew now that this was pointless.

"No."

"But, Sir…"

He leaned forward, resting his elbows on the arm rests of the chair. "I can't let you go over there. All of this is being done to keep you away from that place." Then he corrected himself. "*All* of you away from that place. Do you know how much damage he could do with just your sample?" He shook his head. "And I won't have Atalanta put in jeopardy either. It's too dangerous."

I couldn't help myself. "Dangerous, yes, but if it works it could…"

Now he leaned in really close and dropped his voice to a furious whisper. "You are barely trained and too inexperienced. You will be going into a pit of vipers with no idea what they have up their sleeve. You will have your DNA taken and, if you are lucky, you'll be killed outright. There are some really sick fucks on that ship and, one way or another, they will destroy you." He took a deep breath to calm himself. It didn't work, but he pretended it had. "Permission denied. And I mean it, Jane. Do you understand?"

I understood perfectly. I felt sorry for him and sorry that I was going to go anyway and cause him to suffer. He wasn't wrong, but he also, I thought, wasn't right.

"Sorry, Sir." I started to move away.

"Jane." I turned back. "I'm glad you want to help. There are few things more important than upholding your sense of duty. You won't be on the sidelines forever. Just give it time." He smiled at me. He was starting to calm down and I was glad. But I was late for a meeting that would allow me to…betray his trust. Too fucking bad. I would rather have him be *alive* and hating me.

I nodded and took off.

15:30 – Training Room (Arrow), *P.S. Scylla*

I walked in to see Felix, Atalanta, Arrow and Wilby waiting for me. I had left, after much argument, the 5 Marines outside the door. They were very unhappy, especially George, but they hadn't been willing to push it too hard. A small demonstration by Felix involving a crushed trash can had convinced them that we would all be just fine in the room by ourselves.

Felix stood across the room from Atalanta or was it Atalanta standing far away from Felix? (what the hell was going on with them, anyway?). Arrow looked like she would rather have been anywhere but where she was, trapped with fools, and Wilby just looked annoyed. The only person projecting serenity was Atalanta who, not coincidentally, was the only one besides me who knew the play.

Wilby, ever the gentleman, started off with, "Why am I here? And make it quick."

Fine by me. I stood near the center of their little semi-circle.

"You all were at the meeting in the loading bay. The General told you what he knows to be the truth, but he didn't tell you everything he knows."

Wilby was unsurprisingly unsympathetic. "Why not, and how would you know?" Atalanta didn't even blink but Arrow looked at the floor, as did Felix.

I was unfazed. "I'll explain later, if I need to, but the long and short of it is that before the Director tries to take our samples by force he has to eliminate his biggest obstacle."

There was quiet for a second. Arrow wrapped her arms around herself. "The General."

I nodded. "He apparently made it very clear, too clear, at that meeting the other day that he would rather die than see us violated that way. A mistake, he admits, but there it is." Wilby started to interject a comment but I rode over him. "I don't have to tell you how important the General is to our survival. We cannot just let him be murdered." I felt the emotion threatening to spill out, but I fought it.

"I like the General just fine, Jane, but it seems like everyone is getting all riled up over something that doesn't really matter. So, they have our genetic samples. We were *made* from samples. We all were. If it didn't bother us before, then why now?"

"Because we've finally allowed ourselves to understand the consequences," Arrow said, her quiet voice carrying a surprising amount of power. The feminine version of her father's voice, I thought. She looked at Wilby intently. "You'll never know how many of your children died on the planets when they were consumed." She crossed her arms on her chest. "And the sad thing is that you wouldn't have known even if we hadn't lost Pace. Doesn't that bother you, Wilby? At least a little?" She walked closer to him, her voice still soft but persuasive. "Even if you'd never planned to have a child of your own, you would want to know if there was one, wouldn't you? You couldn't be as heartless as you pretend to be. Or are you?" And suddenly her protective mask dropped. She looked into Wilby's eyes not as Arrow Queen She-Wolf, but as Arrow the young woman. I shot a quick glance to Atalanta whose eyes were huge with surprise. No one ever got into Arrow's head.

Even Wilby wasn't immune to this plea from Arrow. "No," he said quietly, "I'm not heartless." Arrow nodded and retreated to her original spot.

It was time for me to keep the meeting moving. "I have a plan that should allow me to get in to the main lab on the *Hastings* and destroy all of their DNA samples. The whole treasure trove." Felix and Wilby looked up in surprise. Arrow nodded to herself, apparently too lost in her own thoughts to be surprised. Atalanta just watched everyone.

Nobody said anything, so I kept going. "A two part plan. Part 1 is recon and depends on Atalanta." Felix shifted his stance uncomfortably. Plans that involved Atalanta usually involved things he didn't like to think about. I pitied him, but didn't have anyone else I trusted that had her…assets. "Someone will fly her over to the *Hastings* where she will find Dr. Bayliss and get him to tell her how to get to the lab and how to get in. Hopefully she'll even score a tour."

Wilby looked over at Atalanta. "You know what that will involve, don't you?"

She cocked her head to the side and gave him a look that told him what a complete moron she thought he was. He shrugged and turned back to me.

"Part 2," I continued, "Involves my going over in the regular shuttle run for the people 'defecting' to the *Hastings* and the *Trafalgar*. I will be a volunteer."

"That's insane," Felix burst out. "Way too dangerous, Jane." He walked towards me, agitated. "You don't have either the training or experience to manage a mission like that."

"But, even with that," I countered, "I'm the best person to go. They want me. And since I am the only Macro/Micro we know of, inexperienced or not, I have the best skill set."

"You don't need a Macro. You need a Micro." Wilby looked pale as he said this. "You should be sending me."

Felix turned on him. "Would you go? If you were asked?"

Wilby cracked his knuckles thoughtfully. "I don't know."

Felix shook his head. "I'll go. Arrow can pilot the shuttle."

Arrow looked up. "Ian is our best pilot."

I shook my head. "No Armstrongs can know about this." I turned to Felix. "And Arrow can't be anywhere near that shuttle. They want her as much as they want any of us." That was an unfortunate turn of phrase because now every eye focused on Arrow who seemed to shrink back from the scrutiny.

It was Wilby again. "Why?"

Arrow was staring at me, willing me not to tell about…what? Which secret was dearer to her, Samuel being her father or the fact that she was a supernormal? Who was I kidding? I knew which one she'd pick.

Arrow straightened her shoulders. "I'm a pre-cog. So, I'm a super like all of you." She gave me a look that was less than friendly. I didn't have time to worry about her annoyance.

Felix didn't look all that surprised; in fact he looked as though that concept had satisfied certain theories he'd had regarding Arrow. Atalanta looked from Arrow to me and frowned. Well, I was going to get in trouble there, but it couldn't be helped. Atalanta was not going to understand why I hadn't told her, since it was obvious to everyone that I had prior knowledge. Wilby was astonished.

"You actually get visions of the future?" Wilby had, once again, dropped his mask of indifference.

Arrow rolled her eyes at him, though I thought I could see part of her lip curling up in amusement. "I saw you helping us. What do you think of that?"

Well, that shut him up. There were times when I almost liked her.

"Anyway, back to the main point." I cut through the distractions, or tried to. "The way I figure it, this could work with a top-tier Micro more than with a top-tier Macro," both Felix and Wilby, the top-tier gentlemen in question, started to speak, but I kept going, "but with a Micro, I just don't see being able to destroy the samples."

"How were you going to do it?" Felix asked.

"Pull the wall down."

Felix started playing with his beard, a sure sign he was plotting.

Wilby shook his head. "That's a desperation move and way too noisy. Plus, you pull down the wrong wall and you could damage the structural integrity of the ship, killing everyone, including yourself. The only chance you have of surviving this insanity is to get in, destroy the samples and get out without anyone knowing. You pull that wall down and they'll come for you. Then you'll have a lot of people to kill in a very short time. You won't make it, Jane." Wilby looked away, cracking his knuckles again. "You'll have to take out a bunch of people, you know, either way. Your lab techs, Docs and any Doctors you run across. It will have to be subtle and silent, but it will still be killing. There will be no way around it. Are you prepared for that?"

Now all eyes turned to me. This had been one of the biggest points for me when I had come up with the plan. I'd given it some thought. A lot of thought. "Yes. I can do it. I *will* do it."

Wilby flung up his hands in exasperation. "What is the General to you, anyway? Aside from the loyalty thing, which I do get, why are *you* pushing this?" I didn't say anything. Then I saw enlightenment in his eyes. "So you're sleeping with him?"

I'd known that Wilby would figure it out. For a moment I felt like a pre-cog. And I had my answer prepared. "Yes."

If Wilby was surprised by the quickness of my answer he didn't show it. "You must love him, then." His tone was casual, but his eyes were intense.

I hadn't expected him to ask me that, but only hesitated for a second. I needed this issue to be done. "Very much." Arrow looked away, frowning slightly. I wondered if she was thinking of Ian.

Wilby thought about that for a minute. "What do you want me to do?"

I let out a sigh of relief. "I need training on how to kill the lab techs without letting anyone know and I need to figure out how to destroy those samples quietly if I can, noisily if I have to." I looked from Wilby to Felix. "Between the two of you, you should be able to come up with something brilliant." Felix snorted.

"And me?" asked Arrow.

"I need to be more…lethal."

"Great," Arrow said sarcastically. "Because *that's* not vague."

"Atalanta's already booked a shuttle for the morning trip to the *Hastings* and will borrow ID from another pilot to protect our pilot from getting snatched."

"I'm taking her," Felix said firmly. Atalanta just looked at the floor.

"Are you sure that's a good idea, Felix?" I asked, dismayed.

"Yes," he said with equal firmness.

And with that the group started talking, arguing points with whomever was closest. I was watching and listening when Atalanta appeared at my side and we stepped over to a corner of the room. I couldn't stand it. "What the fuck is going on with you two?"

"He moved out two days ago. I…asked him to go. It was just too hard."

"Geez, 'Lanta, why didn't you tell me?"

"You'd come back because you wouldn't want me to be alone, but I don't want that." She rubbed her forehead like she was trying to stamp out a headache. "I don't see any reason to separate you from the man you love because I am unhappy. None of this is new. This is how Felix and I work."

"But do you want him taking you?"

"I do, Jane." She looked up at me, fear in those lovely dark eyes. "Who else in the entire universe would be more determined to bring me home?"

I saw her point and nodded, knowing that my opposition would mean nothing anyway. I wasn't going to keep Felix from protecting Atalanta any more than anyone else was going to keep me from trying to protect Samuel.

I looked up and raised my voice. "Are we in at least tentative agreement on the plan?" Everyone nodded except Wilby, who shrugged. "I think we should break for dinner then come back for training. I have limited time—I have to be back by a certain time or he'll notice."

"So he, the General, isn't going to know about this?" Wilby was confirming.

"Not until after." I said flatly.

"Told you to pound sand, did he?" Wilby smiled. The smile was actually borderline sympathetic.

"Emphatically." I looked at Arrow to make sure she knew what her father thought of this plan. She returned a 'what the fuck do I care' look that was very Arrow.

Wilby laughed with gallows humor. "Great. Our best tactician thinks this is a stinker." He rubbed his hands together gleefully. "I love a hopeless challenge." In a rare display of normal behavior, Arrow smacked him in the shoulder.

Felix wasn't paying much attention, worriedly pulling on his beard. Atalanta walked over to him and took his hand. He pulled her hand up and kissed it, then wrapped his arm around her waist. Funny how I never noticed that they are almost the same size. They looked good together.

Felix smiled at Atalanta. "Let's take our Marines to dinner, then."

16:30 – Training Room (Arrow), *P.S. Scylla*

Felix, Atalanta and Arrow stood off to the side while Wilby prepared to work with me. Felix was holding plans of the *Hastings* and going over them with Arrow.

Wilby cleared his throat to get my attention. I looked away from the others and to him. "The trick to taking out multiple people without detection is timing. You don't want to have them falling one right after the other. By the time you get to the third person you'll be dead."

"Right."

"What you do is plant a sort of medical bomb inside them, calculated to go off at a time of your choosing." Wilby moved towards me and touched my lower rib cage. "Take tissue from inside the bronchial artery that brings blood to the lung. Can you feel it?" I nodded. "Scrape together the tissue here," and he pressed to indicate the proper spot, "and if you make it big enough you can let it go and then count down from 120. When that clot hits your victim will go down, either in death or with a massive stroke, which will serve the same purpose." He moved his hand to the back of my neck. "Next slightly sever the spiral cord at the neck. Don't cut it, just nick it. This will distract and paralyze your victim."

"Why not just cut it?"

"Speed. Don't worry, he will fall and that will break it for you." He moved his hand to my throat. "Next, crush a windpipe. It will take the person a minute or two to die from this and they won't be able to scream." He placed his hand on my heart, grinning at me, daring me to move his hand off my chest. I'm fighting for my life and getting groped at the same time. "Next a simple heart squeeze which will induce a heart attack." I grounded myself on the ship and 'moved' his hand so that it smacked him in the face. He laughed and continued, not missing a beat. "And finally, make a knife," he indicated this with his fingers, "and cut the jugulars of anyone else. It's quick but very bloody."

"Ok." I took a nervous breath.

"Now we're going to go over placement of all this in sequence so that you can do it without thinking. You can practice on me, but don't kill me." I nodded.

"All right, then. Bronchial artery…"

17:30 – Training Room (Arrow), *P.S. Scylla*

Felix knelt next to me on the floor. We both studied the plans of the *Hastings*. Wilby was lounging in one of the chairs. Arrow and Atalanta were near each other but not actually speaking.

"These are the rooms set up with proper electricity and plumbing for genetic labs. Atalanta will confirm this," he grimaced but kept going, "but we will assume that this is where they will be. This room," and he indicated it on the map, "is the most likely one to be fitted with the refrigerated vault that they would use to protect and store the samples."

"What kind of lock?"

Felix shook his head. "We may not know until we get there, though I am hoping Atalanta will get a visual that will give us a clue." Atalanta nodded. "Either way, quiet will be best, but it may not be possible. Unfortunately," he rubbed his beard thoughtfully, "you won't be able to bring any weapons or devices with you. With that vault door to muffle the sound, all you would need would be enough time to lob something in and get it closed before it went off."

"Like a needle grenade."

Both Felix and Wilby's eyes widened in surprise at my bit of knowledge. If they only knew. Wilby smiled. "A needle grenade would be fun." He sat up. "Do the soldiers working for the Government still carry those? It used to be regulation."

Felix raised his eyebrows. "I don't know."

Wilby's eyes glittered. "I think I'll have a talk with our Marines when we're done here. They should know." Wilby looked so pleased I thought of warning George. Then again, Marines should be able to look after themselves. And who knows? He might enjoy it.

Felix shook his head, I think he was pitying the Marines as well. "Barring that, you can always attempt to pull the wall down (carefully!), as you had originally suggested, or just pull all the vials out and smash them on the ground. Not subtle, but very effective."

"Or," Wilby started, but then he stopped. We all looked at him. He was thinking. "I'll be right back." He quickly left the room. Five minutes later he returned with a bag full of small bottles of water. He set about 30 of them out on the table in a pyramid shape. Once done he stepped back to admire his work.

"Watch this." And using his wonderful control I could feel him concentrate on the bottles. No, not on the bottles, I thought as the water inside them started to bubble. The water itself. Soon they were bubbling away and shaking as though threatening to pop their caps. Wilby stopped and grinned at us, immensely pleased with himself. Felix walked forward, smiling himself.

Arrow spoke for the first time in a long time. "You can boil liquids?" Even she sounded impressed.

Wilby's grin got wider as he turned to me. "If you can make the samples boil, they will be ruined."

"And it's silent." Felix was clearly delighted.

"*If* you can do it. Not all Micros can." Somehow Wilby managed to say this without sounding too much like a dick. Too caught up in the project to spare time for his own affectations, I supposed. "It's time to find out. Jane?"

I stepped forward. "What does it feel like?"

Wilby thought for a second. "Pick a spot on one of the bottles. Picture the water molecules moving around placidly." I started to protest that there was no way I'd be able to feel molecules, they were way too small, but he stopped me. "It's just a trick to get you in the right headspace. No one can actually feel molecules."

I stared at one of the bottles. Nothing. Then, almost without thinking I reached out and swirled the bottle. Yes, now I could feel something. Wilby looked almost proud of me for a second. "Now focus on a section of the bottle and imagine the molecules banging against each other, creating friction. This friction, if there is enough of it, will create heat, with enough heat your liquid will boil."

I reswirled the bottle. I put it back on the table and tried to feel the molecules again. I felt something that was moving in the right direction, so I assumed it was what I was looking for. I felt the wonderful liquidity of the water as it swirled around. And, just to see if I could, I told it to stop swirling. And it did.

"Holy fuck," Wilby said to himself. I ignored him and told the molecules to fight each other, which they did. I felt them bouncing against each other, but it was too slow so I made them go faster and faster. I felt the water bits (as I was calling them in my head) wanting to turn into steam bits. I moved everything faster to make that happen. Within a few second the water bubbled, then boiled, then blew the top off and shot it across the room. I then let the water bits alone and they resumed their previous quiet state. It was only after I'd stopped and was no longer caught up in doing it that I realized what I'd done.

Felix shook his head, awe written all over his face. "Well done, Jane."

"Thanks, Felix." I almost glowed with his praise, but tried not to gloat too much when I turned to Wilby with my hands on my hips. "Was that something a Micro, a *true* Micro can do, Wilby?"

He looked at me for a second, shock written all over his face. Atalanta laughed and not too kindly. "Leave him alone, Jane. Poor boy has had a terrible shock."

Wilby exhaled, almost snorting. "Yes, Jane. That was something a real Micro can do."

Felix looked at Wilby. "Do you want to work on transference tomorrow morning?"

Wilby nodded. "You need to be able to spread this to many vials at the same time. Similar principal, just…wider," he explained. Made sense to me. And by then I was sure Wilby would have recovered his usual snarkiness. It was sad, but I actually preferred him that way now that he wasn't. There must be something wrong with me.

Felix turned to Arrow. "You're up." Arrow rose from the floor where she'd been sitting in one fluid cat-like movement. I noticed a case in her hand. She must have gotten it at the dinner break and brought it in and I hadn't noticed it. Shit. The look she gave me as she walked towards the table told me that she knew I'd no idea it was there. She raised her eyebrows at me; all the reproof I needed. I felt like a fool, which seemed appropriate. I'm never going to get it right for her, am I? Well, at least I can boil water for coffee with my mind. Nice party trick, right?

Arrow started to place the case on the table but stopped, frowning. "There is one thing that is important, but that we don't have time to address." She looked at all of us, one by one, ending with me. "These people *created* supernormals, which means we have to assume that they have a defense against them."

I felt my insides go cold. "The gasses."

She nodded. "I would have every room and corridor rigged with a panic button of some kind. It may not be obvious, though, because not everyone would be told where it was. The good news is that the rooms are probably wired individually—otherwise one breach by supers would knock out the whole ship."

"You said 'knock out'?" Atalanta prompted.

"Whatever they may do later, this system would only make sense if it was designed to help capture, not kill."

"So, what do I do?" I asked, trying not to sound panicked.

Arrow grimaced. "Learning to recognize and fight off gasses and drugs takes months and isn't as consistently successful as I would like. We have hours, not months and I can't have you befuddled by anything I might try on you today." She took a deep breath and almost smiled in a gallows humor type of way. "So, just run."

I couldn't believe my ears. "Run? That's the best you can do? *Run*?"

"If I am right and they gas by rooms or even sections, make sure you run out of the room you're in as soon as you feel any effects."

"Do I have time to do that? How fast will the gas hit me?"

Arrow looked as if she'd tasting something bad. "I don't know." Or she knew and she didn't want to tell me. She played with the handle on her case. "I really wish I could do better, but I've gone over and over it and I just can't."

I didn't say anything. This was not good. I didn't really fault Arrow. Some difficulties *can't* be overcome in 24 hours.

Arrow took a second, as if to collect herself, then looked up. She placed the case on the table and opened it. We all crowded around to see it. It was a surgical kit. What looked like 20 different knives, clamps, clips, plier-looking things, etc. I looked at Arrow.

"This is a standard surgical medic's kit that you will find in virtually every Infirmary or Lab. You wanted to be more lethal?" She picked up a large scalpel. "You don't need to bring any weapons, Jane. They're already there waiting for you." She put the scalpel back down in the case.

"Now," Arrow said. "Let's see how many of these knives you can keep at our throats and for how long." I looked at her, dismayed. One knife, sure, maybe two on a good day, but four? I was assuming she didn't want me to hold a knife to my *own* throat. Maybe I was assuming too much.

I concentrated and four small knives rose out of the case, then two of them wobbled and fell. The other two would only move together and both fell when I tried to separate them. Damn it.

"Again."

And I tried again. And I sucked.

23:00 – The General's Quarters, *P.S. Scylla*

I was waiting for Samuel as he came in. I'd been in his quarters for almost half an hour. A half hour I'd dearly needed to get clear of my training, both good and bad; the knives had remained a disaster. I had more work with Wilby and Arrow tomorrow, including an actual fight practice with Arrow; because nothing boosts your confidence like having your ass kicked.

We wouldn't see Felix or Atalanta until after they'd returned from the *Hastings*, which only gave us about two hours before Felix was supposed to take me and the other volunteers (assuming there were any and I hoped there would be simply for sake of camouflage) back there. I did my best to let it all go, though I did find myself compulsively reheating Samuel's old coffee.

I'd taken a shower to clear my head and it had helped a bit.

Then I saw him and my focus problem was fixed. I was flooded with memories of this morning (god, was it only this morning?) and how long it had taken me to get myself together. Yes, I had to talk to him about it, it was true, but I was nervous. Would he be mad? Would he ask me to leave? I'd never been in a relationship long enough to have a problem like this. I stood leaning against his desk, waiting for the right time. Samuel dropped his jacket on the floor and walked up to me. He frowned.

"What's wrong?" he asked quietly.

I shook my head slightly and stayed mute. He moved closer and reached for my cheek, caressing it. His touch sent shivers through my body as it always did. I took his hand in both of mine and kissed the palm, then held it. Now he started to look worried.

"Something is wrong, Jane." He sat on the desk, but I kept his hand. "Tell me."

I gulped. My heart was racing, but this time not for the usual Samuel reasons. "I wanted to talk to you about this morning."

I could feel tension explode through his body. He tried to pull his hand back, but I held onto it. He looked away. I moved closer to him, standing between his legs. I tried to remember my plan. I was going to just put it all out there. Say what I really thought and hope for the best. But my heart quailed now. He could hurt me with a look, let alone words. And I could him as well.

"I've never…had anything like that before." I could feel tears building up behind my eyes. Damn it, why am I such a wreck? "Being with you that way, was the most," I searched for the words on my internal script, "beautiful, powerful experience of my life."

He looked up again. His hand relaxed in mine. He didn't say anything, though he swallowed convulsively.

"It felt almost like…you were reaching into my…soul." I saw the look of surprise on his face and took a step back. "That's just what it felt like," I said apologetically. As soon as this is over I think I'm going to throw myself out of the nearest airlock.

He pulled me back to him. He looked down, biting his lips as if mastering himself. "I was."

"Oh," was all I could say because I couldn't see. I hadn't expected him to respond to that, or if he had it would have been with a knowing smile or something. But I'd never thought… I looked back at him, as soon as I could see again, having blinked the tears back. He watched me expectantly.

He was waiting for the 'but' so I plowed ahead and gave it to him.

"The thing is, Samuel, that I'm (and we all are) worried and nervous about the future…" I said hesitantly. He pulled his hand away now and I didn't stop him. He crossed his arms on his chest and stared at me, his manner defensive. "…and I'm barely keeping my shit together as it is." Now I couldn't look at him. I was too embarrassed. "I just don't know how much my soul can handle right now."

Samuel got up and started pacing, his posture tense and angry. I'd already hurt him.

I continued, "I thought that maybe, sometimes, we could do it, you know, instead of deep and meaningful, just…you know…dirty." It had sounded so much better in my head, and without the stammering. I sounded like the biggest fucking idiot in the universe. He stopped pacing an expression of complete shock on his face. I looked away again.

Suddenly I heard him chuckle. I saw him leaning against the desk, his tension suddenly gone. He rubbed his face with his hands and continued to laugh. At me. I felt my cheeks burning red. I certainly did not feel like being laughed at. I started for the door.

"Jane, wait." Samuel headed me off. "I'm sorry. I shouldn't have laughed, but you really scared me back there."

I just stood there, unmoved. He stepped to me and put his arms around me. He might as well have been embracing a statue. "I promise that someday, when you're older, you'll look back at this moment and laugh yourself."

And thanks for reminding me that I'm just a kid. I tried to disentangle myself from him, but he held on. He lifted my chin with his hand and made me look at him. "Do you understand the inherent danger in telling a dirty old man that you *want* dirty?" And he gave me a devilish grin.

I'm afraid a couple more tears ran out of my eyes as my whole self was flooded with relief. He wasn't mad. I happily surrendered to his embrace. Then I realized I hadn't answered his question and I nodded.

He kissed me then growled in my ear, "*How* dirty?"

I ran my hands down his chest, then below his belt. "Show me what you've got."

He chuckled low, but *this* laugh was music to my ears.

Excerpt from Wilby's Journal, July 16, 2869

Jane has pretty much lost her mind. She seems to be oblivious to danger and (though reluctantly) capable of risking others to protect someone she cares about. I know she would rather go by herself, but she needed our help so she asked for it. And the really sad thing is that not one of us said no. So I guess that means we are all crazy by association.

And I never thought I'd say this, but it bothers me that we are going behind General Armstrong's back. He's the master tactician, not Jane or even Felix, though Felix is no slouch.

What if we make everything so much worse? What if one of us dies? What if we outright fail?

And there again, I know we're all thinking these horrible thoughts but we're still preparing. We're still going through with it. And why? Because she's right. She's fucking right.

How can she be both crazy and right at the same time?

Fuck it. I need a drink. And a distraction. I think I'll hit the Officer's Lounge. It's a little late but I should be able to pick some of the low hanging fruit—and hopefully more than one.

ENTRY 6-2-12

An Excerpt from Arrow's Journal, July 17, 2869

Today is the day of Jane's Mission. Felix, Wilby and I prepared her all day yesterday and I think she's in as good a shape as she can be under the circumstances. All my wishing that she had ten more years under her belt is helping nothing, unfortunately. I'm worried, but I always worry.

It bothers me that I can't tell Ian, but I see Jane's point on that. I sprained my wrist fighting her (not that I would ever let on) and he wrapped it for me and brought me soup (!). He's always so gentle with me, which is funny to me since I'm gentle with no one. You'd think I would hate it, but I don't. From him I don't.

I had a dream last night. One of those *dreams, but just images this time: Jane was marched down a corridor under guard. Soldiers. Needles drawing blood, blood on walls, people, strangers, collapsing. An open vault door. Jane running...and falling. Felix, afraid—for her, I think—carrying her in his arms to the shuttle. She doesn't move, but he buckles her in anyway. Fear all over his face.*

I woke up in a panic, trying to get more images to clarify, but the dream evaporated. Ian calmed me down like he always does and we went back to sleep.

So frustrating *not to have any control.*

06:00 – The General's Quarters, *P.S. Scylla*

It was early but I'd been awake for a while. Samuel had been, too, but he'd remained silent and I'd let him be. We weren't upset with each other, just wrapped up in our own separate worries. And as much fun as 'dirty old man' sex had been, the best thing that had come of it was the few hours of sleep that had followed.

Samuel sat up and leaned against the headboard. I took this as a cue that he wanted company and sat up next to him, taking his hand. "I don't understand why they haven't attacked yet," he said, truly perplexed.

"Are we ready if they do?"

"Close enough," he shrugged, "The more time we get the better, but the Scientists know that. What are they waiting for?" He shifted how he was sitting, irritated, then looked quickly over at me, as if just remembering something. "We're having gravity drills today."

"Gravity drills," I repeated, not really sure what that meant.

"I'll be turning off the generators as a test, see how it'll affect our ability to fight."

"Oh. When?"

"Afternoon. 14 hundred. Felix will work with the Macros. I'm curious to see how you all adapt."

I was, too, but knew Felix would be helping no one but me at 14 hundred. We would still be on the *Hastings*.

I felt incredibly guilty and tried to make not looking at him seem natural. My thoughts for the last few hours had been the same over and over. What if Samuel was right and this was a terrible idea? He knows so much more than I do about almost everything. It will hurt him terribly if I go and scare him to death. And if I'm captured, then what? Then he will come get me and then he'll be at risk, which defeats the purpose, well one of the purposes, of this whole mission.

And I was deeply afraid of fucking it up, of failing. The plan was ballsy, sure, and had the benefit of only risking Atalanta, Felix and me. Felix could take care of himself. More than I could myself, certainly. Atalanta had been to the *Hastings* several times before without a problem, so that was more a known thing than my trip to the lab. Bayliss was a pushover for beautiful eyes and perfect breasts, so that should be OK. I was the biggest liability we had. Strangely, that made me feel a little better. I didn't want to get my friends hurt. I just wanted to get it right. For all of us. And especially for him.

Which brought me to my second loop of thoughts. This one was tougher to get through. This would be the last time I woke up with him. And if he kissed me before I left, that would be it as well. And I would never be his 'baby' again. I felt a huge wave of emotion hovering in my mind, threatening to drown me, but that couldn't happen today. I had to shut it out; I would have all the time in the world to fall apart after. The sad thing was that I knew it was going to be devastating for me even if everything went perfectly. But this was for him.

And it was, in a way, his fault. Those needle grenades he'd thrown in the vault on Bane, destroying all that DNA, had given me the idea. That's right, I thought. Blame the man you are trying to protect—even though he adamantly doesn't want you to do this. Good one.

I couldn't help it, I looked over at him and found he'd been watching me.

"What are you thinking about, Baby?" His voice was gentle. I loved that voice as much as I loved everything about him.

"You," I answered honestly. Not *completely* at all, but honestly.

Samuel drew me onto his lap and smiled. "And what were you thinking about me, Jane?"

I paused. I didn't even know what I wanted to tell him, but I felt compelled to say something, make some statement about us. Let him know without saying the actual words…

"I was thinking..," and I swallowed. Keep it together, girl. "…that there is no one in the universe more precious to me than you." For fuck's sake, do not cry.

Samuel looked away. His face was flushed. He also clenched his jaw convulsively and I guessed that he was 'keeping in together' as well. "Jane, I…"

But I stopped him with a kiss. He returned the kiss softly at first, but then with more passion. I didn't know what to do. I always wanted Samuel, but today…? I gently broke the kiss and stood up. He looked up at me, confused, hurt. "Shower," I explained. I walked into the bathroom and flipped the water on.

I could see him in the bathroom mirror, his expression blank. That would not do. I stripped off my clothes, then peeked out the bathroom door, my hand extended. He looked up again. "Shower?" I asked, beckoning. He nodded and got out of bed.

I left him an hour or so later, having said goodbye with a kiss, saying we'd see each other tonight. With luck we would, but everything would be different then. I pushed my emotions down even further. I had no time for them now and I had to meet Arrow.

07:00 – Training Room (Arrow), *P.S. Scylla*

I'd arrived at Arrow's door and was surprised to see the four other Marines standing outside. Why were they there? I thought Atalanta and Felix were prepping on their own. I left George and went inside.

Felix looked grim. Wilby was cracking his knuckles again. Arrow was stretching in preparation for our training fight. Then, from behind Felix stepped Atalanta. I held my breath in shock. As beautiful as I had seen her, I had never seen her actually *try* to be beautiful. Her dress was dark red and cinched tight at the waist, showing some shapely leg. Her generous cleavage was both covered (enough) and accentuated. Her heart shaped face was subtly made up, her full lips reddened and her glossy black hair was a cascade of sensuous curls.

"Dear god, 'Lanta," I breathed. Has there ever been anyone this lovely?

Atalanta gave me a smile, but didn't preen as she normally would have. Today was about business. Felix continued to look grim and I could tell he was watching Wilby, giving him 'don't fuck with me' looks every time Wilby chanced to look in Atalanta's direction.

Atalanta stepped closer to me. Wow, she even smelled amazing. "What do you want me to say to *him* after you leave."

I thought for a second. "Nothing—unless you have to."

She shook her perfect head. "That's a mistake, Jane."

"But he'll worry..."

She cut me off, exasperated. "This isn't about the two of you. He is the *General* and he needs to know if someone is making a tactical play that affects either his personnel or his ship. This could potentially affect both." She looked up at me, annoyed but not without sympathy. "Big picture, Jane. We want to win the battle *and* the war."

I looked at Felix, Arrow and Wilby who all nodded. "You're right. Tell him about the mission after Felix and I are already on the *Hastings*." Atalanta started to protest, but I cut her off this time. "He can't stop us if we're already there."

"OK." Atalanta caught Felix's eye and they headed for the door.

I intercepted her as she was leaving and spoke softly. "Would you, please, tell him *everything* if..." She stared at me, fear in her eyes. Her lips moved as she formed a protest, but then she just nodded. They left.

I stood up, ready as I was going to be for Arrow. She stood in front of me, all lithe muscle and skill. She gave me a rather ominous smile. This was going to be ugly.

08:30 – Training Room (Arrow), *P.S. Scylla*

I sat on the floor, recovering from having my ass handed to me by Arrow. I was sweaty and physically tired but surprisingly relaxed. Or almost relaxed. Arrow sat near me, chugging a bottle of water. I reached a hand out for my own bottle and Arrow quickly threw it across the room. I stopped it where it was and floated it over to me, cracked it and took a giant swig.

Then out of the blue, Arrow chuckled to herself. "Wilby?" He had been sitting in the corner of the room, bored, making a house out of scalpels. A floating house of scalpels. He looked over at her, eyebrows raised.

Arrow flicked her eyes from the pile of bottles to me suggestively. "What were you planning on doing about transference?" Wilby floated all the scalpels to the floor.

He twitched his mouth to the side, considering, then abruptly stood up. He put on his best smart-ass smile. "Jane, this exercise is called: Repel 'em, keep 'em up and boil 'em." And with that all the water bottles flew into the air, hovered for a second, then came straight at me. Thankfully I'd already grounded myself to train with Arrow.

I held the bottles off, then as I felt Wilby drop control of them, I maintained their position. They fanned out around me like half a pin cushion. I moved very quickly, the water inside the bottles needed to still be in motion to help me find the 'water bits' I needed for the boil. I focused on one bottle and locked in the water's motion. I widened my gaze, getting a spot, grabbing a 'bit' in each bottle. Once I had that I made 'bits' fight 'bits,' as I had the previous night. Thirty seconds later I had all of them boiling. Thirty seconds after that the tops blew off—and I got doused with water. Hot water. I shrieked and all the bottles fell to the floor.

Arrow actually laughed (whether with appreciation or with amusement at seeing me drenched was unclear) and Wilby's response took the form of silence.

We just sat there for a while. Wilby cracked his knuckles again. Arrow looked thoughtful.

"Nervous?" Arrow asked. This was to me.

Terrified, actually. "No." I answered.

Arrow looked me over approvingly. "That's good. Saying it is the first step to believing it."

I wished I had Atalanta calming me down, selfish as that sounded even to me. If I were rich I would pay her buckets of money just to stand around and keep me calm—and that was aside from her decorative value. I was still surprised at my own reaction to her appearance earlier. She was so lovely it was like a punch in the gut. But I'd seen the downside of these things. Pure beauty like that was as much curse as blessing. I wouldn't wish for it. The knot of worry grabbed my stomach again as I thought of someone trying to hurt my friend. No, I thought, Atalanta can take care of herself.

"Where are they now?" I asked, thinking of Felix and Atalanta.

Wilby checked his watch. "They should be on the *Hastings*." He looked worried, too, and his constant knuckle-cracking was bugging me. Arrow amused herself by watching my fists clench every time he let out a crack. I was considering breaking one of his fingers when I realized that the combination of fighting training and hot water meant that I stank. An escape!

"Do I have time for a shower?" I asked, rising.

"Sure," Arrow said, amused. "Don't go to the General's, OK?"

I knew she was right, but only officers had private showers. Oh, well. "No, I'll hit the community showers by my quarters."

"Where are you going to put your Marine?" Wilby asked. "Nice boy."

I shook my head. "I thought he liked girls. He certainly liked Atalanta from the way he stared at her."

Wilby laughed. "Oh, he likes girls, Jane, but everyone likes me." I rolled my eyes at his massive ego. "Besides everyone looks at Atalanta that way. *You* look at her that way. You should have seen your face earlier."

I shrugged. It seemed stupid to deny it. "I appreciate beauty."

Wilby snorted.

"I think it must be a burden sometimes, which sounds funny. It know it is for her." I looked at the two of them. "Is it for you?"

Arrow looked up, startled. "What are you looking at me for?"

I cocked my head to one side. Wow. Someone on this ship who was gorgeous, though in an angular, almost architectural way, who didn't know it. Would wonders never cease? Now I was amused. "Wilby," I asked. "Is Arrow beautiful?"

Wilby glared at me out of, I guessed, a mixture of annoyance at being put on the spot and a touch of jealousy. So only Atalanta was allowed to be pretty besides him? Twerp. But he wasn't going to lie. I was so happy this had come up.

Wilby looked Arrow over in all her toned, graceful severity. She met his eyes without fear of his comments. No vanity. "Arrow, you are a stunner." I saw her cheeks flush slightly. So, maybe, a little vanity after all. Good for her. He'd even managed to keep 90% of his usual sarcasm out of his voice. Good boy. I walked over and patted him patronizingly on the shoulder.

"I'll be back."

"Enjoy your Marine. Don't be afraid. He's surprisingly gentle for such a big guy." Wilby called after me. I sighed and got out of there.

10:00 – Training Room (Arrow), *P.S. Scylla*

I was showered and dressed and in a pretty good frame of mind. I'd had some success at suppressing my terror and was pretty much ready to go. I left George at the doorway to the room. Wilby and Arrow's Marines were waiting outside, but looked agitated. One of them, a Corporal, by his stripes, tried to buttonhole me as I headed for the door.

"Where are Allen and Nofsinger?" the Corporal demanded.

I stared at him in surprise. "With Felix and Atalanta? Where else would they be?"

The Corporal started to say something else when the door opened. Wilby stood there, looking white as a sheet. What was wrong? Without a word he reached out, grabbed my arm and pulled me in, the door shutting behind me.

"Wilby, what the..." But then I looked around and just stopped.

Atalanta sat on a chair, supported by Felix on one side and Arrow on the other. Her clothes were torn, her face bruised. There were dried blood in tracks down her legs. For a moment I felt the universe spinning out of control. Not Atalanta. Not her.

I felt myself breaking down inside. I wanted to scream, faint, anything. How could anyone have hurt her? Who would do that?

"Jane." Atalanta's voice was soft. I looked up, barely able to see. "Put all that away now. We have to focus. There'll be time later."

I nodded like a small child. "What happened?" I'd managed to keep most of the tremor out of my voice. I don't know how but I did.

Now Felix met my eyes. In them was a fury that even I'd never seen before. I had never wanted to hurt anyone and I'd hurt both of them by putting her in danger. "It was Bayliss."

"He did this?" I couldn't keep the surprise out of my tone. I knew he was a toad, but a rapist?

Felix looked at Atlanta for permission and she nodded. She then closed her eyes and leaned back in the chair. It was Felix who spoke.

"We got to the *Hastings* and she found him almost immediately. She got the tour, got to see the vault door (standard physical vault lock) and was able to confirm that the lab was situated where we thought it would be. From what she's told me it was all going to plan. Too much to plan. So she was preparing to," and Felix looked uncomfortable, but only for a second, "reward him for all this attention, especially since he'd taken her to restricted areas, when she blacked out."

"Blacked out," Arrow repeated. Atalanta nodded, eyes still closed. Arrow looked from Felix to me, worried.

"When she woke up she..." and then Felix had to stop.

"The first one was almost finished when I came to. They must have timed the drug. I guess it's more fun if the girl is awake and struggling." Atalanta's voice was cold, so cold.

I wanted to throw up. I looked at Wilby and he looked as ill as I felt.

"How did you get away?" I asked numbly.

"I made them love me, then made them help me escape. Five were killed in the process. The sixth…" She looked at Felix.

"Was mine." Felix's mouth was set grimly.

I clenched my fists to try to control myself. Wilby turned away. Arrow's face could have been made of stone.

"Bayliss?"

"He gave me to them." She closed her eyes again.

"I figure that she'd been spotted on her last visit. They knew Bayliss knew her and they used him. The tour allowed them time to get together, procure the drug, etc." Felix's voice was devoid of inflection. I felt wave after wave of guilt. But I couldn't let it get to me now.

I looked at everyone. I'd been so sure that this was right and now I felt completely lost. Samuel had warned me of risk to Atalanta and I hadn't listened. "Do I still go? Or was this a mistake all along? What do I do?" I was pleading, I knew, but I didn't care.

There was silence for a minute, but it was Atalanta who answered me. "You have to go, Jane, especially now."

I nodded. "It's only fair. I understand."

She opened her eyes and sat herself up painfully. "This isn't punishment. You have to go and destroy those samples."

"Why?"

"Because Bayliss told me that the Scientists aren't coming for our DNA. They don't need it." Atalanta swallowed, still managing to look appalled even in her current state. "Our super DNA was the only DNA they saved. That's why they're only demanding the normal DNA now."

Arrow was incredulous. "So they abandoned all the centuries of Pace-normal DNA and only saved the supernormal samples?"

Atalanta laughed without humor. "Bayliss said that those were the samples they could have the most fun with."

I could see us all recoiling in horror. She was right. I had to go.

"I'll go for Jane." Wilby said quietly. "I can do it."

I shook my head. "I'm going. Besides, we need someone to inform the General once Felix and I are at the *Hastings*." Wilby didn't looked pleased about that and I didn't blame him. Atalanta started to protest but I didn't let her. "*You* can't do it. There is a difference between letting him know what is going on and scaring the shit out of him. He'll take one look at you and lose objectivity. Wilby can tell him just as well. Arrow, can you keep her out of sight until we return?"

Arrow nodded.

"Wilby, are you all right with talking to the General?

"Yes." Wilby still looked unhappy, but also relieved.

"I can take Atalanta to my quarters for the duration." Arrow said quietly.

"Thank you." Oh, right. My mind was racing. Something wasn't right now—ah that's the problem. "I'll need to borrow someone's ID." Wilby and Arrow looked up in surprise. Felix just watched Atalanta. "They don't want supers, so I need to be a normal. I won't get into the restricted areas otherwise." I turned to Wilby. "Maybe one of the General's staff?" Wilby nodded. "And what about the needle grenades?"

Wilby looked displeased. "No longer standard issue, unfortunately. Soldiers were denied the ability to carry any type of grenade or incendiary once on board ship. Too dangerous."

"They have a point." Arrow commented. "Hell of a time for them to get smart."

I looked at my watch, then back up. Felix was watching Atalanta who still had her eyes closed in the chair. I was so used to having him to guide me, it was strange being without him, his encouragement, even though he was right in front of me. I understood it and didn't blame him, but I still missed his reassurances. "Felix? Where are your Marines?"

Felix didn't look up. "Safe. They will wake up with a headache in a few hours. I didn't hurt them but I couldn't have them in our way. In fact," he stood up, reluctantly letting go of Atalanta's hand, "it is time to add the remaining three to our collection." He started for the door, but turned back, "Wilby? Care to assist?"

Wilby immediately moved to follow him, but stopped in front of me for a second, speaking in a low voice. “That wasn’t just a gesture. I would’ve gone.”

“I know.” I looked up and gave him a half smile, which was all I could muster. He paused a second then continued following Felix.

“Shuttle Bay at 13:00, Jane,” Felix called over his shoulder.

“Yes, Sir.”

Then it was just the three of us in the room. I didn’t want to look at Atalanta, but I didn’t want to not look at her either. I didn’t want her to think of me as the coward I thought I was. But when I did quickly glance in her direction I saw Arrow give me a subtle head shake. Atalanta, eyes still closed, was crying. Crying silently so no one would hear. Arrow wiped her eyes on her sleeve.

My eyes were dry. They were dry because that moment of suffering, of seeing this beautiful girl violated and defaced and hurting had crystallized my sadness, grief and guilt into white hot fury. My nervousness was erased, my sadness postponed. I needed revenge.

“Come on, love, let’s go.” I recognized the voice as Arrow’s but the words threw me for a loop. And her tone was so gentle, so…maternal. I was again glad for my anger because I couldn’t afford to be sad for Arrow, too. Not right now.

Arrow helped Atalanta up. She surveyed Atalanta’s appearance and turned to me. “Lower right cabinet. Grab a hooded jacket and trousers.” I did this and we managed to get Atalanta dressed, carefully, and to cover up most of her injuries. “Are you good enough to go to my quarters?” This was to Atalanta and still in that soothing voice. Atalanta nodded. Her face was still swelling, but the hood and her hair covered most of the damage.

They took initial steps towards the door. “Arrow?” I asked. Arrow paused, but didn’t turn around. I assumed she didn’t want to jar Atalanta. What I realized much later was that she’d been anticipating my question. “What did you see about today?”

Arrow’s shoulders slumped a bit. “Just images. Destruction. Dead Scientists. Blood.”

She was holding something back, I just felt it. I walked in front of them so that I could see Arrow’s face. “Did you see *this*?” I indicated Atalanta.

“No,” Arrow said. She looked up at me, her big dark eyes full of her own guilt. “I need to get her to bed.” She frowned, as if she’d almost forgotten to be inspirational. “Remember your training and keep your head. You *will* come back, Jane.” She and Atalanta started moving again.

I called after them. “Alive, Arrow?”

She hesitated. “I think so.” She hesitated again. “Yes.”

Well, that instilled confidence. Fuck me. I then settled into wait the over two hours I had to kill before I went to the shuttle. Two hours to run over the plan again and again and to build my anger up to the sky.

13:00 – Shuttle Bay, *P.S. Scylla*

I made my way to the shuttle, dressed as inconspicuously as I could. I had ditched my usual School uniform for civilian clothing and had tucked my hair under a scarf wrapped around my head. I could see a small line of people carrying belongings waiting in front of the shuttle. I heard the small whine of the shuttle as it ran through its pre-flight check. I assumed Felix was already on it in his new persona.

I took my place in line.

"Jane!" Someone, Ian, shouted at me from across the Bay. Fuck. So much for the brilliance of my disguise. I started walking away from the line as though I had wandered into it by mistake and tried to disappear into a corridor. I heard running footsteps and felt Ian catching up to me. Fuck again. I waited for him. I needed to head him off at the pass or I would miss the shuttle altogether.

He rounded the corner into the corridor and stopped. "Jane, I can't find Arrow—and what the hell were you doing in that line?"

I advanced on him so quickly that he actually backed up into the wall. "Arrow is fine. She's busy for the next few hours. I am going to the *Hastings* but I will be back." I leaned very closely to him for emphasis. "Do me a favor and forget you saw me here. It will be very bad if you don't."

He was taken aback, as well he might be. "I don't understand? What are you doing?"

"I am trying to protect us. You breathe a word of seeing me here and you'll screw it up. Do you understand *that*?"

Ian looked at me, confused and hurt and I felt like a real bitch. I looked over his shoulder and could see people starting to load onto the shuttle.

"I'm sorry, Ian. We didn't want any of this to splash on you."

"It's splashed. Arrow's helping you?"

I nodded, still watching my opportunity go by. I tapped my foot nervously. He looked back and understood.

Ian blinked, clearly thinking. "OK. I won't spill and I'll go help Arrow." He looked down at me. "You should have come to me. He's my *father*."

"At the end of the day, I wanted him to have someone he loves that hadn't betrayed him." Ian stared at me in astonishment, but I didn't have time for questions. I squeezed his arm in apology and took off.

I made it to the shuttle just as the hatch was closing. I pretended to be picky about my seat as I looked for Felix. I felt him before I saw him, but there he was. There was no overt acknowledgement, but I felt a little of his tension dissipate when he saw me.

I looked around me to see who the other 'volunteers' were. There were 5 of us all together. I watched their faces and saw mostly fear. They are rats fleeing our sinking ship, I thought. I didn't know whether to pity them or not. I knew I would have thrown in my lot with the General even if I wasn't involved with him. How could they choose the people that wanted to control every aspect of their lives over freedom?

I finally chose my seat and strapped in. I felt my fears coming back in full force. My hands were starting to shake. I had to stop it. I pictured Atalanta's bruised face and my anger returned and so did my focus.

Felix got clearance to leave and the shuttle bay doors opened on the *Scylla* to let us out. We lifted up and cleared the bay, launching into space. I looked at my companions again. They looked less afraid the further we were from the *Scylla*. Well, I thought, I guess we are taking them where they want to be. In keeping with my 'character' I hid my disgust.

13:30 – Shuttle Bay, *P.S. Hastings*

I was the last one out. I saw the soldiers, Pac-Mil regulars, waiting to check people in on the Bay deck. I paused, looking back at Felix who sat, immobile in his pilot's chair. It seemed he didn't have anything to say so I turned to go.

"Andrea?" Felix said.

It took me a split second to remember that that was me. "Yes, Captain?"

"Make him pay. Make him *suffer*." Then he looked up at me. His hatred and despair showed in his eyes. Felix didn't have to worry. Bayliss was going to get his punishment. I owed both of them that.

I nodded and stepped out of the shuttle.

I went to the end of the line of people queuing up to be checked in and pulled out my borrowed ID. Wilby had done well. The woman I was impersonating was my age and bore a passing resemblance to me. Before I knew it I was in front of a bored soldier.

"Name?" The soldier looked me over. I wondered if he was sorry he hadn't been one of the ones to get Atalanta. Bet he was.

"Andrea Martin, Lieutenant, jg., *P.S. Scylla*."

He checked my ID and handed it back to me. He looked over his shoulder at another soldier. "Everyone from the *Scylla* goes directly to Lab 1. You can take her with the others." There was a loud beeping overhead. "That's the shuttle from the *Nelson*. We need to clear the Bay. And we need that shuttle out of here."

A stab of panic shot through me, despite my focus. "I'm returning, Sir. I'm just here to give my sample. The Shuttle Captain has orders to wait."

The Soldier frowned. I had to think of something quick.

"Captain Armstrong sent me, Sir, to do my duty, but the General doesn't know I'm here. He'll know if I don't return."

The Soldier looked skeptical. "Captain *Armstrong* sent you?"

"Yes, Sir. He'll be coming as soon as he can to donate as well. But he and his people, myself included, only have their clearance to travel within the fleet if the General doesn't know." Sure, why not. Paranoids love conspiracies. And everyone is always willing to believe that fathers and sons hate each other deep down.

I could see the Soldier's interest waning, which was what I wanted. "Fine, I'll shift your shuttle over." He waved over the other soldier. "Lab 1. She'll be returning immediately after."

I nodded my thanks and found myself being escorted with 4 other people from my ship. This time I was lucky and it was no one I knew or who was likely to know who I was. I started counting corridors and turns. Yes, we were right where I wanted us to be. The outer room that lead to the vault. We were lined up and I was still last.

A Lab Tech, then another came into the room. The single soldier stayed by the door armed with an LPG. The door to the vault room was closed and, apparently, locked, but I could feel two presences on the other side.

I calmly grounded myself on the new ship. Its shape was different, but the feel of a ship's hull was familiar to me now. I picked out the bronchial artery on the first Lab Tech. I mentally marked the spinal cord at the neck on the second. All I had to do, I reasoned, was wait for all of the *Scylla* people to have their samples taken and leave. I would make my move when it was just the 2 Labbies and the soldier.

The first *Scylla* normal sat in the chair and had her ID re-checked, then scanned. Then the Lab Tech inserted the needle and drew blood with practiced ease. The *Scylla* normal was given a bandage and told to wait against the other wall. Which meant that we would all be here together when it was my turn. I mentally smacked myself on the head. Because we only have one guard. Was I going to have to kill *all* of these people? I was going to do what I had to do, but I really didn't want to do that.

Before I knew it the fourth person was sitting in the chair, having his blood taken. It was eerily quiet in the room. Time was short. The second Tech was processing the samples on the far counter. I moved my mind gently over to the soldier, felt for his gun and coughed as I gently slipped the safety back on.

Then I reached into the bronchial artery of the first Lab Tech and created the large clot that would buy me two minutes. I waited to be called.

"Andrea Martin?" I nodded and walked to the chair, noting one of the normals who was staring at me in shock. He knows I'm not Andrea, was the thought flying through my head. He knows Andrea. I mentally knocked his elbow into the wall behind him. Hard enough to distract him.

"Ow," he cried out.

Lab Tech 1 looked over at him. "Are you all right?"

"Banged my elbow." Then he looked right at me. Fuck, I hadn't hit him hard enough. "Your name is…" And I pinched the proper nerve at the base of his neck and he dropped unconscious. I wasn't looking directly at him when I did this, which I hoped would buy me a few seconds.

Then I nicked the spinal cord on Lab Tech 2. He fell to the floor. The soldier raised his weapon and I turned his head, breaking his neck. He struggled on the floor, trying to get air. Lab Tech 1 made a kind of strangled sound and collapsed as well.

I looked at the normals who stared at me in terror. I had only a second to decide what to do with them. They had made their choice to leave the *Scylla*, so taking them back was out. Fuck them. But I didn't want to kill them either. "I'm going to knock you out, like I did that guy," I said, indicating the normal on the floor.

"Knock us out? He isn't dead?" one woman asked.

"He's alive—they," and I indicated the other 3, "are dead. Choose."

The woman looked at the others. "Don't kill us."

One by one I dropped them to the floor. I stalked over to the separating door. I felt the inner lock and quietly started moving the internal pieces, but realized I didn't have the time. I banged on the door loudly.

"Something terrible has happened! HELP!"

The door flew open and a Scientist came out to help. I broke his neck reflexively. I tossed his body into the first room and ran into the room with the vault. I knew someone was in there, but I was intent on the vault door and had just shoved him into a cabinet.

"Jane!" a familiar voice groaned. I stopped and turned around, eyes wide. Pinned against the wall was Dr. Bayliss. "Jane! I'm so glad to see you."

"And I you." I turned to the vault door, leaving him pinned. "A moment, please."

I felt for the lock, scanning it and trying to be quick but not careless. Yes, I could feel the tumblers and gears. I started moving them, just as Wilby had taught me.

"Jane, what are you…" I pinched his lips together and continued. Click and click and click. I had the line almost complete. There. The latch released. I spun the wheel and the door swung open. The huge door—it had to be 3 feet thick.

There, inside the vault, wrapped in a haze of cool vapor, rested tens of thousands of blood samples. The samples were lit up, like they were in a display case for sale and covered the wall in scores of tiny rows. I felt behind the layer I could see and sensed only wall. So this was it, was it? Their treasure. Their legacy.

I picked Bayliss up and lifted him into the vault, re-pinning him, this time to the inside of the vault door, which was the only wall not covered with samples. I released my hold on his lips.

"Jane, you have to get me out of here. You have to take me with you." His pasty face was pale with fear, whether it was fear of staying or fear of me was anyone's guess. "This place is evil." He started to weep.

"Why should I save you when you let them do that to Atalanta?" My voice was casual. Deliberately so.

He exhaled and pulled his head back as if I'd struck him. "They wanted her. They said they would send me to a Pace 3 ship if I didn't bring her to them. Sig's ship." And the Pacey 3's were not fond of Bayliss, or any Scientist. I had a feeling that Sig would have a knack for punishment as well. A good threat to a true coward. "I had no choice."

I re-grounded myself and picked a vial, trying to feel the molecules in the blood sample. The molecules were larger than I had expected. Good. I made that vial do a little swirl, just make sure I had it. It swirled, though on so small a scale that only I could have detected it.

"You let them rape, repeatedly, the most exquisite woman anyone has ever seen. They made her cry. They made her *bleed*." I made the molecules fight each other. "Her only crime was being beautiful." I made my transfer, now all the vials' molecules were moving. Moving faster and faster.

"But I heard that they're all dead, right?" Now he was definitely more afraid of me than them. "They got what they deserved…for actually doing it to her." His voice became panicked. "I'll apologize a million times, Jane, if you take me back. I know Scientists aren't known for understanding consequences." His face turned bleak for a second. "That's what Sig always says." He looking back up, pleading. "But I do understand and I'm so sorry. I want to tell her myself how sorry I am."

It was then that I transferred to Bayliss as well. Inside I could feel every molecule, blood or otherwise move, then move faster, then start to bounce—bounce off arteries, off tissues, off organs, off his brain.

His face was turning red, his skin was flushing as I boiled him from the inside. The vials were starting to shake with the pressure. I could feel bubbles, bubbles everywhere, inside the vials and now inside Bayliss.

"Jane?!?" Bayliss screamed.

I had tried to think of something devastating to say, something clever and cutting, but I didn't have it in me.

I just looked him right in the eye and said, “You hurt my friend and now you’ll die for it.”

At that moment all the vials exploded, spraying the room with hot blood.

Blood ran out of Bayliss’s ears, nose, eyes and mouth. I let him fall to the floor, dead. Good. A klaxon sounded, loud. That had to be the alarm on the vials. Time to go.

I went out through the first room, stepping over the bodies. I picked up the dead soldier’s gun and unlocked the safety. I took a breath and keyed open the door to the hallway. I peeked around the corner. A soldier was walking. I felt his form at the end of the hallway and moved the LPG into the line of fire. I pulled the trigger. I felt, and heard, the man fall. I darted out into the hallway and ran for it.

Turn and turn. And wall. I stopped, dismayed. They’d closed the emergency airlock. My first thought was gas. It was overruled by the sound of a dozen booted feet behind me. I turned to the airlock door, made a ‘fist’ and ‘punched.’ The boots were getting closer. Punch. I could see light on the other side of the door. They wouldn’t gas me with their people in here, I thought. Actually, they might. Gas first, ask questions later. I punched again. Now the hole was almost big enough to get through.

The soldiers surged around the corner and landed in perfect formation, LPGs pointed at me. I held out my arm and swept them back around the corner.

I punched again and the door broke in two. I put my foot through the hole and felt the pulse of an LPG coming at me. I ducked and turned around. The soldiers I had swept away (stupidly, I realized) were regrouping and coming back. I fired at them with my gun, trying to think of what to do. They were starting to advance. I used the door as a shield. They were moving closer.

I fired again then looking at the jagged edge of the door in front of me. Concentrating, I yanked half of the door from its track, now using the other half as a shield. I turned the door on its side, sharp metal pointed horizontally at the soldiers. I gathered my strength…and shot it straight at them as fast as I could. Within a second it had swept the soldiers up en masse, burying itself into the ship’s interior wall. There were screams as the people on the outside had been cut in half, the ones behind being crushed. I hesitated a second, horrified.

But time was passing and more people would come.

I ran. Turn. Turn. There was no one in these hallways. I saw the doors that were the entrance to the Shuttle Bay at the end. No one guarded it. They’d cleared all their people out. That was bad for me. I felt something change in the air. Something…

I took a deep breath, hoping it wasn’t my last, and blew out the doors. I started to run. My vision blurred. I felt the shape of the hallway and kept trying to run even though I couldn't see. My muscles started spasming. I dropped to one knee and everything went dark.

23:00 – Infirmary, *P.S. Scylla*

I woke up on the *Scylla*. For a second I enjoyed the feeling of the engines, the right engines, the shape of the hull, all the things that came with my physical home. I felt groggy and my limbs were heavy, but I felt otherwise all right.

I felt Felix hovering at the far end of the room and reached out a hand to him. "You saved me."

He stepped out of the shadows. He was a ghost his former self, thin, pale and with deep circles under his eyes. He sat on the bed and took my proffered hand. "The Bay doors blew out and I saw you collapse." He swallowed convulsively. "I got to you as fast as I could and carried you to the shuttle. I got the hatch closed and…"

"How did you get out? How did you get clearance?" I pulled myself up to a sitting position.

And for a moment I saw a hint of a smile on his wasted face. "Following your example I blew out the outer doors, instantly depressurized the Bay and, I'm guessing, some portions of the ship itself."

He squeezed my hand. "I…couldn't tell if you were alive. You were so deeply drugged. I thought for a while there that I was just bringing your body back. It wasn't until you were in the Infirmary that I knew you'd be all right."

"How long was I out, Felix?"

"Eight hours." No wonder he looked exhausted. Funny how he thought I was his responsibility and I thought he was mine. Then he looked over at me. "Did you do it?"

I stared at him, surprised.

"There was a lot of emergency communications within the *Hastings*," he said, "we'd been monitoring all their comm traffic, but that could've just been the shuttle Bay getting blown out. Probably was, come to think of it. It's not as if they would advertise what you'd tried to do. So, we didn't have anyone to ask and the only person who knew was unconscious."

Hm. I supposed so. I gave Felix a half smile. "We did it. I got them. Everything in the vault."

"And Bayliss?" he asked this quietly as if trying not to get his hopes up.

"With the vault," I answered promptly. Felix looked up, life in his eyes for the first time. I continued. "I boiled him. Like the vials. Like the water bottles."

"So he suffered."

"He suffered."

Felix sat there for a second, as if trying to process the fact that the object of a decade long hatred was finally dead. "Thank you."

"How's our girl?"

"We brought her here to get checked out. She's in pain but Doc Wells doesn't think any of her injuries are permanent."

I smiled a little, relieved. While I was glad that the physical injuries would resolve, those weren't the injuries I'd been worried about. I took a deep breath now. "What did Samuel say when Wilby told him, Felix? Did Wilby tell you?"

Felix sat there in silence for a minute as if trying to keep from having to tell me. "Wilby told me. The General said nothing. Nothing. Wilby told me that he said his piece and then just stood there while the General stared at him." Felix pulled on his beard thoughtfully. "He said he'd never seen *anyone* so angry, let alone the General. He sat there, just staring for about thirty seconds, then picked up his report log and threw it into one of the command monitors."

"Sounds scary," I said softly. My poor Samuel.

"It was, apparently," Felix admitted. "Then the General brought the ship to battle stations and, as far as anyone can tell, didn't say another word until we came back on the shuttle."

I sat up more. "What did he do? Did he see me?"

Felix's face was full of pity. "He only came in once, to make sure you were going to be all right. Then he spent the next 8 hours out there," Felix indicated the area on the other side of the Infirmary doors, "waiting for you to wake up."

I frowned. "And when I did?"

"He left."

"Oh." I sat there, puzzled by my own calm reaction. I knew that the General's reaction was bad, bad for him and bad for me, but that was only intellectual. I didn't actually feel it. Had I buried my emotions so deeply that I'd lost them? Then I took a second to think about whether that was a good or bad thing. Why was I in a hurry to feel anyway, when the only things I could look forward to were miserable? But what was wrong with me?

I looked at Felix and found him watching me. "What did the Doc say about me?"

"He said that you are fine, but that we should watch you for signs of shock."

"Shock." I repeated. "I can't feel anything. I mean, I can sense things, I can ground, but I don't feel sad or relieved or guilty or anything. I feel nothing." I paused. "I killed a lot of people, Felix. I should feel something, shouldn't I?" I was worried now. Was I some sociopath that I could kill and feel nothing? "Is that shock?"

"Yes," Felix gave me a worried look.

I swung my legs over the side of the bed. Felix jumped up, alarmed. I patted his shoulder. "No, this is good, Felix. I can't emote all over Atalanta like this, which means I can stay with her tonight. If you want."

"I don't think you should be leaving…"

"And I'll try to see Samuel. I at least owe him the opportunity to yell at me. I don't know how long this will last, so I should go now." I smiled at him again. I stood up, wobbling a bit. Felix grabbed my arm to steady me. I quickly, and successfully, grounded myself with the ship and felt steadier.

"This is a mistake, Jane. You aren't right, yet."

"I'm good enough." I looked around me at the Infirmary. "I don't want to stay here. I don't want to be where people can come and look at me. I feel trapped here." I saw my boots sitting on a shelf in the corner. I grabbed them and started putting them on. This feeling of nothing was so strange. I felt drugged. I knew I wasn't myself, but I still needed to get out of there. I could feel Felix stressing out now, clearly about me. He was thinking hard.

"I can't take you to Atalanta," he started.

"Why?"

He kept going, "And, as your friend, I can't let you talk to the General like this."

And just then I felt a crack in the wall that was keeping me from feeling anything. The General. I saw his face before me. The crack widened. Felix looked even more worried now.

"She needs you, Felix." The voice was Wilby's. I looked over at the door and there he was. He looks uncomfortable, I thought. Pain isn't his thing. Felix sort of froze in position. He needed to go, but didn't want to leave me.

I straightened up. "You're right. I shouldn't be going anywhere. I'll just stay here tonight and figure out what I'm doing tomorrow."

"You promise? You'll stay here?"

"I promise. Don't worry about me." I gave him a smile I didn't feel at all. The crack widened again, but I concealed its effects. "She needs you." Felix looked relieved and gave me a quick kiss on the cheek. He almost ran out of there. I looked over at Wilby.

"You should go get some rest, Wilby." I sat back down on the bed, kicking off my shoes. "Been a hell of day." He didn't go. He was watching me warily, like an experiment that was about to blow up in his face. "You've been really great. This couldn't have happened without you."

He looked away from me for a second. "Both the good and the bad things that happened. Yes, I helped."

The pressure was building in my chest and I tried to blink away tears that were forming without looking like I was. I just needed him to go. Go before the whole wall fucking collapsed.

"I'll get some sleep now, I think." With that I got in the cot and pulled the covers up. He just stood there. I felt like I had seconds before I fell apart. "Please go."

Wilby took a couple of steps further into the room. "He wouldn't have been so angry if he didn't love you so much." His voice was gentle but his words killed me.

The wall crumbled. I cried quietly at first into the pillow, but soon gave up and sobbed aloud. For my beautiful Atalanta, for Felix who suffered with and for her, for the more than a dozen people I had so casually killed and would never even know the names of, and for the loss of my beloved Samuel. Samuel, who would never forgive me.

Suddenly Wilby gently, but firmly, pulled me up so that I was sitting on the cot. He sat close and held me. It was almost worse having a man do that that wasn't Samuel, but I was too overcome to protest. He held me and rocked me gently and I wept.

"It's going to be all right, sweet baby," Wilby said softly.

Not 'baby', I thought. "Please don't call me that," I whispered between sobs.

"I'm sorry, Jane," Wilby said quietly, sensing he'd hit on something painful.

So am I, I thought. Sorry for everything.

Wilby held me for a long time, until I was cried out. I felt him there as I was dropping off to sleep at last. He must have left soon after. I woke up alone in the dead of night and wept some more.

Entry 7-2-13

Except from Felix's Journal, July 18, 2869

Well, Jane did it. She saved the General and killed Bayliss. I thought I'd feel better when he was dead and I guess I do but…
…they hurt my girl. She suffers and I can't stand it. How could they do that to my beautiful sweet, sweet girl? How?
I can't breathe.

06:00 – Infirmary, *P.S. Scylla*

I'd forgotten where I was. For a second I felt I was in the General's Quarters and he was there with me. Everything was OK. Nothing bad had happened. I hadn't betrayed his trust, hadn't gotten Atalanta hurt and he still wanted me. I lay there for a minute or two, eyes still closed, enjoying the unexpected relief from misery. Then I realized that he *was* there. I could feel him. I smiled to myself. My Samuel.

But then I remembered that everything had changed. The mission was over and I was in the Infirmary. Samuel was filled with tension. He was tired, stressed. No, wait, he really was there. I opened my eyes with a start and immediately sat up on the cot. He was standing at the foot of it, watching me. This wasn't a dream.

The General stood at parade rest. He was in uniform and looked very put together. This was completely at odds with his internal readings, which were all over the place. Even in the dim light of the Infirmary I could see his eyes were bloodshot and his jaw was clenched. In his face I could see his anger, his disappointment. I pulled my knees up to my chest defensively and waited for him to start. He just stood there for what seemed like an eternity as if trying to figure out what to say.

"I need to confirm the report Felix gave me about your actions yesterday on the *Hastings*." The General's voice was professional and cold. My heart sank. His anger wasn't a surprise, but I guess I'd held out some hope that he'd see past it. Until that moment.

"Yes, Sir."

"Yesterday, against my express orders, you sent Felix and Atalanta to the *Hastings* for recon."

I nodded.

"During which time she was repeatedly raped," he didn't try to conceal the pain in his voice when he said this. I felt my chest tighten with guilt and sadness. "And was forced to take out, one way or another, the six Scientists that had done this to protect herself."

"Yes, Sir." But she succeeded in her mission, I thought loudly in my head. She did her job. She didn't fuck up. It was my fault for putting her there. But I didn't want to defend either her or myself. I wanted this interview to be over as soon as possible.

"You then went back to the *Hastings* with Felix and got in to the labs under the pretext of being a normal who was there to give her sample." I nodded again. "You then took out two Lab Techs, a dozen soldiers and a Scientist, two actually, and proceeded to destroy the DNA samples held in their vault."

"I boiled them in their containers, Sir." The General looked at me with a hint of surprise. Maybe Felix hadn't told him how I'd done it.

"And you murdered Dr. Bayliss."

"I boiled him, too." The General dropped his pose of parade rest and turned slightly away from me. Felix definitely hadn't told him that.

"Why?"

"He'd arranged for Atalanta's assault. He set her up." I didn't mention what he'd done to Felix with his piss-poor engineering. I didn't know what the General knew about that and it wasn't my story to tell. "Felix didn't tell you that did he? Sir."

The General rubbed his hand across his face. "No."

I figured it was time to give the full accounting. "Atalanta told me, when she came back from the *Hastings*, that the Scientists weren't going to come for us, for our DNA." The General look over at me sharply. "According to Bayliss, the only samples they'd saved were the ones with super DNA. They said it was the DNA they could have 'the most fun with'."

The General looked a bit sick to his stomach. "So why go, Jane? They weren't coming for us. You knew that and you went anyway."

I found it hard to believe that he didn't know why I'd gone anyway, but I played along. "I figured that if I could destroy their stores then we could be done with them. Officially."

The General sighed. "That's what I thought you'd say. Well, thanks to you, now we have to be. Even if they never admit what you destroyed, and you can bet they won't, you killed two Scientists, Jane. That means war."

"They deserved it."

"I'm not arguing with you on that." The General looked beat, in more ways than one. "You've set the stage for this, you know. With this…mission of yours, with your insane conspiracy." His blood pressure was up again, his adrenaline reenergized. He clenched his fists, as if trying to force himself to calm down.

"But you wanted to secede, S-Sir." I couldn't call him Samuel now. Not now. I didn't want him to take his name away from me.

"I did." He looked so defeated as he turned and headed for the door. "But if they attacked us and we fought back, we would have seceded under provocation and under *my* authority. Anything after that would have fallen on my head." He paused in the doorway, not looking back. "Whose head does it fall on now, Jane?"

I shrunk back further against the headboard. "On mine?" I said softly. Could that be true? Is that true??? My fault? Dear god, is anything bad that happens from now on…? I just sat there, staring into space as my mind spun out of control.

He paused a second but didn't answer. Then he walked out the door.

<u>10:00 – Atalanta/Felix/Jane's Quarters, *P.S. Scylla*</u>

I stood outside my quarters and pressed the entry button. I knew Atalanta and Felix were in there but I didn't want to surprise anyone. The hallways were essentially deserted. The General had called a meeting in the Loading Bay. I assumed that he was announcing our secession. I had had no intention of going and I was pretty sure Atalanta and Felix had skipped it as well. The General's words still flew around in my head. They filled my mind with fear and a sort of future guilt, even as I tried not to think about them. The door to the room slid open and Felix stepped out, letting it reclose behind him. Now I had to focus on my friends.

Felix still looked bad. He was exhausted and wired. His hands had a small tremor and his body was all tension.

"I need to talk to you," he started without preamble. "We need your help."

"Of course," I said, wondering what help I, of all people, could offer.

Felix looked up at me, eyes filled with worry. "She isn't better." I started to say something but he cut me off. "Physically she's improving, but otherwise she's getting worse."

I nodded impotently, imprisoned by my own guilt. I found myself hoping desperately for direction, from Felix, from anyone, that would free me from the pain of having gotten Atalanta hurt. Free her from her pain and thus, me from mine.

"I need you to help me do a 'tap' on her."

And what the hell was a 'tap'? I let my raised eyebrows ask the question for me.

"It's a thing with MEmps. Under normal circumstances they take in emotion but then process it and let it go. This applies both to emotions they pick up and to their own. It's like a cup of water. Emotions fill up the cup and some evaporate naturally and some get (to follow this terrible metaphor) consumed by 'drinking' them off in small sips. This keeps everything in balance."

"But that isn't happening now."

"No. She's overloaded, Jane. It's too much for her and she's, well, you'll see." He stood there a moment, trying to keep his emotions under control. I could feel him trying to center himself on the ship…and failing.

"So, what is a 'tap'?" I asked gently. It was killing me seeing him so…reduced. He was always so good at everything. Not being able to fix this is torture for him, I thought.

"MEmps can channel away excess emotions if they want to into another person. It was an unintended by-product of being able to project feelings in the first place. They use the other person as a 'tap' to relieve the pressure. Draining the cup back to normal."

"I'll do it." I said quickly.

Felix allowed a flicker of a smile across his face. "That's what I said, but she won't let me. But I thought that if there were two of us to share the burden, she might be convinced."

"Why would she say no to you?" I asked, perplexed. "She knows you would do anything for her."

"She does," he replied sadly. "But I did a tap for her once before and they are hard to get through. It…it isn't just feelings. MEmps were bred from Telepaths, you know. It can be images…it can feel like it is actually happening to you."

"You helped her tap out her molestation, from her childhood." I took a step back in awe of his bravery. I found the very concept terrifying. "Didn't you?"

He closed his eyes in remembered pain. "I was unprepared, though I had the best intentions. It scared me and I…didn't handle it well. She felt terrible—she'd never done a tap before—and swore she'd never do another."

"But she needs one."

"Desperately."

"What will happen if she doesn't let us do it?"

His expression was bleak. "I honestly don't know." The tremor in his hands was increasing and he was rubbing them together as if to hide it. His misery was awful to watch.

Unable to take it anymore I stepped forward and wrapped him in a hug. He just stood there, immobile. Not fighting me, exactly, but not surrendering either. "Try grounding again, sweetheart," I whispered to him. I could feel him doing it and his tension drop a tiny bit.

I tried loosening the muscle tension in his shoulders with my mind. Gently, gently. Slowly he relaxed some. Eventually he hugged me back. I rocked him the way Wilby had rocked me the night before. We didn't say anything for a while. Finally he pulled away from me and wiped his face dry of unacknowledged tears. He pulled up one of my hands and kissed it, then let it go and keyed open the door.

Atalanta sat on her bunk leaning up against a wall of pillows. She was awake and looked as though she had never slept. Her face was pale and sheened with sweat and her bruised jaw was black and blue turning into green. She was breathing fast like a hunted animal. She looked like she was dying.

"He's been persuading you," she said, her voice a ghost of its former melodiousness.

"He persuaded me, 'Lanta."

She closed her eyes for a second then opened them again. "No. For two reasons. One: I'm going to be fine. It's just going to take a while for me to get back on my feet. And two: Having you do a tap is just as bad as having Felix do it. Contrary to what you might think, Jane, I don't want you to suffer for me. You don't deserve it and neither does Felix."

I sat down on the bed next to her. "Let me be the old Atalanta that I met two years ago. Let me tell you what *she* would be saying to you right now."

Atalanta gave a small frown, the tiniest sign of impatience. "Jane, this is…"

I assumed a bitchy air (trying to keep the mood lighter) and cocked my head to look at her. "You look like shit. You seem to be dying. Your friends want to share the tap. Stop being an idiot and let them help you." I turned to Felix. "How was that?"

I saw that phantom smile again. "Not bitchy enough," Felix replied.

"Fine time to pick on me," Atalanta said, still barely above audible. "You two will *share* the tap?"

"Yes," we both responded at the same time.

Atalanta sat against her pillows, her breathing still too fast, and thought. She turned her head a little to look at me. "You don't owe me anything, Jane. I chose to go. I got unlucky."

I thought about it for a second. "It's not just that." I looked at both of them seriously. "You two are the first real friends I've ever had. That's a debt I will never be able to pay off." I laughed at myself. "Sounds sappy, but it's true."

Atalanta looked away, her eyes moist. "A tap isn't like you think, Jane. Once it starts it's in your mind and you can't escape it."

"Felix and I understand," I said firmly.

"You don't. But I will think about it. Come back in a couple of hours."

"Ok." I patted her foot as it stuck up under her blanket and walked to the door. Felix followed me the short distance.

"Just a note on your gravity class today…" Felix started.

"My what?" Who the hell would put me in class *today*? Don't I get a fucking day off?

"The General has insisted that *all* Telekinetics take the gravity (or zero-G) classes. Macros get more of a priority because we can do more with the lack of gravity. Telepaths and MEmps will get training as well, but it will be more along the lines of the training normals get."

"I thought you'd be teaching this." I said unhappily.

"I will be, once things are resolved here. You'll have Wilby today."

"But Wilby's a Micro," I protested.

"No kidding."

"Sorry. I thought you just said this was a Macro thing."

Felix sighed. "Wilby knows what he's doing. How many times does he have to prove it to you?"

A bunch more, I thought, but I didn't say it. His skills were impeccable; I just didn't know what to make of him. It wasn't that I thought he was a bad guy anymore; I just wanted to actually like him. I contented myself with a nod and keyed open the door.

"Oh, and Jane."

"Yes?"

"Skip lunch." And there was that shadow smile. The door closed and Felix was gone.

14:00 – Shuttle Bay, *P.S. Scylla*

"Welcome to Gravity Training, boys and girls." Wilby stood in front of us and looked smug. Typical. He wasn't the selfless loyal, dare I say it, *caring* fellow he had been over the last few days. Wilby was back. Well, I thought, it was probably a relief for him.

"As you have probably guessed, we are in the Shuttle Bay because it is easy to depressurize and because it already has hand holds and hooks to help you control yourselves. Eventually we will be doing gravity drills within the ship itself where things will be more difficult."

I looked around at my classmates. Some Macros, some Micros, including the ever inquisitive Gladys, whom I really hoped would keep her trap shut today and me, the freak hybrid. Wilby picked up a something off a table next to him.

Gladys. "What's that, Sir?"

Wilby smiled. "There is a technical name for this that I have mercifully forgotten, but we all refer to this as a 'vomit net'." He smiled and looked right at me. That's right. What was it? Incompetent, dangerous drama queen that pukes all the time? That's Jane. Prick.

"The most important things to remember in zero g is velocity control. The smallest mistake can send you out into nowhere with nothing to hold on to. These sessions should enable you to get used to these conditions.

Zero g is part of being in space." Wilby signaled to a deck hand. "Take the first few minutes to play around and get used to it. It can be fun, but don't let the giddiness of this fool you. You will need to fight without gravity. Being able to do this well can save your life and the lives of your team."

"We will be fighting whom exactly?" Gladys looked worried.

"That is not the subject of this lesson. I will tell you when I am cleared to do so. Otherwise I think you can direct your questions to the General himself."

Gladys looked like she'd rather eat glass. The interior shuttle bay door opened and Captain Ian stepped in. Wilby smiled, a little sourly.

"Captain Armstrong has volunteered to assist in today's lesson." Ian grinned at Wilby, positively delighted at his discomfiture. I wondered if life was just more fun for Wilby if he had a beef with everyone. Probably. Ian stood next to Wilby.

"Per the General's instructions, there will be two parts to today's drill. One where you practice moving yourselves through zero g and the second where you move Objects through it." We all looked at each other with anticipation. I caught Ian's eye and he winked at me. Ian looked awfully happy these days, for which I was cautiously glad, but this apparently intimate wink made Wilby look even more put out. Oh, Wilby. Drama.

An overhead klaxon sounded loudly. Within seconds I felt lighter. I looked down and my feet were off the ground. I heard the sound of retching and turned my head just in time to see Gladys vomit into the air. With a graceful movement, Wilby zoomed over and scooped up the puke with his net. My stomach felt a little queasy, but I was ok. Per Felix's advice I had skipped lunch. Thank god for Felix.

I felt movement to the side of me and looked over to see Ian move efficiently through the air and turn a somersault to land/float right next to me.

"Showing off, Sir?" I murmured.

He flashed me a beautiful smile. "I love zero g. I always wanted to be able to fly."

I looked at him in amused dismay. "But you're a pilot."

"Even a fantastic pilot, and I *am* a fantastic pilot, Jane, can't fly without a ship."

It was bizarre seeing Ian like this—smiling and full of play. Who the hell was actually happy on *this* ship?

I leaned closer to him. "Are you on any medications we should know about?"

He threw his head back and laughed. "I'm fine, Jane, and I'm going to be one of your flight instructors, once everything calms down." His face held a microscopic frown for a second above those bold blue eyes. Yes, I thought, if we are all still kicking when things 'calm down.'

"Flight? I'm going to learn to fly?" How fucking cool was that? Then I pictured myself vomiting all over the instrument panel of the ship and it seemed less cool.

"Fighters. It'll be fun."

"Sounds it." Than I had a thought. "Whose idea was this, Sir?"

"The General's."

I nodded. "When did he mention it to you, if I may ask?"

He looked at me, eyes twinkling. "About two hours ago."

My spirits lifted a bit. He was still looking out for me, even if he was upset.

"People! Less talking, more acclimating." Wilby glared at Ian and me.

Ian turned his head away from Wilby before rolling his eyes. I laughed quietly. It felt like it had been forever since I'd laughed, though I was pretty sure it hadn't been. Really felt like it though.

"Let's work on velocity and control." Ian gave me a wicked look. "Catch me." And he took off.

I hesitated for a second and decided that since I was here, with this class, as a Macro, I should be grounded and act like one. I centered myself on the ship and "swam" my way to the floor for a push off. I looked like an idiot, swimming awkwardly when Ian could fly, I knew, but I was hoping that would pass with time. It could happen, right?

I pushed off the floor way too hard, apparently, and went shooting through the air like a bullet. I could see the wall of the shuttle bay coming right at me. Fast.

"Jane! Repel it!" I heard Wilby shout.

I obeyed instantly, out of instinct more than thought, and held out my hand. I pushed away from the wall and immediately found myself bouncing like a pinball in the other direction. Another wall was coming at me.

"Slow your velocity!" Wilby shouted.

My hand was out again and this time I didn't repel as hard, but I still shot off in another direction. I heard someone laugh below me. I didn't blame her, whoever it was, but I had other problems. The third wall was coming at me. I put out my hand again.

"You're a *Telespatial* for fuck's sake!" Wilby cried, exasperated.

Oh. Right. I quickly felt the shape of the room itself, felt my own velocity and the movement of the others, most of whom were hovering watching the show. Suddenly it all made sense. I had the feel of the room and the bodies within it. I slowed myself. I stopped. I gently 'pushed' on walls one at a time to turn myself around. This was *awesome*. I pushed off the ceiling and floated down to Wilby and Ian. Wilby's expression seemed torn between annoyance and relief that I'd finally gained some measure of control.

"Sorry, Sir." I said formally. Wilby nodded. It was then that I looked around at the other students. Gladys still looked green and was off to the side holding on to the wall for dear life. One of the Macros was nursing what seemed to be a bruised shoulder. Two other students were outright missing. I assumed they were in the Infirmary. I bet they hadn't screwed up as spectacularly as I had, I thought with a sort of deranged pride.

"Next." Wilby floated in front of the survivors and Ian. "A race. All eight corners." He briefly sketched out the pattern we were to follow. "And ready, steady, GO!"

We all shot into the air. Wilby and Ian hovered in the center of the room, monitoring, though I could tell that Ian would much rather have been participating (and winning).

There were six others racing with me. I got to the first corner in third position, which didn't bother me. I had seven more corners to catch up—and watch my competitors implode. As for me, I was flying.

One Macro smashed his head into a corner, trying to beat Gladys. Wilby helped him down and got him out to the Infirmary. Another Macro hooked Gladys's arm and spun her. She went from light green to puce and threw up again. She grabbed the nearest set of handholds and climbed down, defeated. Four left. We were heading for the third corner and I was speeding up. I had control and it felt wonderful. Another Macro, Garrett, was ahead of me. I increased my velocity and snaked by him. I touched the third corner and zoomed for the fourth. It was then that I felt myself slow down. And stop. I watched as Garrett passed me. Oh, I don't think so, my friend.

I gave him a strong downward push and he plummeted towards the deck. I touched the fourth corner and turned to 'catch' Garrett before he smacked into the floor. Garrett gave me a look of pure hatred and I heard Wilby laugh. Garrett launched himself back to touch 4 (to catch up) and I made (metaphorical) tracks for 5.

The other two opponents tried racing each other and collided, each spinning out of control. With Garrett on my tail I moved one, the girl Macro, in front of him, throwing off his trajectory. 6. Garrett angrily pushed her aside and she flew into a wall. I saw her drop down in full retreat.

Just Garrett and a Micro left now. 7. The other Micro was no threat. He was fast but had no control and seemed to reach the corners with more force than precision. He was back at 6, but Garrett was catching up. I saw 8 right in front of me. I was suddenly shoved to one side and went careening into space (as it were). Garrett was 10 yards from the goal. I reached for him and spun him like a dervish. Like I'd spun Wilby. Garrett went towards the ceiling, completely out of control. I touched 8.

Garrett stopped himself and threw up. Wilby again masterfully caught the vomit with his net. Garrett's green color could not hide the look of loathing he gave me. I made myself float down to Wilby and Ian who were grinning ear to ear. It was strange, good, but strange, to see them with the same expression on their faces.

"Nice work, Jane." Wilby said, watching the last of my fellow competitors stumble out. "You seem to have a hidden competitive streak."

"Not hidden, Sir. I just don't compete unless I have the skills to back myself up."

"Fair enough." Wilby sighed.

"What's wrong?" I asked.

Ian, smirking, answered for him. "He was going to do a second drill, but you took out all your classmates."

"Oh, sorry." I wasn't really sorry, but it seemed the right thing to say.

Wilby shrugged as he turned and started floating to the door. "See you tomorrow."

I felt cheated. I didn't want to stop playing. "Hey, Wilby?" Wilby turned around. "Do you like Zero G?"

"Sure," he answered warily.

I floated closer to him. I flicked Ian a glance. I figured Ian was up for anything. I touched Wilby on the shoulder. "Tag. You're It." And I zoomed away.

Wilby looked at me, apparently torn between annoyance and amusement. Ian started backing up. Wilby sighed again. "*Really*, Jane."

I floated higher and higher, giggling. "Can't catch me."

Without warning Wilby pushed himself into the air. I shrieked and 'ran' for it. He then turned and chased after Ian, catching him handily. Now that Ian was It I positioned myself behind Wilby who kept trying to shake me. Ian was edging closer and my battle with Wilby was messing with my maneuverability.

"Hey, Jane." Ian said softly. "Look who's watching."

There was a viewing window I hadn't noticed before and there, staring at us, was the General, expression suspiciously blank. I paused a second, floating, and Ian swooped in and tagged me.

"Bastard!" I protested as Ian cackled in merriment, Wilby chuckling as well. There was no time to worry about the General. This was War.

16:00 – Hallway outside Training Room 7, *P.S. Scylla*

Wilby, Ian and I walked down the corridor, heading out from our shuttle Bay romp. Ian was going back to the Command Deck, Wilby to another class, this one for Micros. I was pretty sure it was time to deal with Atalanta's problem. While my resolve to do it was unshaken, I was a little nervous about how bad it would be. Well, I thought, it doesn't matter does it? It is what it is.

Wilby waved goodbye as he peeled off down another hallway. I thought I saw someone standing in the doorway of one of the empty Training Rooms at the end of the hall. I scanned and realized that the man standing there was the General. A few steps later and Ian recognized him, too.

Ian looked away from his father to me. “Good luck,” he muttered as he, too, turned off the main hallway. I walked to the door of the room, but the General just stood there, as if arguing with himself about something. He read as calm and collected, which was bullshit. He still said nothing and I started to walk on.

“Jane, may I see you a minute?” His voice was professionally cool. The General’s voice.

“Of course, Sir.” I answered wondering what this was about. It was unfortunate that he had happened to see me with Ian again, innocent as it was. But then I thought, maybe it wasn’t unfortunate at all. Maybe a little unwarranted jealousy was a good idea for him. I felt myself getting pissed off. I also had to admit that I had read an awful lot into ‘Jane, may I see you a minute’ and that I actually had no idea what he would say to me.

I walked into the training room and the door shut behind us. The General reached for the door pad and locked it. It was pretty dark in there, just the standard work light on. Light or dark didn’t matter to me, of course. I knew exactly where he was. Even he couldn’t hide that.

He was very close to me now. I could smell that Samuel smell I loved. I could hear his breathing. It was faster than normal. Bit by bit I felt him releasing the projection so that I could really read him. I felt the certain type of tension in his body that I had learned meant he was angry. He was also very aroused.

My body was automatically responding, almost against my will. I mean, I wanted him (and more and more with every second) but what would it mean? It can’t mean forgiveness, I thought, or we would be at his place. I was confused, but also knew that it would only take a small push to not care.

“Samuel…” I started, but stopped when he kissed me hard. Without even thinking about it I surrendered to his touch, to his mouth. He pulled down my trousers and touched me. Dear god. I reached for his belt, but he grabbed my hands and put them over my head as he leaned me against a wall. He transferred my hands to one of his and unbuckled with the other. He was still angry, I realized. This wasn’t like Samuel. It was insanely hot, however.

Within a few seconds he had taken me, pushing my body hard against the wall. He kissed me again and again as he moved inside me. I came soon but he paid no attention. He was all urgency, no gentleness. He seemed to be using my body to exorcise his rage; this was not ‘making love’ though I was hardly going to quibble. I came again when he did.

He pulled me off the wall where he'd had me pinned and held me. We stood there a while. He seemed to be thinking of what to say as he caught his breath. Finally he spoke.

"Did I hurt you?"

I shook my head against his shoulder. It felt so good to be in his arms, even if it meant nothing. I wished I had any idea what he was thinking.

He stepped back from me, letting me go. I pulled myself back together, clothing-wise. He did the same.

"I'm sorry. I saw you…and couldn't control myself." He didn't look at me when he said this.

"You saw me with *Ian*, Samuel. That's why you couldn't." This jealousy thing needed to be out in the open and put to bed, no pun intended. And why not now when things were already a mess? At the name Ian Samuel looked up at me, crossing his arms on his chest protectively. I tried to drive home the point. "Ian is a friend, Samuel. He doesn't want me and I don't want him. I want you. Only you." Samuel nodded tensely and started for the door. I was fairly certain that he hadn't believed me.

But then my mind jumped to our early morning conversation and how much what he'd said bothered me. "Did you mean what you said this morning? About everything from now on being my fault?"

Now Samuel froze and, to his credit, looked deeply ashamed of himself. "No. This fight has been coming since Pace was destroyed. None of it is our fault, Jane."

"It was a really nasty thing to say." I tried very hard not to sound choked up when I said this, which I came pretty close to managing.

"I know." Samuel looked at the floor. "I haven't been myself lately." He was almost at the door now. He turned back as he keyed off the lock. "This," and by 'this' he meant angry exorcism sex, I guessed, "won't happen again." He went to leave when I spoke and stopped him.

"Bet your ass it won't." He stared at me in surprise. I continued, "We have to talk, Samuel. Right? *Talk*."

"I know we do," Samuel responded quietly, reluctantly.

"Ok then."

And he went out, leaving me in darkness.

<u>17:00 – Officer's Lounge, *P.S. Scylla*</u>

I'd put off visiting Atalanta long enough to eat. I'd brought my rations into the Lounge to enjoy the view. Not that I actually noticed the view at all as I ran over what had happened with Samuel in my mind. I sat down on one of the many window seats ringing the outside of the Lounge and tried to eat. At least zero-g had been fun.

"May I join you?" It was Ian. I sighed internally, but looked up with a smile. He was carrying his rations, too, and sat near me on the seat. "Good spot?"

"Sure."

He took a bite thoughtfully, swallowed and asked softly, "So, how's the General?"

I dusted off my hands of crumbs. "Fucked if I know, Ian." Just then Arrow appeared with her dinner. Ian made room for her on the seat. I mentally shook my head. All we needed was the General to complete the most fucked up family dynamic ever.

"How is Atalanta?" Arrow asked.

"I saw her this morning and it wasn't good." Arrow and Ian looked up in alarm. "But I'm going there right after this and Felix thinks things will start improving soon."

"Is there anything we can do?" Arrow was worried. Ian reached over and squeezed her hand reassuringly—the hand on the far side of her so no one could see it but me. Ian gazed at her with such love, such adoration. I suddenly felt very sad. I missed *my* Samuel (not the current angry mean Samuel) so much. Too much. I had to get out of there.

"Not right now, but I promise I will let you know if there is," I said as I rose hurriedly. I saw Arrow shoot Ian a worried glance, but he shook his head. I opened my mouth to say goodbye when a klaxon sounded. Battle stations. Ian was out of his seat in an instant, charging for the Command Center, Arrow and I right on his heels.

We quickly emerged onto the Command Deck which was frothing with activity. Marines flanked the room, weapons drawn. Staff officers spoke to each other just below yelling. Captain Ian was almost to his chair. Everyone was getting more and more hyped up, though it wasn't clear to me why. The sounds of talking were building.

"People!" Sound stopped. It was the General. Alert but calm. In control, projecting strength. "Status," he ordered as he walked towards the center of the room, towards Ian.

"Scanners indicate material change in movement capability in *P.S. Hastings* and *P.S. Trafalgar*, Sir." The middle-aged soldier's voice had steel-like precision.

"What change, Lieutenant?"

"They have activated their FTL Drives on both ships."

Ian looked quickly to his father who rubbed his face with his hand thoughtfully. "Where the hell are they going? Should we even *let* them go?"

The General gave his son a sly look out of the corner of his eye. "Time until they are able to jump?"

"Estimated 9 minutes until both ships have Faster Than Light capability."

The General was still standing next to Ian's chair, which Ian had vacated in favor of his father. Arrow and I took steps closer to hear what they were saying.

Ian was thinking out loud. "Well we figured they would need to do something since we seceded this morning. But they're not going to Earth. Not now." The General shook his head. "Because they've realized they don't really want to go there anyway."

"Right," the General agreed.

"Could they be heading off to start their new colony?" Ian asked skeptically. Arrow shook her head and the movement caught the attention of Ian and the General. Now *I* would have been embarrassed, but this was Arrow. The General raised his eyebrows, indicating that she should explain.

"No money. No colonists. No equipment." Arrow looked disgusted. "Even they aren't deluded enough to think they have enough of anything to start a new colony now." Personally I felt that the one thing the Scientists were never short on was delusion, but I figured she was probably right.

The General heaved a sigh. "What is the one thing that the Scientists have always made sure they've had?"

Ian grimaced, "You mean aside from everything?"

"Control," I said aloud without meaning to. The other three looked at me. The General looked away first, however, nodding.

"I think they're jumping out of system to prepare their counter attack. They want to have absolute control of where and, more importantly, *when* the fight takes place. We can be sure they have secret resources we know nothing about and we don't really know how hard they've been hit." He paused and the other two looked briefly at me, the one woman hit squad. "So we don't know when they'll be coming for us or what they'll be bringing with them when they do." He leaned in closer to Ian. "One of us needs to be on deck at all times." Ian agreed tensely.

"*Hastings'* FTL Drive active, Sir." We watched on the viewer as the *Hastings* moved suddenly then seemed to vanish. "*Trafalgar's* FTL Drive also active, General." The *Trafalgar* did the same.

Arrow stepped forward, staring at the clusters of smaller ships that were now so much more noticeable since the bigger ones were gone. "They abandoned all their sub light allies, Sir."

"At least they're running true to form," Ian observed wryly.

"We'll need to step up training," the General said, more to himself than to us. Then he looked seriously at Ian, then at me. "This is no time for play." He let his glare linger on me a little longer than it had to. Son of a bitch was still jealous.

I returned his gaze levelly, not backing down. He looked away first. Ian watched us curiously. "I'll take first watch."

The General nodded absently, clearly thinking. He turned again to the Lieutenant. "Ilene, get Sig on the line and route him to my Quarters. I'll be there in 5."

"Yes, General."

Ian gave his Dad an inquisitive look. The General looked thoughtful. "We need to repair the *Hephestus*. Just enough to make it space-worthy again." Ian nodded, instantly understanding.

Not so me and, I thought, Arrow didn't get it either. "Why?" Then both Armstrongs looked at me and I quailed a bit. "Sirs?"

The General gave a wry look to his son, who answered me. "Evac for as many non-combatants as we can manage. We'll also need a ship to lead the sub-lights away from the rest of us."

"To protect them," I said, not sure if I was making a statement or asking a question.

"That and to make sure they can't turn on us." Arrow finished. Both the General and Ian smiled at her proudly. It was weird how different those two smiles were, I thought.

"I think Sig will help." The General turned to his son. "See you in 8 hours." Ian nodded as the General left the Command Center.

Ian gave me a meaningful look and deposited himself in his chair. I had to go.

18:00 – Atalanta/Felix/Jane's Quarters, *P.S. Scylla*

I stood outside the door for a minute, gathering my courage. I took a deep breath and rang the entry bell. Felix let me in and we both walked over to Atalanta's bed. She looked even worse. Her skin was kind of grey and she was still breathing way too fast. She met my eyes as I sat down then looked away. Wasting no time Felix took one of my hands and we each took one of Atalanta's. Felix looked at me seriously.

"Just don't try to fight it. It won't do any good and it will make it worse for you. Trust me." I did trust him. I nodded, afraid but determined. Felix turned to his love and said, "Atalanta. It's time."

She closed her eyes.

Suddenly I wasn't myself. I was beautiful. I was sexy and my body moved like music. I was Atalanta. I felt fear grip me as I realized just how bad this connection was going to make future events, but I held true.

I walked down the corridor with Bayliss. I was on the *Hastings*, I realized belatedly. We paused in a side corridor and I pressed myself against him, kissing him and rubbing the front of his trousers. He was excited. I was surprised that I wasn't. Not at all. He pressed a button to open the door of the room we were in front of as he reached to fondle a breast. We moved inside and…nothing. Blackness.

I woke up with a stranger on top of me, fucking me, no, raping me. I could feel my actual self (Jane) screaming in protest. My Atalanta self struggled and cried. The first rapist ejaculated and pulled out. The second one hovered, naked from the waist down and erect. His expression was so ugly I felt my Jane self backing up on the bed. I sensed Felix's strong hand pulling me back. I watched in horror as the second man moved closer, as if mentally savoring the delights ahead. His face was contorted with lust/hatred. I/Jane screamed again.

He rammed into me. It hurt. Even more than the last one. I felt real tears coursing down my cheeks, matching Atalanta's remembered ones. The pain was awful. Why didn't we fight? Then I felt the shackles. I was bound hand and foot. The second one ejaculated, slapping me across the face as he did so. Then he got out of the way for the third. I/Jane was sobbing now. I felt like I would go mad.

The third one approached, his expression full of lust as well. But then I saw his face change, soften. The ugliness faded. He kissed me/Atalanta hard but not as hard. He thrust into me/her and I had to guess, started his version of 'love-making'. She had done it. Just like that she had made him love her. It hurt less, but it was still obscene.

The fourth loved her/me enough to caress and kiss me, not even penetrating. The fifth and sixth came over and petted me.

"Don't you want me to touch you?" I said purring. I don't know how she managed that tone, but she did. One of them nodded, then they all did. "I can't do it if I'm tied up like this. Could you help me?" I pulled myself up as far as I could and kissed the closest one. He responded eagerly and I pulled back, indicating my restraints with my/her beautiful eyes. He unbound my arms while another set my legs free. I/Jane would have run, but I/Atalanta didn't.

"I have a special place where we can be together. Somewhere I've never taken anyone. Would you like to come with me?" I looked at all of them one by one and one by one they all nodded. They stood up, mechanically putting their discarded clothes back on. I started to rise but fell back down. I looked up and the first rapist held out his hand to me. I hesitated, but took it and was able to stand. Oh, but it hurt. My face, my body, everything. I continued to hold his hand as we walked out into the corridor. All six of them crowded around me, protective.

Suddenly a soldier turned a corner ahead. Our little group didn't look right to him. "Hey. Stop!"

I turned to the first rapist. "He wants to hurt me. Help me, please!" I squeezed out some tears that weren't faked and the first man turned and charged the soldier who, surprised, killed him with his LPG. I looked at my other 'protectors' and all but one of them charged the soldier as well. He started shooting, but couldn't hit all of them. Two of my six died by LPG, three more stayed to beat the soldier to death. The sixth man grabbed my hand and followed me as I continued in the path I knew (as Jane) that led to the shuttle bay.

Behind us I heard booted footsteps and LPG fire. I assumed that the three left behind were now dead. I started walking faster. Turn, turn and turn. There was the familiar hallway to the shuttle bay. The doors were open to it. And there was Felix looking terrified.

There was a guard mid-way through the hallway. He was checking ID's. I held tighter to my rapist's hand. We walked up to the guard who frowned at us.

"What business do you have in the Shuttle Bay, Dr. Morrisey?" And his eyes moved up and down my form invasively. But then his frown faded and he smiled. I looked up at my rapist and kissed his hand.

"We have to go to her special place, Jeff." His look of adoration made my/Jane's skin crawl.

"All right. Go ahead," the guard waved us on through.

I walked, a bit unsteadily, down the corridor. Felix was waiting, every muscle tensed, for his moment to act. We reached Felix finally and I saw his face as he took in the wreck that I was. Now, I/Atalanta had to fight not to sob. Felix's suffering was painful to see. Then he looked at the man holding my hand. He quickly looked back at me. I nodded curtly.

The three of us walked into the shuttle bay, but only two of us got on the shuttle itself. Felix didn't even leave my side, but I knew the other was dead. Felix carefully led me up the ramp into the shuttle, retracting it as soon as we were fully inside. I heard him calling for clearance. I started walking towards my chair when I passed a shuttle wall that happened to be reflective. I stopped in horror as I saw what they'd done. Bruised jaw, torn dress, blood tracks down my legs. I/Jane wept for desecration of my friend. I/Atalanta finally sobbed and collapsed on the floor.

Felix was beside me in a second and I could feel his arms around me. I clung to him, wracked with sobs. I felt him pick me up and strap me in the chair. Then he left me to fly the shuttle. This seeming abandonment made me cry harder. The look on Felix's face would have broken anyone's heart.

"We have to get out of here, love. I won't leave you, but we have to get out of this place."

I nodded and looked away…

Suddenly I was Jane again, just for a second. I looked over at Felix, whose eyes were closed, his face wet. I turned to Atalanta and found her eyes open, staring at me. It may have been my imagination, but she didn't look as grey. Her lovely eyes were clear again and her breathing seemed normal.

"Thank you," she breathed softly. She started to say something else but the scene shifted and I wasn't on the *Scylla* anymore. I was at the School on Pace 4. I was Atalanta, but a perfect unmarred Atalanta. No, I was wrong. I wasn't inside Atalanta because I was looking at her. I was *Felix*. It was dark and Atalanta and I/Felix were in her dorm room. We were both undressed and our bodies were touching. This must have been before Atalanta and I were room-mates I/Jane thought idly.

She was kissing me. I/Felix was overwhelmed with love for her. I loved her so completely it was hard to breathe. I kissed her back with feigned passion. I touched her breasts, I touched everything. She was very aroused and clearly desperate to be with me. But as Felix I felt no sympathetic arousal. Nothing at all. Love, yes. Oceans of love, but no desire. I/Jane was so glad Bayliss was fucking dead.

I/Felix moved to her stomach, then lower, using his mouth to bring her to orgasm. It was very strange, though interesting, I had to admit, to be ah…part of that in such an intimate way. Atalanta came, gasping and shuddering. She pulled him back up her and rested her head on his chest. She was so happy. And I was happy to have done that for her, but there was nothing beyond that for me. As Jane my thought was that she was feeling that they'd overcome a hurdle and that things would be OK now. But I was Felix and I knew that no hurdle had been overcome.

She reached down to caress my member (also an interesting experience) but there was no response. She tried again, but there was still nothing. She looked up at me, cruel enlightenment dawning in her eyes. She sat up and started shaking her head with tiny almost convulsive shakes.

"That was all for me, wasn't it. Nothing for you. Nothing." She looked at me accusingly.

"All I want, love, is to make you happy." I felt the lump in my/Felix's throat.

"I know that, Felix." She got out of the bed and started putting her clothes on. "I know you are the most generous man in the world and I love you for it. But it can't all be about me." She looked over at me, still on the bed. "I can't be with you if it's all about me. I don't want that."

My eyes, both Felix's and mine, filled with tears…

And I was Jane once again. Neither Atalanta nor Felix would meet my eyes.

"You must think I'm the biggest bitch." Atalanta said softly. She looked at Felix but he wouldn't look at her either.

"I don't, 'Lanta. I was *there*." She looked over at me at that and nodded. Without warning the scene shifted yet again. I felt a knot of fear in my stomach as I guessed whose life we would be experiencing next. What would it be? I wondered. Then I knew. I felt momentary embarrassment, but I pushed it aside. Selfish of me to be worried about that now.

Then I realized I was on the *Scylla*, in the General's quarters. That morning he had made love to me so beautifully, so devastatingly. But I was me this time and I felt my body responding the way it did when it had happened. It was glorious and heartbreaking to feel him on top of me again, like it was all new. He touched me, moved inside me. But this time it was even more debilitating because I didn't know if he would ever be with me that way again.

Then I felt something unexpected. I felt Atalanta getting turned on by the experience. The General, Samuel, groaned as he came, bringing his lips close to mine. I kissed him with all the passion I had, but it was strange. I *felt* it. Felt the lips on mine. I opened my eyes and realized I was kissing Atalanta and she was kissing me back. Shocked I pulled back, blushing. What the fuck was that? I thought.

The bigger surprise was the lust, yes lust, on Felix's face. Atalanta turned away from me and reached for him. And he kissed her. It may have been *my* lust but it was *in* him. He pulled her to him, exploring her mouth hungrily. My god, I thought. Real passion for Felix after all this time. Unfortunately, my surprise, or my shock more like, was too distracting and the vision, or whatever it was, faded.

It was just the three of us on the bed, holding hands. We were as we had been before. I looked over at Atalanta who was weeping but smiling at the same time. Felix wore an expression of complete astonishment. He stared at me in wonder.

"I had no idea that that was what it felt like." I felt the lump in my throat return on his behalf. He kissed my hand before he let it go. "Thank you."

I nodded, too blown away to speak. Felix moved closer to Atalanta and held her, resting her head on his chest as he had done before. Atalanta snuggled closer to him and closed her eyes. It looked like she could sleep now. I couldn't imagine *how*, after all that, but she looked at peace.

I got up and faked a smile at them before leaving. I left them to wander the hallways aimlessly, trying to process whatever the hell had just happened. Trying to sort out all the emotions and all the consequences. If re-living her rape had been horrifying for *me*… I made a random turn and I remembered Samuel earlier asking if he'd hurt me. My poor Atalanta. I had to stop because I couldn't see.

ENTRY 8-2-14

Excerpt from Director Doyle Jacobi's Personal Journal, P.S. Hastings, *July 19, 2869*

Arrogant mutated bastards. Who the fuck do they think they are coming to my ship, destroying my samples (centuries of work!) and killing my Scientists. Scientists. *They seem to have conveniently forgotten that they have been bred, like cattle, to serve. Well, we have been bred to rule.*

I will take their goddamned DNA samples and I then I will blow every one of their goddamned mother fucking ships out of the sky. After all it's only the code that has value. We will create them again and better and their genetic successors will be kept in their place.

They will pay for what they have done. Oh, yes.

Fuck them all. They clearly have no fucking idea who they are fucking dealing with.

06:00 – Officer's Lounge, *P.S. Scylla*

I woke up at the usual time and for a second couldn't remember where I was. I opened my eyes and saw a large window showing the beauties of the Pace-Pallon system in glorious starry night. Ah, yes. I'd curled up in the most private of the booths in the Officer's Lounge. The booths ringed the room, carefully tucked into the side of an inner wall. They'd been designed that way for maximum privacy and I'd been pretty sure I'd heard someone using one of the other booths for an assignation during the night.

But I'd enjoyed disappearing into a secret place. The General's was clearly out of the question and I hadn't wanted to intrude upon my roommates. They would have thought that was silly, of course, but that was why I hadn't asked them. I'd slept only a little, my mind still going over and over the events of yesterday. In terms of having lived through Atalanta's rape, my revulsion on my own behalf had faded. A function of it having not really been my memory, I supposed. My distress on *her* behalf was almost as strong as it had been the day before. Only seeing Atalanta improving and being happy would help alleviate my horror and guilt.

But the thing that continued to keep me up, once I'd addressed these other more pressing concerns, was, selfishly, missing Samuel. I'd thought I would have been prepared to be without him. Intellectually I'd been ready. But I couldn't escape this pressure in my chest, this almost physical sadness. Could he be as upset as I? Or was he too overwhelmed with everything else to be much affected? He did, I had to allow out of fairness, have the prospect of an attack to deal with. And an evacuation. And training all of us to fight. Maybe I should cut him some slack, I thought. But I still missed him terribly. Rationalization only went so far.

I heard (and felt) people moving in the main part of the Lounge, probably preparing for the new day. I sighed. Time to get up.

07:00 – Command Center, *P.S. Scylla*

I passed through the Command Center, out of habit, on my way to Arrow's class. At this point my old goal of trying to catch a glimpse of the General was a source of ambivalence. I wanted to see him, but then again I didn't know if I would be able to bear it, separated as we were. Ah, fuck it. It was a short cut.

The General, I saw, was talking to Sig about something I couldn't hear. Both of them were tired and tense, though it seemed to be less noticeable on the giant Sig. They both nodded and Sig clapped the General on the shoulder and took off. The General stared into space for a second, deep in thought. He looked over suddenly and saw me watching him. His expression, which had been hard and focused, softened, his brown eyes sad. I wanted to go to him and was about to take a step in his direction when one of his staff spoke to him. His focus snapped back and the moment was gone.

I headed for the door on the far side of the room. I saw Ian talking with a soldier and he looked up as I passed. He finished whatever he'd been saying to the soldier and called after me. I stopped. Even Ian's usual smile was tense. I leaned in for confidentiality.

"What are Sig and the General up to today, Captain?"

"Sig's crew worked all first watch and the *Hephaestus* is almost ready for the refugees." I opened my eyes wide in surprise. Ian continued, "Sig says that Pacey-3's are always underestimated." He shrugged. "I'm as surprised as you are—actually more so because I knew exactly how badly damaged that ship had been."

"We're doing evac today?" That seemed so soon, but it probably wasn't. The Scientists could be back any second. A day could cost hundreds of lives.

Ian nodded. "Non-essentials, civilians and," his expression was one of distaste, "Objectors."

"You mean cowards," I said, bristling.

"That's unfair, Jane." Ian said, watching a nearby readout as he spoke. Then he looked at me, his face serious. "And, yes, that is exactly what I mean." He glanced in his father's direction. "Sig will assign one of his Captains to take the *Hephaestus* to a far corner of the system and lead all the sub light ships there as well."

I frowned. "*Sig* is assigning?"

Ian's jaw clenched for a second. "The General's initial choice refused to go."

I looked from Ian to the General and back again, exhaling in surprise as I did so. "He's got to stop trying to protect us like that."

Ian snorted. "Yeah, good luck convincing him."

"Right," I responded absently as I watched the General speak with his officers. Ian smiled to himself as he saw me do this.

"You should talk to him, Jane."

"I know, Ian." I never took my eyes off of the General. "But as painful as it is to be apart now, part of me wonders why we would even bother to try again. Even if he wanted to—and I don't know if he does."

Ian looked surprised. "What do you mean, why bother?"

Now I looked at Ian, suddenly concerned that he'd forgotten certain obstacles that were coming. "The Terrans, Ian. Everything has to change when they come. For Samuel, me and for you," and Arrow, I added in my head only. "There are things we can get away with as Paceys that Terrans will not understand." Like being in love with your half-sister. Or a senior commanding officer dating a subordinate who is nearly 4 decades younger than himself. I softened my voice for Ian's benefit, trying to keep my anger about the unfairness of this to myself. "You know that, don't you?"

He nodded, his expression looking choked.

God, I am such a bitch. Why am I always saying things to him that, while true, hurt him? I rested my hand on his sleeve and he turned his blue eyes on me. "I'm sorry. I get so freaked out about this coming…juggernaut, that I always seem to take it out on you in the guise of 'helping.' I'll stop." I felt terrible. But even so, I couldn't help feeling that he was trying to forget about the Terrans and what it would mean. Or worse, that he would refuse to give up his relationship when it came down to it. While Samuel's being with me would make him a joke, Ian's affair with Arrow would make him a pariah. I didn't want that for Ian. Or Arrow.

Ian sighed. "You're not wrong, Jane. And you haven't been, which makes it worse." He leaned against a console, crossing his arms over his chest. "Can't say you aren't a bit of drag at times, though."

I shook my head ruefully. "You're being generous."

"No, I'm not." Then I saw the corners of his mouth twitch into a smile. "And, speaking of truths, you know you suck at tag."

I took a step back outraged. "No way, Ian. You cheated!"

"You'll never prove it." His eyes twinkled at me. I swatted him on the arm. He laughed. "Hey, don't you have Arrow now?"

I looked up at the clock. Yes, I did. I waved and took off, leaving Ian still smiling behind me. At the last second I looked back as I turned the corner and saw the General's eyes following me out.

07:30 – Training Room (Arrow), *P.S. Scylla*

"Everyone take one of these, please, and put them on." Arrow held out her right arm which was covered with about a dozen white rings that looked to be the size of a small dinner plate. I looked more closely at Arrow herself and noticed that she had one around her neck. I took one and put it on cautiously. It was slightly thicker than a necklace and seemed to be made of a light metal that, once put on, conformed a bit to the skin around my neck. In the front was what looked like a button in a slightly darker metal.

I had no idea what these things were, but they were a lot more comfortable to wear than they looked. Not as comfortable as *not* wearing them of course, but, from Arrow's serious expression I was guessing that there wasn't going to be much choice.

All the rings were handed out and had been put on. Arrow stood in front of us.

"These 'rings' are to be worn at all times. They are pretty much anything proof. Even wear them in bed, if you can manage it. They are required, though, for all the time you are conscious. No exceptions."

"What are they?" Gladys asked.

Arrow smiled grimly. "They are state of the art automatic gas masks. Scientists made them for their own use. And there is nothing too good for the Scientists, as you all know."

Gladys started to speak but for once I beat her to it. "Gas masks, Arrow. How?"

Arrow had pulled out a small aerosol vial from her pocket. "This is a mild sedating gas. Nothing like what they will be throwing at us, but good enough for a demonstration."

She took a breath, then sprayed. The instant the gas left the container the mask/necklace expanded, immediately forming a seal starting at the bridge of her nose, down over her cheekbones, then down to where the necklace had originally just been touching the skin around her neck. The protective material that stretched from nose to collarbone (essentially) was almost clear and we could see her mouth move as she spoke. "The mask expands in half a second, completely filtering air intake. It will take out pretty much any toxin—but it does not *create* oxygen, so do not try to go into space with it. Instead of being a dead guy in space you will be a dead guy with a gas mask in space. Not a vast improvement."

"And the Scientists generously donated these because…" I asked, wanting the story. There had to be a story.

"These came to us from the cargo hold of the *Hephaestus*. Apparently some enterprising Marine had nicked cases and cases of these things during the evacuation from Pace. A Corporal found them weeks ago and his commander, realizing the need to protect everyone who was staying on the *Scylla* (Marines included) gave them to us this morning." Arrow gestured to the button on the front of her mask. "This button can either expand the mask manually or retract it," she pressed it and the mask became a necklace again.

"So the Scientists don't know we have these?" Gladys asked, trying to look at her own necklace mask by craning her neck.

"They don't. As far as we know," Arrow responded. She straightened up. "Now, I want you in two groups. Micros over to my left, Macros to my right." We quickly did as she had ordered, waiting for her direction. "We will start with drills without extra abilities, then move to drills with them. Ready?"

I nodded as did many of my classmates. And we got to work.

11:00 – Training Room (Mallory), *P.S. Scylla*

Two hours plus with Arrow had been exhausting but worth it. It was nice finally being allowed to fight with our talents. I'd managed to throw a couple of my peers into walls and be knocked around by them in turn. The thrashing had banged up my poor shoulder again, but that seemed to be the norm these days. Arrow was driving home the point of exploiting an enemy's weakness, though I wasn't sure how the Scientists would know about my bum shoulder unless Arrow had told them about it. I grimaced to myself. I bet she'd considered telling them just to prove a point.

Mallory was handing out shoulder holsters (for two weapons) to all 6 of us in her weapons class. This time we were all Macros (we're counting me as a Macro in this particular case). We dutifully put on our holsters and waited for the explanation.

Mallory moved to the front of the classroom and held up a medium sized gun. "You will be issued 2 weapons today that, like your gas masks, must now be on you at all times until this crisis is over." The gun was bulky and the metal that comprised it was almost translucent. Her face lit up with a wicked smile.

"This is a modified projectile weapon. It shoots bullets that have a hollow tip or point. These bullets will create maximum damage on impact." She looked at us seriously. "I must caution you that you will be firing this type of projectile on a ship. Most likely *our ship*. Puncturing an outer wall will be deadly for your assailants but also for you and your team." She placed the large weapon in her left holster.

The she picked up a smaller, much longer and more elegant gun. It was easily twice as long as the other and looked like it weighed a third as much. Mallory looked at it lovingly. I wondered if she had created it. Wouldn't have surprised me.

"This," Mallory indicated the second gun in her hand, "is, for all intents and purposes, a dart gun. It shoots small projectiles or darts with the strongest sedative we have. And why could this be a good thing?"

I looked around for Gladys, but remembered that she was a Micro and thus not here. I filled the vacuum. "Because it may be more important that we *stop* them rather than just kill them?"

Mallory smiled at me. "Right. Today we will practice with both weapons. Projectiles are something you will be able to manipulate. This is why after *much* discussion," and I guessed from the way she'd said that, the discussion had been a nightmare of arguing, "it was decided not to issue you Macros LPGs." Then, out of the blue, she grinned at us. "LPGs are the last refuge of the, shall we say, untalented." A few of us chuckled.

Mallory holstered the dart gun. "First we will work in here, then we will continue the lesson in zero g."

Ooh, now that was fun. Mallory handed out the projectile guns and we dutifully holstered those as well. She quickly put on some protective gloves. Next she held up the two projectiles themselves, one in each gloved hand. She kept the larger of the two higher in the air first.

"This is an old-fashioned hollow point bullet. The hollow point allows the bullet to expand once it hits soft tissue or flesh, creating much more damage than a traditional bullet of the same size would be able to. These bullets will generally stop within a body and not pass through and out the other side. This only applies to flesh or similar material. These bullets will not expand and stop if they are fired into, say, walls or a ship's hull."

Mallory looked at us all very seriously. "Now I am not saying that our hull is so paper-thin that one bullet would blow it out, but if enough of you are careless we could be in a lot of trouble. So be extra fucking careful, right?" Her use of the swear word (the first I'd ever heard her use) drove the message home, I thought. I wondered how long she'd been saving it.

Mallory continued. "This bullet has also been coated with a neurotoxin that will paralyze and kill. This bullet is used only to kill. Do not shoot it unless you intend your target to die."

We all nodded. She raised her other gloved hand. In it was a small, thin dart-like bullet. It was a medium brown metal and looked very light, as if it were made of wood. "This is a dart with a sedative originally developed for surgery on horses. It hits hard and very fast. It buys you two hours from the time of each hit. It doesn't mean that you won't have to kill the person that you've shot with this dart, but it does buy you time to figure out what to do." She looked closely at the little dart, smiling, and I got the impression that this was her pride and joy.

"The dart gun has been calibrated to shoot in bursts—3 darts at a time. Just be careful that you aren't pressing the trigger convulsively. You will blow through your darts faster than you can imagine. Each of you will be given three extra clips of darts, but you've fewer darts than you think. Be careful with them."

Garrett spoke up now. "What happens if we hit our target multiple times, you know, in the heat of the moment?"

Mallory shrugged. "This is, unfortunately, very likely given the dangers we anticipate facing and the huge amounts of adrenaline involved. Doc Wells figures that a normal-sized human male could survive 5 darts and a female could handle 4. Your two hour window becomes much longer, however, and we weren't able to determine how much longer."

"And if we hit more than those 5 or 4 times?" I asked.

"Then your target will be so sedated that they will 'forget' to breathe." Mallory put the two bullets on her table and pulled off her gloves. "All right, then. Let's suit up."

12:00 – Shuttle Bay, *P.S. Scylla*

The 7 of us (including Mallory) walked into the shuttle bay. We were still suited up and armed, gas masks around our necks. All this gear was cumbersome, but I couldn't fault any of it. We all looked like sexless robots, true, but I, personally, did feel safer wearing all the shit.

Over time my aim with the LPG had greatly improved (which also meant my aim in general was vastly better) once I'd given up trying to mess with the pulse to control it. It had turned out that I wasn't such a bad shot when forced to do it the old-fashioned way. You know, by *looking* and *aiming*. In today's lesson the bullets had been pretty easy for me. We had practiced with bullets before and my targeting with them was pretty great, if I did say so myself. The other Macros had found the bullets problematic, unfortunately. They were just on the border of being too small. They actually were too small for one of the Macros and she had returned to aiming and shooting. No messing. The nice thing was, though, that these were still decent weapons even if you couldn't manipulate them.

But if the bullets were a bit of a problem, at least they had had some small amount of weight, some heft. The darts, however, were impossible. They were tiny and weighed almost nothing. Even Garrett (the cheater in racing) had had almost no luck with them. He had come up with the rather clever (I admitted grudgingly) idea of shooting a bunch of them and then massing them together as a group. This gave them sufficient mass for Macro control. Unfortunately, this also made them lethal, which defeated the whole purpose of the dart. Mallory had suggested that he stick with controlling bullets, which he was pretty good at, and firing the darts the way a normal would. This suggestion, which was a disguised order, had not gone over well with Garrett, but no one had cared about that but him.

My experience with the darts had been altogether different. I was only now starting to realize how lucky I had been to be blessed, if that was the right word, with both Micro and Macro abilities. It was right where the two overlapped that lay the skill to manipulate the darts. I wasn't perfect at it by any means. I am, apparently, not a natural at weapons. Shocking, I know, but true. But I did fine. At least I could *do* it. I just needed practice, but I was getting the sense from all the training we were being force fed, that I wasn't going to get it. I had felt the tension in Arrow earlier and I felt it again in Mallory. They were pros and didn't let it get to them, but it was definitely there.

The far door opened and in walked Felix. My face immediately broke into a huge grin. I scanned him as he walked towards us. He wasn't so thin, his color was good. His tension level was the same as Mallory's and Arrow's, which I took as a good sign. He caught my eye and smirked at me, knowing I was scanning him. I chuckled silently. It was so good to have him back.

"Welcome, kids, to zero g part 2. I am looking forward to seeing how much of Wilby's teaching you absorbed yesterday, though he told me that the Macros did very well." Then he grinned. "Much less vomit than the Micros." We smiled back at him. Yeah, we vomited less! I guess you always need something to be proud of.

Felix waved to the attendant in the viewing booth. "Today we will start with manipulating the projectiles in zero g. Now projectiles have consistency within a gravity environment and they have consistency within a non-gravity environment. These two environments are vastly different from each other however."

Where was Gladys? Why do I have to do all the work? I asked, "How are the LPG's affected?"

Felix nodded, pleased by the question. "Negligibly. Their targeting and pulse don't depend on gravity, being energy based. You'd feel a difference if you fired one, but most people adapt very quickly."

The Klaxon sounded and we all started lifting off the ground. It was a marvelous feeling. Like swimming but with the ability to breathe. Like fish.

Felix floated skillfully in front of us holding the projectile gun. "The main difference between firing in a gravity environment and this one is the difference in the bullet's arc. With gravity the bullet travels straight at first, then falls until it eventually strikes the ground (unless it hits something in the meantime). What should happen with no gravity?"

"Since there is no gravity to pull it down a bullet should travel in a straight line indefinitely." I responded, mostly just thinking aloud.

Felix smiled at me. "Correct. And there's a difference between our zero g, which has oxygen so that we can breathe, and what is out there in space. Actually there are a bunch of differences, but for our purposes: your projectile weapon must have oxygen to allow combustion so that you can fire. No oxygen and your projectile gun is useless." He checked the gun, making sure it was loaded. “The nice thing is that your range can be infinite, especially if you are firing at a fixed target. The danger is that in a fight like this there tend to be arms in play that belong to no one. Depending on how far-ranging your battle is you can get hit by a bullet that was fired 10 minutes ago by someone on your own side. You must keep your sense of objects tightly honed for this or you will get hurt.”

The far entry door opened and in swam Wilby.

Felix acknowledged Wilby's entry with a smile. "Another thing to think about. There are no dead bullets when bullets are treated with chemicals. The toxin on the hollow point bullets is just as deadly on a spent bullet. Same for the darts. Our attackers' bullets, assuming they have moved beyond LPGs, may have the same dangers, so you must be careful of those as well." He looked at us at seriously. "Imagine how stupid you will feel, or, to be more accurate, your team will feel when you survive the actual battle and then die because you touched a bullet."

I found myself unconsciously nodding agreement. Yep, pretty stupid. Pretty dead, too.

Felix pushed himself over to a compartment and pulled out three guns, pushing one over to Mallory and floating another to Wilby. He then pulled out two large...blast shields, I guessed. He pushed one to Mallory and picked another one for Wilby who snorted and arrogantly waved it away. Felix shrugged and pushed it back into the compartment. "For today's purposes we are sticking to our old friends the hard wax bullets." I had to admit I was very happy about this and, judging from the smiles of relief I was seeing around me, I wasn't the only one. "In two sizes." I saw Garrett's face fall. Still too small for him. I knew it was technically beneath me to crow over his distress, but the bastard cheated at racing. He deserved what he got.

"So..." Felix gestured and Mallory and Wilby moved themselves to apparently predetermined spots within the shuttle bay. "Start at one end and try to make it through to the other. Carry your gear and your weapons, but keep them holstered for now.” We started maneuvering ourselves to the far end of the enormous bay. "And remember, kids, know where the hell everything is. Lose track of what is in the air and you've lost."

We were in line now. I was third. I felt the adrenaline pumping and my hands started to shake. If I could get the feel of this, I knew I had a decent chance of running the gauntlet successfully. I took a deep breath and grounded myself, first on the ship, then on the bay itself. I sensed clearly the human bodies in the room, their trajectories, no matter how small, and the gentle, almost undetectable flow from the air circulators. I felt the whip-like precision of Mallory checking her weapon's magazine for the wax bullets, the focus that cut through Wilby's feigned indifference as he did the same. Felix was between them, more relaxed than anyone in the room. He made being both relaxed and completely ready for anything seem possible. Mallory had set up her blast shield to one side, within easy reach.

"Weapons ready." Felix said quietly, voice carrying easily. He looked at Mallory, who nodded, then Wilby who did the same. "Ten second burst on my mark."

Felix looked over at us. "Macros, go." We hesitated. He meant all of us at once? We looked askance at him and he raised his eyebrows, indicating that our asses should already be out there. No one moved. Well fuck that, I thought. I'm not going to miss playing in zero g. I pushed off the wall and into the line of fire. Others belatedly started to follow.

"Fire." Felix said calmly. Suddenly the air was full of projectiles. Some had already passed my position by the time I got there, but most seemed to be coming right at me. The first wax bullet was coming at my head and I ducked instinctively. Suddenly I felt Felix's blood pressure spike. I took that to mean that he wanted to yell at me for missing something obvious. Right. *Telespatial.*

The onslaught of bullets was almost upon me and I quickly swept my arm in front of me, sweeping all the bullets away from me...and into my fellow Macros. I heard the cries of outrage as they were all hit, hit forcefully by the wax bullets—*hard* wax bullets. I'd made it easily through the line, of course. I'd taken out my entire team to do it. I snuck a look at Felix, who was rubbing his forehead with his hand. Mallory was shaking her head slightly, but Wilby was (silently) laughing his ass off.

Fuck. I'd done it again.

Soon everyone was through and sort of clustered on the other side of the course. Not clustered near me, of course. Well, I thought, through my own self-annoyance, at least my survival instinct is still intact.

Felix floated in front of us. He looked pained, which seemed completely appropriate. "Let's try that again. And this time we'll try not to take out our own people before the bad guys do." Felix finally looked up at me.

"Sorry," I said pathetically. I looked over at my team-mates, who were all covered with splatter marks from the hard wax bullets I'd so generously sent their way. Their expressions were hard. Garrett looked like he would happily throttle me. Oh, good, I thought. Now I can defend myself from the bullets *and* my team mates.

Felix gestured us back into line and Mallory and Wilby got back into position as well. My 'friends' had pushed me to the back. They wanted to have more bullets to throw at me, I guessed. Well, I may have fucked up, I thought, but I had no intention of letting them shit on me if they tried anything.

"Ten seconds on my mark." I heard Felix's calm voice say. I regrounded myself, sensing everything that moved in the space. Felix seemed about as calm as ever, but Wilby seemed to be …energized? Was that what anticipation looked like? Interesting.

"Fire." The room was starting to fill with both sizes of wax bullets. We all pushed our way into the onslaught. A bunch of the darts were heading my way. I checked the position of my compatriots then simply pushed the darts below me so that they missed both me and my fellows by a comfortable margin. It was then I got hit in the chest with about 35 of the larger wax bullets. My head snapped around to see my "team-mates" pushing everything they could at me. Felix looked pissed, but was saying nothing. Wilby, however, was watching me like he'd bet on me in a sporting event. I saw all this in a flash and actually processed it much later.

What I did was something else. I saw the other 5 Macros looking back over their shoulders as they approached the end of the course. I 'reached' for every single bullet (either live or spent) in the room. Once I had them I brought them into the center of the space, swirling them once violently like tornado. I then shot *all* the bullets at my team-mates, super-fast. I was deliberately going for speed and the effect was rather frightening. Wilby told me later that it had looked like a swarm of angry hornets. I heard the collective intake of breath as the bullets charged them.

I waited until they were about 6 inches from the faces of my victims and then I stopped them. And this time I didn't move a muscle (no raised hand, no nothing)—so they'd had no warning the bullets were going to stop *at all*. The bullets and darts obediently fanned out around the clustered, terrified Macros and hovered, perfectly in place. I waited until I had seen fear in all their faces, especially Garrett's, then I deftly gathered them in a bunch and lowered them down, never breaking eye contact.

Everyone took a breath. The Macros separated from each other and no one said anything. Wilby had a big shit-eating grin on his face.

Felix looked torn between amusement and disgust at my theatrics and had started to say something when the entry door opened. We all turned and saw a dozen Marines enter in perfect formation, through the zero g. I wondered *how*, since they were Pacey-normals, and then I saw that they were wearing…jet packs. Cool.

Felix flicked me a look but said, "May I introduce Colonel Aleph Gold and the Third Squad of the First Battalion of the Pace-Pallon Independent Marines, here for our second drill."

The Macros, myself included, moved to the side to let the Marines and their Colonel have center stage. Wilby caught up to me as I floated, still keeping an eye on my fellows. He moved himself closer and said in a low voice, "*So* much more fun when it's happening to someone else." The he winked at me and floated over by Mallory. Would wonders never cease.

Colonel Aleph Gold (whom I now remembered from that big meeting the General had given when the Marines had first joined us) floated confidently in front of us (the Macros and teachers) with his Marines floating imposingly behind him. "This is an experiment in what Felix has termed 'large object movement and enhancement.' My Marines are experienced at fighting in zero g and are really fucking good at it." The Marines behind him all smiled cockily. "We have been used as a force and as an effective weapon for as long as there have been Marines at Pace. Felix thinks that Macros can turn Marines into weapons of even greater power, plus add an element of surprise to the enemy that they so badly deserve." And here the Colonel's grin matched that of his men. He glanced over at Felix who continued the introduction.

"The goal of this exercise is to enhance the abilities of the Marines. While I think it is a given that we Macros have an advantage in, shall we say, unusual talents," he smirked at us and we smirked right back, "I think is also fair to say that the Marines are by far our superiors in terms of training and experience in actual combat. I am hoping that we can combine these two advantages to our mutual benefit."

Colonel Gold called out, "Sergeant Lee!" And my old bodyguard swam forward. Still a very physically impressive specimen, I thought. Wonder if he still liked us as much after Felix had drugged and stuffed him in a closet (or something like it) while our little mission to the *Hastings* had gone down. I assumed that Felix had covered his tracks so well that the Sergeant had no idea who had done that to him. Mostly because Felix was still alive.

Felix pushed himself up next to Sergeant Lee. George.

Colonel Gold did something with the controller in his right hand and lowered to stand on the floor. He looked up at his Marine. "Deactivate Jet Pack, Sergeant!" George pressed a button on his remote and tucked it efficiently in a pocket. I could tell he was starting to drift a bit now that he wasn't under power.

"You all will probably be very comfortable, given the average size and mass of a Marine, moving them around. That is the good news." Felix looked at us seriously. "But while all of us will allow for some errors in training, that being part of what training is for, you need to remember that you are moving *people* and need to act accordingly."

"People who are a lot bigger than you are," added Wilby, who gave a knowing look the Sergeant George who pretended not to notice. I sighed. *Really*, Wilby. You want to pick on a former conquest now?

Felix caught George's eye and George nodded. I felt Felix re-ground himself and then George started to move. George himself was holding still, statue still, but still he moved and fast. Felix moved him quickly all the way to the back of the enormous shuttle bay, then brought him back to us impossibly fast. George's face was impassive (I suspected years of training in not looking terrified were coming into play) but his body read in a full blown panic. He got about halfway to us when the Colonel yelled out to him.

"Present arms!" George's gun was out in a flash. "Aim!" And suddenly we were facing a large, speeding man pointing a loaded gun at us. All the Macros, myself included, automatically moved back as he zoomed towards us. Then Felix held up his hand and George stopped on a dime exactly where he'd started. The Colonel smiled. "Stand down, Sergeant." George put his gun at his side. I could see a slight tremor in his hands, but other than that he might have been made of steel. Outwardly, anyway.

Felix grinned at us all. "I think you can see the psychological advantage of this sort of thing. Throwing one of us," he indicated the Macros, "at an enemy could be scary, but throwing a fully armed Marine like Sergeant Lee here would be absolutely terrifying." Felix smiled at George, effectively dismissing him. George switched his jet pack back on and floated back to his own people, clearly relieved to be done with the demonstration. "We split up the work by doing the moving for him. If I have control of his movements, the Sergeant can fully focus on targeting. Also, I can get him places unfavorable to jet packs, like tight spaces or anywhere in Engineering (remember that). And while jet packs are *virtually* silent, a human under Macro guidance *is* silent. All of these things can be an advantage under the proper circumstances."

While Felix was speaking, I'd been eyeing the jet packs covetously. I raised my hand and Felix indicated that I should speak.

"Will our normals be issued jet packs, Sir?" I was thinking of Arrow and Ian, Atalanta and Samuel and many others.

Felix looked over to Colonel Gold who responded, "We have some spares but not enough for everyone. We are starting with officers and key personnel and then we'll go down the ranks until we run out. I have people distributing them now."

I smiled, relieved. "Thank you, Sir."

Felix's eyes swept over the Macros. "Who wants to try first?" Garrett's and my hands shot up. Felix nodded to Garrett, giving me a look that might have been a recommendation not to show off in his class again.

Garrett stepped forward. The Colonel called out, "Sergeant Bellefleur!" and a very tough looking woman Marine stepped forward.

And we all got to work.

We all exited the Shuttle Bay about 2 hours later. The Marines marched out first, then most of the Macros and Mallory, then Felix, Wilby and I. I'd hung back to check in with Felix since I hadn't spoken to him since the Tap yesterday, but though he gave me a welcoming smile it was clear he was all business. He caught Wilby's eye.

"Briefing," Felix said tersely. Wilby nodded. They started off in the direction of, I assumed, the conference rooms when Felix stopped, realizing that I was not following. He looked at me and beckoned with a head jerk. I hesitated, surprised. He shrugged. “You’ve been requested.” He didn’t need to tell me by whom when he said it like that. I followed.

So the General had asked for me to attend a briefing. On what? There was so much crap going on it was hard to know who was telling who what.

“So today you’re going to get an update on the *tapetia mortis*. Remember them?” It was less than ten minutes later and the General’s voice was dry and almost amused. Almost. Thing was, I’d personally been so distracted that I *had* forgotten about them. And that is one of oh so many reasons I am glad he is the General and I am not.

The General was standing at the front of the small conference room. The rest of us—and there were about 20 of us including Ian and Sig, who seemed to take up the space of several people—sat around the conference table. The General radiated calm and purpose, which meant he was projecting for all of us. I was grateful that I couldn’t read him. Too painful.

The General pressed a button on the conference table and the screen on the wall lit up with a simulation. It was one of the ‘hives’ on Pace 4. But it looked like the creatures were moving in slow motion this time. Felix raised his hand to speak, but the General merely nodded and spoke himself.

“As you can see the creatures have slowed down considerably. It has become more and more noticeable over the last few days. If our ‘preparation for re-launch’ theory is correct it means they are getting closer to being able to do it.”

We all took a second to digest that unpleasant concept. The General smiled grimly at us and our discomfiture. “Since we have seceded we have eliminated the need to get consensus, at least with our Scientist brethren,” and he said that word the same way one would say ‘turd,’ “to figure how to act, or even if we are going to act at all.” He took a deep breath. “While this has simplified things, it hasn’t actually created a clear plan of action.” He looked pointedly at Sig who spoke without leaving his chair.

“We have a couple of options.” Sig’s voice was like gravel compared to the General’s rich tones, but there was no lessening of his authority. He just had that quality, I guessed, that leaders have. Was that just born in you? Then I forced myself to focus like a good girl. “One is that we ask the Terrans for help when they come. They are bound to have much more firepower than we could ever have. They also have actual scientific officers who may have better ideas for how to deal with the threat.” Sig didn’t look too thrilled with this option, however, as he continued, “The problem is that we are putting ourselves under Terran protection which means that…”

“...we have to go along with whatever they decide,” I finished, thinking out loud as usual. Most of the heads turned when they heard my quiet voice finish the thought. I felt my cheeks turn pink, but I didn’t look away. "So if they decide to leave the *tapetia mortis* as someone else's problem and we don't want to, we're screwed. Right?"

Sig smiled at me, showing many of his jagged teeth. "Right." He leaned on one of the arm rests of his chair. "I think it is safe to assume that we give control over most everything once we accept Terran help. Now this may be acceptable to everyone here." His eyes searched the faces in the room. "Or it may not." Sig leaned back in his chair. "Or we can try to take care of it ourselves before they get here." Sig's implication seemed to be that Pacey affairs weren't any of the Terran's business anyway. I quite agreed with him.

Sig continued. "Unfortunately, as we've seen from earlier tests, we don't have enough nukes to take all of the hives out. And," and he caught the General's eye, who nodded, "our targeting is probably not good enough to destroy all the 'pods' of creatures as they try to leave the system." The simulation changed, showing the new Objects shooting into space and collecting into clumps as they gathered speed to leave the system. Sig drew a breath to continue when someone spoke.

"Excuse me?" All eyes, including mine, turned to the sound of the voice. It was Felix, looking thoughtful. Sig gestured for Felix to continue. "Why not have Macros 'throw' the pods into the sun?"

There was silence. Stunned silence. "But those pods have to be *massive*," Ian protested apparently struck by the sheer audacity of that concept.

"You can *do* that?" Sig asked, shocked.

Felix was watching the pod on the simulation carefully. "Jane and I could do it, I think."

I looked sharply at Felix and…everyone else looked sharply at me. I would follow Felix anywhere, but I wasn't thrilled at being volunteered for something I was pretty fucking sure I couldn't do. The General was the only one looking at Felix and deliberately not looking at me.

Felix turned his attention from the simulation to me. "Mass is irrelevant, Jane. You know that." I could tell he really wanted me on board, but I really didn't want to say I could do something I couldn't do. Not when I could screw it up for others. It was just too fucking big. I couldn't even conceive of grasping it mentally, let alone *moving* it. I said nothing. Now I felt the General's eyes on me, but I kept mine on Felix. Felix wilted a bit when I didn't respond. "But I don't have enough of the right caliber Macros to take care of all of them, even with Jane, especially if you count all four planets." He sat back in his chair.

I caught Ian moving his eyes from Felix to me and back again as if we had suddenly sprouted horns. Yes, dear boy, we aren't just freaks, we're super-crazy-freaks!

The General interjected thoughtfully. "We'll talk about this option again, Felix. There may be applications even if we don't have the personnel to handle the whole thing that way."

Felix nodded gratefully.

Sig moved on. "There are several Pacey-3's who have suggested tractoring asteroids for planetary impact." Several at the table looked up in horror. Sig lifted a large hand to forestall their protests. "Even though there wouldn't be the fall-out that would come with the nuclear solution, the debris would make the planets uninhabitable in our lifetimes and the lifetimes of generations to come."

A staffer spoke up, "But it would kill the *tapetia*?"

Sig looked grim. "It would kill everything." Sig sighed heavily. "And there is a last idea, from some of my miners." He gestured for the General to do something. The General changed the simulation and we were now looking at Pace 3.

"Fracture Pace 3 to the point of destruction (or near enough)." The simulation showed Pace 3 rocked by several explosions and breaking into 4 large pieces, one of which flew away, the other 3 kind of hovering together awkwardly. "If we damage, sorry, *break* Pace 3 badly enough to fundamentally change its shape the orbits of the other planets will be radically affected, thus wiping out all life on all 3 remaining planets."

"And you can do *that*?" Felix asked, the words surprisingly devoid of anything but awe and, I thought, fear.

Sig looked at him, his face unreadable. "Possibly."

The General took a moment to let us take in all that had been said. "This is a lot to take in. Please think over what's been said here. Any ideas are appreciated. And it goes without saying that anything said in these briefings is classified. Dismissed." People got up to leave and filed towards the door.

The General turned off the simulation then looked at Felix. "Felix, take Jane and Wilby on another flyby tomorrow, if there's time, and scan a hive to check it against the simulations. Take Sig while you're at it. Man has entirely too much time on his hands these days."

Sig gave the General a dirty look, which the General returned cheerfully. Sig shook his head as he lumbered out. Wilby and Felix had artfully made sure that the General and I would be the last ones to leave and so we were suddenly alone. I didn't know if that would be a good thing or a bad thing. My stomach was in knots either way. He didn't look too comfortable either.

"Sorry about sending you to scan those things. I know you hate it, but I need your input." He sounded like he was trying to be extra professional.

"Glad to be of use." I said meaninglessly. I just wanted to get out. I had finally made my way around the chairs and was at the door. I reached out my hand to key it open when his voice stopped me.

"Jane?" I turned around. That had almost been Samuel's voice.

"Why didn't you like Felix's idea?"

"You mean the idea of taking something as large, conceivably, as the *Scylla* and trying to throw it into the sun with my *mind*? What's not to like?" Since we were alone, I didn't bother to mask the sarcasm.

The General snorted. "Felix thinks the two of you could do it. In my experience, Felix is rarely, if ever, wrong."

I shrugged. "He isn't. And I trust him with my life, but...but that is *impossible*."

His face clouded, his flicker of amusement erased. "'Impossible' didn't stop you before."

I took a step back, recoiling at his flash of anger. He quickly keyed open the door. Not quickly, guiltily, I thought, and he left. And so the rage continues.

18:00 – Shuttle Bay, *P.S. Scylla*

I'd already grabbed my dinner rations and was passing by the door to the Shuttle Bay when I saw people just standing around. No, they weren't just standing around. They were in line to get off the *Scylla*. Ah, yes, the refugees going to the *Hephaestus*.

Suddenly curious, I quickly slipped into the Shuttle Bay. The line stretched all around the huge space. I found myself shocked that there were so many people evacuating. A couple hundred, easy, I thought. I saw Ian off to the side, checking the memo board he was carrying. Even though they were loading onto our largest shuttle, it was clear that there were too many people to all fit in in one trip. Ian walked up behind a small group of people, clearly a family, and stuck his arm between them and the next person in line.

"Everyone after this, please move to the hallway. You will be on the next shuttle out." There were some groans but Ian was unflappable. "Please move to the hallway now." Ian turned to me and the temporarily rejected refugees started filing out. He looked incredibly bored. "Fun stuff," Ian said dryly.

"Looks like," I responded. I was searching the faces of the remaining people in line as they slowly started filing onto the shuttle. I dropped my voice. "So who are the non-combatants and who are the cowards?"

He scanned the people, too as they moved by. "Hard to tell. Cowards tend to look just like everybody else."

I sighed. "Until they don't."

"Right," he agreed. There didn't seem to be any more to see or to say, so I gave him a friendly pat on the arm and took off, leaving him to his drudgery.

I was still surprised that so many people were leaving. While I knew that some of them, most of them actually, had been *ordered* to go for their own protection, that's not what it felt like to me. It felt like rats deserting a sinking ship. I had a strong sense of foreboding just then. I tried not to credit it, since Arrow was the pre-cog and not me, but I still found the feeling unnerving.

I did my best to shake it off and move on.

18:10 – Officer's Lounge, *P.S. Scylla*

I wandered in to the Lounge carrying my dinner rations. I had decided that I liked this room since it had sheltered me through the night. It seemed more my space than my other two recent homes aboard ship, since it belonged to no one in particular. And it followed that if it belonged to no one in particular it couldn't not be mine. Or something like that. I headed to one of the booths and spied Atalanta sitting in the big one in front. She looked up and smiled as she saw me so I went to her.

She looked better, much better. She looked like she had just gotten over being ill, rather than looking like she was actually dying. Her hair was drawn back and she was what I would have called 'comfortably covered' from head to toe. I supposed it was as close to turning off her beauty as she could get without actually wearing a disguise. It didn't really work, of course, but it sent the signal to let her alone unless invited, which I was. I sat next to her in the window seat.

"You look better," I said smiling.

She smiled back. Not a big smile but it seemed genuine all the same. "I'm doing well. I can process it now, thanks to you and Felix." Atalanta reached over and squeezed my hand. "Thanks." She looked out the window at the stars. "Sorry it was so awful."

Awful, yes, but it was also other things that made me feel a bit awkward. "It was certainly more…intimate than I had expected." I blushed. Fuck, I have got to figure out how to control that.

Then I saw a mischievous twinkle in Atalanta's beautiful eye. "Never gone down on a girl before, Jane?"

Only Atalanta would think it was *funny* to remind me that I'd been 'inside' Felix (in his memory) when he'd done just that to her, I thought as I turned beet red. I put my hands to my cheeks involuntarily. Like fire. Atalanta chuckled. She continued her torturing, "And that was a hell of a kiss you gave me. The General is a lucky man."

Dear god. Shameless, she was. "You know that if there is a hell, you're going there when you die, simply for teasing me like this."

Now she laughed. I had to admit I was glad she could laugh. Wasn't so thrilled she was laughing at *me*, but whatever.

She simmered down a bit and gave me an apologetic look. "I'm sorry, but I had to joke about it." She bit her lip, thinking. "You and I seem to be linked somehow. Your inborn barrier to being scanned or 'read' by MEmps hasn't applied with me for a long time. I don't know why. But I think you and I have more intimate knowledge of each other's lives than most friends. I want you to be Ok with it."

"Are you Ok with it?"

She shrugged. "I have to be. Being a MEmp means being assaulted by very personal feelings all the time. Sometimes it's useful but most times it's just intrusive."

"I don't want to be a problem for you, 'Lanta."

"You're not." Now she looked away, as if embarrassed herself. "Women don't like me, generally." I didn't know what to say to that since I hadn't liked her either for almost the first two years I'd known her. I didn't want to make her feel bad but I didn't want to lie either. She gave a sad smile at my guilty silence. "I know I've made myself easy to dislike. It was easier than trying to convince potential girlfriends that I didn't want to fuck their boyfriends."

I raised my eyebrows at this. "And did you fuck their boyfriends?"

Atalanta smirked a bit. "Not at first."

I shook my head in wonder. Not that I doubted her for a second. If anyone could get anyone to drop their pants (male or female) it would be Atalanta. Well, and Wilby.

Atalanta hesitated for a second, then asked delicately, "Why did you give me a chance, Jane?"

I answered immediately, patently relieved that there was a question I could answer that didn't make me uncomfortable. Rare for this conversation. "Felix."

She laughed to herself. "Of course. Felix."

"He told me not to confuse being a bitch with being evil." I watched her face to see how she took that less than gallant statement.

Her big brown eyes opened wide with astonishment, then she dissolved into silent laughter. I had to laugh, too. After a minute she pulled herself back together and became semi-serious again.

"I think, Jane, that our friendship is always going to come with this…knowledge of each other that most friends don't share. I wanted to joke about some of the funnier things that happened to let you know that it is all right with me. But *is* it all right with you?"

I thought for a second, even though I knew my answer. I liked being her friend. I'd never had a close female friend before. Or a close friend period before Atalanta and Felix had adopted me. I knew we were closer than most, but, except for a few uncomfortable moments, I found it reassuring. I smiled at her. "It's all right with me."

She exhaled, relieved and happier. We each took a bite of our dinner.

Atalanta looked at me slyly. "By the way, your old man has some *moves*."

I almost choked on my chicken. She continued, "Those extra decades of experience have really paid off. That man knows what he's doing."

"Leaving now." I was already up, gathering up my rations.

"Some good quality lovin' there, Jane," Atalanta called after me.

"Going to hell," I called over my shoulder. I heard her laugh as I got out of there. And this, I thought wryly, is my best friend. Sheesh.

<u>11:00 – The General's Quarters, *P.S. Scylla*</u>

I'd stationed myself outside the General's door leaning against the wall. I had no idea when he would, or if he would, be home, but I was all right with waiting. I'd closed my eyes relying on scanning alone to figure out travelers through the hallway. This served two purposes: one, it gave me practice identifying people by their body signatures and two, it pretty much assured that no one would bother me. I had no interest in having to either smile at or ignore every single person that passed in front of his quarters. I'd been waiting almost two hours when I felt a signature so familiar that I found my heart racing before I'd said his name in my mind.

"I didn't change the door code, Jane." Samuel said his voice rich and sad.

"I know," and I did. I'd checked earlier, desperately looking for some kind of sign that he didn't hate me. It had been nice to find he hadn't changed it, but I hadn't been able to draw any deeper conclusions. "I didn't know if I'd be intruding."

He sighed, his shoulders slumping. "No." He keyed open the door. "After you."

I went in warily. Most days I had no interest in being an Empath, but this was not one of those times. I felt I was walking into an ambush. He probably felt the same.

I hung back just inside the entry and he walked over to the desk, dropping his jacket as he did so. Samuel looked beat, not surprising considering the threat hanging over our heads. "I'm only supposed to be gone long enough to shower and change, so I'll start."

He turned around and leaned against the desk, folding his arms on his chest. "So you got the idea from my story about the needle grenades." He gave a hint of a wry smile.

"I did."

"So this is my fault, basically."

"No. I made a choice as did Felix and Atalanta."

"And Wilby and Arrow and Ian." Samuel's mouth was a flat line of disapproval.

"Ian found out accidentally at the end right before we left. We tried to keep him out of it."

"Why, exactly?"

"I thought you'd have enough people you cared about disobeying you and I wanted you to have Ian when everything went down. Especially if things went wrong."

A shadow of pain crossed his face at the reminder that things could have gone very badly indeed. "And you would call what you organized and did 'disobeying' me?"

"No, Sir. I would call it a betrayal of trust."

He stopped leaning against the desk and started pacing. "You know when you are in the real world and have an actual boss, you would be in deep shit for what you did, for the risks you took..."

I cut him off, enraged that he would take refuge in career advice when he should be yelling at me. "Why the fuck would I care about that now, Samuel?" He stopped pacing in shock at my sudden anger. "What is wrong with you? Why aren't you screaming at me for being stupid and irresponsible. For getting Atalanta hurt and for putting Felix in danger. For putting myself in a position where you might have had to rescue me, putting *more* people in danger. It was an insane move." I advanced on him, so frustrated and guilty. I wanted a response. Punishment. Something. "Why aren't you raging at me?"

He said nothing for a full minute. "I've been nothing *but* angry. I was so furious with you the night you were brought back I only saw you when you were still unconscious. And I was mean to you in the morning. And then when we were...together yesterday, I was still so mad."

I'd known it. I hated that I'd done this to him. I asked, "Are you now?" fully aware that I deserved every bit of his fury. For scaring him and, worse, for making him helpless while he was afraid.

"I don't know. I can't tell what I feel anymore." He looked over at me, his brown eyes so sad. "I know why you did it."

"Do you?" I challenged him. I was suddenly, selfishly, desperate to make sure he knew why. To make him say it. I suddenly had the image of a dog bringing home a goose it had caught to its master. I shook my head to dispel the thought.

"To protect your friends and this ship and..." he stopped.

"And?" I prompted.

"Me." He said it very quietly, as if embarrassed. "Why for me?"

"You are the only leader we have who wants to protect the supers, Samuel. Everyone knows that. I convinced the others on that argument, almost that *sentence* alone."

"And that was your only reason." He looked into my eyes searchingly. "I mean *your* reason, Jane."

I had to stop and think for a second. My reason was just a ball of emotion, fear and love, in my head. If it was almost incoherent to me, how on earth would I translate it for him? Then I re-ran his questions in my mind. Why him? Why him *personally*, was what he meant. Did he really think he was only worth something as a leader, but not as a man? Now I was annoyed at him, but on his own behalf (which seemed more than a little nuts, but I rolled with the contradiction).

He needed reassurance, then fine. "You are *mine,* Samuel, whether or not we are together or whether you even want me anymore, and there was no way in hell I was going to let them hurt you, no matter what I had to do or personally sacrifice." I leaned forward for emphasis. "*No matter what I had to do*." I put all the passion I felt into the words. They sounded melodramatic to my ears but they were perfectly true.

Samuel's face had flushed a bit as I spoke. He seemed to be at a loss. He rested his chin on his hand as he considered saying something. He finally spoke, looking everywhere in the room but at me. "I kept going over and over what you'd done in my head. I thought I was going to lose my mind when I realized you were gone and what you were trying to do." His expression was bleak. "I couldn't bear the thought of losing you, especially not that way."

So he'd rather lose me by dumping me later, I thought sadly.

"But," he continued, still looking elsewhere, "I kept coming back to the same thought, once you were back safe. No matter how insane this plan was and how dangerous the execution of it proved to be," he looked at his shoes, "I can't believe anyone risking all that just for me."

I looked up in surprise. He had to be kidding. How could he really not know how wonderful he was? "I would do it all again and more to keep you alive and safe."

I saw his jaw muscles working. He was trying to stay unemotional, but I read his body and I knew he wasn't. It was nice that he wasn't projecting at all and was letting me see everything. Samuel spoke again. "Even though you obviously assumed I would leave you because of it. That's why you'd said goodbye to me that way the morning you left."

I nodded. "I knew you would leave me, yes. But it didn't affect my decision. You have to be alive to hate me." Then I glared at him fiercely. "And don't try to make me promise never to do something that stupid again. I won't, Samuel. I just won't." He looked a bit taken aback by the vehemence of my response and said nothing.

We stayed in silence for a bit. Samuel was clearly pondering something. He cocked his head to the side and regarded me.

"Jane, do you love me?" he asked quietly.

I felt dizzy as my universe seemed to heave under my feet. My vision blacked out for a second as my mind struggled to process his question. Of all the ways I'd thought of this conversation going I'd never, ever thought he would ask me that. Not so baldly.

And you don't ask that question unless you know the answer, I thought as my mind continued to reel. I fell a half-step back, leaning hard against the wall. He rose from the desk as if to help me but I waved him away. What the fuck do you say to the question you want to hear least in the whole world? And the thing that made it so sad was that in the end love didn't matter. Not if the Terrans could take it, take *him*, away just like that.

"Why?" It was all I could think of to say and I was pretty sure that he wasn't expecting this response. I was right.

He blinked at me a second uncomprehendingly. "Because I..."

This time I had to interrupt him more forcefully. "It doesn't matter, does it?"

"Of course it matters."

I could feel emotions, mostly anger and loss, building up in my chest and the tears (the fucking tears) behind my eyes threatening to spill over. "I will give you everything I have, Samuel. I *have* given you everything, but I won't give you that. Not the words. Not if you're going to leave me behind when the Terrans come. I keep that. If only that."

Samuel leaned back on the desk, understanding dawning on his face.

I continued. "So don't say anything unless you mean us to stay together. To me those words are a promise of sorts." I laughed at myself humorlessly. "I have this stupid idea that it will hurt less when you go if the words are never said."

"Even if you feel it."

I looked at him defiantly. "*Especially* if I feel it."

He nodded to himself as if confirming his own comprehension. "Should I send you away now? Would that be better?"

Now the tears spilled down my cheeks. "Not for me."

He pushed himself off the desk and walked over to me, arms outstretched. "Not for me either, Baby." I let out a small sob, too overcome to move. He crossed the rest of the distance and folded me in his arms. I clung to him, pressing my head against his chest, feeling his heartbeat.

"God, I've missed you." he said softly as he kissed the top of my head. I couldn't answer, I just pulled him closer.

He then held me at arm's length and looked at me as I wiped my tears away with my sleeve. "So all I have to do to keep you is say the words?"

I looked up at him in hopeful horror. "You can't, Samuel. What about your future command? What about being the joker with the teenaged girlfriend? You're telling me you weren't right about all that?"

"No," he admitted. "I still think those will be problems. But I can't lose you again."

"But Samuel..." I started to pull away from him but he held on.

"I love you, Jane." Samuel gently cradled my face in his hands, peering deep into my eyes. "Don't leave me. I *love* you."

I searched his face, not daring to believe it. But he smiled and kissed me. I didn't respond for a second, my mind telling me that this was a dream or a trick or something. But it wasn't. He loved me. And he wanted me to stay.

All the fear, all the worry I'd carried around since we'd first made love here in this room evaporated. Finally, there was only joy. I kissed him back savoring everything that was mine and, incredibly, *ours*.

"I love you, too." I whispered. "I love you so much it hurts."

"Baby," Samuel whispered back. He buried his face in my shoulder and exhaled deeply as if the weight of the world had been lifted.

ENTRY 9-2-15

06:00 – The General's Quarters, *P.S. Scylla*, July 20, 2869

We hadn't talked much and had slept a little. For now everything seemed to have been said. We'd made love some and beautifully and sleeping in the safety of his strong arms had been bliss itself. Of all the happiness Samuel had brought me, this was the most powerful. I dreaded the alarm and the start of an uncertain day, but still treasured this warmth; this hard fought moment of joy.

My mind ran on well-worn tracks as I rested against his chest. I gave an involuntary sigh and then froze, afraid I'd disturbed him.

"Baby?" Samuel asked softly into my neck.

"Sorry," I whispered.

"What are you thinking about?" He turned on his back, shifting me with him effortlessly, bringing my head onto his chest.

"I was feeling a bit guilty."

"About being happy?"

I looked at him in surprise. Samuel shrugged. "You, *we*, survived and millions of us didn't. If Ian hadn't come for us we wouldn't have either. It's natural to feel badly about that."

I sat up a little and leaned against him. "But it's more than that, Samuel. Everything changed for me when the *tapetia* landed in the Quad. Our world is gone and our people devoured, but I have, I don't know, more things to be personally grateful for than I ever did before."

He looked at me with a half-smile. "Like what?"

"Like *friends*. Like Atalanta, whom I couldn't stand before all this, and Felix, Ian, Arrow and even Wilby." And I pulled myself closer to him, my face in front of his. "And you, Samuel. You most of all." I gently caressed his rough cheek with my fingers.

Samuel brushed the hair out of my face. "A crisis focuses things, like an LPG to the head does. Things can become much clearer very quickly."

"I think you wouldn't have liked me without that certain deadly threat hanging over your head," I said, part teasing, part truthfully.

"I always liked you, Jane. It took the end of the world to make me realize how much." And he kissed me.

07:00 – Shuttle Bay, *P.S. Scylla*

We were meeting early to train and it was a very select group this time: Felix, Arrow and me. Ian was there also, but I had the feeling that he had merely tagged along. Felix looked tired, not unwell, but like he'd already had a very long day. His shoulders were hunched as if good posture had become too much effort. I sidled up to him.

"Are you all right?"

"I'm at hour 36 of a 24 hour project for the General." His smile was wry and he didn't look unhappy, but he did look exhausted. He rubbed his eyes and took a breath.

"Anything I can help with, Felix?" I asked, but he smiled as he squeezed my hand, shaking his head.

Time for business, then, apparently, because Felix immediately stepped in from of us. "In light of the General's order that supers be paired with normals and since Arrow's super abilities aren't as technically useful as weapons in a fight, I thought I would try to exploit the Jane/Arrow pairing the best I could."

"Jane and Arrow," Ian repeated. "Not Arrow and *you*," he said to Felix. Then Ian looked at me, embarrassed a little. "Sorry, Jane, no offence."

I shrugged. "I'd pick Felix over me, too."

Felix gave me a look as if annoyed at my lack of self-confidence. It wasn't that. I had confidence enough. Felix was just better. It didn't bother me as long as he was around to *be* better.

Ian watched Arrow who was loading the practice guns with the hard wax bullets. I could tell she was listening, but had nothing to new to contribute. She had added a side holster to the two shoulder ones. The side holster held her LPG and the shoulder ones carried the two projectile weapons we'd been training with. She also had the body armor, jet pack, the gas mask necklace and a helmet. She could have disappeared under the weight and heft of that crap, but the fierceness of her eyes made her intimidating despite the fact that she was only a half inch taller than Felix.

Felix sighed. "The General made the assignments." So, I thought, the General wants me to protect his daughter. Of course I would, but geez. No fucking pressure. "And," Felix continued, "I've been assigned other duties."

All three of us, even Arrow, looked up at that one. Felix stared back at us with affected innocence. It was clear that he wasn't going to tell us shit. Disappointed, Arrow went back to her methodical weapons check.

Felix pulled a man-shaped dummy out of one of the compartments in the Bay and set it out in the center of the deck. He tossed Ian a projectile weapon (hollow point style) and a blast shield. He pointed to a spot on the floor and Ian walked over to it, checking his weapon for the wax bullets as Arrow had done.

Felix stood in front of Arrow and motioned me over. "Let's keep it simple for this first try. You," and he meant me, "will deflect incoming fire, get Arrow into the air, then direct to target." He looked at Arrow and smiled. "And I don't need to tell you what to do." Arrow gave a tiny head shake in agreement. I was, as always, impressed with her focus. She was absorbing everything around her but her focus never wavered. Felix waved his hand to get the attention of the solider in the viewing booth.

"And remember also, hitting helmets and armor does us no good. We need flesh. Face and neck will be best." Felix started walking towards the side of the Bay, past Ian. "Rip off helmets or goggles. We can't count on any of these people being stupid enough to touch a spent bullet later and die from it."

The klaxon sounded and we all rose in the air.

"Ian, begin firing," Felix ordered and Ian did so. He was a very good shot and managed to hit Arrow in the chest before I could do anything. Arrow glared back at me.

"Sorry." I had to protect myself *and* Arrow. Right. Ian kept firing, but now I had it. I didn't raise a hand or even make a movement, I just thought the bullets in a different direction. At the target dummy.

Arrow, tired of waiting for me to do something, started firing at Ian, forcing him to duck behind his blast shield. I felt darts coming at me from behind. Felix was firing now in bursts, the tiny darts spewing out at us. I diverted the stream of darts from Arrow and me…into Ian who moved his shield just in time to avoid being splattered.

"Jane! Use me!" Arrow hissed.

Belatedly, I lifted Arrow up as she continued to fire at Ian while I also kept diverting darts to Ian. Arrow flew through the air at tremendous speed. Ian looked up at her, distracted for just a moment and I yanked away his shield. Arrow pretended to shoot him in the face and he raised his hands in surrender.

Felix was still firing. I let the bullets swim by us, allowing the still elevated Arrow to keep firing. I moved her behind Felix while I stayed in front. I wanted Felix concentrating on Arrow. I knew he was too much of a pro to forget about me, but I still wanted his attention more on her. I was collecting his darts and Arrow's bullets. I was keeping them kind of spread out so that their mass wouldn't give them away, but knew it was only a matter of time.

Arrow could see what I was doing and kept firing, doing her best to keep Felix occupied. Then I'd saved one bullet too many and his head whipped around in time to see 100 bullets and darts racing for his face. He put out a hand to stop them, and I quickly flipped Arrow over and down almost flat on the ground, her gun barrel now under his chin. Felix raised both hands in surrender and all the bullets (since neither Felix nor I cared about them anymore) floated off aimlessly. Felix was sweating and breathing fast, but he grinned.

I marveled at how Arrow had made that move look very graceful and planned, and sexy, despite the fact that there had been no plan, just improvisation. But I wasn't the only one who had noticed the sexiness in Arrow's fighting. Ian's handsome face had a look on it for Arrow that made me glad Felix didn't know about their blood relationship. The look Arrow gave him in return made me *really* glad. Did they not know that Felix could see this?

Felix, however, kept his smile. He thinks this is cute, I thought. And it would be…with different people entirely.

"Good, now let's try it again." And Felix moved himself over to me, happy for his friends, but his smile faltered when he saw my face and the ambivalence there. He floated closer. "What's wrong?" he asked softly. Ian jetted over to Arrow to talk to her. Felix looked from me to Ian and Arrow and frowned.

"Nothing," I said quietly. Felix's face registered surprise. I shook my head, lest he think I was jealous. "It's not what you think." Felix, bless him, did not push, but still looked puzzled.

Felix raised his voice again, still watching me, "Original positions, please."

And we did it again and better.

<u>08:50 – Training Room (Wilby), *P.S. Scylla*</u>

I arrived for Wilby a few minutes early to find the room already in use. Two men were fighting, well, sparring would be the right word, I supposed. One was Wilby and the other was, surprisingly, the General. I knew they were fighting in some kind of a martial art style, but I had no idea what it was. I'd never been one for the 'fighting arts' unlike Arrow or Felix. It was a lapse in my education that Arrow had been trying to correct for as long as I'd known her, but I just didn't like all the work involved.

But I was curious to see the men fight so settled myself in a chair in the corner to watch.

Wilby made a fist and punched for the General's gut, but the General blocked him easily with his forearm, then used that same arm to twist Wilby's away from his body. Wilby, clearly expecting this, switched his weight to his other leg and brought his other fist into the General's side. Contact. The General made no sound or movement to indicate that he'd been hit, but it had to have hurt. He then swept one leg under Wilby's, knocking him down. Wilby landed on the floor, but was up again almost immediately, spinning a roundhouse kick for the General's solar plexus. The General moved out of the way, barely, and grabbed Wilby's foot as it went by, twisting it and forcing Wilby down again. But the General held onto Wilby's foot too long and Wilby pushed himself up off the matt and kicked the General down to the ground onto his back.

I gasped (internally, not to distract anyone), but the General was up again before Wilby could press his advantage. They circled each other warily. (This particular fight I figured out much later was the genesis of my lifelong, shall we say, *appreciation* for watching men fight. Does it for me every time. And it was doing it for me now.)

Then suddenly Wilby moved, the General countered and one of his powerful arms was at Wilby's throat. They held position for a few seconds then relaxed. My man had won the point. They separated, breathing hard, only now showing that that had been serious effort for both of them. The General picked up two towels from a nearby table and tossed one to Wilby. He wiped his face with the one he'd kept.

"Four out of five?" The General said as he caught his breath.

"Next time, Sir. I have a class in a couple of minutes." Wilby looked at me out of the corner of his eye slyly. "Hello, Jane."

"Morning, Sirs," I said as I got up and walked over to them, but Wilby walked away from the General and towards the door.

"I'll be back in ten." Wilby smirked and then was gone. That seemed odd only for a second then I realized that the bastard had scanned me and knew I was…excited by the fighting. How fucking embarrassing. Oh well. I kept walking towards Samuel.

"So, you fight, Sir?"

He briefly rubbed the towel on his face again. "Yep." His eyes twinkled at me.

I was right in front of him now. "You want to fight me?"

Samuel gave me a playfully challenging look. "Show me what you got."

What I had was nothing, fighting-wise. This he knew, of course, since Arrow had reported to him my general hopelessness. I considered trying to throw a punch, just to amuse him (because it would) but changed my mind.

I walked up to him and stood on tip-toes, wrapping my arms around his neck. My mouth was inches from his when I said, "Defend yourself, Baby."

"Yes, Ma'am," he said, smiling, then kissed me deeply. This was not something I wanted to stop doing, but reality would soon be intruding. He broke the kiss and hugged me for a second. "Class."

I nodded, separating myself from him. "Cla—"

Suddenly the Klaxon sounded—the one for Battle Stations. The General quickly grabbed the armor and weapons he had taken off to fight and we both headed for the Command Center. I helped him get dressed as we went and we arrived to find the Center a sea of activity. It seemed that everyone was moving, running with purpose to some task they had to perform, except for the Marines who stood like lethal statues around the perimeter of the room. Theirs was a contained energy, like a coiled serpent, in the midst of the movement of staffers and students.

The female Lieutenant, Ilene Something, looked up at the General's entrance. Ian and Arrow arrived right on our heels. Atalanta was already there. Sig looked up from one of the screens he'd been reading. He met the General's eyes and nodded, then stood up, waiting expectantly.

"Status," the General ordered. I backed up to stand near my friends and found myself next to Wilby who was, I could tell from the way he was convulsively flexing his fingers, trying not to crack his knuckles.

"Two contacts, General." The lieutenant frowned. "The *Hastings* and *Trafalgar*. One on either side of us."

They're back, I thought. My stomach knotted with tension. Even though I'd known, we'd all known, that it had only been a matter of time, I was scared and, judging by the strained faces around me, I wasn't the only one.

The General, however, was calm. And I think he actually *was* calm, not just projecting it. I was impressed and a bit jealous. Maybe I'd be able to do that someday. Maybe.

"Get me Felix," the General said to his comm officer.

"Sir?" Felix's amplified voice came across the speakers.

"Screen is in position?" Wilby looked at me for an explanation. I had to shrug my ignorance.

"Yes, Sir." Felix sounded confident. Whether or not it was feigned, and it probably wasn't, I felt better.

"Stay in position and wait for my orders."

"Yes, General."

"Armstrong clear." The General turned to his comm officer yet again. "Get Captain DeStephani on the line."

The mention of Captain DeStephani's name wrought a shocking change in Wilby, who stood up ramrod straight, as if he'd been electrocuted. Atalanta's head whipped towards Wilby and she looked as surprised as he did. What the hell just happened, I wondered.

This time the comm call was visual, though why I didn't know. A man, the Pacey 3 Captain Sig had assigned, appeared on one of the screens over the General's head. Now I was watching Wilby, too, though it appeared that Wilby was oblivious. Oblivious to anything but the face on that screen. He was a large man, as all Pacey-3's tended to be, and not bad looking in an extremely rugged super-masculine way. Aside from sheer mass and obvious physical strength he seemed fairly ordinary except for his eyes, which were unexpectedly green and piercing. It seemed silly to 'feel' intelligence only through eyes, but I felt it, or saw it, rather.

"Captain DeStephani here." The Captain's voice was lighter than I had expected. But, given his appearance it would have had to be. In my mind the voice that fit that body would have sounded like an erupting volcano. But that voice had turned Wilby's face white as death. I shot a look to Atalanta whose eyes were huge with surprise and, I could see, worry. No, I could *feel* worry. She was sending her feelings. How? She wasn't making *me* feel worry, it was *her* worry… Belatedly I realized she was telling me what to do. I gently took Wilby's hand. He looked at me as if he'd forgotten my very existence and tried to politely disengage from me, but I held on.

Sig smiled at the Captain. "Nunzio! I'm sure you know we've got company."

Captain DeStephani smiled. "Yes, Boss." The sound of the Captain's first name seemed to make Wilby even more upset and his hand spasmed in mine. I stepped closer to him, both of my hands now holding his one.

"So, go ahead and give your report to my friend the General, here." Sig waved his attention to the General who didn't seem to mind the informality but wasn't going to go there himself.

The Captain straightened up a bit as if sensing he needed to for the General's benefit. "The sub light fleet is in position, General." I noticed that he had not mentioned exactly where the fleet was, but I was sure that the people who needed to know that already did.

"And you know what to do if things go South for us here?" The General's expression was grim.

"Disappear." The Captain's expression mirrored the General's for a second, but his face became the picture of the resolute. "As long as these are my people, Sir, they'll get through." Somehow I believed him. Wilby's eyes were closed and his hand was trembling between mine. Atalanta was looking very alarmed and I was wondering what the fuck this was. I'd never even contemplated Wilby being this upset.

"Thank you, Captain." The General's control never wavered. "We'll see you after."

Sig's bonhomie became serious, too. "Godspeed, Nunzio."

"Godspeed, Boss. General." I took one more look into those clear green eyes. There was someone really interesting in there, I thought. Interesting to Wilby, though?

Sig and the General both nodded mechanically. "Armstrong clear." And the connection went dark. Sig and the General bent their heads together to confer, but I had a more pressing concern. Atalanta bore down on us and between the two of us we were able to pull Wilby aside.

His eyes were open. He took in the worried expressions on Atalanta's and my faces and came as close to blushing as I'd ever seen him. He pulled his hand out of mine more forcefully than he had before.

"Wilby?" I asked quietly.

"I'm fine," he came close to snarling. He's embarrassed, I thought. I glanced at Atalanta who had reached the same conclusion. We'd seen him weak. Brought to his knees by…something. *Someone*, I corrected myself. He needs to be left alone. I took a respectful step away from him and Atalanta did the same. I saw Wilby take a deep breath and try to calm his heart rate, but his hands still shook. I pretended not to notice, which was silly, of course, since he knew I could read him. But I pretended nonetheless. I couldn't think of anything else to do.

"Shuttle launch! Multiple shuttle launch!" The Lieutenant said urgently.

Now all eyes were back to the screens and the General. "Ship of origin, Lieutenant."

"*Hastings*, Sir. Two assault shuttles, *Fisher* Class."

"Estimated arrival, Ilene."

"Estimated arrival 13 minutes, General." The Lieutenant betrayed no emotion, even in her voice.

"Colonel Gold." The General raised his voice, but did not take his eyes off the screens. The screens that now showed two small red dots moving slowly towards our much larger blue footprint.

Colonel Gold had, apparently, been standing in the threshold of the Command Center. I hadn't noticed him, most of us hadn't, I guessed, but all his Marines had. All of them watched him, waiting for orders. "General," Colonel Gold answered forcefully.

The red dots were getting much closer to the large blue thing that represented the *Scylla*. The General stopped whatever it was he had been going to say, holding up a hand as a gesture to wait.

"External camera's, port side, Arbrogast. On the main screen." The General barked.

"Yes, Sir." Whoever Arbrogast was pressed some buttons and suddenly we were looking out of the port side of the ship through…what? Instead of seeing clean clear space like I was used to when I looked out the windows in the Lounge, I saw what looked like debris at semi-regular intervals around the ship. Or around as much of it as this view would let us see.

The General took a quick look around, noting our puzzlement. "Debris screen, kids."

So that had been the huge project Felix had been working on. And, from the conspiratorial smile the General gave his son, I guessed that Ian had been in on it, too.

The assault shuttles were getting closer, close enough that they had become small dots on the main screen in real time. I tried to read the General, but it was futile. But I *saw* him holding his breath. Why? The shuttles moved closer and closer. Now they looked like shuttles, albeit very tiny ones. They were getting closer to the debris field. He shook his head quickly, as if in frustration.

"Focus cameras on debris field at 100x magnification." The General had had to breathe to speak, but held his breath again once he was done. The camera zoomed in closer and now we could all make out the space trash and the shuttles coming at it.

And suddenly, effortlessly, the debris shifted, some up, some to the side, making a nice large hole for the shuttles to fly through. The General exhaled and looked at Sig who nodded ever so slightly.

"They have supers," the General said quietly, but in a voice that we all heard.

For a split second the words seemed to mean nothing to me, then the implications came crashing in. Fucking Scientist supers?!? How fucked were we now? I looked at Atalanta, who seemed to be having similar thoughts, but then from her I saw Ian nodding to Arrow who didn't look at all surprised. So everyone had guessed but me? And Atalanta? I looked up at Wilby who seemed to have recovered from his personal shock just in time for this greater one. He hadn't guessed either. Well, I didn't feel as much like an idiot, but I still felt we were all fucked.

"Al." Colonel Gold looked up. "Defensive Plan Beta." Colonel Gold nodded.

"Beta, yes, Sir." He turned to his Marines. "Defensive Plan Beta. Scramble!" His voice was harsh and loud, but the energy and the speed with which his Marines left for their positions was somehow comforting. You know, in a 'we're still all gonna die' kind of way.

"Supers, to your positions!" The General looked us over as we started to move, though not with the well-trained sense of purpose of the Marines. "Take care of your partners…" and he looked at me though the strength of his voice didn't change, "…and Godspeed." I nodded and ran for Arrow. Arrow gave Ian a heartfelt glance as he disappeared out the Command Center door.

"Where is he going?" I asked Arrow.

"Engineering. Protecting the FTL generator and power plant," Arrow responded as we started moving towards our assigned positions. We were almost to the door, Atalanta close behind me when I heard the General again.

"Atalanta. With me."

Atalanta stopped in her tracks and I stopped with her. She turned back in shock and consternation to look at the General. He caught her eyes and jerked his head in his direction. It was an order. I felt (because she sent it to me) her frustration at being kept behind. I tried to conceal my relief but she felt it and Atalanta's annoyance was now directed at me, too. I gave her a look of apology but she ignored it and started for the General.

"Felix got me out of the way," she muttered to herself. Now she was hopping mad. I sympathized, never having been happy being 'protected' either.

"Jane!" Arrow hissed, calling me to order. I took one last look at Atalanta and followed Arrow out of the room.

Within about 2 minutes we were stationed in the main corridor from the exterior Bays (Shuttle, Loading, Cargo, Auxilliarys, etc.). We were behind a line of Marines, led by Colonel Gold himself. I wished Felix was there. Out of the corner of my eye I saw Wilby at the far end of the hallway with his partner, a woman I didn't know.

"Jane," Arrow whispered, "What's going on out there?"

I grounded myself quickly, on the ship, then on the hallway for good measure. I extended myself into the Bays. I felt the assault shuttles outside of…the Loading Bay. One of the shuttles was backing up a little, then the other backed up, too. Why would they do that unless…

"Incoming!" I screamed, "Loading Bay!"

I said it before I felt the small missile released, but…there it was.

Overhead the address system roared, "Single Missile Launch! Take cover!"

Arrow and I huddled down as the ship rocked with the explosion. I looked up to try and assess the damage in the hallway and found I couldn't see it. The Marines had assumed crash positions that had covered the supers like human shields. I looked up into the face of a young Corporal, whose body shook as a piece of debris hit him in the back. He saw my face full of worry and grinned.

"Hell of a way to make a living, right Ma'am?"

In spite of myself I grinned back at him. Then my head whipped to the Loading Bay door.

I could feel the exterior Loading Bay doors fly out into space. One of the shuttles moved quickly in and landed. I felt the other shuttle move away and…I lost it. Fuck. Then I felt the pressure in the bay change…they had put up some kind of screen?? A barrier to keep the vacuum out? Then I felt people debark from the shuttle and into the Bay, heading for the door. The door to us.

I felt heat. Like welding torches. And where was that other shuttle going?

"They're at the door!" I yelled, making no effort to keep the fear out of my voice.

As one, everyone, super and Marine alike stood up and turned to the Loading Bay door. We aimed. I could tell the door was hanging on its track by a thread, but then our attackers paused.

I looked at Arrow in confusion. Why pause now? Arrow shrugged unhappily. She was right. A pause now couldn't be good.

The address system came on again, "Pulse weapon fire incom—" and the ship rocked again with another explosion.

And then we all started to float.

Arrow looked as close to panicked as I'd ever seen her. "They've hit the Generators, which means they sent that pulse into Engineering…" Her eyes were wide with fear for Ian.

I started to respond, when the interior Loading Bay door blew open.

The Marines (and their jet packs) moved forward and fanned out, some moving higher. I quickly fired my regular gun 6 times into the air, stopping each bullet as I did so, creating a cluster of bullets. The first attacker stepped through and everyone opened fire. But I hesitated in dismay as he fell and more attackers came out. They were Marines, too. They looked just like *our* Marines. I glanced up at the Corporal who had just protected me, but, other than a tightly clenched jaw, he didn't show an obvious signs of surprise. He'd known, and I was pretty sure they'd all known who was coming.

But, I wailed in my head, how were we supposed to tell them apart? Well, Jane, my inner voice said, if they're shooting at you, they probably aren't friendlies. My inner voice could be such a sarcastic bitch sometimes.

Suddenly there was a large blast and we were all knocked into the inner corridor wall. I looked up and found that most of the outer wall had been blown out to let more of the enemy in faster. The hallway became ablaze with LPG fire, bullets and darts (though I suppose the projectiles didn't really blaze all that much). I re-separated and 'threw' my bullets into the faces of the attackers. I pushed myself up in the zero-g to get a better view and found myself looking down at a sea of helmets.

"Arrow!" I shouted over the noise. "Up here!"

Arrow jetted herself up.

I pointed at the helmeted men. "I'll rip, you shoot, yes?"

Arrow nodded and I started ripping off helmets one by one. Arrow shot every bare head I cleared for her. But there were so many of them. I spared a quick look down the line and saw Garrett and his partner, Mallory, apparently, start to do the same thing.

Then I heard an unfamiliar voice yell, "Target the civilians!" And then all the hell of the enemy fire turned on the supers, on us. On Arrow and me, on Wilby, on Garrett and Mallory, on Gladys, Beno, and on all the faces I knew even though their names escaped me in the heat of the moment.

The address system. "*Trafalgar* firing SLPGs!" and the ship shuddered as a large laser pulse hit. It wasn't near us, but that didn't make it a good thing.

The Marines did it again. The friendly Corporal put his body between me and the onslaught from the Scientist Marines.

Another of our Marines powered up to block for Arrow. And the other *Scylla* supers had protectors. We kept firing around them and the Marines (our Marines) kept firing, too. We didn't want anyone to get past us. No one.

But then I felt something and froze. That couldn't be. Not possible. But I looked up and there it was. There was a woman, dressed similarly to a Marine (of any variety), crawling up the wall. Then she started across the ceiling. I was so stunned it took me a second to raise my gun. I fired my darts, instinctively not wanting to kill this...super with a talent I'd never even *heard* of. The darts made it within about a yard of the crawling super when they gracefully diverted away from her. She kept going, unconcerned and undeterred. I watched the path of the darts and followed it to a gloved hand...of a small man who floated four feet from the ground. No jet pack. He caught my eye, waited a bit for me to absorb his presence, and flung the darts at me incredibly fast. I could hear Wilby's, "You're a *telespatial* for fuck's sake!" in my head as I stopped the bullets and redirected them away, away from me and the new super.

The floating enemy super looked at my Marine and my Corporal's neck was broken.

This asshole is a hybrid like me, I thought, amazed. And how could any supers work for *them*? Were they raised for the purpose, like we were? But I had no time to think as the floating super looked up at Arrow's Marine and broke his neck as well. The crab woman was almost across the ceiling. To Arrow. No. No. No. Not Arrow.

"She's going to kill you, Simon," a quiet voice said. A tall woman floated next to the super that had killed the Marines. The tall woman looked up at me. "And me." The quiet voice had been enough to distract the floating super and I broke his neck without a second thought and shot the pre-cog in the face with the dart gun. Score one for pre-cognition.

"Incoming SLPG, starboard!" the address system screamed and the *Scylla* rocked again with the blast. Port side but far away I thought unconsciously. They aren't shooting near their own people. Thank god for small favors.

Arrow was firing at the crab-lady, but her bullets were going astray. Another Scientist super had risen in the air, a Micro, I guessed, and was flicking the bullets away one by one as they were fired. Arrow was in trouble. Though she was outwardly calm, I could feel her body in full panic. I wasn't far from that myself as I shot up through the air. Another Scientist super had risen in the air and was advancing on Arrow. I was firing everything I had but it was all deflected. The deflections were interfering with my ability to 'hold' onto the supers to kill them.

The newest super, protected by the Micro's deflections, advanced on Arrow who kept firing despite the fact that it did no good. Then her gun made a clicking sound when it fired. She was out of bullets. The newest super smiled at Arrow. "Where is Captain Armstrong?" Arrow's face showed her surprise, but she said nothing. The super smiled again. "Engineering!" he called into his wrist communicator. Then *I* ran out of bullets. And the 'interference' stopped. I broke the neck of the Micro. His body started floating aimlessly around with all the other dead bodies, some Marines from either side (far as I could tell), some supers.

The Telepath (for that was what he was) turned to me and cocked his head. "Where is General Armstrong?" And his eyes opened wide in shock at the wealth of information he got simply from saying that name to me. I tried to shut my mind down, but I knew I'd failed. The Telepath's shock turned to delight. I couldn't let him do whatever it was he was going to do that made him so happy. I 'reached' into his chest (and I did thrust my physical hand out, though he was a few yards away) and grabbed his heart, turning it in his body, ripping it from its blood supply. I felt more supers behind me and turned, just as I heard the dead Telepath's wrist comm respond with, "We've got him! Heading back to *Hastings*, Commander!"

I saw Arrow raise her arms, preparing to fight hand to hand and I started for her, but the crab-lady grabbed her and, it looked like, injected her with something. Arrow collapsed into the crab-lady's arms.

"Aspect change on *Trafalgar*! Incoming *port side*!" The pulse was coming must closer. I could feel the heat as it raced through space towards the ship. Our side of the ship. The ship shook hard with this impact and the lights went out for a second, but quickly came back up. I needed to get to Arrow but was distracted by something new in front of me.

Four Scientist supers floated up towards me as the crab-lady crawled back on the ceiling carrying Arrow. She looked so tiny, I thought. So fragile. This can't be happening. I looked down, aware I had but seconds to get help. I saw Wilby and Mallory still fighting. Garrett was down and Wilby's partner was as well.

"Wilby! Mallory! Save Arrow!" I screamed at the top of my lungs. They looked up and saw how close the crab-lady was to the Loading Bay wall and the shuttle. I had to focus on the four Scientist supers. But what *were* they? Big burly thugs. Well, there was only one way to see if I was going to make it.

I held out my hands, like I was going to clap and smashed them together with all my mental strength. Thug 1's head crushed. I did it again and Thug 2's head did the same. Thug 3 flicked his fingers and sent a burst of…wind? I didn't know but it threw me across the corridor and slammed me into the wall. I'd tried to stop myself from hitting hard and I had some success, but it hurt. I pushed myself away from the wall and saw Wilby and Mallory chasing after the crab-lady and Arrow. I summoned my strength to crush the head of the 'wind-super' when he summoned more 'wind' and threw me like a rag doll down the hallway the long way. I absorbed a little less of the impact this time, but some. I think I'd broken another rib or two since I'd landed in a sort of corner. All this I figured out later. I got up and shot myself across the long hallway, picking up several Marine bodies as my shield. I had four bodies in front of me as I rammed my way down the corridor. I didn't have time to waste with these fuckheads, I kept thinking. Arrow. I had to save Arrow.

Using as much force as I could summon, I smashed the dead Marines into the wall, burying the 'wind-super' under them. I felt his body crunch satisfactorily and let them all go to float. The last of the four Scientist supers watched me do this, then I felt pressure on my chest. *In* my chest. I felt 'fingers' wrapping around my heart. It was a revolting, terrifying feeling.

"Come with us, little girl, or this baby's coming out." He grinned toothily at me.

I could see, out of the corner of my eye, Wilby fighting for Arrow with the crab-lady. Mallory was floating aimlessly, though I could tell she was alive. I focused on my thug. I ripped out his femoral nerve. He screeched in agony and then I crushed his head. He died quickly, but not quickly enough as I felt my heart spasm with his death throes. My arm hurt. My chest hurt. I felt myself losing control of my orientation. I saw Wilby fall, a great bloody slash across his chest. Blood was floating everywhere in the hallway, I noticed, in a detached way, as I started to float around in it. My vision started to cycle in and out of black. The pain in my chest was growing. I wished I could help Wilby. And *Arrow*. And *Ian*. Oh, Samuel. How could I have let you down this way? A tear ran down my nose impotently. The room went black again.

When I came back I could hear the whine of the Scientist shuttle engines warming up. We'll all be in vacuum in a minute, I thought sleepily as my chest pain grew almost unbearable.

"Marines! Carry the wounded! Blast doors coming down any second." It was Colonel Gold, I thought. So brave, those Marines. I felt myself lifted and everything went black.

11:00 – Command Center, *P.S. Scylla*

"Sir, you *can't* go," I heard Felix say softly but with a sort of desperate conviction. "I know they have Arrow and your son, but *you* can't go."

I opened my eyes. My chest felt weird but didn't hurt. My hands were shaking and I looked up to see Doc Wells standing over me. I realized I was in the Command Center, not the Infirmary, which meant that we weren't done. This nightmare wasn't over. It all came rushing back to me then. Arrow and Ian. I didn't see Wilby. We had partial gravity, which meant we floated a little. Some of the Gravitic Generators must still be down.

"Wilby?" I asked the Doc.

"Stable. I gave you a shot of adrenaline and I think you'll be fine with some rest." The Doc's mouth was a line of grief for all the ones he'd lost. I didn't have time for that now. Later. I pulled myself to a sitting position and found I was on the floor. I needed to talk to Samuel. I needed to make an apology that would mean nothing to him. I'd failed.

Lieutenant Ilene jerked up in her seat. "Incoming message to General Armstrong."

The General's voice, usually so melodious and calm was ragged and full of grief. "Put it through, Ilene."

A face and shoulders appeared on the large monitor overhead. It could only be the Director, Director Jacobi. He smiled his triumph. I saw Atalanta cringe.

"General Armstrong, this is Director Jacobi of Pace-Pallon." Like we didn't know. "I will be sending two lab techs to your ship to take samples of all your supers, as well as your Marines. These samples will be taken from both the living and the dead."

It was clear he expected a response, but the General had none to give. He already seemed to know what the Director was going to say. The Director looked annoyed at the General's silence but moved on. "You will allow this and you will not attempt to replace any of my people. They will come in single person craft, keyed to their genetic codes. Any attempt to delay or tamper with this process and your children, *both* of them," and now the smile was all cruelty, "will be spaced. You have 30 seconds to reply." And the screen went dark.

I felt the ripples of extra stress and something that had to be the physical manifestation of wonder flowing through our people in the Command Center. Felix looked at me, as did Atalanta. I met their eyes sadly. So, the secret was out. Felix's eyes opened wide, finally understanding my reaction to Arrow and Ian earlier today. Atalanta just looked thoughtful. The General just sat there, wrapped up in his silence and misery. I wanted to go to him, but I wouldn't have even if we'd been alone. I was too afraid of his disappointment. But I found his fear paralyzing. I took a breath and tried to stand. I wobbled, but grabbed onto one of the consoles to steady myself.

"30 seconds are up, General." The Director was back, still smiling, so proud of himself for finding the chink in the General's armor. "What is your response?"

"I need proof of life," the General said calmly. Well, he projected calm, but he was as far from it as a person could be.

The Director's smile turned into a small snarl but he jerked his head to one of his people and the scene shifted. Then there, in front of the Scientist's Official Seal sat Arrow, tied up but otherwise undamaged, and Ian who looked like he'd had the shit kicked out of him. His clothes were torn and he was cut and bloody. And his right arm was hanging wrong. He'd put up quite the struggle. I was proud of him, suddenly. It seemed a strange thing to think at that moment, even to me, but he'd *fought*. Which was more than poor Arrow had been allowed to do.

A voice spoke to Arrow and Ian. "Do you have anything you wish to say?" Arrow looked at Ian, but he shook his head. I didn't blame him. I wouldn't have known what to say either, but Arrow looked right at the camera.

"Sir. Let us go." Then even *her* strength relented a bit and she swallowed. He voice dropped a bit, "There'll be another day, Dad." I saw the General's eyes close in his agony. I felt my heart (my metaphorical heart, this time) breaking for him. And if I couldn't bear it, how could he? The General took a deep breath to calm himself. But, no, I realized, he wasn't calming himself. He was angry. Really angry. He'd stopped projecting and I could read it all. He was using his anger to keep going, I thought. He was gathering his strength to get them back. He reopened his eyes.

"Tell *Trafalgar* to continue to hold its fire and send your techs. Armstrong clear." The General signaled for Ilene to cut the comm, which she did. The Director had opened his mouth to say something as the screen went black again. He turned to Felix.

"We'll take the debris ship," the General's voice was flat, and he stood up as he spoke. There was still that anger. I found it somehow encouraging until I played back his words in my head. '*We'll* take'? No. Felix had been right from the first; the one person who *couldn't* go was the General. Felix had frozen in place. He clearly didn't know what to say. He'd already made his objection and couldn't make it again. Sig, who I hadn't noticed before, which was shocking considering his immense size, was closely watching his friend Sam. There was great sympathy on that scarred face. Then all at once Sig nodded and stood up.

"I'll join you, Felix." The General turned his exhausted eyes to his friend, his eyebrows raised. "They've got Appleseeds, Sam." Sig grinned, showing all his teeth. "And Appleseeds are *exactly* what we need." The General just stood there a second, clearly reluctant to give this up. Sig dropped his voice, "I've got this. OK?"

It only took a couple of seconds (though it seemed to take much longer) but the General finally nodded and Felix exhaled, probably unaware that he'd been holding his breath during the entire exchange. Felix started for the door to the Command Center, Sig following. I saw Atalanta slip out of the room wordlessly as I took a couple of steps and followed her. Doc Wells reached out a hand to stop me and opened his mouth to protest, but I gave him a murderous look and he said nothing. My steps were getting steadier the closer I got to the door. Doc Wells looked from me to the General wildly.

"Sir, you can't let Jane go. It could kill her." The Doc took a breath to say more but a quelling look from the General shut him right up.

Despite the anger he was clinging to the General looked almost broken. This blow had taken everything he had. And now I was going to add myself to the danger. He started to say something, to stop me, I think, but visibly paused, as he saw the challenge in my eyes.

"Jane…" the General started but I cut him off, something I'd never done in public before. But time was short.

"Sir. I have to go. Arrow was my responsibility and I failed." That was what I said, but what I mean was "I failed *you*" which was true. "We've been there before and we will bring them back." I looked at him intently, willing him to just give up this useless battle with me. "You *must* stay. And we *must* go."

The General knew there was no way he *could* stop me, short of having me shot. And he didn't have the energy to try. He looked so…defeated.

"Bring them back, Jane." He wasn't begging, but he was. I hated this. Hated that they'd made him suffer like this. That they could exploit the best things about his character to hurt him. Well I knew something about hurting, too. And they would pay.

"Before you know it, Sir. I promise." My voice was stronger and more confident than I'd thought it could be. I nodded for emphasis and he nodded back reflexively. I knew I was coming back with his kids or I wasn't coming back at all. Nothing less. My literal 'do or die' determination must have shown in my eyes because for a moment I saw Samuel, not the General, looking at me from his prison of pain. I looked away, blinking back the unwanted tears. And I left.

12:30 – Debris Shuttle, Space outside *P.S. Scylla*

I all but collapsed into my shuttle seat as I strapped myself in. I was shaking. My chest hurt, but I did my best to ignore it. Sig was across from me, even his constant good cheer dimmed a little in the light of the dangers we were about to face. Felix was warming up the disguised shuttle and Atalanta was running diagnostics. She kept shooting me worried looks which I tried to ignore without being rude.

I felt the shuttle hum and knew it was nearly ready. Felix plopped down in front of Sig and me.

"We are moving the Debris field with us. Or as much of it as we can grab." I looked over at him in surprise. Sig didn't look surprised at all. Maybe he was incapable of it. "The General is having our functioning Macros move over the parts you and I can't see."

"That's a lot of debris, Felix." I said, my voice full of wonder and concern.

He nodded. "There needs to be enough of it that they will have plenty of opportunities to miss us if they start shooting at it." Sig nodded. Felix continued. "Jane, you'll help Sig get the Appleseeds and Atalanta and I will get Arrow and Ian. Assuming they haven't moved them."

I turned to Atalanta. "You know where they are?"

"They're in the formal conference room. I recognized the seal. It had been part of Bayliss's tour." She said the word with distaste, but rolled over any deeper associations. "It's in Sector A, two sections away from the Shuttle Bay, not," and she smiled, looking at Sig, "that we're going to the Shuttle Bay."

I looked over at Sig for an explanation. He pointedly stared around him at the shuttle itself. It was then I noticed how different it was from any other shuttle I'd ever been on, not that I'd been on that many. The seats were enormous. The shape was wrong. I reached out to sense the hull and that was wrong, too. And there was a…drill, I thought, on one side that led to an airlock with a seal…? Then I got it. This was a Pacey-3 *Mining* shuttle. Oh, excellent. Sig's full grin was back. Felix pulled out a memo pad with the same *Hastings* schematic we'd used on the last mission. He pointed to a cargo bay.

"We will drill in and make a seal here."

I looked at Felix, confused. It was nowhere near where Arrow and Felix were. But Sig was still grinning. Sig spoke, "Felix and the little lady here," and I flicked an amused glance to Atalanta who shrugged with a small eye roll, "will have an easier time moving Arrow and Ian than you and I will have moving the Appleseeds. And the Appleseeds are," and he pointed to what looked like a vast Weapons Vault next to the cargo bay, "there. Just waiting for us."

"And Appleseeds are…?" I asked, slightly annoyed that everyone else seemed to know.

Now Sig's grin seemed to take over his whole head. "*Johnny* Appleseeds. Successors to the old Terra Davy Crocketts." I sighed, not knowing what Davy Crocketts were anymore than I knew what Johnny Appleseeds were. "Portable nukes."

Oh. Now I grinned, too. Sig continued. "We're gonna need every advantage we have. And the Scientists aren't going to need theirs." Now his grin turned dark. Dangerous. "So I'll need your help getting into the Vault and then with the lifting. All goes well and we'll have quite the little arsenal to replace ours."

"*Replace* ours?" I asked. "Where is 'ours' going?"

"Wait and see."

Felix's mouth quirked at Sig's attempt at mystery and he indicated the Sig should take the pilot's chair. Sig did so, strapping himself in. Felix stationed himself by the co-pilot's window. Sig checked some of the readouts. "We're warm."

Felix nodded. "Let's move." The ship moved forward slowly, very slowly. Just to get momentum going, then, surprisingly, Sig cut the engines and dropped the power to almost nothing. Felix looked at me. "Sense the left side debris and I'll take the right. Match velocity to the shuttle's. I'll give her a push when she slows, if she does." I could feel him grounding himself and I did the same. "We have to be debris only. Any power and they'll shoot us down before we get close."

"Ok." I concentrated on the pieces of trash on the left side. I was able to feel their weight, their heft and make their trajectories match through transference. Then I matched their velocities to the shuttle's. I distantly felt Felix do the same with the pieces on his side. We were a fleet of trash moving towards the *Hastings*. Slowly, slowly.

"Contact. Two one-man craft heading for the *Scylla*." Sig's voice was a whisper. They couldn't have heard us through the vacuum of space, but I appreciated the thought. So the lab techs were on their way. The clock was ticking.

I flicked my eyes to Atalanta, who sat calm and still, not getting in anyone's way. She was armored and armed like the rest of us (we'd all replenished our ammunition as we'd left the *Scylla*) but it suddenly seemed like a really bad idea that she was here. Especially after what had happened the last time she'd been to *Hastings*. She sensed my worry and smiled at me.

"Don't worry, Jane. It isn't the same." Her voice was soft and soothing. But my doubts remained. "I'm armed this time." She smiled with anticipation. "Trust me, it'll make a difference."

Felix smiled himself, though he never took his eyes off his charges in space. "My girl's got *skills*."

I was surprised, to say the least. I mean, she was the best MEmp I'd ever heard of, but that hadn't served her so well last time. "You mean secret supernormal skills?"

Atalanta looked at me with fond exasperation. "No, Jane, I mean 'shoot to kill' skills. You know why you never saw me in a weapons class?" I shook my head. "Because I can hit any target with any weapon at any time. Mallory passed me out my first year."

How cool was that? "You never cease to amaze me, 'Lanta."

She preened a bit. "It's a routine compliment, but I'll accept it."

Felix snorted from the co-pilot's seat. "Always so modest, love."

Atalanta smiled expansively. "But I have so much to be modest *about*, dear boy."

I watched them banter as of old and it made me feel better. But what really made me happy was the surreptitious looks of surprise that Sig kept giving the two of them as he guessed that Felix and the 'little lady' were a couple. He looked a bit confused. Well, tough, I thought. They only seem odd on the surface.

We continued creeping along. The *Hastings* was getting closer, but slowly.

"Hey, Sig. Whose this Captain DeStephani we saw today?" I asked with feigned casualness. I saw Atalanta was paying attention now.

"What? Nunzio?" Sig chuckled softly. "He's my second in command for the Pacey-3 fleet, such as it is. One of the best guys I know. Been grooming him for years to take over."

"Were you thinking of retiring?" I asked, trying to keep the conversation going.

Sig paused, still staring out, watching the debris and the approaching ship. We were finally getting really close. "You don't retire on Pace 3, Jane." His voice, still soft, was grim. I let the subject drop. He checked his plot. "We're too far to the left, Felix. We need to adjust and now."

"How much?"

"10 degrees, give or take. Starboard."

Suddenly the darkness outside lit up with a burst of energy. A piece of debris vaporized to my left. I instinctively shuddered away from that side of the ship, even though it made no real sense to do so. Felix looked out the viewport. "Ship LPGs." He looked at Sig and started to say something but stopped himself. Sig knew what he was doing. Another burst and one of the farther bits of trash was gone. Then another closer to us. And another. Had they read our power signature, small as it was?

Sig spoke, "Jane, accelerate your half so it becomes a bigger threat."

I felt my part of the debris field and gave it a shove towards the ship. I gave it a good bit of speed, hoping that watching it rushing at them would be distracting enough that we could get through. The SLPG's went crazy now, shooting (and hitting, generally) tons of debris pieces on the left side.

"They're more accurate than we thought they'd be," Felix muttered.

"It'll be enough," Sig returned quietly.

Felix, as if suddenly remembering the course change Sig needed, gently nudged both the shuttle and his side of the debris field starboard. The side of the ship loomed in front of us. We were suddenly surrounded by flashes of light as the SLPGs went crazy in a last ditch effort to keep anything from making contact with their ship. Closer and closer to the hull. I wanted to back up. This seemed like the absolute wrong way to get on a ship. You know by *hitting* it. But that was what we were going to do.

Sig again. "Create uneven hits with the debris field, kids. We don't want to be the first ones to touch the ship." Felix and I nodded in unison.

The first debris piece hit the ship, not hard because we weren't going that fast, but I could see the metal of the ship's skin buckle a bit. Then more and more of the survivors of the SLPGs hit, debris covering the whole side of the ship in an uneven pattern. But the debris didn't bounce off like it should have. It stayed. Or rather it *stuck*. Our ship hit the *Hastings* and stuck as well. Sig pressed something, apparently clamping our ship to theirs and got up from his seat. I looked a question at him as he passed.

"The debris is magnetic," he said as he went by. I nodded, impressed. Sig and the General had thought of everything. "And don't worry about the SLPGs for now. They'd have to shoot their own ship to shoot us off." I had to admit that that was good to hear.

Sig walked over to the airlock and seal that led to the drill. He pressed buttons, listened, adjusted then stood back to watch. We crowded around him to do the same. The drill was large but shallow. It started turning slowly and almost silently.

"Get ready," Sig ordered. We donned any helmets we'd put down and drew our guns. The drill cut through the hull like butter, pushing its way through into the ship and opening the medium-sized hole wide. Sig checked something on a readout. "Atmospheres match, as does oxygenation." Atalanta looked at him. "The bays are intact and pressurized." He opened the soft seal on the airlock, took a breath and went charging through. I was next, then Atalanta, then Felix. The cargo bay was unused and dark. We ran through it quickly. We only paused at the door long enough for me to sense when the corridor would be clear. When it was we went silently through the door, Felix and Atalanta going to the left, Sig and I to the right. We figured we couldn't take any longer than 20 minutes maximum to do this. That seemed really long to me, but I didn't argue. This wasn't my show.

Sig and I paused next to the Weapons Storage Bay. The outer door had a lock, but the real devil would be the one inside, the one to the Vault itself. I held up 4 fingers to Sig, indicating the four people I felt just on the other side of the door. He nodded.

I concentrated on the lock. Retina scan and password. No good. I was starting to sweat. Ok. Think. I took out my gun (not the dart gun) and indicated that Sig do the same. He put his LPG away and did it. I held up 2 fingers for me and indicated 2 for him. He nodded. I really hoped that that was clear because I wasn't well versed in secret silent military language. I imagined the door as a big sheet of paper. I used my 'hands' (instead of just fingers) to roll it back just a bit from the door frame. I put the barrel of my gun into the slit I had made and gestured for Sig to do the same. I grounded. I thought.

"Fire 2," I whispered. We fired. Suddenly 4 bullets were in the air. And I felt all four bodies drop. The shots hadn't had to be good, fortunately. Thanks to the toxin on the bullets they just had to hit the victims somewhere. I quietly lifted the door out of its frame and held it while we got in. Then I rested it back against the frame and hoped no one would notice its mutilation.

There was the Vault door. Similar to the one that had protected the DNA sample vials. Sig covered the battered door to the corridor while I got the Vault open. I loved combination locks. Really, I did. I swung the Vault door open and exhaled sharply. Sig, hearing this, came over and did the same.

The huge vault was full of 'Appleseeds.' Full to the brim. Sig clapped me on the back, almost knocking me over and causing an involuntary wince, jarring one of the broken ribs my adrenaline had allowed me to forget about. He held his hand up in apology and I shook it off. We had work to do.

I turned to the shared wall between the outer Vault entry room and the cargo bay where our ship was. I ran over Felix's drill thing in my mind. I pictured it. And I felt myself tensing up. I needed Felix. I was starting to breathe faster, feeling some panic. I could see Sig watching me and see his alarm starting to build. I took a breath to calm down.

"Sig," I said softly. He came over to me. "Put your hands on my shoulders." He looked askance at me, but I didn't have time to explain. "Please."

He put his massive paws on my shoulders and I concentrated again. Yes. I made the drill in my mind and imagined it cutting through the bulkhead like butter. I used Sig's drill as my model. And in 10 seconds we were looking into the cargo bay. Sig gave my shoulders a happy shake, and one that was surprisingly gentle for him.

"Let's load," he said.

13:45 – Cargo Bay, *P.S. Hastings*

I had 'lifted' all but the last half dozen nukes into the back of the Pacey-3 shuttle. We were nearing the 20 minute mark and no sign of Arrow, Ian, Felix and Atalanta. Even Sig was starting to look worried. I got the last 6 in the air and out of the Vault and was getting them through the cargo bay when I heard LPG fire. Sig jerked his head to indicate that I should continue getting the Appleseeds into the ship and headed for the cargo bay inner door.

I deposited my charges gently and ran back out to Sig. I sensed the hallway. People were running. I knew all those body signatures.

"They're coming!" I whispered. Sig keyed open the door and we heard footsteps. Running. And more people running after them. I peeked out and there they were. Arrow and Atalanta running and Felix behind 'lifting' Ian in front of him.

"Cover me!" Atalanta screamed. Sig and I obediently opened fire, causing their pursuers to slow down and find cover. I aimed my projectiles to hit every face I could see. Atalanta stopped running and fired her LPG at a sensor in the wall. The blast door next to it whizzed shut. She turned and ran to us. Arrow was already in the cargo hold, waiting for Ian. Atalanta bolted through the door as well. Felix was going as fast as he could, but 'carrying' Ian was slowing him down. Suddenly a laser pulse flew by my head. And singed Ian's boot.

"Jane!" Felix handed Ian over to me and I got him in the hold. Sig and Felix returned fire, preparing to withdraw. Felix fired. And then I saw Sig jerk and list to one side. Felix caught his breath, but kept firing. I had gotten Ian into the ship under Arrow's care and had come back in time to see Sig start to fall. I 'caught' him and pulled him into the cargo hold.

More soldiers were coming down the hallway. Felix knew they'd be on us if he stopped firing.

"Felix!" I screamed over the gun fire. "Pull the ceiling down and get out of there!"

Felix nodded and raised his LPG to the ceiling. Couldn't remember what was up there, but it didn't really matter. He cut an arc, a surgical cut down the belly of the ceiling from one end to the other. The soldiers stopped shooting long enough to raise their eyes fearfully. Then the ceiling opened up…and so came the flood. The swimming pool they'd put in. That's what it was, I thought. Then I grabbed Felix and ran for it.

We flew through the soft seal into the shuttle and pressed the autoclose buttons (thank god there was something that simple) and detached from the ship.

"Detonate 1," Sig said softly from the floor. I looked over and saw Sig, his whole side ruined by LPG fire, lying with his head cradled gently in Atalanta's lap. She was stroking his hair. She looked up at me and I felt, pain/loss from her in a wave. And I knew from that that Sig, our friend, was going to die. Numbly Atalanta looked back to Sig and resumed stroking his hair.

Felix, now strapped into the pilot's seat flipped a switch. We watched the *Hastings* rock. Felix started backing our shuttle up and away from the *Hastings* as fast as possible. Felix flipped another switch, but now we could see what he was doing since we were further away. The magnetic debris was exploding. Felix flipped two more switches. More explosions.

"Do the big one, kid." Sig voice was barely audible, but Felix heard him anyway. He waited ten more seconds to give us the best clearance and flipped the last switch.

All the remaining pieces of debris detonated at once. For a second it looked like the ship would be all right. But these last bombs made *holes* and the ship just…crumpled in on itself. Then there was a flash of light (as, I presume, the FTL drive went up) and the ship was just more debris. I realized that I now knew where all our nukes had gone. So clever of Sig to think of stealing theirs. It's not like they were going to need them.

Felix exhaled in relief, but Arrow said nothing, too worried about Ian. But all I could think about was Sig, who had come along to get the nukes and to make it Ok for Samuel to stay behind. I looked at Atalanta whose face was wet with tears. She shook her head. Sig was gone. Felix saw Atalanta's face and knew it, too, and his victory was bittered.

Grief-stricken I reached over and closed Sig's eyes, then sat on the floor next to Atalanta who still cradled his enormous head on her lap. I held her hand as Felix took all of us home.

Excerpt from Ian Armstrong's Journal, August 6, 2869 (sixteen days after the action of this entry, but inserted here for relevance)

I've been told that it isn't always clear when something ends. Sometimes you don't notice; you're distracted or overtaken by events. Sometimes you have to look back to know the moment when it happened.

I took me two weeks to see it. Arrow. I lost her the moment she called Samuel 'Dad.'

It had felt strange when she'd said it. She'd never said it before that moment. But I was hurt and I was scared that they were going to hurt her and Dad was so upset.

But she'd never brought herself to call him that before because it would mean an acknowledgment of...of too much.

I'd known it was only a matter of time, I just hadn't known it would be a matter of just one word.

ENTRY 10-2-16

Excerpt from Wilby's Journal, July 20, 2869

It's horrible that we lost Sig. He was a good man, in the same league with the General, and there aren't too many people like that. We needed him. We still have much to do. Damn it, we needed him.

He was like a father to...never mind.

I just hate for us to keep losing Pacey 3's. Some of them are really quite exceptional.

14:35 – Shuttle Bay, *P.S. Scylla*, July 20, 2869 (continued)

Felix powered down the shuttle and we sat there, waiting for the Bay to repressurize. We sat in silence. Atalanta and I hadn't moved from our positions on the floor and Sig's head was still cradled in Atalanta's lap. Her tears were dry now, but our sorrow was still there. Arrow had her arms around Ian who was at least sitting up now. He was conscious and pretending he was ok, but not one of us was fooled.

I felt the Bay's pressure normalize. And then I felt something else. People. The bay was filling with people. I looked at Atalanta. I could tell that they were moving excitedly.

"They're happy." She tried to smile. "We won, you know." She looked down at Sig. "*Someone* should be celebrating, I guess."

"Popping the hatch," Felix said, more as a warning than anything else. The hatch started to open slowly and I could hear people screaming and cheering. I looked at Arrow, who only had eyes for Ian and Atalanta who clearly didn't want the emotional assault of all those minds.

I squeezed Atalanta's hand and stood up. "Felix, you and I should go." Felix looked at me, clearly as anxious to avoid the crowd as all of us were. I looked at the two remaining women. "We'll send Doc Wells as soon as we can get out of the shuttle bay." I looked back at Felix and shrugged. "Maybe they won't notice us and we'll get away clean." Felix gave me a look that did not express high confidence in my hope.

The hatch opened fully and Felix and I stood in the opening. People cheered. Some were drinking, some were dancing. I didn't need to be an Empath to feel the relief and the jubilation. The hatch closed behind us, leaving our friends to the relative quiet of the shuttle.

Someone I barely recognized as one of the General's staff ran up to us. "The *Trafalgar* surrendered! Right after the *Hastings* blew up!" She hugged me roughly and I looked over at Felix whose face reflected his own relief at this news. Thank god. No more shooting.

The crowd swept us out. We had painted-on smiles at first, but soon their enthusiasm was so overwhelming that I found myself smiling and laughing for real. Another person hugged me, then hugged Felix. Then it became an orgy (but not the really fun kind) of hugs, kisses and semi-hysterical joy.

I thought of poor Sig in the shuttle. I looked at Felix and for some reason felt he was thinking that, too. Then suddenly I found myself wrapped in Felix's embrace. I clung to him myself. And even though we were the least joyful people there, he was the only one in the room I actually wanted to touch. He finally pulled back and I saw his face was wet. Mine was too. The party continued without us and around us. We were now able to walk calmly out of the shuttle bay and into the corridor. The revelers didn't notice.

I pressed the button for the Infirmary on the comm on the wall. "Doc Wells, please, this is Shuttle Bay 1." I stood next to Felix, his arm still around my waist.

"Wells, here." His voice came over the comm. Even amplified he sounded stressed.

"Doc, can you send a Team to the Shuttle bay? Captain Armstrong has been injured and needs immediate attention. He's in the shuttle with Arrow and I can't tell how badly he's hurt." Then I swallowed. "And we need a Corpsman. I'm afraid Senior Engineer Van Houton was fatally shot during our escape."

There was a pause at the other end of the line. "Acknowledged. Team and Corpsmen on their way." Another pause. "Is that Jane?"

I looked at Felix in surprise, but Felix shrugged. "Yes, Sir."

"Jane, I need you to report to the Infirmary immediately."

Suddenly my guts clenched. And I realized that not one of the hundred revelers I had just seen had been a close friend. Not one. "On my way, Sir."

I looked at Felix, fear in my eyes. "I'll stay with the shuttle," Felix said. "Go." He gave me a shake and released me. I ran.

I arrived at the Infirmary a few minutes later, the lift having given me a chance to catch my breath. My chest was hurting again. A lot, actually, but I wasn't in the mood to admit it. I wondered how much damage that Scientist Micro had actually done to me. But it didn't really matter now. I raced in the door to see Doc Wells waiting for me. He was incredibly stressed out and approaching adrenaline burnout. He held up his hand to stop my progress and I waited. Waited for what had to be very bad news.

"The General has been seriously injured. He was supervising the repair of the Gravitic Generators." I hadn't even noticed that the gravity was fully back on. "Something went wrong with a stabilizer. It flew into the gear box and he caught it before it could destroy Generator 3, but his leg got caught..." I felt my face drain of color, but I tried to keep it together.

"Can you save the leg?"

"I think so, but..." And I could feel the *real* bad news coming. "I can't do anything right now. I've detected an enormous clot in the leg. I don't have the facilities here to break it up." He looked anguished at this admission. I didn't understand why this was so bad. He could see that I didn't get it. "If that clot comes loose without breaking up on its own, it will travel to either his heart or his brain. And if it does that he will either suffer a massive stroke or just die outright."

Well, I got it now. My arm was hurting again and my chest was worse, but I knew (ironically) that this was the last person I wanted to know that. My mind was reeling. I felt terrified like I could see my own mortality in front of me there with Samuel's. Samuel!

"I need to see him."

Doc Wells nodded, vaguely disapproving. "He's expecting you."

"Thank you."

I followed him through the rather labyrinthine set of rooms that made up the Infirmary complex within the *Scylla.* Finally we turned a corner and I saw Samuel lying on a gurney. It was awful. His face was grey and wasted with pain. I looked down to his left leg. They'd cut his pants away and the keg was bound with a clean bandage, but it was the wrong shape somehow. And there was evidence of blood on the floor. Over to the side I saw the bloody mess of the cut-away trouser leg as an orderly was throwing it away. I closed my eyes to try to get myself together and took a breath.

He was staring at me when I opened them. "Jane." His voice was thin and weak, a shadow of its former self.

I forced myself to smile and walk over to him. "Sir." Then my eyes filled with tears. "We brought them back. Felix and Atalanta and I."

"Ian's hurt?" I guessed he had been told. I nodded. He continued, "And Sig is dead." I nodded again. My heart was pumping unevenly. It was getting harder to ignore. It hurt and I was afraid he would see it and worry more. I did my best to tuck the pain away but it was hard—all I could think about was Samuel, my Samuel. He can't die. What was the point of …existing without him? I felt panic rising in my chest, adding to the physical pain. *He can't die.*

He reached a hand up off the gurney. It shook with the effort to raise it. I hesitated, not wanting anyone to see even this small intimacy. He lifted it higher, his hand shaking more and his eyes were pleading. I took his hand. It made me feel better to touch him. Like he hadn't slipped away. "Thanks for saving my kids," his voice was weaker. I looked up at Doc Wells who had been watching us with apparent fascination.

"Isn't there anything he can have for the pain?" I asked quietly.

"Yes, but he wouldn't take anything until he'd seen his kids." Doc Wells paused. "And you. He insisted."

Then there was commotion in the outer rooms. It had to be Arrow and Ian. Samuel tried to straighten up on the bed, but failed. He squeezed my hand and let it go. I stood up. A gurney burst through the opening. Ian was on it, suffering but conscious. Arrow followed, emanating worry. Samuel put on a smile which seemed real.

Ian tried to sit up, but was forced back down by the nurses wheeling his cart. "Dad!" Then he took in how awful the General looked. "My god, what's happened?" Arrow's eyes were wide and she froze in place. I pitied her. It was too much for anyone.

Samuel looked over at the nurse that seemed to be in charge of Ian. His voice was harsh as he spoke through gritted teeth. "How badly did they hurt my son?" Even now, even in the agony he must be in, he was still angry. What a man, I thought.

"Broken arm, looks like two broken ribs, concussion, lacerations, bruising and probably some internal bleeding. I'm taking him to scan," she sniffed, obviously disapproving of Ian's choice to see his father before a scan, "after he sees you."

I looked at Arrow, expecting a question, but she looked too numb to say anything. So Samuel asked, "Are the injuries life threatening?"

The nurse sniffed again, this sniff signifying her lack of respect for a man who tries to get himself killed but can't do it properly. "I do not believe so. Doc Wells will make the final determination, of course." She frowned thunderously. "Now, to the scanner, Captain." She started to roll Ian a way when Samuel raised another shaky hand. Ian looked from the hand to his dad's face.

"I'm glad you're back, son." Samuel smiled.

"Me, too, Dad." And Ian smiled back. It was a sad, fearful smile.

And *this* is how grown men say, "I love you," I thought as my eyes refilled with tears. Idiots. Ian was wheeled away. Samuel turned his eyes to his daughter who still seemed frozen on the spot. She was staring at him, her eyes dry. But I knew, because I knew her better, that she was trying to control herself.

"Sweetheart," Samuel said softly.

This was too much for Arrow and she stumbled over to him, reaching out and hugging him gently. He moved both shaky hands to rest on her back and she let out a quiet solitary sob. What a long way they've come, I thought, only to come together at what might be the end? Then I stopped that line of thought. How could I even think something so awful. But there it was. The horror of it was starting to crash over me and I knew I had to get out of there before I disgraced myself by completely losing control. I looked at the floor and walked (at least I think I walked, I may have run) out of the room.

And I ran, literally, into Felix and Atalanta. Atalanta's eyes opened hugely as she read me. "Jane, what's wrong?" I couldn't breathe. My chest hurt. I was wringing my hands and tears were pouring down my face. Atalanta put her arms around my shoulders and made a shushing sound. I felt waves of calm flowing into me that were so strong I felt drugged, almost high. I closed my eyes, leaning into her. I could tell she was looking at Felix. They were trying to figure out what to do without speaking. I found I was sitting now. Atalanta must have moved me. I was between my two friends on some chairs.

"Is it the General?" Felix's voice was gentle and calm. It was nice, I thought, in my semi-drugged state. And my chest feels a lot better. I can't burst my heart right now.

I nodded. "His leg was shattered in an accident. There is a massive blood clot in it," Felix stood up, all pretense of calm gone. "Doc Wells can't break it up without killing him and he'll die or stroke out if the clot moves to his heart or brain." I felt Atalanta's body stiffen. Felix only paused in his pacing for a second as he took this in.

Then Felix stopped pacing and looked at me. "Have you *seen* it? The clot?"

I shook my head. It hadn't occurred to me to try to see it. It might have in time, but no one knew how much time we actually had. Felix helped me up, Atalanta staying right by my side. We walked slowly into Samuel's room. He was asleep. Apparently he had finally allowed the painkillers. I was glad for him. I couldn't stand to see him suffer. Arrow was on a chair, curled up, the picture of misery. Atalanta left and sat next to Arrow, putting an arm around her. Arrow stiffened at first, then leaned on Atalanta, resting her head on her shoulder.

Felix and I went to Samuel and stood over the shattered leg. He moved behind me, putting his hands on my shoulders. "Now ground," he commanded softly.

I did. On the ship, then the room. I started on the exterior of the leg. It was a mess of shattered bone. I wanted to withdraw, but Felix tightened his grip on my shoulders and I kept going. I found the artery and traced it. There it was. A massive ugly clot. It blocked the blood and the blood pounded against it. I touched the clot with my mind but it was solid. I didn't, couldn't touch it without dislodging it. I knew it. But I had to try. I gave it a tiny touch, trying to scoop out part of it to break it up, but nothing moved. I couldn't do it. I was flooded with despair. I couldn't help him. I withdrew and stepped back.

"I can't do it." I whispered. "I don't have the control." The chest pain was back with a vengeance. I felt a tremendous weight on me. I was sweating now. I wanted to throw up. But what could I do for Samuel???? Then I knew. Wilby could do it.

"Wilby," I whispered to Felix.

Felix nodded. "Is he here?"

"Wilby!" I called out loudly. "Wilby, we need you!"

Doc Wells was suddenly in front of me. His expression was daunting.

"We need him, Doc. He can save General Armstrong," I heard Felix say. My jaw hurt.

"Wilby is recovering from his injuries. I can't risk having him exert himself right now." The Doc was unmoved, I could tell. I couldn't have cared less.

"Wilby!" I cried out again. My arm was numb now.

Now Doc Wells was angry. "I will not let you endanger one of my patients, Jane!"

I looked up at him, which I had to do since I was now bent over in pain. "You get Wilby in here or I swear to god I'll rip your balls off and shove them down your fucking throat."

Doc Wells recoiled at the vehemence of my threat. It wasn't empty, though I doubted I had the strength right now to actually act on it.

"I'm here," I heard a voice say. I looked up. It was Wilby in his infirmary gown. He looked at all of us in confusion, then saw me and his expression turned to one of horror. "Jane!" I turned away from everyone and threw up on the floor. Wilby rushed forward. "She's having a heart attack." The pressure on my chest was terrible. I couldn't breathe at all now.

"Felix. Tell Wilby what to do. Save Samuel," I said, but I couldn't tell if I'd actually made any sound. Doc Wells was running at me and I put up my arm to ward him off. I felt a cool hiss in my arm as I fell towards the floor. Then nothing.

The next few hours/days were a blur of pain, drugs and semi-consciousness. I only had two thoughts: Samuel and pain. Then the pain stopped and I found myself wanting to sleep. But I knew I couldn't yet. Not until I knew.

Then I heard a voice, Atalanta's I thought, say, "Wilby saved the General, Jane. He destroyed the clot molecule by molecule. Wilby saved the General. You can sleep now, love. Sleep." I felt relief wash over me and I slept.

21:00 – Infirmary, *P.S. Scylla*, July 23, 2869

I woke up suddenly. It was night, apparently, in the Infirmary, and everything was dim and quiet. I didn't hurt. Aside from being tired I actually felt pretty good. I tried sitting up in the hospital bed and found that didn't hurt either. Wonder of wonders.

Someone was in the room with me. Samuel. He had been sitting in a chair, apparently waiting for me to wake up. He stood up carefully and leaned heavily on a crutch as he walked. I moved over and he sat on the bed next to me. Then he gently, oh so gently, reached for me and held me against his chest. My arms reached around his back. I wanted to pull him tightly to me, but found I didn't have the strength. My arms fell back down but he didn't let go. I was so happy. He was alive and he was with me.

After a while he drew a ragged breath and took my face gently between his hands. His eyes were full and so were mine. I could sense someone at the doorway. Doc Wells. Samuel brought his mouth to mine and I realized that in that moment I didn't give a flying fuck if anyone else saw.

When he finally spoke to me his voice was so soft it was barely audible. "I'm constantly amazed, Jane, at how you can love me so…fiercely."

I looked into that wonderful lined face and took a second to find my voice. "And how do you love me, Samuel?"

He blinked away the moisture in his eyes. "Completely." And he kissed me gently again. Then he laid me back down and pulled the covers up for me, kissed me on the cheek and stole away. I don't know when Doc Wells had left but I scanned for him and he was gone, too. But I didn't care. I had everything I wanted. All I needed now was more sleep.

10:00 – Infirmary, *P.S. Scylla*, July 24, 2869

It was the next morning and I was doing much better. I'd slept long and well and seemed to have regained some limited strength. I was dealing myself solitaire with the playing cards Atalanta had left me. The nurses had wheeled over a table for the purpose and some had stayed to watch Atalanta clean my clock at poker. It was a tribute to my weakened state that it had taken me several hands to realize that I was playing poker with an *Empath*. So I'd lost and lost big.

Someone familiar was at the door to my room. Wilby, I recognized. I felt a surge of gratitude as I looked up. He was in regular clothes, apparently having been discharged, and looked, well, like Wilby. It really was criminal how handsome he was. He walked in immediately, his confidence and cockiness almost back to normal levels. I was glad. He wouldn't be Wilby without that touch of…asshole.

"I'm early for your therapy and scan." Wilby saw Atalanta's recently vacated chair and took it.

I looked askance at him, having no idea what he was talking about. I kept playing, dealing the cards quickly and moving them around. I was fast if not actually good.

"Doc Wells has been using a specialized therapy that has repaired your heart muscle. I was curious to 'feel' the progress and he's been letting me scan you every day during your recovery."

"Well, that was nice of him," I said non-committally. I wasn't sure how I felt about Doc Wells. He'd helped to save my life, obviously, but I *still* wanted to rip his balls off for trying to stop Wilby from helping Samuel. Though, now that I thought about it, I wasn't entirely sure he'd known that that was what he was doing when he tried to stop me from getting Wilby.

"He's a good doctor." I shrugged. Wilby sighed.

I looked at my cards. I'd lost at solitaire again. I really hoped that wasn't symbolic. Then I suppressed a giggle at my own ridiculousness. Wilby saw my hesitation in dealing, checked the cards and gathered them up in his hands to shuffle.

"I owe you for saving Samuel, and me."

Wilby shuffled and cut the cards, then shuffled again. "Don't worry about it."

I heaved a sigh of relief. "Good. Then I won't." Wilby looked up in surprise and I held his gaze until he realized I was teasing him. But I had to be serious for a second. "I don't have the words to tell you how grateful I am, Wilby."

He paused in his shuffling, his jaw clenched. I wasn't the only emotional one. I didn't want to make him even more uncomfortable (as payment for all his help) but I had to know.

"What was it like? Breaking that monster up?" I tried to catch his eyes, but he was refocused on the shuffling.

"I…" He took a breath. "I've never been so terrified." Now his eyes met mine. Yes, I could see the remembered fear. "That thing was so huge and the work was so slow. It had to be. And any second the clot would move and the General would be dead." He put the cards down and leaned back in his chair.

"How long did it take?"

"A little over 4 hours," Wilby said bleakly.

Now I leaned back in shock. That seemed an eternity to balance on the head of a pin like that.

"Atalanta helped, though." His face had a look of wonder on it. "Has she ever done that calming thing for you?"

I had to laugh at that. "More often than I care to admit."

"Well, I wouldn't have made it through without it." He paused for a second, as if going over something in his head, then resumed his shuffling. Finally done with his exhaustive shuffling he plopped the deck onto my table. I cut it, he put the stack back together and handed it over.

"More solitaire?"

"Nope. We're playing Rummy 500."

Now he sighed petulantly. "But I hate playing cards."

I was unmoved by his protestation. I started dealing. "Good. Then maybe I can actually win a game. Atalanta knew every card I put down before I did it."

Wilby snorted. "You played with *Atalanta*? Who's a, oh what is that word, it's on the tip of my tongue…?

"MEmp?"

Now Wilby was laughing at me, but I couldn't really mind since I *had* been an idiot to play with her. "Yeah, that. And you played, I'm guessing, poker?" I nodded, chagrined. "You played poker with a woman who can not only read all your emotions but manipulate them as well." He laughed some more. "Not, apparently, that she needed to in your case."

I shook my head. "Pick up your cards, smart ass."

Wilby, still laughing to himself, picked up his cards.

We started to play. He discarded. I picked up from the pile, etc. I opened my mouth to say something, but stopped myself. Wilby gave me a look out of the corner of his eye as he continued to play. I took another breath to speak, but didn't yet again.

"Oh, for the love of god, Jane. Spit it out."

I took a second to marshal my thoughts. "So...how about that Captain DeStephani?"

Wilby blinked in surprise for just a second, then recovered to purse his lips in what I hoped was affectionate annoyance. Well, I was at least half right. Hopefully more than half right, but I couldn't tell. But then my nerves quailed seeing his rather bleak expression. "It isn't any of my business. Sorry, Wilby. Forget I asked."

He sighed. "I guess I owe you some kind of explanation for my strange reaction the other day. Well," he corrected himself, "I don't *owe* an explanation, but I'll give you one anyway because I know I looked like I was losing my mind. Which," he admitted, apparently reflecting on it, "I guess I was."

He put his cards down and looked at me. "I met Andrew on my Tour. Pace 3, obviously."

I had to interrupt. "I'm sorry, 'Andrew'?"

Now Wilby had to smile. "His first name is Nunzio, which he hates. Unfortunately for Andrew Sig figured that out and, being Sig, never called him anything else." His face fell for a second, reminded that Sig was lost. "Anyway I was assigned to Andrew's ship. He was being groomed to be Sig's second, but he was still proving himself. He seemed like a good guy and the work was incredibly hard and very dangerous. I was there to help so I helped."

"And you fell for him." I said it as a statement of fact. He twitched his shoulders as if still uncomfortable with the idea.

"I'm not like you, Jane. I don't just throw myself into an attachment like that. I don't *want* attachments like that. Too many complications. Too much suffering in the end."

"But isn't the joy you get worth it?" I asked.

Now his handsome face was bitter. "I'll ask *you* that question in a year." I started to ask him what the hell that meant but he kept going. "But I found myself in love anyway despite all my best efforts not to be." Wilby sighed. "A lot of people get married during their Tour..."

"Like Samuel."

Wilby nodded and continued. "...but Andrew had ten years on me and a career that was about to take off. And while I liked Pace 3, much more than I thought I would, I didn't want to live there permanently. Plus, I knew the Government would never let me choose…anything for myself." Then he looked at me, again serious. "You don't know how lucky we are to be free of that, Jane. Scary as it is to be free."

I nodded half-heartedly, being much more interested in the love story than politics. "So what happened with Andrew, Wilby?"

"It was time to move on to Pace 1, so I kissed him goodbye and left." And now Wilby looked incredibly down. I'd never seen him look miserable like that. He tried to smile, to make light of it. "Took me forever to get back in the game."

"But you did."

Now his smile was rakish and much more genuine, though his eyes were still sad. "With a vengeance."

"But..." I started but he continued for me.

"But why was Andrew's appearance on that screen such a profound shock?"

Wilby shook his head. "He'd been listed as dead on the casualty lists since Pace fell. In my mind he *was* dead, until the General said his name."

I rocked back against the bed frame. Well, that would certainly do it. "But why?"

"My guess is that Sig thought he was too valuable to be officially alive. No Scientists can demand anything from someone that was supposedly consumed by the *tapetia mortis* on Pace 3." Wilby rubbed his face with his hands, then ran them up through his hair. "A bit hard on those of us not in the know, but it was a smart move. We probably should have done something like that to protect our top people." His voice trailed off on his own train of thought.

"So what happens now? Now that you know he's alive?"

"No idea. Nothing."

"And you still care for him." I suppose that should have been a question, but I knew it didn't need to be.

"No." Now Wilby was up, pacing, agitated.

"You do, though."

"Jane, cut it out."

"I saw your face. I felt it in your body. And Atalanta read you like a book. You love him the way I love Samuel."

Wilby, really distressed now, leaned against a wall and closed his eyes. "Why are you torturing me?"

I pushed the table aside and got out of bed to go to him. I took his hands. "Because you're already suffering. It seems stupid not to try to have the good stuff, too." He looked down at me but I felt like he wasn't seeing me at all. He was looking at Andrew through the haze of memory. "Don't you miss him? I mean physically miss his touch?"

He pulled his hands from mine and buried his face in them.

"Maybe he misses you, too, love." But now watching Wilby like this was bringing me some well-deserved remorse for upsetting him. Maybe I'd pushed too far. I probably had, but I wanted to see him actually happy. He deserved it. I knew he was more right that I cared to admit about my ability to rush into emotional attachments without thinking them through, but things for Andrew and Wilby *were* different now. Paceys weren't confined anymore. We had choices. Didn't he want to be happy, even with the risk of unhappiness? But, then I thought, maybe he didn't. Maybe any risk was too much for him.

He'd brought his hands down from his face and seemed to have himself back together a bit. I joined him on the wall and leaned my head on his shoulder. "You are my friend, Wilby. And I want you to be happy." I sighed. "My way is the hard way and it definitely isn't the smartest way."

“No shit.” Wilby snorted.

"So you pick your way to be happy, whatever that is, and I'll be happy for you."

Wilby said nothing for a minute, still clearly thinking about Andrew. "I *hate* this."

I nodded, our philosophies on love being so very different, I could sympathize but not completely understand.

"So," Wilby asked quietly after a long pause, "Is being your friend always this much fun?"

I had to laugh. And I laughed for a while, remembering Ian saying something very similar to me. "It's all downhill from here."

"Great." And Wilby put his arm around my shoulder for a brief side hug. I hugged him back. And we'd all been so happy to find out Wilby wasn't heartless. Poor lamb.

13:00 – Infirmary, *P.S. Scylla*

My therapy and scan consisted of an injection and Wilby staring at my chest, theoretically looking at my heart's internals; the leer that came with the stare was gratis, apparently. It took about five minutes out of my long day. After that I had been allowed to walk through the ship in order to build up my strength. Atalanta had joined me partway and I'd filled her in on Wilby. I hadn't seen Samuel since last night. I was sure he was busy, he was always busy, but I was so far out of the loop that I had no idea what he might be busy with.

So now I was back in bed, having recently woken from a wonderful nap, beating solitaire. I was bored, but kind of all right with it. A little boredom was welcome after all the excitement of the last week.

I felt a presence at the door. Doc Wells. He came in, moved the chair a respectable distance away from my bed and sat down without invitation. Curious, I scanned him. Now if this was Samuel, I would say this man was pissed off…

"I'm expecting to discharge you tomorrow. Your progress is excellent, better than I had expected, and you would only need to come back here for monitoring every morning for a week."

"That's good to hear, Sir." I started collecting my cards. "How is the Captain?"

Doc Wells' expression lightened a bit. "Even better. He went home today. His broken bones are almost healed and we didn't need to do surgery. We were able to stop the internal bleeding without it." Then he grimaced. "His *sister* was so relieved."

I felt myself bristle at the nasty way he'd said that. Who the fuck was this asshole to judge them? But deep inside I knew he was only the *first* asshole to judge them.

"Wilby was able to help him, too. He has a real gift for healing, ironic considering that all of you supers have been trained to do nothing but kill your entire lives." His tone was light, but his every word was laced with contempt. Geez, was he having a bad day or was he just like this?

"So, where will you go when you are discharged, Jane?" The Doc's question was pointed but I couldn't imagine why he cared.

"Why, Sir?"

"Because you won't be cleared for sexual activity," and here I blushed, dammit, "for the week you are in outpatient therapy. I thought that might affect where you went." I just looked at him stunned. He continued, "It should be two weeks, but I thought that would be cruel considering we have so little time, less than a month I'm guessing, before the Terrans come."

OK, I thought as I tried to control my temper. The fuckhead knows I'm with Samuel, obviously, then why would he make this 'magnanimous gesture' giving me more time to have sex with my own boyfriend. Because of the Terrans. Because he thinks we are going to break up when they come. Fine, then. Let's just cut to the chase.

"Samuel and I are staying together."

Doc Wells sucked in his breath quickly. What on earth had he expected me to say? "That's an incredibly stupid choice, Jane."

I started looking around the room for my shoes. By the door. I needed to get out of here and away from this jerk. "Samuel and I made the choice together. Why don't you talk to him about how stupid it is?"

"I did." Doc Wells grimaced angrily. "He admitted it would be difficult, but wouldn't change his mind."

Oh, now that was too much. "I don't see how this is any of your business." I paused. "Sir."

Doc Wells leaned forward in his chair. "I have been Sam's friend for 3 decades. He is the best commander I have ever served with. I was thrilled when he came to the School after he retired. He's a good man."

"I know."

"But his relationship with you will ruin him." I looked at him in astonishment. "Not right away, but in dribs and drabs. Neither of you can really see it now because you are in the bubble. And it will carry you for a while, but then it will burst and you will go on your merry 18 year old way and he will forever be a joke."

"People will understand over time that we're good together," I started, but it sounded weak and clichéd even as I said it aloud.

"The couple dozen people that know you two may get it. Or they may not. And everyone else will think it's funny. That the General brought along his own fresh piece of ass to keep him amused. And they'll assume that he'll replace you with a new one when you get too old. They'll be waiting for it. And if they see you look at a man your own age, they will think you are cheating because the 'old man' is too old to satisfy you. And he looks at a woman his age, they'll say that he wants more than sex from *her* since he can only get sex from *you*."

I could hardly breathe—and was really glad my heart was already in good shape. His words were mean and merciless and they hurt. The way he put it was all so coarse and sordid. I wanted to scrub it off my skin and out of my mind. But the worst part was that I didn't know how to defend myself against what he was saying. I mean, it all sounded so…plausible. And so awful.

"Listen, I knew Ruth, his wife. They met and fell in love in a bubble, too. They were happy on Pace 1, in her world. But then he got command and she realized she would be living on a ship in order to be with him. That made the bubble burst." He sighed. "The sad thing was that she had known that that was who he was going to be. But she, and he, couldn't bear to acknowledge the future reality because they instinctively knew their relationship wouldn't survive. So they pretended it was never going to be a problem and the bubble burst anyway *because it always does*. She never forgave him for going into space. She was a fool. Like you. And like him."

I was too shocked to speak. Here he was casually shitting on my dreams, on the dreams of someone he claimed was his friend. And then I had another horrible thought. Is this what I do to Ian and Wilby? Am I this cruel?

I no longer felt I had the power to go, but I really wished he would finish and leave.

"Would you love him if he weren't 'the General'?"

I met Doc Wells' cold brown eyes. "Yes." That at least was something I was sure about.

"I believe you. I know that probably surprises you, but I do. No one would have done all the things you've done for Sam without real love." He seemed to think I should respond, but rolled on when I didn't. "The problem is that Sam won't survive *not* being 'the General.' It is his first best destiny." Doc Wells dropped his voice. "Anyone who selfishly takes that away from him doesn't love him enough to deserve him."

I couldn't even think now. I had a dozen emotions running through my head, but the top two were fear and fury. How dare he lecture me like this? How dare he try to rip Samuel away from me with his nasty words? I opened my mouth to speak but he held up his hand for silence.

"On another note, I understand that you were under tremendous stress the other day, both physical and mental. But I *am* your superior and, while we tend to keep things fairly informal here, your insubordination is not going to be tolerated." Just when I thought I'd run out of shock, he was taking time from attempting to ruin my life to yell at me for *insubordination*? Was he fucking kidding? He continued, "Let me put it another way, Jane." He stood up as if to leave. "You ever fucking threaten me like that again and I'll have you up on charges—which will embarrass the hell out of your boyfriend since he'll have to punish you to the maximum so as not to show favoritism. And I know you are just a girl, but I am fully willing to fight back."

I looked up at him, no longer cowed, no longer afraid, just mad. "I could have killed you ten different ways within the first thirty seconds you were in here. I could still do it."

Doc Wells exhaled his contempt. "It wouldn't make me wrong about anything I said, though, would it." He headed for the door. "And I could have let you die on the table." Those words sent a chill through my body. "I wouldn't do that." And he turned back, abruptly serious. "I actually *wouldn't* do that. Ever, no matter how much I dislike a patient. But being a doctor and a good one is the focus of my life." Now his voice was soft, almost pleading. "Like being a leader is for Sam."

He took a deep breath apparently collecting himself. His heart was beating very fast. It had cost him to say this to me. That made me feel a little better, if only a very little.

"So where will you go when I release you?"

It was then I noticed Samuel in the doorway, leaning on his crutch. I don't know how long he'd been there. I'd been too absorbed in this unexpected attack to notice anything else.

"She's coming with me, Julius." The look Samuel was giving Doc Wells would have vaporized a mere mortal. I think he'd heard quite a bit of our conversation. I didn't know if I was glad or not. No, not. I didn't feel the need to spread the Doc's vitriol to Samuel. Bad enough I'd had to hear it.

I felt Samuel looking at me, but I didn't meet his eyes. My anger was waning now that he was there. Now I just wanted it all to stop. I wanted to unhear everything I'd heard.

"You had no right to speak to her like that, Julius." Samuel's voice was low and full of fury. "Now get out the fuck out of her room."

The Doc started to speak, but changed his mind. His face was flushed and his eyes bright. He hesitated a second, but registered the murderous expression in Samuel's eyes and quickly left the room. Samuel watched him go. "All the social skills of a live *tapetia mortis*," he said to himself.

I sat perfectly still on the bed, hurtful words running rampant though my head. Was he right? Did we only make sense in the bubble? Was I really going to have to give Samuel up to prove how much I loved him? Dear god was he *right*? I felt my world was crashing in on me.

"Jane?" Samuel asked softly.

I just sat there like an idiot. He limped over and put down his crutch. Then I felt him gently lift me out of bed and hold me to him as he leaned against it for support. I found his strong arms as comforting as I always did, but I also felt the poison of the Doc's words working their way through me. I buried my face in Samuel's chest.

"Just put it out of your mind, Baby. Just forget everything he said. It's going to be all right." I felt his chest resonate as he spoke and I held him tighter.

I'd had 12 hours or so of happiness, I thought. That brief period where everything was actually all right. He hadn't died, *I* hadn't died, his kids were safe, the Scientists were defeated and we were going to be together. And even though I could hold and be held by him now and rejoice in it, there was no stopping that poison as it worked its way further and further into my mind and heart.

ENTRY 11-2-17

Excerpt from Captain Nunzio Andrew DeStephani's Journal, August 1, 2869

I once had a man from Pace 4
Who lived his life like a whore
His heart I would lock
Though I'd marry his cock
But he left me begging for more

I can't believe I just reduced a love affair to a dirty limerick, but it was the best I could do.

But maybe I'll see him today after all this time.

No, I will *see him. But does he want to see* me*?*

08:00 – The General's Quarters, *P.S. Scylla*, August 1, 2869

Samuel had just left, having given me the required chaste kiss and a completely non-regulation smile (of the dirty old man variety). It had been a long, rather dull week of therapy and no sex. But I was supposed to be cleared this morning and I was relieved. There had been several, *several* times when temptation had almost been too much, but we'd made it. Thank god it was almost over, though. Because the more time passed the choice between living a full life without being able to make love to Samuel and being able to make love to him damning the consequences, well… Let's just say that another week would have finished at least one of us.

So Samuel went off to work every day and I got to play with a new toy. Not *that* kind of toy. No, a more useful toy. A Flight Simulator.

I'd gotten used to the display, the targeting and my favorite, the small 3-D projection that floated over my left hand showing my ship's location in relation to the 4 planets and sun of my system. I was just a dot there, but Paces 1-4 glowed with color and slowly turned on their axis around their own personal fireball. My abilities with the controls were all right. My ability to get back in the carrier ship, in this case the *P.S. Newton,* was, however, abysmal. The fighters, and we only had twelve so the carrier ship was mostly empty, were loaded into tubes and 'dropped' into space for launch. Any idiot could get out of the ship. But it actually took some skill to get back in without getting yourself killed. More skill than I currently possessed, apparently, because I hadn't made it back alive yet. The worst, though, was the time I'd crashed so badly that I'd incinerated the *Newton*, too.

Now, to be fair, these…errors on my part should have been private and the mortification mine and mine alone. But only a few of us were being trained and our sessions with the simulator were being monitored remotely by both Felix and Ian. Felix, of course, was quite skilled and Ian was, arguably, the best Pacey pilot alive.

The real problem for me was that as good as this simulator was, and I had been assured it was quite good, it couldn't give you the *feel* of flying through space. That was impossible. But I wasn't necessarily in a hurry to rush out into a real fighter either. I had two main worries: One—that I wouldn't be able to get back on the carrier and Two—that I would throw up all over the cockpit. To tell the truth I wasn't sure which of those two options would be worse. I was going to get to sit in, and hopefully (?), fly one of the *Caracara* class fighters today after lunch. I had the simulator (with the large exception of the landing snafu) down cold and Ian and Felix wanted me and the other Macros they were training to try the real thing. More fools they.

But first we all had to gather for a briefing. Apparently the *tapetia mortis* were getting closer to launch.

10:00 – Small Conference Room, *P.S. Scylla*

The room was packed. I was there with Felix and Ian, several of *Scylla*'s staffers, Colonel Gold and a few Pacey 3 Engineers. Ian's arm was still in a sling and he looked terrible. He was unshaven and barely put together and his handsome blue eyes were bloodshot. The break with Arrow, the *inevitable* break with Arrow, had come too soon for him. But it had had to come now that everyone knew. My heart went out to him, but this was neither the time nor place to try to comfort him.

The General stood in front of us, waiting for us to simmer down. But the person I was most interested in (aside from Ian) was the large man with the piercing green eyes sitting at the front of the table. The General cleared his throat and we all gave him our attention.

"Ladies and Gentlemen, we all are mourning the losses of so many of our friends in the recent action. And one of the greatest losses to us personally is that of Senior Engineer Sig Van Houton." The General's face was appropriately, almost professionally sad, though I knew he had been deeply upset by the loss of his friend. I'd felt it myself. "But since we've come to rely on the expertise and ideas of our Pacey-3 compatriots, I have asked for help from Sig's second in command, Senior Engineer Nunzio Andrew DeStephani, who is now in charge of all things Pace-3." The General smiled and gestured to the large man with the green eyes who smiled at us. We gave him a small round of applause to welcome him and he acknowledged it with a nod. "Andrew, if you would?"

Andrew raised his eyebrows at the fact that the General had gotten his name right (I'd told him) and stood up. God, he was big.

"Thank you, Sam." Andrew scanned the room quickly and plunged in, "We believe that we have reached a critical time in the evolution of the *tapetia mortis*."

He pressed a button on the conference table and a simulation popped up on the wall monitor. "According to our flybys, the crab-creatures are in the process of creating their new Objects. These Objects will be used to carry the creatures back into space then, eventually, to another set of worlds to devour." The simulation showed a mountain from Pace 4 with a *t-hive* built against it. At the top of a mountain the creatures had apparently created a sort of bowl. That bowl was filled with Objects. Like a giant nest.

"When the time is right, the Objects will be dropped into the *t-hive* and then the pressure within it will shoot them into the atmosphere and beyond."

Felix raised his hand. Andrew nodded permission to speak. "How long do we have?"

"Not long. To be safe the General and I think we should be prepared to act very soon."

"How soon?" I asked, surprised. I hadn't meant to speak, but then I never did.

Andrew gave me a serious look. "Within the next 6 days."

There was some comment among the people in the room. It seemed unreasonably soon to me, but I had to admit that, as usual, there had been so many other things occupying me that I hadn't kept the *tapetia* problem in the front of my thoughts. Samuel and I almost dying was so *distracting*.

We watched the Objects roll into the simulated *t-hives* and shoot up into the air as if out of a gun. It was very fast and soon the 'bowl of eggs' was completely empty. The room was silent for a while, the horror of imagining this escape weighing on us all. Andrew continued, "They aren't quite this far along, but they're getting there. They never stop and never sleep, they just keep going. Thankfully, for our sakes, they don't move that quickly. But they are inexorable."

Then Andrew smiled, though his manner was still serious. "But we have a plan." Despite what he was saying I found I liked his smile. I could see someone, namely Wilby, loving that smile. He clicked something else and the display changed.

Now we were looking at our Pace Star System. The sun and all four planets moving around it. Then we moved closer to Pace 3. Andrew's smile broadened a bit, at seeing his clearly beloved home. But then his expression hardened.

"Pace 3 has a massive fault line running through the southwest hemisphere." The simulation zoomed in to Pace 3 and the fault. Pace 3 was beautiful in a wild and very dangerous way—the way a volcano was beautiful. All black and fiery red. "If we concentrate all of our nukes along this line," the fault line was now illuminated in green, "we should be able to force it open." The green fault line cracked and the planet fractured into 1 small piece and 2 larger ones. "The gravitational pull on Pace 3 will be so radically altered that the orbits of the remaining 3 planets will be violently disrupted."

The view on the simulation pulled back as Pace 3 disintegrated. The remaining 3 planets were forced to shift their orbits and changed as they did so. The topography of Pace 4 became smooth. The green jewel that was Pace 1 turned grey and dead. Pace 2's buildings and structures were wiped away as though by a giant hand. I watched with shock as all evidence of human progress was erased from our worlds.

"It's like we were never there," I said bleakly to myself. Felix caught my eye, but then looked away. I think he'd been thinking something similar. I turned my head to check Ian's reaction, but he appeared too wrapped up in his own thoughts to have a response. I wondered how much of this he was actually hearing and seeing. He was worrying me.

Andrew clicked again and several ships appeared around Pace 3. The largest of them had to be the *Scylla*, then there was a very menacing looking Pacey-3 ship and half a dozen fighters. *Caracara* class, if I wasn't mistaken. Oh, I got it now. I shot a look to the General who shrugged, but gave me a small smile.

"As you can see here," Andrew continued, "the *Scylla* will shoot the bulk of the Appleseed nukes into the fault line. My ship, the *DSVH*, will send the rest and get in closer to help coordinate." I looked at him questioningly. He seemed to think I thought he was overstepping or something because he immediately explained, "My ship can get much closer than conventional metal."

I shook my head. "What does *DSVH* stand for, Sir?"

Now Andrew actually grinned. "*Doctor Sig Van Houton*." He laughed a little. "Sig never got over having that title withheld so we gave him a ship when it was christened a couple of years ago." We all chuckled a bit. Yes, from what we'd seen of Sig that seemed quite in character. But then Andrew was back to being serious. "The fighters, the few that we have, will be piloted by Macros to help with any unexpected problems, and will be led by Captain Armstrong." Ian managed to summon a smile and nod, but then retreated into his own thoughts.

Andrew scanned our faces again, taking in our reactions. "It is a radical solution, but we," and here he indicated the General and himself and, I guessed, Sig, "believe it will work and will stop the *tapetia mortis* from doing this to anyone else." He looked over at the General who spoke.

"Captain Armstrong will be taking command of the *Trafalgar*, assisted by Major Meir, but will be periodically on the *Newton* to supervise Macro fighter training." The General looked back at Andrew, who had nothing more to add. "I think that's all. Dismissed."

Everyone stood up except Ian and me. I watched them file out, the General leaving last of all. He watched me and Ian as he limped along leaning on his cane, but there was no jealousy in his expression this time. All I saw was concern for his son. I nodded at the General as he reached the door. Then he was gone and I turned to Ian, who still just sat there. I rested my hand on his good arm.

"How can I help you, Ian?" Though I was pretty sure there wasn't anything.

He said nothing for a while, then looked right at me with those incredibly blue eyes. "Take care of Arrow."

I nodded. "Do you *want* to go to the *Trafalgar*?"

He let out a laugh. "I volunteered." Then he looked away. "Too many people have suspicions. I need to disappear. It was Dad's idea, though it was a logical choice." He rubbed his face with his good hand. "I have to get out of here, Jane."

"I know, love."

The door opened and in walked Andrew. He didn't seem to notice us as he looked, then spied his flight jacket on a chair. Ian and I just stayed silent and waited for him to go. Then Ian stood up and I did the same.

"Great focus on that guy." Ian said quietly. I took his arm and we followed Andrew out the door. Once we were in the corridor I heard the crack of knuckles. And my first thought was, that's the sound Wilby makes when he's nervous. And then I thought, my god, Wilby is *here*.

I looked quickly around for him and there he was, off to the side, leaning against a wall. Crack. He's really nervous, I thought. Crack.

Then Andrew froze. He was thinking, like he'd been reminded of some long forgotten memory. It seemed he knew what the 'crack' meant as well as I did. His head whipped around and he saw Wilby.

"*Wilby!*" Andrew whispered. At the sound of his name Wilby stood up straight, but didn't move, as if paralyzed by fear. Andrew, however, moved quickly in broad strides and swept Wilby up in what had to have been a bone-crushing embrace. Ian and I stopped in our tracks and, I'm ashamed to admit, stared. Wilby just stood there for a minute, unmoving, unresponding.

Then I heard Andrew say, still softly, "I've missed you so much, Wilby. So much." And all at once Wilby surrendered and wrapped his arms around that impossibly muscled back.

"You were dead. You were dead, Drew," Wilby said, his voice unsteady. I saw tears in his eyes and realized, rather belatedly, that Ian and

I needed to go. We started to walk away, but out of the corner of my eye I saw Andrew hold Wilby's face in his hands and, very tenderly, kiss him.

12:10 – Officer's Lounge, *P.S. Scylla*

Ian hadn't wanted to eat so had left me for his quarters almost as soon as we'd given Andrew and Wilby their privacy. All the privacy a busy hallway outside our main conference room could afford, I should say. Wilby in love. What an idea. I was happy for him. Ian wasn't, but that seemed understandable. Lost love found would be the last thing I'd want to see, too, were I in his shoes. Then I had the unwelcome thought that that might be me soon, too. Fighting the stirrings of panic in my soul, I sent the thought away. I just wanted to focus on the good. That was all.

I'd made a quick stop into the Infirmary to get cleared by the dickhead Doc Wells. It had gone pleasantly enough. He'd insinuated (well, said outright) that I was a bitch and I'd threatened to turn his penis inside out. Sigh. But he'd cleared me anyway. My guess was that he hadn't wanted to deal with the fallout from Samuel. Knowing how pissed off Samuel would be if I hadn't been cleared made me think this was a smart choice on his part.

I wandered into the Officer's Lounge for lunch, rations in hand. I saw Atalanta in her usual spot and made my way over to her. Apparently lost in thought, she didn't notice me until I was right next to her. Her pretty face was creased with a frown and she stared off out the window, her food untouched.

"'Lanta?"

She looked up at me and smiled, patting the seat next to her. I took it but continued to watch my friend. She took a breath and visibly shook herself to dispel her mood.

"How was your check up?"

I grinned. "Apparently my recovery was so good the old son of a bitch *had* to clear me."

"I'm glad."

"Me, too. It's been a long fucking week. It will be so good to get back to the fun stuff."

Atalanta's face fell and I realized that it would have been difficult for me to have picked anything more insensitive to say. "I am such an idiot, 'Lanta..."

She held up her hand to forestall any apology. I felt terrible anyway, though. Silence fell, neither one of us seeming to know where to go after my genius statements extolling the extreme difficulties of going over a *week* without sex.

Atalanta spoke. "Would you have fallen in love with the General if you'd known you could never have sex with him?"

This seemed a very loaded question. I thought for a second, trying to anticipate the answer that would make her feel best. But Atalanta caught my eyes. "Be honest. Please."

I exhaled. "You mean feel attraction but never be able to act on it?" She nodded. "Yes. But it would be torture."

"And if you couldn't feel the attraction. Would you have fallen for him anyway?"

Now I really was stuck. If I was honest and I knew she wanted me to be, neither of us was going to be satisfied with my answer. "I don't know. Sex has always been such a huge part of our relationship. Do I love Samuel as a person separately from sex? Absolutely. Without question. One of the reasons making love to him is so wonderful is because I love the man he is. But..." And here I hesitated. "But I can't imagine romantic love without that kind of intimacy. So, I don't know."

"That's about what I thought you'd say." Her face was sad.

"You mentioned peaks and valleys in your relationship with Felix. We're in a valley, I take it."

"A fairly deep one." Atalanta shrugged. "I just need to wait for it to pass."

"And I come in here all happy, flaunting my relationship with Samuel. I'm such an asshole."

She let out at small laugh. "I'm happy for you, Jane. And for him. And you aren't 'flaunting' anything. My life wouldn't be improved if you were as unhappy as I am." She played with her food, still not actually eating any of it. "It's one of the drawbacks of being a MEmp, especially as connected as we are. I can feel your love for him, your desire for him. It comes pouring out of you."

I recoiled in horror at the unhappiness I was unintentionally inflicting upon her. This was so unfair. So awfully one-sided. Ok. But maybe fair can be fair.

"So give it to me," I said. Atalanta's eyes went very wide. I nodded emphatically. "I'm serious. Share with me. You've done it before." She looked at me. I guessed she was gauging my sincerity. Thankfully I *was* sincere.

So she let me have it. I felt a wave of love mixed with longing. Powerful, overpowering longing. All for Felix. A more detached part of my brain measured it against my love for Samuel. No less strong, just different. I felt intense compassion and a protective streak as strong as my own, but that felt very different, too. And at the base of it, nestled in with the love and desire, was anger. Anger at Bayliss for creating Felix this way, anger at their eternal standoff, even a little anger at Felix for making her love him. For trapping her. And then the accompanying guilt for even thinking something like that.

Then the onslaught of emotions retreated and I was able to focus on the room, on Atalanta again. My eyes were full. But she turned away from me when I tried to catch her eyes.

"I didn't mean for you to see all that." She looked like she wanted to cry. "Much worse than you thought, right?"

I put my food down and moved close to her, desperate to calm her distress. I put my arm around her small shoulders and hugged her. "I don't think you're horrible, love." I had to laugh at myself. "I think your 'packaging' makes it easy to think of you as either all good or..."

"...Queen bitch." Atalanta finished tearfully.

"But you're not. I know what a good person you are. And though I was surprised at some of what you felt, none of it seems crazy to me. And you feel guilty because of it and that seems right, too."

"You wouldn't feel that way about Samuel."

I didn't say anything to that. In fact I didn't say anything long enough that she pulled away from me to stare at me. Now I was embarrassed. Now I had to look away from her.

"I couldn't forgive him for wanting to give me up when the Terrans arrived." Her face had the abstracted look it sometimes got when she scanned. Her expression cleared.

"But you never called him a coward to his face?"

I shook my head.

Atalanta bit her lip. She was holding something back. She looked like she was about to say something but changed her mind.

But I thought I knew what she was thinking. "You don't think it was cowardice. You think it was prudence." And suddenly I didn't know whether to be angry or to give in to despair. I wanted to scream at her that she was wrong, that she was punishing me for seeing too much of her heart. That she was just being vindictive and that it was nothing more than that.

But then she projected her emotions on me again and I found none of that. What I felt was remorse for having upset me, worry that I wouldn't forgive her and fear that *whatever* happened to Samuel and me that I was going to end up hurt. She pulled her emotions back from me again. I was still upset, but I wasn't mad at her, needless as that would have been. I was just scared. I couldn't imagine losing him. The thought of it was simply terrifying to me. Without him all I saw before me was hopelessness. Losing him felt to me like a death.

Atalanta was watching me and clearly growing more and more alarmed as my emotions ran away with me. I felt her take both my hands and I was flooded with calm. My despairing train of thought was immediately broken and I was able to breathe easier.

"Thanks," I said, feeling more than a little drugged.

"No problem." Atalanta shook her head. "Man, we are so much fun to have around."

"You know it." I smiled at her and she released my hands. As she did so a thought occurred to me. An old idea I'd had that had been put aside when we'd started planning the destructions of the DNA samples on the *Hastings*. But Atalanta was herself again, Felix was all right and Samuel and I were happy (at least for now). There was no time like the present.

"I actually had an idea. It's a little out there, but see what you think..."

I started outlining my plan and if anyone had been watching us they would have seen Atalanta jump back in her seat in surprise. But then she leaned forward again, listening and thinking. I had definitely caught her attention.

14:00 – Fighter Maintenance Bay, *P.S. Newton*

I'd come over on the shuttle with Felix, Garrett, and two Macros I didn't really know: Julianne and Anan. Ian was waiting for us, his arm now out of its sling, having just come over himself in his own fighter from the *Trafalgar*. He looked very handsome in his flight suit. Or he would have if everything about him didn't scream out his misery.

"Today each of you will feel what it is like to fly one of these *Caracara* class fighters." Ian spoke quietly but his voice, like his father's carried well. My gut clenched. I was never going to get back in the carrier. My hand dropped involuntarily to the inner pocket of my jacket where my stash of vomit bags was safely tucked away.

"These ships are the cutting edge of Pace-Pallon technology," he said, saying the words with distaste. "Which means that they were built almost 30 years ago and they were the *only* ones we've built in those same 30 years." He sighed. "Which also means that they are wildly out of date compared to anything the Terrans will have should you be offered the chance to fly with them." Some of us looked up, surprised. He held up a hand to calm us. "It doesn't really matter. The principals will be the same. You will adapt and probably more easily than you think. Master these ships and you'll be fine." He looked over at Felix.

"Unfortunately," Felix continued, "We need you to master these right away. Some of you were at the briefing this morning and know that we expect to be called to action within the next 6 days. Probably sooner. At the minimum you *must* be able to control your ship. Anything beyond that will be good, but the control is crucial." The he looked at us with tremendous seriousness. "If you can't control it I, we," he corrected, "can't let you fly. For your safety and the safety of the mission. Understood?"

We nodded, some of us looking distinctly nervous. Not Garrett (the cheater), of course. I scanned him. Nope he wasn't hiding it either. Well, maybe he was good at this. I was suddenly overcome with the urge to be a genius at this flying thing. Please god don't let me throw up.

Half an hour later we were each sitting in our very own fighters. While someone might describe them (accurately) as a chair sitting on an engine, they were far cooler than that. The exterior of each ship was black, painted with some kind of light-absorbing material. The small wings swung around the barrel of the main body from nose to tail, giving them an almost disc-like shape. The cockpit was an elongated bubble of clear Tenorium, providing a 360 degree view of everything. Inside the displays lit up like a miniature jewel box. The ships were incredibly cool.

The four Macros (myself included) were sitting in their fighters while Ian and Felix prowled around us answering questions. Once I was strapped in I gazed at my display and felt the surprisingly comfortable seat beneath me. Much more comfortable than Samuel's office chair. The 3-D planets were still on my left with small icons of our major ships. My ship wasn't on the display because it was still within the *Newton*. I was outfitted with a flight suit, like Ian's, though I didn't have the masculine swagger I felt it needed to really pull it off. It was airtight and had its own oxygen and, uncomfortably, toilet facilities built in. I'd left my vomit bags behind. Apparently the only place vomit was going to go was *in my suit*. This was an incredibly gross incentive to not throw up.

"Now the first thing we are going to do," Felix's amplified voice came over the comm built into my helmet, "is ground. We will ground on the *Newton*, then our fighter. And Jane?"

"Sir?" I answered, surprised he was addressing me directly.

"Be careful. Make sure you are set before you attempt anything. It is a ship, but it is also a weapon in more ways than one. Understood?"

"Yes, Sir." This little and frustratingly vague extra warning was not helping my nerves. He must be worried about the Telespatial thing. Why else single me out? Great, now *I* was worried about the Telespatial thing. Fuck me running.

Felix continued, "Macros can have a problem with being part of smaller Objects that move. Some of you had a bad time on the shuttle when we evacuated," that would be me, I thought, "and had difficulty, at least initially, grounding at all once we were on the *Scylla*." Me, again. "As I've discussed with all of you individually, the best solution I found for being able to use our gifts in a moving object was to ground progressively, starting with the biggest thing and ending with the smallest, in this case, your fighters." He chuckled. "This took a lot of experimentation…" Then we heard a snort that had to be Ian, who must have been witness to some of this potential disaster. "…but this is the solution that has worked for me on a craft this small."

Felix paused so that we could absorb this. "So I want to you to ground the way I said, then try, *gently*, to raise your ship while you are in it."

"Without power?" I asked, dubious.

"Without power," Felix confirmed.

Well, what the hell. I did as I was bid, grounding on the *Newton* first. The *Newton* was a much smaller ship than the *Scylla*, but I found it easy enough to ground on. Then, for good measure I grounded on the Fighter Repair Bay within the Newton. Then the *Caracara* fighter itself. I took a second to feel the rather elegant streamlining of the wings, the smooth shape of the cockpit. I took its measure and attempted to gauge its weight.

I felt other ships around me moving, taking baby steps to leave the Repair deck. I took a breath, now no longer nervous, and once again felt the 'body' of my small ship. Anticipating the weight I gathered myself to lift…and shot my ship through the air on a collision course with the ceiling of the Bay.

"Jane!!!!" Felix and Ian screamed. My gloved hands reached up and pushed on my clear cockpit ceiling. I could see it coming at me so fast. Crazy fast. Almost instinctively I 'reached' for the ceiling and pushed back on it—and managed this time not to send my ship careening hopelessly in the opposite direction. It stopped. It stopped about two yards from smashing into the roof. I then held her (the ship) there in hopes of one day catching my breath. I slowly pried my hands down from the cockpit roof and saw them, not surprisingly, shaking violently. I wondered how much adrenaline my body was producing. Enough to light up a small town, I thought.

After a few seconds I gently lowered my ship back down to the ground, touching it down. Perfectly, really, not that anyone cared. I looked over at Felix and Ian whom I could see through the Tenorium cockpit window. Felix had his fingers on the bridge of his nose and his eyes closed, an unfortunately typical expression for him when he was training me. Ian had his hand over his mouth and his eyes wide. He was quietly laughing and shaking his head. The other ships were safely on the ground and everyone was staring at me.

For once I didn't blush. Was that a good thing? Was I so used to fucking up that I'd just accepted it? I sighed. Apparently I might as well.

"Ok," said Felix glaring at me, "since we all seem to have grasped the grounding concept we will load the ships and prepare to drop."

Fifteen minutes later I was in the drop tube waiting my turn to go into space. The ships were turned vertically and dropped 'down' out of the carrier. The tricky thing was getting the ignition sequence timed properly. You could have the auxiliary systems warm in the tube, but sub light Iris Drive (so named because the throttle opened and closed on the energy source like an iris) had to activated *after* the ship left the tube. Turning it on while it was in the tube would be, I had been assured, very, very bad. So the pilot had to turn on, at the very tail end of an unpowered drop, the Iris drive and gain control of the ship as soon as possible.

Now the consequences of timing it badly were, admittedly not great under normal conditions. Floundering around with no power while trying to get your engine started just made you look like a fool, something no watching pilot would ever let you forget. It was only under battle scenarios that getting late control of your ship could get you killed. Ian had told us the story of how pilots during the Revolution of 30 years ago had to start firing weapons the second they'd cleared the drop tube and before their drives had been activated just to stay alive. Fighters of the opposition had just been waiting to pick them off one by one. The few seconds between the drop and ignition were the most dangerous for any fighter.

The ship ahead of me in the queue dropped and mine was automatically moved forward. I quickly ran over my ignition sequence, which was, thankfully, pretty simple. I still felt grounded.

Launch Control came on the speakers, "Prepare to launch at 3, 2, 1 and DROP."

It wasn't so much a drop as being shot out of the tube downwards at great velocity. But I'd practiced this hundreds of times. I flipped the switches, turned the dial and watched the countdown until Iris's full activation.

"Iris drive activated in 5 seconds, Launch Control," I said into my microphone. I could feel the heat building in the engine. Building and then… "Iris Drive active, Launch Control, *Caracara* 5 under power." I pushed the throttle a bit, not wanting to overdo it so soon after nearly killing myself in the Repair Bay, and the ship moved like a dream. I moved away from the *Newton* to let another person drop. "*Caracara* 5 cleared the *Newton*, Launch Control."

"Launch Control copies, *Caracara* 5. Godspeed."

The ship was moving, but my euphoria was abruptly gone as my vision blurred. I couldn't tell where I was, everything spun around me. I was nauseous from motion sickness. I tried to take deep breaths to shake it, but it wasn't helping. I forced myself to speak into the microphone.

"Felix, this is Jane. Having a problem. I need a minute." And I was taken by the spinning again. I tried to 'reach' outside the ship and was knocked back by the vacuum whipping by me as if at light speed.

"What's wrong, Jane?" Felix asked, concern in his voice.

I took another deep breath, begging the universe to make it stop. "A minute."

Ian's voice came over the speaker. "*Caracara* 1 and 4 shadow *Caracara* 5. Safe distance."

"Yes, Sir," Garrett and Anan replied. Within a few seconds I could feel the two ships on either side of me. Not too close. I was grateful for that. I couldn't see my displays, couldn't control my ship anymore. Couldn't even control it enough to stop it.

I had to fix this, but all I wanted to do was stop the ship and throw up out her window. Think, Jane. Think. There *has* to be a way to center. Well, a part of my brain said, there doesn't *have* to be anything. Maybe you just can't do this. I felt my heart pounding in my chest. Wait. Wait a minute. What if I could ground on my own body? I'd never even considered doing that. I'd never attempted to ground on something as comparatively small as a human body—much less my *own* body. But I had to try.

I closed my eyes and tried my best to tune out the dizziness and the disorientation. I put aside the nausea. And I focused on the ship with an intensity that literally made my head hurt. Then I moved my focus to the beating of my own heart and of all the tiny systems within my body—from the blood flow to the creaking of joints, to the pull of muscles.

I imagined myself as inviolate.

In my mind I had turned myself into a human-shaped piece of impenetrable stone around whom all other things (from ships to objects to whole planets) revolved. It was an odd feeling, really. I mean, nothing about me had changed, but I felt more…permanent somehow.

And then, like coming out of a fog, the dizziness faded away. I opened my eyes and I could see everything before me again. My stomach settled and I was re-oriented to my ship and the universe at large. I felt space flying by, but it felt good. I'd gotten it. I was OK. I exhaled hugely.

"Sorry, Felix. I was having a problem but I've fixed it. I have control of the ship again and am all right to continue the exercise."

There was a slight pause but then Felix came back on, "Acknowledged, Jane. What happened?"

"A grounding issue, Sir. But I figured it out. I'll explain later."

"Very well. Garrett and Anan, please return to previous positions."

"On our way," Garrett responded as his and Anan's ships peeled away from mine.

"Jesus, Jane. Do you have to scare us *all* the time?" That was Ian, sounding a little peeved.

"Sorry, Captain. Just trying to keep it interesting."

Ian mumbled something profane into his pickup that I didn't quite understand. I smiled to myself wryly. I would really hate to have me as a trainee.

But now that I was finally feeling good I wanted to *fly*. Really fly. I moved the controls tentatively, feeling her out. I concentrated on keeping my movements smooth and reveled in feeling the ship cut through space like warm butter. This was…amazing.

It was like the simulation, but it was also nothing like it at all. It was like the difference between understanding the *concept* of sex and actually *having* sex. The vibration of the engines was comforting, the feel of moving through space was exciting, like a strong swimmer gliding underwater. Yes, this was really fucking cool.

"Hey, Felix, how fast does this baby go?" I asked happily.

"Jane," Felix said, sounding very put upon, "Promise me you won't try anything on your own. Promise?"

I exhaled petulantly. "*Fine.*" Then I realized how that sounded and corrected myself. "Of course, Felix. Sorry." I thought I could hear Ian give what seemed like a grudging chuckle.

Ian spoke, "Now we will go around the *Newton* once, Perimeter Program Gamma, and then practice landing on the actual Flight Deck. Ships will land in the following order: Caracara 1, 3, 4 and…" and I could almost hear the wince, "5. Do not start your approach until you are cleared by the Air Boss."

The Flight Deck on the *Newton* was more a large tube on the bottom of the ship than anything else. Only one end was open during 'recovery' but the other end could be opened in a split second if necessary, in the event of a miss. What was supposed to happen was the fighter would come in and catch the arresting wires, the Alpha Bolters, and this would stop the ship, line it up with its Loading Track (which would, once the ship was ready, take it back to the drop tube) and allow the pilot to safely debark.

The brief time between drop and ignition was the most dangerous time for a pilot if someone else wanted to take them out. Trying to land your tiny ship back on your carrier was the most dangerous time for the pilot to take *herself* out. Of this I was well aware since I'd never managed to do it even in simulation. I started my Perimeter Program, leaving a nice distance between myself and the other ships. I wasn't so much worried about hitting the other ships when I tried to land. I knew there was no possible way that Ian and Felix wouldn't have the whole area evacuated before I got there. I could have been offended, but I really, really wasn't. The only thing worse than getting myself killed was taking out other people while I was doing it.

Before I knew it, it was my turn.

"*Caracara 5* is cleared the Flight Deck. Start your approach," said the voice that I assumed belonged to the Air Boss. I nodded, even though there was no one there to see it and took a breath.

I swung around the *Newton* and saw the opening to the Flight Deck in front of me. I turned my Iris Drive down to almost nothing, just enough for a little momentum. I felt the *Newton* coming at me and slowed my ship even more. Then I turned off the Iris completely. It was almost as if I could feel Felix struggling not to say something. This was not the way we were supposed to do it. But he kept quiet. In the back of my mind I appreciated the amount of effort it must be taking for him to let me fuck up on my own. I needed a bit more velocity so I 'grabbed' onto the mouth of the Flight Deck opening and 'pulled' my ship into it. We floated gently over the deck and I dropped the ship down to roll right over the Alpha Bolter until it clicked.

I looked around me. I was still alive. I hadn't done it the 'right' way, but I had done it and hadn't destroyed anything or hurt anyone. I was so happy I laughed like an idiot, sitting there in the cockpit. I saw the Control Tower (that was on my left) door open and Felix and Ian walk out. By now the giant Flight Deck door was closed tight and the room was repressurized. Ian was grinning. Felix was smiling, a bit wryly, I had to admit, but at least it was a smile. I popped the lid of my cockpit and scrambled out, removing my helmet as I did so. I saw the other students walking behind our two instructors. No one was limping or bleeding and everyone was still there so I assumed that everyone else had also done well.

Felix spoke to all of us. "That was good, people. Now, let's do it again."

The other students started walked towards the Drop Tubes and I caught up with Felix and Ian. I was still grinning like a crazy person. I dropped my voice as I spoke to them. "I did it. No one got hurt and I didn't screw up. Isn't that amazing?"

Ian barked a laugh, "It's a fucking miracle." I looked over at him a little hurt by his tone, but then I saw a shadow of his usual brilliant smile and realized that even though it *was* a miracle, he was teasing me. The shadows had left his eyes for just a second and he looked like himself again. It was a fleeting look, like the sun appearing from behind a cloud. And then his face sunk back into sadness.

Now Felix looked at me seriously. "What happened out there, Jane?"

I shrugged. "I had to figure out how to beat the Telespatial problem on the fly."

Felix nodded unhappily. "There wasn't any good way to know if that would even *be* a problem…"

"…without trying it in the actual ship. I know, Felix. But I solved it," I said, a smile on my face again.

"How?" Ian asked, his annoyance with me seemingly dissipated.

So I answered both of them. "I grounded on my own body—starting with my heartbeat. And it worked."

Felix, grinned at me, shaking his head in approval. "Clever girl." Now the three of us started walking towards the Drop Tubes. "I do have one real criticism, though."

Ian raised an eyebrow at the idea of only 'one' correction being needed, but didn't add anything.

Felix ignored him. "In terms of your landing: I think that this time you can treat the ship as though it is made of metal…"

Ian finished for him, "…not eggshells."

I grinned at them. "Fair enough, Sirs."

And we went back to work.

18:00 – Arrow's Quarters, *P.S. Scylla*

I entered carrying dinner rations for Arrow. It had taken about ten minutes to get her to open the door. Well, it had taken her ten minutes to realize that I wasn't going away. Her expression wasn't at all welcoming, but I hadn't expected it to be. Arrow looked pretty close to normal; it was only the deep dark circles under her eyes that told of her pain.

I handed her the rations and she accepted them with a shrug. She carried them to a corner, apparently the corner she'd abandoned to answer the door, and she gracefully sat back down on the floor and leaned against the wall. I sat next to her. She said nothing, just stared into space. I opened up her ration pack and waited for the self-heating element to warm her food.

"You know I saw all this. Before." Arrow said quietly.

"You did?" I watched her face. Her expression was bleak. "What did you see?"

"I saw us together, torn away from our ship. I saw it right down the exact bones they broke in his arm when he attacked them for trying to touch me." Arrow swallowed. "And I saw him come to me in the middle of the night, afraid that someone might see. I knew every word of his goodbye even before he'd said a thing."

The food beeped, indicating that it was ready to be consumed. She opened the top, took out the fork and stabbed a bite.

"So, he's," and I noticed then how she was avoiding saying his name, "off to the *Trafalgar* now?"

"I think he may already have moved over. But he's commuting to the *Newton* for fighter training," I said. Arrow nodded, chewing. "I saw him today."

She swallowed her bite. "How did he look?"

I looked at her, trying to gauge the answer that she was expecting. I went with the truth. "He looks like shit."

Arrow almost snorted. "He has never been good at hiding how he feels." She stabbed another bite. "It's one of the things I …like about him. But it won't help the situation now." She took the bite. I watched her eat and had the feeling that she was really hungry, from the way she devoured the dinner.

"When was the last time you ate anything, Arrow?" She shrugged. "Did you eat yesterday?" She shrugged again. "The day before?"

"I haven't been hungry, Jane. I don't see any point in eating when I'm not hungry."

Now I was worried and a little angry that she was neglecting herself. "How many days, Arrow?"

"I don't know. Three or four." The rations were gone and the little tray picked clean.

I stood up. She needed more food. "I'll be right back." I headed for the door, but her voice stopped me.

"I'm not afraid of physical pain, you know."

"I know."

"But this…" she looked away. "This is so much worse."

Her eyes were dry but mine were filling with tears for her. I marveled, in an almost detached way, how she could still manage to look elegant sitting there on the floor. Even with her heart crushed. I was so sorry for her.

"I'm getting more food." I keyed open the door and prepared to step through. "And I'm your dinner date until you start eating on your own."

"If you want," Arrow said with affected nonchalance. But then she looked up at me. "Why?"

"Two reasons: I don't want you to starve to death and I have the feeling that you'll only remember to eat if food is actually put in front of you. And because Ian asked me to look after you."

"Ian," she said softly, and her perfect posture seemed to disintegrate with the name. Her misery was so acute that I took a step back towards her, but she held up her hand to stop me. "Food," she commanded. So I went off to get it.

She didn't say much when I returned a few minutes later, but she did eat another whole ration box as well as the cocktail I'd brought her. She'd started to look sleepy, especially after imbibing the spirits, but had point blank refused to go to bed. Symbolically, I supposed it made sense. I don't know if I'd want to sleep in Samuel's bed (or, I qualified, since this was Arrow's bed, *any* bed I'd shared with Samuel) if I'd known I'd never be with him again.

I brought her a pillow and dropped it on the floor next to her. She lay down on it and watched me get her a blanket and cover her up.

"So what's going to happen with you and Dad?"

"We're supposed to stay together, but I don't know." I really didn't want to think about this now, but it was a fair question.

"Love like that is rare, Jane." Arrow's voice was getting softer and fuzzier as she started to drift off to sleep. "At least you have the option of being together." She sighed sleepily. "God, if I was in your situation, there's nothing I wouldn't do to stay with the man I love."

"But I don't know if our being together is the best thing for Samuel." Arrow said nothing in return and I looked over. She was asleep. I sighed and picked up the discarded ration box.

"Goodnight, sweetheart." And I turned out the light and left.

I went to the Officer's Lounge for a drink to clear my head. I needed to put my worries aside and not spoil tonight with Samuel. I'd missed being with him and I knew, mostly from the various near misses, that he'd missed me just as much. This wasn't the time for worry.

I ordered another drink. Better.

20:00 – The General's Quarters, *P.S. Scylla*

I was leaning against the desk waiting for him. The drinks had helped and I'd successfully beaten back my worries and was actually feeling really good by the time I was expecting him home. I had something to say, a favor, really and I didn't have any idea what he would say to it. Trouble was that I didn't want to talk at all and I was pretty damn sure he didn't want to either.

The door opened and there Samuel was. He'd already loosened his uniform jacket and he dropped it as he walked through, his limp hardly noticeable. He leaned his cane against a wall.

"Samuel," I breathed as he took me in his arms and kissed me. For a second, well, for longer, I lost myself in the kiss and in feeling his body against mine. I was starting to care less and less about my question as he pulled off my top and bra.

"Samuel?" No response. No *verbal* response. His mouth was on my neck, then my collar bone. Oh my. "Samuel, Baby." He'd moved on to my breasts and concentration was difficult.

"Just give me a minute," he said, pausing only to speak, then returning to work. He was moving lower. My god, I thought, it would be criminal to stop this. My question can wait.

"Take as long as you need," I gasped as he pulled my trousers off. He chuckled and kept going.

A little while later, both of us now much more relaxed, Samuel sat in his chair, facing slightly away, and I sat on the desk next to him, resting one of my legs on his shoulder. I ran my fingers through his hair and kissed his ear. He pressed my face to his with his hand. My newly healed heart was full. He was so beloved to me in this moment, it was hard to take.

"Did you need to ask me something, Jane?" His voice was soft as he leaned back in the chair, holding my leg with one hand.

Oh right. Yes, I did need to talk to him. "A favor. A really unusual favor."

"What is it, Baby?"

I had to fight the urge to laugh—not at him, but at the absurdity of the whole concept. But I'd meant to bring it up and I was still going to do it. No matter how crazy it sounded. "I thought maybe we could go to my place in a few minutes and make love again."

Samuel turned the chair around to face me, my foot now on his thigh. His eyebrows were raised as high as they would go. "Because smaller, more cramped environments with no privacy are…sexier? I've had sex in crew quarters—when I was part of the crew. It's not exactly palatial." He cast a quick look around his room as if reevaluating it. "Don't you like my quarters?"

I smiled. "I love them. They're my home." He smiled. "This is something else." He gestured for me to explain and I paused a second to marshal my thoughts. "You know about Felix. I mean, his genetic design problem."

Samuel's face became serious. "It was in his file. I looked it up, and his program and what they did to him." He looked away for a second, then looked back at me. "It was the kind of thing I wished I didn't know once I knew it. It must be awful for him."

"It is."

"And he's in love with Atalanta of all people."

"He is. And she with him."

Samuel nodded, exhaling at the thought.

Now here was the crux of it. "When Atalanta was trying to recover from her…attack," and I felt Samuel's internal wince even though I'd avoided saying 'rape,' "she and Felix and I sort of connected empathically. We were able to effectively drain off the worst of it so that she could get a handle on what had happened to her."

"She can do that?"

I nodded. "But in order to do that Felix and I lived her experience…"

"Good god, Jane," Samuel said, moving closer to me and putting his hand comfortingly on my knee.

"It's Ok now." I put my hand to his cheek and smiled. "And then Atalanta and I lived one of Felix's memories," and I looked away for a second, sadly.

"One of his memories with Atalanta?" Samuel asked, watching me.

"An intimate one." I sighed. "At least, for her."

He leaned back in his chair, clearly imagining the scenario. He shook his head. "And what did they see of yours?"

I blushed a bit. "Us. Together."

Samuel leaned forward again. "You mean, *together*?"

I had to smile a little bit though my cheeks were still red. "Very." Samuel stood up and took a step away. When he turned back I was surprised to see he was blushing, too. And this was probably *not* the time to tell him that Atalanta was impressed by his skill in the sack.

He closed his eyes as if trying to get the thought out of his head. "And you are telling me all this because..?"

I stood up, too. "Because Atalanta and I have some sort of empathic connection. When you and I were together my…love for you and my wanting you transferred to Atalanta and through her…"

"…to Felix." Samuel's eyes were opened wide at this revelation. He leaned on the desk and I leaned next to him.

"It was only a few seconds (mostly because I was so surprised it happened that I took myself out of the memory) but Felix got to *feel* passion for the first time in his life. Just for a minute, maybe. Just long enough to kiss, for the first time, the woman he's been in love with for years."

Samuel said nothing, clearly putting the pieces together.

"Think about us, Samuel." And he looked at me. "We couldn't make love for, what, ten days..."

"Eleven," Samuel corrected.

"…eleven days and I was going crazy."

Samuel snorted. "I was, too. But Felix can't feel any of this."

"But Atalanta can. And she can get sex anywhere she wants," Samuel shrugged his acknowledgement of the obvious, "but that isn't a good fix because she really only wants Felix."

"Wouldn't just any couple fucking do it for them?" I recoiled a bit from his choice of words and he shrugged an apology. "Sorry, it just seems such a personal thing to ask of anyone."

"They're not asking. *I'm* asking. And, no, it wouldn't be the same for two reasons. One: my link with Atalanta and Two: these are two people in love. It isn't just sex for them. They need, they deserve more than that. Atalanta knows, because she can read me, how much I love you, and…"

"Has she read me?"

"Yes," but, not wanting him to think I'd been prying I hurriedly added, "but I've never asked her about it."

Samuel smiled and put his arm around my shoulders, pulling me to his side. "Ask."

I felt a lump in my throat, but hid my reaction by resting my face on his chest.

"So how far are you willing to go to get me to do this? Dirty looks? Withholding sex? Hiding my boots?"

I laughed, "Withholding sex would be punishing me just as much as you. No," I said, more seriously, "no punishments. No recrimination. I knew there was a good chance this would be too out there for you, but I had to ask. Saying no is all right."

"You mean that?" He pulled my head gently away from his chest to look in my eyes.

"Completely." And he kissed me. But I had one more card to play. "Just one more thing to think about, though, Samuel."

He cocked his head to one side and looked at me very suspiciously. "Uh huh."

I once again felt hysterical laughter building up. So inappropriate, I scolded myself. "I wasn't the only one who risked her life for you. Felix risked his *twice*."

Samuel just stood there for a second then shook his head and started to laugh. "You're unbelievable, Jane."

I pretended to take offense. "I'll take that as a compliment, even though you didn't mean it in a nice way."

He reached out and pulled me to him. "Maybe I did and maybe I didn't." And he kissed me deeply. Really deeply. I felt the issue at hand retreating from my brain again. "Just give me a minute to think," he said as his hands started to move down my body.

"After your 'minute' will you say yes?"

"Yes."

I caught his eyes and smiled gratefully at him. "Thank you, Baby. Really." I captured his hands and held them.

"My minute isn't up," he complained.

"Let's take your minute somewhere else."

"You mean *now*?" I nodded. He sighed. I snuggled up to him as we stood. "Love is a crazy thing, Jane."

"No shit, Samuel."

<u>19:00 – Hallway outside Atalanta/Felix/Jane's Quarters, *P.S. Scylla*</u>

I stood outside my quarters. I was a little nervous, which I guess shouldn't have surprised me. Samuel was two minutes behind me and even more nervous. I was actually a little worried that he would be too nervous to perform. I really didn't want that to happen to him. He'd only had one real condition: He'd been adamant that this event, assuming it even worked, would happen but then just disappear from memory. Never discussed outside of the established couples, never alluded to and above all, *never* the subject of gossip. That seemed more than fair to me.

I pressed the entry bell. The door opened almost immediately. There was Atalanta, a little dressed up but kind of pale. Still beautiful, so beautiful. She invited me in with a gesture.

"Are you all right?" I asked.

She nodded. "Nervous. Stupid, isn't it? Even if he's a virgin, *I'm* certainly not."

I smiled at her. "I think this is an unusual situation for all of us, 'Lanta. I think a little anxiety wouldn't be surprising." I looked around the room, noting the dim lighting and the privacy curtain that was pulled all the way across. "He's not here?"

Atalanta shook her head quickly. "I'm expecting him in about 5 minutes." She bit her lip.

I took her hand and squeezed it. “It’s going to be OK. We’ve stacked the deck in our favor as much as we can.” She nodded. “He has no idea?” She shook her head.

There was the door chime. I looked quickly at Atalanta who let go of my hand and disappeared behind the curtain. I keyed the door open and there was Samuel, looking uncomfortable. He leaned a bit on his cane but came in quickly. He put his cane down by the door. I quickly pulled him to my half of the room and secured the privacy curtain so that no could see our side when they came in the door.

Then we just stood there awkwardly. He took a step towards me and leaned in to whisper in my ear, “This may be the most absurd thing I’ve even been a part of.”

I smiled my agreement but was concentrating on other things. I reached up to caress his cheek, then ran my fingers through his hair. I pressed my body against his and spoke softly. “I know this is strange, but I’m happy to be with you anywhere, Samuel.” I smoothed away some frown lines in his forehead with both sets of fingers. “There is nothing in the universe that I love so much as you. Anyplace. Or any time.”

He paused a second, thinking. “It’s kind of scary, wanting someone so much.”

I stood on my toes to kiss him gently. “Scary or wonderful?”

“Both.” His mouth met mine again, but this time more urgently. No, not urgently. With deliberate passion. He was going to give them, and me, bless him, their money’s worth. As my body responded I scanned Samuel, though I hardly needed to. Everything was terrific with both of us. But then I reached out my scan to Atalanta and was surprised to find her as aroused as I was. I had a brief moment of concern that we were already too into it, but then realized I wasn’t going to change anything. Samuel knew what he was doing and I was sure as hell not going to mess with his *moves*.

I pulled off his shirt, for the second time that night, and was preparing to take off his trousers when we heard the door open. We both froze like children caught doing something naughty.

It was Felix.

“Atalanta, what’s…who’s here?” Fuck, he’d seen the cane.

Samuel pulled me to him. “Don’t panic,” he whispered. And suddenly the potential silliness of the situation overwhelmed me. I started to laugh silently. Then Samuel started to silently laugh, too. But he got a hold of himself.

“Atalanta? What’s going on?” But she said nothing. I felt her move towards him, her body swayed as if to music. She rested her hands on his chest and I felt her kiss him. Kiss him with all the longing of years of waiting.

This was it. This was the moment of truth. Samuel felt me hold my breath, instinctively knowing what was going on. He kissed me again, so passionately that he lifted me from the ground. And I knew that it would be what it would be. I needed to love my man and let the chips fall where they would. I surrendered to his kiss, to the need in his body while he surrendered to mine.

But just then, just as I was about to abandon myself completely to sensation I felt something change in Felix. Something I'd never felt in him before. Everything was working. *Everything.* Then I felt tears coursing down Felix's cheeks and Atalanta's as well.

"Help me, love." Felix whispered, an echo of fear in his voice.

"Always," she whispered back.

Samuel had my clothes off by now and I hurried to get his off. He carried me to the bottom bunk and laid me down on it. He looked me in the eye as he leaned over me. "Just you and me, Baby. They will take care of themselves."

I nodded and he kissed me, then slowly and teasingly moved over me. Focus became very easy all of a sudden.

It was a strange and wonderful experience being made love to while being connected to Atalanta and Felix. The feedback loop we'd experienced during the Tap was even more noticeable now, every touch echoing and feeding into the next.

Of all of us I definitely got the best of the bargain. I felt Atalanta's orgasm, my own several and finally, exquisitely, Felix's. When Felix came it drove me over the edge and, through me, Samuel. Well, I don't really remember that part. I must have blacked out because I opened my eyes to Samuel shaking me.

"What happened? What's wrong?" I asked quietly.

Samuel exhaled in relief and brushed the hair out of my face. "I think the three of us 'loved' you into oblivion, Baby."

I snuggled up to him, feeling rather giddy. I looked into his eyes, delighting in how happy he looked. How contented.

Contented but, apparently, not done. "Can we continue this at home?" Samuel asked in my ear.

I nodded. "It'll be a tough act to follow."

He grinned at me. "All we can do is try."

We snuck out soon after, leaving the other couple asleep, wrapped up in each other. I wasn't an Empath, that was for sure, but I didn't need to be to know what they had together. They had joy. Thanks to Samuel *that* was something I knew a lot about. I pushed my worries out of my mind and followed Samuel home.

ENTRY 12-2-18

An Excerpt from Arrow Peter's Journal, August 2, 2869

I had another of those *dreams. I'd been expecting one for days considering that we're about to attempt to destroy a planet. But my dream wasn't about that at all. It was all personal, or close enough. I saw Ian handing over his uniform jacket and LPG to someone in a uniform I didn't recognize. I saw Jane and father embrace with tears and then say goodbye. I saw Wilby alone, broken. I saw Atalanta weeping into Felix's shoulder.*

But even though my dream wasn't about the mission, I have this feeling of foreboding. I wish I had more information. Jane has been pretty good about 'real' intelligence, though gossip would be a better name for it. She seems quite determined to do this dinner thing and looks unreasonably happy when I eat a lot. Funny girl.

I thought the worst had already happened to me…losing him. *But I guess the universe always has the power to disappoint you more. I wish I hadn't dreamt my dream. I am so tired of all the suffering.*

I can't wait to stop missing him. I wonder if I ever will.

06:00 – The General's Quarters, *P.S. Scylla*

I woke up in Samuel's arms, as usual. It had been three days since our nocturnal adventures with Felix and Atalanta and everyone seemed to have survived just fine.

Still half asleep, I re-ran my conversation with Felix from the day after everything had happened. I'd run into him in the Locker Room on the *Newton* as I was getting ready to fly. Things had felt different that day on the carrier. The fun of the previous day had been replaced, overnight, apparently, with the realities of having to train inexperienced pilots to fly in a ridiculously short amount of time. My fellow Macros had dressed out and left the locker room quickly. They looked worried. So when I'd initially seen Felix I hadn't known what to expect. Emotional fallout from the previous night? General worry about the flight program? Fear of the larger plan going wrong? It could have been any of that.

But, it turned out, it wasn't.

As soon as Felix had walked in the room and spied me his face had lit up with a beautiful smile. He then grabbed me in a fierce hug that could have crushed my ribs. I hugged him back, filled with relief that this event had made him happier (which was the point). I always forget, I'd thought in a detached part of my brain, how small he actually is, as his forehead rested against my collar bone. It's his brains and character that make him seem ten feet tall. Felix pulled back from me, still holding my arms. His eyes were wet and, I realized, so were mine. "Are you all right? Are you both ok?" I asked.

Felix nodded and his smile returned. But, upon reflection, his smile had looked different to me, somehow. He was thinking of *her*. How truly wonderful.

I'd put my arm around his shoulders. "How did you know it was me, us, I mean?"

Felix had laughed a little. "The cane." He pursed his lips together. "And, you know, it's a *really* small room."

And my cheeks went bright scarlet. Which was ridiculous, really, since I would have been a fool to think that a mere privacy curtain could render a tiny room like that actually private. Plus the fact that Samuel and I had managed to hear *everything* going on between Atalanta and Felix. Yet my cheeks could have given the sun a run for their money. He put the back of his hand to my cheek, cooling it.

"Thanks, Jane."

I'd smiled at him. Then I'd had a thought. A reminder. "You know that if you see Samuel..."

"...it never happened." Felix had snorted. "Trust me, if there is a straight man in the universe less likely to admit that he 'shared' his first sexual experience with his female best friend and our male boss, I don't know who that would be."

"You mean, aside from Samuel?" I'd said dryly.

Felix had laughed. "Aside from him."

Back in the present, I suppressed a chuckle, not wanting to disturb Samuel.

But my mind had run on to Atalanta and all traces of humor disappeared from my thoughts. She'd shown up to our quarters at 20:00 last night. She'd gone out of her way, earlier in the day, to make an appointment to see us then. My theory had been that making this appointment had served two purposes: 1) to make sure we'd both be there and 2) to make sure we had our clothes on. I couldn't argue with that logic.

She'd walked in our quarters at 20:00 on the dot and had given each of us a hug and a kiss on the cheek. Samuel and I were leaning against the desk with Atalanta standing in front of it. I *knew* she was happy, but her expression was serious. I didn't understand why.

"I've been trying to think of a way to thank you both for helping Felix and me. It meant more than I can say." Her eyes were full momentarily, but she blinked it away. Samuel said nothing and looked...uncomfortable. He was probably thinking that he'd specifically asked for this topic to never come up, but here it was. He was too polite to shut Atalanta down, of course, but he looked like he'd rather be anywhere else.

"You don't have to thank us, 'Lanta." I said sincerely.

She shrugged her perfect shoulders and took a deep breath. "I would like to link the two of you, empathically, for just a minute."

Samuel had been looking at the floor but at this his head snapped up. I was surprised myself. "Now before you say no, Sir," and Atalanta was looking only at Samuel, "I think you might want to consider it. Empathic closeness can be a real gift when two people care about each other the way you two do." She turned her big brown eyes on me.

I had to think. Samuel had said that he'd wanted me to be told exactly how he felt. But that would have been Atalanta reading him (and filtering it) before telling me. This would be direct.

"How?" I asked this purely for Samuel's benefit and Atalanta knew it. Also, it would buy him more time to think.

Atalanta addressed Samuel with her answer. "I can use my link with Jane to read you, Sir, and then project through, and into, Jane. I can read Jane very clearly and project that to you." She looked back at me. "If you want."

Samuel said nothing for a minute, his expression unreadable. I wondered if he was letting Atalanta read him at all. I doubted it. He looked at me and I instinctively slid over to him putting my arm around his waist. I looked up at him.

"What do you want to do?" he asked softly. "Is this even a good idea?"

I had to shrug at that. "The few times I've done this I've always ended up with more than I bargained for, so I don't know if it is a good idea. But…"

He gently brushed my hair off my forehead and smiled. "I'm not afraid of you, Jane. I want to know everything."

I felt emotion welling up within me. Love and fear. I didn't know if he'd like his 'everything,' but the truth was that I wanted to see inside him, too, and fair was fair. I looked at Atalanta and nodded.

A minute or two later and Samuel and I were sitting close together on the tiny couch in the corner. The couch was so insignificant that I'd forgotten it was there, but I didn't mind its size. Samuel's leg and thigh were pressed against mine and I found that comforting. Atalanta sat in front of us, having rolled over the desk chair. Not a lot of seating in this place, I observed to myself. And then I had to wonder what was wrong with me that I was thinking about *seating* at a time like this.

Atalanta rolled closer and took Samuel's right hand and my left.

"I will start, Sir, by…"

But Samuel interrupted quietly. "Sam, please." She looked at him, a bit surprised. He shrugged. "I'm letting you into my head, Atalanta. That sort of thing makes this…name formality seem ridiculous, don't you think?" Her cheeks actually dimpled into a small smile.

"Yes, Sir." She took a breath. "Now as I was saying, Samuel, you will 'read' Jane first. So please everyone relax and," and this was directed at Samuel, "try not to deflect or project yourself. It won't work if you do that." Samuel's eyebrows went as high as they could go and still remain on his face. He looked from Atalanta to me then back again. Atalanta smiled again. "I figured it out all by myself, Sam." His eyebrows dropped back down, mollified.

I felt butterflies in my stomach, wondering what he would read from me. I wasn't worried about him not reading the love; I was worried about all the other stuff. But it was too late now.

Atalanta whispered, "From her to him," under her breath.

I felt something small, like a breeze blowing through my mind, but that was all. It didn't hurt and wasn't at all upsetting. Samuel, on the other hand, jerked back on the couch as though he'd been punched in the gut. He looked around him but his eyes were unseeing, at least of our reality. He was seeing my thoughts. Feeling my feelings. I imagined him running through bits of my life, good and bad, but knew whatever I was imagining was only a guess. I looked at Atalanta but her eyes were closed with concentration. A minute or five (or much more) passed and Samuel's body returned to its normal posture and he could see us again. He looked worn, exhausted. He sat very still for a second, then dropped Atalanta's hand and pulled me to him in a crushing embrace. His breathing was ragged and it was clear he was very upset. What had he seen? What did he get from that? He released me after a while. I was impressed and grateful that Atalanta hadn't tried to hurry him along.

Atalanta held out her hands out for ours again. We took hers. I was really nervous now. I looked over at Samuel but he was staring into space, lost in what he'd seen in my mind.

And this time Atalanta whispered, "From him to her."

I closed my eyes and was suddenly thrust into his thoughts. Images and feeling were flung at me at light speed. I saw a beautiful woman, the female version of Ian smiling at me/Samuel. Ruth, my brain identified. Love and attraction swept through me as we looked into her clear blue eyes. Ian's eyes.

The scene changed and I/Samuel was holding a small baby who also had those eyes. My/Samuel's love for his son was intense and, apparently, its great intensity was a surprise to him/me. Baby Ian cried and I/Samuel held it my chest and rocked it. This love was so different from the romantic kind, but I felt its tremendous and undeniable power.

Then the vision had shifted again to the face of the same woman. Time had clearly passed, her smile was gone, her mouth had turned into a line of anger and disappointment. I/Samuel looked at the door where a bunch of bags sat. My bags. I/He was going off to space and leaving her behind. I felt regret, sorrow, but also a huge wave of relief as we headed for the door.

Then I/Samuel was standing on the bridge of a ship. We looked out the window as another ship, the *Wayne* I knew somehow, passed calmly by. And then *our* ship blew up. An explosion of white fire bucked and rocked us violently as the *Edo* tore herself apart. I/Samuel was knocked to the deck. We looked down and our chest was ripped open in a riot of blood. Pain. Brain-numbing pain.

Then I/Samuel was looking through a 'nursery' window at the tubs that held new as yet unborn babies. The one in front of us held a copper-skinned little girl. My god, I thought. Arrow. Now there was only anguish as I/Samuel pounded uselessly on the glass for my/his daughter.

The vision had shifted yet again. A sexual encounter with a woman I didn't recognize. Another with a woman I did recognize, I thought. Mallory? She was much younger and they were on some ship. But while I felt my/his lust I also felt nothing more than friendship for her. Not the love I'd/he'd felt for Ruth. But for me/Jane having sex as a man (with all the appropriate anatomical differences) was, while undeniably sexy, surreal. I'd stay a girl, thanks.

Then I/Samuel was walking through the main doors at the School. The place seemed foreign and I/Samuel was nervous. First day as Keeper, I guessed. I/Samuel walked through the double doors and saw two people: a sixteen year old Jane (and here I felt an immediate attraction and then an effort to stop feeling it) and Arrow. Seeing her made my/his stomach physically ache as it turned into knots.

Then I/Samuel was in Arrow's quarters. Some time had passed. Arrow looked up, surprised that I/Samuel was in her room. She stood up, a smile on her face. An easier smile than I had ever seen her give since I'd known her. "I know who you are, Sir. You're Captain Armstrong's father. He talks about you a lot." I/Samuel felt deep sorrow running through me/Samuel as she said this, but my/his desperate need to tell her the truth. To have her acknowledge me/Samuel as one of her parents. I'd/he'd worked so hard to find her, given up so much, not that she knew that. I/Samuel sat in her desk chair as she sat on her bed. The memory became less coherent with the emotions involved, but we stayed in it long enough to see Arrow's head shake in frantic, desperate denial. A drowning woman. And I/Samuel am the father who had tossed her into the deep end. The guilt and regret were overwhelming for me/Samuel. I/Samuel wished I hadn't said anything now, but it was too late to take it back. So much regret.

Then we'd shifted again and it was Jane looking at him shyly saying, "Samuel." The attraction was back. A longing. I/Samuel looked down at my/his hands. One was around the spirit bottle and the other clenched spasmodically. I/Samuel wanted to touch me/Jane. To touch and be touched. Loneliness and fear had hung over even the attraction.

Then it was a different day and I/Samuel was saying to me/Jane, "…and you are late for your date." I/Samuel had turned to watch Jane leave and had taken a drink from the bottle, suddenly awash with jealousy and sexual frustration. I/Samuel stood up, located the trash can and threw the spirit bottle into it with enough force to make it shatter. I/Samuel then left the room, slamming the door behind him.

There were more images and more scenes, but they'd been moving too fast for me to process now. There was Sig grinning. Great sorrow came with that image. Faces of people I didn't recognize. Friends, probably. An older couple with horses—my/his parents? Fellow soldiers. Even Doc Wells at a facility that was completely foreign to me. The feelings surrounding *him* were ambiguous at best.

There had been the sheer terror of me/Samuel sitting in the Command Center just after Wilby had told me/him that Jane and Felix had gone to the *Hastings*. I/Samuel just stared at Wilby once he'd finished speaking. Some of my/his terror abruptly became fury. My/his heart raced, chest felt tight. I/he couldn't think except to scream "Jane! How could you do this!" in the privacy of my/his own head. I felt the lump in my/his throat. I/Samuel couldn't break down in front of everyone. So I/Samuel used all my strength to hurl my electronic notepad into a command display, destroying it. That at least took the edge off. I/Jane expected the scene to change, but it didn't yet. I/Samuel sat in my chair and stewed. "I have to tell her I love her," we thought. "How can she go off to die—for me, no less, no matter what she says—without knowing that?" Then my/his emotions changed to a combination of love and despair. "It won't work on Terra, she knows that. And she may not make it back from this anyway." The despair was building, choking. "What am I going to do without her?" I/Jane needed for this to stop. It was heartbreaking to feel how much I had made him suffer and how hopeless our future together was. But the visions weren't done with either of us.

I/Samuel looked up at the large overhead monitors in the Command Center as we watched the proof of life that was Arrow and a very beaten Ian. I/Jane remembered very clearly what had been said and tuned it out. Something inside I/Samuel's soul was stretching thin with the anguish of seeing his kids in mortal danger. I/He was outwardly calm, but the inside of my/his head was high as a kite with terror, adrenaline and anger. Anger at the Scientists, at the Director himself and…me (his Jane) for letting Arrow get taken away. The real present day Jane was once again full of guilt and I felt real tears falling down my cheeks. I'd forgotten how much I'd let him down. It was awful.

Mercifully the scene switched yet again to our quarters and I heard my/Samuel's voice say, "I love you, Jane." I/Samuel gently cradled Jane's face in his hands. “Don’t leave me. I *love* you." It had been a life-changing moment for me, a realization of a dream when I had had only his words to go by, but this time I *was* Samuel. I could feel what he felt and what he felt took my breath away. So much love, desire, caring, protectiveness, friendship and this constant longing to be closer still. It had been so powerful that it was hard for any of us (either in the memory or in the present) to think. Was it possible, I/Jane had thought breathlessly, that he could actually love me as much as I love him? But the onslaught of emotions kept coming and increased yet again when the memory me told him I/Jane loved him, too. So much it hurt. The real me had been sobbing then, as the emotion had to be released somehow. I felt the link fade away and realized that I was back in our quarters and that Samuel was holding me again. I had opened my eyes and Atalanta was gone. I clung to Samuel a tightly as I could. I never, never wanted to let go.

And all the while I’d been nestled in the safety of his strong arms I’d kept thinking, “He loves me as much as I love him. How? Why? How could he love me that much? I don’t understand…” But it had been a glorious, if inexplicable, revelation.

Back in the present now, I stretched a little as I stared at the ceiling. We hadn’t discussed anything in the intervening time. We hadn’t done much except just be together. There had been no desire even for sex (which was a first for us). It seemed for those few hours almost…redundant. I knew we would need to talk about some of what we’d seen and I was starting to wonder what choice bits of my life he’d been privy to. I shuddered at the thought, but I still wanted to know.

He, Samuel, pulled me closer to him sleepily, but, I realized as I scanned him, he wasn't asleep. I pulled myself onto an elbow, but without actually separating myself from him. It was something I'd noticed recently, for while touch and always been important to me where Samuel was concerned, it was doubly so now. Ever since he'd held my hand in the Infirmary before he’d almost died. I guess part of me must still be afraid of him slipping away. I knew it was silly, but there it was anyway.

"How long have you been awake?" I asked as I leaned in to kiss him. He was watching me with those beautiful (to me) brown eyes of his. He looked worried. His body read worried, too. Tense.

"I haven't slept yet." He sat up and leaned against the headboard. I moved with him, resting my head on his chest. "Revelations of yesterday aside,” and he shook his head in wonder at those revelations, “I realized that I had been putting something off and that I couldn't any longer."

Suddenly afraid I started to pull away from him, but he wrapped his arms around me, gently, and made me stay. He kissed the top of my head. "Nothing to do with us, Baby. But I’m worried about how it will affect you." He shook his head. "And all the Macros."

Well, I guessed that was better. But it couldn't be good. Any man who wasn't completely exhausted after last night was really concerned about something. "Well, Samuel," I said, keeping my voice light, "you might as well spill it."

"I am going to set up daily hyperspace drills for the *Scylla*, starting this afternoon."

"Oh." I sat up fully now, resting my hand gently on my favorite spot on his chest. Thinking. This was scary for me. I didn't have any idea how I would react to the whole physical universe I centered myself on becoming 'other.' Samuel was right: All the Macros were going to have a problem, even Felix, who always seemed to be able to rise above anything. But Felix had never gone faster than light any more than the rest of us had. I'd asked. He'd even managed to look a little pale when I brought it up. It was bad enough for an 'ordinary' Macro, but the Telespatial aspect of my gene mod was causing me even more worry. What would going into hyper mean? I shuddered involuntarily and Samuel sat up next to me, his arm now around my waist.

"I realized that we just don't know what sort of disturbance the destruction of Pace 3 will cause to the system. I'm going to get the sub light ships out of the system today..."

"...the fighters are all sub light..." I interjected.

Samuel nodded. "But the *Newton* isn't. All six of you need to get back to the carrier as soon as the nukes have detonated. *Newton* will get you out of there if it has to." He rubbed the stubble on his chin with his hand thoughtfully. “And getting all of you on the carrier is one *more* thing for your teachers to worry about. Not that they don’t already have too much.”

And, I thought, speaking of my flight instructors… "Ian said something about rules with hyper travel. Like you can't do it in-system..? Something like that."

Samuel sighed. "Normally, yes. But we're destroying the system, Jane. There’s nothing worse we could do to it."

Then I thought of Wilby and Andrew. "And the *DSVH*?" How will it get out?" I looked at Samuel, alarmed. "We only have 5 faster that light ships."

"Seven." Now he grimaced, but I could tell by his body language that he was amused.

"*Seven?*"

"I had a brief, though very enlightening, conversation with Andrew before yesterday's briefing." He chuckled. "Remember the other day when he’d said that the *DSVH* was a new ship, just christened a couple of years ago?"

Samuel paused and I thought about it. Hey, wait a minute. "But we haven't built any new ships in 30 years. How...?"

"The *DSVH* is a *Terran* mining ship." I looked at Samuel in shock. "The Pacey 3's traded minerals, some rare stuff apparently, for it and were able to refit it specifically to their needs. They bought two faster than light ships, the *DSVH* and the *Canary*. No one knew because, as Sig was fond of saying, no one gave a rat's ass about anything Pace 3."

"But if the Government had found out..." I said, awed at the audacity of the scheme and once again impressed with Sig. Poor Sig.

"It would have been civil war. There was no way Sig would have rolled over for those...people." Samuel sighed. "Every day I'm reminded how much we lost when we lost him."

"He was the Pace 3 version of you." I said more to myself than to him. Samuel looked at me sharply but his face softened when he saw what a compliment I thought that was. Truly, it was the biggest compliment I could give.

The side of his mouth turned up in the beginning of a smile. "Would Sig have been on your conquest list if I'd been unavailable?" he teased.

I shuddered again, but this time for effect. "God, no. Who wants to make love to a mountain?"

Samuel laughed. "So I guess Andrew is off the table, too?"

I turned so that I could sit on his lap, effectively straddling him. "No table, my love, just you."

I kissed him and he kissed me back.

<u>09:00 – Large Conference Room, *P.S. Scylla*</u>

I flopped into the seat next to Andrew. He smiled at me, his piercing green eyes soft. Yes, I thought, protestations to Samuel aside, this man is adorable. I didn't blame Wilby for falling for him. I probably would have myself if I weren't head over heels in love with Samuel. And if Andrew were at all interested in women. As it was he was a good briefing buddy.

I looked around the room to see who else was there. Most of the usual suspects, but a few surprises. Namely, my fellow pilot-Macros, Garrett, Julianne and Anan. What the heck were they doing there? I felt Andrew draw a breath to speak and turned my attention back to him.

"So I hear I have you to thank for my reunion with Wilby." Andrew said softly. I raised my eyebrows. Andrew gave a short laugh. "Wilby is…wonderful, but skittish about emotional entanglements. He never involves himself like this without a push."

"And he told you that I was the one who pushed him."

"He did. He told me last night."

I sighed. "I have the wonderful ability to diagnose (and, I must say, brilliantly solve) everyone else's problems." I looked over at Andrew. "Is there something called an 'interference gene'?"

Andrew chuckled. "No, dear girl, I think that's all on you." He put his massive hand over one of mine. "But thank you anyway."

I squeezed his hand back even as I looked up, sensing the General's arrival. He'd come from a pre-briefing meeting with Felix and Ian, giving them the news of the extra training. He looked grim. Felix and Ian walked in and went to their accustomed seats—Felix on my other side and Ian across the table. They didn't look happy either. In fact, they both scanned as stressed and angry. Or was that stress and fear? I couldn't tell. I wished Atalanta was there. I spoke to Andrew, even as I turned my attention back to the General who now looked even more grim.

"I always seem to have confidence in my solutions for other people's problems—whether or not my confidence is actually justified."

Andrew followed my eyes as I watched the General. "And for your own problems?"

"Hopeless," I said softly.

"Good morning, Ladies and Gentlemen." The General stood in front of us at the head of the table. "Let's get right to it." He pressed a button on the table and the display came to life. It was a *t-hive* from Pace 4.

"This is not a simulation. This is actual footage of the Irrfan *t-hive* on Pace 4." The General paused as the camera started moving closer to the actual *t-hive*. We got much closer. Then I saw something and gasped. No one turned to look at me because everyone had seen the same thing I had. The *tapetia mortis* had built their bowl at the top of the *t-hive* mountain and it was full of Objects. Huge Objects full of the larger creatures. My god, I thought. They're ready to launch. I was sure I wasn't the only one who now looked at the General with fear in her eyes.

"The Pacey-3 Techs," and here the General gave a nod to Andrew who returned it, "that have been monitoring the *t-hives* estimate that we have less than 48 hours before they launch. Perhaps much less." He took a breath and as he did so he mentally radiated purpose and strength. I felt it, too, even though I knew his talent. I saw some people at the table lean forward, some of their fear diminished, their resolve stiffened.

On others it had no effect. Not on Felix or Ian. I couldn't tell about Andrew, but I watched him looking around him at all of us curiously. I wondered if he suspected that something was up.

"We go tomorrow." The General said firmly.

Suddenly, the General's projection was forgotten as the room erupted in worry and verbal protests. I leaned back in my chair, silent. Andrew stayed quiet as well. Not so Ian and Felix.

"General," Ian said, his voice almost quiet with suppressed anger, "we aren't ready. We need more time to train on the fighters."

Felix interrupted angrily, but without trying to hide it. "We're fine. The kids know what they need to know to do the job."

Now Ian turned from his father to Felix. "It takes years to master a *Caracara*, Felix. It's a miracle no one has been killed so far."

Felix shrugged this off. "Accidents happen with every training class. It's part of the risks of training." Felix was referring to a nearly-ugly incident yesterday when Julianne had clipped part of Anan's wing during a formation. It had been scary there for a minute or two, but Julianne had regained control of her ship and the damage to Anan's had turned out to be mostly cosmetic. All the same everyone would have been much happier if it hadn't happened.

Ian opened his mouth to respond even more angrily when his father interrupted. "This brings up my next point. We need the fighters, and god knows we don't have nearly enough of them, for two things: Debris control and additional missile guidance. We need to keep the area around the *Scylla*, the *DSVH* and the *Newton* clear once we start blowing Pace 3 all to hell." He was starting to pace, a sure sign that he was upset. "I have gone over and over it. The targeting systems on those 3 ships will be useless against something really big, especially since most of their fire (with the exception of the *Newton*) will be dedicated to the nukes. A Macro in the right place at the right time can do more than most conventional weapons."

"Then leave the kids at home, Sir. Felix and I will be there," Ian said.

"You may be the best pilot in the universe, Captain, but you're not a *Macro*," Felix said cuttingly. Ian looked as if he'd been punched in the face.

I felt my chest tighten. I'd never seen these two actually fight. Ever. And I'd never seen Felix be…mean. Not to a friend. Unconsciously I looked at the General. I guess I wanted him to fix it. How I didn't know. The General flicked a glance in my direction but then turned a glare on Ian and Felix.

"Enough." The General didn't shout, but his powerful voice hit like a small shock wave. Ian started to say something but the General gave him a quelling look and Ian stayed (wisely) silent.

"I've heard all of this over and over. We are out of time. The plan we've devised depends on the use of Macro-piloted fighters. But," the General sighed, "Captain Armstrong does have a point: the best thing would be more time, months more time to train. We don't have it." The display had frozen on the close-up of the 'bowl' of Objects, sitting there looking like a giant nest.

"So," the General continued, "I've decided to make participation in the Macro-fighter mission voluntary." Felix looked up quickly. Ian looked over at me then looked away. He didn't look any happier. If possible he looked worse. "I will not order any *student* to go. It's too dangerous."

"But what will happen if none of us chooses to go, Sir?" But it wasn't me this time. The quiet voice belonged to Julianne who sat at the far end of the table. Ian cast a quick glance to his father, silently getting permission to answer for him.

"We will adapt, Julianne. We'll do the best we can." Ian responded quietly.

Julianne fell silent. I wanted to say something but suddenly found myself embarrassed. I didn't want the people I cared about (who all knew of my relationship with Samuel) to think I was only supporting going because I was sleeping with him. And while it wouldn't hurt me to agree with my lover, I would have gone anyway. We needed Macros in fighters. End of story. But yet I stayed quiet, coward that I was.

The General spoke again. "So, I need each of you to answer. Will you fly?" He looked at Garrett. "Garrett?"

"I'll go, Sir."

"Anan?"

"Me, too, General."

"Julianne?"

Now Julianne hesitated. She looked afraid and she knew that we knew she'd made that mistake the day before. I thought she was going to drop out, but she raised her chin defiantly.

"Count me in, Sir."

And then the smallest of hesitations before the General turned to me. "Jane?"

"Of course, Sir," I responded.

"Of course," Ian muttered, "why even ask?"

I got angry so fast I'm surprised I was able to speak. "*Excuse me?*" Ian's head popped up and his eyes narrowed.

"You heard me, Jane."

I tried to calm myself for about a split second then gave up. Why should I have to fucking calm down? "Yes I did, Captain. And I heard some other things, too. Maybe you can clear some things up for me since you seem to know everything." My voice was not loud but was full of venom. Ian folded his arms on his chest defensively but said nothing. "Do we or do we not need these Macro-fighters out there when we blow this planet up?"

Ian said nothing. There was silence in the room. I didn't have any idea what anyone else was doing, my focus was entirely on my friend who was being a real asshole right now.

"I'm sorry." I said, "Perhaps I didn't speak clearly enough. *Do we or do we not need these Macro-fighters out there when we blow this fucking planet up?*"

"Yes, but…" Ian said but I cut him off.

"You're right that we're not ready," I dropped my voice down low, which was hard to do considering how pissed off I was. Like white hot pissed off. "At least compared to professional pilots who have been training for years." Felix looked up sharply when I said this. I tuned him out, still staring down Ian. "But we may be ready *enough*. And we need to do the job anyway. So quit your goddamned whining and do your fucking job."

Ian met my eyes for a few seconds, then looked away. I could feel the anger running through his body, but figured he was done mouthing off for now. I was no less angry. How dare that son-of-a-bitch throw my relationship in my face like that? I knew he was hurting over Arrow and terrified that one of his 'kids' would get killed flying. I understood that intellectually, but it didn't affect the fact that I wanted to kick the crap out of him.

I have no idea how long silence reigned in the conference room. Ten seconds? Ten minutes? I didn't really care.

"Well, I think that is enough for today," the General said blandly. "We'll meet here at 07:00 tomorrow for a detailed run through and a final briefing. I expect us to execute at 11:00. Dismissed."

I just sat there as people filed out. The General had moved in Andrew's and my direction and gave me an unreadable look. I searched his face to see what he thought—and there it was. A twinkle in his eye. "Andrew, do you have to get back this morning? I'd like to go over the deployment numbers."

Andrew nodded. "Sure thing, Sam." Then he turned and pretended to tip a hat to me. "Ma'am." Andrew smirked and followed the General out. I looked back around the room. Oh, goodie. It was just Ian and me.

"Jane…"

"I cannot *believe* you pulled that shit, Ian. What kind of a crappy thing was that to do?"

"I know, Jane. It *was* crappy." Ian, to his credit, looked ashamed.

Well that took the wind out of my sails pretty effectively. My anger had immediately dropped from white hot to low boil, which was actually all right with me. I didn't want to be angry at anyone, let alone Ian.

"I can't sleep," Ian said, his voice anguished. "I go over and over the training, over and over everyone's performance. And I try to convince myself that putting these inexperienced pilots into these ships isn't taking weapons that should be used *for* us and turning them into weapons that could be used (unintentionally) *against* us."

I sighed. "And then your father dumps trying to get everyone on the carrier at speed so that we can all get into hyper before 3 blows."

Ian ran his fingers through his hair nervously. "I just can't see putting these kids into the mix making anything better. I can't see it, Jane."

I shrugged. "We could turn this into a numbers game. 5 Macros out there tackling debris and guiding stray missiles versus the dozens or more that could die if a very big rock hits one of our ships."

He rested his face in his hands. "I don't want to play the numbers game."

"Neither do I. Especially when you and I and our friends are the numbers in question. But," and I looked him in the eye, "We need to make the best of our bad options. I am going out there because it seems the best thing to do for all us Paceys. I didn't," and I tried to keep the bit of residual anger out of my voice, "discuss it with Samuel. He didn't ask me to back his play. I knew that I would decide for myself and he knew it, too. He doesn't want me to be at risk any more than I want to be at risk. And that goes double for you."

Ian snorted derisively. "Because I'm his son."

"Yes, because you're his son and he loves you. Isn't that enough? He can always get another girlfriend, but his first born is irreplaceable."

Ian looked up at me, apparently a bit unnerved by the 'girlfriend' comment. I waved whatever he'd been about to say away. "Never mind, Ian. We have a shuttle to catch to the *Newton*."

I got up to leave, but waited for him by the door. He caught up with me and…offered me his arm, which I took gratefully.

"Sorry," he said quietly.

"Apologies for ripping you a new one in front of everybody."

Ian shrugged, a ghost of a smile on his face. "I deserved it. And Dad really enjoyed it."

I laughed in surprise. "He did?"

"Yeah, you saved him from having to do it himself. He has a certain look he gets right before he puts me in my place. It was coming." His mouth quirked into a smile. "I'm sure he'll be grateful." I smiled back at him, glad we were being friendly again.

Arm in arm we headed for the shuttle to the *Newton*. Whew.

<u>11:00 – Space outside of *P.S. Newton*</u>

The four Macro-piloted *Caracara* fighters flew blindingly fast past the *Newton*, perfectly in formation. It was easy to put my concerns over the upcoming hyperspace drills out of my head when I was flying like this. I was pretty sure this was the most fun you could have with your clothes on.

"Evasive Pattern Zeta," Felix's voice calmly ordered over the comm. "By the numbers." Which meant 1, 3, 4, and 5 (me). I had the sneaking suspicion that they had given me the highest number to try to reduce casualties. That sort of thing was only starting to bother me now, now since flying was something I was really enjoying and wanted to be good at. "Execute," Felix said tersely.

Zeta was a scatter pattern. I'd had to work to memorize it since it was one of the few that didn't involve just following everyone else. While I preferred those, I could see that there would be times when something else was needed. I flashed the image of the diagram in my mind and turned my ship away from the *Newton* at maximum acceleration. All four of us were heading for the system limit but in vastly different directions. This was clearly a plan of last resort; of escape. The more I thought about it, the less I liked it. I was just approaching the end of my run when I heard Felix's voice break into the silence urgently.

"Return to Base! Code Red!"

I felt adrenaline flood my system, despite the fact that I knew full well that this was only a drill to make sure the fighters could get back on the *Newton* quickly. I turned my ship on a dime and sped (or the space fighter equivalent of it) back to the carrier. Before I knew it I had the carrier distantly in sight. Apparently I was the first of us back.

"Julianne! Slow down!" Felix yelled. Alarmed, I checked my display. One tiny dot was careening almost out of control, heading toward the carrier. "Julianne! Status!" Felix's voice was all controlled fear. "Julianne, talk to me." Now Felix was pleading.

Then we all heard it. "I think I can make it in…" But Julianne sounded terrified.

Then I heard another voice on the comm in my helmet. "Prepare to launch *Caracara* 2 at 3, 2, 1 and DROP." Launch Control. And *Caracara 2* was…

"Iris drive activated in 2 seconds, Launch Control," Ian said over the speakers. Two seconds. Fuck that was cutting it close. "Iris Drive active, Launch Control, *Caracara* 2 under power and moving to intercept." I felt both comforted that Ian was now out here with us and even more worried because his presence meant this was serious.

I looked at my display. Apparently Julianne's ship had had the furthest to go in 'Zeta' but she had made up for it by going incredibly fast. Too fast.

"Ian," I said into the microphone. "I'm going to match velocity, see if I can't slow her down."

There was only a second's hesitation, then Ian said, "Be careful."

"Yes, Sir." I turned my ship back again, watching my display. Man, she was coming in fast. I got to a good spot then turned around yet again and began accelerating to match her speed. I could feel her coming now. So fast, but I knew just how fast that was and I matched it.

"Weapons hot." It was Ian's voice.

"Weapons hot acknowledged, *Caracara* 2," Launch Control responded.

He was going to shoot her out of the sky to protect the carrier. I took a breath to try to calm the panic in my stomach. I sensed her engines; her Iris Drive was fully opened. I 'reached' out to close it by force and let out a yelp of pain as the heat of the engine 'burned' me like the pulse from the LPG had.

"Jane!" Felix called.

"I'm OK." I blinked away the tears that had involuntarily formed in my eyes with the mental pain I'd just stupidly inflicted on myself. "I'm going to try to pull her slower."

"Roger that," Felix responded, not sounding too happy about it. But what choice did he have?

"We have to get her to either change course or eject within the next 30 seconds or I'll have to take out her ship," Ian said, his voice coolly professional. "She has to slow down, Jane. If she ejects at that speed it'll kill her. The eject pod compensators weren't designed for it."

"Understood." I put in a course into autopilot that would allow me to come close to the *Newton* but not hit her. Then I concentrated again on Julianne's ship. I regrounded (because I had already grounded before I'd even launched) then reached out and grabbed her ship as if with a giant hand. And I pulled back. Hard. I felt her engines whining in protest even as her progress slowed. I kept one hand on my own throttle so that I would stay with her.

"Julianne," this was Felix, "you must slow down. Right now!"

Then we finally heard her over the comm. She was gasping as she cried, "I can't do it. Something's stuck. I don't understand…" We all heard her take a ragged breath. "Don't let me hit the ship."

Far off in the distance I could see (in real time, not just on the display) the *Newton*. We were getting too close. I pulled harder and we slowed more. Still not enough. The engines were screaming now. I could feel something building inside. A power surge, something. Whatever it was it was very bad.

"Julianne, this is Jane. Get ready to eject."

All I could hear over the comm was the sound of Julianne crying softly as she watched her mortality coming at her.

This wasn't going to work.

"Julianne, put your hand on the eject cord," I ordered. "Have you done that?"

Just crying.

"*Julianne! Put your fucking hand on the fucking eject cord!*"

"Ok," Julianne said softly.

"Jane," Ian started to say, but I cut him off.

"We're too close, right?" the silence confirmed it. "I can't slow her more without blowing up her ship. The engines are close to…bursting. You take the ship and I'll take Julianne once she ejects."

"But…" Felix started.

"I'll catch her." Not even waiting for approval I turned my attention back to Julianne. "Julianne," I had wanted a count down, but the Newton was looming larger and larger. "NOW!"

The top of Julianne's ship ripped open and a small person-sized pod flew out of it. I let go of the ship itself and concentrated fully on the pod. I grabbed it firmly, slowing my ship as I did so. Then I slowed both of us to a crawl.

"Target locked," it was Ian. "Firing SLPG." And the night lit up with the SLPG fire and Julianne's empty ship exploded into a ball of fiery white. There was a pause. "Target destroyed."

Felix's voice came back on, his voice dead. "All ships return to the carrier immediately. By the numbers."

"I'm bringing her back," I said as I kept hold of the pod, slowing my ship down still further.

"Jane…" Ian started, but didn't finish his thought.

"Don't worry, I've got her."

But no one responded. No one wanted to. I felt panic yet again as I scanned the pod for Julianne's body signature. Nothing. Nothing at all. I hunched down in my chair. We'd been going too fast for the compensators. Ian had warned me, but I'd thought I could beat it. But I'd been wrong. All I was doing now was bringing her body home.

After a minute, I heard Felix over the comm. "You did all you could, Jane, but there are limits."

Yes, I thought miserably. I have limits.

15:00 – Officer's Lounge, *P.S. Scylla*

I sat, looking out at my favorite view but not actually seeing it. My food, some kind of reconstituted chicken thing, was in front of me, but I'd forgotten about it. I hadn't ever really failed—not permanently. I'd always been able to correct my fuckups before, but not this time. I had turned Julianne's body over to the Corpsman and left the Shuttle Bay as quickly as I could.

The only people I felt worse for were Felix and Ian who had spent the whole shuttle ride back in dead silence. I couldn't decide whether the silence was an improvement on the fighting. Well, at least it was quieter.

The other two surviving Macros, Garrett and Anan, had sat in silence as well. This reminder of mortality was too painful for speech. The thing was that I didn't blame either Ian or Felix. I knew that both of them, whether they had agreed with the training program or not, had done their very best to train us well. But despite that Felix looked wracked with guilt and Ian stared into space with the knowledge that his nightmare had already come true before the actual mission had even started. I pitied them deeply, but I didn't blame them.

That part of my analysis was fairly rational. But all rationality ended when it came to my role in the 'rescue' of my fellow pilot. I didn't deserve the out I was giving my friends. *That* I was sure of. I should have been better, done better. For Julianne.

I put my hands over my face, trying to shut out the thoughts of blame.

"Jane?" It was that voice. How had I not sensed him? I looked up and the General was standing next to me.

"Sir?" I said, trying to keep my voice level.

"I need to debrief you. Please report to the conference room when you're done eating." His words were very official, but his voice was gentle. I could feel emotion building in my chest, but I tamped it down.

"I'll be there in a minute, Sir, if that's all right. I'm not hungry."

He nodded, frowning, and left. I waited a minute, trying to collect myself. Then I got up and threw away my uneaten food, heading for the conference room.

I walked like a zombie to the conference room and went in, ready to take whatever it was he had to say to me. I really had no expectations, except that I didn't think it would be good. But when I looked up, expecting to see the General, I found it was Samuel waiting for me. He didn't even wait for me speak, he just pulled me to him and held me. Unable to contain myself anymore, my tears fell onto his uniform jacket. He rocked me a little and stroked my hair. We stayed like that for a while (I couldn't tell how long) before anything was said. But eventually Samuel spoke.

"Do you know the hard part about loving someone who is just beginning?"

I shook my head against his chest.

"Seeing all the things that they have to go through as they learn." He sighed. "I know you did everything you could to save Julianne. I know it because Felix knows it, Ian knows it and because I know *you.* I was hoping, though, that you wouldn't have to learn this lesson so soon."

"What lesson?" I said, my voice muffled by his chest.

"That you can do everything right and people can still die. Right in front of you." He pulled me even tighter. "That you can lose."

I felt more tears pouring out of my eyes. Samuel continued, "Do you know why I didn't want you to go the *Hastings* that first time?"

"Because going was insane?"

He gave a short bark of a laugh, "Well, yes, that was the main reason. But another one, almost as important, was that I was afraid something would go wrong. That you would be responsible for your people getting hurt or dying. It was your idea, your mission and your responsibility."

I looked up at him. "I'll never get that picture out of my head, Samuel. What they did to 'Lanta…"

"I know, Baby, trust me, I know." Now his face was a study in sadness as he seemed to be remembering the many he had lost over the years. But then Samuel turned his brown eyes back on me. "These are brutal lessons, Jane, and it's killing me watching you learn them." I reached up and caressed his cheek.

"I'm sorry I'm making you suffer. I don't want anyone to suffer, Samuel." My eyes filled with tears again and he hugged me close.

"I admit that things are happening for you much sooner than they would have if Pace hadn't fallen. But," and here he held my face gently between his strong hands, "these are the types of lessons that come to the kind of person you are. The kind of person who runs towards danger. Who always tries to help, no matter what the risk." And he kissed me gently, "The kind of person who would always choose to risk her life for others. *That* person will always have a difficult road ahead of her. But she will follow it anyway because that is the extraordinary person that she is and is becoming."

"I don't feel even remotely extraordinary." And that, my friends, may be the truest thing I've ever said.

"It's not for you to *feel*, Jane. It's just who you are. It's one of the reasons I love you and…one of the reasons loving you can be so terrifying." Samuel kissed me gently again. "I have to get back now. And," he bit his lip as if embarrassed, "I have the hyperspace drill going in about an hour." I started to protest, but he cut me off. "My people need the practice and so do the Macros. I'm sorry, but we need to do it." I nodded.

He was right, of course. Samuel kissed me on the forehead and turned to leave. "All the Macros are reporting to the Infirmary for the drill. Everyone will be monitored." He shrugged. "Should be interesting." I nodded again and he was gone.

Thank goodness I'd already skipped lunch. This was going to suck.

16:00 – Small Ward, Infirmary, *P.S. Scylla*

I looked around me at the white room. It was plain with a curtain for a door, a small iron bed and a chair or two. There was a set of cabinets holding, I guessed, some kind of medical supplies and a glass case carrying technical instruments and devices. There were also, I noticed, arm and leg restraints attached to the bed frame. I was alone in the room and I paced nervously.

Lieutenant Ilene's voice came over the address system, "Hyperspace drill will commence in 3 minutes. Go to Battlestations!" A small red light glowed on the wall and somewhere a klaxon sounded. Everything was muffled here in the Infirmary, but nothing was completely shut out.

I felt someone on the other side of my curtain door. Felix. I looked up at his entrance.

"I'm right next door." I nodded but must have looked pretty freaked out because he walked further in the room. "Just ground and stay grounded. The General said this will be a short jump, just a few minutes.

We'll do the best we can and then adapt from what we've learned." He rested a hand on my shoulder and caught my eyes. "Right?"

I was feeling unequal to speech and merely nodded tensely back. Felix gave my shoulder a shake and headed back to his room. "See ya after, kiddo." He smiled and I nodded for the third time. Then he was gone.

Time was ticking away and I was unsure what I was supposed to do. The tech that had assigned me the room hadn't given me any instructions. Of course, any instructions would have been a guess anyway since no super on the *Scylla* had been through this particular scenario before. I tried lying down on the bed. Then I stood up again. Then I sat down. That seemed best. Oh, fuck, I was supposed to be grounding. I took a breath and grounded on everything I could think of including my own body the way I did when I was flying. Calm. I need to be calm.

And there was Lieutenant Ilene again, "Jumping into hyperspace in 5, 4, 3, 2, 1."

The universe stretched. It was matter and it wasn't. Things were coming at me, but they weren't. Matter pitted my skin, points of light raced by me, confusing me. I flung out my arms to protect myself but there was no protection to be had. I felt the *Scylla* constantly breaking apart and reforming and space was…the wrong shape. It moved wrong. The ship felt wrong. Everything was wrong. Before I knew it I was in full blown panic. I heard something smash and covered my head with my arms, curling up into a ball. I felt the space around the ship closing in on me. Closer and closer. I tried to 'push' it away but it was unstoppable. And as it was about to consume me I felt myself scream.

And then it was over. Space was normal. The ship was normal. All was quiet except for the thunderous pounding of my still terrified heart.

"My god." It was Felix and I felt him standing at the doorway of my room. My eyes were still closed as I scanned him. He seemed a little off, like he'd been ill but was otherwise Ok. I felt him walk over to me, his boots crunching (?) on the floor. "You're cut, sweetheart. Can you look at me?"

I opened my eyes to look into Felix's own worried ones. "Are we done? Are you all right?"

"We have to go back in a few minutes but this part is done." He rubbed his unusually pale face with his hand. "It wasn't pretty, but I'll get better at it. I'm sorry that was so rough for you."

"Rough?" My brain seemed to be working very slowly.

"Jane," Felix admonished gently as he gestured with his hand to the room around us.

My eyes widened in shock. The room was destroyed. Chairs ripped apart, instruments smashed. Not one piece of glass was whole and shattered fragments covered every surface including the bed and including me. I suddenly noticed that my face and arms hurt. I was cut, especially on my arms. I'd even managed to shred the door curtain into tiny rags.

"Fuuuuuuuck," I said slowly.

Felix rose from the bed. "We're going back in ten minutes. I'm going to get a Tech to sedate you."

"Bless you, Felix."

Felix disappeared out the door and a minute later I heard two sets of footsteps coming back. Crunch crunch went the boots.

"What the bloody hell happened here?" a shocked and annoyed voice cried out. Oh. *Him.* I looked up and there was Doc Wells, rather red in the face with indignation. I thought he looked like an old Earth turkey.

I sighed. "Nothing, Doc. Why?"

Felix was looking agitated. "Doc we are going back into hyper in six minutes. Please sedate her immediately so that we can get back without more damage."

"How long do you want her out for?" Doc Wells looked as though he thought years might be nice.

"20 minutes. And I'll stay here with her until she wakes up."

"Fine." Doc Wells prepared his spray shot thing (whose technical name I have apparently forgotten) as I stood up and shook the blanket to get all the glass off the bed. I lay down and Felix sat next to me. I could feel him going through his grounding ritual. Doc Wells injected the ampule and everything went foggy and then foggier.

"Felix," I said, or whispered, I'm not sure. "Felix, center on your heartbeat. Maybe that will help." He took my hand and I felt something. His pulse. Fast, but steady and strong. Hey, wait a minute… And then world went black.

<u>20:00 – Officer's Lounge, *P.S. Scylla*</u>

I'd stopped in for a drink before heading home since I wasn't expecting Samuel to be free until later. My daily dinner with Arrow had been even quieter than usual. Arrow wasn't much of a talker under the best circumstances and I, though physically recovered from our hyperspace adventures, wasn't feeling expansive either. I wished I'd been able to go into hyper again (despite the fact that the very thought made me shudder), but the drill had been over. No other chance to try and beat it. And Julianne's death hovered over me, too. This had not been the best day.

Arrow looked better, though. Food and forced companionship can work wonders apparently. She'd told me that she was back to her old workout routines again and she was no longer living on the floor. She'd put her mattress against the wall and was sleeping on the flat-bottomed metal frame. That seemed worse than the floor to me, but it wasn't my call. She still never smiled, but I wasn't so worried for her anymore. She was tough. She'd just needed some time and some food.

Now in the Officer's Lounge I walked up to the bar and was surprised to see Andrew sitting there with a drink in front of him. He smiled when he saw me and beckoned me over.

"Join me, Jane. My shuttle doesn't leave for half an hour."

My friend-crush on Andrew was in full bloom, so I was happy to oblige. I ordered Samuel's favorite brand of spirits and regarded the giant next to me. He downed his drink and I, not to be outdone, downed mine in hopes of making my bad day retreat into a haze of spirits. But boy, did it burn. It was painful moments like this that made me wonder if I was supposed to be sitting at the grownup table. Oh, what the hell. We ordered more.

I felt a slight fog of a buzz and relaxed. Andrew's sharp green eyes were on me again.

"What?" I asked, smiling.

"So who's the secret lover? A boyfriend? Girlfriend? An assortment of each?" Andrew downed his second drink as if it was water. I temporarily refrained from downing mine. Calling me a lightweight would be an understatement.

"Boyfriend." I really wanted to tell him. I wanted to talk about Samuel. And there just weren't any opportunities, what with the secrecy, to show him off. It sucked, but that was the way it had to be.

Andrew leaned in. "He who shall remain nameless, eh? Why? Terrible scar? Sticks to walls? Or is he one of the purple people with the tails—though I think that could be pretty interesting under the right circumstances."

I laughed. "All of the above." I took a sip of my drink then looked at Andrew, suddenly possessed by a startling thought. "Wilby didn't tell you? Not even the sex?" I put my glass down, a little astonished.

"You sound shocked," Andrew looked a little put out, "that Wilby could keep a confidence."

I looked away, realizing I'd offended him. "Sorry, I was thinking of the Wilby I met years ago. The one I threw against the wall and made spin around until he threw up." Andrew had been taking a sip and choked on it. I hit him on his massive back to help him get clear. He regained control and stared at me.

"You did *what*?" Andrew cleared his throat again. "Why?"

"He made me hurt my boyfriend." Andrew raised his eyebrows at me. "Different one."

"Not the dick nerve thing?"

I blinked rapidly.

Andrew grimaced. "Classic Wilby. He must have liked you. It's his favorite way to clear the old and make way for…himself." He gestured to the barman for another drink. "I guess you haven't forgiven him. Funny, I thought from the way he talked about you that you two were close. I must have misunderstood."

I shook my head. "You didn't. I love Wilby," Andrew looked at me askance and I hurriedly added, "Not like that. But I've spent most of the time I've known him hating him. The love is fairly recent."

Andrew shrugged but seemed to be mollified by my reply. "So what changed your mind?"

I had a gulp of my second drink. "A bunch of reasons. But two big ones. He volunteered to take my place on a mission."

Now Andrew's face was serious. "Was it dangerous?"

I snorted. "More than even we knew."

"Did you let him?"

"No. I was risking too many others already." I frowned, remembering.

"And the second time?" Andrew prompted.

"He recognized I was…ill," that seemed less sensational than 'having a heart attack induced by an evil traitor Micro,' "and saved my life, then saved the life of someone else very dear to me." The spirits were definitely getting to me and I felt my eyes fill with tears. Samuel. I blinked them away. "So did you ever meet the asshole Wilby or did you only fall for the brave honorable Wilby I only met about a month ago?" If I hadn't been tipsy I doubted I would ever have asked such an indelicate and invasive question, but I figured spirits had been an excuse for asking things one shouldn't ask for thousands of years, so who was I to fight tradition?

Andrew chuckled and then the chuckle turned into a quiet, though hearty, laugh. I consumed a bit more of my drink as I waited for him to recover.

"Yes, I first met the 'asshole Wilby,' as you call him." He stared at his glass, thinking. "But I have always been a good judge of character. I can read people very quickly and am almost always right." Andrew sipped. "A useful talent in command."

I nodded, hoping for much more. Wilby never talked about himself and he *certainly* wouldn't voluntarily talk about Andrew, so I figured that this would be my only opportunity for dirt.

He gave a short bark of a laugh. "I had to trick him, you know."

"You," I responded, not bothering to keep the surprise out of my voice, "tricked *Wilby*?"

"Yep." Andrew shot back the rest of his drink and gestured for another. "Tricked him with sex."

"Oh," I said rather unthinkingly, "that would work."

He smiled to himself. "Everyone knew Wilby's reputation before he'd even come to Pace 3. He'd already screwed his way across Pace 2 by the time he'd gotten to us. So, I let him seduce me and then, over time I seduced him right back." His private smile deepened as he remembered.

"Sounds like fun."

"It was," he said softly, almost to himself. "The best kind of fun." He shrugged. "It was pretty close to love at first sight for me. For Wilby it took much longer." He picked up the glass of spirits, his expression just a little bitter. "Much."

There was silence for a minute. "But he loves you. He just gets afraid."

"I know." Andrew downed his drink. "But he thinks *I'm* fearless."

Something about the way he'd said that made me say… "But you're not?"

Then Andrew turned his green eyes on me. "We just aren't afraid of the same things." Now I laughed to myself. Yes, I really understood that one. "So was it love at first sight with your mystery lover?"

"Not at all. Just plain old like and respect in the beginning."

"And what changed all that?"

And I answered before I'd even thought about what I might be giving away, "He asked me to call him by his first name." Andrew looked at me questioningly. And I had to shrug. "That little intimacy changed everything. Changed my life. Changed his." I pictured Samuel smiling at me and I smiled in response. "He became everything to me. My whole life." I finished my drink. "You probably think that could only be said by an inexperienced young idiot."

Andrew frowned at me. "Why would you say that?"

"Because sometimes that's what I think."

Andrew leaned back against his bar stool thoughtfully. "Speaking as someone much older than you…"

"Isn't everyone," I muttered. Andrew gave me a dirty look and I subsided.

"…*much* older than you," he continued pointedly, "I have found that life experience changes everyone. It changes who we choose and why we choose them. The next time, assuming there is a next time, you'll carry your previous relationship with you and it will affect it, for good," and here he grimaced, "or ill. *But*," he said with enough emphasis that I turned to look at him, "all that aside, I think we love how we love. I fall in love quickly, but completely. Wilby falls in love reluctantly, but…," and here he paused as if searching for the right word, "generously." Andrew smiled at me. "And how do you fall in love, Jane?"

I sighed through my tipsy state and came up with the only thing that seemed right. "Fiercely."

<u>22:35 – The General's Quarters, *P.S. Scylla*</u>

I walked into Samuel's Quarters rather unsteadily. I had offered to walk Andrew to his shuttle, but he had ended up making sure I got partially home all right. Even in my altered state I had had the presence of mind to have him take me to the regular crew quarters. I'd thanked him, waited a bit, then walked slowly home. I couldn't be sure he'd seen me skip going in to my official room, but I didn't think he had. Either way, I didn't feel like worrying about it now.

The door closed behind me and I saw Samuel working at his desk. I took a couple of steps and then realized that leaning against the closest wall would be much safer. That would teach me to drink with a man who weighed four times as much as I did. He probably wasn't even buzzed and I was pretty much as soused as I'd ever been.

Samuel watched my initial progress across the room and the subsequent surrender to the safety of the wall with barely hidden amusement. He got up, walked around the desk and leaned on it.

"So, Jane. What have you been up to this evening?"

I was feeling pretty good, so I decided to tease him. "Having drinks with a very attractive man."

"Yes, I know. I saw you as I passed by the Lounge."

"*Very* attractive."

"Uh huh." He picked up something from his desk and brought it to me with a glass of water that had been waiting there. "Here, take this." It was a small pill.

"What is it?" I said eyeing it distrustfully.

"It'll keep you from waking up with a hangover."

"Thanks," I said gratefully. I took the pill and he put the glass back on the desk.

"So, you were saying that you had drinks with a very attractive man."

"I did."

I could tell he was trying very hard not to smile. He wasn't really succeeding. "Andrew knows about us, you know. I told him."

"What?"

Samuel laughed. "You think you are the only one that's allowed to tell people? He asked me point blank after the briefing today so I confirmed his suspicions."

What a stinker Andrew is, I thought. Pretending not to know like that.

Samuel was walking closer to me, his manner both playful and seductive. "So you want me to be jealous of Andrew, I take it? My friend. A man who likes men even more than you do?"

I regarded my lover as he drew closer. "Maybe a little. Just for a minute."

Now Samuel's smile lit his face. "Ok." And then he projected. Blinding jealousy and angry lust. It was so strong I took an involuntary step backwards. "Like that?" he asked.

All I felt was a burst of fear but I looked into his eyes and saw he was still smiling. Andrew wasn't the only stinker I knew, apparently. "Maybe not."

Now Samuel was in front of me, almost touching me but not quite. "Then how about this." And suddenly I was flooded with love and desire. I found my emotional (and physical) equilibrium gone and I leaned against the wall.

"I didn't know you could do that," I breathed.

"I'd never tried until now." He expression was tender now, all traces of amusement erased.

I reached out a hand to his face and he kissed my palm. "Samuel."

"Baby," he said softly as he kissed me.

It was wonderful, as it always was, feeling his body against mine, his mouth on mine. Unfortunately for me, though, the spirits were catching up with me and the room was fading from view. The last thing I remembered as I passed out for the second time that day was Samuel picking me up in his arms and putting me to bed.

And his amused chuckle was the last thing I heard as I drifted off.

ENTRY 13-2-19

Excerpt from Captain Ian Armstrong's Journal, August 3, 2869

So here we go, out of time and unprepared. Today we will (if all goes well) wipe out the tapetia mortis *forever. No more systems for them to destroy. No more whole peoples to devour. I don't know if they have enough soul to suffer but I hope they do.*

We lost Julianne yesterday. She shouldn't have been flying. Felix hopes for the best and I expect the worst. A perfect couple I guess. Jane can fly. And Felix and me. But, as Felix pointed out so kindly, it's only the Macros that count.

I didn't care for Pace 3 when I was there. Too hot. Too toxic. I shouldn't be sorry to see it go, but I am. It's as much a part of us Paceys as the pretty places we'll never see again.

I don't feel right. Too much change. I wish I had someone to talk to about everything. Jane would listen, but Dad wouldn't like it. I don't know why he'd bother worrying about it. Jane and I are very much in love with other people.

04:00 – The General's Quarters, *P.S. Scylla*

I awoke suddenly. It was very dark in our room. I sat up in bed and realized I was alone. Samuel was gone. Trying not to panic I got out of bed and walked around. Everything looked different. Wrong somehow. The furniture was there, but blank, empty. The desk was cleared of papers. The picture of his dog was missing. No books. No clothes in the closet. I looked back at the bed. No bedding, no pillows, only a mattress. What the fuck was going on? Something was changing outside the window and I walked towards it cautiously.

Light. There was light outside the window. Too much light and it was growing. I stepped to the Tenorium and gasped as I saw the sun coming up. Within a few seconds it was up and I was looking out into a field. My mind was boggled by this, since as far as I knew, I was on a space ship in *space*, but I watched as the world outside lit up. The sky was the wrong shade of blue. The field was green with touches of blue flowers. The clouds were the wrong shape. The sun was too bright. I tried to feel the turn of this world but failed. But I knew where I was. Earth. Terra.

The panic I had been tamping down surged to the fore again. Where was he? I searched the small room and the bathroom but no Samuel. He was gone. They'd taken him. I was having a lot of trouble breathing. I felt myself starting to hyperventilate, but made no effort to stop it or calm down. I hoped I would pass out from it and wake up back...where? Back home? Where was that exactly? I climbed into the center of the bare mattress and huddled in a ball.

"Samuel?" I whispered. But there wasn't enough volume in my cry to let any pain out.

"Samuel!" No answer. He really *was* gone. Panic attack in full swing I took what felt like would be my last deep breath and screamed, "*Samuel!!*" I felt hands on my shoulders and someone screamed in terror.

"Jane!" I knew that voice. *That* voice. "Jane, wake up, Baby!" Someone, he, was shaking me. I opened my eyes and I was back home. Back on the *Scylla* in our place with our things. I looked up and there he was. Samuel. Samuel looking scared for me. My throat hurt. I must have been the one to scream.

"You're Ok, now, Jane." He pulled me to him and hugged me hard. I could feel his arms shaking with adrenaline. His heart was beating fast, so fast. I buried my face in his chest. I needed to cry, to let it out somehow, but as upset as I was, I didn't want to let go and sob.

I sat up and looked in his wonderful lined face. He was worried. I don't think I'd had a nightmare with him before. I felt bad for scaring him and knew he had questions. But they could wait.

I knelt in front of him and kissed him. This kiss was not gentle, it was desperate and full of the fear of losing him. Surprised, it took him a second to respond, but respond he did. I moved my mouth to his ear and he shuddered. I moved down to his neck, then down his chest, reveling in his muscles, kissing his scars. I had made it down to his stomach and was reaching for the waistband of his underwear when he grabbed my hands. I froze. I had been here before with him, though it seemed like a lifetime ago. I tried to pull my hands away but he held them tightly.

"What did you see in your dream, Jane? Tell me?" Samuel's voice was gently pleading.

I hadn't raised my eyes from his body. He released one hand and tilted up my chin so that I had to look him in the eye. I shook my head. He let go of my chin, frowning. I put my free hand to his forehead and smoothed away his frown lines. I swallowed and finally spoke.

"I'm afraid, Samuel. I really need you now." I looked up at him, my eyes begging for his touch. For this connection. I put both hands on his chest and brought my mouth up close to his, but I hovered. I wanted him to want me so I waited. I knew he was turned on enough, but was trying to decide if this was a good idea. He rested his forehead against mine for a second.

"I need you, too." he said softly. He kissed me deeply, but then broke off to look me in the eyes again. "We'll talk after, yes?" I nodded and he kissed me again, pulling me to him. His touch, his mouth, his everything was sublime but it wasn't until he was inside me that I was able to shake the dream. And it wasn't until he groaned my name as he came that I was able to find my own release. The tears I had been waiting for streamed down my face and I let out a sob. Samuel rolled on his back and pulled me on top of him, his strong arms wrapped around me, protecting me. Right then I felt safe.

I rested my chin on his chest. "You are so beautiful to me, Samuel."

He smiled at me and brushed my hair out of my face. "I think you may be the only person in the universe that would call me beautiful, Baby."

"Well, you are." I said stubbornly. He might have been right, but he was still beautiful in my eyes.

He sat up a bit, amused. "If that isn't proof of love, I don't know what is."

I sat up, facing him. "Does love render me beautiful, Samuel?" I said, teasing him.

"You don't need love to be beautiful, Jane. You never did."

Well that seemed a bit much to me, but I tried to enjoy some of the compliment. I was not beautiful. I didn't think I was repulsive, but you can't live with Atalanta for years and not know beautiful. Funny how it was all right for me to compliment him, but not all right for him to compliment me. I sighed internally. Maybe all girls are nuts deep down.

Samuel was watching me think. He reached out for me, tucking me under his arm. "I know you won't believe me, but I was attracted to you from the first moment I saw you."

"I know," I said without thinking.

I felt his body stiffen. Oh, hell, I thought. I had, thus far, been so good at not discussing what we'd seen in each other's memories and I'd had to go and just blow it like that. Fuck.

"What did you see?" He was nervous. I sympathized. I was afraid of what he'd seen in my head, too.

I rested my head on his chest again. "Nothing bad, Samuel. Most of it was nice. Some of it was...wonderful."

"And the rest?" Tension.

"Interesting, but ultimately irrelevant."

"You have to tell me more than that, Jane," Samuel said, exasperated.

"I felt your love for Ruth," Samuel looked uncomfortable, "Your joy when you held baby Ian for the first time. Some girl you were with. Your...affair with Mallory." Now Samuel looked *really* uncomfortable. I turned my body so that I could face him. "I assumed that you weren't a virgin. Besides, that wasn't the weird part." Now Samuel looked me in the eye, dread written all over his face. I had to contain my grin. "Well when you…" I was at a loss for the proper verb. While he liked and, clearly, had wanted her, he hadn't loved her, so…

Samuel sighed. "When I fucked her?"

I felt a blush on my cheeks. Really, Jane? Five minutes ago your lover gave you a screaming orgasm, but *this* makes you blush. "Yeah, that. But I got to feel what you felt." He looked at me surprised. "I was in your body, I *was* you." I looked at him in wonder. "Holy shit, Samuel, if that's what sex feels like for you."

He stared at me dumbfounded. "I have no idea what to say to that," he said unnecessarily.

But my mind had already run on to another memory, a much more emotional one. "And then there was how much you suffered when they took Arrow and Ian." I felt his stomach clench and he closed his eyes in remembered pain. I dropped my voice lower to get to the worst of it. "And how angry you were with me."

Samuel's eyes snapped open. He looked at me. Was his expression guilty? I was too upset to be able to tell. He opened his mouth to speak but I beat him to it.

"I don't blame you. I really let you down." Now I was overcome again, wrapping my arms around myself protectively. "I tried to protect her, I really did. And I tried so hard to get her back. I just couldn't." I buried my face in my hands.

Suddenly Samuel's arms were around me and he was rocking me gently. "Jesus, Jane. I'm sorry. I was so flat out terrified I barely knew what I was doing." He took a slightly ragged breath. "I *was* angry at you. Because," and here he pulled my hands away from my wet face and made me look at him, "I was so helpless. They took my *children*, Jane." His remembered pain and terror filled my eyes anew. "And then I couldn't even go get them. Sig sacrificed himself so that I would come to my senses and stay on the ship." He looked away from me, now very clearly deeply ashamed. "And then I selfishly, so selfishly let you go get them. I still can't believe I did that."

"I didn't need your permission. I had to fix my mistake. No one could have stopped me."

"Not even me," he breathed.

"Especially not you."

"I saw the look in your eye right before you left."

"What look?"

"The one that said you weren't coming back without them, even if you died trying." Now I had nothing to say to that. It was true, of course. Samuel's eyes were now full of anguish. "I saw that look and I let you go anyway," he whispered. "What kind of person does that to someone he loves?" He looked at me, his self-loathing evident in his eyes.

"A father, Samuel. Trying to save his children." I couldn't take his pain, I needed to be closer. I sat on his lap, facing him, a leg on either side of his torso. "You aren't *my* father. You are the man responsible for my training. You 'let' me go because you wanted your children back safe and you thought I could help accomplish that." Then I had an ugly thought. "You weren't sending me to the slaughter because I had screwed up, were you?"

"God, no," he said.

"Ok, then, Baby. Don't worry about that anymore." And I nestled up to him, resting my cheek against his stubbly one.

He ran his hands through my hair. "I know you did everything you could for Arrow. I thought about it a lot after they were back safe and I realized I felt as bad for you when she was taken as I did for Arrow herself."

"Why on earth?"

"Because you would rather suffer anything than let someone you care about down." He rested his forehead against mine, closing his eyes. "You don't want anyone you love to hurt." He kissed me gently on the lips. "What is it you are so worried about, Jane?"

And there it was. This question was what I hadn't wanted him to see in my mind—or in my nightmare for that matter. I couldn't bear to discuss whether or not we should stay together once our 'rescue' came. What would be the point? Nothing good could come of that conversation. Only pain and potentially empty promises. He put his hands on my shoulders and gently kneaded the now iron-tight muscles. Fuck, what a giveaway. How the hell can I handle this? I let the silence drag on, really and truly stumped.

"There were two memories of yours that stuck out the most to me." Samuel said, apparently getting that I was not capable of moving this conversation forward. "My favorite was the first time we made love."

I reached out to touch his face. "When I realized that I was in love with you."

He nodded, swallowing convulsively. "I was there. It was…" Now words failed him, too. "She gave us quite a gift."

I nodded. But I was, despite my emotion, waiting for the other shoe to drop. The second memory.

"And then there was Julius yelling at you." Now Samuel's mouth took a grim line and I felt his hands become fists with his anger. I was angry at the fuckhead myself, but I didn't think it was for the same reasons. "I'd heard most of it before, from outside the room. But being you while I heard it was something else." Yes, Samuel, I bet it was. "How could you let him poison your mind like that?"

I said nothing. I was not ready to discuss this. I wasn't ready to burst any bubble. Samuel was confused by my silence. He was frowning at me and I could feel adrenaline flooding his system. Fuck, I've scared him. What am I supposed to do? I reached my hands out to smooth away his frown but he caught and held them.

"You want to leave me?"

I took a breath. He said 'want' to leave him. I could answer without promising or lying. "No. I never want to leave you, Samuel."

He looked at me askance. He could tell I was splitting hairs. Why the hell couldn't I have fallen in love with someone stupid. An idiot would totally have let me get away with that.

Before he could ask another question that I didn't want to answer I spoke. "I love you, Baby. Do you doubt it?"

"No."

I looked into that wonderful lined face with those beloved brown eyes. "Sometimes I think an 'I love you' is far too weak a phrase for how I feel about you." His worried expression softened a bit and he caressed my cheek. But he was no fool and he hadn't forgotten. "I have worries and you know that now."

"Why didn't you tell me?" Samuel said, his voice sounding hurt.

"You are saving the world all the time, my love," I smiled at him, but he didn't smile back, "and I didn't want to have that conversation."

"Why?"

I bit my lip. "He said I didn't love you enough to deserve you if I took you away from...being the General."

"And you believe him?"

"I don't want to, Samuel." I must have looked pretty forlorn because he wrapped me in his arms and rocked me again, kissing my hair.

"Do you know one of the reasons I fell for you, Jane?"

"No crow's feet?"

Samuel snorted. "You saw me as a man first and the General second. It was something I was desperately missing, even though I hadn't realized it until you gave it to me." He held my face gently in both hands. "I don't want to just be the General, Jane. Not again. I need more than that. I need you."

And he kissed me, hard, feasting on my mouth. I surrendered to him, flush with relief that the conversation was over and that he still wanted me. I needed more time to think. But now what I really wanted to do was not think at all. Fortunately, my Samuel was way ahead of me on that. God help me but I loved him so.

07:00 – Hall Outside Small Conference Room, *P.S. Scylla*

"I cannot *believe* you!" It was Wilby's voice. He was really pissed. The General, Felix and I were rounding the corner to the Conference Room but paused. Wilby was standing in front of Andrew, hands on his hips, face pale with rage.

"Wilby, try and understand…"

"*You* try and understand. After all this, after all we've been through, and you are leaving me behind."

Andrew took a breath, apparently trying to control his temper. "I can't risk you. It's dangerous enough for me, I won't have you…"

But Wilby overrode him. "You can't have me what? Share the danger? Am I so…delicate that I need fucking protecting? We are together. Finally. And you just drop me off to be *babysat* while you…" He trailed off.

"While I what?" Andrew's voice was softer, sadder now. The conference room door opened and people started slowly streaming out from an earlier meeting. Samuel, Felix and I stood there, waiting for the room, trying not to intrude.

Wilby just stood there for a second. His anger was dissipating and fear was coming to the fore. "You can't just leave me behind, Drew."

Andrew shook his head. "I won't risk you. You are too important to me."

Wilby walked up to him and put his arms around him. He looked small compared to the giant who held him. "If you're going to be lost, I want to be lost with you."

Andrew leaned down and cradled Wilby's head against his own. "I would feel the same way if I were you, but you have to stay. I'm risking enough people as it is. I can't risk you, too."

"You have to come back," Wilby whispered. I felt Samuel's arm steal secretly around my waist and I looked up at him. There was worry in those brown eyes. I gave him a small smile and leaned a little against his shoulder. Felix pretended not to notice.

"I will, my beloved boy, I promise," Andrew whispered back. The conference room appeared to have cleared out and the three of us headed for the door as Andrew kissed Wilby passionately.

Samuel released my waist with a squeeze and went to the head of the table as usual, pressing buttons, calling up the display for the final briefing. More people were starting to stream in. Felix leaned in to me and whispered, "That was pretty daring of you guys." Ah, he'd seen Samuel put his arm around me. I raised my eyebrows at him. Felix grinned mischievously. "That is by far the most demonstrative thing I've ever seen the two of you do in public. If it had been anyone else I would have suggested getting a room, but as it was…"

I chuckled, looking over at my rather formidable boyfriend. "I think you made the right choice, Felix." We took our usual seats. Andrew walked in a second later and sat down next to me. He looked flushed. "You all right?"

He nodded curtly. "This is all so much harder when you have someone waiting for you," he said quietly.

Unconsciously I found my eyes seeking the General. "I know, love. I know." Andrew followed by glance and reached over and squeezed my hand. I smiled gratefully at him and squeezed back. What a dear fellow he was. Wilby is a very lucky man. Then I corrected myself out of fairness to my friend Wilby. They're both lucky.

The General straightened up and took his place at the front of the conference room, ready to start. Talk died down respectfully.

"Ladies and Gentlemen, let's do a brief rundown of today's activities..."

10:00 – Command Center, *P.S. Scylla*

I walked into the room. Our briefing had just let out and I had decided to wait here until it was time for my shuttle. I wanted to at least see Samuel before I left. The Command Center was seething with activity. As usual for one of our missions there were grim faced Marines ringing the room, armed to the teeth. I didn't think they'd be much use against giant flying pieces of rock, but everyone helped in their own way, I supposed. I spotted Wilby standing in the corner of the room, looking upset. I immediately made my way over to him.

Then there was a hush. The General, having finished his last minute conference with Andrew, paused on the threshold. He looked around, a small smile on his lips, then walked in with purpose to the main chair. All eyes followed him and I felt (or imagined) a sigh of relief coming from everyone that he was there.

"Status, Ilene," The General said calmly. Was he projecting calm? I scanned him and found that even though he clearly was projecting for the benefit of his people, he was projecting emotions that matched his physicality. He *was* calm—energized but calm. He was completely comfortable, controlling the destiny of these lives, shouldering this awesome responsibility. He wore it easily. So impressive this man, I thought.

"All clear, Sir. Sub light fleet is out of sensor range." Ilene looked over at her boss and smiled. His confidence was in her eyes. How he was able to do that, I didn't know, but he'd done it. It wasn't just a trick of his gene mod, it was *him*.

"Mallory, missile status," he said, that rich voice carrying stability and trust.

"All tubes loaded and ready, General." Mallory looked tense, but unafraid. Arrow sat next to her, staring at the display. I was surprised to see her in public, but felt pretty sure that the General had wanted her where he could be sure she was safe. It was bad enough that Ian had to be in the line of fire.

"Excellent," he said as he gave Mallory a quick smile, too. I felt the tension in her notch down a peg or two.

"Shuttle for *DSVH* departing, Sir." Ilene reported.

The General nodded. So Andrew was on his way—without Wilby. I looked up at Wilby. His eyes were closed and his lips were moving. Was he praying? I don't think I'd seen anyone do that before. I scanned him and found he was, not surprisingly, a ball of tension. His chest was tight, like he wanted to cry. I took his hand. "Wilby?"

He looked down at me, his eyes moist. "So this is love, Jane?"

I brought the back of his hand to my lips and kissed it. "This is love, Wilby."

Wilby nodded. I think he didn't trust himself to speak, but he wrapped his arm around me and leaned my body to his side. All this emotion was getting to me, too, and it was nice to be close to a friend.

"Prepare to execute Tango 1 in," and the General consulted the clock above the monitors, "54 minutes."

"Yes, Sir." Six different officers had responded confidently to that order. The General nodded again, standing up from his chair. He started walking around slowly to the various stations, leaning over shoulders, asking questions. His voice was pitched low enough so that only the people near him could hear him. Occasionally he rested a hand on someone's back encouragingly. It was getting close to my shuttle time, but I just stood there, fascinated as he worked the room. He corrected (gently), bolstered confidence when it was needed and teased when it would foster trust.

The General was happy. Now, when everything hovered on the brink of danger, he was prepared in every way he could be and no one could accuse him of taking any of this lightly, but he was actually happy. He must have felt me watching him because he turned to catch my eyes and, when he thought no one was looking, he winked at me.

Suddenly the room seemed to move in slow motion for me. It was silent and the people moved gracefully. All I could see was Samuel in his element. And all I could hear were Doc Wells' words, that Samuel wouldn't survive not being the General. That it was his first best destiny.

And I admitted to myself for the first time that Doc Wells was right.

The room returned to normal speed and I summoned a strained smile to answer Samuel's wink. He turned away, pleased, and resumed his circuit of the room.

But inside me something had shattered. In that moment I knew I had to let him go. I really did. Not pretend to negotiate for more time or for more declarations of love. I had to send him on his way. Even thinking this made it hard to breathe. How the fuck was I going to tell him? Where the hell was I going to get the strength to break *both* our hearts? This wasn't a case of not being sure how he feels for me and hoping that it wouldn't hurt that much if he didn't really love me. Not at all. I had been there, felt it inside his head. This was no passing fling for him any more than it was for me.

My breathing shallowed and I started to sort of fold in on myself. What I wanted to do was curl up in a ball on the floor, but I couldn't. Wilby's arm tightened around my rib cage.

"Jane? What's wrong?" Wilby whispered. I shook my head. I could tell from his expression that he was scanning me. Scanning my heart. Ah, the irony!

"Sorry. It just all got to me for a second. I'm fine." I straightened up with a great deal of effort.

All I'd ever wanted was to love Samuel and to protect him. This was going to hurt. *I* was going to hurt him.

Then I was abruptly furious. *This is so goddamned unfair! Who the fuck are these Terrans that they get to judge us like this? How dare they make us suffer when all we want to do is be together? SO FUCKING UNFAIR!* And then, in the relative quiet of my head, I screamed as loudly as I could.

"Jane!" Wilby whispered fiercely. "What the fuck is wrong?"

I took a big breath to try to cool down. I was going to have to fly soon and the mission wasn't going to care whether or not my personal life had just been painfully obliterated. I forced a smile, which was ridiculous, of course, because he could feel that it was forced. "I'm Ok, Wilby. I have to go."

Then, mercifully, came the announcement. "Shuttle for *Newton* departing in 3 minutes," Lieutenant Ilene said.

Well, that was me. I gave a confused/annoyed Wilby a kiss on the cheek and headed for the door. The General's head turned at the movement and he looked at me, his eyes softening for just a second.

"Godspeed, Jane," he said and I could tell he was fighting to keep the professional tone.

"Godspeed, Sir," I said and this smile, though sad, was real. Let's pray I see you again, my love. And I was through the door.

10:55 – Locker Room, *P.S. Newton*

The Macro-fighters (and Ian) were all there, suited up and nervously awaiting final orders. Felix and Ian stood in front of Garret, Anan and I. We all carried our helmets under our arms.

"Just some last minute thoughts before we head out." Felix looked serious, which seemed to me entirely appropriate. "Remember your training and do not panic. Our job is to stop debris from hitting our ships and to redirect any errant missiles to target. Captain Armstrong and I will be out there to guide you, but a lot will be going on and you will mostly have to rely on your own judgment. No," and here he looked directly at me, "heroics. No stupidly dangerous stunts." I returned his gaze innocently and tried not to blush. "We've already lost a good person flying." His expression saddened for a second. "The Captain and I want all of you to come back home safely." He looked at Ian.

"One more thing." Ian was calm and focused. I found it very reassuring. He gets that from his dad, I thought. What is Ian's first best destiny, I wondered. Ian continued. "If you get the call to head for the *Newton* and it looks like you can't make it safely, head out of system as fast as you can. We should be able to come back for you once the gravitational pull has revised itself. It is unconscionable to put others in danger if you know you can't make it." Now *Ian* was looking at me. Good grief. Well, I was used to somebody always thinking I was a loose cannon. Why should today be any different?

"To your fighters." Ian nodded a dismissal and we all started for the door. I squeezed Felix's suited arm as I passed and he gave me a small nervous smile. I caught Ian's eyes and found they were twinkling at me. "Let's go have some fun, Jane." And he winked at me. I painted on a smile, but inside my heart dropped a bit. Like his father. Like his father. I took a breath. Ian is the best pilot alive. He can take care of himself. Better than I can do it, certainly. My protective instinct is on overdrive these days, I thought. It would probably calm down if we weren't in deadly danger all the time. Wouldn't that be fucking nice.

A few minutes later I was sitting in *Caracara 5* awaiting my drop.

Launch Control came on the speakers, "Prepare to launch at 3, 2, 1 and DROP."

My ship dropped. I flipped the switches, turned the dial and watched the countdown until my Iris Drive's full activation.

"Iris drive activated in 5 seconds, Launch Control," I said into my microphone, going through the ritual responses with Launch Control. I could feel the heat building in the engine. Building and then… "Iris Drive active, Launch Control, *Caracara* 5 under power." I pushed the throttle and moved away from the *Newton* to let another person drop. "*Caracara* 5 cleared the *Newton*, Launch Control."

"Launch Control copies, *Caracara* 5. Godspeed."

I had already centered on my ship and my own heartbeat. It felt good to be flying again. It felt funny to feel attachment to an activity that I hadn't even tried a week ago, but there it was. Garrett (*Caracara 1*) and Anan (*Caracara 4*) were already under power. Felix (*Caracara 6*) dropped next, then Ian (*Caracara 2*). I had increased magnification on my display so that I could see our ships a little better. We were still dots of light, but I could tell the shape of the *Scylla*, the *Newton* and the *DSVH* quite clearly. But the biggest shape of all was Pace 3. Her fault line, the one all this was being aimed at, was on our nav computers and our displays, highlighted in green.

"All ships acknowledge Ok to go," the voice of Lieutenant Ilene came over my speakers in my helmet.

"*P.S. Newton* ready." That was the voice of Launch Control.

"*DSVH* ready," Andrew's voice said. Funny how there was no 'P.S.' in front of his ship's name. Sig's idea, I was sure.

"*Caracara 1* ready," Garrett reported.

"*Caracara 2* ready." That was Ian.

"*Caracara 4* ready," Anan said, sounding nervous. Finally, I thought. An actual human amongst all this bravado.

"*Caracara 5* ready," I said. My nerves were making me want to giggle, but I was able to control myself. No giggling.

"*Caracara 6* ready," said Felix sounding cool and collected. Back to our testosterone parade, I smiled to myself.

"*P.S. Scylla* ready," Lieutenant Ilene said as she finished the run down. "All ships report ready, Sir." And that 'Sir' is my Samuel, I thought, wishing I could hear his voice. Oh, well. Lieutenant Ilene must have received some go-ahead from the General because she spoke again. "*P.S. Newton*, move into position. *DSVH* proceed to target at assigned range. *P.S. Scylla* holding position."

Now Ian's voice. "Preparing to execute *Caracara* Debris Alpha, *Scylla*."

There was another small pause. "Execute, Captain."

"*Caracaras* 1 and 6 to Position 1, *Caracaras* 2, 4 and 5 to position 2 and await further orders." Ian's orders were no surprise, it was all going as we'd discussed. Anan and Felix were on the left of the *DSVH* and Ian, Garrett and I were on the right. We had fanned out in hope of improving our chances of catching as much debris as possible. All 5 of us were between the *Scylla* and Pace 3, but it wasn't just as simple as being blockers. Both the *Scylla* and the *DSVH* were going to be launching missiles. We needed to protect *and* stay out of the way.

"Fighters go 'weapons hot'," Ian ordered.

I flipped the switches and read green on my display. "*Caracara 5* Weapons hot." The others all said the same.

"All ships report ready to fire, General." Lieutenant Ilene could have been a computer voice for all the emotion she was showing, but now, instead of finding it inhuman, I found it reassuring.

"Andrew? Ready to go?" It was the General. He sounded good, confident.

“Ready and willing, Sam. Let’s do this.” I could hear the smile in Andrew’s voice. These leaders were peas in a pod.

One last pause in which I imagined the General taking a deep breath. “Execute Tango 1.”

“*DSVH* firing on my mark,” this was Andrew’s voice. “Fire!”

Suddenly an onslaught of missiles flew out of the side of the *DSVH* and disappeared into Pace 3. The missiles themselves had seemed small when Sig and I had been moving them, but now they seemed miniscule.

They were tiny pinpoints of light on my display and barely visible (from this distance) to the naked eye. We all held our collective breaths, waiting for detonation. And there it was—tiny pinpricks of light blooming in the bowels of Pace 3. Pace 3 seemed unchanged, but that was expected. This was a *planet*, after all. It would take more than a few nukes to break it apart.

"*Scylla* firing…now." An even larger group of missiles flew out of the larger ship, streaking through space mindlessly to their target. They detonated in the same place, that same weak spot on Pace 3. I felt something from the planet. Something had cracked.

"Anybody feel that?" I asked excitedly.

Felix overrode me, "General, we have movement in the planet. The fault is widening slightly."

"*DSVH* firing," Andrew said and his grin sounded bigger. I watched the missiles leave his ship and cross the darkness to their target. They had almost to the fault line when…

"Object launch! Multiple Object launch!" A small frantic pause. "Pace 2!"

Oh my god, I thought, as I felt my stomach drop in horror. The General's voice said, "Felix…"

Felix spoke up quickly. "Jane, with me." I obeyed without thinking, turning my ship away from Pace 3 to Pace 2. Well, I thought, I finally have my chance to go fast. Felix and I pushed our ships to the limit, arriving at Pace 2 faster than I would have thought.

"I'll head out to the system limit and catch strays. You go in closer and shoot them as they come out." Felix's voice was all controlled tension.

"Is it just one *t-hive*, Felix? Or is it all of them?" Please god, let it be just one.

But before Felix could answer, I heard Lieutenant Ilene say, "Just one, for now. There is only one stream of Objects."

"Acknowledged, *Scylla*. Thank you." I said, relieved.

"On my way," Felix said as I watched him pull away. I zeroed in on the planet and then I saw it. An Object shot into space. I turned to my targeting system and fired, destroying the Object into a burst of red flame. Die, you fuckers, I thought unpoetically. Thirty seconds later another Object flew up out of the atmosphere. I shot it and it disintegrated beautifully. I waited for the next one.

"We've lost missile control! Redirect it, fighters!"

My body tensed, though I did not stop my watch for Objects. Another one came, another one destroyed.

"It's heading for the *Scylla*! *Caracara 4*, redirect!"

"I've got it! It's too close to the planet—I can't get it into the fault," Anan said tensely.

"Just get it away from the ship, Anan!" Ian ordered.

"Roger, Captain."

I destroyed another Object. I couldn't stay here anymore. I had to get back. I started moving my ship closer to the atmosphere.

"Jane, what are you doing!?!" Felix shouted.

"Are you done yet? We need to blow the hive and get back." I kept moving my ship closer to the atmosphere.

"Jane, these ships can't handle atmospheric entry, they'll burn up."

"No!" Anan screamed from back at the planet.

Then there was a cacophony of voices, all speaking over one another. I tried to piece it together. Too confusing.

One of those voices was Felix yelling at me that I was getting too close. I couldn't really hear it, but I didn't need to. I stopped my ship at the very edge of the atmosphere and concentrated. I looked at the Pace 2 surface map I had called up on my targeting system. If I could find that mountain… I'd never scanned a planet, well, at all, but certainly not from this far above it. An Object whizzed by me. Fuck. I'd missed it. It exploded above me in a ball of red fire. Ah, Felix was here. I wish those idiots on the comm would shut up and explain what was going on.

I sensed the mountain and tried to feel for bubbling of the *t-hive*, but it was too far away. All I had to do was wait, though. Wait for that fucker to spit out another monster. I held my breath, waiting. An Object shot into the air. I had it. I told the targeting computer exactly where to shoot and turned up the firepower. Felix took out the Object that had just passed me as I fired holy hell (or as close to it as I could get) onto the planet.

I felt something exploding, then I felt the mountain collapsing. A lucky shot on my part, but I wasn't about to complain. The Objects stopped coming. The *t-hive* was damaged enough that it couldn't function. Good enough. I let out the breath I'd been holding.

The comm was deadly silent now. I hadn't been able to focus on it and the silence was unnerving after all the chatter. I knew I didn't need to tell Felix that we were Ok to go back and I was glad. I didn't want to be the one to speak first. What had happened?

"Pace 2 *t-hive* has been neutralized. *Carcaras* 5 and 6 returning to Pace 3 orbit," Felix said quietly. "What happened back there, *Scylla*?"

There was a pause then the cool voice of Lieutenant Ilene came on. "An errant missile was diverted from the *Scylla* into a corner of Pace 3. The resulting debris was so massive that the *Scylla* wasn't going to be able to evade. *Carcaras* 1 and 4 pushed the debris aside just enough to save the ship. *Caracara 4* was unable to maintain control of his fighter and collided with the debris."

Felix swallowed. "Acknowledged, *Scylla*. We're returning to help."

I was surprised that I had no real reaction to the news of Anan's death. I mean, I knew I was sad, but I didn't really feel it. Maybe I would later. I guessed my brain knew I just didn't have time for that now.

Our fighters approached Pace 3 again. Now there were 4 fighters, the *Scylla*, the *Newton*, off more or less on its own, and the *DSVH* in close. Something about it felt too close, to me, but I was pretty sure that was because Andrew was on it and I wanted him safe. Across the galaxy would have been preferable for me.

We were in visual range and I gasped. Part of Pace 3 was shorn away. It looked like an angry mass, twisted and broken. I felt my ship accelerate, but I hadn't done anything.

"Felix?" I said, trying to hide my panic.

"The gravitational pull is changing," he said. "The mass is shifting, pulling us towards it. All fighters, reverse thrusters." I did so and my ship slowed down a bit, but still moved towards the wrecked planet.

I felt the *Scylla* move. Move closer as gravity started pulling it in, too. If it was affecting a ship as large as the *Scylla*, what must it be doing to…

"Andrew, get out of there!" The General ordered.

"One more volley should do it," Andrew said, the humor in his voice completely gone now. I could feel the *DSVH* being sucked in to the ruined planet. "Firing!"

What seemed like thousands of missiles streaked out of the *DSVH*. A second later what had to have been the last of the *Scylla's* nukes followed.

"You have nothing left to shoot, Andrew! Get the fuck out of there!" Samuel was yelling now. No. No. No. I thought. Get away from there Andrew. "Fighters, Code Red!"

Thankfully my ship had stopped moving forward. I had control. I turned her around to head for the *Newton* and reached out to make sure that Felix was following me. But he wasn't. His ship was heading inexorably for Pace 3. He was caught.

I turned my ship around again and reached out for Felix's ship but stopped myself just before I got 'burned' again.

"I can't get out," Felix said, sounding panicked. I'd never heard him panicked before and it chilled me to the bone. I flicked a glance at the display. The missiles were almost to target. If it was going to work at all, this was the time. Ian and Garrett's ships were almost to the *Newton*. But Felix?

I had to act now. "Felix, kill your Iris! Now!" And he did, thank god.

I reached out and 'grabbed' his ship. I knew I had no time so I picked it up and 'threw' it into open space as hard as I could. I had been doing it wrong I knew and I felt my shoulders and back scream with pain as I tensed up. But I didn't feel anything break. Felix's ship flew away from Pace 3, spinning like a top.

I turned my senses back to Pace 3 as I moved away from it. The *DSVH* was retreating, fighting with every bit of power she had. She was moving, but so slowly. The *Scylla* had pulled herself free and was no longer being affected. Move, Andrew. Move out of the way, I kept chanting to myself.

Then the missiles detonated. For a second it seemed that time stopped. I held my ship in position so that I could see; see the end of one of our planets.

The small (comparatively) fireworks of the detonations blinked out. Then, with infinite slowness, Pace 3 broke. One 'small' piece floated off to one side. The remaining monolith cracked violently apart, sending a small shock wave out, buffeting the *DSVH* and, to a lesser extent, the *Scylla*.

I felt my ship moving sharply to the left, then to the right, then up, then that pull inward. My god, I thought, if it's affecting my ship all the way out here…

"Andrew!" The General screamed.

And then I saw Pace 3 smash the *DSVH* like it was a child's toy.

The detachment I had felt when Anan died was nonexistent now. The *DSVH* and all her crew were gone, smashed into the planet they loved. I let out a sob, realizing belatedly that because of my helmet I couldn't even wipe away my tears.

Then I felt the universe (well, the system) shift. Everything was realigning. It was a small thing, in the cosmic sense, but it was there. I felt all the remaining planets shift, just a bit. Just enough to kill everything on them. Pace 2 was in the wrong place now. Pace 1 had shifted the most. Pace 4 was close to unaffected. Did we do it, I wondered. I had to know. Had to know that Andrew and his crew and Anan hadn't sacrificed themselves in vain. I turned my ship towards Pace 4, my birthworld.

In the back of my mind I registered that Felix's ship had righted itself and that he was under power again. That was a relief. I was waiting for him to say…

"Jane, what the fuck are you doing?" Felix's voice was full of grief and anger at me for doing my own thing as usual.

"I have to see if we did it, Felix. I have to know. We all have to know."

"Jane, you…"

But a voice cut him off. That voice. "Let her go, Felix. She's right. We need to know." My eyes closed in sympathy. The General's voice was full of pain and he wasn't bothering to hide it. My poor Samuel. I couldn't even bear to think of Wilby, poor Wilby, watching his lover die from the Command Center. No, I told myself, we aren't done. You can't think of that now.

I pointed my fighter in the direction of Pace 4 and soon felt Felix's fighter following behind. Pace 1 was in front of us, all grey and dead. I'd never seen it beautiful, I thought sadly. And now it was gone. We cleared Pace 1 and Pace 4 lay before us. It was a wasteland, like Pace 1 only with more wreckage. I could see footprints of whole cities that had been wiped off the surface in a split second. The mountains were obliterated. It was flat. Wiped clean as if by god himself.

"No *tapetia*." Felix said, wonder and horror in his voice. "Everything's gone." He took a second to get himself under control. "We did it."

"Acknowledged, *Caracara 6*. All fighters return to the *Newton* immediately." Lieutenant Ilene's voice was gentle and soft. And so sad. What a victory.

Within an hour Felix, Ian, Garrett and I were back in the locker room on the *Newton*. I had gotten my helmet off, but had made no move to beyond that to change back into regular clothes. Oh, Wilby. Everyone was too wrapped up in their own thoughts to talk and I found it a relief. I wished I could also have relief from my overwhelming sense of guilt regarding my friend. I'd pushed him to be with Andrew. And now… I buried my face in my hands. Andrew was so wonderful, how could he be gone? He'd seemed so…indestructible. But then so had Sig. Wilby would never forgive me and I didn't blame him. Andrew, I wailed in my head. How could you be gone?

"Pace-Pallon fleet this is the *T.S.S. Beagle*, do you copy?"

I froze. We all froze. The voice was alien to us and the words almost incredible as they had come over the comm speakers. I looked wide-eyed at my companions.

"Pace-Pallon fleet, this is the *T.S.S. Beagle*," the voice repeated but this time more urgently. "My God, what the hell happened to your system!?!"

"*T.S.S. Beagle* this is General Samuel Armstrong, Pace-Pallon Fleet Commander. A lot has happened in the six months since you've been here. I'll be happy to fill you in upon your arrival." Samuel's voice was professional again. Probably the shock of having the Terrans just show up like this out of nowhere and after so long. "What is your ETA?"

"This is Captain Alan Piper, General. We estimate 3 hours. What type of assistance do you require?"

I could hear the General sigh. "All kinds, Captain, all kinds. Welcome back to Pace-Pallon."

<u>14:00 – Command Center, *P.S. Scylla*</u>

Felix, Garrett, Ian and I walked into the Command Center about an hour later. There were none of the cheers that everyone had been so happy to give after we'd defeated the Scientists. The loss of the *DSVH* was too big, too raw for anything other than grief.

The General rose from his chair as soon as he saw us and crossed over to Ian hugging him hard. Ian's eyes were full as the word "Dad" escaped his lips seemingly involuntarily. General released his son and clapped Felix and Garrett and me gently on the shoulders. It was just a little contact, but it helped. Then I noticed Arrow, still sitting next to Mallory. Her eyes were huge, but she didn't move. Ian froze, so very aware of her look but unable to meet her eyes. She looked away and only then did he glance at her. It was only a second, but that…lost connection just added to the sadness of this day. This day when we had risked so much for future worlds. For people who would, because we'd succeeded, never know what we'd done for them.

I had to turn away. I just wanted to go back to our cabin and feel like shit. I had no intention of being around for the Terran invasion. I nodded sadly to the General and had walked almost to the door when Atalanta appeared as if out of nowhere. Her lovely face was streaked with tears as she ran into Felix's waiting arms. He whispered something to her that made her clutch him even more tightly. She looked over at me.

"You saved his life," Atalanta whispered.

"I owed him," I mumbled, not wanting gratitude of any kind. She had taken a step towards me but read my mood and stopped. She gave me a smile and I was glad to be able to send my own gratitude and affection back to her.

I turned again to leave and felt someone behind me. My heart pounded out of control and I felt sick to my stomach. Wilby.

I turned around slowly. He was staring at me with a look of such hatred, such pure loathing than I took a step back involuntarily. I heard Atalanta gasp.

"*You*," Wilby said, putting a wealth of blame and fury into that one word.

"Yes, me," I whispered.

He advanced on me with such overt menace that Felix stepped forward, putting his body in front of mine. Wilby stopped a couple of inches from Felix and glared at him.

"This doesn't concern you, Felix," Wilby sneered. "That bitch knows what she did."

I flinched at the word, even though I'd accepted the blame for Wilby's pain. Now Felix was mad. And despite the fact that Wilby towered over him, Felix was not someone you wanted angry.

"Back off. It wasn't her fault what happened to…" Felix swallowed, unable to say Andrew's name, "the *DSVH*."

Wilby didn't take his eyes off me. "She knows what I blame her for."

I took a step forward. "Wilby, I…"

And he spat at me. It hit my right boot. I stared at it, astonished that he had done such a thing. Better than him hitting me or ripping out a nerve or something, I guessed, though I was still a bit horrified. But he'd made his point. I was determined not to look up again, accepting his wrath, when Wilby was suddenly thrown out the door and slammed into the corridor wall. Like I said, don't piss off Felix.

Felix stalked out into the corridor, Atalanta following. I followed, hovering at the doorway. Felix had left Wilby trapped against the wall. He walked right up to him and pitched his voice angry and low. "I cannot even begin to understand your loss, Wilby, and you and Jane both," and he glared at me, "seem to have agreed that she has contributed to your suffering. But," and Felix stepped closer and I saw a flash of fear in Wilby's eyes, "you will not threaten or disrespect her like that *ever* again. Understand?"

Wilby said nothing, his momentary fear had been replaced by anger again. Felix watched him for a second, then walked back in to the Command Center with Atalanta and I trailing him. And just as the door closed I heard the 'umph' of Wilby being dropped to the floor. Felix took a breath, trying to shake his anger. I looked sadly at Felix who shrugged and I headed for the door—the far door that was far away from Wilby.

I heard Atalanta say softly, "He's lost the love of his life, Felix."

"I know, but I couldn't let him do that to her."

I reached the door and turned back quickly to see Atalanta weeping into Felix's shoulder. Weeping for Wilby. I practically ran back to our quarters. I needed to weep for Wilby, too.

18:00 – Officer's Lounge, *P.S. Scylla*

After a good bout of crying over the loss of Andrew I had found myself hungry and on my way to the Lounge. I had effectively hidden myself from the Terrans by staying in Samuel's Quarters for most of the afternoon, but hunger had driven me out. Even then I had waited as long as possible to leave and was now ravenous. I paused on the threshold. My plan was to grab rations and retreat to my little hidey booth in the corner of the room, but I stopped in surprise when I saw who else was in the Lounge.

Off in a corner were Felix, Atalanta, Ian, Garrett, Gladys, Stuart, Beno and a couple other supers that I recognized but whose names escaped me. No Wilby, but that wasn't a surprise. I watched them for a second. They weren't saying much. The loss of Anan and Julianne would be felt more keenly with this group than anywhere else. Coming to a decision (fight or flight) I grabbed my rations and headed over. It was funny that Ian had grouped himself with the freaks since he was the only non-freak I'd ever known. But I guess being a Pacey made you a weirdo whether you had been seriously modified or not. Arrow wasn't there, I noticed. But she wouldn't be if Ian was.

Felix looked and smiled a welcome as I approached. I found a seat and plopped down.

"So this is where the freaks hide out?" I said with a small smile.

"We're just waiting to hear what the General is able to get for us." Stuart said softly. It was weird hearing his voice after so long. I had been so preoccupied with Samuel that I'd pretty much forgotten Stuart's existence. Classy way to treat an ex, Jane, I thought. I saw him frown. He was scanning me, I knew, and I glared at him. I knew he wouldn't betray my Samuel secret but I really didn't care for Telepaths scanning me without permission. Stuart looked away, cheeks reddened by my silent rebuke.

"Get for us?" I looked at Felix.

"The General is meeting with the Terran Captain now." Felix raised his eyebrows and shrugged. "Negotiating."

I blinked in surprise. "Negotiating?" Apparently I just liked repeating everything Felix said. Sheesh.

"Terms for our 'reabsorption' into the Terran culture." Felix said the word 'reabsorption' the way someone would say 'vermin.'

I felt my stomach clench with worry. I hated that we were dependent on the mercy of these people, whoever they were. And who were the Terrans? They were like some scary ghost story, all vapors and menace. Too much was unknown for my taste.

"And," Felix continued calmly, "We were discussing names. The General told us weeks ago that we'd all need to choose our own surnames. Terran custom." Felix shrugged his opinion of Terran customs. "Ian is ahead of the game on that one," Felix smirked at Ian who appeared lost in thought, but smirked back politely. Ian has the best last name, I thought, suddenly sad again. I would have been happy to be Jane Armstrong. But that would never be. I felt Atalanta watching me and I closed my eyes for a second to get myself under control. Ok. Eyes open again I looked around at the little assembly.

"What have you come up with so far?" I asked. Some people had suggested last names from literature, some Pacey, some very old Terran. Bennett, Shaw, Tio, Miller, Hornblower. Or from history: Napoleon (that got a laugh), Aldrin, Motola, Lathrop, etc. People were arguing, but in a friendly way, pushing their favorites and dismissing the stinkers.

My mind was racing. None of these names was great, and everyone had to pick for themselves, but I suddenly felt very strongly that giving myself a cool last name that gave nothing away about myself was not the way I wanted to go. If I was going to be treated like something unnatural, unholy even, then I wanted to be upfront. I knew that this reaction wasn't entirely rational. No Terran had ever actually done anything to me. I'd only ever met one and he had been fine. But my imagination had turned them into giant six-headed racist monsters who would hate us for everything that we had no control over being.

"You know what," I said aloud, "Fuck them."

Everybody at the table stopped talking in shock at my outburst. All eyes turned to me, demanding an explanation.

"I don't want to spend the first minutes, days or weeks I meet a Terran waiting for them to figure out who or what I am. They may not like that I am, or that any of us, is a super, but that's their fucking problem. I want it out there. Right up front. And anyone who doesn't like it can go fuck themselves." Yes, I do have a way with words, don't I?

Felix looked at me, serious but also amused. Stuart was watching me, too, eyebrows raised. Yes, Stuart, I've changed a lot since I almost ripped your dick off.

"So," Felix said, "What will you call yourself?"

"Pace. Jane Pace." The name had come out of nowhere into my mind, but it was right. Yes, I thought, that was my name.

Felix leaned back in his chair thoughtfully. Atalanta nodded slowly. "She's right. We are who we are. Atalanta Pace, hm. I like the sound of that." And she smiled, a heart stopping beautiful smile. Wow. She snuggled up against Felix. Which would prompt any person, male or female to say...

"Ok. Felix Pace it is." And he smiled, too. I shook my head in wonder. I hadn't meant to suggest that Pace become *everyone's* last name, but found I liked the idea now that my friends were doing it. We were as close to a family as any of us had ever had. Sharing a family name made sense. The others now spoke in turn, faces wreathed in relief at finally making a choice.

"Garrett Pace."

"Gladys Pace."

"Beno Pace."

A pause. "Stuart Pace."

Then the three supers I didn't really know spoke up.

"Astrid Pace," A Macro, as I dimly recalled.

"Berenice Pace," A Micro, a young one.

"Peter Pace," a twenty-ish Telepath said. "God that sounds terrible, but..." Peter smiled sheepishly.

Then another voice was raised. "Captain Ian Armstrong." Ian's face was flushed a little. He sounded defensive. What a strange thing to feel left out of a club most people would give anything *not* to join.

"Ooh, I want one of those," Gladys said excitedly. "I want a title like that."

Her unbridled enthusiasm brought smiles to most of our faces, Ian's included, though his smile was grudging. "It's not a title, it's a rank. And I'm sure Dad is working on that for all of you right now."

"Cool," Gladys said, her enthusiasm undimmed. Ian relaxed a bit and people seemed to remember that there was food to eat. Atalanta stood up, kissing Felix on the cheek as she did so. She made her way over to me, leaning down to speak softly in my ear. My lips quirked in amusement as I realized, from the wide-eyed expression on Beno's face that he was getting quite an eyeful of her generous cleavage. My mouth surrendered to a full grin when I saw the murderous look Felix gave him. Beno wisely concentrated on his food.

"I'm going to see Wilby," she said.

"Felix is Ok with that?"

She rolled her eyes. "He has to be. Wilby needs someone and for once it can't be you." I nodded gratefully, sending the emotion to her as strongly as I could. "Besides, I can barely remember it happened," she said, referring to their affair at the School. "It seems like a lifetime ago."

I cast a quick glance to Stuart. "I know what you mean."

Atalanta gripped my shoulders then moved off, all music and beauty. What a dear she is.

I sighed and started to eat. Jane Pace, I thought. Now I am Jane Pace.

22:00 – The General's Quarters, *P.S. Scylla*

I knelt on the little couch, looking out the Tenorium at the vastness of space. Everything looked different now. There was no 'sun' as such, only impersonal stars. What had been Pace-Pallon was out of sight, but not out of mind. I was still stunned and saddened by the loss of Andrew, but had, at least temporarily, cried myself out. I wished Samuel was home. I knew, had known since the morning, with dreadful certainty that I would have to break things off, but I also knew that today was not the day to do it. Tomorrow would come soon enough and we'd had enough heartache for one day. Poor, poor Andrew.

But right now I needed Samuel. I needed the kind of touch and distraction that only my lover could give me. And, after a day like today, I was pretty sure he would need it, too.

The door opened and Samuel came in. He moved slowly, clearly tired from a god awful day. He dropped his jacket on the ground and moved towards me, not stopping. I stood up fully as I looked over my shoulder as he neared. My heart swelled with love and pity.

Samuel came up behind me and wrapped me up in his strong arms, burying his face in my shoulder. I relaxed into him, reveling in the comfort of his touch, his body.

"So you are Miss Pace, now?" Samuel's voice was husky. Oh, god, that voice. Even at this incongruous time I felt my insides melt. It was a kind of miracle that he could do that to me with merely a word or two.

But I had to laugh at the whole 'Pace' as a last name concept. "Along with all my new brothers and sisters." I reached up my arm, cradling his head against my own and pressed myself against him. "Nice to meet you."

"Really nice to meet you," he growled as his hands moved to cup my breasts. Oh, my. This was a wonderful start.

"Samuel?"

"Hm?" he said, implying that I was distracting him from more important matters as his hands moved lower and lower down my waiting body.

"*Nice* is the last thing I need right now." I could feel him hard against me and was overwhelmed with desire. There was a pause as his hands stopped moving.

"That's what you want?" he whispered breathlessly.

"Now," I whispered back, my voice unsteady with anticipation.

He held onto me with one hand and let go with the other. I felt him unbuckle, then lift the skirt I had put on a hour ago in anticipation of his coming home to me. Without further preamble he pulled me to him hard and we were together.

“Like this?” His voice was almost a groan.

“God, yes,” I replied semi-incoherently.

Suddenly it was all a flurry of passion and sensation and, soon, glorious orgasms. My Samuel, I thought as he held me, waiting for my body to stop shuddering, he never ceases to amaze me.

I took a moment to catch my breath then turned around, pulling my skirt down as I did so.

He looked at me, as if worried that he hadn't been loving enough. "You know I love you, Jane."

I snuggled up to him, resting my face on his neck. "I know it in a million ways, Samuel. I see it in everything you do." Then I grinned up at him. "Is that an egocentric statement or what?"

He smiled back. It was good to see a real smile on his face. "Egocentric or not, it's true, Baby." Then his smile became a smirk as his natural honesty forced him to qualify his statement. “Or true enough.”

"I love you, too." And I gently pulled his head down to kiss him.

ENTRY 14-2-20

An Excerpt from Atalanta's Journal, August 4, 2869

Everything is awful. Arrow, when I can even get near her, seems to be disappearing more and more every day. I can barely read her at all. Ian is worried about his people and the burning loss within him makes me want to cry. Jane is avoiding me, even though I know something is terribly wrong with her and Samuel. Samuel reads like someone waiting for the worst to happen and I don't think it has anything to do with our 'reabsorption' into Terra.

Everyone is still in shock over the loss of Captain DeStephani and his crew. Especially Wilby, who seems to be wrapping himself in rage to keep himself from feeling. Last night I'd tried to comfort him the way Jane would have, but he pushed me away.

Why won't Jane talk to me?

Why can't I help anyone? I can *help. I wish someone would let me.*

21:00 – Officer's Lounge, *P.S. Scylla*

I sat at the bar on my second drink. I tried to put all thoughts of the last time I'd sat at this bar with Andrew, but I still felt he was there. Laughing at me, teasing me about Samuel and talking about Wilby. Wilby had gone from active to passive hatred and pretended I didn't exist. I supposed this was an improvement. It certainly was easier on Felix, my apparent protector.

I had done my best to avoid everyone today. Especially the Terrans who seemed to have invaded our ship like a cancer. They were everywhere with their slightly off accents and their unfamiliar uniforms (black to our gray). I hated them. Hated them for what they were going to make me do. Hated them for being constant and unwelcome reminders that it was past time to talk to Samuel. *They* were why I was drinking after a completely useless day.

I needed courage. The courage to hurt the man I loved and break my own heart in the process.

I quickly downed my drink and headed home.

22:00 – The General's Quarters, *P.S. Scylla*

Samuel walked in and stopped dead. He looked down at the floor by the door. A bag sat there, a bag containing all my few possessions. He looked up to see me standing there, leaning against the desk waiting for him.

"Jane," he whispered, his face now creased with pain.

I had been leaning there for an hour, going over and over my speech. But with every breath the panic I felt at finally doing this had built exponentially. I don't want to hurt you, my love, I kept saying over and over in my head. But it was time.

"Jane, don't do this." Samuel's voice was so quiet that it was almost inaudible.

"Samuel." I took a deep breath to try to calm my nerves. It didn't work at all. "You know what I'm going to say. Why make me say it?"

"Because I won't believe it unless you do."

He wasn't going to make this any easier for me. I didn't blame him. If someone was going to hurt me like this I'd make them to have to say the words, too.

"I have to let you go, Baby."

Samuel exhaled and slumped forward as if someone had stabbed him. I put my hands on my shoulders, crossing my arms in front of me. I felt achy, like my body was hurting to reflect my inner misery.

"Don't," he pleaded.

I hugged myself tighter. "I have to. You have given more joy, more passion, more of yourself than I could ever have imagined a man doing. And I love every part of you, from your very cells to your soul." He sucked air in quickly in surprise. I had never told him this so forcefully before, I supposed. "I love and I want you *more than anything*." I rubbed my neck trying to relieve the horrible tension. "And I would move heaven and earth to stay with you in the bubble if I loved you less."

Samuel let himself lean against the wall. "You wouldn't love me if I wasn't the General?" Of all the ways I could hurt him, this thought was just one. But it still hurt, I could tell.

"I would love you no matter what you were. I love watching you work and I feel safer (and I did even before we were together) knowing that you are there protecting us. But to me that's a wonderful *part* of who you are. I love all." I sighed sadly. "But you need it. To be this truly remarkable man *you* need it."

"You don't know that…"

"I do." I had to cut him off. He was fighting the inevitable and I owed him the fight. Maybe it would help. "Loving you has made me *more*. Made me know my own strength. Given me people to protect and a purpose. I am more because of you, Samuel." Then my voice faltered even though I didn't want it to. "How can I be the one who made you *less*?"

He closed his eyes, saying nothing. His posture slumped even more. I found I was clenching my fists to the point my fingernails were cutting into my palms. I stretched out my fingers. They were shaking.

"I've been thinking about this a lot, Samuel. More than I ever wished to. I'm relieved that you see that having a teenaged girlfriend would make keeping a command impossible. That is what you think, yes?"

Samuel kept his silence, his eyes still closed as if to shut out the pain.

"So I had to ask myself what would happen if the situation was reversed, sort of."

He opened his eyes and looked at me warily.

"Let's say that we could stay together if I never used my abilities again."

"You would do that?" he asked quietly.

"Of course." I smiled sadly at him. "And we would be happy. We would be in the bubble. And then something would happen. Something horrible that I could have prevented if I could lift. A boat sinking. A bridge collapsing. A shuttle crash. Hovercar accident." And now I met his eyes. "And in that moment I would have to choose between the healthy, whole man that I love and people who are dying. Who do I choose, Samuel?"

He closed his eyes again, his breathing increasing as if he could fight this off. "It isn't the same."

"It's the same enough. You know that. Don't you?"

Now the silence stretched for an even longer time. Samuel sighed painfully. "You seem to think that I have given to you and received nothing in return. That isn't true at all, Jane." He ran his hands through his hair and looked at me, his brown eyes burning. "You gave me someone to love. Someone wonderful. Someone who could have had anyone and chose me. You remade me into a man again." He gave a short humor-free laugh. "You're too young to understand what it means to come alive again. It's redemptive. And you did it. You wanted *me*. I'll never know why. But you did."

I couldn't stand it anymore and I crossed the room to him. He tensed up as I neared him, but didn't back away. I felt tears building, threatening to fill my eyes, but I wasn't ready to give myself over to them yet.

"I do, Samuel. I want you. I always want you." Then the despair I'd been fighting and fighting swarmed over me. I couldn't breathe. Maybe he would let me comfort him now. Maybe not. But even if he did, who would be there for him tomorrow? He would be sad and alone. And so would I. It was too much. I let out a sob and sank to the floor, crumpled in a ball. As awful as I'd thought this would be, feeling it now was so much worse. I recoiled from myself in horror. How could I hurt him? How could *I* be the one to hurt him? These thoughts just made me cry harder.

Suddenly I was off the ground and standing, folded in those strong arms. Samuel had lifted me up like I was nothing and buried his face in my neck. He stroked my hair.

"I feel like I'm dying," I whispered.

"I know, Baby." His beautiful voice was soft in my ear. I clung to him, desperate not to have to let go. "Don't go tonight, Jane."

What? I held his face in my hands so I could look in his sad, sad eyes. "I don't think that's a good idea."

"It isn't. But do this for me. Please?"

I'd made him suffer too much. I couldn't say no to his request. I nodded. He exhaled with relief and pulled me tightly to him again. He dropped his jacket to the floor and walked me to the bed. We lay down still embracing each other. I pressed myself to him, trying to soak up all the contact I could before our separation tomorrow.

We lay like that in silence for the better part of an hour. I felt his heart rate increasing over that time. His breathing was faster, but when I scanned him it was clear that it wasn't sexual. His silent thoughts were making him more and more upset as time passed. I said nothing, not wanting to intrude—or not knowing what to do. Either way, I said nothing.

Samuel sat up, swinging his legs over his side of the bed. I let him go, keeping physical contact only by placing my hand gently at the small of his back. He sat there for a second, his breathing becoming labored. I sat up, my eyes full again. Knowing he was suffering so was torture.

Then Samuel sobbed into his hands. And again and again. I froze, horrified at his distress. I'd never seen a man I loved cry before and it was painful to watch. He didn't want to cry and he was fighting it so hard. I'm a monster, I thought, tears streaming down my face.

I was at his side now. "Samuel," I pleaded. "Samuel, don't…" I put my hand on his shoulder and he flinched. I froze again, then removed my hand quickly. He'd never resisted my touch before (well, not since we'd been together) and it hurt. It surprised me that there was any more room for hurt in this moment but apparently there was. But I was undeterred.

"Samuel, sweetheart. Tell me I'm wrong. Tell me I'm wrong and this all goes away." I was pleading. Begging him to fix this. To end the suffering for both of us. "*Please*, tell me I'm wrong."

His sobs had, mercifully, stopped. He raised his face from his hands. He looked exhausted and worse, beaten down. "I wish I could, Baby."

I nodded. More tears for me, but I struggled and got myself somewhat under control. I wanted to touch him. I was afraid he would push me away again, but need overcame fear and I reached a shaking hand out to touch his face. He was frowning, I noticed, and now I used both shaking hands to smooth away the frown. He hesitated for a second, then leaned in tentatively until his mouth was an inch or so from mine. He started to speak but stopped.

I looked into his eyes and saw his need for connection. I felt it, too.

"I want to be yours one last time, Samuel. Beloved Samuel. Is that all right?"

His eyes were full again as he nodded and kissed me deeply.

09:00 – The General's Quarters, *P.S. Scylla*, August 5, 2869

I walked slowly towards the door, Samuel following equally slowly behind. I carried my bag loosely in my hand. We were both worn out and looked it. I'd been astonished to see how defeated I'd looked in the bathroom mirror. Samuel, if anything, looked worse. His eyes looked dead and he walked as if his whole body hurt. My poor Samuel, I thought with despair.

We spent the night, post love-making, in silence, just holding each other. I think we were both afraid that anything we tried to say would just end up hurting the other more. Every subject was painful—or at least any were that I could think of. So silence was best.

I paused near the entry, just standing there, staring at the floor. This was it. Even in my exhausted, deadened state I balked at actually walking out the door. I could feel him standing behind me, watching me.

"I want you to keep this for me," Samuel said softly. I turned around as he slipped off his uniform jacket and held it out to be to put on. Dropping my bag, I slipped my arms into the holes. It was enormous on me, but it was warm from his body and I pulled it around me. I closed my eyes as I smelled the lining. That wonderful Samuel smell.

"Thank you," I whispered.

He stepped close to me and rested his hands on my shoulders. "I need you to do something else for me, Jane."

I looked up at him, curious, resting my face on the jacket collar.

Samuel sighed. "Over time memories of us will fade. And in a few years, or months even you will start to forget how we were together. This is natural. It happens to everyone. But you'll start to doubt."

I didn't believe him. I mean, it had happened with Stuart, but this was so different. He shook his head when he saw that disbelief on my face. "You won't believe it, what we had. Not really. You won't forget the times and places and the danger; you won't be losing your mind. But the immediacy will be lost."

"I don't want to forget, Samuel."

He shrugged. "You would hurt too much and for too long if you couldn't forget at least some of the emotion. It's how we get over things like this." He took a ragged breath. I put my hand on his chest, feeling his heart pounding. This was important to him. I climbed out of my own hell to pay attention fully. "So you may not remember how we felt, but you can remember my words." He cupped my face gently, so gently, in his strong hands. "This was real, Jane. We really loved each other, in every way. We changed each other's lives." He let go of my face to give my shoulders a gentle shake. "This was *real*."

I blinked away tears as quickly as I could so that I could see him clearly. “I am so in love with you, Samuel.”

“I’m so in love with you, Jane.” Samuel leaned down and kissed me. But the passion, though there, was chaste. This was the end.

I reached up with both hands and once again and for last time smoothed away his frown lines. He took one of my hands and kissed it gently on the palm. I held his gaze for a second, saying goodbye silently since I didn’t trust myself to actually pronounce the word. He nodded, understanding.

I picked up my bag, turned, and walked out the door.

11:00 – Captain Phan’s Office, *T.S.S. Beagle*

I sat down at the table. A small woman in the uniform of the Terran Military sat there impassively. If I had to guess I would say that she wasn't a huge fan of my brand of freak. I couldn't have cared less. The man sitting next to her was more intriguing. He was watching me intently. Too intently. He had a sort of flattish face and pale, almost colorless grey eyes. Looked to be nearing 40, though that was just a guess. Pacey's tended to get to their forties and fifties and stay looking like that for 50 years or so. It was part of our genetic design. We could look that way until about 110 then age more regularly. But I didn't like the way he was looking at me. Looking *into* me, really. I scanned his breathing. It was regular, almost measured. Like he was scanning me. Holy fuck..?

"I am Captain Karen Phan of the Terran Military Special Task force," the woman said, her voice cool and professional. I’d been so focused on the man, I’d almost forgotten she was there. "This is Lieutenant Soames Cherwell." Lieutenant Cherwell gave me the coldest smile I have even received; it was a movement of the muscles of his face, nothing more. I nodded. What was up here? "Our CO, Colonel Manthorpe is recruiting for a new division of the Task Force that will be made up of extra-sensory personnel. According to our reports you have been given extraordinary skills. Depending on your level of interest we may be offering you a position within this Task Force."

"Doing what?" I was not in the habit of being rude to people, but I wasn't in the mood to sell myself for a job. Not today.

"Information gathering and whatever mission we feel your talents would best be served by," was the prompt answer. I saw Cherwell write something on a pad in front of the Captain. It was one word, 'angry.'

Fuck. A Telepath. Or at least an Empath. All right then. I fixed Cherwell with a challenging glance. His grey eyes didn't even blink but his eyebrows raised. Now it was time to separate the men from boys or, in this case, the Empaths from the Telepaths.

I carefully pictured Cherwell standing in a field (why a field, I didn't know, but it was what came to mind) and out of nowhere came a *tapetia mortis*. It paused in front of him. I let the pause grow, building on any possible fear Cherwell might be having. Then I let it go and it consumed him, screaming, until there was nothing left. Nothing.

Cherwell let out a small sound of pure terror and stood up so quickly that he knocked his chair over. A Telepath, then. I cleared the image from my mind and smiled at him.

"Christ, Soames, what is wrong with you?"

Cherwell didn't answer, he just stared at me, a look of loathing on his face. Well, back at you, dickhead. He closed his eyes for a second, getting himself back under control. It had been worse because he hadn't been expecting it and I knew I would never be able to catch him off guard like that again, but I'd made my point.

"She's a sociopath," he said a little breathlessly.

"No. I'm not." I said this to the Captain, but then I looked Cherwell in the eye. "Stay out of my head." My voice was as threatening as I could make it.

I could see the hint of a smile in the Captain's face. "Well, you've been spotted, Soames. You can relax now."

"Have you been able to recruit any of my fellow Paceys?" I asked.

"Some. Felix Pace has accepted a Captaincy and will lead your particular group."

"And you've told him far more than you will ever tell me about what you are planning for the Task Force. Correct?"

The Captain nodded, a little surprised at my abruptness of manner.

"What are you offering me?"

I saw Cherwell looking at me again. I guess the temptation to scan me was too strong. I pictured a *tapetia mortis* chasing him down into a ravine. I pumped the image of him with terror and made sure the creepy clacking sound of the feet and shell of the *tapetia* crawling was as loud as I remembered it. Cherwell looked away. He looked ill and scared.

"Last warning." I glared at him.

"What *are* those things?" Cherwell asked breathlessly.

"*Tapetia mortis*. They killed about 50 million of our people. They left nothing behind." Cherwell's eyes were wide and I'd effectively reinforced his fear. Good. I hoped we were done. I didn't like having the *tapetia* in my head any more than he liked having it in his. Effective, though.

Captain Phan continued, clearly trying to keep things moving and annoyed at the distractions. "Standard salary. Apartment on Terra 1, our largest space station. Rank of junior grade lieutenant. Other things. I have a packet of information you can look over while you make your decision."

"No room-mate. Non-negotiable. My own place."

The Captain paused. "I can guarantee that."

"And I report to Captain Felix Pace. He's my direct supervisor?" Saying Felix's name with both a rank and last name was strange, but I knew I'd better get used to it. I was feeling a little better. If I could keep Felix, I could make it work, I thought. I couldn't care less about the details.

"Captain Pace, yes. And he would report directly to Colonel Manthorpe."

"All right then." I stood up to leave. I saw the Captain's jaw drop.

"You don't need to know anything else?"

I shook my head. I just wanted to leave. "Felix Pace is the best at…what he does." Or at being who he was made to be. Our genetics have become our profession, I thought bitterly. "You're lucky to have him."

"He was very highly recommended, as were you and several others from your...school." She was looking over her papers. Funny. They used actual papers for things. "We were strongly advised to keep the lot of you together. That you were a team."

I found myself having to focus hard on the *tapetia mortis* image again. It was Samuel who had done this. A final gift to me, to us, his 'kids.' I felt a lump in my throat. I fought it hard. The last thing I needed was to be thinking of him with a Telepath in the room.

"We *are* a team. A very good one."

I took a few steps for the door. "Miss Pace?" I turned back. It was the Captain. "This is a military organization. We have certain protocols and certain conventions that one follows. You have not been dismissed."

I sighed. "Captain Phan, with all due respect, my home system was destroyed two days ago and I'm tired. How about this. I'll accept your offer starting tomorrow and I'll leave when I want to today. All right?"

"All right, Miss Pace." She cocked her head at me appraisingly. "I hope you live up to the Admiral's recommendation of you."

I looked at her, curious. "What Admiral, Captain?"

"Your Admiral Armstrong. A Pacey like you. He accepted his commission an hour ago. I thought you knew him."

My Admiral Armstrong. No, not mine. "I know him." I kept my voice and expression neutral and filled my head with as many violent images as I could think of so that any scans would be nullified. I wanted to comment further, but couldn't think of anything to say that wouldn't give away my feelings.

"One last question, Miss Pace?"

"Your marital status is listed as single, is that correct?"

"It is."

She regarded me closely, but I don't think I gave anything away. She nodded and I left.

I walked slowly back to the shuttle waiting area. The large grey room sported lines of hard fixed chairs and its large window showed a glorious view of what looked like a storage area for the maintenance crew. Garrett, Beno, Gladys, Stuart and a couple of others sat waiting. Felix had probably caught the earlier shuttle back and I assumed Atalanta had been with him. I nodded to my fellow Paceys and sat down, closing my eyes so that I could think. Samuel. So like him to be this generous. To keep protecting us even when he couldn't be there himself. Samuel. My chest was tight with my emotion, but I fought its release. There needed to be just a few minutes each hour that I wasn't crying. Or maybe that was too much to ask.

Then I felt someone walk into the room. Even with my eyes closed I knew it was Wilby. I kept my eyes closed for a second longer. It was a coward's move. I felt I owed him the opportunity to shun me, but I didn't want to be reminded of guilt and the loss of his friendship. But it couldn't be helped. Then I heard Wilby laugh.

My eyes snapped open. Wilby was walking with a Doctor (clearly a medical doctor from the uniform) and smiling at him with that Wilby smile. Wilby was charming the Doctor. And it was working. Yes, I thought, he has many weapons, the handsomeness being just the most obvious one.

The Doctor clapped Wilby on the shoulder, smiling, "Welcome to TerMed 1, Lieutenant Pace."

Wilby dazzled with another blinding smile. "It is a privilege, Doctor Mohindra."

Wilby headed for the seats, his smile fading as soon as the Doctor was out of sight. His eyes scanned the people in the room coldly. He looked, deliberately, right through me and took a seat on the opposite side of the room.

Garrett turned around so that he could talk to me. His set of chairs was facing the same way as mine so he really had to twist around. "Did they offer you the Task force?"

I nodded. I didn't want to talk to anyone, but Garrett hadn't done anything to me recently, so what the hell. "Lieutenancy, you?"

"Same." Garrett looked relieved. I didn't enjoy the loss of his arrogance the way I would have if we were still on our ship. We'd been separated out now. There were Paceys and there was everybody else. He was us. "Where the hell is Captain Armstrong?"

"Why? Is he here?" I looked around but didn't see him.

"Yeah. He's supposed to pilot us back. He came earlier but had to wait. Some personnel crap."

Suddenly my stomach clenched. *Personnel crap.* No. No. No. I tried to keep my voice steady.

"Did he say who he was meeting with, Garrett?"

"Same person we all did. Captain Phan. Why?"

I stood up and was moving even before I answered. "They have a Telepath. There is a Telepath in that meeting." I ran out of the room, Garrett followed, clearly knowing something was badly wrong, but I was pretty sure he had no idea what. I felt also, to my surprise, Wilby following too.

I ran up to Captain Phan's door and lifted my hand to key it open when it flew open on its own. Ian was coming out the door, but stopped when he saw me. His eyes were wild, face flushed. He was angry, grief-stricken. Beyond upset. His jacket was off. I looked in the room to the horrified expressions of Captain Phan and Lieutenant Cherwell. The missing jacket looked like it had been flung at them. It lay lost and forgotten on the floor, his LPG next to it.

Ian stepped beyond the door so that it closed automatically behind him.

"Ian, the Telepath... I didn't know you were in there. I would have warned you..."

"It's Ok, Jane," Ian said, his eyes alight with a manic intensity that I found disturbing. I looked over at Garrett and Wilby who also looked shocked at Ian's demeanor. "The other shoe dropped. I'm free." He looked at me and smiled crookedly. My heart was full of pity for that smile.

Ian started to walk away, going who knows where. I grabbed his arm, stopping him. "Where are you going, Ian?"

"No idea. But our universe is bigger than it was. I have options now. And," his face became momentarily tight with grief, "I no longer have anything to lose."

"Ian," I said. He was thinking, still absorbing the end of his career. "Ian!" He turned those beautiful eyes on me. "You must promise me you'll keep in touch with me." He looked at me uncomprehendingly for a second. "With me and with Samuel."

Ian shook his head. "With you, yes. I give you my word. You can tell dad for me."

Now I shook my head. "I can't, Ian. Not anymore." Wilby looked up sharply at this. I guess he hadn't known Samuel and I were doomed from the start. But Ian had known.

"Oh," Ian said softly. "When did you do it?"

How did he know I would have been the one to leave Samuel? "This morning." Well, last night, but it didn't matter.

"I'm sorry, Jane. Truly sorry." A tear forced its way out of my eye. This poor man had pity for *me*? How was that possible?

"No, Ian. *I'm* sorry. The universe has screwed you over."

Ian actually laughed for a second at my bluntness. But then his expression changed, becoming infinitely sadder. He leaned close to me, dropping his voice so that only I could hear. "Tell her something for me. Please." Oh, god, did I not want to have to tell Arrow anything. I didn't think my heart and soul could take any more suffering. But I couldn't say no. Not after what had just happened to him. I nodded. "Tell her I haven't changed at all here," and he put his hand over his heart, "but that I have to disappear now. I need to start over. And tell her," and Ian stopped speaking for a second, swallowing compulsively, trying to get his emotions in check, "that I want her to have all the things I can't give her."

I nodded numbly, closing my eyes, trying to ward off his pain. Two more tears leaked out as I did this. But then I looked up at him.

"But what about your father? It will kill him to lose you, Ian. You know that."

Ian's expression hardened a bit. "The last thing the Admiral needs is a connection with his son who has been accused of incest," I flinched at the word, "and disgraced." He looked down at me, his expression gentle and sad. "He's given up too much to be able to serve. I'm not going to make it any harder for him." Losing his son *would* make it harder for him, I thought, but I didn't think I'd be able to convince Ian of that so I kept quiet.

"Where will you go?"

"I'm going to talk to the Captain of the *Canary*. Pacey 3's have always been independent. There might be a place for me there."

I was awash with sadness as it hit me that I was losing another friend. My eyes were filling with tears in earnest now. Ian swept me into a hug. I hugged him back. "Keep your promise to stay in touch, Ian. Take good care of yourself."

"I will, Jane. You, too." Ian relaxed for a second in my embrace and buried his face in my neck. Like his father. Well, that was confusing and made me even sadder. Ian let me go and turned to Garrett. They shook hands. Then Ian shook hands with Wilby as well. Wilby touched him on the shoulder reassuringly, but said nothing, looking distressed. Wilby's eyes then moved to me and he frowned. It was the first time he had looked at me without anger since Andrew's death, but I had no idea what he was thinking.

Ian took one last look at us, as if officially saying goodbye to his old life, and started walking away.

"Godspeed, Ian." I said softly.

He turned a corner and was gone.

The three of us remaining stood in silence for a minute. I wanted to be alone. I couldn't take all this suffering. Everyone I loved was miserable. I wanted Samuel. I was safe in his arms. I felt the convulsive sobs building in my chest. I knew I would be doubled over with grief within a minute so I started walking. I turned down hallway after hallway, looking for…something…a safe haven. I found myself soon in the bowels of the ship (the bowels of the *Beagle*, ha ha) and on a deck of crew quarters. A door opened to my right and a young man stepped out of a room. He was fully dressed but his hair was wet. My brain seized on it. A shower room. Good. I darted in and found a line of shower stalls, each curtained off to itself.

The shower room was quiet. No water running. It was empty. I didn't know if that was a good thing or a bad thing. A full, noisy room would have provided more cover, I guessed, but it didn't really matter. I practically ran to the last stall and pulled the curtain shut behind me.

Ian. Samuel. Wilby. Too much sadness. I let go my iron control and let out a sob. A huge ugly sob as I sunk to the floor, curling up into a ball. I let my body take over and let it out. How could my heart break again and again I wondered as the racking sobs kept coming, pinning me to the floor.

I heard booted feet walking into the shower. Surprise stopped my crying, which was a relief. I scanned and found it was Wilby. More surprise. I sat up and backed hard against the wall. I felt like a cornered animal. Trapped in a fucking shower stall. I was abruptly angry. I deserved Wilby's ire, but did he have to follow me to give it? Wasn't making me feel like shit whenever he ran into me enough?

He pulled the curtain back roughly and just stood there. I could see Wilby's anger drain right out of him as he looked at me. His shoulders slumped. Oh, Wilby. Fresh tears coursed down my cheeks. He saw my grief and tears ran down his cheeks as well. He closed his eyes and took a breath. He walked over and sat down next to me on the floor. He exhaled hugely as he leaned against the wall. He ran his hands through his hair and leaned his head against the wall as well.

"I had to be mad at someone," Wilby said quietly.

"I know," I responded. And I did. That was why I'd let him be mad at me. I hated the Terrans for the same reason. But while his anger appeared to be gone, or at least diminished, mine was still in full force. I hated my new bosses and didn't care.

He closed his eyes. "I don't think I can bear it," he whispered. I couldn't either. I scooted close to him, putting my legs over his so that I could pull him to me. He resisted for a second, then pulled me closer still, his arms tight around me. I felt his body shake as he fought not to abandon himself to feeling. I stroked his hair.

He pulled back just a little from me, wiping his face on his sleeve. Then he used the same sleeve to wipe my tear stained face dry as well. He looked lost, crushed. Then his eyes met mine and he leaned in and kissed me. I couldn't breathe for a second; I was so astonished. His tongue touched mine and I felt my body respond unthinkingly. He pulled me onto his lap and deepened the kiss even more. What *was* I thinking? I wasn't. I wanted to be touched. I wanted the connection. I felt his erection under me and knew he wanted it too. But in the back part of my brain I knew that as good, as relieving as this felt, it wasn't *his* touch I so desperately wanted. And it wasn't *my* touch he wanted either. This wasn't right.

I pulled my mouth from his reluctantly. He looked at me, his expression hurt and confused.

"I can't," I whispered.

"But you want me," Wilby said. His expression was so sad, so…vulnerable, that I almost changed my mind right there. But I didn't want to use him. Even if he wanted me to.

"I want you," I agreed. "But I see *him*."

"I don't want to see him," he said, desperation in his eye. *His* him, Andrew. "It hurts too much."

"But this," and I touched his lips gently, "is only a distraction, love."

"An incredibly hot distraction," he said, a shadow of a smile on his handsome face. My body was agreeing, but I disciplined myself not listen to it.

"I would expect nothing less, Wilby. But I need a friend and so do you. Not this. Not now."

Wilby looked away, thinking, then nodded slowly. I shifted my position so that I was next to him again. I held both his hands and rested my head on his shoulder. He wrapped his arm around me.

"What are we going to do, Jane?"

"Fucked if I know, Wilby. Just keep going, I guess."

He pulled me tighter and we stayed sitting in silence for a long, long time.

14:00 – Command Center, *P.S. Scylla*

I was back on our ship wandering the halls aimlessly. I had nothing to do, just people to avoid. The most obvious was Samuel. I just couldn't bear it, seeing him. I didn't know how I felt about kissing Wilby. Confused, I guessed. I had never thought of sex as something comforting, something that deepened a connection—until Samuel. I didn't think I felt guilty about the kiss, but I wasn't sure. I was unattached and Wilby, poor Wilby, was single himself. No, I didn't feel guilty, I just felt sad and kind of out of control. I missed Samuel's arms around me. It's where I went when I was scared and I was scared now.

I'd written a note to Samuel, the Admiral, and left it with Lieutenant Ilene. I felt I owed him some information, but was very mindful that others would be reading it. Which sucked. The note read:

Admiral Armstrong:

Congratulations, Sir, on your commission with TerNav. I am sure the arrangement will be mutually beneficial.

I do not know if you have been informed that Captain Ian Armstrong has, due to the presence of an undercover Telepath (Lt. S. Cherwell) during a personnel interview, had certain aspects of his private life exposed and has declined military service and departed for places unknown. In all probability he will be traveling, at least temporarily, on the P.S. Canary. *He has promised to keep in touch with me.*

I think this may be the best course for him at this time. He wishes to 'disappear' and start again. Per his request, I will inform your daughter of his intentions.

I thought you deserved to know.

Godspeed,

Jane Pace, Lt. (j.g), TerMil

It sounded so cold. I hated writing like that, but figured he would understand why I did it. And I needed him to know, in case he didn't already, that the Terrans had supers that were scanning people without permission. Or at least without identifying themselves. But the part that would affect him the most was the fact that Ian would keep in touch with me—not with his father. I wasn't happy about that either, but it wasn't my choice. Another heartbreak for my beloved Samuel. I was loitering now in the Command Center. I'd walked most of the ship already and was, frankly, really tired of it. But when I sat down I couldn't stay put. Fuck it, then. More walking.

And just then in walked the second person I was avoiding, though for very different reasons: Atalanta. I was trying so hard to save her my suffering. I missed my friend, but had been keeping her at arm's length for her protection. I mean, what kind of friend puts another in the position to suffer? Not me.

I could tell, from the extremely pissed expression on her lovely face, that she would not have agreed with that axiom *at all.*

"With me. Now," she ordered. I sighed and followed her reluctantly. And I followed her all the way back to our quarters. We walked in and she saw my bag on the floor by my bunk. There was no surprise at seeing evidence that I had moved back in. She just looked even angrier.

"Are we friends, Jane?" Atalanta's arms were crossed on her chest. Man, was she pissed.

"Of course we are, 'Lanta," I murmured.

"Don't you 'Lanta' me, Miss Pace." He big brown eyes were burning with fury. "All this shit is happening to you and I have to hear about it from *Wilby*?"

"Wilby talked to you about me?" Oh, good lord, what did she scan from that? I shuddered to think.

Atalanta snorted. "Sort of. I mentioned your name, you know, asking about you since actually asking *you* seems to be impossible and suddenly I am covered in his pity, sadness, worry and…guilt." She looked a question at me, but I wasn't going to touch that one. That mistaken kiss was dead and buried as far as I was concerned. "I asked him about Sam and he told me." She paused, her face mirroring her hurt at losing my confidence. "You've broken your own heart and you didn't tell me? You didn't want my help?" Her eyes looked glassy. "Don't you like me anymore?"

Fuck, I'm just hurting people I love right and left today, aren't I? I crossed quickly to her and hugged her tightly. Suddenly I couldn't wait to leave this Ship of Suffering. Maybe we'd all have half a shot at actual happiness if we were somewhere else. Or maybe just a shot at different suffering. I stroked Atalanta's hair.

"You know I love you, 'Lanta. You can read me like a book. And I've backed away from you because of that. I'm miserable. I'm falling apart. People are hurting, leaving. And Andrew…" I took a breath to try to evict the lump from my throat. I was so fucking sick of crying. Better. "And it seemed selfish to make you have to take on my grief along with your own. I didn't want to be a burden." I kissed the top of her head and gave her a squeeze. "I've missed you. I didn't mean to hurt you."

Atalanta nodded against my collar bone. Short people, I thought erroneously. "You don't mean to hurt anybody, Jane. But you can't disappear every time something bad happens. I can't just be your friend in only the good times."

I released her from the hug and leaned against the top bunk. "So, how do we do that?"

"I will have to learn to turn the 'volume' down on your emotions, the way I do with everyone else. It won't be easy because what I get from you is so strong, but I should be able to do it. With time and practice."

"Is that what you want? Is it worth it to go through that bother?" This seemed rather chancy to me and there would be too much time with her in my unfiltered feelings. I knew, or guessed, that it would be a long, long time before I felt anything other than desolated. And there this poor girl would be—wallowing in it with me. I shook my head at my own thoughts.

"You are worth it to me, Jane." I looked up at her, her voice was strong as if she'd been sure I wouldn't believe her. She was right. After all that had happened in the last two days, this was the least likely time in my life for me to believe anything like that. I sat hard on the bottom bunk, saying nothing.

Atalanta walked over gracefully, kneeling in front of me and taking my hands. She closed her eyes and, instead of the calm she usually sent me, she sent love, concern and…pride to me. Holy fuck, she was *proud* of me? This was so unexpected, so generous and kind—and I just couldn't take it. I pulled my hands from hers and brought them to my face. I didn't cry, I just concentrated on breathing.

"Jane..?" Atalanta said softly, tears in her voice.

"My future is black without him," I whispered from between my fingers. I felt her sit next to me on the bunk, putting both arms around my shoulders. I sat, trying to breathe, and she wept for me.

02:00 – Atalanta/Felix/Jane's Quarters, *P.S. Scylla*, August 6, 2869

I lay in my bunk, dozing but not actually sleeping, wrapped in Samuel's jacket. It still smelled of him and it made me feel better. I was going over my visit to Arrow earlier in an effort to distract myself from other miseries as well as the fact that sleep was eluding me. Arrow hadn't cried, hadn't even acted surprised. She took the news and had said nothing at all. She hadn't been rude, she hadn't been angry. She'd been…null. It hadn't been clear to me how to help her, so I had told her that I was her friend and that I would be there for her. She hadn't responded except for a short sharp nod. So then I'd left. I wondered when Arrow was going to stop getting kicked in the teeth by life. Soon. Hopefully soon.

Felix slept. I could sense it, but Atalanta was awake, reading. Well, she was holding a book reader in front of her but her eyes hadn't moved (you know, like she was actually looking at words) for the last half hour. The privacy curtain was closed to keep her light from bothering me, but it didn't matter since I was awake.

Then I heard it. Someone was keying our door code. I sat up, my heart in my mouth. Please, please, please let it be him. The door opened and our visitor paused on the threshold and made a shhh sound to Atalanta. Dear god, it was Samuel. It was!

A hand moved the curtain aside and there he was. He stepped into my half of the room, tucked the curtain back in place as he did so. He was wearing the new black uniform, the TerMil one. It suited him, I thought to myself. Or rather, I thought this later, because now all I saw were his eyes. Burning with sadness, loss and longing. He knelt next to my bunk. Was I supposed to touch him? It was all I wanted to do, but I didn't know what he wanted so I waited. His eyes flicked over the jacket I was wearing. His eyes softened a bit when he saw how wrapped up I was in it.

"Thank you for my note," Samuel said softly, his voice sounding uneven. "He won't communicate with me? He said that?"

I nodded. Oh, Samuel. "I'm sorry. He thinks he will taint you by staying in your life."

"He's my *son*," he said, voice full of hurt.

"I know, Samuel. But he's wounded and, I think, he feels he deserves it." Samuel looked at me sharply. "I think he's punishing himself by giving up more than he has to."

"It's not just that," he said, a touch angrily. "He can't forgive me keeping them apart." I opened my mouth to protest and he held up a hand to stop me. "It isn't rational and I'm sure he knows that. But things would have been so different if I hadn't said anything to Arrow in the first place."

"You couldn't help being Arrow's father!"

"But she didn't need to *know* I was. My being her father hasn't made her life any better. Only worse." Samuel dropped his head down, miserable.

"Hey," I said and he looked up. "This is all very fresh and incredibly painful. What was it you told me about the immediacy fading—it counts for this, too, doesn't it?" He nodded. "Give it time, Baby, and quit beating yourself up. They love you and they'll come around."

He stared at me a second as if trying to believe that were true and nodded. "I'm transferring to the *Beagle* tomorrow. It's my last night on a Pace ship."

"Will you miss it?"

He gave a quiet laugh. "You know, I don't know. I'll miss the good things, but so much other stuff has happened here that I'd rather forget, so...?"

I smiled at him. "I was thinking the same thing earlier." His brief moment of mirth disappeared and I felt him shift his weight as though he were about to rise. I felt panic flood my system. "Thank you, by the way, for keeping all us freaks together. It means a tremendous amount to me." I bit my lip, trying to keep myself together. "I wasn't expecting anything good to happen and you surprised me. I am so grateful, Samuel."

He shrugged. "I love you, Jane."

I was moving towards him before I even realized it and I kissed him. He froze, startled by my attack and conscious, very conscious, of the fact that we had already said our goodbyes. I couldn't have cared less. His few seconds of hesitation seemed to stretch and I wished, oh I wished that the last lips I'd kissed hadn't been Wilby's. I put the thought aside easily, though, as Samuel kissed me back. My god, it was even more amazing, sexy, meaningful than anything else. This was *Samuel.*

I pulled off my sleeping clothes and his old jacket and pressed myself naked to his chest. I ran my fingers through his hair, reveling in the ability to touch him again. He groaned as he moved his mouth to my neck and ran his hands down to my backside.

I started working on the collar of his uniform but the closures were difficult. Sensing I was having trouble he hastened to help.

"Fucking jacket. I could barely get the damn thing on this morning," Samuel said as he struggled with the closures, getting some open, some not. I sat there, naked and impatient.

I felt a bubble of laughter building up. "Well, can we at least get your pants off?"

He looked up from his jacket and gave me a wicked grin. "Baby, I can always get my pants off for you." I let out a giggle, then clapped my hand over my mouth, mindful that we weren't alone. I did a quick scan and realized than Atalanta wasn't in her bunk anymore. She was in Felix's and Felix was awake. Very awake.

I looked back at Samuel. His jacket was miraculously on the floor. Thank god, I thought, as I leaned in to kiss him again. His shirt was off in a second, his pants followed a few seconds after that. I pulled off his underwear and no longer had any doubt as to whether he wanted me as much as I wanted him. He devoured my mouth then moved deliciously down my body. Then I felt the…lust, passion, desire from Felix and Atalanta flooding across the room. Holy shit, I thought. Samuel's not the only one around here with moves.

Now vibrating with need I flipped Samuel down to the bed so that I could straddle him. I moved my mouth down his chest, tasting his scars, his nipples. I put my mouth on his, then sat up and slowly lowered myself down onto him. Holy fuck, that felt incredible. *He* felt incredible. Immediacy indeed.

"Jane," Samuel groaned. And then I started to move and neither of us could speak.

It was about 3 hours later and I was tucked safely under Samuel's shoulder, my arm sprawled comfortably across his chest. Atalanta and Felix were dead asleep, having been worn out by us a while ago. The only thing that was keeping me awake was the knowledge that Samuel was about to go.

"Do you miss sunlight?" I asked softly.

"Sunlight?" Samuel's voice was surprised. Then he considered. "Not really. I never think about it when I don't see it."

"I guess you were destined for space, then." But this thought made me sad and I quieted. Somehow he sensed this and his arm around me tightened.

"Why?"

"I was just thinking that your leaving would be so…poetic if the sun was rising as you kissed me goodbye." The lump in my throat was back.

"Stars are beautiful, Baby. Give them a chance." His voice sounded funny, too. He took a couple of breaths, as if gearing up for something, and rose, kissing the top of my head as he did so.

I stayed in bed, watching him get dressed, which he did quickly. Before I knew it he was the General, no, the Admiral, again. I got to my knees and straightened his collar.

"This suits you, my love."

He kissed my fingers. "You'll remember what I said. Promise?"

I nodded. I felt emotion catching up to me again, but I didn't want to spoil our goodbye, our second goodbye, with tears.

"You'll remember me, Samuel?" I whispered. I sounded so needy, even to myself, but I couldn't help it.

Samuel leaned in and kissed me. His eyes were full. "Always, Baby."

He pressed my cheek to his, then released me. Then Samuel was gone.

I lay back down in bed then got up again immediately. I searched around and found Samuel's Pace jacket on the floor and slipped it on. I settled myself back on my bed and stared at the bottom of the bunk above me. And I thought, *Samuel.* Despair.

05:00 – My Quarters, *Terra 1 Space Station*

It was early but I was wide awake, once again staring at the ceiling of my small apartment. The misery of losing Samuel had been replaced, over time, with a numbness, an emotional deadness, that I cherished.

There was movement next to me in bed and I looked over. Even the back of his head is handsome, I thought idly.

It'd been a little over a year since we'd left home for good. It was funny that so much could change and still stay the same.

I closed my eyes again and willed myself to sleep.

September 16, 2870

END OF BOOK TWO

www.ingramcontent.com/pod-product-compliance
Lightning Source LLC
LaVergne TN
LVHW020652110826
845149LV00012B/1963

* 9 7 8 0 9 8 5 8 6 0 3 4 9 *